I0822335

THE KING'S PALADIN

By Randy Cloward

No part of this story was written by generative artificial intelligence (AI). This novel has been verified to have been written by the author between the months of May 2021 and June 2024.

Library of Congress number: **2025922611**

ISBN: 979-8-218-86410-1

Warwick & Stein,
New York

First edition
Publishing date: November 2025

Cover art by Pablo Heredia
Interior digital art by Stefan Alden
Edited by Cori Latsch
Audiobook by Jon Krajecki

For Laura.
An angel among humans.

Part I

Part II

N
S
Haberlorn
Tillsboro
Mountaintop
Fortress
Witch's
Woods
Outer Woods
Thearbuc's Cabin
Brodel's Hut

Lake of Dreams
Skerlin
Portal
Cave Entrance
Goldmines
Briardale
Mazeron
Emoras-Graum

The following events happened on this planet earth, thousands and thousands of years ago. Before magic was lost to the world…

Names and phrases of the time have been translated to the closest modern-day vernacular.

Chapter 1: A Secret Meeting

It was evening. The sun was calmly making its way back down towards the horizon which cast a warm glow across seemingly endless miles of green valleys and turned distant snowcapped mountain peaks a soft red glow. A light breeze blew crisp evening air through open windows, indicating the warm evening was coming to an end and making way for a cool night. An old man sat at a wooden table, reading a large, leather-bound book. He pulled his dark woolen cloak close to his face as the cool air bit at exposed skin, then turned his attention back to the book.

The man was visibly older with a long, black and gray beard that reached below his chest, and shambled hair draped past his shoulders from his woolen cloak. His dark leathered hands were thick with calluses and cracks as they skimmed along the pages, and his face was weathered by time and gravity, which made a permanent scowl that could not be hidden by the unkempt beard.

As time went on, the sun continued to dip lower and the room grew darker. The man casually glanced at the open window, then with a rotation of his wrist, a soft ball of light appeared glowing from the palm of his hand which illuminated the book and area around him. More moments passed as he continued studying the texts, then with a soft wave of his hand a page lazily flipped to the next without him touching it. He calmly glanced over to the fireplace where the last flames of a dying fire were flicking at the bottom of a kettle, and the ladle in the pot slowly stirred the stew as he made circular motions with his finger from across the room.

Eventually the man stood up and shuffled towards the open window and gazed out to the lands beyond. His cottage was in the low foothills of the mountains and a vast valley stretched out before him. It was almost dark now except for the faint lights coming from people's cottages that dotted the valley floor and surrounding foothills. The air was getting cold, and the sound of crickets resonated through the fields beyond the cottage. Toward the west end of the valley the shadow of a large castle rose high into the night sky. Dim lights could be seen glowing through the tower windows that stretched towards the heavens and were topped with golden cone shaped roofs that proudly reflected the last bits of evening sunlight.

Beyond the valley a purplish red glow began to appear in the surrounding forests, indicating the faeries of the forest were waking up for the night. In their soft yet dangerous glow he could see the shadows of large trees from the vast forests that stretched beyond these lands, further than anyone knew. He always enjoyed the soft glow of the forests at night. It was like a dim but permanent sunset on the horizon. But it also served as a constant reminder of the dangers that surrounded the kingdom, as the vast forests were home to countless beasts, monsters, and all types of magical creatures that made traveling through them extremely dangerous. But he knew how. He had traveled through the outer forests many times throughout his long existence.

He had traveled far and wide, but this was home. The foothill village of Briardale in the great kingdom of Mazeron. No matter how far his travels took him, he would always find his way back here. It was the only place he had ever lived and the only place he had ever wanted to live. He gazed into the peacefulness of it all until the last bit of sunlight faded from the sky. But now it was time, and he could not stay. There were things to be done tonight. Important things.

"It's time," he muttered to himself quietly, dousing a candle. He closed the shutters, grabbed the large book from the table, tightened his cloak for warmth, and hurried out the door.

Outside, the wind was picking up. Growing steadily, it howled through the mountain canyons above. He did not waste any time and quickly hopped onto his horse, stowed the large book, and rode swiftly and quietly away from the cottage, blending into the night like a shadow on the hillside.

The chill wind bit at his face and his eyes began to water from the cold as he rode downward from the foothills. The horse's heaving breaths and thumping hooves were the only sounds he could hear beyond the rushing cold wind. Behind him, the snowcapped mountains towered against the black sky like giant gods watching over the valley, silently judging the lands below with conceited indifference.

Feathered by the moonlight, they rode for hours into the night. Downward from the foothills and to the valley floor, then towards a grouping of lights off in the distance that indicated a small village was ahead. Once there, a small dirt road led directly towards the flickering lights and before the moon had risen high above the towering mountains, they were there.

The village consisted of all dark and weathered wooden structures that were hugged by overgrown grasses and weeds. He stayed off the main roads and wound quietly through the dark passages and alleys between the buildings, making sure not to be seen. As he rode, he could hear the faint sounds of laughter and chatter in the distance from a village pub or gathering house as people shared each other's good company, food, and drinks into the late hours of the night. Then turning a corner, he approached the only stone structure in the village. There were no windows, and it was illuminated only by the soft moonlight. He dismounted and tied up his horse, unstowed the large book, glanced behind him to make sure he hadn't been followed, then hurried down a dark alleyway towards the front of the building as a shadow shuffling through the night.

Looking back behind his shoulder one last time he turned the corner of the building and ran hard into a sturdy and tall, human-shaped figure that was cloaked in black and almost completely hidden by the dark night. The old man stumbled backward from the impact and gasped as fear quickly washed over him, then turned to gaze upon the hooded figure that towered menacingly above him. There was no face inside the darkness of the cloak. Just blackness as it gazed down silent and intimidating onto the old man.

"Oh my, I didn't see you there," the old man said breathing heavily and holding his chest. The large, cloaked figure did not reply but slowly nodded his cloaked head downward as it stood strong and still in the dark night.

Beyond the shadow there was a large wooden door illuminated only by a single flame. The two stared at each other for a moment, then after composing himself the old man rolled up his sleeve past his forearm and exposed a tattoo of a pipe and round orb above the wrist. The cloaked shadow glanced at the tattoo, nodded, then motioned towards the door. As he waved his arm the sound of a large beam unbarring the door and locks clicking could be heard on the other side of the door. After a quick nod the old man hurried past the cloaked figure and with a shove pushed the giant wooden door open and entered the stone building.

The heavy door swung open and inside gave way to a great hall. Large sturdy wooden beams lined the center of the room, and a fire roared inside of a large fireplace at the far end of the hall. There were roughly a dozen men inside the dimly lit room, all concealed in dark red cloaks, the same as the old man standing inside the doorway. They all turned towards the door as it slammed shut, cutting off the howling wind from the outside.

"He's here. Barreston is here." Voices could be heard, bouncing off the stone walls as the cloaked men whispered to one another. Then one of them approached.

"Barreston, we've been waiting. Everyone is here," the man spoke quietly with a slow nod.

"Is it here?" Barreston asked with a sense of urgency, pushing past the other man. The other man paused for a moment, confused, and did not answer. "The book? Is it here?" Barreston asked again. "Tell me!"

"Yes, yes," he replied. "Ehvsund arrived with it not long ago" he said pointing to a younger man sitting at the head of a large wooden table.

"Were any of you followed?" Barreston interrupted sounding worried. The others slowly shook their heads and replied with confused looks. "Are you sure?" He demanded, raising his voice.

"None of us were followed," Ehvsund answered. Ehvsund was noticeably younger than the other cloaked men who all had long beards extending from their cloaks. He was clean shaven and had his hood casually pulled back, exposing golden hair, unlike the others who's hoods hid most of their faces.

"Then bar the doors," Barreston ordered as he shuffled hurriedly into the great hall, still holding the large book in his arms.

"What has gotten you so riled up?" Ehvsund asked bewildered. "What is so important about this book?" he said while casually flipping the pages of a similar large book that was sitting in front of him. "This was not as easy to acquire as you made it seem. You know who, would not part with this worthless thing at all for some reason. I had to resort to, let's just say more aggressive methods to acquire it. Why is this old thing so important?"

"I am not sure yet," Barreston replied, slamming the book he had been carrying down onto the wooden table. It made a loud thud as it landed next to the other large and tattered book. "I found this book of magic recently. Deep in the woods just south of my cottage, concealed in a stone tomb. It is a book of spells but look." Barreston opened and began flipping through the large pages of the book. Some pages had partial, complex spells written on them while other pages seemed to be complete gibberish, and other pages were blank altogether. "I was trying to make sense of the blank pages, half spells, and utter nonsense. Then it began to feel oddly familiar, and it dawned on me. Long ago, during some questionable snooping, I came across a similar book. This book!" He said pointing at the other old, tattered book that Ehvsund had in front of him. Barreston paused as he examined the books, the others waiting and watching intently. "I didn't think anything of it at the time, but it must mean something," Barreston trailed off, rubbing his beard.

He began flipping through the large pages of both books, scanning the text and mysterious characters as he went. The other wizards huddled around him, also looking for some sort of meaning to the books. But many of the words were not legible, pages were left blank, and only half spells adorned the other pages. The group took significant time studying the books but nothing of importance ever seemed to present itself.

"He brought us all here for this?" one of the other members eventually scoffed from behind a dark hood. "I thought there was some sort of emergency, or someone needed our help. We should at least be practicing summoning crops if the upcoming summer season is especially dry again. This society was formed to help the kingdom." The others nodded that they agreed.

There were many secret societies of sorcerers and wizards in the kingdom, but this was the pinnacle of them, this was The Secret Order of Smoke and Orb, and they were not keen on wasting time or gathering just for fun or comradery as some other secret societies in the kingdom were. The members of Smoke and Orb were mainly focused on using their magic abilities to help the people of the kingdom. They were a powerful and talented group. All very educated in the ways of magic and dedicated to their craft. But calling them all out to a secret meeting in a faraway village in the middle of the night for seemingly nothing was beginning to not sit well with most of them.

"They're just two old books, friend," one of the others stated as he began to walk away. "Nothing worth all this fuss."

Barreston and Ehvsund ignored the negative comments and continued to diligently examine the two books for some time as the others wandered away and gathered at the other end of the hall to whisper among each other and use simple magic to make the flames of the fire dance and take shapes.

Page by page they flipped through, examining, pondering, then moving onto the next page. Then finally something caught Barreston's eye.

"Stop!" He said urgently as Ehvsund flipped the page. "Go back." Ehvsund turned the page back then Barreston gently pushed him aside. "Stand back."

Barreston pushed the two books together and overlapped the left page of the right book onto the right page of the left book. The pages fell together, and at the bottom of the page written in thick ink the word *Abborell* was spelled out, written across both pages. Barreston's eyes bulged wide as he saw the pages from two books fit together as one.

"Ehvsund, old friend, look!" He said in a hoarse whisper. Barreston then flipped the page of the right book to the left, and the left book page to the right. As the pages fell into the place, they started to recognize the pattern as a large spell, strewn across both pages. Their eyes lit up as the pages floated into place and when they finally came to rest, the book began to glow a soft blue light that illuminated the room. "My goodness," Ehvsund gasped.

The sudden bright, illuminating light from the book captured the attention of the other wizards and they all turned quickly to see the glowing books laid out in front of Barreston.

"It's a spell," Barreston announced, his finger scanning the page as he read the ancient characters. "And not a good one…" he trailed off, wrinkling his brow.

"What is it?" One of the others asked.

"Nothing!" Barreston snapped, then quickly grabbed the corner of the next page and flipped both pages over. Once again, left over right, right over left. The light glow around the books changed colors from a soft blue to a dark red as the pages landed in their place. The men all gazed in amazement as they slowly gathered around and huddled over the completed spell.

"These are powerful spells," Ehvsund said eventually, still in awe.

"Too powerful," Barreston replied, slowly turning the pages again.

They began flipping through the pages and scanning the different spells for some time. Each time the pages were flipped the light illuminating from the book would change colors, and they realized the spells were growing more powerful and atrocious with every page turned.

"This one doesn't look so bad," Ehvsund broke the silence while pointing at a drawing of a pyramid.

"That is absurd," Barreston replied. "What would anyone do with a giant stone pyramid? You would need a lot more sand for that spell than Mazeron has to offer anyway. It would have to be done in a desert," he said trailing off before continuing on to the next page.

As they continued flipping through the pages, one by one, the mood grew darker and more anxious as every page revealed increasingly destructive, and some just pure evil spells.

"We shouldn't be reading these," Barreston eventually whispered with a worried face, as the pages turned and the glow surrounding the books changed colors again.

"Anybody want to make it rain fire?" Ehvsund said with a forced laugh. "Harness the same type of energy that powers the sun to explode down onto another kingdom?"

"Oh, my, god," another said with a trembling voice as he read more text and the books continued to reveal their powerful magical secrets.

"Close it!" Barreston commanded urgently. "Nothing good can come from this amount of power."

"Now we know why they were kept separate from each other," Ehvsund replied, ignoring Barreston's command.

I said close the books!" He could feel the books pulling their accumulative magic inward, gathering it without permission. "Close it now!"

As he reached over the others to slam the book closed, suddenly a loud ball of energy exploded from the book and shot towards the ceiling. The group of wizards turned away and shielded their eyes from the blinding light and when they looked back a large blue sphere was floating over the books above them. They waited in silence for something else to happen, but the sphere floated motionless, emitting a soft hum and occasional pops of electricity. They waited and waited with intense intrigue, but the sphere seemed stable.

"I think it's a portal," Ehvsund announced, reading the text from the glowing page. "Imagine where it could lead to."

"We must try it," another said excitedly. Almost all of the others slowly nodded that they agreed. They were letting their excitement and curiosity of new magic get the better of them. Barreston knew better than to mess with the books and now realized why they had been kept apart and guarded, but the curiosity was getting to him too.

"It is our business to try," Ehvsund added. "We are wizards. Imagine the possibilities this could unlock."

Barreston did not reply but continued to think in silence as the sphere floated calmly in place. "So be it!" he said finally. "But any sign of trouble we close the book. Just a test, just this one spell."

The others agreed and soon the group gathered back around the books and individually the began scanning the text as they each began memorizing the spell. Luckily this one was fairly simple and didn't seem to be destructive. After some time Barreston spoke again.

"You know what to do. Let us begin…"

In moments the cloaked men began to chant in unison. Slow and quiet at first but steadily growing louder and faster. The same chant over and over. Their low voices echoed off the stone walls, reverberating louder and louder, the echoes acting like a second group of chanting men filling the room even more with sound while their ominous shadows flickered in the torchlight.

The sphere began to pop and buzz, getting louder as the men chanted. Then it began getting larger and giving off a bright magical light that lit up the room. It floated higher until it towered over their heads, still growing until it was a large magical orb. Then different sounds began to emerge from the orb, indicating something was beyond it. The mysterious sounds that sounded like growls and roars began to get louder and louder, closer and closer, until it was louder than a thunderous crashing waterfall.

Then suddenly and through the chaos, Barreston, at the head of the congregation, noticed something out of the corner of his eye and looked up from the books. In the great magical light that the floating orb was giving off he could see a shadow of a person near the doorway. There was a shadow but there was no person there to cast it. It crouched near the door, then moved.

"Spy!" his powerful voice broke the chant. The others turned to look and saw it immediately. It was there. A shadow that looked like a thin figure crouching near the wall by the doorway. It turned to run one way, then quickly turned back and darted for the door. The cloaked wizards turned and began to move on the shadow, breaking the spell and causing the sphere and light to collapse on itself behind them. The room went dark once again save for the faint flicker of torchlight which caused the shadow to disappear.

The cloaked men were rushing fast and were almost where the shadow had been when the bar on the door was thrust off by the invisible assailant and the door swung open with great force, slamming hard against the wall. As the men approached the door nothing else was seen except a few quick foot impressions in the wet dirt as the invisible intruder fled into the night.

Ehvsund ran out into the windy, dark night, but nothing could be seen besides a few distant trees illuminated in the moonlight. Then with a motion of his hands thrust quickly towards his torso, a blast of energy exploded from his hands and shot a great fireball out into the night. It hit a tree creating a loud explosion that lit up the night sky, but nothing else could be seen or heard from the fleeing spy. The men stood quietly in the doorway gazing into the blackness, listening for a sound, but all they could hear was the heavy wind blowing outside.

"Come back in, come in," Barreston said urgently as the others closed and barred the door, blocking out the howling wind from outside. "A spy," he said, thinking out loud while rubbing his beard. "We need to get these books out of here. Gather around."

The others huddled together near the roaring fire and after some nervous discussion about who might want to spy on their meetings, they created a crude plan to keep the two magic books apart from each other so they wouldn't fall into the wrong hands. The consequences of such things, they realized, could be catastrophic and whoever had been spying in on their meeting now also knew of the magic books of Abborell, as they named them, and the powerful and horrific spells that they contained.

"No one but us can possess these books," Barreston said later in the night as the others left the hall either by secret passage or the front door to throw off any unwanted onlookers. He was the last to gather his horse and leave the old stone building, which was quiet and lifeless once again.

The small village was quiet now as Barreston rode back towards his cottage in the foothills. No laughter in the distance or any sign of life at all. Just the howling wind and the moonlight. He was lost in thought about the events of the evening as he rode. The peacefulness had left him, and he found himself more troubled than he had felt in a long time. Who was the intruder? How many secret meetings had he seen? Why did he choose the Secret Order of Smoke and Orb out of all the other secret societies out there?

There were many secret societies in the Kingdom of Mazeron. All based on the furtherment and study of magic. Most would meet and study in secret because there had been a noticeable and growing disdain for magic throughout the kingdom for many years. Barreston wondered if for some reason another secret society had a reason to spy or come after them, but he could not think of any enemies they may have. Maybe the books had something to do with it? He patted the side satchel on his horse, making sure his book was still safely in his possession.

There very well could be a possibility that another secret society had ill intent and wanted to use their magic for evil and destruction. There were always threats like that in the kingdom, especially back in the early days of magic use. But the combined power of good men using magic had overpowered them and banished all evil magic from the lands long ago. Any time magic was used to hurt others or cause destruction they were quickly dealt with.

Barreston contemplated those days long ago, before magic use was a prominent part of life and how dangerous these lands used to be. People and the kingdom were defenseless against anything stronger than themselves. Plundering the villages was common. Dragons did as they pleased, consuming livestock and seemingly making nests wherever would cause the most destruction. Giant ill-tempered trolls roamed aimlessly through the foothills and wreaked havoc whenever their mood turned sour.

But as more people settled into the lands and magic became more commonplace, they worked together to create a safe and prosperous kingdom. The trolls whose small minds couldn't comprehend or make sense of magic were frightened of it and fled deep into the mountains. The dragons who were aggressive beasts by nature were still flight creatures when it came to flight or fight, so a well-placed fireball would send them fleeing from the area. They quickly learned not to settle in areas otherwise occupied by humans.

The sun was coming up over the horizon now, and behind the magnificent, towering, snowcapped mountains the light was touching the sky once again as Barreston and his horse slowly trotted up the dirt road back towards the settlement of Briardale and his cottage. Soon the sun had climbed higher into the sky it began beating down hot and heavily on his back. Sweat began to drip from his forehead, and he could feel the heat radiating up from his horses dark hair, so he steered towards one side of the trail and tried to gain some shade from the trees that lined the path.

Then something stung the exposed skin on his hand and began to itch. Moments later it happened again on his neck, then again on his other hand and his forehead. Any exposed skin was getting stung. It was the Leedles. They were small gnome type creatures only about five inches tall that were extremely ill tempered, territorial, and shot tiny arrows from little bows at any person or animal that would come across them. There were not a lot of bugs in the kingdom of Mazeron because of the frequent winds, and there were no mosquitos, but there were the Leedles. Heat and humidity made them extra angry, and any exposed skin would feel the sting of their tiny arrows. Most clothing would be sufficient at deflecting their attacks and would cause the arrows to just bounce off, but exposed skin was always at risk.

He swatted with his hand, motioning them to leave him alone, then brushed away a tiny arrow that was sticking out of his thumb. Usually, the arrows would just prick you and fall to the ground, but some of them would stick in until you brushed them off or pulled them out.

"What a nuisance," he grumbled aloud as he continued on. Their tiny screams and yells at his presence were barely audible to him. "We should use our combined magic to disintegrate every one of you monsters!" He shouted at them aloud as he thought about tossing a fireball in their direction and roasting a few of them. But he knew from experience that it only made them angrier and would just bring in more reinforcements. I wonder why they are always so mad? He thought as he pulled his sleeves down to protect himself from further stings. He continued watching them from atop his horse as they hurled pebbles and shot tiny arrows at him. Some were dressed in tiny tunics; some just had a cloth around their waists. He wondered if there was some sort of hierarchy in their insignificant little lives or if some were just more evolved or less lazy than others. It really didn't matter. They were a nuisance that were just part of life. Soon he picked up the pace so they couldn't get to him as easily. A brisk walk or a canter usually would suffice as their tiny legs could not keep up. The gallop created a breeze that blew refreshingly into his face and the stings stopped as he and his horse continued on more quickly now towards Briardale, and not long after were eventually back to the trail leading up to his cottage.

As he approached the cottage there was smoke coming from the chimney and the smell of food wafted through the air. A faint smile brushed across his hardened face as he tied up his horse and walked calmly to the edge of his property in front of the cottage.

He was high upon his hill staring out into the land, watching the sun stretch across the fields as it rose higher into the fresh morning sky.

Yes, after decades of hard work these were safe and prosperous lands now. He stepped to the edge of the path and gazed off into the distance. This was Briardale. A peaceful settlement in the foothills that overlooked the valley of the kingdom. He gazed across large orchards of perfectly lined fruit trees and scattered cottages that dotted the foothills. Most of the inhabitants of Briardale were fruit farmers that tended to their own orchards. They were a self-sufficient, usually reserved bunch, and one living in Briardale could go for multiple moon cycles without seeing any of their neighbors, if they chose to do so.

The foothills of Briardale

They were largely left alone up here and would gather news of the kingdom when they occasionally went into the villages in the valley below to sell their fruit.

Barreston turned his gaze from the foothills of Briardale to the vast green valleys below. He saw a faint haze rising from the fields as the sun evaporated the night's dew. Noise could be heard echoing across the mountains as the gold mines sprang to life for the new day. The gold mines were the lifeline of these lands and the kingdom. People traveled from faraway and mysterious lands to trade goods for the gold the mines produced. Not only were the mountains surrounding the kingdom massive and beautiful, but they were also filled with what seemed to be endless large veins of gold.

But the world was small for most of the citizens of Mazeron. Because of the vast forests and massive, prominent mountains that surrounded the kingdom, most of the villagers would not venture to other lands in their entire lifetime. So as far as any of them knew, this was the center of commerce and civilization in their little world. Nowhere else had gold and trade as plentiful as the kingdom. All different races of beings would come here to trade goods for gold, and no one in the kingdom went without. Unless it was by their own poor choices and undoing.

In the distance toward the west side of the valley towered the castle. On a clear day, from Barreston's cottage in the foothills of Briardale you could make out the individual guards walking the ramparts. The flag of Mazeron, green with a white galloping deer, blew lazily in the morning wind atop the tallest towers, which were topped with a cone shape made of the kingdom's finest gold. The golden caps could be seen from miles and miles away, like a lighthouse guiding weary travelers from faraway lands safely to the kingdom.

Below the towers was a large balcony which sat atop the main body of the castle between the battlements. This is where it was common for the king to address the citizens or give news on the kingdom's happenings. Barreston would see the king standing out on the large balcony from time to time, silently gazing onto his kingdom in the mornings. King Victus, as he was named, was a strong king both mentally and physically, and he ruled the kingdom with justice and fairness. He lived in the castle with his wife, a beautiful and intelligent queen, and together they had one son.

On this morning, Barreston witnessed the guards walking along the battlements as usual, their metal helmets were glinting in the morning sunlight. On the main balcony of the castle stood a tall, thin, black shadow. It stood motionless with hands on the rails, overlooking the courtyard in silence. It was the king's wizard, Maub. Barreston shuttered at the name. He had never fully trusted the wizard, and from the moment he first met the man he had a bad feeling about him. A distrust, whether it was misplaced or not, came from deep within his stomach, which was usually correct on most matters.

Maub, the king's wizard and head counsel, was an almost-seven-foot tall, craggy old man with long crooked fingers extending out from a long black cloak. The shoulders and back area of the cloak were adorned with thick black raven feathers, making the old wizard's silhouette resemble a black vulture.

He was known only as Maub. No one knew what family or lands he came from or anything about his history, but everyone seemed to know of him by the time he was called into the position of the king's wizard.

Before that, he would show up in magic circles of all types throughout the years. The wizards knew him, and the mages, sorcerers, covens, and druids. It was rumored that even the fairies in the woods that lit up the forests in the night with a bright glow were visited by him frequently. Everyone knew who he was, but he rarely spoke to anyone past normal formalities and was never seen in the company of anyone else, except the king of course.

Barreston remembered him at many secret and public meetings throughout the years. He was a shadow. Watching from the wings, learning what he could, and honing his own skills in private. He wasn't the type of wizard to display his magic in proud shows of power. Instead, he hoarded it like a secret. Everyone seemed to know that he was immensely powerful, but it was rarely if ever actually seen.

The king first noticed Maub's powers when he saved him from a rare assassination attempt. Years ago, King Victus and his queen were in their carriage being taken through the village markets to the outskirts of town, towards the orchards of Briardale, which was a common area for them to picnic on pleasant afternoons. It was a normal outing; the king's coach would often be seen throughout the kingdom, and because he wasn't particularly fond of attention or telling the villagers how they should be living their lives, most people were disinterested in his presence, and his happenings went largely unnoticed.

Then, suddenly, out of the crowd a massively large and burly man pushed through the bystanders and started towards the coach with a dagger in hand. People instantly noticed and ran towards him attempting to subdue the man, but they were brushed aside and heaved to the ground as he picked up speed towards the carriage. It was just an instant, and he was there, ripping the door open, drawing back the dagger, about to plunge it deep into the chest of the startled king, who was frozen in fear at the sudden but fierce surprise attack. The king closed his eyes tightly, extending his arms in defense, waiting for the blow. But nothing happened. When the king opened his eyes again the man was gone. Simply vanished into thin air like he had never existed in the first place. The onlookers glanced at each other with confused looks, each trying to affirm one another that they were not losing their minds and that the man had actually been there just a moment before.

Then they noticed him. There stood Maub. Half crouched at the edge of the street, staring at his hands raised up in front of his face as if he had never seen his own hands before. Bewilderment and amazement in his eyes. The crowd immediately pieced together what had happened. The large craggy, intimidating wizard that they all knew had made the attacker vanish, and he had saved the king. It wouldn't have been such a big deal if the attacker was changed into something like a chicken or a frog. That was normal magic because the molecules and matter were still there, just rearranged. But the complete disappearance of mass was astounding and, until then, thought to be impossible.

Everyone froze in place with fear and intrigue in their eyes. Many scrambled away. Among the chaos Maub stood still. Then there was a yell from the carriage and a snap at the reins as it began to speed away from the scene. The carriage slowed as it passed Maub, who was waiting for them as they approached. Words were exchanged between wizard and the king, then the wizard climbed into the coach as it sped away, and they were gone. From then on, Maub would be known throughout the kingdom as the king's wizard and head counsel of the castle.

"I still don't trust that wizard," Grumbled Barreston as he turned from the peaceful morning view and made his way back towards his cottage on the hill. He walked up the three steps to a large wooden door and went inside, where he was greeted with a soft hug by a young woman.

"Out late again, I see," she said cheerfully, making her way back to the fire and stirring a pan of mush. "Another meeting?"

"Yes. And an odd one too," Barreston replied as he quietly put the book back onto a large bookshelf, concealing it in plain sight for the time being. "How were your travels to your parents?" he asked.

"Uneventful," she replied. "They are well. They were happy to see their grandson after so many months."

"He's growing fast," Barreston said, looking down at a small child crawling around the room on the floor, exploring everything he could get his hands on. He was right. The child already had wide shoulders and a thick core. "He's shaped like a brick!" Barreston laughed.

The child was his grandson, and the woman was his recently deceased son's widow. You lose so much in this life, he thought, and he could not help but notice how heavy his heart was when he thought of his departed wife and son.

Barreston's daughter-in-law, whose name was Elisha, and her son lived with Barreston here in the foothills. When his son passed away unexpectedly it was decided that they would live with Barreston because, although he was older, he was a very wise and powerful man, and they would be safe here with him in Briardale. It was also the hope that the child would also be a magic wielder like Barreston and would need his guidance and mentorship throughout his life.

Magic was fickle though. You were either born with the ability to wield magic or you weren't. And even if they were born with the gift, the person would have to study and practice tirelessly to learn how to use it. It was rarely seen, if ever, for someone to just *be* a powerful magic user. Barreston's only son unfortunately did not have that gift. Sometimes it would skip a generation. Sometimes it would skip multiple generations then show back up in a bloodline centuries later. It was a recessive, unexplained gene. Some bloodlines never had it at all, and some that did would choose not to advance or use their abilities and it would simply fizzle out of a bloodline.

For those reasons, magic users had always been a minority in these lands. And now that it had become such a normal part of life for most people in these modern times, interest in the subject was dwindling.

Not only was it dwindling, but recently there had been a noticeable disdain creeping into society on the subject, and toward the users of magic in general. It had become common if you visited a pub near one of the mining villages to hear conversations about it. Men poking fun at and jeering at the subject of magic and the often-odd wizards that use it. Calling it the old ways, outdated, and odd. Barreston recognized the contempt for what it was, mostly jealousy mixed with a bit of fear. It was human nature for people to be scared of things that they didn't understand. He hoped that as time went on people would be more accepting of those who weren't all exactly like the main group. If they understood how much progress and safety the use of magic had provided these lands for centuries, then they would not have such a bitterness towards it. But people tend to forget things very fast. Because the days of dragons, trolls, and marauders terrorizing the countryside were over for the time being, people had developed the notion that it could never happen again.

So, Barreston and his little family knew the importance of magic use in society which is why he worked so tirelessly on his abilities and dedicated his life to the craft. It was obviously his hope that his grandson, too, would inherit his abilities, but that was yet to be seen.

For now, he would continue studying his magic book of Abborell and other magic texts as usual. The more he understood about the books, he figured, the less likely something catastrophic would happen and give the magic wielders of the kingdom a worse reputation. But that seemed inevitable to happen anyway.

Chapter 2: The Incident

Weeks later, it was a calm and peaceful evening outside one of the popular pubs in the center of town, near the castle. The cobblestone streets were scattered with random people in no hurry to get anywhere. Villagers were walking home from their daily duties and tasks, enjoying the warm summer night air. The inside of the meeting house was rowdy and loud with festive chatter fueled by ale and food.

Out of nowhere there was a loud explosion from within the pub accompanied by multiple quick, bright, and colorful flashes of light and smoke. The front doors swung open violently with a crash, and a man dressed in all black came hurrying and stumbling from the pub, as if he was being chased. Another explosion of bright colored light and sparks followed him, and a loud commotion came from behind him within the pub as he fled. He rushed down the steps and jumped on the nearest horse, then began to ride fast down the main street towards the castle at a fierce pace.

As he rode away, a giant rooster-tail of colorful sparks and white flashes of light shot high into the night sky behind his fleeing horse. The bright colorful sparks flew high into the sky and illuminated the street, then began to fall lazily back to the earth like a beautiful and colorful snowfall.

As the sparks fell and surrounded the villagers who were passing by, they became amused by the colorful display, and many began to dance and play in the beautiful sparkles that were raining down, spinning and twirling in the magicalness of it all. As they became more engulfed in the falling sparks they began to laugh and wiggle, as if they were being tickled by an invisible ghost. Then, in the peak of their laughter and playfulness, they one by one suddenly exploded into a magical burst of colorful light, and where once stood a person, now stood a sheep.

Dozens of villagers began turning into sheep as the sparks rained down onto the street. Some began to notice what was happening and tried to run away, but it was too late for them. They were already engulfed in magical colors. Within minutes, the streets were littered with wandering, grazing sheep and shocked onlookers who witnessed it but were lucky enough to be far enough away to not be affected by this wicked display of magic.

In the morning light of the next day the damage was surveyed by the king and authorities, known as the King's Guard. The destruction went on for blocks. The fronts of many buildings had been destroyed by fire, and dozens of sheep wandered aimlessly around the streets. Smoke from the ashes blew lazily into the wind, burning the eyes and throats of the villagers as they awoke to see the havoc that had been caused the night before. Everyone looked for answers and speculated about what had caused this interruption to their usual peaceful existence, but there were none. No one knew who the mysterious rider was or what the reason or motive behind all this destruction was. Some figured it was an accident. Some thought a more sinister plot was at work.

But the people of the Mazeron were a proud people and would not let this destruction and unease stand. By midday a cleanup effort had begun, and word was sent from the castle into the villages to fetch all magic users far and wide to help in turning the unfortunate villagers back into their human forms, if that was at all possible.

Word reached Barreston high up on his hill in Briardale later that day, and he readied himself immediately. Despite the horrible news, he was quite literally excited to be able to help others with his abilities and soon he was off towards the castle.

The cleanup happened quick. Within two days, the wizards and sorcerers of the kingdom had changed most of the unfortunate villagers back into their normal selves, save for a few stragglers that had wandered far off into the neighboring grasslands. None of them could remember a thing about what had happened, and they had no recollection of what it was like to be a sheep whatsoever.

The rebuilding of the damaged buildings would happen slowly and over time, but that could wait. For now, the king had announced it was time for a celebration and had called for anyone that had helped to gather at the castle in two weeks' time for a ball in recognition of all their help. Before they left the scene of the accident they were to sign their names on the castle's guest registration, which was being kept my Maub in one of the lesser damaged buildings.

Barreston entered the dark room to sign his name on the guest list. Maub sat silently at the far end of the room, guarding the large book. The candlelight flickering in his eyes made it an ominous sight for a supposedly happy occasion. Barreston approached in silence, expecting Maub to say something. A "thank you" or a speech of some sort. But the old craggy wizard only motioned with one hand toward the book for Barreston to sign his name and the location where the official invitation could be sent.

The guest list was already long, Barreston noticed as he penned his name. He was pleasantly surprised to see how many wizards were still in these lands. He recognized many of their names. A good bunch, he thought to himself as he put his signature down with a swoop of the pen. Replacing the pen back in the jar of ink, he gave Maub a small smile, and their eyes met. Even on this occasion, he still only felt mistrust and deceit in Maub's eyes. He wondered how, out of all the good wizards out there, the king decided to choose Maub as the castle's head wizard and counsel of the kingdom. Barreston then turned back toward the door and left the building feeling uneasy about the encounter.

Days later, Barreston's usual peaceful existence was interrupted when he was awoken by a pounding on his front door. It was hard and consistent. Trying to figure out what was going on and still being half asleep, he could hear someone outside yelling, "Barreston, open the door quick. I have news from the castle."

Barreston got out of bed, dressed quickly, then walked through the front room where Elisha was sitting with the baby with a concerned look on her face. Unexpected visitors to their cottage, way up here on the hill, were a rare occurrence. Barreston opened the door and there stood Ehvsund.

"What are you doing here?" Barreston asked harshly. "Were you followed?" He grabbed Ehvsund and pulled him inside quickly slamming the door behind him. "Is it the book? It's the book, isn't it? There's something wrong with the books. Who stole the book!?"

"No, no Barreston," Ehvsund said, correcting his collar. "Calm down, the books are safe. I'm afraid the news I have is much worse.

"What could be worse than years of our collective hard work vanishing before we even have the chance to test it?"

Barreston replied, talking once again about the two magic books of Abborell and one of his biggest fears of late.

"Well, that's basically it," Ehvsund replied. "The castle, the king. They've… They've… They have banned magic! All throughout the kingdom!" Ehvsund was shaking his arms and raising his voice as he said it, then he shoved a piece of crumbled paper into Barreston's chest. Barreston took the paper, unfolded it, and then began to read…

By order of the King.

As a result of recent tragedies, all use of magic is henceforth banished from these lands.

Refusal to obey order will result in immediate imprisonment or death.

This includes ALL magic. No exceptions.
Including but not limited to...

Magic use for healing

Magic use for farming

Magic use for mining

Magic use for protection

Magic use for fun

Magic use for destruction

ALL MAGIC IS BANNED.

All magic items and books containing text pertaining to the study and use of magic shall be turned in at the castle immediately where they will be safely destroyed. Instructions for book drop off are at the castle gates. Failure to hand over magic texts and items will result in imprisonment or death.

This is for the safety and protection of all citizens of the great kingdom of Mazeron.

The king thanks you for your cooperation and understanding.

"What is the meaning of this? How could this happen?" Barreston said angrily, beginning to shake. A feeling of being trapped and helpless like he had never known washed over him and the room began to spin. "I need to sit down," he exclaimed, then slowly stepped backward and onto a chair where he sat silently staring at the letter, unable to find the words or answer to make this problem and feeling go away.

"No doubt a short-sighted response to the incident that happened last week," Ehvsund said, trying to calm down the old wizard.

"Surely they can't be serious," he exclaimed, still trembling. "They cannot possibly mean everyone. Not me, not us. I know how to wield my powers safely, all of us in the group do. We are good people who have lived our entire lives never causing any harm to anyone. They cannot possibly mean us. This is just a warning for novice magic users like whoever caused that tragedy. Not us," Barreston was rambling, shaking, and rubbing the sweat from the brow as he spoke.

Ehvsund stood silent, still near the door. He could see the pain on Barreston's face. The man had dedicated his entire life to magic. It was quite literally his identity. What would he do without it? He looked so old and helpless right now, even though Ehvsund knew Barreston was an incredibly powerful wizard. He knew the story of Barreston's son's death and how Barreston almost single handedly took out a group of Marauders that sprang a surprise attack on the area, looking to loot and plunder the foothills before vanishing back into the safety of the high mountain passes where none would pursue.

Barreston's son was a fierce fighter, one of the best. But he was not a magic user and was simply overpowered by the group of Marauders before he could escape or get to safety. He held them off long enough for Barreston and more help to arrive, where in a blinding rage at his son's murder, Barreston laid waste to most of them with incredible destructive forces of magic that no one in these lands had ever seen before. The other villagers of Briardale were saved from the attack but at a great cost to Barreston and his family.

"Send word to the members of Smoke and Orb," Barreston finally announced. "We will meet in the woods at Fayes cross at midnight in three days to discuss this predicament." Ehvsund agreed, then a plan was put into place to alert the others, and he departed as quickly as he came.

Three days later, Barreston sighed heavily as he finished penning a letter to the king that explained how poverty, cruelty, and instability were the baseline of human existence, and without good people using superior strength to constantly push away from that baseline, society would automatically return it. He warned that with magic leaving the kingdom the void would be filled with instability, violence, and destruction then went into great detail to explain how much magic had helped the kingdom throughout the years and begged him to rethink his decision. THE MEEK WILL GO EXTINCT; he penned as a final warning before folding and sealing the letter.

Still sitting at his desk in the cottage, he looked out the open window. The sun was beginning to dip into evening again. The time had come to meet the others from Smoke and Orb, deep in the woods at Fayes cross. He stood up, gathered his robes, his staff, and made his way outside towards his horse. Those meaningful words were still resonating in his mind.

"The meek will go extinct," he muttered under his breath. A warning that would resonate through time. He walked over to his large outdoor wooden picnic style table that sat under a large tree near the stables and hovering his staff over the table the words began to burn into the wood for all future generations to see. The meek will go extinct, he whispered as the words burned down the center of the table. He grinned slightly, pleased with his work, then turned back towards his horse and started his ride.

He rode the usual dirt road downward toward the valley, but halfway down this time he took a sharp left on a small deer trail which traversed the lower section of the mountain for some time. The trail took him steadily downward, and he could see it below leading into the thick green forest of pine trees.

As he rode, he thought of the first book of magic ever found, which was discovered centuries ago, buried in the ground. No one knew who wrote it or how it had gotten there. It was the first magical text ever known and it had introduced magic to the world. Not all people had the gift to use it, but those who did were able to study the book and pass its teachings along, creating other magic wielders in the process. This led to the discovery of more magic texts and objects, which is what led Barreston to recently find the second magic book of Abborell. Once you were a magic wielder you could feel the presence of it in the air and all around you. Like air or gravity, it was always there. It could also be felt when someone else was using it. Magic bent time and physics, so if someone else was using it, it would be felt by others like a ripple in a pond.

The sun was already getting low, darkening the sky as he approached the forest. But when the trail finally dipped into the trees, it became instantly dark under the thick canopy of trees. Shadows played tricks on his mind as he rode. Suddenly, out of the corner of his eye, he saw an animal or man crouched eerily at the forest floor, which startled him. But upon further inspection it was just a tree stump in the waning evening light. Sticks cracked and wolves howled in the distance, while the wind rustled leaves, making it impossible to tell if there was animal or person stalking him or just the leaves in the wind. It was an ominous trek, and he was forced to stay alert and cautious as the trail wound through the ever-darkening, thick forest.

Eventually the thin trail through the woods brought him to what looked like an incredibly large tree, with burly branches that rose into the sky like thick tentacles. But upon further inspection he could tell that it wasn't a tree at all, but the remains of some sort of monster of the woods. A remnant from a battle long ago and a reminder of the dangers that lurked in the forests. Barreston marveled at the size of the beast that had since been retaken by nature, then turned off the trail and went past it, delving deeper into the thick woods. It was almost pitch black now, the forest floor barely illuminated by faint whispers of moonlight through the canopy of the trees.

Then ahead of him Barreston saw a faint light flickering in the distance. He turned his horse slightly and together they wound slowly through the forest towards the light. Moments later, another faint light appeared, then another. They were small candle flames in the distance, lined in a straight row. He came upon the candles lining the path then followed the now illuminated and wider path through the forest. The illuminated trail dipped downward, deeper into the forest, then leveled out again as he continued through the night. Then suddenly the forest opened before him and there he stood atop his horse in a large clearing amongst the dense trees.

He could see the outlines and shadows of other cloaked men, huddled in the darkness at the far end of the clearing. Lanterns faintly illuminated the perimeter and in the center of it stood a large stone cross with the ends of each point being exaggerated in size compared to the thinner center of the stone cross. It stood the height of three men. There was a circle etched into the very center of the cross with lines that resembled rays of the sun extending from it. This was Fayes cross. The location where Barreston had discovered the second book of magic, buried deep in the base of the stone monument. The cross, they believed, was to represent the crossing of two worlds and the light rays extending from the center signified a portal between the two. It wasn't until the Order of Smoke and Orb had conjured a portal that fateful night that the monument started to make any sense.

Now this was one of the society's secret meetings areas. They felt confident that no one besides them had stepped foot in this clearing for hundreds of years, as it was hidden well, deep in the forest.

Barreston dismounted along the perimeter of the clearing, tied up his horse near the others, then made his way towards the far side of the clearing where the other cloaked men stood silently waiting. One of them approached him in the darkness, his face concealed by a thick woolen hood and the darkness of the night. As he approached, he knew it to be Ehvsund.

"None of the men were followed," Ehvsund said in a whisper. "Not to our knowing anyway." Barreston nodded as they made their way towards the others. Then approaching the group of wizards, Barreston spoke.

"Brothers of Smoke and Orb," he announced as he approached the group. The others gathered around in the faint glow of the moonlight. "As you all know we have a predicament with the castle." The others nodded slowly beneath dark hoods in agreement. "I'm not going to lie to you," Barreston continued, "I do not know if it can be fixed. What I am proposing is we limit our practice to this location only, and only with concealment spells in place. The books of Abborell are too important to forget about now and we must continue our studies of them." A thick silence hung in the air as the others contemplated the risks of what Barreston was proposing, and he felt their uneasiness.

"It's too risky," one of the other wizards stated aloud. The others nodded that they agreed.

"We're just as curious about the books as you are, Barreston.," another said., "But I just don't know if it's worth the risk. At least for now."

"The risk is minimal," Barreston replied quickly. "No one will be able to sense the ripple of magic from out here, and even if they did, we will be long gone by the time they can get here. We can cast concealment spells around the perimeter, and no one will ever know we are here." The others contemplated in silence what Barreston was proposing while he awaited their decisions.

"I suppose just a little magic, every so often won't hurt," Ehvsund finally broke the silence. After another moment the others started to nod and mumble that they agreed too.

"Then we are in agreement!" Barreston announced. "I recommend we discuss the healing center tonight. Any thoughts on location?" He asked.

"We can't have a magic healing center anymore, Barreston," Ehvsund replied with an exaggerated tone. "We can't use magic in public anymore!"

"We can try another spell out of the book?" another wizard chimed in while turning about and picking up one of the large books of Abborell that had been sitting on the ground in the darkness behind the group of wizards.

"Why did you bring that?" Barreston asked quickly, pulling back with wide frantic eyes.

"I thought… I thought you wanted me to," the wizard replied.

"The books can be sensed, you fool!" It could lead them right to us!" Barreston was visibly angry. "Not to mention we cannot let the books fall into the wrong hands. Any other hands but ours! The books need to be hidden, immediately," Barreston's eyes darted back and forth as fear and anxiety began to rush through his body. The others began arguing amongst each other and a commotion began to build. "We need to get out of here," Barreston announced, already heading towards his horse. "Hide that book!" he yelled back as he walked away.

Then, as he turned to flee, Barreston suddenly began to feel odd. A presence was surrounding him like a silent buzz, and the hairs on his arms began to stick up. He paused and looked at Ehvsund who was already looking back at him with a distressed look on his face. Barreston's heart began to race, and his eyes darted back and forth to the other men. All were stopped in place, looking about with confusion and fear upon their faces. Barreston looked at his hands as they began to feel numb. The feeling of an invisible energy was in the air all about him.

Then out of nowhere his head was thrust back violently, and he felt an extreme force like he had been hit with a club in the center of his back. The breath left his body and before he could contemplate what was happening, he was staring upward at the sky. Confusion rushed over him and frantically looking about while trying to catch his breath he realized he was floating in the air on his back, slowly being raised towards the sky. The initial impact had caused him to drop his staff and he could still barely breathe. Jerking his head around wildly to get a grasp on what was happening, he could see the others were in the same position. Helplessly being lifted into the air until they stopped about a tall man's height off the ground.

Barreston tried to flail his arms, grasping for anything, but they barely moved. It was as if he was immersed in a heavy invisible liquid that was keeping him from regular movement. His head turned slowly to the side, then he caught sight of a shadowy figure out of the corner of his eye, emerging from the dark woods beyond. At first it was a shadow, then a man came into the dim light. He advanced methodically and slowly through the group of wizards suspended helplessly in the air. He stared heavily at each one of them with black hollow eyes as he passed, saying nothing but peering deep into their souls. His head bore no hair and his face was painted, blue on one side and red on the other that gave an eerie, and frightening otherworldly look to him.

"You aren't supposed to be practicing magic," the man said slowly and flat. "You may…" He paused. "…have heard about it." The calm in his voice was chilling and threatening.

He turned toward Barreston. "I know… *you* have," he said, staring with his soulless black eyes. Barreston saw hate in the hollow eyes. A burning hatred. But why? They had never even met before as far as Barreston could recall in his frantic thought.

Confusion rushed through his mind. How was he being so overpowered when he himself was such a powerful magic user? Who was this man, capable of overpowering all of them at once? And why did he have such hatred towards them?

These questions burned through each of their minds as the man turned calmly and walked away from the group of suspended wizards. Then, when he was barely visible in the moonlight, he stopped. The Brothers of Smoke and Orb were still suspended helplessly in the air, each watching the man and exchanging glances, looking for any sign of hope that one of them had a plan or the power to get free of the thick hold that was bearing down upon them.

Slowly the man crouched down low to the forest floor and picked up the magic book of Abborell. "This, as you know, is illegal," the man said in a monotone, flat voice. "There must be consequences."

Then the man crouched down, just a shadow against the forest and began slowly and methodically rocking back and forth, starting slow at first but steadily increasing his pace until he was quickly rocking back and forth, silently. The wizards were overcome with fear at the bizarre display, then abruptly and without warning, like a predatory animal attacking its prey, the man turned and with lightning speed he bounded violently toward the wizards. It all happened so fast in Barreston's rushing mind, and within moments, there was nothing.

Earlier that evening, back at Barreston's cottage on the hillside in Briardale, a thick fog was slowly making its way down the mountain through the canyons and towards the foothills as the warmth of the afternoon gave way to the incoming coolness of the night. A soft evening rain had left the ground damp and the air smelled of fresh raindrops as the evening began to set in.

Elisha was reading a fairytale story to her infant son when suddenly out of the silence she heard some commotion outside, then saw shadows rushing past through the crack in one of the shutters. She paused and listened. She heard the faint sound of footsteps. Lots of them, all around the cottage. She quietly jumped up, holding the baby close and peered out of the crack in the shutters to see what was going on.

There were men outside of the cottage. She counted at least eight of them. They were soldiers but she did not recognize them as the king's guards, who she was familiar with. Instead of the prancing deer of Mazeron logo, which was the normal symbol of the kingdom worn by the soldiers, their breast plates were adorned with a dragon wrapped around a wizard's staff instead. A symbol which she did not recognize.

Dressed in light armor and metal helmets with their swords drawn, the soldiers were huddled together outside of the cottage, talking amongst each other in whispers. Beyond them on the path leading up to the cottage she noticed something on the trail. It was the height of a man, almost shaped like a man, but it was made of a dark fog or smoke. It bellowed thick from the center of the shape then whirled away in the wind as it rose from the mysterious being. She knew immediately that this apparition was someone using a cloaking spell. Whoever brought these soldiers here did not want their identity to be known. The apparition stood motionless on the trail, watching the soldiers. She stepped back into the room and paused to think about the situation. What was going on? Why were they here and dressed in armor like they were going to battle?

Then there was a strong pounding at the door which shook the whole cottage. "By order of the king, open the door or we will break it in!" A soldier yelled loudly as the door pounded.

Scared, she stepped back from the door, holding her baby tightly to her body. This wasn't right. They weren't here to talk. Instinct set in immediately and she knew what to do. She and Barreston had been over this a dozen times. She turned and ran to the back of the cottage into her bedroom and placed the baby on the bed. Then she turned to a chest on the floor and hurled it from its resting place with impressive strength to the corner of the room. She kneeled down and placed her hands on the floorboards until she found a small groove. With one finger, she lifted open a secret door. Inside was one of the magic books of Abborell, some random items, and a tunic which glittered brightly like a thousand diamonds, even in the fading sunlight. She lifted the tunic and held it up high. It turned from silver into waves of every color of the rainbow that washed over it as it moved through the light.

At the other end of the cottage there was a loud crash as the door was smashed to the ground, and she could hear the heavy footsteps as the soldiers came rushing in quick. She grabbed the tunic then ran back to the baby. Heavy fast footsteps were coming down the hall now. She slipped the tunic over her head. It glittered brightly even in the shadowy room. She grabbed the baby just as three soldiers entered the room, then she vanished into thin air only a moment before they entered and looked directly at her. She stood motionless, watching them peer about the room. Terror gripped her and she was almost unable to breathe as they looked right at her from just two arms lengths away. She was certain they would walk over, grab her and take her away right then. But the soldiers turned and walked out of the room slowly. It worked. The tunic worked. They couldn't see her!

Still holding the baby tightly to her chest, she crouched low and walked slowly toward the open window at the back of the cottage. The soldiers were yelling with obvious frustration in the front room, and their booming voices of anger made her heart race. Slowly she put one leg out the window, and with one arm steadying herself and the other holding her baby tight, she dropped from the window and landed on the ground safely outside. It was still light out but the fog rolling in from the canyons above was moving quickly towards the cottage.

As she was creeping away from the cottage she heard the soldiers enter the room again. There was the sound of loud commotion and crashes as they threw things around the room, searching for something or someone.

"I found something!" one of them said. Elisha knew they had found the secret compartment that she had left open. Anxiety set in. She knew the contents of the compartment were of great value to Barreston, and most of them pertained to powerful magic. Now it was all in the hands of these soldiers. But the only thing that mattered to her right now was getting out of here and getting the baby to safety. But where would she go? There were only a few other dwellings nearby. She needed to get to someone for help, and she needed to get there fast.

Quickly she walked away from the cottage, trying to stay quiet while being as swift as possible. She was almost to the dirt road behind the cottage that led through the orchards when she heard a yell from back at the cottage window.

"Footsteps, here! Out the window!" one of the soldiers shouted. Elisha looked down and her heart sank. There in the damp ground were perfect footsteps leading right back to the window. By the time she looked up, the soldiers were already leaping out of the window. She turned and began to run as fast she could towards the nearest dwelling. She could see it through the orchard trees and haze up ahead. She ran like she had never run before, but glancing back through the haze and incoming fog she could see the soldiers were gaining on her.

Finally, she made it to the steps in front of the nearby cottage. Glancing back again the soldiers were close behind, already coming up the pathway to the cottage.

"There she is!" they yelled out almost in unison. Confusion overwhelmed Elisha. How could they see her? Frantically she glanced about and quickly realized her undoing. In the cool evening air and after the days light rains the thick haze had set in. Wherever she moved a swirl of humidity would follow and gust around her. Invisible or not, they had her. Her heart sank.

But even in the moment of deepening grief she knew what to do. The soldiers were still far enough off. She ran quickly to the side porch of the house, took off the invisibility tunic exposing her position for all eyes to see, then quickly laid the baby on the ground and draped the tunic over him. He instantly disappeared as she laid it across him.

Almost that very instant her pursuers came charging from the front of the cottage and saw her standing there with wide eyes. They gave no thought as to why. She turned to run, and they quickly pursued. They caught up to her on the road not far from the cottage and pushed her hard to the ground, then surrounded her. Any chance of escape was now gone.

"What do you want from me!?" she cried out in despair. There was a pause while the soldiers exchanged glances.

"Where is the baby?" one of the soldiers asked sternly.

"I don't have a baby!" she yelled back in defiance. The soldiers each took their time looking about and listening for any signs of a baby until they were forced to agree with her statement. They stayed silent as Elisha lay on the ground. Her eyes darting back and forth, still looking for a way out. The soldiers waited and still said nothing, almost like they were mocking her. She was about to speak when the apparition that she saw outside of the cottage slowly advanced up the dirt road towards them. It was holding Barreston's large book of magic. The second magic book of Abborell. Suddenly the soldiers jumped into action in the presence of the apparition. Then a voice came from within the whirling smoke around the being.

“You are being charged with usssing magic and being in possessssion of magic itemsss,” the apparition hissed through the whirling smoke which caused its voice to ominously draw out the S sounds. “Which have been deemed illegal by the king, King Victussss.” the hissing whispers continued.

Confused and set back at the absurdity of it all, Elisha stuttered with her reply. “That… that just happened three days ago!” she said trembling. “We… we haven’t had time to make the journey back to the valley to turn the items in. I don’t even know magic. I have never used magic in my life!” A slice of hope resonated through her mind at the possibility of getting out of this dangerous mess, knowing now that she was in fact innocent of the charges being levied against her. Then the smokey apparition approached, getting uncomfortably close. It spoke slowly, drawing out the “S” sounds, which made the presence of the being even more frightful.

“Magic, as you know, can be passssed down from generation to generation,” the apparition said slowly. “Where is the grandssson of Barresssston?” The apparition held a long pause, waiting for Elisha to reply, and to give up her son’s location. Then he continued. “Should the grandson possesss, such powers, he himself is illegal, and you are breaking the king’s lawsss by being in possession of him.” It paused again, waiting for the charges and severity of the situation to sink in. “You will be sssspared, if you take us to him,” the smokey apparition finished. The hiss of his voice sent chills through her body. She knew he was lying. She could tell by the situation that he intended on killing them both. So, she said nothing. The smoke-like apparition and the soldiers waited, beginning to show more and more impatience, but she stayed silent through the tension.

“Kill her!” the apparition finally hissed, as it turned away quickly and floated back towards the soldiers. They looked at each other in silence.

“An unarmed woman?” one of them asked finally. “We can’t do that. We won’t do that! You said we were here to arrest her for breaking the law.

"I haven't seen her break any law," another soldier chimed in.

Then, the smokey apparition moved toward one of the soldiers and handed him the large book of magic he was carrying. He turned and faced the soldier who was speaking out. Confusion and fear immediately rushed over the soldier's face, and he turned to run but froze in place before he could even fully turn around. The man's eyes darted back and forth as the confusion set in. Invisible ties bound him, and he could not move. Then the apparition drew the soldier's sword from its sheath. There he stood among the orchard trees and fog, an ominous black cloud wielding a large sword. There was visible terror on all the men's faces. Then the sword swung through the air at the disobedient soldier, and in an instant, he lay on the ground motionless.

"Take her. Find the baby!" the apparition hissed angrily. There was no hesitation from the soldiers this time. They made their way hastily back toward the cottage to search for the child. Her hands were bound, and she was escorted away by two of the soldiers. The apparition stayed standing among the orchard trees, motionless, with the large book of magic in its arms.

Elisha made a quick glance at the neighboring cottage as they passed by, making sure the child was still unable to be seen. She just needed to buy some time, she thought to herself. Soon she would be able to get back here to save him or someone would come along to get him. Her heart sank at the thought of him not being found. Unfortunately, it was a chance she had to take. Just buy some time and increase the odds of survival, she thought. There were no other options to be had. As it is more often than not, life makes the decisions for you.

That evening as the sun was setting, a man working the orchards followed the sounds of a crying baby and found him lying next to the invisibility cloak. After an extensive search, late into the evening and finding no one else around, he decided he had no choice but to take the baby home to his wife where the two would care for him, for the time being. Because of the invisibility cloak that was found near him, what had been going on in the kingdom lately, and finding Barreston's cottage ransacked, they had a pretty decent idea about what had transpired and were smart enough not to advertise the child's existence too loudly or to the wrong people. Weeks of quietly searching for any sign of Barreston or possible parents in the area went by until eventually they had to give up looking, and decided for the boy's safety they must raise him as their own. They named him Aleric and the three became a family.

Over the next few months after the disappearance of Barreston there were many similar attacks on the secret societies and magic wielders throughout the kingdom. They all happened at night and in secret, so the stories rarely got out and most villagers knew nothing about what was going on. Well-armed soldiers bursting into dimly lit, stone walled rooms, filled with cloaked men who were attacked by surprise and in the chaos arrested and taken away.

Rumors and whispers of people mysteriously disappearing all throughout the kingdom soon became commonplace. It wasn't long until people began to piece together that most of their friends and family who were missing were those who possessed magic abilities. Some people began to think that all of them just decided to up and leave to boycott the kingdom, or simply flee to safer lands. Maybe they were creating their own society somewhere else where they could practice their magic freely? Some hoped. Still, even though many of the wizards and sorcerers were odd and peculiar it was not like most of them to just up and leave without saying goodbye to loved ones.

Months later, as more time went by with no contact from any of the missing villagers, it started to become painfully clear. Every magic user in the kingdom had disappeared without a trace. Were they locked up somewhere? Were they killed? There were rumors of distraught villagers going to the castle in hysterics, blaming the King for the disappearances. Then that person would go missing in the night too, just days later. These rumors spread like wildfire, and everyone seemed to know someone else who had the exact same story. It wasn't long before most everyone in the kingdom decided to stay quiet on the subject and not ask questions out of the fear of disappearing themselves. There was a very real fear that whoever spoke positively about magic or was thought to be doing magic would be reported to the castle by their neighbors. Fear seemed to be a powerful motivator in turning neighbors and friends against each other.

It happened fast in the end, but looking back it happened slowly over time. It was slow yes, but more importantly it was consistent. Then eventually it happened. The use of magic, even speaking of it, was removed from the once magical and prosperous kingdom of Mazeron.

Chapter 3: Kingdom In Ruin

Rain was coming down hard in the early hours of the morning. Everything was a hazy gray and blue at this time of day, before the sun came up over the horizon. The tinking sound of heavy raindrops was loud as it hit helmets and armor made of steel. Aleric stood guard below the castle's ramparts as the rain trickled down his cold face. He was exhausted and tired from a long night shift, and soggy from standing in the rain and mud. He adjusted his stance, leaning in toward the doorway, trying to take more cover from the steady pounding of rain. Another guard stood beside him at the large door. Other guards around the castle walked methodically to and fro, manning their posts.

So many guards, all doing nothing, all night long. Aleric thought to himself. Pretty much every young, capable man in the kingdom was a guard these days. Guards everywhere. The kingdom had grown incredibly strict since the gold mines were abandoned and crime became more prevalent throughout the land. It was pretty much the only decent job left in the kingdom, so in all this cold and wet misery he was still thankful to have it. He gazed eastward toward the horizon.

"The sun is almost up," Aleric said to the other guard. "Almost time to go home and get out of this wet armor."

"I think I am going to rust solid," the other guard replied with a forced laugh.

"Hush you two!" a voice bellowed from the ramparts above. "You aren't relieved yet."

Someone is always watching, Aleric thought. No privacy or personal space anymore. He rolled his eyes and continued with the watch, glancing at the horizon from time to time. Once the sun came up above the horizon, the guards would be swapped out for the afternoon, and he would be free to leave this wet misery.

Then, out of the foggy haze ahead, came a large shadow through the rain, and he could hear the grumbling of men approaching. They got closer, their feet splashing in the mud. It was two guards carrying a limp man by the shoulders, dragging his feet through the mud as they walked. The captor's head was limp and facing the ground. Blood slowly dripped from his nose.

"We've got another one," one of the approaching guards stated. "Open the gates."

Aleric and the other guard turned and pushed heavily on the giant wooden doors, opening them with a creak on old, rusted hinges.

"Found this on him after an anonymous tip," the incoming guard said, tossing a small sphere to Aleric. "It's magic."

Aleric held the ball up to his face as purple and red smoke swirled inside of the sphere. Images of people's faces and various landscapes faded in and out of the smoke as he watched in awe.

"I've never seen magic," Aleric said slowly, his eyes bright with amazement and a sudden feeling of excitement inside him that he had never felt before.

"We'll take it to Maub," the other guard said in a deep voice, snatching the sphere back from Aleric. "That's a big no-no, isn't it?" the guard said exaggeratively to the prisoner hanging between the two guards before punching him squarely in the side of the ribs. The man let out a grunt of pain and gasped for air as he tried to catch his breath.

"Take him away," the other door guard commanded. Then he ushered them through the large doors and watched them fade away into a dark, damp corridor beyond.

"Can you believe some people still try to cling to that old magic nonsense, even after all these years and even when they know the consequences of it?" the guard asked Aleric. "They should all know better by now," he stated. But it fell on deaf ears. Aleric was still in awe at the magical sphere and how it showed different images. He could have sworn he felt something when he held it.

His thoughts were interrupted when moments later he heard men approaching again. Through the fog, more shadows emerged. It was two more guards, again escorting a prisoner. They approached quickly this time. The detained villager was pulling and trying to get away, but he was unable to overpower the strong guards. They stopped in front of Aleric and the large wooden door. One guard kicked the back of the detained man's leg, and he fell painfully on his knees into the mud.

"Another thief," one of the approaching guards spoke.

"I just needed some food!" the man wailed in distress. "It was just an onion!"

"Shut up, you!" the guard replied, kicking the man down into the mud. "They never learn," he said, shaking his head. "Open up!"

Again, Aleric and the other guard pushed the heavy dungeon doors and watched as the other two guards dragged the man down the corridor until they disappeared into the darkness. A faint scream echoed through the corridor, coming from the belly of the dungeon chambers beyond. They closed the door again and continued to wait.

After what seemed like forever, small sunbeams showed through the clouds, indicating the sun was up and that the storm was finally dying out. A ringing bell could be heard in the distance, echoing off the castle walls. Shift change. Behind Aleric, the door slowly swung open again and two new guards emerged. Aleric nodded at them, then turned to make his way back to the stables to fetch his horse. All the other guards were doing the same. They were all soaked, soggy, and cold from the storm that lasted the entire night. Their heads and their spirits hung low as they trekked through the thick mud in the gloom.

As he was untying the reins of his horse, he saw the king's wizard Maub standing atop the castle's balcony, as he usually did in the mornings. It used to be King Victus standing up there. But come to think of it, he hadn't seen the king out there in over two years. The king had become a shut-in since the abrupt and unexpected passing of his wife. Then there was the mysterious disappearance of his only son shortly afterwards. Some say that the young man ran away, not wanting to be king of such a dreary and hopeless kingdom. But others thought he was murdered. Too many people went missing in the kingdom of Mazeron these days.

Aleric mounted his horse and began to ride towards home. The horse's hooves splashed heavily in the thick mud, making travel slow and causing the horse to struggle to stay balanced. They were still on the main road leaving the village near the castle when they came upon a crossroads. Trotting slowly through the crossing of the two dirt roads Aleric saw a group of the king's guards emerging from the woods in the distance.

Most of the guards were walking but some were on horseback. There were about ten of them walking slowly down the road. As they came closer, Aleric noticed that some were limping, and most had dried blood on their faces and armor. He could see visible wounds wrapped with blood-stained cloth as they came clamoring towards him. In visible distress at the sight of the wounded guards, Aleric rode to them.

"What happened?" he asked urgently.

"What do you think?" one of the soldiers replied angrily. "Brigands!" he continued with a scruff voice. "They got the jump on us again. Lost almost fifty men this time."

"Best to just let them be," another wounded soldier muttered from below his breath.

"Can I be of any help?" Aleric asked. "You are wounded." The man in the lead made a motion like he was swatting away a fly with his hand.

"Leave us alone, boy," he grumbled. "We're going to be in worse shape soon enough once we report to Maub that we lost fifty more men on this lost cause."

"He'll have our hides," one man agreed.

"He'll turn us into frogs," said another.

"If magic is so dangerous that it had to be banned, why does he still get to use it?" another asked in an annoyed tone.

"Shhhh!" the first man shushed the other. "You know you can't be saying stuff like that out loud." The two of them looked around at the other men nervously, who awkwardly pretended to ignore them and stayed silent.

Aleric watched as the damaged group trudged on by. Dragging legs, limping, blood dripping from wounds, dented and missing armor. They were a mess of a sight to see, he thought to himself as continued on.

"Glad I wasn't sent out there," he mumbled under his breath. He turned his horse around and continued their journey back home.

On the slow ride back to his cottage he thought about the brigands and those unlucky men sent out into the woods to be ambushed. No one knew who the brigands were or where they came from. They seemed to just show up one day, setting up camp in the thick forests, then never left again. They would raid and plunder almost every merchant who would come through the mountain passes. Now, years later, there were almost no merchants coming into the lands to trade with the kingdom and villagers anymore. The forests had always been dangerous with the various beasts and monsters that called them home, but now with the brigands as well it was just too dangerous.

The brigands would raid the goods coming into the lands and the gold heading out of the lands. The king had thrown garrison after garrison at them, but they were dug in deep, and the forests were thick and unknown. No one knew how many of them there were, but they seemed to be everywhere and nowhere all at the same time. Usually, the only evidence of them was burnt and destroyed merchant wagons scattered along the sides of the roads through the forest and mountain passes. They had successfully cut off all trade from the kingdom, but they were just one of many things that had choked the prosperity from the land.

Aleric felt hopeless at the sight of the wounded men. He knew that would be him soon enough. He was an asset to have guarding the castle because he was one of the strongest of the guards, but he knew it wouldn't be long until he was sent out there to fight. The fighting wasn't a problem. He was well trained in combat, better than most. It was being sent out to get ambushed in the woods and killed before he even had the chance to fight that bothered him.

He felt trapped. Trapped in these lands surrounded by impassable forests and mountains. He had to work for the castle. There were no other options open to him to put food on his and his wife's table. They barely made it as it was, and working for the king's guard was one of, if not the best jobs in the kingdom. Most of the other villagers were stricken with poverty, and he wanted to avoid that at all costs. But even if it cost him his life?

As he rode, he thought about the days when these lands were prosperous and wondered what he could have become if he was born in a different time. He had heard many stories of the good old days and would often contemplate different ways of improving his situation or getting the gold mines active again.

The mines eventually became dormant because the miners relied on short, stubborn, magical creatures called Stone Gnomes who could use their magic to move freely through the rock like it wasn't there to find the veins of gold deep within the mountains. The Stone Gnomes were notoriously lazy, and mining was back breaking work, so they had developed a symbiotic relationship with the miners. They showed the miners where the gold was, then the miners would mine the area and retrieve the gold out of the mountains, then reward the Stone Gnomes with goods purchased with the gold. Mostly tasty foods, which is what they enjoyed the most. Apparently, this relationship went on for centuries. But when the king banned magic just decades ago, they began to be mistreated. Once magic users disappeared from all over the land, the Stone Gnomes feared for their own safety then retreated to their natural habitat, deep within the mountains. Now that the kingdom was suffering without them, there were attempts to bring them back, but no contact was ever made.

It was a chain reaction. Without the gold, poverty became rampant. Crime and thieves became prevalent throughout the kingdom. Thievery was so prominent that there was a rumor that there was actually a 'Thieves guild" where they had joined forces and had some sort of system for stealing then liquidating and laundering the stolen goods in exchange for food or money. The castle had tried to stem the plague of robberies and thieves, but just like the brigands, the effort was thus far mostly fruitless.

Aleric clenched his fists together in frustration around the reins as he thought about his life and the circumstances that brought him here to be soggy and cold, miserably stomping through the mud in the early hours of the morning. He remembered his father always saying that life wasn't fair, but this was just ridiculous.

His parents had passed away when he was young, forcing him to work and start life when he was still just a boy. When they passed away, they left him their cottage, so he always had a roof over his head even if he had to work hard to keep it. Over the years he had to sell off the surrounding land to make ends meet. So, what were once farm fields around the house was now a nice little village of wooden and stone cottages. Most of which were leased by the villagers and who paid rent to the castle. Hardly anyone actually owned their land anymore. Aleric was one of the only owners in his village. Somehow all of the farms kept slowly getting acquired by the castle, and being able to own your land had become more and more scarce. This only added to the difficulty of life in the kingdom, as everyone seemed forced into a lifetime of hard work and toil as they were unable to get ahead or rest constantly trying to keep up with the increasing rent for their entire lives.

It was humid and gloomy, but the rain had completely stopped by the time he approached his village. The humidity always made the Leedles extra angry for some reason and they were out this morning with a vengeance. He swatted away tiny arrows that bit and poked at exposed skin and had to put his helmet back on for more protection from the little nuisances as he rode through the fields leading up to his cottage.

Finally, he arrived back at his cottage. He tied up his horse out front, dismounted, took off his helmet, and began to unclip the steel armor he wore. He did it outside so he wouldn't track the mud and mess indoors. He was of average height and had a strong and lean build. The kind of strength without a lot of bulk that allowed for athletic agility and quickness, which made him the ideal knight and king's soldier. His dark hair was longer and went down past his ears to the middle of his neck and his skin was naturally pale on his upper arms, but he was mostly tanned from farming and working in the sun as most people in Mazeron were.

He pushed open the door of the old wooden hut and walked inside, still sopping wet and cold. As he entered the small cottage, he was greeted with a rush of warmth, the smell of good food in the air, and a big kiss from his beautiful wife Briss. Suddenly all the misery from the night's shift disappeared at the sight of her. The cottage was warm and comfortable and the big smile on her face was everything he needed to know that the night's work was worth it. Anything to keep food on the table and a roof over their heads. Things could be worse, he thought to himself as a grin took the place of the scowl he had been donning all morning.

Briss was quite a bit shorter than Aleric. She was wearing her usual bright green colored pants that accentuated her long, smooth red hair. Besides her bright hair and clothing style she also had a bright and lively personality. She was full of life, always with agile quick spins and movements and full of laughter and life. She had a visible love for life that seemed to get beaten out of everyone else by the time they were her age, but somehow, she had been able to hold onto hers. She was the only light in Aleric's life, and he treasured her with every fiber of his being.

"I made your favorite hen," she said, bobbing her head and making her hair dance and swoosh about playfully.

"What, why!?' Aleric said shocked and taken back.

"Just joking, these are just her eggs," she laughed out loud, handing a warm plate of food over to Aleric. She was always laughing and being fun.

"How was your shift? She asked as the two sat down at the table. "Have you seen King Victus at all lately? Odd he is rarely if ever seen these days."

"I held a magic item today," Aleric replied. The magical orb and the feeling it had given him had been in the back of his mind all day. "One of the guards took it off of a prisoner."

"Really?" Briss lit up with intrigue. "Tell me about it! I know everyone hates that stuff and we are supposed to hate it too, but I think it's interesting. I think people just say they hate magic because everyone else says it. Imagine living back in the magical times and all the excitement it had."

Aleric began telling her about the magical orb over breakfast and the two enjoyed each other's company through the morning as Aleric slowly began to thaw out from the cold night. Aleric and Briss had known each other since they were basically kids and still always had plenty to talk and laugh about. They had met shortly after his parents had passed away, which made his loss of them magnificently easier to cope with, and the two had been basically inseparable ever since.

"I'm going to the orchards of Briardale tomorrow," Briss said excitedly at one point. "To pick some apples for your favorite apple pie."

Picking fruit in the orchards of the foothills was one of Briss' only simple pleasures and she treasured the days she got to go up there. Aleric smiled at the thought of it, and they ended up talking and laughing together until the afternoon came.

Eventually Aleric mentioned he needed to sleep for a while, then needed to sharpen his swords out back in his shed sometime before the sun went down. It was a simple life that they shared, but it was also hard, and almost all their days were taken up with chores, work, and survival. It was for them just as it is for everything else that lives on this planet; existence was grueling.

The remainder of the day and evening went by fast. Too fast, Aleric thought to himself as he laid down to bed that night next to Briss. This was his favorite time of day. Holding and laughing with Briss as they lay together in the warmth of their home. Together they talked and laughed, flirted, and loved each other. They made shadow puppets on the ceiling in the faint candlelight, and Briss would sporadically try to tickle Aleric because she knew just where to tickle to get the strong man to squirm and loved the sound of his laughter. They spent the entire evening being silly and fun together. Briss felt safe in Aleric's arms, and he felt love and happiness with her in them. Then eventually the two fell asleep in each other's arms in the small bed on the cottage floor.

The next morning, they were awakened by the peaceful sound of birds chirping outside their window, who were also beginning another day in the lands of Mazeron.

"Another shift already," Aleric grumbled as he rolled out of bed. His muscles were stiff from yesterday's work and sword practice. "I want nothing more than to stay here in the warm bed with you," he said, forcing a smile. Briss smiled back and pulled the covers close to her face, hiding from the chill morning air. After dressing and eating, he kissed her goodbye and was out the door.

Most of the guards lived at the castle barracks, but most of them had no one to go home to either. They were a rough, dirty bunch, and Aleric found them uncomfortable to be around. Many of them were boorish and rude. Luckily, he lived close enough to the castle to make the trek every day, and even though it ate up a lot of his daylight riding there and back, his life was significantly better once he got home. Once again, Aleric strapped the armor to his body. The steel was cold from the night air but at least it was dry today.

He rode at a mellow pace on the dried dirt path towards the castle towering in the distance. The sun was shining a soft gold, and the fields were alive with birds and deer attending to their daily duties. He had to admit that even though life was difficult here, it was magnificently beautiful. Every inch of the land was green, and the sky was so big and blue that it seemed to go on forever. The snowcapped mountains in the distance were so large and prominent that they would captivate anyone who gazed upon them, no matter how many times they had done so. In the distance, the gold conical roofs of the castle were reflecting almost as bright as the sun.

Halfway to the castle he noticed something in the sky, far off in the distance. Squinting against the sunlight, he could see a tiny shadow circling near a grouping of clouds. He knew immediately what it was. A dragon. Over the years they had been coming closer and closer to the villages, some wreaking havoc on the crops and livestock along the countryside. They were filthy, dangerous, unpredictable creatures. Sometimes they would make their nest for a night in a field. When the morning came, they would be gone but the area that they nest in would be destroyed. The only thing left would be remnants of dead crops and a disgusting snot-like substance with a red hue that would burn anything it touched and smelled strong, like eggs gone bad.

Soon enough he arrived back at the castle, put his helmet and gauntlets on, and took his place as a dungeon guard once again. The day passed just like any other day. A steady stream of guards hauling unfortunate villagers and rough-looking criminals to their new home in the cold belly of the castle. Most were petty crimes. Saying something wrong or not being friendly enough to the king's guards. There were no trials or judges for the most part. Just a dark dirt and stone passageway that led to a cold, dark, dirt and stone cell. The arresting guards would always tell Aleric what the charges were, even though it didn't matter to him, and they probably weren't ever reported to anyone else. He always wondered about the families they were leaving behind. No wonder so many people in this kingdom were destitute, he thought to himself.

It was later in the afternoon when a shadow suddenly blocked the sun out of Aleric's eyes, just for a second. He looked up but nothing was there, not even a cloud in the sky. He could have sworn it got darker for just a moment. Then he heard commotion coming from the distance. Aleric and the other door guard glanced at each other in confusion. For a moment nothing happened as they stood in silence listening. Then they heard a scream in the distance. This time they were certain they had heard something. Moments later, a group of guards went running quickly past them, clearly in a hurry to get somewhere. The two dungeon guards stayed at their post, watching in confusion as villagers and guards began to run in every which direction. The sound of screaming was steadily growing until they both knew something was going on, but they still didn't know what.

Then the shadow appeared again, and they looked up just as an enormous dragon soared by, completely blocking out the sun above them. It was dangerously low and looked like it almost hit the castle's golden tops as it flew past. There was chaos and panic everywhere. People running in no particular direction to get away. Aleric could see the smoke floating lazily from the dragon's nostrils as it soared back into the sky. He knew how dangerous these animals could be and this was the closest he had ever been to one. Probably the closest any of them had ever been to one.

The dragon circled the castle lazily in the afternoon sun, seemingly without a care in the world despite the chaos it was causing below. Then it took a sharp turn and dipped towards the castle. It approached quickly, then abruptly turned upright to slow down right in front of the largest tower. With a few flaps of its massive wings, it landed and came to a rest clinging to the side of the stone tower.

Everyone froze. Watching in anticipation. The dragon clung to the side of the castle, quietly and calmly. It turned its massive head towards the sun and stretched it out lazily in obvious satisfaction as the sun warmed its cold blood.

"It's just a giant lizard!" Aleric exclaimed. "He just wants to bask in the sun." The crowd stayed silent, watching, waiting for some sort of destruction or show of aggression. The animal was so incredibly large that it could destroy the whole castle just by being clumsy.

"We need to get it off of there before it damages the tower!" one of the commanding guards eventually said to the others.

Orders were given and not long after a small group of archers had been assembled for the task. They began firing arrows at random

at the dragon, but they bounced off the armored scales and the big lizard didn't even seem to notice them. The soft underbelly was securely pressed against the stone tower of the castle as it basked in the warm afternoon sun. Aleric watched the amusing scene unfold with a grin on his face. They continued in futility for some time, but the dragon did not budge or even seem to care about the hail of arrows being shot at him.

"Get the catapult!" one of the captains eventually yelled out in frustration.

"You can't use the catapult!" another officer yelled back in reply. "You'll blow the whole tower to pieces!"

"We need to get up there and poke it," Aleric said aloud with a chuckle. "Or else he's not going anywhere until the sun goes down." The other guards looked at him in silence for a long moment.

"Well then, get up there and get at it why don't you!" the captain finally managed.

"Fine," Aleric replied blankly after a long pause. He could see the old king running in frantic circles up on the balcony, which added to the absurdity of the scene.

"Where's Maub when you need him?" Aleric laughed as he took his gauntlets and helmet off, getting ready for the climb. Then he reached down and grabbed a handful of dirt to rub between his hands, and he started off, climbing upwards on the stone tower.

The tower was made of thick, uneven bricks, so handholds were easy to come by, and some bricks allowed the full length of his fingers to grab securely on to them. His feet were too large to fit into the cracks, but the tips of his leather shoes fit well, making nice footholds, so the climb started out easier than expected.

Aleric was already two levels off the ground when the dragon started moving upward to reposition itself, then stopped again in a sitting position atop one of the towers. The dragon's tail swung lazily above as he rested in the warm sun and it crashed heavily into the tower, knocking many bricks loose, which tumbled to the ground, almost hitting Aleric on their way down. The heavy impact left a large hole in the tower wall. The dragon's claws were also doing damage to the tower. It was a miracle that it was even holding the massive weight of the animal. Every minute that it sat atop the tower it was causing more damage to it.

The crowd below watched intently as Aleric climbed up towards the dragon. The wind began to blow harder and harder the higher he went, making every next push more difficult than the last. He squinted as the cold wind dried out his eyes but could not let go of the finger holds to clear the water running from them.

Finally, Aleric had almost reached the dragon. He was looking for a solid place to grab on to before reaching for his sword, when suddenly the dragon's tail came swinging by once again and he had to duck quickly, grabbing tightly to the bricks to avoid being flung off the wall like a helpless bug. Still not even being noticed by the large dragon.

"How did I get myself into this one?" he grumbled to himself, regaining his balance. Then he found a nice foothold and felt secure for the moment. Keeping his left hand deep between the bricks, he let his right hand loose and slowly and carefully unsheathed his sword. Then he reached up, and pushing upward as far and hard as he could, he stabbed his sword into the bottom rump of the dragon near its rear end.

A roar of fire and smoke bellowed from the animal's mouth as it leapt into the sky and took flight. The entire gold cone of the tower was shoved from its resting place and hurled heavily to the ground with tons of burnt bricks and debris crashing among the gathered crowd below. Aleric held tight to the wall as he was pummeled by the crumbling tower, but he managed to hold on.

Then it was silent. He waited another moment before lifting his face to look around. The dragon was flying away into the distance, and he heard a sudden roar of cheers from the onlookers below. A great sigh of relief flowed through his body as he realized the dragon was leaving and that he was, in fact, still alive.

But the relief was short lived. The dragon was not soaring lazily, floating on the wind like it had before. It was flapping its wings frantically and hard. Gaining speed as it flew quickly towards the nearest village. Aleric's village!

"No, no, no," he begged quietly to himself. "Please no." But then the worst happened. The dragon in the distance dove from an incredible height and at magnificent speeds down towards the village. As it leveled out, a giant stream of fire bellowed from its mouth as it strafed the village. Soaring back into the sky, it was followed by a trail of deep black smoke, slowly rising into the sky from the burning buildings of the far-off village.

"Briss!" Aleric screamed. "No!" He started down the tower as quickly as he could. There was already a wagon assembled with other soldiers on the ground below, waiting for him with intense anticipation as he climbed down.

"Just go!" he yelled in an angry voice. Quickly the reins snapped and the group of soldiers in the wagon were off.

Soon after, Aleric reached the flat ground once again and was finally off the tower. His hands were trembling from the adrenaline, fear, and exhaustion of the climb. He turned and ran fast and aggressively towards the stables and in just a few moments was atop his horse, and then they too were off.

When he came upon the village it was a war zone. Almost unrecognizable. Buildings were on fire everywhere, the streets filled with debris. People were running and screams filled the air. The dragon was still circling above. After quickly assessing the situation, he went from attack mode to just save Briss mode. The dragon was too large and could cover too much ground to form any sort of effective assault on it, even after the other guards arrived. He needed to find Briss and get her out of there before the dragon leveled the entire village. Aleric turned his horse and sped towards their cottage.

He didn't recognize anything with the billowing smoke and destroyed buildings surrounding him, but he knew the roads well and went directly there. Upon arriving, he saw his house still standing and untouched. He let out a huge sigh of relief and started quickly up the path, calling out for Briss. Then, as he approached the cottage, the dragon came down out of the sky and landed in the field directly behind their cottage, just beyond his shed.

Aleric crept to the corner of his cottage and watched quietly as the dragon sat in the field near his back shed where all his weapons were kept. The dragon seemed to be content again and began lazily licking its front claws, slowly cleaning them in the warm afternoon sun. Aleric looked around again and remembered that Briss had planned to go to the orchards of Briardale today to pick fruit. Then he saw an opportunity...

The dragon was so close to the shed and unaware of any danger. It was just flicking his tongue toward the sky and licking its claws. Aleric had the element of surprise and decided he had to take it. If he could get to the shed without being noticed, he could arm himself. Then, with just a few large bounds from the shed he could bury his longsword deep into the dragon before it even knew he was there. Even if the dragon saw him approach, he knew it was heavy and couldn't take flight instantly, so he would have at least a few moments to make his attack. Once the dragon was injured, he and the rest of the guards could finish the job when they arrived, and together they could put an end to this madness and destruction and the entire kingdom would hail him as a hero. The thought of being a hero quickly clouded all other judgment and soon his mind was made up.

He didn't have to wait long until the dragon turned slightly away from him and lay down in the field. It was a bizarre sight, he thought, seeing the vicious animal at such peace with so much destruction and chaos all around it. Aleric crept forward, exposing his position, then ran fast and quiet to the cover of the shed that was in the field behind his cottage. He got to it just as the dragon turned his gaze back around, luckily it did not see him.

Inside, the shed was filled with Aleric's various weapons. He would train extensively with them almost every day. Long swords, short daggers, bows, crossbows. Anything that was spikey or sharp was in here, including a large spring powered crossbow on wheels that shot metal arrows that were almost as tall as he was. He went for that first and loaded an arrow into it. Then he continued to arm himself with a long sword and shorter sword that was about a forearm in length.

Slowly, Aleric cracked open the back door of the shed and peered through the gap at the large, violent, and unpredictable animal. It was still there in the field, basking in the sun. Its long tongue whipped the warm afternoon breeze. Aleric opened the door a little more then slowly moved the giant crossbow into place. It was pointed right at the animal, which was less than half the field away. He paused to ready himself. It was eerily quiet around the green grassy field, and the sky above was a magnificent blue as he gazed outside and observed the area one last time before making his attack.

He breathed a heavy sigh, paused again, then charged into the field at a full sprint, pulling a long, thin rope behind him. He was deep into the field when the rope pulled tight and the crossbow mechanism in the shed fired. With a clank of the spring the large arrow sped fast from the shed, flying so fast that he could barely see it speed past him, or have time to think before he heard the heavy thud of the arrow bouncing off the animal's thick scales.

Aleric was already deep into the field, with his sword drawn and ready to make his attack when the dragon felt the arrow bounce off its thick scales. It turned swiftly and spotted the approaching knight. Aleric stopped dead in his tracks at the animal's gaze and his stomach sank as he realized the grave error he had made. He paused for just a moment to think. Was there time to retreat and reload another arrow? But before he could decide, the dragon was up off the ground and moving towards him. Aleric turned and ran like the wind. He ran past the shed and continued on towards the cottage. As he ran through the field and tall grasses, the dragon trailing behind him stepped on the shed and crushed it into a million pieces of debris without even slowing. Then with heavy flaps of giant wings, the dragon was airborne, still in chase of the fleeing knight.

Aleric ran back towards his cottage as fast as he could. The dragon was gaining on him, flying low and fast close behind. As he ran past the cottage, Aleric saw a large basket of freshly picked apples sitting at the back door and his heart instantly sank. Briss! No! He felt a panic so intense that his heart could barely be contained inside of his chest. She was home after all, but she had gone in through the back door of the cottage, which was not her usual pattern.

Behind him, the animal was approaching the cottage. It lowered its left shoulder and barreled into it with all of its weight and flew through the structure like it wasn't even there, destroying most of the cottage in the process and sending its wooden beams and planks into sharp pieces, soaring violently and dangerous through the air.

In the chaos and just in time, Aleric leapt away from the debris and rolled to the ground, covering his head as pieces of wood and debris rained down on him. The dragon flew low over his head with magnificent speed then took off high into the sky with effortless flaps of its large wings. Aleric lay there on the ground covered in debris, fighting against unconsciousness. His cottage was in pieces behind him. The other cottages nearby billowed smoke and were engulfed in flames. Eventually he snapped out of the haze and was faced with the reality of the situation once again.

"Briss!" he yelled in a panic, pushing debris from him and rushing toward what was left of the house. He had completely forgotten about the threat of the dragon and only cared about finding Briss. He started throwing boards and rummaging through the rubble. He looked back and forth, thinking she would come safely out of hiding somewhere, but she did not appear. He couldn't find her.

"Briss! Briss!" he yelled out her name over and over again. Maybe she got out before the dragon hit? Maybe she wasn't even home in the first place or escaped when she saw the animal land near the shed? His heart was starting to feel better about her not even being home when he moved a pile of wood debris near where the chimney had once stood and saw her pinned under a large beam.

His heart sank. This couldn't be happening. Just moments ago, he was having a normal day, guarding the castle. How did this happen!?

He hurried toward her, heaving planks, beams, and debris like it was tiny wood chips. Finally, he got to her, but he could already tell that he was too late. He pressed his cheek close to hers, but she was gone. He collapsed to the ground in a frenzy of emotion. So much anger and sadness that the world around him became blurry and he was close to blacking out. Tears trickled down his face as the rain set in again.

He was there, collapsed to his knees in a pile of rubble, holding Briss' hand, when he heard and felt a heavy thud coming from behind him. He knew the dragon had returned. He didn't even have to turn around to know it. He could smell its foul stench and hear its furnaces raging inside of its fiery belly.

Aleric was still holding Briss' cold hand when the dragon slowly began approaching from behind him, readying for the kill. Then suddenly a violent rage began to course through Aleric's body. It was something he had never felt before and something he could not contain. He let go of Briss' hand and began to tremble with rage. Rage from a lifetime of losing battles, rage at the world, rage at now losing the one person that mattered to him in this wretched, painful world.

When he finally looked up from the ground, Aleric's eyes were glowing a bright yellow and orange glow. His pupils and any detail in them were long gone, and all that was left was hollow, glowing eyes of rage. He let out a yell like a clap of thunder that stopped the dragon in its steps and resonated through the valley like the crashing of mountains.

Then, in an instant, Aleric was on his feet, turning about and charging the animal. Taken aback and startled by the enormous roar and sudden attack, the dragon flapped its wings and quickly flew backwards and away from the charging knight, then landed again nearby in front of another cottage. But Aleric did not slow. He charged towards the dragon with fierce speed. Upon seeing the attacking knight getting closer, the beast readied for another attack and also charged forward.

The two warriors approached each other; Aleric was fueled with a burning rage and a feeling of strength and energy like he had never felt before. He effortlessly bound high into the air towards the cottage's roof, then using one leg to push off it he flew higher into the sky, and with incredible speed toward the beast he came down hard on the dragon and plunged his sword deep into the side of its neck. It was an incredible show of strength and agility that no one had ever seen before. It was not even humanly possible, but the whole attack felt second-nature to Aleric, like an effortless instinct, as the magic that had been inside of him his entire life began to explode out.

The dragon flailed in agony, whipping its tail into the cottage and taking out an entire wall. Then it rolled onto another structure and crushed it as well. His eyes still glowing bright with rage, Aleric did not slow. In an instant he was on the beast, plunging his sword into it repeatedly, backing away to regroup and dodge sporadic hot breaths of unpredictable fire, then continuing the attack again.

But the animal would not give up. It broke free from the attack and took to the sky once again. It flew high and out of reach quickly. In a rage, Aleric thundered another yell of anger that could be heard for miles. The dragon heard the battle cry as well and decided it would not be outdone by a tiny human. The animal turned slowly from high in the sky, aimed itself directly at Aleric, readied its internal furnaces that bellowed its deadly fire, then dove straight down from the incredible heights, picking up speed as it came in for the final attack.

Aleric stood his ground among the rubble, burnt down cottages, and the chaos that surrounded him. His eyes were still burning a bright, raging amber colored glow. He dropped his long sword to the ground and drew the smaller sword and held it upright. He gripped the sword so hard that his hand began to vibrate and shake. Then the blade began to vibrate, violently, until soon turned into a hot red glow. He could feel the heat from the sword swelter across his face. The metal of the blade started to droop, and the sword began to melt away. It folded over on itself until it was a glowing, hot handful of steel. With both hands, Aleric molded it into a sphere of hot metal.

The dragon was approaching fast, at lightning speed from high in the sky, then it leveled out over the nearby fields and came in fast for the strafe attack. As it inhaled one last large breath, readying its furnaces within, Aleric reared back, then with inhuman strength threw the hot steel ball at the dragon with incredible force. The glowing ball of metal flew through the sky and hit the dragon right under the chin, penetrating the dragon's skull. The animal was dead instantly and as its wings went limp it came crashing down to the ground with enormous, heavy and violent force. Aleric ducked as it flew over his head and came crashing down behind him, and skidded across the field, finally coming to rest in a cloud of mud, fire, and debris. He turned to see the fallen beast and stood motionless before it with his eyes still glowing bright in the pouring rain.

The other guards had arrived just before the battle and witnessed the whole thing. Other villagers had also witnessed the fight from their hiding spots in the village. Through the haze and rain, Aleric saw them. Their silhouettes in the gray haze, silently watching as he stood before the giant fallen beast. He gathered his longsword and leaned heavily on the hilt for support while he caught his breath. It was covered in mud and dragon's blood, as was his face. Eventually cheers started to echo in from the distance as more of the villagers discovered that one man had single-handedly taken down a dragon.

Eventually a small group of villagers came towards Aleric extatically to offer their congratulations. But when they came close, he turned and glared menacingly and angrily at them with his hollow, glowing eyes. They were frightened and walked backward quickly, leaving him there alone in the rain. For some time, the villagers watched in awe and confusion from a distance as the strong knight stood there motionless in front of the large slain beast.

Finally, Aleric turned from the animal and slowly walked back towards the wreckage of his home. He dropped his sword to the ground and returned defeatedly back to the rubble. He kicked and tossed pieces of debris slowly and carelessly side to side. The onlookers had closed in, forming a circle around the dead animal and the destroyed cottage. They watched in silence as Aleric knelt down, picked up Briss' body, then walked away slowly into the haze and rain, until they were just a fading silhouette that eventually disappeared into the gray.

Chapter 4: An Agreement

Five days had passed since the mysterious magic-wielding knight had single-handedly defeated the ferocious dragon. But the knight had disappeared, and there had been no contact or sighting of him since. Word of the epic battle had spread throughout the kingdom like wildfire. Everyone had questions and wanted to hear from Aleric. To find out what had happened and how it was that he knew magic. Many people had witnessed the battle unfold, but the tale grew larger and more exaggerated with every mouth that told the tale.

Despite Aleric's disappearance, work about the kingdom went on as usual. Scaffolding had gone up and repairs were underway on the castle's tower that had been damaged by the lounging dragon. But Aleric's village had so far been left untouched and unrepaired. Smoldering rubble from the torched village blew light gray smoke into the sky for days. Burnt debris was scattered everywhere throughout the village, and Aleric's cottage was nothing more than a large pile of wood in a field, near a rotting and stinking dragon corpse.

There was much talk about the magic knight throughout the kingdom. It seemed like it was the only thing on everyone's mind and the only thing that anyone would speak about. Who was Aleric? How did he know magic? Would he be arrested or rewarded for what had happened? The not-knowing was almost too intense for the quiet townspeople to bear. Some believed he had already been arrested and locked away. Some said he had fled the valley for good, to avoid that exact fate. But no one really knew what had happened to the knight. They needed answers, they needed closure.

Night set in on the fifth day of the knight's disappearance. Outside it was dark, still, and quiet. But inside the barracks of the king's guards, it was loud and awake with the sounds of the guards eating dinner and winding down for the night after the long workday. Patrols had stepped up after the dragon attack, and more men had been brought in from the villages to work on repairing the castle, so the barracks were more crowded than usual.

The eating hall was deafeningly loud with the booming voices of the many guards when the front door slowly creeped open and a strong breeze of cold air blew heavily into the room. Aleric stood in the doorway like a ghost. The door slammed shut with a loud bang in the now-silent room. All the guards stopped and stared, making sure their eyes were not deceiving them and that the person in the doorway was in fact who they all thought it was.

Aleric was still wearing most of the armor he had been wearing five days ago when they last saw him climbing the castle's tower. He was drenched, wet and filthy. Mud and grass spots covered his armor, and his exposed cloth shirt was dripping wet and stained gray. His sword hung loosely from his belt, still stained with mud and dragon's blood. He said nothing as the men all stared in silence. Finally, he began to walk through the meeting hall without looking at or acknowledging anybody, making his way toward the bunk rooms where the guards would sleep. After he exited the hall, the men all just looked at each other and whispers began to arise from the silence.

Aleric made his way to his bunk. Although he rarely ever stayed in the barracks, he did have a chest and a bunk here. He made his way down the center of dozens of beds that lined each side of the room until he found his own near the far end of the room. He sat down in silence and stared at the floor. Back at the front of the room a few of the men were peeking around the doorway watching him and wondering what he was going to do next. Eventually he unclipped his metal armor and dropped it carelessly to the ground. He sat in dirty clothes just staring blankly at the floor, saying and doing nothing. His long hair slowly dripped drops of rainwater on the floor.

There he sat. Silently, in thought, still staring at the floor. He had nowhere else to go but here. He knew he was responsible for Briss' death. If he had just put her first, gone inside to her instead of going after the dragon then everything would be different right now. The harshness of this reality weighed on him like an invisible lead blanket, making even the most routine movements and breathing difficult. It wasn't long until one of the guards entered the room.

"Sir. I mean Aleric, sir," the guard said sheepishly, trying not to make eye contact. "The king, he would like a word from you in the castle." The man paused, waiting for Aleric to reply, but there was no response. There was no emotion at all. "He expects you now," the guard demanded more confidently.

As he finished speaking, three other guards stepped through the doorway and stood menacingly with hands on the hilts of their swords. They were making it known that they would escort Aleric to the king if he did not choose to come willingly.

"Calm your nerves, boys," Aleric replied in an annoyed tone as he stood up and opened the chest at the foot of his bed. The guards took a step forward in preparation, but he only pulled out a clean shirt and quickly changed from the wet stained shirt he was in. "Let's go then," he said, walking past the guards, shoving one of them with his shoulder on the way past.

They left the barracks and went into the open windy night, then onward toward the castle. The three guards were trailing Aleric by a noticeably safe distance. If he wanted to run he could have, and they could say they tried to stop him. But it was clear by their positioning that none of them were ready to take on the knight, should he try to flee. He walked with a slow calmness before them, through the courtyards and to a small side door that led into the castle.

"The king requests you in the dining hall," one of the guards exclaimed. "You know the way."

Aleric was ushered inside, then the door slammed loudly behind him. He was standing in a dark, dimly lit room that he knew to be one of the castle's smaller libraries. Books lined the walls, and a large wooden table stood before him. A single wooden chair sat empty at the head of the table, barely visible in the darkness. There was a single sconce illuminating a wooden door at the far end of the room, and he made his way towards it cautiously in the dark empty dark room.

He was almost at the door when suddenly a voice came out of the darkness behind him.

"Where did you learn how to do that?" it asked, ominous and stern.

Startled, Aleric turned in the darkness, and in the chair that he could have sworn was empty just moments before, sat Maub. Cloaked in black against the darkness of the room, he was barely visible. He wore his usual black cloak and intimidating feathered cape that made him resemble a raven in the darkness. He stood up from the chair and swiftly walked towards Aleric. The old craggy wizard towered over him, staring at him, inspecting him.

"Tell me now," the wizard demanded as he approached.

Aleric noticed the threatening tone in his voice. He knew he was in trouble and would be arrested for using magic. He knew he shouldn't have come back here. He didn't know what to say. He didn't actually know how he did what he did, and he couldn't explain if he wanted to. He stood in silence as the wizard stared hard into his eyes. Aleric was cornered in the room with nowhere to turn to escape.

"You *will* tell me," Maub demanded, raising his voice. He was so close now that Aleric could feel the wizard's foul breath on his face. Then, just in time a line of light beamed into the room as the door at the other end opened. Aleric and Maub both looked over. The king stood in the doorway.

"Ah, there you are! You've met Maub, I see. I knew he would want to meet you. Come, come. We have much to speak about!"

Aleric glanced back at Maub who was still standing tall and menacing over him, glaring at him with intense eyes. Aleric turned away defiantly, as if he didn't notice the wizard at all and followed the king out of the room.

"This way." The old king motioned and led the way from the library down a stone-walled corridor. This part of the castle was well lit, and a few guards could be seen standing in the various corridors and hallways of the quiet night as they made their way through the castle until they came to the dining hall. "Sit down," the king said in a friendly tone, motioning to a chair at a large table. As he took his seat, Aleric got the first up-close look of the king in years.

King Victus was an older man by now. He was tall and slender but hunched over from age. His hair had gone gray but had retained its thickness and was noticeably longer, shambled, and unkempt. Aleric noticed he was not wearing the king's crown, which was made of Mazeron's finest pure gold and jewels. But he did notice it lying on its side on a nearby chair, as if it had been tossed there carelessly.

On the king's right arm, he wore a gold wrist and hand piece of jewelry known as the Medallion of Mazeron. It was a thick gold band that went around the wrist and had a glowing blueish green medallion on the inside of the wrist. Attached to the wrist band was a gold chain that extended over the top of the hand and onto the middle finger, so it was secured to his arm and near impossible to steal. This gold and glowing medallion is what made the king, king. It was said to possess magical powers and lent those powers to whoever wore it. It opened every door in the castle, including the front gates with just a waving motion in front of the door. If the king of Mazeron were to ever be overthrown or ousted, the new inhabitants of the castle would simply find themselves locked out of most of the rooms without the magical cuff.

It also unsheathed the sword of Mazeron, which was usually worn by the king at all times. A large, magnificent sword that was also said to be magic would, with the combined medallion, guide the wearer in battle and aid them to victory. The sword could not be drawn from its sheath without the medallion. It was also said that the magical medallion could not be stolen. That it had to be given by the king or taken by one who defeated him in battle. The medallion had been handed down through the Victus family for generations, longer than anyone even knew. The central medallion of the piece glowed soft blue as the king took his chair at the large table. Aleric knew the glow of the medallion well, but he had never seen it this close before. Historically, when the king finished a speech or showed pride in the kingdom, he would raise his right arm high into the sky with a closed fist, exposing the magical, glowing stone to the villagers which would draw cheers and applause.

The next thing Aleric noticed about the king was how much his age was showing. Large bags under the eyes made him look tired and defeated. His hands seemed to shake, making the once strong man seem frail and nervous. Aleric looked about the dining hall and noticed the room was larger than his entire cottage. They were sitting at a long wooden table that could seat probably fifteen people on each side. A magnificent candlelit chandelier hung above them and a set of stone steps at the far end of the room gave way to the upper floors and the castle beyond.

“Sit down,” the king said politely, gesturing to an open seat at the table as he pulled his seat closer. There were a few other men there, all older, who were also sitting at the long table.

Aleric recognized most of them as the king's counsel and various commanders of the king's guard.

"Now," King Victus continued, "you have a lot of explaining to do." The tone in his voice noticeably changed and he stared heavily into Aleric's eyes, studying him intently as he spoke. Aleric noticed more guards assembling atop the stone stairs and felt an unease wash over him. He shouldn't have come back here. He knew they were going drag him into the belly of the dungeon when this interrogation was all over. He was going to end up just like all those villagers he saw pass through his doorway, being dragged into the cold dark depths of the dungeon. He sighed heavily, stalling; he still didn't know what to say.

"How do you know magic!" Maub stood from his seat and yelled, obviously having lost his patience already.

"I… I don't know," Aleric replied softly. "It just happened. I barely remember doing it. I had just lost my wife; I went into a frenzy," he said, throwing his hands into the air.

"He's lying," Maub said slowly, sitting down once again. "No one can wield magic like that without years of practice and studying. It doesn't just happen."

After that Maub laid into Aleric with a series of questions, one after another. Who were your parents? Where did you grow up? How long have you been practicing magic? Aleric answered all of them truthfully but still gave no insight on how it could be that he wielded such powerful magic. The king and his counselors sat silent through the interrogation, staring, and studying Aleric and his responses to the questions. The group of guards watched intently from the floor above. Hands on their weapons and ready to give chase if Aleric tried to flee the room.

During the interrogation Maub became visibly frustrated, yelling and flailing his arms about in disgust. They were getting nowhere. Eventually the tall menacing wizard paused, and the room fell silent. A tense silence.

"Well," Maub finally continued after some time, "we don't know how you know magic, where you learned it, or how you even have the power to use it. But we do know that it is illegal!" he said, raising his voice. "You know the punishments for it. Guards! Take this man away!"

The guards looked at each other with wide eyes, they all knew what Aleric was capable of, and now they were supposed to apprehend him?

Aleric quickly grew angry upon hearing the words that he was to be arrested. He hadn't felt any emotion besides sadness in days, but now he was angry. Suddenly, he looked up at the guards with his eyes glowing a fiery yellow light. The guards stopped in their steps. Aleric sat motionless, glaring. Waiting for anyone to approach. It was their move…

"What, do you want all the magic for yourself, Maub?" the king finally spoke, trying to break the thick tension. "If you have magic, Maub, then what's the harm if one more person does too?

"He can hurt people!" Maub yelled visibly irritated. "He broke the law! You know what can happen. It is for the kingdom's safety. *Your* safety!"

The king ignored the ranting wizard. He was busy looking over Aleric as he sat motionless with glowing eyes.

"Tell me, boy," the king continued. "Do you think you can use your magic whenever you want? Or just when it comes around?" There was a long pause.

"I can control it," Aleric replied in a distinctly lower voice that carried an ominous echo with it. The king was taken back by Aleric's voice, it having almost completely changed, but he regained his composure quickly. There was a glint in the king's eyes and a half grin on his face.

"Do you think you can use your magic to find my son?" the king's old eyes lit up with eagerness as he awaited Aleric's response. "Can you sense where people are with your magic?"

"I don't think so, my king," Aleric replied. "I believe these powers are limited to just strength."

"Oh," replied the king, turning his face to the ground, "I see." The king turned away and sat back down in his seat. He looked upward to the makeshift roof that had been built to temporarily block out the rain and wind while the castle's roof could be repaired from the dragon's damage. A calm but cold breeze ran through the room from the open roof far above them.

"Be that as it may. This kingdom still needs you," the king eventually spoke.

"What?" Maub yelled, rising to his feet once again. "This man broke the law!" he cried out, pointing a long craggy finger at Aleric.

"Just because it is illegal doesn't make it wrong!" King Victus snapped back loud and stern at the wizard.

"It… does… so." Maub said slowly, slamming both hands onto the table. There was an obvious change to his tone as he grew angrier. But the king ignored the outburst and began to speak again.

"We may have been wrong about this whole magic thing all along," he said, stroking his white beard. "Look what has become of the kingdom. We are outnumbered, outmatched, and overpowered by the morally corrupt! I've learned a painful lesson over these last decades." The king's voice grew louder, and he stood from his seat as his words became more passionate. "The only way to keep evil and destruction at bay is to overpower it with force. Good force!" he said waving a finger into the air. "We can't just sit back and *hope* people do good to each other. They don't! They tear each other apart! Destruction, poverty, and instability have flowed in like water since we have been incapable of forcing it back. We've all suffered from it!" he yelled aloud. "My son, my wife..." He trailed off from his passionate speech, then sat back down in thought. "The kingdom of Mazeron needs you, boy," he said solemnly. "I need you. Your people need you. Will you help us?"

"We have laws!" Maub interrupted, throwing his arms up in disgust.

"Then we'll change the laws," King Victus yelled back.

"I have to agree with Maub," one of the council members interrupted after silently observing the conversation. "This man knew the laws of the land, and he broke them." The king paused at the comment and sat deep in thought for some time before responding.

"Being able to blindly follow laws made up by foolish old men does not make someone moral," he announced quietly. "In fact, maybe being in defiance of unjust laws does," he said, raising an eyebrow. King Victus turned back toward Aleric. "What is your answer, Paladin? Will you serve your kingdom?" he asked. There was a moment's pause. Everyone was staring at the king and Aleric with anticipation.

Aleric took a moment to think about what was being asked of him and his eyes returned to their normal, non-glowing state as he sat, deep in thought. First he thought about Briss and how he had let her down in such an immense way. What would it feel like if he let the people of Mazeron down in the same way? The responsibility seemed too overwhelming. But as he continued to think about Briss he thought about what he had left in this life. She was gone, his home was gone. He had nothing left to live for, but this would give him purpose. The thought of that surprisingly made him feel better for a quick moment. He realized then that he had nothing left to give the world but himself. But that might just be enough.

"I will serve," he replied quietly. The room stayed thick with silence for some moments until finally Maub stood up and stormed out of the room quickly without saying another word. He shuffled away with long angry strides, his long robes flowing behind him, then slammed the large wooden door with a bang behind him as he exited.

"Guards!" The king yelled out. He paused while the guards assembled and turned their attention to the king. "Take this man to his room," he yelled out with a smile on his face. King Victus walked calmly over to Aleric who was still seated. "You'll live here in the castle with me," he stated. "That shouldn't be a problem I would assume since the word is your house was destroyed. I'll pay you 5 gold coins per week. Together we are going to clean up this kingdom!" There was excitement in the king's eyes and his face seemed more youthful and full of life, and with a grin on it rather than the usual scowl. "Do we have a deal?" the king outstretched his arm to Aleric who stood up from his seat and grasped the king's outstretched hand in return.

"Deal," Aleric replied with a smile.

"Wonderful!" the king said laboring to his feet and shuffling over to pat Aleric's shoulder. "Let's get started right away. Fetch some wine! he yelled out to the porters. "I have so many ideas."

Later, after a long night of wine and lots of discussion about what overwhelming tasks he should take on, Aleric was shown to his new quarters within the castle. It was a large suite in the east tower. There was a feather bed in the room and in a separate room it had its own privy and a large steel tub.

"They bring hot water for the tub every third day," one of the guards said excitedly. "Wish we had that kind of treatment at the barracks!" he said with a chuckle.

"No kidding," Aleric replied, walking around, marveling at the room. "This place is almost as big as my cottage was," he said in awe. After some quick small talk, the accompanying guards began to exit the room.

"It is good to have you back," one of them replied as he closed the door, leaving Aleric finally alone once again.

Then he turned and fell to the bed with a giant sigh of relief. Just hours before he had nowhere else to go but back here. He was almost certain he would end up in the dark belly of the dungeon. He never would have thought he would have ended up here high in the castle with his own private room and soft bed. He was still feeling the weight of the world from the loss of his wife, and the tragedy still hung heavy upon him, but tonight there was a small sense of relief. Maybe things will be okay one day after all? He thought. He was exhausted and hadn't had any decent rest since his last night with Briss almost a week ago. A brief and rare moment of comfort washed over him as he lay in the bed, and then finally he was asleep.

For Aleric, the next few days were spent lazily getting to know the castle grounds, resting, and getting settled into his new quarters. At one point the king sent two guards with him to help gather up important belongings from the rubble that was once his home. But most items just reminded him of Briss which upset him deeply, so after a few hours of scouring the wreckage, they left with almost nothing except a few tokens to remember Briss by and his weapons from the destroyed shed. The king had promised Aleric that the guards would have his cottage rebuilt as soon as possible. Although grateful for the offer, Aleric couldn't help but think it wouldn't be much of a home without Briss.

Returning to the castle that evening, Aleric found the dining hall filled with various unfamiliar people, all dressed in the finest attire of the time. The king immediately pulled Aleric in and began introducing him to the various nobles and landowners that were left from throughout the kingdom.

"Here he is!" the king yelled aloud, announcing Aleric's arrival. "This is the man I was telling you about." The king was visibly excited and acting youthfully again, and Aleric soon found out this entire event was planned for him. He knew it was just an excuse for the wealthy members of the kingdom to get together for drink and company, but he enjoyed the attention nonetheless.

"Cheers to the king's paladin!" different guests would announce loudly throughout the night.

"To the king's paladin!" the others would shout as they raised their glasses.

It was good for him to stay busy, he thought to himself in a rare moment of downtime. Even in the short down moments between conversations his mind would wander back to his wife Briss. Staying busy, he thought, was the only way to make it through.

The party ran late into the night and despite the seemingly endless advances and flirtations by the various noblewomen of the party, Aleric eventually escaped to his room alone and fell hard and exhausted onto the soft bed. There he lay once again, alone in the thick silence. This is the part he hated, the lonely times when his mind was free to wander. Unintentionally he dwelled endlessly on how the loss of his wife Briss was entirely his fault. The what-if's were endless as he played out the events of that day over and over in his head. What if one little thing had changed at any moment in time? None of this would have happened. It was all so avoidable. The things he wanted to say to her, the apologies he needed her to know. They would never happen, he thought to himself. She is gone.

Chapter 5: The Mischief Mage

Weeks later, the rainy season was coming to an end and the muddy paths and streets throughout the kingdom were drying out and giving way to warmer and sunnier days. The king ensured Aleric that plans were being drawn up immediately on how he and the king's guards could get the kingdom back on track and rid the valley of all the menaces that were choking the once thriving kingdom.

Aleric awoke late one morning in his room. Surrounded by stone walls, it was cold from the night air, and he pulled the blankets up to protect himself from the cool breeze coming through the open window. He could hear the villagers in the courtyards and streets below going about their daily business. There was a knock at his chamber doors. He got up and opened the door. It was one of the castle's many servants.

"The king requests your company in the South wing, sir," the man said.

"Ok, when?" replied Aleric in a slow and low voice, still half asleep.

"Now," the man said. Then walked away down the hall.

Aleric closed the door, got dressed, and headed toward the South wing to one of the meeting rooms within the castle. He opened the thick wooden doors and entered the room. In the solid stone room sat a long wooden table with a dozen chairs surrounding it. On the walls hung two cloth tapestries and some sconces, but otherwise they were bare and void of any windows. This particular room was their normal meeting place and was used solely for that because it was it was on one of the center floors and at the far end of the castle, so no unwelcome visitors could eavesdrop from the roof or surrounding rooms.

As Aleric entered the room, Maub was standing at the head of the table, tall and lanky in black cloaks that draped down to the floor. With both hands leaning on the table, he glared at Aleric as he entered. The king was sitting next to him, looking timid and small next to the towering wizard. Aleric entered with confidence and took his place at the table, near the door. Aleric, King Victus, and Maub were the only three members in the room today which was odd and out of place for these meetings. Usually there were advisors, commanders, and plans being made as a group. Quiet and timid the king started to speak.

"I still think we should start with…" He was cut short by a quick gesture of Maub's hand that caused him to flinch.

"It has already been discussed, my lord," Maub said slowly, raising his eyes mischievously toward Aleric. "Remember?" The king nodded slowly like a disciplined child. Then Maub spoke loudly. "We have weighed the options; we must now put plans into motion. We must act. We must *do*!" The king lowered his head and stayed silent as Maub spoke. He was pale and flush and looked to be somewhat sick. Still, Aleric thought, the quietness seemed out of character for the king who was usually excited and commanding in these meetings.

A feeling of distrust washed over Aleric, and he studied the tall ominous wizard as he spoke. Aleric had always been wary and distrusting of Maub. But over the past few weeks he had started to get used to the wizard's unusual and sometimes random behavior and had come to the conclusion that the wizard was not bad, just odd. Aleric did, however, take notice of the peculiar glance that the wizard gave the king before speaking to Aleric again.

"We have your first mission, Paladin," Maub said loudly. "An easy one to start, but an important one, nonetheless. There has been an anomaly in the far lands beyond the villages. One which has plagued the outer farmers for years that no one can explain. One that it is choking the entire kingdom's food supply."

"What is this anomaly?" Aleric asked, becoming interested.

"Weather will change suddenly and without warning. Winds and tornadoes come out of nowhere. Hail in the middle of the summer, fires during the wet season. All destroying crops and forests across the outer lands."

"Why bother? There are hardly any farms out in those lands," Aleric replied with a confused tone. "That area is probably not inhabited at all."

"Exactly!" Maub cut him short. "And we are going to fix that. And people will benefit from it," he said excitedly, throwing his arms about. "There is some sort of magic at work out there and you are the only one who can counter it. Some sort of magic artifact or token that has been lost, wreaking havoc out there. It will be an easy task for our fearless powerful Paladin." Maub paused and waited for a reply. "Right?" he challenged.

"Sure," Aleric said with a small roll of his eyes. He stood up and moved towards the door. "Leave a map under my door before morning that shows the area this supposed weather anomaly is happening. I'll ready my horse and set off at dawn to investigate."

"Very well then," Maub said with a small bow towards Aleric. "Your service is…appreciated." The odd wizard forced a thin grin on his face. The king sat motionless and silently nodded as the conversation went on around him and without him. As Aleric turned towards the door, he did not notice Maub's mischievous grin. Aleric turned, and with a respectful head nod towards the king, let himself out. He stopped just before the door.

"I'm curious, Maub," Aleric said, turning back around. "You've had magic this whole time. Why do you need me? Why haven't you fixed these problems?" There was a long intense pause as Maub glared back at Aleric. There was hate in the wizard's eyes, and he was clearly not used to being challenged in any way. Finally, his face relaxed.

"I am old, Paladin," Maub replied, his tone more friendly than his expression. "Magic ages the body and wears out over the long years. I barely wield enough power these days to light a candle. Sadly, I am not what I used to be. I give counsel to the king these days. That is all." Maub grinned a forced smile. After a moment, Aleric nodded in understanding then exited the room, closing the door behind him.

After that, Aleric spent the rest of the day doing work around his new living quarters. Still trying to make his area of the castle comfortable. But the task was fruitless without Briss.

"You need a woman to make a house a home" he mumbled aloud, staring at an almost blank wall in the center of the cluttered and cold room. He decided he should get out of the cold, lonely room for a while and spent the remainder of the day napping in a nearby field under the warm spring sun then began assembling his gear and getting his horse ready for the journey ahead.

The next day felt like it came almost immediately after he closed his eyes the night before, and he started the day not as rested as he would prefer for a long voyage. The king and Maub were mysteriously absent from breakfast, which wasn't too uncommon, but he thought they would have at least been there to see him off on this important day. But the map had been left under his door as requested, so he knew the task was still expected to be done. He ate alone in the large dining hall, gathered extra apples, carrots, and rations for the road, then went to the stables.

The morning air was pleasant and cool as he rode away from the castle. He rode west toward the edge of the kingdom and the surrounding forests. Most people, along with Aleric, did not really know what lay beyond the forests. He had never been very far into them. Hardly anyone had. No one recently anyway. There were often travelers coming and going in his youth, he remembered. But not so much these days.

He pulled out the map which was pretty much blank in all the areas past the forests, but it did outline the mountain range that ran through the kingdom and far beyond, so he was able to get a decent idea of how far he would be traveling. A basic red X marked the general area in which he was to go looking for the magic, or whatever was causing the mysterious weather patterns that had been reported.

"Reported by who?" he mumbled aloud and scrunched his face in confusion. "There must be farmers out there." He shrugged then continued to ride on.

Aleric, looking strong, shiny, and proud in his armor atop his tall horse, reached the forests before the end of the day. He paused on the overgrown dirt road and gazed ahead as it barreled into the tree line and disappeared into the dark thick forests ahead.

"Here we go," he said aloud, patting the horse on the neck. He continued into the thick woods as the sun was starting to get low in the sky.

It was an eerie feeling to him being in the thick woods after being in the valley of the kingdom for so many years. This time of day when the sun was low in the sky made every shadow seem like a predator, lying in wait for the kill. As he traveled through the darkening forest he saw movement in the distance, then turning quickly he realized it to be only a tree stump or blowing leaves in the waning light. This happened over and over throughout the evening. His mind was playing tricks on him, but confidently he rode on, deeper into the woods.

Soon the darkness settled over the forest, and he thought about stopping for the night, but Aleric was not tired. The moon hung full and bright in the sky above and illuminated the path just enough to continue on. He was already getting used to traveling through the thick forests, and his spirits were unexpectedly high for being in such an empty, ominous place all alone. But the sounds of owls and snapping sticks in the distance reminded him that he wasn't alone in these woods at all. In fact, they teamed with life. Eyes reflected in the moonlight, watching him closely as he slowly trotted by. The sound of wings could be heard in the distance as different flying species hunted in the darkness of night, and he could see the glow of the nighttime fairies in the distance through the trees. Always at a distance. At least he hoped they would always stay at a distance.

He could have gone all night at this pace, he thought to himself. But eventually the ground beneath the horse's hooves became noticeably wet, indicating a swamp or river was nearby. It was too late to be navigating a river crossing in unknown lands in the middle of the night. So, he decided it would be a good time to stop and camp until morning. After finding a nice clearing just a few feet from the path, he dismounted the horse and began gathering firewood and preparing to cook a meal. Soon he had a nice bundle of firewood, and after piling it in a nice teepee shape, he began rummaging through his pack, looking for his flint to light the fire with.

"What in the world am I doing?" he said aloud, throwing up his arms. Then leaning over to the stack of firewood he held his palm open. Suddenly his eyes began to glow their ominous amber color, and a ball of light appeared in the palm of his hand. He blew with his lips and out of his hand, a fire bellowed loud and fast into the firewood, igniting it into a nice warm fire immediately. He grinned as his eyes dimmed, then scooted closer to the warmth of the fire. "I could get used to this," he said aloud to the forest, then continued warming his hands.

After a small meal Aleric doused the fire and was left surrounded in almost complete darkness. It was a warm evening, so his heavy blanket was enough shelter. He curled up next to a large tree and with the long days ride weighing on him, he fell deep asleep in just moments.

This travel routine went on for days as Aleric trudged through the vast forest. The canopy of the forest was thick, and the trees were so massively tall that some days he barely saw the sun at all. Eventually he found the river that was indicated on the map, and he followed it for days as the directions stated. It was peaceful to travel near the river, he thought. Plenty of water for drinking and bathing and the woods here seemed to pose no threat towards humans, or Paladins.

On the fifth day, after following the river on a barely noticeable trail, finally a small bridge appeared in front of him. It was thin, only as wide as one horse. He thought it was odd for an area that was supposedly heavily traveled at one time that the bridge wasn't made large enough for even a wagon to cross. He looked about and studied the area. There were no footprints anywhere nearby, and the entire bridge was entangled in greenery and leaves indicating it had been abandoned and unused for quite some time.

"What kind of wild goose chase am I on here?" he mumbled out loud as he dismounted his horse and began to guide him across the rickety old bridge. It creaked as they crossed but held steady and there was no incident, as he almost expected.

After crossing the bridge Aleric got back on his horse and they continued on. Not long after the bridge crossing the trail took a sharp hook right, and all of the sudden the thick forest opened into vast fields of tall green grass surrounded by cliffs on either side. Finally, the sun shown down bright and warm upon his face and his spirits immediately improved upon leaving the confinement of the thick damp forest.

The afternoon wore on and Aleric whistled lightly as they trotted slowly in the hot sun. He put off stopping for lunch now that it felt like they were actually getting somewhere after days of being confined in the forests. Later in the day the trail began to wind left and right again instead of its earlier straight and narrow route. Winding through trees and large rocks then back into the grassy fields surrounded by tall cliffs. At one turn he thought he heard and saw something in the trees, but upon swinging his head and horse around swiftly he found nothing there.

Then, not even an hour later it happened again. A shadow in the trees to his right. He turned quickly, then it was gone. This time he was sure he had seen something. A cloaked shadow, not far off into the trees. He dismounted quickly to investigate. Walking to the edge of the trail and pushing through the brush, he peered into the deep forest beyond and called out to whoever may be listening. But it was silent, not even the sound of birds could be heard. After noticing nothing out of the ordinary he walked back to his horse, but this time took him by the reins and walked him cautiously forward along the open trail. No birds? He thought to himself. Something felt unsafe now. It was in the air. He grabbed his longsword from the horse's satchel and put it in the sheath on his waist and wore it like he did the rest of his armor, save for his helmet.

Through the eerie calmness they continued, walking slowly and cautiously, eyes darting back and forth looking for anything concealed in the trees. Aleric was still feeling uneasy when he noticed a herd of deer running quickly along the steep hills past the fields to his left. He watched them in awe as they pranced easily on the steep terrain. They were going very fast though, more than a deer's regular trot. Too fast, as if they were fleeing a predator. He waited and watched but they were not being chased as far as he could see.

Then, out of the corner of his eye there was a sudden bright light in the distance. He realized it just in time. With instinct alone he jumped fast and far off the trail then rolled into the brush as a massive fireball exploded right where he had been standing. Hot air and debris blew across his face as he rolled away from the explosion. It narrowly missed his horse who in a sheer panic reared up and took off down the trail at a full sprint, leaving him behind without a thought.

Peeking up from the tall grass and brush at the edge of the trail, Aleric saw the shape of a cloaked man on top of a cliff, at the opposite end of the clearing. Suddenly another fireball came crashing down from the cliffs. It exploded just feet away and the force was so hard it shoved him sideways as a blast of dry heat and bits of rock and debris bit and stung at his exposed skin. Aleric rolled into the thicker brush and laid still for a moment to gather his thoughts. Then it hit him harder than if the fireball had. He had been ambushed by a powerful magic wielder. The thought gripped him with fear, and he knew he had to act fast, so he crawled through the brush and rolled into the trees at the edge of the clearing just as another fireball exploded into a tree next to him, leaving a charred stump and scattered bits of burning wood. He knew he would eventually get hit if stayed here, exposed from the attacker's high ground.

Quickly, Aleric rose to his feet with a loud grunt then ran directly into the concealment of the woods. He ran as fast and far as he could, then after a significant amount of time had passed, he stopped to listen. It was silent in the forest. Dead silent. But not for long. Soon he heard footsteps coming from somewhere in the woods. He peaked slowly from behind the large tree that he was hiding behind and peered towards the sound of crunching leaves. There in the distance through the trees was a hooded figure creeping through the woods. He couldn't make out many details of the attacker besides the deep red cloak he wore and a long tangling gray beard that went down to the man's chest.

How did he get down here in the valley from the top of that cliff so fast? Aleric thought to himself, feeling utterly unprepared and outmatched. How could I have gotten myself into this situation, going head-to-head with a mage when I only found out that even have magic just weeks ago? His thoughts were taking over his instinct and the despair of the hopeless situation was setting in, paralyzing his ability for action.

Then he noticed the footsteps in the leaves had stopped. His intuition finally kicked back in and immediately he jumped and rolled to the next tree, just as the one he was hiding behind exploded into nothing but wood chips and burning twigs. In an instant, Aleric darted out from behind the tree and returned fire. Forcing a blast of hot energy towards the attacker, just as he had done in his fight against the dragon. But this time it was fruitless. With a simple motion of his staff, the cloaked mage deflected the energy blast into the forest with ease. Panic set in as Aleric realized he was woefully outmatched, so he began to run again. The cloaked figure chased quickly behind him with an awkward shuffle in the long robes.

Aleric was lost here in the thickness of the woods. He had no idea how to counter or make a stand against his attacker. All he could do was run, and that is exactly what he did. He ran back towards the direction he came, back towards the fields.

He exited the woods, bursting into the clearing, panting and almost out of energy from running with the weight of his armor. Aleric turned back towards the woods and saw his assailant not far in the distance, still coming for him.

The cloaked mage had a tanned, weathered, wrinkly face with solid white eyes and an intense stare glaring back at Aleric with hate and determination. He could tell the man was older but the speed at which he shuffled through the woods, pursuing him, was beyond his comprehension.

Aleric began to run again, completely out of ideas and with his attacker closing in on him fast. Then, as he ran across the trail, he almost crashed right into the side of his horse as it came running by, still running aimlessly about in a panic. With impressive agility, Aleric leapt forward, grabbed ahold of the reins, and in one motion using the forward momentum of the horse to swing him around was quickly atop the horse. Quickly, he tucked his head down low against the horse's body as they raced away from their attacker. As they sped away Aleric braved a glance behind them to see the cloaked figure standing motionless in the middle of the trail, watching them ride away. Suddenly one more ball of fire crashed into the trees in front of them, just as he thought they were safe. A scream of rage came from behind them from the cloaked mage, filling the air like thunder. That was the last Aleric saw of the mage before the trail turned a sharp left and back into the safety of the woods.

After that, Aleric rode for hours until he felt that he had sufficiently lost the mysterious attacker, and then they rode some more. He continued on because he was fairly certain that the cloaked man had somehow transported himself from on atop of the cliffs from where he first ambushed him, to down in the woods in just a matter of moments. Magic wielders like this were not to be underestimated as no one knew the limits and capabilities of what was possible with magic. Aleric pondered the possibilities with anxiety coursing through his veins. Could this man transport to anywhere that he wanted, and just appear again after he rode all day and night? He shrugged the thought out of his head, realizing there was nothing much he could do about it, then pushed his fear aside and kept riding. Eventually Aleric and his horse both became too tired and were forced to stop.

They had ridden all night, and it was almost morning by now. The morning light illuminated the lands with a soft gold hue before the sun came up over the horizon and began giving heat to the day. Aleric turned from the trail and delved into forests and the cover of the thick trees. He guided his horse far off the trail then began to make a camp in the thick woods to get some rest. His knees and hands still felt shaky from the adrenaline of the fight and following hard ride. There would be no fire for a warm meal today. He did not have much of an appetite anyway but forced down some bread, fed the horse, then curled up under a tree again and tried to get some rest. Aleric decided he would continue on later that night under the cover of darkness, to avoid being seen and ambushed again.

Although he was exhausted from the long ride, an uneasiness kept him from sleep. His mind began to wander as he lay there in the loneliness of the woods. For the first time since he had moved into the castle and been praised throughout the kingdom for slaying the dragon, he started to doubt himself. Doubt his strength, doubt his powers and his ability to use them. The cloaked mage had deflected his magic so easily. His confidence began to slip, thinking that he might be found out to be a fraud and would inevitably let everyone down. Suddenly he felt despairingly alone and wished he was home, comfortable in a warm bed with a warm family around him. Not lying under this tree in the damp dirt in who knows where, middle of some forest. He would trade all his recent glory just to be home safe and comfortable. Even just some friends for some company would be nice. But none of this was an option, he concluded. Even if he did want it so badly. Somehow that put his mind at ease and his teeth and fists slowly unclenched and soon he was in a deep, healing sleep.

Aleric awoke later that day, refreshed and with high morale simply at the fact that he was still alive. There was no sign of the attacker or pursuit of any kind. To his best recollection, from his hidden spot deep in the woods it felt like midday had come and gone but evening was not yet approaching. He sat in silence while the haze from his deep sleep wore off and enjoyed the calmness of the forest. The horse was grazing peacefully nearby when suddenly Aleric heard a faint sound in the distance. Like music dancing on the wind and flowing through the trees. It rang in his ears like a bell, and he instantly recognized it as a musical instrument of some sort, coming from somewhere in the distance. He stood up quickly but cautiously, then made his way through the forest, walking his horse towards the sound.

The sound was still far in the distance, but he could tell he was getting closer to it. Soon he arrived at the edge of the forest and a large clearing of a field opened before him. He stayed hidden within the trees as he peered out into the vast field that was surrounded by trees on all sides. At the far end of the field sat a small cabin made of wood. A single level cabin with smoke lazily wafting from the chimney. A field behind the cabin showed crops lined in neat rows. Past the cabin flowed a thick, slow-moving river that meandered away into the forests beyond.

Then he heard the sound again. On the West end of the field, adjacent to the cabin and just a few yards from the edge of the forest he saw a girl, sitting and playing a harp like instrument that was small enough to fit in her arms. She plucked the strings gracefully with thin agile fingers and the sound was carried off by the wind into the distance. A small herd of deer peacefully grazed near her, glancing up occasionally to watch her as they ate.

Aleric's recent fears and anxiety subsided as he realized this was a peaceful place where he could possibly get a meal and regroup before going back through the thick and unknown forests. Still, being a cautious person, he waited and watched the harp playing girl a little longer before deciding to make his presence known to her and the occupants of this cabin, hidden deep within the woods. Aleric sat down on the forest floor, legs crossed and listened to the peaceful sound of the harp and the wind blowing lightly across the fields and through the forest trees.

Then he noticed movement in the trees beyond the far end of the field. He couldn't make out what it was, but there was definitely a shadow of a figure moving through the woods. Moving fast. He stayed hidden within the trees, watching intently, prying through the thick forests to catch a glimpse of what was over there. Then he saw it…

In an instant he was back on his horse and riding at full speed through the woods, still behind the tree line and concealed in the forest. Together Aleric and his horse dodged trees and bounded over branches with intense speed as they raced toward the harp playing girl in the field. Aleric's eyes began to glow bright amber again, just as they had when he fought the dragon. He lowered his head down close to the horse for speed and his powers began to resonate through the horse. Together they picked up speed. Faster now, absorbing The Paladin's powers, the horse was almost flying over the branches and felled trees while hardly making any sound in the process. They had almost run the whole length of the field, and the young girl was just feet away when they bounded through the forest's edge and burst into the field.

Startled, the terrified girl dropped her instrument and turned to run. But before she had any time to get away The Paladin leapt from his horse, and flying through the air with fierce speed his body hit like a crashing meteor into the giant beast that was charging from behind the girl, that she hadn't even seen or knew was coming for her. Paladin and beast collided with massive force and a loud crash of armor. The two rolled and tumbled to the ground until they both came to a stop, lying in the tall grass, just feet apart from one another.

The stunned girl, frozen in fear, surveyed the two. Animal and metal knight lying motionless in the grass. The animal was heaving large breaths, lying on the ground. She did not recognize what type of animal it was, but it was large. Very large and smelled foul like the stench of death. She turned to the knight whose armor was crumpled and broken, and he lay motionless on the ground. Filled with fear she turned and ran towards the cabin. Aleric's horse also fled, but in the opposite direction.

The animal rose first. It was the height of a bull and its hair was long, black and dripped a foul-smelling sweat. Its face resembled a wolf, and it had fangs exposed from its upper and lower jaws. Its eyes were a soulless, fierce orange like a snakes. Cautiously it approached the motionless knight. Slowly it stalked towards him, then confidently and almost arrogantly stood over Aleric's motionless body.

Then suddenly a hard kick to the animal's knee knocked it off guard and The Paladin rose to his feet in an instant. His eyes were glowing bright amber as the beast stumbled to catch its balance. The Paladin had no weapon because his sword was stowed on the horse who had fled. The Paladin glanced back and forth, looking for a way out of the situation as the beast circled him, closing in for the kill. Standing ready, circling with arms up, he knew he had to make the first move.

The Paladin charged the beast and with three giant steps he lowered his shoulder and slammed all his weight into the oncoming beast's chest, body checking it and pushing it's front legs off the ground. It was just an instant; The Paladin unsheathed his dagger and with one hand jabbed it hard, directly into the beast's raised chest. Then with the other hand he hammered the butt end of the dagger deep into the hide. The beast let out a horrible shriek that told The Paladin the dagger had penetrated deep.

But not deep enough. With unworldly strength the beast swatted The Paladin with his giant muscled arm, and he went tumbling like a toy into the bush, knocking him momentarily unconscious and rattled. He couldn't think clearly or move as the beast came upon him to finish the attack. He just knew the beast was there and that he was finished. Aleric's eyes lost their glow and there was nothing left to give. A blankness washed over his face and all the fear left his body. Too tired and defeated to care.

It was then in the final moments when a man came from seemingly out of nowhere, leaping through the air from the tall grass he landed next to the beast and with a quick motion of one arm cut a long, thin, razor-sharp sword right down the beast's side. The beast pulled back away with a shriek of pain and confusion from the sudden attack. Then again, the man leapt through the air, pushing off the beasts back with enormous strength he landed on the other side of the animal before it even realized where its attacker had gone. The man took another swing so fast that it seemed like the sword weighed nothing. It found its mark once again along the beast's throat and it fell lifeless to the ground.

The man stood ready and silent with his wide, thin sword still raised to ensure the threat was gone. Aleric was slowly rolling over in the tall grass, trying to make sense of what he had just witnessed. He laid there as his vision became less blurred and ears slowly stopped ringing. Finally, he was able to make out the person. Standing before him was a thick man with a leather tunic. His bare arms were bulky with muscle. He held a long-flattened sword that was noticeably shinier, thinner, and wider than standard swords. The man had a thick, dark black beard that made his teeth look extra white, and he wore a wool knitted cap atop his most likely hairless head. The man's massive tree-trunk like structure and stern look was intimidating at first, but as Aleric began to help himself up from the ground the man's stern face softened and he gave him a noticeably friendly smile, showing his bright white teeth behind the dark black beard.

"Aaaaye, you're ok!" He said walking towards Aleric with an outstretched hand. "Let me help you up" he said grabbing Aleric's arm and yanking him from the ground with impressive strength.

"What was that thing?" Aleric asked as they both glanced at the massive corpse. It was already starting to decay and decompose. Most of the flesh was vanishing before their eyes, blowing away like black dust into the wind until just black bones like charcoal were left.

"I've never seen anything like it," the man said, studying the quickly decaying corpse. It sure looked like the mythical Morghvile to me though."

"You don't really think those exist?" Aleric replied.

"Well," the man pointed at the corpse. "Sure looks real to me."

"We're all in a lot of trouble if the Morghvile are real," Aleric said forcing a chuckle. The Morghvile were creatures of legend that only the mad ever reported seeing. Maybe just no one else ever lived to tell about them? Large, fanged beasts from another world that specialized in hunting and shredding their victims. They knew only two things; hunt and kill. Their bodies were homed in for it. Long snouts could sniff out their target from miles away and their long legs ensured they caught up to them quick.

"All I know is that you saved my little girls life." The bearded man continued.

"Well, you saved mine, so I guess we're even." Aleric replied with a grunt, brushing the grass and dirt from his crumpled armor. There was a pause as the man stared at Aleric.

"I like you. You're ok! Come inside, let's get you cleaned up and talk about this mess." Together they began to walk slowly through the golden colored fields and towards the cabin. Aleric was limping in obvious pain from the fight. In the distance, smoke rose lazily from the chimney of the cabin until it disappeared into the wind over a calm river. Aleric looked around as they walked but could not see his horse anywhere in the field. Oh well, he thought. We'll deal with one problem at a time.

As they approached the cabin, Aleric could see the young girl that had been playing the small harp at the edge of the forest and two others standing on the porch with her. An older man and woman.

"This is my family" the bearded man gestured as they stopped at the steps at the front porch of the cabin. "My daughter Thei, who you saw out there in the field. My older son Baylen, and his wife. My name is Thearbuc." He announced, outstretching his hand to Aleric. "And you are?"

"I am Aleric," he replied shaking Thearbuc's hand. His hands were thick and calloused and his grip alarming tight.

"Please, come inside," Thearbuc motioned toward the cabin door with his booming friendly voice. Thearbuc seemed so friendly and confident that Aleric wondered if the man had ever had a self-doubt or negative thought about anything in the world ever.

The two entered the cabin. It was bright inside from the low hanging sun shining through the windows and there were scattered candles lit throughout the room. A small fire with a pot of boiling stew hung in the fireplace at the far end of the room.

Sitting down on wooden rocking chair, Thearbuc spoke first. "So, what are you doing all the way out here?" he asked in his usual friendly tone.

Aleric sat down across the room and started from the top. He told Thearbuc the whole story from the dragon slaying and magic use, to being hired by the king to clean up the kingdom, then being sent out here in the far woods to be ambushed by a powerful mage. After Aleric finished the story there was a long pause.

"A paladin huh?" Thearbuc finally replied after listening to the story intently. "That's a bold statement. Haven't even heard that word in these parts for oh, about 20 or 30 years." He paused, stroking his beard deep in thought, then continued. "We rarely get travelers out here anymore. And now you show up, right when that Morghvile looking beast did. Well, let's just say I don't think that is a coincidence." His voice was sterner now and he studied Aleric as he contemplated the story he had just been told.

"You may be right." Aleric replied rubbing his chin, also thinking about the events of the day. "Maybe it hunted me here from the forests? There are a lot of beasts roam these woods."

"Mmmm," grumbled Thearbuc. "I just don't know. We've lived out here for a while now and have never seen anything like that. But yes, from time to time we do have to defend ourselves and our home out here. There are many different creatures from magical to evil that call these forests home. None like that though." There was a long silence while both men contemplated the situation. Then Thearbuc spoke again.

"And this mage… I think know of this mage you speak of" he said curiously. "The mischief you mentioned, the weather anomalies, destruction of fields and crops, fires out of nowhere. There's even been rumors of farmers going missing. Well, farmers have gone missing. The only rumor part is why they left and where they went. I think your mage has been in these parts for some time now. In areas where I hunt, I have seen random small tornados and hailstorms in the distance. Hail in the middle of summer. I've seen fields and forests burnt when there hasn't been lighting storms in months." Thearbuc paused again, deep in thought. "I think I may know about where he is..."

“Can you take me there?” Aleric asked in a low and serious tone, sitting up in his chair with a faint glow appearing in his eyes.

“Whoa!” Thearbuc leaned back, noticing the glow in The Paladin’s eyes. “So, you are a paladin,” he said somewhat nervously. “I think I know what you’re getting at. You want to go after this mischief mage, don’t you?”

“I do,” Aleric replied blankly with his eyes returning to normal. “With the element of surprise, I know I can get at him. I won’t be caught off guard again.”

Thearbuc paused, still thinking. “I’m not trying to be rude here but I’m not sure you can take him alone,” he said with a thin grin forming. “Plus, I owe you and I never turn down a fight. I’m going with you! Let’s go get your Mischief Mage. I have a lot more to lose if he ever comes across this place anyway. Can’t have him out there in my fields causing trouble.”

“Just like that?” Aleric asked confused. “No argument?”

“Gah.” Thearbuc replied. “I’ve been itching for a fight. Been out here getting old for far too long. Old and bored I am.”

“But your daughter?”

“Meh, she’ll be happy to be rid of me. She is that age. Plus my son and his wife will be here to watch over her.” Aleric stared at Thearbuc for a moment. He could tell his mind was made up. “I want to feel alive again!” Thearbuc announced sitting up. “I want the kingdom to be prosperous again and be able to move back. To be around LIFE!”

“Very well then,” Aleric stated cheerfully. “Let’s prepare then leave at dawn.”

“Cheers to that!” Thearbuc said raising his stein to Aleric’s. “Tomorrow, we hunt!”

They clanked their steins together and began talking about less important and more joyous matters. Aleric noticed right away that Thearbuc was talkative and friendly. A truly great person and family man. His wife had mysteriously gone missing as many people of Mazeron did. So, to keep his family safe from the ever-failing kingdom he had gathered them up and moved them out here to the forests. “Better to take our chances out here with the beasts and animals over the real beasts and animals in the kingdom,” he said more than once.

The merry night wore on, then after supper they began to discuss a plan and gather supplies for the upcoming adventure. They didn't know how many days it would take to find the mage, so they planned for a long trip and packed enough to be well supplied for many days in the woods.

In the morning Thearbuc bade his children goodbye. Leaving the older son in charge, the two left the cabin and marched through the fields back towards the forest. As they marched away Thearbuc veered away from the fields and into the tree line of the forest.

"One quick stop," he announced loudly. "You'll love this…" As he said it, he turned into the woods and there stood a large wooden shed. Aleric was taken back as he did not notice the shed through the woods until they were almost upon it. "Come in!" Thearbuc said opening the latch and swinging the door open. "This is my blacksmith shop. Load up!"

Aleric gazed in awe as he looked about the shed. There were weapons everywhere. Probably the most he had ever seen before in once place, and most were a shiny silver as opposed to the dull brownish color most weapons of the day were.

"What is this metal?" Aleric asked looking at a particularly beautiful longsword. "I noticed your sword is the same color."

"It don't have a name," Thearbuc replied, smiling about finally being able to show off his work." It's a blend of metals, I invented. Makes them stronger and lighter."

"That is why your sword can be lighter and thinner, and still cut so sharp," Aleric said in amazement, touching the shiny sword.

"Well. I didn't make all these for nothing," Thearbuc interrupted, grabbing two sharp daggers and a hatchet, and stowing them throughout his boots and belt. "Load up!" The two spent some time choosing their weapons then after some time left the cabin with enough weapons to arm a small brigade, then began their march again.

The sun was already hot on their faces even though it was just peaking over the morning horizon and the occasional sting of the Leedles reminded them they were always around. The tall grass was wet from the nighttime dew and made their feet and clothes below the knees wet. Some spots in the field were still muddy which made travel slow until they got to the edge of the fields then finally entered the forest once again.

The march through the woods was surprisingly pleasant. They both enjoyed each other's company and had a lot in common as far as their childhoods in the kingdom and their views on the state of things now.

Thearbuc spoke more about moving his family into the woods to get away from all the arrests and impositions from the king. He felt the bad times and tyranny brewing and didn't want anything to do with it.

He also spoke in depth about how he had always been a weapons master. His parents had him learning combat skills almost as soon as he could walk, he joked. Thearbuc knew someone strong and noticeable like him would inevitably get into trouble with the king if he had stayed. So, they moved to the woods after his wife had disappeared mysteriously, and there in the deep forests he raised his daughter with the help of his older son and his wife while honing his combat skills and living the most peaceful life he could.

Thearbuc was a true weapons master, Aleric learned. Swords, bows, maces, and all sorts of miscellaneous weapons. He had mastered them all. He would invent and build his own weapons in his shop then train extensively with them. He spoke more in depth about how he had created the metal for the weapons himself. A super light alloy that was almost unbreakable, even when forged thin.

"These are all made of the same steel," Thearbuc said, motioning to the many daggers and hatchet that were draped about him.

"And what is that then?" Aleric asked with a slight laugh, pointing at the large wooden club that Thearbuc wore on his back.

"Sometimes you just need a simple club." He replied with a white toothed grin behind his dark beard. Thearbuc was well armed to say the least, Aleric thought to himself. You wouldn't want to stumble across someone who looked as fierce as Thearbuc while alone in the woods. It was odd how friendly and nice he was once you got to know him, despite his fierce look.

The day wore on as the two marched through the vast woods. They didn't expect to find any trace of their Mischief

Mage for many days at least but as they were walking, they began to smell the faint smell of smoke in the air.

"Burning wood," Thearbuc announced just as Aleric's senses were telling him the same thing. "Look. There through the woods," he pointed. Up ahead there was a lingering haze hovering in the air which made it difficult to see through. "It's smoke."

Cautiously the two rushed ahead. The smoke got thicker as they ran until finally, they broke through the thick trees of the forest and into a clearing in the woods. But the clearing wasn't a natural one. All around them were burnt stumps and remnants of destroyed and burnt trees. The burns were fresh and the remaining stumps still smoldering. They gazed in disbelief. Looking around they saw a vast area of forest and trees gone. Burnt into almost nothing, leaving only debris and destruction.

"Has there been any lighting storms around here lately?" Aleric asked Thearbuc, with a faint bit of hope.

"No sir," Thearbuc replied slowly looking at the charred remains of a burnt tree stump.

"It must be him. We're getting close," Aleric said eagerly with a flicker of light in his eyes. After a moment of observation, he motioned ahead and they continued on through the haze and burnt trees, cautious and more alert than before.

Then just minutes later, through the haze of the smoke the sky lit up with a flash of lighting and the sound of thunder clapped heavily through the surrounding forest. They jumped at the loud clap of thunder then stopped quietly to listen and watch. The two looked at each other, waiting and wondering what would happen next. Then, it happened again. A booming thunder shook the forest and sent birds fleeing from the treetops.

"Over that hill" Aleric pointed. "It's coming from that direction." Quickly and quietly, they crept upwards onto the hill and out of the depths of the forest. There was smoke blowing through the sky ahead in the distance as they climbed. When they approached the top of hill they began to crawl towards the summit, then they peered over the edge. Ahead of them lay a large field surrounded by the trees of the forest which continued on as far as their eyes could see. In the middle of the field stood the robed man Aleric had seen before. He instantly recognized the dark red robes that the ambushing mage wore. "The attacker from the woods," Aleric whispered. "That's him."

The mage's back was turned, facing away from them so they could not see his face. He raised his hands slowly and with his palms facing upward, he quickly rotated his wrists then there was a sudden loud crack of thunder immediately followed by massive balls of hail and sharp sticks of ice that came crashing down from the sky and into the trees and plants, destroying everything in the fierce storms path. Moments later a small tornado came crashing through the forest and into the field. Trees were instantly turned into small shards of sharp shrapnel and violently pulled from their roots to be thrown through the air.

Aleric and Thearbuc observed the destruction in silence from the top of the hill until they were forced to duck away, back behind the safety of the hill to keep from getting hit by flying debris. They crept back down the hill towards safety as the sound of the storm raged on in the distance.

"What are we going to do?" Thearbuc asked. "I've never seen such powerful magic!"

"Don't I know it," Aleric replied scratching his chin. "We stick to the plan. We need to get to the forests edge without him seeing us." Thearbuc nodded that he agreed, and they set out.

Quickly but quietly, they made their way around the hill and into the forests beyond. They crept quietly through the trees, behind the mages' attention and stayed away from the rolling hills that would likely expose them. At one point they were so close to the mage that they felt like they could just make a charge at him from the woods and into the field. But they knew better by now. The mage was clearly incredibly powerful. Like an orchestra conductor he conducted his symphony of destruction before them. Lightning, thunder, hail, and fiery winds raged on, beating on the forest without mercy. There was no chance at defeating him in a straight up fistfight. They had to outsmart him…

It seemed like it took forever, having to creep around the forest so slowly and stealthily, but eventually Thearbuc and Aleric were in position. The mage had concluded his symphony of destruction for the time being and the forest and fields before him lay destroyed. Nothing was left except a fiery blaze that bellowed black smoke high into the sky. The mage stood motionless in the center of the field. His chest heaving with heavy breaths as he stared blankly at the meaningless destruction; marveling in it. He looked down at his open hands, admiring the power they wielded.

Aleric understood immediately what this was. Power like that was addicting.

Then, with eyes like glowing embers, Aleric stepped out of the forest and into the clearing. Still unknown to the mage he raised both hands high above his head and wielding a large fireball of energy he thrust his hands inward to his torso and with a kickball type motion threw it speeding towards the Mage with complete silence and pinpoint accuracy. The force of the throw went through his entire body, and pushed him backward to where he crouched to one knee as the ball of energy flew fast and silent towards its target. The Mage stood motionless as the projectile approached, seemingly unaware of the imminent explosion about to explode around him.

Then with frightening speed the mage turned towards the attack and with a wave of his wrist it was abruptly deflected violently out of the air without even touching it. The fireball raced towards the forest and exploded into an enormous blast of heat and energy upon hitting a nearby tree, but the mage stood unharmed.

The mage and The Paladin made eye contact. It was just an instant. Then simultaneously The Paladin turned to flee, just as the mage charged after him, fierce and fast as The Paladin fled back into the woods. Again, the mage was unnaturally fast for the way he shuffled with his long robes, and he was already gaining on the knight fast. In just moments the mage had made the length of the field and entered the trees into the thick woods in pursuit.

Then, hiding just to the side within the concealment of the forest, Thearbuc who was lying in wait sprang their trap. He let go the massive, heavy club through air with barely a sound and from just yards away. The Mage didn't sense this one coming until it was right in front of him and just before the club reached his body, he threw his robed arms up as it hit him and managed some sort of defensive spell at the last moment. With a flash of quick blue light between him and the club he was thrown heavily to the ground as collided with his body. The impact of the club took him off his feet, but his magic kept the full force of the club from him.

The mage rolled on the ground grumbling in pain as Thearbuc approached, drawing his sword for the kill. But suddenly he stopped short of the mage, sensing something wrong. The two made eye contact through mage's long hair and hooded robe and Thearbuc saw the rage and hate in his blank white eyes. He knew instantly that an attack was imminent, and he wouldn't be able to make the distance in time before the mage struck. Realizing his mistake, Thearbuc turned to run but before he could take two steps, he felt a blow in the center of the back and was thrown with amazing force, hard to the ground. It was only an instant and everything went black.

In the distance Aleric saw him go down and he turned to flee. The mage turned from Thearbuc's motionless body and made chase. The forest was thick, so Aleric was forced to run along a faint deer path through the woods. The brush was too thick to break through and hide in. He wound through the forest at amazing speed but could still see the mage in the distance, through the trees gaining on him. He was out of ideas. It was clear now after two attempts that the mage could overpower Aleric's magic with ease. He knew this was going to come down to a fistfight with someone far more powerful than himself and it would all be over very quickly.

Then the path turned a sharp left and breaking through the trees Aleric stumbled into a small clearing at the base of a large cliff. Directly in front of him lay a giant dragon which he almost ran straight into it when charging from the forest. Stopping his speed with flailing arms and a cloud of dirt he tried hard to stop before crashing into the dragon. Then, staring face to face with giant teeth and scales he paused for a moment, waited to see if the dragon would awake, then half crouching began to sneak away from the dragon as quietly as possible before it could wake or see him.

But the dragon heard the commotion, and one eye opened lazily as he awoke from his slumber in the warm sunny clearing. Another quiet moment passed then suddenly the mage came crashing out of the forest and into the clearing. Not seeing the dragon in time, he ran straight into its face with a thud, then stumbled backwards, marveling and gasping at the huge beast that lay in front of him.

The dragon, an enormous animal startled from its sleep, was frightened and quickly began to take flight. Massive wings thrust air downward so heavily that it nearly pushed Aleric and the mage to the ground. Dirt and debris whirled everywhere in the downforce. The mage, directly below the dragon taking flight, was shielding his eyes from the debris with his arms and cloak.

In the hectic confusion of the dragon's sudden force, Aleric saw his chance. To him it seemed to happen in slow motion. The mage was distracted from the chaos of the dragon, so with one fluid motion he withdrew his longsword and gripping it with both hands, bent his knees and spun in two full circles, gaining momentum with each spin, like a shot-putter, then let the sword go. At alarming speed, it struck the confused and preoccupied mage directly in the torso with so much force that it threw him into the air, and by the time he returned to the ground he was motionless.

The frightened dragon flew high and away, then suddenly out of all the chaos the forest was eerily quiet again. Aleric stood in silence, watching the mages body for movement, but it was still. Aleric was still breathing heavily when Thearbuc came crashing into the clearing, just as Aleric and the mage had before. He stopped instantly upon seeing the scene. The dead mage lying in the leaves and Aleric standing proud, breathing heavily, trying to catch his breath, and the large dragon flying away into the distance.

"You're. Alive!" Aleric panted, barely able to breathe from the fight and chase through the woods.

"Barely!" Thearbuc replied, wincing in obvious pain.

"Is he dead?"

"I think so," Aleric replied. "He must be."

Thearbuc was still not completely sure they were safe, so he quickly pulled the long sword out of the mage's body, then took a few steps back and readied the sword for another attack. The two stared in silence but the mischief mage did not move. Eventually they approached the body and rolled it over so they could see his face.

The mage had a long nest of a grayed beard. Nappy like the hair that was receding on his head. He had a tattoo on his face. A swirl between his eyes that extended into what looked like antlers coming from the center of eyes and extending up across his forehead. His eyes were pure white. No pupils or color. Just glossy, faded white like Thearbuc had noticed before in the forest when they had made eye contact.

Aleric felt for pockets to search and found a piece of paper tucked in the mage's red cloak. One arm fell to the side exposing a tattoo on the mage's forearm. It was a dragon wrapped around a wizard's staff, extending from just below the elbow to just above the wrist. The two men looked at each other in confusion. Tattoos were known but were very rare these days. They used to signify that a person belonged to a secret order or secret society. Only the other members of the society would recognize the symbols, and it was how they would recognize each other as members. Aleric had heard stories of when these secret societies were a more prevalent part of society, but he had never seen evidence of one in person.

He opened the folded piece of paper that he found in the mage's robe pocket and gasped as he read it.

"What is it?" Thearbuc asked, seeing the worry come across Aleric's face. Slowly he handed the paper to Thearbuc, and he too read it. Written across the top the crumbled piece were the words "Keepers of the dragon's flame." Below that was a perfect visual description of Aleric. It described the color of his horse and the flag he would be riding with, his armor and his weapons, all described in detail. "Will arrive near the half-moon." Was also written towards the bottom of the note.

"The half-moon was just two days ago." Thearbuc announced, like Aleric hadn't already known.

This was a trap. An assassination attempt, Aleric realized, slumping to the ground with a heavy sense of dread guzzling through his stomach and washing over him. Someone knew he would be coming this way and informed the mage to be lying in wait. But who? Yes, everyone in the kingdom knew that he was going to be working for the king, but hardly anyone outside of the castle knew he would be coming out here into the far forests. In fact, no one outside of the castle knew. The assassin, whoever wanted him dead, must be inside the castle, he thought. But why? Was the king not actually the friend he thought he was and had sent him out here to get rid of him? The ideas and hunches swirled through his head but couldn't find a definitive answer or make sense of it all. Could he trust anyone at all?

"It was that nasty old wizard, Maub." Thearbuc chimed in, seeing the frustration and contemplation on Aleric's worried face.

Aleric thought for a moment. "I don't know. He's just a weak old man by now. Weird but harmless."

"We might never find out." Thearbuc said scrunching his face.

"Oh yes we will," Aleric said with a quick flicker of light in his eyes that helped bring back some strength to his wounded ego.

Eventually Thearbuc helped Aleric to his feet, and they moved away from the lifeless mage and back into the woods. They walked slowly for some time, barely talking, until they felt they were in a safe enough spot in the woods to spend the night. Almost nothing was said the rest of the evening. Aleric's spirits were low. The thrill of the chase was over, he didn't have a friend in the world besides this woodsman he had just met, and someone wanted him dead. His mood was dreary at best.

Exhausted from the trek and the days battle they made camp and a warm fire, then they each sat down for the night, each leaning up against a separate large tree. They were too exhausted to be careful of being found and didn't even discuss taking turns on the watch during the night. Eventually the sun faded away and the forest around them grew its purplish glow as the sky turned to black. The fire danced in front of them as their thoughts went blank and they slowly began to fade into a deep sleep. They didn't see the beady set of eyes watching them through the trees. The reflection of the fire dancing in the reflection of the eyes. Two bright dots in the darkness. Watching…

CHAPTER 6: The Forest Walker

Thearbuc and Aleric woke the next morning feeling refreshed and in higher spirits. Conversation between the two started again over a hefty breakfast. They took their time eating and enjoying the relaxation of the morning in the now, seemingly safe forest. It was almost midday by the time they decided to break camp and begin the journey back to the kingdom. Thearbuc had agreed to accompany Aleric back to Mazeron because he felt he still owed him a gratitude of debt for saving his daughter, and he hadn't ventured to the kingdom for quite some time and wanted to see how things were for himself. He was also interested in Aleric and the king's plan of cleaning up the lands and wanted to help towards the common goal if he could. He realized that he and his family could also benefit from a more stable and prosperous kingdom, so he was willing to help his paladin friend towards if it could also help him and his family.

At midday they began their trek back through the forests, towards the kingdom. The journey was pleasant because the terrain was fairly flat, dry, and the forest air this time of year was still too cold to bring out too many Leedles, who usually stuck to the warmer fields when the forests were cooler. They would see a few of them here and there but they were less angry and calmer this time of year, so they weren't much of a nuisance. The two had good conversations as they marched on. They made plans and shared dreams about what they would do if they succeeded in making these lands prosperous again someday and Thearbuc showed obvious excitement at the thought of moving his family out of the lonely forest and back to the kingdom. He continuously brought up how lonely life in the forest was to the point that Aleric would roll his eyes and think to himself "we need to get this guy a girl."

Later in the afternoon, coming up over a small ridge then traversing across, Aleric spotted something down in the hollow below. Thearbuc saw it too and they both instantly dropped to the ground and took cover in the tall grass. They glanced at each other in hiding, then together slowly crawled up the ridge to peer down below to see who or what it was they had seen moving.

Down below them and amongst the many fallen trees and tall grass they saw a person who was sitting on a log. No, it wasn't just a person. It was a young person, a teenager or young adult. He was sitting like a bored child with his elbows on his knees and was swinging his feet back and forth because they were too short to touch the ground.

"What is someone so young doing out here in the forests all alone?" whispered Thearbuc.

"Look closer," Aleric said with intrigue in his eyes. They squinted in the sunlight and noticed small flickers and flashes of light of all different colors, slowly radiating from the boy's body. A pop of blue here, then pop of red there. Like colorful sparklers slowly lifting into the air from his shoulders and body. The sparkles and lights danced and played as they rose into the air until eventually disappearing into nothing.

"What is that?" Thearbuc asked.

"Its magic!" Aleric replied whispering with excitement in his voice. "Powerful magic. I've heard about these people, my parents used to tell me about them. Their magic is so powerful that you can actually see it radiating from them." The two paused and waited for something to happen, but the boy kept still, swinging his feet in the air atop the large fallen tree.

"He looks like he's a kid, he must not use it that often," Thearbuc mentioned in a whisper. "Magic can age the body. So I've heard…"

"I've heard the same," Aleric whispered.

"Let's go talk to him. Introduce ourselves!" Thearbuc said livelier, but still whispering.

"Not so fast. A magic user that powerful could be dangerous, even if he looks friendly enough," Aleric said pulling Thearbuc's arm back to the ground.

They talked it through from the cover of the hill and tall grass then eventually decided that it wasn't worth the risk to cross paths with another person out here who wielded such powerful magic. Especially just a day after they had fought the so-called mischief mage. Best to let him be, they agreed.

Carefully and quietly, they crawled back down the hillside and continued their journey lower on the back side of the hills so as not to be seen by the boy down in the hollow on the other side. Soon they found the trail again which led them through more fields and hills, then eventually back into the covering of the thick vast forests. This trail would eventually lead them to the river that they could follow straight back to the kingdom in a matter of days. The mysterious boy in the hollow was forgotten about and they continued their lively conversation and plans for the kingdom and told each other fun stories of mischief and fun from their younger days as they marched on through the thick woods.

As they delved deeper into the forest, the trees became thick on both sides of the trail and the trail itself became thin and hard to follow. They walked single file, and the thick trees brushed their shoulders as they trekked along. Then the trail began to twist and turn through the trees, making it impossible to see where the trail was headed or anything more than a few feet in front of them. At one point the trail led them around a sharp bend, then directly in front of them and seemingly out of nowhere there stood a person in the center of the trail. They both gasped and jumped, startled at the sudden and unexpected appearance of a person. Immediately they both instinctively reached to draw their weapons. As they were drawing their swords, they realized it was the same person that they had seen down in the hollow, just earlier that day. Confused they stared at the young man who looked to be no older than a teenager. He had light brown, combed hair, and wore a sweater type shirt with a hood that was draped across his shoulders and tied with a shiny belt buckle at the waist. There was a moment of intense silence and confusion while they waited to see what was going to happen next.

"You weren't going to say hello?" The boy stated non-threateningly with his hands on his hips. "There's no one out here for days and you pass up a friendly traveler?" Aleric and Thearbuc said nothing, studying the boy as he spoke. "I was waiting for you. I had hoped you would say hello. I haven't spoken to anyone in…" He trailed off. "In I can't remember how long.

"Who are you boy?" Thearbuc asked, in his usual direct manner.

"I saw you two last night," the boy continued. "I saw what you did with that mage. I didn't want you to see me until I knew you were good. When you didn't attack me down in the hollow, I knew you weren't here to hurt me." The boy was starting to talk faster and in a shaky tone, showing he was nervous near the two large men. Thearbuc and Aleric listened quietly, hands still on the hilts of their swords at the ready as he spoke. "That mage you killed. He has been some trouble around here for some time now. He would come and go; I could tell he was powerful so I would just hide from him. I could tell he was bad." Finally, the boy stopped his nervous ramblings.

"How old are you boy" Asked Thearbuc again. "What are you doing out here all alone? What is your name?"

"I don't know that either," the boy replied as loud pop and sparkle of red and blue light floated from his shoulders. "How old I am I mean. As you can see, I am plagued, I mean gifted with magic. Always have been. Just born with it, I guess. I was young when they outlawed magic from the kingdom and my parents knew there was no hiding what I had. Obviously, look you can just see it!" He chuckled. "They would have come for me eventually and I would have disappeared like everyone else who could use magic, so my parents sent me away. I've been out here alone ever since. My parents used to come visit me for weeks at a time, but they say there are eyes everywhere in the kingdom now, watching everyone, and they fear for all of our safety if they come out here anymore." The boy trailed off and paused for a moment as a look of sadness washed across his face. "My name is Brodel!" He said perking back up.

"Well, Brodel, that is quite impressive," Thearbuc stated. "You surviving out here all alone. Especially with the beasts and bandits that roam these woods."

"I have a cottage. I mean a hidden cottage," Brodel replied. "I can show you. I trust you two." He paused for a moment then spoke again. "You!" Brodel said, pointing at Aleric. "You are a magic wielder too. I can tell." Aleric gave a look of confusion but didn't say anything. "I can just sense these things," Brodel continued. "Follow me," he said as he turned and started down the path. Aleric and Thearbuc exchanged glances, shrugged their shoulders, then followed the boy.

Brodel continued to talk fast and nervously as they stood on the path in the thick woods. He was clearly ecstatic to meet other people. Ones that he trusted, and especially another magic user. Eventually Aleric chimed in.

"Well, we have had a long day of travel. We'd love a warm meal and safe place to rest for the night. We'll just follow you," he gestured.

Brodel led the way and along the trail the three walked and talked as they trekked through the forests for hours and hours. About the kingdom, the forests, the comings, and goings of different wanderers through these mysterious lands. More hours rolled by and both Aleric and Thearbuc began looking at one another with confused looks. Silently expressing that they both thought the destination would be a lot closer.

"What brought you so far away from home this day Brodel?" Thearbuc asked in his notorious "not beating around the bush" style.

"I could sense your magic. His magic!" He pointed to Aleric. "It's like a ripple in a pool of thick liquid. I can feel it when other people use magic. When you and that mage were casting spells, I felt it and came to see what was going on or help if I could. You were too far away though and I got there too late. You were both asleep by the time I made it out here. Not very smart to not keep a watchful eye open in these forests," Brodel said bluntly looking over his shoulder with a grin as they continued on.

"We're here now," he said not long later, walking off the path and into the thick of the forest. He walked up to a dense thicket that showed no light from beyond and waved his arms in front of his face with his palms facing outward. Then a small yellow light illumined an opening into the thicket. He ducked into the opening and abruptly was gone. Disappeared out of sight completely. Aleric and Thearbuc looked at each other with wide eyes, shrugged again, then followed into the dense thicket.

They crouched low, almost crawling for many yards in a tight opening that wound through the thicket. The path was so small that the branches brushed their shoulders and scratched their faces. After a while the thicket opened up to two steep walls of rock on both sides of them. It was a tight fit for Aleric and Thearbuc's wider shoulders, but at least they could stand up straight again and walk sideways through the tight space. Brodel fit just fine and walked quickly through the path between the rock, slowing down occasionally for the others to catch up.

Then they made their way through the steep rock walls as the trail wound in front them, only showing them a few feet of visibility at a time. Then finally the rocks opened into a clearing that showed the large, beautiful blue sky above. The clearing was filled with brown and green grass and dotted with scattered fruit trees. Groups of tiny gnats hovered in slow lazy circles throughout the clearing, easily visible in the low evening sun.

In the center of the clearing stood a stone cottage. The cottage was gray stone with a bright gold colored wooden door and a thatched roof. A chimney rose from the side and a small porch led up to the front door. Beyond the clearing were trees and more cliffs that made this area the perfect tucked away hiding spot from any prying eyes that may be searching for it.

"Come on in," Brodel said, showing the way. "Oh wait, the traps. Hang on," he said as he waved his arm in a swooping motion in front of him. The sparks and flashes radiating from his body grew in number and more rapidly emitted from his body, then various clicks and sounds were heard around the clearing. Aleric and Thearbuc couldn't see anything, but they knew Brodel was disabling various booby-traps with the use of his magic. "Ok it's safe now. Come on in," Brodel said walking up towards the door. The three entered the cottage. The smell of stale air hung in the room. The cottage was cluttered with trinkets and odd worthless looking items, stacked and strewn about everywhere. There was a large stone fireplace at one end of the room with a cozy chair near it. And books. There were books everywhere. Book and trinkets. It was an unkempt museum.

"I try to keep them organized" Brodel stated pointing to a shelf filled with more trinkets. "But there are too many now to bother. I just have them thrown around now. But I know every piece, so if anything goes missing, I will know." He turned and gave Aleric and Thearbuc a quick hard stare, then paused. "I know you wouldn't do that though," he said with a light laugh.

"What is all this stuff?" Muttered Aleric who was gazing in awe at the mess of different trinkets "I have a weird sense about it all."

"It's magic!" Brodel replied. "All of it. Magic items. That's why you can feel it. Just not as much as me probably. I can sense magic in everything. Well, I think in everything. I have collected every magic item in here by seeking it out myself. Some were buried, some were lost and laying around. Some were…he paused. Some were in people's homes." He shrugged. "I'm fascinated by all of it.

Brodel's hut

I play with all of it. I try to figure out what everything does. Some I haven't figured out yet, but a lot this stuff I know what it does."

The three continued to scan the room picking up trinkets and looking around with mild fascination. Aleric took a seat in the soft chair near the fireplace and began fumbling with a trinket. Then Brodel spoke again.

"I wanted to give you this for getting rid of that mage for me," Brodel said turning to Aleric. "He came sniffing around here too many times. I think he could sense that I was here, but he couldn't find my door. I hide it with magic. Here take it," he said tossing a thin shiny tunic to Aleric who caught it in the air and examined it. The cloth was sparkly silver at first but then started to reflect the light and morph colors into different shades of greens, purples, and reds as he moved it through the light. Aleric didn't even know it, but he was holding the very same tunic that saved his life the day the mysterious soldiers came for him and his mother.

"What is it?" Aleric asked. "It's beautiful."

"Invisibility cloak," Brodel replied quickly. "If you are really taking on the task of cleaning up the kingdom like you say you are, then you're going to need it. There's been a lot of weird magic lately. It's new, I can sense it. I think you are up against something that we don't know all about yet. I tried following it before, but it bounces around, and I can't track it. It is too powerful or coming from somewhere else. Like another dimension, or maybe it's being hidden by a spell? I don't know, maybe I'm wrong. Either way I want you to have the tunic. It could come in handy in your quests!"

"What is this one?" Thearbuc interrupted, picking up a clear but dusty bottle laying on its side.

"Don't touch that!" Brodel cried out, running to Thearbuc quickly and snatching the bottle out of his hands. Then the bottle began to fill with gray smoke, which swirled lazily within the bottle at first, but then turned dark like a storm. Lights began flashing inside the bottle like lighting. Brodel set the bottle back down softly and the dark fog within began to dissipate back into gray before disappearing altogether, leaving the bottle empty and calm once again.

"That holds a demon. Or a devil," Brodel said, sounding relieved. "If he gets out, he can take control over most people and make them do terrible things, destroying themselves along the way. It got out once. You have no idea how hard it was to get him back in there." He breathed a sigh of relief as he said it. After a moment Brodel spoke up again. "I just picked this one up a few days ago," he said, showing a small trinket to the two others. It was the size of the palm of his hand and resembled a thin metal crown. "Maybe a bracelet?" Brodel asked aloud? It was dirty with no shine, and besides a few small red stones adorning it, it wasn't very interesting.

"What's so special about that one?" Thearbuc asked.

"I don't know" Brodel replied. "I haven't found out what it does yet, but I can feel it. It's magical somehow. "Here, why don't you have it" Brodel said tossing it to Thearbuc.

"Ok why not," Thearbuc said, examining the dull colored armlet before putting it into one of his pockets. "Looks fancy enough," he said raising his hands as if-whatever." If it doesn't do anything, then maybe I can just trade it or maybe my daughter would like it?" Thearbuc turned to sit in the nearby chair and promptly kicked his toe onto the heavy wooden table. "Gah!" he yelped. "Stupid table!" Aleric laughed but Thearbuc was hiding how badly it hurt that he had stubbed his toe against the table and wondered to himself if his toe was in fact broken.

After that, the three settled in for a rest while a warm dinner was prepared by Brodel and in the meantime good company was kept. Aleric and Thearbuc both realized very quickly that even though Brodel looked young he did not act it. He was very wise, far beyond his years. Aleric was the first to realize what an asset he could be to the kingdom. Another magic user, and a powerful one at that. Aleric and Thearbuc both kept finding themselves marveling at Brodel. They watched the flickers and sparks of all different colors radiate from his body then softly float into the air until making a pop or crackling sound and disappearing into nothing into the air.

"Why don't you come back to the kingdom with us tomorrow?" Aleric asked out of nowhere. "Things are changing in Mazeron, and I think you will be able to help us. Not to mention I think you may want to end your exile from these woods, no? Brodel paused while he thought about it.

"I don't think so," he replied. "I don't think I can. My parents told me I have to stay here no matter what anyone says, or I'll be a goner. I could suddenly disappear at night like all the other magic users have. It's not that I don't trust you two, it's more like a policy we have."

Aleric sat silent for a moment while the young boy awaited his reply. Brodel waited with anticipation, wondering what to expect out of the rejection. Anger, frustration, or understanding from the large, strong paladin. Aleric stared back at him blankly for only a moment then lowered his eyes to the ground. When he looked back up to Brodel his eyes were glowing like bright embers again. Brodel saw no pupils or any discernable features. Just an empty glow, hollow into the depths of his powers.

"Trust me boy," The Paladin said. "They won't be able to mess with us even if they wanted to." The words were stern, but The Paladin's voice was calm and unthreatening. Just like it did with Thearbuc, this stoic show of power and force put Brodel more at ease. He quickly realized if he was on The Paladin's side that no one would be able to mess with the two of them. Brodel also picked up a hint of desperation. The Paladin needed another magic user by his side. Someone who he could learn a thing or two from and not be the only one person around with these inherited gifts. He thought more about for some time before making his decision.

"Alright. I'll go." He replied eventually, still somewhat unsure after a long pause. "I trust you and what you are doing. But the first sign of trouble I'm out of there and you'll never be able to find me if I don't want you to. Even if you look. So don't even try!"

"I believe you" Aleric replied as his burning eyes faded back to their normal green color. "Nothing of the sort will happen and our intentions are nothing but pure."

The night grew colder and dark outside as time passed later into the evening, but inside the hut was warm and welcoming. Ale was poured, and the conversation became louder around the warmth of the roaring fire. The mood was nothing but positive and welcoming as the three newly formed friends talked late into the night. Their shadows from the candles and the fire danced across the stone walls which echoed laughter and warm conversation through the evening.

It was far into the night when suddenly a terrible screeching wail from out in the woods cut through the conversation and pierced through the mood like a black dagger through their hearts. They fell silent instantly, looking about the room with wide eyes, waiting with thumping, nervous hearts. Then it happened again. The shriek tore through their souls. Horrifying and deafeningly loud like it was somehow inside of their ears. Thearbuc and Aleric both looked at Brodel, with confusion and fear in their eyes, and goosebumps on the back of their necks and arms as they slumped terrified to the ground.

“Shhhhh.” Brodel whispered putting his finger up to his mouth slowly. Just be still and it will be gone soon.”

“What will be gone?” whispered Thearbuc.

“The forest walker” Brodel whispered back, his body visibly trembling. Then the shriek came piercing through the air again and Brodel slumped down to the floor with a look of pain and agony upon his face. He was crippled with fear.

“Brodel, what is it!?” Aleric whispered as he got up and rushed to the boy’s side.

“It’s the forest walker,” Brodel mumbled behind clenched teeth. “It comes by around this time of night often.
It’s an enormous giant being of some sort. Twice as tall as the cottage. It walks on two legs like a person. Its arms are like long lanky like tree branches, but it has the head of a giant deer... A giant deer skull! It’s a skull, with long antlers. They reach as tall as the trees. It moves unlike anything I’ve ever seen. It doesn’t walk, it pauses in one second of time and space, then it flickers like a candle, disappearing for a second, then reappears moment later in another place. Jumping from spot to spot. That’s how it moves.”

The three sat crouched in silence peering through the windows from the floor and Aleric kept a firm comforting hand on Brodel’s shoulder as the poor boy cowered in fear. Through the moonlit darkness of the night a shadow moved through the trees in the distance. Thearbuc and Aleric both saw it, but just for a moment. Large antlers moving through the forest in the moonlight, searching in the darkness. They listened, still frozen in fear as the horrifying sounds of the creature and sounds of crashing trees went further into the woods.

“It goes away, don’t worry,” Brodel mustered. It spotted me once, not far from here. It came after me. I ran and hid from it, but it stalked me through the woods. I’ve never been so scared. It’s been coming back ever since, looking for me. Hunting me.”

They continued to wait silently in the darkness, gripped by fear, as the wails of the creature and sound of crashing trees got further and further away, until they were eventually gone, and all was silent once again.

After some time and each returning to their normal breathing patterns Aleric finally spoke up “We should be turning in for the night,” he finally mustered when it felt safe.

"Agreed." Thearbuc nodded. "I've had my fill of excitement from these treacherous forests for one day."

After that, Brodel showed Aleric and Thearbuc their room for the night. They were both exhausted and fell asleep in moments. But Brodel stayed up. He sat in the front room staring out the window into the clearing beyond the cottage, which was lit only by the light of the moon that made everything outside show in a soft, white, peaceful glow. Then eventually, in the deep hours of the night, there were suddenly more colors than just the glow of the moon. Different bright colors began to form in the meadow in front of the cottage. At first it was just one small ball of glowing blue light, floating in the air. Then there was another, and another. Pink, red, purple, all the colors were emerging slowly from the meadow. They floated lazily like fireflies under a tree at first, but soon began to dart back and forth, faster and faster like they were playing a game of chase with each other. At least a dozen of them had appeared. Brodel watched them dart around with a reverent look and the soft glow of their colors upon his face, then stood up from his chair and walked outside into the clearing and cool night towards them.

He walked slowly and calmly towards the lights because he wasn't afraid. He knew these colors. They were some of the fairies that called these woods home and would give the forests their soft glow through the nighttime hours. As he got closer one of the glowing orbs, one which was a red glow, broke away from the group of other dancing lights and came towards him. Brodel stopped in the clearing between the cottage and the tree. As the red orb approached him it grew from a small ball the size of a fist into a large glowing ball the size of a person.

In the center of the light the shape of a woman began to form. Her skin was a pink hue in the red light that softly illuminated the clearing around her. Her arms were thin, and she had a slender neck up to her short golden hair. She reached out and embraced Brodel with a smile on her face, then pulled back to look him over.

"What's wrong? She asked. "Where have you been lately? You don't seem happy to see us tonight," she said in an upbeat but concerned tone.

"I am." he replied flatly. "I promise. But I'm sad too."

"Why come?" the fairy asked. "What is wrong?"

"Some men came into the forest today," Brodel replied. "They need my help. And I want to help with what they are doing so I have to leave for a while," he explained as a sad look came across his face.

"Well, you can see us when you get back then," the fairy said, still with an upbeat tone. "We will miss you while you're gone though. We will watch over your home mister Brodel. But for now, let us dance and play." As she said it a large grin came across her small face, and she took Brodel's hand.

Together they slowly began to ascend into the sky, her red glow engulfing Brodel until they became one, escaping the confinement of the ground and freed into the cool night air. The sound of laughter and play filled the nighttime sky and the orbs of light twisted and danced through the heavens. Brodel appearing sometimes in the orb of red light only to vanish back into it moments later.

From within the cottage Aleric and Thearbuc sat quietly, watching out the window as Brodel spoke then danced with the fairies of the forest for some time. Their soft glows illuminated their faces through the window as they gazed out in awe and longing jealousy.

"I guess he wasn't all alone after all" Thearbuc finally exclaimed with a soft chuckle. "I'm glad he had the fairies watching out for him out.

"They are pixies," Aleric replied quietly.

"I heard they are called fairies. And you don't want to mess with the fairies, the legends say how dangerous they are. I am surprised they can also be so peaceful. I guess he was safer out here than we thought," Thearbuc said with a shrug. Aleric nodded in agreement, still in awe about what he was witnessing.

"Do you smell that?" Thearbuc interrupted after some time, sniffing the air as a concerned look washed over his face.

"It smells of the stench of death," Aleric replied, sounding alarmed. The smell of decay and death wafted thick through the air, gagging the two. A bizarre humming sound came with it and began to get louder as the stench grew stronger. Aleric's eyes darted back and forth as anxiety gripped him and the smell and eerie buzz became stronger and stronger until it was so strong and thick that it felt like it weighed down on him like a heavy, soured, wet quilt. "Where is my sword?" he cried out urgently as the smell got stronger and stronger and eerie buzzing sound louder and louder, until it was deafening in their ears.

Suddenly they saw through the side window of the cottage a giant shadow burst through the forests outside. It rumbled and shook the cottage as it came crashing through fast and loud. Aleric and Thearbuc dropped to the floor to hide but the shadow did not seem concerned with them or the cottage and charged quickly ahead to the front of the cottage where Brodel and the Fairies were. Aleric and Thearbuc frantically crawled to the window and watched the scene unfold.

Outside they saw the forest walker that Brodel had mentioned before. It was a giant skeleton of a creature with large bits of rotting meat dripping from its bones. Its head was that of a deer skull and its antlers were large and towered up into the blackness of the night.

Immediately it zeroed in on Brodel and charged towards him. Disappearing in one moment, then reappearing again, closer to Brodel. Busy dancing with the fairies, he did not notice the giant, horrifying creature until it had already burst through the woods and was charging towards him. He fell backwards and to the ground at the surprise attack and attempted to crawl away as the creature charged towards him. Aleric and Thearbuc watched helplessly in fear for their friend as they were too far away to do anything so suddenly to help the boy. The forest walker was bearing down on Brodel, just two steps away from consuming him, when suddenly all the orbs of light that were dancing and playing in the meadow rushed towards the creature and surrounded it, darting back and forth, encircling it. Aleric and Thearbuc could not see what the fairies were doing but the walker immediately slowed its attack and reared its large skull of a head back and let out it's piercing yell of agony. Aleric and Thearbuc closed their eyes and clenched their fists and teeth as they tried to endure the sound that seemed to grip and rip at their souls.

The forest walker turned and swayed violently, swatting, and biting at the orbs of light darting around it. Chunks of rotten meat fell to the ground, and the onlookers realized the fairies were hacking away at the monster, taking large chunks off of the beast

The Forest Walker

and destroying it bit by bit. They circled and swayed fast like flying piranhas as they chipped away at the beast. It screamed and roared out again, piecing the air with its evil and horrifying wail. In the commotion Brodel crawled away from the monster as Aleric and Thearbuc burst out the front door to him and pulled him further away from the attack. The walker noticed them and seemingly filled with hate and rage it violently lunged towards them. One last attempt at getting at Brodel, but the two pulled him away just as the gruesome claws scratched down Brodel's leg, then pulled him back away from the scene and into the darkness behind the cottage.

They watched from the shadows as the relentless attack from the fairies went on and on until eventually the forest walker crashed heavily to the ground in a cloud of dust and glowing orbs of light. It moaned in agony and defeat, but the fairies did not let up. Small circles of light came from everywhere from within the forest to join in the fight until the beast was completely engulfed and almost not even visible behind the swarm of fairies. The three friends watched in amazement and horror as the fairies did their violent work. They were quick and efficient. Not long later the orbs of light began darting back into the concealment of the woods, and they saw that all that was left of the forest walker was a few bits of bones and a large skull with antlers strewn across the meadow.

"Unbelievable," Aleric whispered, his eyes wide with complete awe.

"I guess that's why they don't recommend traveling through the forests at night or messing with the fairies," Thearbuc said, trying to force a laugh after witnessing such a violent and gruesome scene.

"You can travel at night. Just don't bother us or try to hurt our friends." A new voice spoke out of nowhere. The three turned quickly and behind them stood the red fairy that was dancing through the sky with Brodel just minutes before.

"Thank you," Brodel said to the fairy, still shaking as he stood up from the ground, brushing the dirt from his pants.

"You are a fairy," Aleric said in awe, gazing over the woman with the red glow. He was awe struck and could not think of anything more to say, he gazed and was lost in the beauty of the creature.

"What is your name?" Thearbuc finally mustered, not knowing what else to say to the magnificent and magical creature.

"We don't have names!" The fairy laughed playfully. "Who would need such a thing?" She ignored the two awe-struck men and went to Brodel and softly touched his hand. "We will await your return mister Brodel," she said softly. Then she gave him a kiss on his forehead, looked at the other two with a mischievous playful grin, then quickly shrank into a fruit-sized orb of light and flew quickly away into the forests beyond the cottage. The three sat in the calm silence with a newfound feeling of bliss and comfort that seemed to come out of nowhere and gazed into the meadows and calm night for some time.

"Let's get inside," Brodel finally broke the silence. The two others followed. Not another word was spoken between them that night. They went calmly and relaxed to their respective rooms and laid down for some of the most peaceful sleep they had each ever experienced. They each dreamt comfortable dreams of love and happiness, colors, and dancing that seemed to go on forever. They wanted it to go on forever. Morning with sleep like this, will always come too soon.

Chapter 7: Dark Passageways

It was midafternoon and the sun was already high in the sky when the three companions finally set out from Brodel's hut to travel back to the kingdom. Brodel, the young magic user, gifted with so much magic you could see it radiating off him. Thearbuc, the weapons master and family man. And Aleric, the king's paladin and muscle, tasked with ridding the kingdom of its many problems that choke it from prosperity. They were a curious group, but the three became instant friends along the trail back to the kingdom.

Aleric led the way, towering atop his horse at a slow trot while Thearbuc and Brodel talked almost constantly on their horses behind him. They were the talkative type, but Aleric only spoke when something needed to be said. They tried to include him from time to time but it quickly became apparent that he preferred his silence over their conversation.

As the hours upon hours of travel wore on, they noticed Aleric was becoming even quieter and speaking less. He seemed to be spending more time thinking to himself, and when he did, his eyes glowed their deep, hollow, amber glow. Thearbuc had noticed on the journey out that his eyes would glow only sporadically or in times of intense emotion. But now it seemed to be happening more often, when he was deep in thought or inside of his own head. He couldn't help but wonder that maybe the paladin was taking over the man.

For the first two days, the journey was pleasant, with a mild, cool breeze and good conversations. But after the third day, the heat of the sun began to beat down hard on the small company, making the trek miserable and strenuous. They had to walk the horses to give them rest more often than they could ride them, and the intense heat along with blistered feet and sore, stiff muscles made all three of them wish they were back to civilization and able to rest.

The blistering heat also brought out the Leedles. The little gnome-type savages seemed to hate the heat even more than the three companions did, and today they came out with their tiny bows and arrows showing it. It was well known that their bad temperament was intensified by the heat and humidity. Dozens of tiny arrows not much larger than a toothpick constantly came at the group as they walked their horses through an open field, exposed to the sun. Stings and bites from the small arrows bit at any exposed skin. The three trudged on, trying to ignore the little monsters as their faint but angry yells followed them along the hot and miserable path.

Eventually the heat and the creatures got to Aleric, and he lost his composure. "Arrrghhh!" he yelled out of nowhere as he threw a fast-speeding fireball into a group of Leedles just off the trail. The explosion sent dozens of them flying high into the air and surrounding bushes. Then the commotion from the other Leedles got louder as they got angrier at the sight of their brothers being attacked. The Leedles swarmed the trio and advanced in on The Paladin, shooting arrows faster, angrier, and more aggressive now. The Paladin let out another battle cry and launched another fireball, blasting more Leedles into the air. One blast after another, his teeth clenched in anger with his eyes glowing like fiery embers.

Thearbuc and Brodel watched the outburst in amusement as Aleric angrily made his way into the field, flailing and throwing fireballs at anything that moved. Tiny Leedles flew high into the air with little smoke trails behind them. Their faint battle cries faded into the distance as they were launched away by the fire-wielding giant. Then Aleric made his way to the far end of the field to a nest of Leedles inside one of the large, spherical rocks they would hollow out and nest in. He pummeled the rock with blasts of fire and energy over and over until their little wooden doors in the rock were obliterated and the inside of the boulder glowed with hot molten rock and fire. Tiny Leedles came rushing from the inferno, jumping into the brush for safety, then re-launching their attack at the invader as more and more came to join the fight.

Back on the trail, Thearbuc had a large grin while watching this amusing show of frustration. His big smile showed bright white teeth behind his dark, menacing beard. Brodel sat atop his horse in silence with a bewildered look as he watched the usually stoic paladin's outburst. Eventually, Aleric tired out. Hands on his knees and breathing heavily, he stared at the destruction he had caused, and the anger and frustration began to wash away from his face. A moment later he stood up, turned, then simply started back towards the trail without even a glance back. He calmly walked back to his horse with the angry army of Leedles following behind, fiercely shouting and shooting their tiny arrows.

"Feel better?" Thearbuc asked with a chuckle as he approached.

"I do." Aleric replied, mounting his horse and continuing forward on the trail like nothing had happened.

Thearbuc and Brodel just looked at each other and shrugged, neither wanting to set off his short temper again.

"What was that about?" Brodel asked in his usual friendly manner, breaking the tension and the silence.

"I hate those things," Aleric grumbled back. The other two decided it would be best to let it go at that, so they pulled their hoods and long sleeves down low to block out the angry Leedles that still followed them, then continued their journey.

"Brodel, you are magic. Why can't you get rid of all those things?" Thearbuc asked.

"It doesn't work like that," Brodel chuckled. "We are all still bound by the laws of nature and physics. We may be able to bend and twist them for a time, but that is all we magic users can do. For example, I could put up an energy field around us that would deflect their arrows, but it takes such an enormous amount of energy, bending the physics and matter around us, that I would not be able to hold it for very long.

"I see," Thearbuc replied. "Why can't we just have mosquitos like everywhere else?" he mumbled quietly to himself. Brodel heard and grinned softly as they trudged along.

The following two days passed more pleasantly as the small company wound through the seemingly endless forests back toward the kingdom. The trail became wider as they went on, indicating they were getting closer, and eventually they found the river which they knew would take them straight back to Mazeron.

During the dark hours of the night, they noticed that the red glow of the fairies, which was usually far off into the distance, had become eerily close to them. To most people caught traveling through the forests at night, the fairies were like crickets. Always in the distance and never right near you. If you chose to make your way towards the fairies' glow, you would only see it move farther away into the forests as you approached. At least you hoped it would. The stories always said that if the fairies came to you, or for you, that you would never been seen again to tell anyone about it. This closeness of the glow they were experiencing was no doubt the fairies watching over Brodel as he journeyed away from the safety of his home.

Meals on the trail were all prepared or conjured by Brodel. His magic was astounding to the other two, and he could pull an entire hot meal out of thin air in mere moments. Large stalks of corn, berries, fruits, and vegetables would sprout out of the ground at the motion of his hands and grow to full size right before their eyes.

"It's just physics," he said jokingly more than once. "All the ingredients are already down there in the dirt and the sunlight and the energy around us. I just rearrange it all. The same way a deer can turn plants into meat. My way is just faster." The fresh food and company made life on the trail far more tolerable than Aleric's lonely trek out. But nonetheless, they were all excited to have the voyage come to an end as they marched ever closer to the kingdom.

It was still morning when the trail turned upwards, toward a hill that peaked above the forest trees. Summitting the hill, they got their first look at the castle of Mazeron, far in the distance. The golden cones atop the towers reflected brightly in the morning sun, and the villages that stretched beyond looked peaceful and calm in the distance as a light breeze brushed softly across their faces. The relief of the trek being almost over gave them newfound energy and they hastily continued onward.

Later in the afternoon they finally broke through the forests and into the openness of the outer villages of the kingdom. It was mostly quiet as they marched along the dirt roads toward the castle. They saw farmers tending to their fields in the distance, and the sounds of various farm animals occasionally broke the deep silence of the open country. Some of the farmers along the way who caught a glance of the small company would stop the work they were doing in their fields and stare as they passed by. There was no doubt that they were staring at Brodel. The small firework display of magic color radiating from his body and shoulders could not be hidden. He seemed to pretend that he didn't mind too much, but Thearbuc saw the uncomfortable look on his face, and they way his eyes turned towards the ground as they passed the staring villagers. Most of them hadn't seen magic in decades, and some still opposed it altogether.

One farmer leaned on his rake, staring at the small company for some time as they trotted past his fields. Then he quickly dropped the rake to the ground and ran inside his cottage like he was fearing for his life. Thearbuc and Aleric shook their heads and looked at Brodel with sympathy. Brodel gave no immediate reaction. Instead, he calmly walked over to the farmer's small field, stood at the fence, and raised his arms. Suddenly the sparks and colors radiating from his body grew faster and brighter, popping loud and fast like a campfire being stoked by a fierce wind. He slowly raised his arms higher, and as he did, the small stalks of corn forming in the farmer's field grew taller and taller. In just mere moments, the entire field was teeming with fresh vegetables taller than all of them. Brodel turned with a grin on his face and walked away from the field.

"It'll take him a month to harvest all that crop," he chuckled. "We'll show these people that magic *can* help the kingdom.

"That'll show 'em, Brodel," Thearbuc chuckled with a hard pat on the boys back as he began down the trail again, walking with his horse in tow.

"I was thinking," Aleric said to Brodel, "It might serve us best if you laid low for a while once we reach the kingdom and meet the king. You'll stay in the castle—we'll insist upon it. We don't know for sure how the villagers will react to you." Brodel and Thearbuc exchanged nervous glances. It was true. Although Aleric had been charged with tasks that other men couldn't do because of his magic ability, they were still unsure how another magic wielder would be received by the king and villagers who had for so long been opposed or hostile towards it. After all, magic was still technically illegal and banned in the kingdom. "No one will mess with you while I'm around," Aleric added, after noticing the concern on the other two's faces. His eyes briefly flickered a bright amber color again, like the last licks of a fire going out, as a reminder and show of force to the others.

"I can handle myself," Brodel replied. Abruptly, he stopped on the trail, the other two turning to look at him, when he abruptly disappeared. Thearbuc and Aleric looked at each other with confused looks. Moments went by in complete silence.

"Not funny!" Aleric yelled into the distance. Still, there was nothing. Brodel was gone.

The two looked back and forth for a sighting of Brodel when a small pebble hit Aleric's metal armor with a loud ting! He reared about on his horse.

"Stop that nonsense!" he yelled. Out of nowhere Brodel reappeared in the distance laughing so hard that he had to put a hand on one knee to steady himself and catch his breath.

"It was your idea to bring a kid with us," laughed Thearbuc quietly.

"No time for games," Aleric replied, unamused, as he turned his horse and continued on. The others followed and the trek began once again.

As they trotted peacefully along the dirt road, getting closer castle and further from the countryside Aleric recapped to them the story about how he found that he had magic in his blood and veered them off of the main road to show them where he had fought the dragon. From this distance, they could see the scaffolding and damage around the castle that the dragon had caused and the wreckage of the village up ahead—Aleric's village.

Not long later, they trotted up the pathway to the wreckage of his once happy cottage. It was just burnt logs by now. No smoldering or dramatic evidence of the battle that had taken place here. Just wood strewn across torn up dirt and mud. The mood grew heavy as he explained what he had done and how his own careless actions led to losing Briss. He pointed to the pile of rubble that was once the shed.

"That's where it all went wrong," Aleric told them, lowering his head.

You could see the large dead spot in the field where the dragon had landed and his bile had torched the grasses, not far beyond the shed.

"Any man would have done the same," Thearbuc said encouragingly. "It was the situation, not you. Just a crummy situation." Aleric stayed silent except for the sound of sniffles as the tears he tried to hold back puddled in the corners of his eyes anyway. The three stared solemnly for some time, then Brodel broke the silence when he abruptly dismounted his horse. He handed the reins to Aleric as he walked by and continued toward the rubble.

The young wizard did not say a word, stopping just short of the piles of wood. He stood there in silence for a moment with his head bowed, facing the ground. Then he lifted his arms slightly up to his head. Suddenly, the sparks and colors of magic surrounding him grew tenfold. He was almost consumed in the brightness, and the other two could barely see him through the sparks. The ground began to shake. The horses stirred, and Aleric and Thearbuc tried to keep them steady. Then, lifting his arms slowly above his head, the pieces of rubble surrounding the house leapt from their resting places on the ground and began to move through the air. Brodel looked like he was almost on fire now, so engulfed in sparks and color. Finally, there was a massive flash of light, followed by silence. The ground stopped shaking, the sound of raging sparks and pops stopped, and there Brodel stood in silence. In front of him was a completely built house.

Aleric and Thearbuc stared in disbelief at the standing structure. They quickly realized that it was not the exact house that Aleric had before but a similar, smaller one. With no front door and the windows askew and in odd places. It was a silly looking house. Still, in front of them stood a house with four walls and a roof.

Atop his horse, Aleric's mouth was stuck open. His heart was beating fast in amazement and gratitude, and he couldn't think straight enough to muster any words. Overwhelmed by witnessing Brodel's powerful magic, he and Thearbuc stared and marveled at what had just happened.

"I can't believe it," Thearbuc said slowly.

"I told you before," Brodel said, turning around. His voice was almost unrecognizable and sounded scratchy and labored. "Just like with the food. The pieces are there, they just need to be rearranged." As he said it, the other two were taken back and gasped at the sight of Brodel. His skin was pale and wrinkles had formed around his young eyes. His cheeks were sunken in like a malnourished old man and his hair had changed to grays.

"What has happened to you?!" Aleric asked with a worried and fearful tone as he jumped from his horse and rushed over to his friend.

"I'll be okay," Brodel managed to say as he collapsed to the ground. Aleric caught him in his arms as he fell. He looked at Thearbuc with a desperate "help me" look in his eyes. The two looked around, they were so far from any help. There was nothing that could be done but to wait.

"Is he breathing?" Thearbuc asked, rushing towards them.

"He is," Aleric replied, still looking around nervously for any idea or help. Brodel lay motionless in Aleric's arms. His face was old and lifeless. Aleric put his hand on Brodel's chest then felt something radiate through his hand and up through his arm and into his chest. The feeling was something he had never felt before, and he was momentarily taken back by it. Then it felt familiar, like a distant memory, as if in the depths of his mind he knew what it was. "Stand back," he shouted, motioning Thearbuc away and laying Brodel on the ground.

Aleric hovered over him and put one hand on his chest and the other on his forehead, then bowed his head, deep in thought. Suddenly his eyes began to glow, and the wind stirred around them. Thearbuc watched in silence as a blue mist began to originate from Aleric's hands and swarm around Brodel's motionless body. Then, in moments, the color began to return to Brodel's face and the wrinkles of age began to disappear. He coughed and grumbled incoherently, but the sign of life, even though it was faint, was giving them hope.

Moments later, the mist and the wind stopped all at once and Brodel rolled over and took a deep, gasping breath. Aleric's eyes returned to normal as Brodel sat up, gasping for air like someone who had almost just drowned. Thearbuc rushed to them to help.

"I didn't know you had healing powers!" he shouted in awe.

"I didn't know either," Aleric said, slumping into the dirt, looking exhausted and defeated himself. The three sat in silence watching Brodel slowly come back to the land of the living. He was in and out of consciousness, but he was breathing and starting to look a little more like his normal, younger self. "Let's get him on the horse and back to the castle," Aleric exclaimed.

By the time the horses were rounded up, Brodel was coming to. He stared blankly at the small home that was newly constructed.

"There's no door," he finally managed to say. There was a bewildered look on his face.

"We can make a door later. You did good," Thearbuc said with a chuckle, patting him on the back. "Now, let's get you to the castle and some rest."

The three rode slowly back to the castle. Brodel rode hunched low to his horse and went in and out of consciousness most of the way there. He mentioned how tired he was every time he opened his eyes, then would fall back to sleep again shortly after.

It was evening when they finally trotted their horses up the long ramp to the castle's gates. The sun was setting low in the sky and the hot day was giving way to a cool evening. The wind was picking up and dark clouds could be seen in the distance, indicating a storm was coming in for the night. The three friends approached the gate with Brodel still barely clinging to consciousness. Two guards exchanged a look of confusion as they saw Brodel slumped down with magic radiating from his body. An obvious magic user in a land where magic was banned, and their job was to enforce it. Aleric approached the guards with his eyes glowing menacingly and the guards sheepishly turned away and began to stare at the ground as the three simply passed by and made their way into the courtyard of the castle.

Nighttime was approaching, so the courtyard was nearly empty. A few guards stood at random doorways and some of the castle stewards walked to and fro, attending their daily duties. One of the king's messengers stood dutifully at the far end of the courtyard. Aleric approached him first.

"We need to speak with the king. Where would he be at this hour?" he asked commandingly. The guard looked nervously at the strong knight with glowing eyes and replied with a shaky voice.

"The king has been ill. He is sleeping. He has been sleeping for some time. He said he is not to be disturbed for any reason or by anybody, including The Paladin," he said.

A confused look came across Aleric's face. That was not like the king. The king appreciated him and would want to hear about his journey. Or so he thought. Anger came over him after hearing the news that he had been shut out from the king, a man he thought was a friend.

"Fine," he replied angrily. We will take care of ourselves." Aleric and Thearbuc helped Brodel from his horse and flung his weak arms over their shoulders so they could help carry him inside. They trudged to the other end of the courtyard, then entered the castle through the large main entrance and into the great hall.

The hall was empty. Huge stone walls and pillars sat cold and quiet in the darkness. Only a few small, scattered candles illuminated the large room.

"Where is everyone?" Thearbuc asked.

"The castle is always like this," Aleric replied. "Cold and lifeless."

"But I heard that the king was always hosting extravagant dinners and parties. Almost every night," Thearbuc replied.

"Maybe once upon a time, but not in these times." Aleric led the way through the large hall and up the stone steps to the towers.

Atop the stairs, the castle's corridors were empty too. Long hallways of closed doorways barely illuminated by small candles made an ominous and eerie feeling. Cold sweeps of faint wind brushed past them from somewhere beyond in the drafty, unwelcoming castle.

"I was expecting a warmer welcome than this," Thearbuc mumbled quietly.

"You shouldn't have," Aleric replied. "These are still dark times in Mazeron. The gold and prosperity have all been taken from the people, wealth dried up, trade choked off, the king and royal family basically absent, and there is no stability for families because the able bodied workers of the households keep going missing or getting arrested for breaking the kingdoms many strict rules." Aleric paused in thought for a moment. "I shouldn't be saying things like that in here. Come, let's get Brodel to a room where he can rest. Where is that steward?" They continued on, mostly carrying Brodel up steps and down long corridors and dark cold hallways.

"I know there are plenty of empty rooms over here near mine," Aleric said as he led the way again down another long, dimly lit hallway. Eventually he stopped and opened one of the many doors. The clank of the heavy door echoed through the stone walls and down the silent hallways and was followed by the loud creaking of old hinges. Peering inside, the room was completely empty besides a dusty mattress of feathers and hay that was lying on the floor.

"This will do fine," Brodel said with a scratchy voice and a cough." Together they laid him down on the hay mattress.

"You need to lay low for a while and I will be right on the other side of that wall. If something happens and they come for you before I have a chance to speak with the king, just yell."

"Thanks. I guess," Brodel mumbled sickly with a roll of his eyes. "Bringing me here to feed me to the wolves," he coughed again.

"That won't happen," Aleric replied, resting his hand on his shoulder. "You will be welcomed in these lands. We just need to get you to the king. Sooner than later." He tried to hide it, but Brodel still picked up on the hint of worry in Aleric's voice. "Eat your rations for dinner and lay low in here tonight," Aleric continued "In the morning I will have this sorted out and we will all eat in the great hall with the king." Then Aleric and Thearbuc left the room and Aleric showed Thearbuc his quarters. Another cold, stone room with dust on the floor and not much else.

"This works fine for me," Thearbuc said with a grin as he saw the straw bed on the floor. He was already taking off his boots when Aleric closed the door

Aleric paused in the hallway for a moment then turned and entered his own room and closed the door behind him. He finally had sanctuary. Four solid walls around him and no other sound besides his own breathing. To him, it felt like he was out on the trail for an eternity, exposed to all forms of danger and harm. He took his boots off his aching feet and collapsed into bed. He wanted to just fall asleep for the night, but he knew he couldn't. At any moment the guards could come for Brodel. He needed to speak to the king about the boy before word reached him through the gossip of the guards. There was also the small matter of being ambushed by the mage that he also needed addressed by the king. He was very determined to find out who had set him up. So, after a short rest, he splashed some water on his face, got dressed, and was once again out the door.

Back into the lonely corridors of the castle he began to roam. He wandered to the east wing, where business was usually conducted, and found no one. Not even the guards seemed to be around tonight. Then he wandered into the king's personal wing of the castle, but still no one could be found. He knew better than to enter the king's living quarters uninvited, but even the personal guards that usually stood watch outside his door were missing, so he decided to venture a peek inside.

He crept to the king's large, red, wooden doors and pressed his ear against them. No sound. Then he gently pushed open one of the doors and peered inside. The sound of wind immediately rushed passed his ears and cold air pushed the door open more. Peering inside, Aleric could see the doors to the large balcony were open, allowing the moonlight and howling wind to flood unimpeded into the large room. Beyond the balcony he saw the vast lands and hillsides of the kingdom gently illuminated by the moonlight. Its brightness showed through the open doors and onto the king's large bed. It was empty. Where was the king? Where were the guards? Where is anybody!?

Getting frustrated, he turned and hurried back down the stone steps and into the great hall near the castles entrance. Besides the dimly lit sconces, the great hall was empty too. He continued through the empty kitchens and toward the food storage rooms near the back of the castle. He had heard there was an entrance into the dungeons somewhere near the back of the kitchen from hearing other guards talk about it, but he had never been here before. Door after door he tried, then, towards the end of the corridor, he opened one of the pantry doors that seemed more worn than the others and entered an empty room of stone walls. No food was stored in this room. At the adjacent end of the room was a wooden trap door in the floor and on the wall next to it was a line of unlit torches. *Found it*, Aleric thought to himself. He took one of the unlit torches, lit it with the sconce, then opened the trap door and stared for a moment at steps leading downward into the blackness, underneath the castle. After a quick hesitation he stepped in and began down the stairs.

Closing the hatch behind him Aleric was suddenly consumed in darkness. The torch barely illuminated the few steps in front of him. The smell of stale damp air hung heavy around him like a suffocating blanket. There was no sound and no other light besides his torch. He made his way down the damp, slippery stone steps that seemed to go on endlessly into the darkness surrounding him. Eventually, after far longer than he expected, he reached the bottom of the stairs, and his feet planted on level dirt ground. He stopped and listened. At first there was nothing. Then a faint sound came through the dark corridors. A low sound, bouncing off the stone walls. It was the sound of voices coming from somewhere beyond.

He continued through the darkness, stopping occasionally to listen then continuing on, trying to follow the sound. The faint sound led him down one long corridor to another, then another, then to a dead end. Then turning back and following some more he came to another dead end. Then another. It seemed like every dark corridor he went down eventually turned into a dead end. He wandered through the darkness for what seemed like hours. Down here time stood still. A distant panic started to come over him and the feeling that nothing else existed in the world beyond these dark walls and being stuck down here forever grew with every dead-end corridor..

But eventually the sound grew nearer and clearer and Aleric knew he was making progress. Finally, he stumbled upon a larger corridor and found fresh footprints in the dirt. Now we are getting somewhere he thought to himself as a feeling of relief rushed through him. He started following the footprints as they led through the maze of dark, stone corridors in the belly of the castle. Then, he turned into new corridor where he instantly noticed a small sliver of light coming through a wooden door that was barely cracked open, up ahead. He slowed his pace and approached quietly then positioned himself along the stone wall and peeked inside.

He saw a large, well-lit room with about a dozen people inside. Some sitting at long tables, some standing along the walls. He recognized the men standing along the walls as the members of the king's guard. But not the main regiment that Aleric had been part of. These were the king's private guards that only lived and worked within the castle. They were a secretive bunch. They were never seen in uniform outside of the castle, so no one knew who they were, and no one even knew who their commander was to ask for a position within their ranks if they wanted to apply. They wore similar armor and uniform as the other castle guards and the same deer of Mazeron emblem adorned their chests and shields, but their tunics were red, and their metal armor had one red strip along the right arm for them to identify each other in battle or daily tasks.

At the forefront of the room stood the wizard Maub. He was at the head of the long wooden table. Standing tall, leaning forward onto the table, and towering over the others in the congregation. He was looking down on and talking to a man seated next to him, but Aleric could not make out what they were saying. He listened and watched intently from the shadows, trying to figure out what was going on in this secret room, hidden deep within the belly of the castle.

"So, you concede that you were in possession of the magic item in question?" he heard Maub ask as the wizard raised his voice, speaking to another man.

"I…I had just found it, sir," the man replied. "It appeared out of nowhere, in my crops, just the day before. I swear it! I just picked it up and took it inside. I don't know how it got back there in my field in the first place!" The man was pleading with Maub. Aleric recognized him as one of the prisoners brought to the castle the day before the dragon had come to the kingdom. The man was still in the same clothes as he was that day, but they were merely rags by now. His arms and face were covered with dirt. He was barely recognizable.

"Maub, sir. Please." The man continued pleading with tears in his eyes. "I just want to go home. Keep the magical sphere, I don't want it. I never did!" he wailed. "I just want to go home. Please don't keep me down here in the darkness forever."

"I will let you go home under one condition," Maub said ominously. "You must sign all your land over to the kingdom as payment for your discretions," Maub paused to wait for a reply, but there was no hesitation from the imprisoned man. He agreed instantly.

"Take it. Take it please. Please let me go. Please let me see the sun again!" he said hastily with a shaking voice. "The land is yours."

"Then let it be done," Maub said loudly, motioning to the guards who brought over a long piece of paper and set it in front of the man. The man grabbed a quill out of the guards hand quickly and scribbled his name. He dropped it anxiously and looked up at the guards with a smile, then glanced at Maub with nervous hope in his eyes.

"Is it done? Can I go home now?" he asked, shaking. Maub looked at the guards and nodded his head with a mischievous grin.

"Yes, it is done," he said calmly, then motioned his hand towards the prisoner. Two guards grabbed the man by his arms and forcefully picked him up and hurried him through a door at the far end of the room. Maub approached, seemingly floating to where the prisoner had been sitting to retrieve the contract, then held it up to his face with a look of satisfaction.

"We're done here. You know what to do with the prisoner. He is no longer…needed."

With that, the guards all shuffled towards another door at the far end of the room and let themselves out without a word to each other. Maub stayed behind and was left alone in the room. Aleric was taken aback by what he had just witnessed. Is this the "court of justice" that he had been defending and participating in all this time? He knew the punishments for possessing magic items were harsh, but this seemed extreme. A hidden, secret trial in the middle of the night? Now it was starting to make sense why hardly anyone owned their own land in the kingdom anymore.

Suddenly, his thoughts were shaken, and a feeling of anxiety rushed through Aleric's body as he began to realize that he was currently in a very bad position. Maub would be exiting out of this door, and he would be found out. And who knows what would happen to him if the strict wizard caught him here spying on his secret court. Everything he had established with the king would be undone, or worse. A lot worse.

Quickly Aleric hurried away from the door with the doused torch in hand then crept quickly and quietly as far down the dark corridor as he could before hearing the old hinges creak and the wooden door open behind him. He froze in place in the darkness, not making a sound, then slumped slowly against the cold wall and let the darkness of the corridor conceal him. Then the dark shadow of Maub exited the room and stopped in the illuminated doorway. The old wizard peered into the darkness curiously then sniffed the air. Aleric knew instantly that he had caught the scent of his doused torch. The smoke hung in the stagnant air for far too long in a place like this. Aleric watched from darkness as Maub's silhouette illuminated from the doorway sniffed the stale smoke that hung in the air. Suddenly, the wizard turned directly toward Aleric and glared into the darkness. Still, Aleric didn't move. Maub was looking right at him, holding the stare. It seemed to go on forever. Aleric was waiting for the wizard to come at him with some sort of violent attack or announce to him to come forward from the darkness. He waited. But nothing happened. Finally, the tall lanky wizard turned and looked down the other end of the corridor.

He can't see me, Aleric thought to himself. Then he began creeping quietly backward, further into the darkness. His fingers fumbled against the stone walls as he crept backwards. Finally, he felt the wall give way, indicating there was another corridor to his right. As he slipped around the corner, he took one last peek at Maub. The wizard was still standing motionless in the illuminated doorway. Then, with the motion of his hands, a bright white ball of light appeared in front of him which illuminated the surrounding area. The wizard turned toward Aleric once again and stretched out his arm, and the orb of light began floating down the corridor toward Aleric.

Panic set in as the orb of light approached. Aleric turned quickly and scurried down the new corridor as fast as he could, doing his best not to make any sound. Glancing behind him, he saw the orb of light coming closer, brightly illuminating the main corridor as it advanced. He looked back and forth but there were no other doors or corridors to escape to. He was out of time. Quickly, he ducked and laid flat on the ground then rolled into the wall, tucking himself tightly against it and putting his hands over his head. Lying on the dirt floor, he closed his eyes and waited. No other sounds besides his own nervous breathing could be heard. Then, he peeked through his concealing hands to see the orb of light floating towards the intersection of the two corridors. It lit the area well, but he was far enough away from its exposing light and was luckily still hidden in the shadows. Then the orb stopped at the intersection of the two corridors and floated in place for some time. Aleric could feel the prying eyes of the wizard looking through the orb, searching for him. Fear gripped him as he lay there, helpless in the dirt. If the orb came towards him, he was done for, if he hadn't been found out already.

He waited. Then waited some more. The moments passed like hours as he waited for what would happen next. His nose began to drip, and the uncomfortableness of the situation was becoming unbearable. If he moved, he would be found out. The tenseness of the situation grew with every second. Then, finally, the orb began to move again, receding away down the corridor until all was enveloped in darkness once again. He listened from his position on the ground and eventually heard the heavy, old, door creak and slam shut then footsteps fading into the distance as Maub left the dungeons.

For the moment, he was not found out, and he took a large sigh of relief at the momentary calmness. The encounter was too close for comfort, so he stayed lying in the damp dirt for some time before deciding that the coast was clear enough to attempt to find his way back out of the maze, here in the belly of the castle. Eventually he stood up and lit his torch again and began to move. With Maub so close by, he would feel Aleric using magic, and he would be found out. So, he lit the torch and began to move through the dark corridors once again.

He had an intense urge to flee the dungeon halls as fast as possible. But another part of him, the primitive part of the brain that gives one their gut instinct was telling him to investigate the now empty and mysterious courtroom here under the depths of the castle. He paused and took a deep breath, knowing it wasn't the rational decision, then quickly turned around and hurried back towards the wooden door Maub had exited from. As he crept inside, the torchlight illuminated the dark room. It was small, not much larger than a bedroom. Curiously small for a courtroom, he thought. There was a large desk at the front of the room with the flag of Mazeron hanging on the wall behind it. Upon the desk were stacks of books and a large rolled up paper. Hurrying as fast as he could while still being quiet, he quickly began rummaging through the books and desk. The books read *Laws of the Kingdom of Mazeron* and *Identifying Magical Items*, but nothing really stood out. Until he grabbed the large roll of paper and unraveled it.

It was a map of the kingdom of Mazeron, which at first sight was nothing special. But upon closer inspection, Aleric noticed that it was extremely detailed, and almost every plot of land in the kingdom was squared off. Many of the lots and farms had red X's written through them. In fact, the entire southeast portion of the kingdom was crossed off in red ink. Almost every farm. Aleric thought back and tried to remember which part of the kingdom Maub's prisoner had come from, studying the map. Sure enough, there was still slightly wet ink where a recent large farming property had been crossed off. He stood back up from studying the map and his head swam. Could the kingdom really be "legally" stealing people's land and farms by using the court system? He pondered the plausibility of the situation. It was hard to argue with a legal court system, after all. No matter how insignificant a crime is, people can't argue with the law, are vastly vengeful, and will always support punishment for breaking it because the person did something wrong, even if the punishment was far harsher than what the crime called for. This could allow the kingdom to steal peoples land for the tiniest infractions if they wanted to. And if it was ever found out most of the villagers would support it anyway.

Aleric's stomach lurched at the possibility that he had been working for and been privy to such injustice and corruption. Could the king he thought he knew really do that to his own people?

Aleric took one last glance around the room before exiting back into the dark dungeon corridors and making his way back into the castle. Soon he had reached the top of the stairs that led back up into the kitchens. Gently pushing the wooden hatch open he peered into the empty storage room. He had made it back. Quickly he threw the missing torch back to the bottom of the stairs and into the darkness, then exited the storage room. Once again, he crept through the kitchens and back through the great hall. Everything was silent and empty, just as it was before. The castle was asleep. As he crept through the castle and the seemingly endless, nervous trek back to the tower and his room, he expected to be found out at any moment. Every moment he expected to hear a voice of alarm from Maub or a guard hiding in the shadows. But to his continuous surprise, no one saw him and there was no alarm sounded.

Eventually, he arrived back at his wing and was standing in front of the door to his room. He opened it cautiously and entered. Still empty. Just as he left it. The only sound was his heart beating heavily in his ears. He couldn't believe he had snuck around the castle for most of the night without being spotted or caught.

He gazed at his bed. The site of it was like seeing a long-lost loved one. He had been on the dangerous road for so very long. Finally, sanctuary and comfort. He fell hard onto the bed with his clothes still on, and in the deep silence of the late night, he fell asleep almost right away.

CHAPTER 8. Assassins In The Castle

Dawn seemed to break instantly for Aleric, who had, in his mind, just laid his head down to sleep moments ago. There were no dreams, no thoughts. Just a few perfect, peaceful seconds before the cruel world woke him up again, calling him back to his many obligations. The sun coming through the window was bright and uncomfortable on his soggy eyes. The sound of the morning hustle from the village below the window was like drums inside of his ears. He wanted nothing besides sanctuary, peace, and rest. But instead, he got the sounds of villagers yelling, horses clomping, and roosters crowing. The unpleasantness of the tired morning quickly vanished as a sudden new fear rushed over him and he realized Brodel was still unattended, alone, and defenseless in the possibly unwelcoming castle. Aleric's eyes shot open quick with alarm at the thought of it.

"Brodel!" he called aloud as he sat up quickly. He had to tell the king about him and introduce the two before the guards got wind of such a powerful magic wielder being inside of the castle. Aleric jumped from his bed quickly then came crashing into Brodel's room, swinging the door open with heavy force and slamming it hard against the stone walls. His fists were up, ready to fight if needed. He was expecting the worst, but as he barged into the room, he found Brodel and Thearbuc already awake, having a peaceful morning conversation.

Brodel turned to Aleric as he barged in and their eyes met. Aleric audibly gasped and was taken back upon seeing Brodel. He was…older. His face had changed, like he had aged into a grown man in one long night. His cheek bones were more pronounced, shoulders broader, and he was most definitely taller. The look on Aleric's face reflected his worried and confused mind.

"I'm fine. It's the magic," Brodel said in a noticeably deeper voice after seeing the bewilderment on Aleric's face. "It wears on the physical body. I'm probably lucky to be alive, and mostly thanks to you I hear. I didn't know you had healing powers."

"Neither did I," Aleric replied, still looking concerned. "Why did you use so much magic that it hurt you?" he snapped.

"One has to find their limits somehow," Brodel replied with a grin. Aleric shook his head. "I told you I'm fine," Brodel repeated reassuringly while gently resting a hand on Aleric's shoulder. "This age is how I am supposed to look anyway. I should thank you!" he laughed. Aleric finally forced a grin and embraced Brodel's shoulder in return.

"Let's get breakfast. He said with a smile. "I just need to get changed."

"Me too," Thearbuc said, exiting the room and heading to his own.

Aleric waited in the hallway for the others and pondered to himself why he had barged into Brodel's room so violently and was so protective of the boy. Well, grown man now. It wasn't like him to go out of the way or be so protective of anyone else, besides Briss of course.

Briss. That is why. He knew it instantly. He had let her down in such a big way. She was someone he cared about immensely, and he let her down as much as was literally possible. He was not about to let that happen again to anyone he cared about. He realized right then and there that he would go out of his way, no matter how miserable it would be, to protect the people he cared about. Not just his friends, but his kingdom as well. Then it dawned on him. That was all he had left in this life. His friends and his kingdom. For better or for worse, nothing else mattered, and he would devote his life to them. It wasn't a conscious choice either. This is just who he was now. The thought of it, although new and unsettling to him, gave him strength and purpose. He was meant to be here to protect people. It was his calling. He had nothing left to give but himself. He was a rock, here to help others survive and be happy, even if he wasn't or ever would be again.

After what seemed like more than enough time to put on clothes and get on with the day, Brodel finally emerged from his room with his usual ignorantly happy look upon his face, even though his eyes drooped more now, and he had stubble already starting to grow on his chin. To Aleric, it seemed like Brodel had no idea what could be in store for him today as an obvious magic wielder within the walls of a kingdom that had long ago made his existence illegal. Was Brodel so carefree because he had Aleric, the paladin, watching over him? Or because he was so comfortable with his own magic ability?

Aleric shrugged off Brodel's nonchalantness as youthful ignorance and asked the boy to follow him to Thearbuc's room so they could all greet the king together.

Aleric went to knock on Thearbuc's door, but it opened just before he knocked and out came Thearbuc looking happy and refreshed.

"You take longer to change than my teenager." He laughed as he pushed them aside with his broad shoulders and then wandered confidently into the hallway. "Now, where's this king?" he bellowed loudly. "I've never been in a castle before."

Aleric rolled his eyes and wondered between Thearbuc and Brodel, who was the most carefree and immature at this serious moment?

"You both are being too lighthearted about this day," Aleric scolded. "The king is missing and that old wizard Maub who hates me is holding secret courts in the dungeons of the castle. If we can't find the king and get him to welcome Brodel we will have to fight our way out of here—past dozens of the king's guards—and be exiled to the woods for the rest of our lives. If we even make it that far." He sighed heavily at the thought of what could happen if the king did not accept them. "Act proper," he said, making hard eye contact.

"What do you mean secret courts?" Thearbuc asked.

"Maybe they aren't secret, but they are definitely corrupt. I went looking through the castle last night, trying to find anyone, and stumbled upon it. I knew that wizard couldn't be trusted. Let's go find the king and hope for the best."

Quickly the mood changed for Thearbuc and Brodel as they realized what they could be in for. They nodded at Aleric then followed him down the long corridor and back down the tower steps, back into the great halls, and toward the kitchens of the castle.

Finally, coming upon the dining hall, Aleric pushed open the large wooden doors with a loud slam, announcing their presence to whoever was nearby. They entered the hall expecting an audience, but again, to their surprise, there was almost no one inside. Just a few of the castle's workers going about their daily duties. No one sat at the table, and it was void of any food or utensils, which was not common for this time of morning.

Confusion washed over Aleric's face as once again he was faced with the question *where is everyone?*

"You there!" he bellowed, pointing to one of the servants. "Can we get breakfast?"

The servant nodded and bowed. "Yes sir, Paladin, sir." And scurried off into the kitchen.

"Pull up a chair," Aleric said, making his way to the large dining table that stretched most of the length of the great dining hall. "You are about to eat better than any of us have eaten in a long time." They each took their place at the table and had quiet conversation while waiting for their meal, or anyone else, to show up in the eerily empty dining hall. Aleric made it a point to tell the others more than once that usually, this time of day the dining hall would be host to guests of the king or at least workers of the castle. But like the rest of the castle since he had returned, it was unusually and eerily quiet and empty.

After some time, the servants returned and pushed a sad case of eggs and potatoes in front of the three friends. Brodel and Thearbuc both glanced up at Aleric.

"Fine dining you say, huh?" Thearbuc chuckled.

"It's all we have sir," the attendant said quietly, stepping back from the table.

"It will do just fine. Thank you," Aleric replied, still looking somewhat confused.

Halfway through their breakfast they were interrupted by the sound of a loud slow creak of old hinges. They turned to see the large door of the dining hall door slowly open. Then watched and waited as it barely cracked open, then in shuffled King Victus. The king looked around with a confused look. His eyes were puffy and hair a mess, like he had just awakened from a deep, long sleep or was recovering from a sickness. His shirt and trousers were ruffled and untucked, which was not how he ever presented himself in public. He stood by the door in silence with a blank look upon his face.

"My king." Aleric stood from the table and went to him.

"Aleric? Is that you?" he replied rubbing his eyes. "Back already?"

"Back already, sir?" Aleric said perplexed. "I've been gone for weeks. I was ambushed by a mage in the woods. We have to talk about it. These men here saved my life, and I have brought them back here to help us." He motioned to Brodel and Thearbuc sitting at the table. He spoke with frustration and confusion that he had been through such a long ordeal and the king barely even noticed he had been gone.

The king turned away from his Paladin with indifference and immediately noticed Brodel. The sparkles and flashes of light radiating from his body had already caught his attention. This was the moment they had all been dreading. The king stared at the boy with a blank face for some time.

"Oh," the king finally spoke. "I see you found more help."

"Indeed, my king," Aleric replied. "Brodel is his name. He is gifted with powerful magic and can help us bring the kingdom back to prosperity." There was a long pause as the tension grew thicker. "He is very powerful, sir. More than I."

"Well, we are happy to have you," the king answered, cutting through the tension with a tired and uncaring voice. "You two and Maub will have to get together and…do whatever it is you wizards do. He was once a powerful magic user, too, you know." The king trailed off and with a yawn began turning back toward the door with a fumble in his step. He put one hand on the door to steady himself and paused for another moment. "I could have sworn you just left yesterday," he said softly to Aleric. "How long did I sleep? No, can't sleep that long. I must be forgetting the days in my old age." He trailed off again as he began to shuffle back out the door. "I need to get some sleep, my head is killing me" he mumbled. You boys make yourselves comfortable in the castle. Let's meet here later this evening, or perhaps tomorrow…or in a few days. Then you can tell me about this mage you mentioned."

"Umm, alright." Aleric shrugged, still confused, as the king shuffled away back into the castle. "Whenever you are ready." The others lowered their heads in silence and thought as the faint footsteps faded into the distance.

"The king does not seem well," Thearbuc stated as Aleric took his seat back at the table.

"Indeed," he replied in a low tone with a troubled look. "His mind must be fading. I've been gone for weeks, and he seems to think I just barely left." He nodded his head back and forth as he contemplated what had just happened.

"At least Brodel seems safe here," Thearbuc stated, looking at the now young man version of Brodel. "I expected a lot worse." All three nodded silently and continued their meal.

"Well, let me show you boys the kingdom today," Aleric said with a more upbeat tone. "I don't want to run into that old wizard without the king around. Who is up for a horse ride through the countryside?"

Soon after the three finished their meals, they followed Aleric out to the stables. As they passed the many guards along the way, Aleric's old coworkers and acquaintances. Brodel noticed most of them giving him hard looks and staring at him. Some of them made aggressive eye contact as they walked by, and some folded their arms and just stared.

"I don't think the kingdom is ready for us," Brodel said nervously. "They've been against using magic for so long now. It is just not a part of life anymore."

"Ready or not, we're here," Aleric laughed in reply. As usual, Aleric wasn't fazed by others, their threats, or what they thought of him. It was a natural disposition he had. A type of arrogance that comes from knowing you are better than the rest.

At the stables, the three chose the horses they would be riding for the day with no help from the stableman and soon were off.

The next few days came and went, and to their surprise, they were never contacted by the king, or anyone else for that matter. As the empty days wore on, they constantly discussed the mischief mage and tried discreetly as they could to see if anyone Aleric trusted recognized the wizard staff and dragon tattoo that adorned the mage's arm. No one seemed to know anything about it or the mage, so the matter remained unresolved for now.

Eventually the castle slowly started to come back to life and the various guards seemed to be returning to their posts, including the guards at the king's wing, where King Victus was reportedly still in his chambers not feeling well. Despite his efforts, Aleric was not allowed to meet with the king.

But overall, this downtime was welcomed by Aleric, Thearbuc, and Brodel. They seemed to have free reign of the castle and its many amenities. They bathed in hot baths and napped in the afternoons, then ate the castle's wonderful food then napped some more. They spent time riding through the countryside and teaching each other combat and magic skills. It was a nice change for all of them, not having to worry about survival. Food and shelter were provided, so all they had to do was enjoy living. This sort of carefree life was usually only experienced by royalty. But for now, the king's Paladin and his two friends were also experiencing this blissful, carefree way of life.

"I'm going to miss this when it's gone," Thearbuc said, chomping into an apple that he had just picked off a tree before laying in the cool grass.

"Who says it has to end?" Brodel replied, shooting a small bolt of magic at another apple that he had set up on a rock for target practice. It exploded into nothing after the bolt was thrown. His magical powers had noticeably matured and grown stronger since he had aged into a strong young man.

"Nice shot," Thearbuc laughed. The warmth of the sun was soft in the cool wind that blew calmly through the natural green grasses of the land.

"I'm sure they'll want us to do some sort of work around here eventually. Right?" Thearbuc turned to ask Aleric.

"I'm about as new to this life as you are," he replied, shrugging his shoulders. "I suppose you are right though. Enjoy this downtime while you can. It probably can't last forever."

The three continued their lazy day, and as the sun began to set, they made their way slowly back to the castle to catch the chef before he turned in for the night. It was a nice vacation they had been having but like all good things, it was not destined to last.

The following evening, Aleric was awoken from a deep daytime nap by a soft knock at his wooden door. He opened his eyes to realize the sun had already set and the day was already long over.

"How long have I been napping?" he mumbled aloud as his blurry vision came back to him. He had been in such a deep sleep that it took a moment to remember where he was and what day it was.

"Your presence is requested by the king," a voice on the other side of the door announced loudly.

Aleric replied that he heard the man and began to get out of bed. Outside the opened window the night was dark, calm, and still. In the town below he could see a few scattered torches and candles from the last merchants still closing down their carts for the night. A slight breeze blew through the window.

Not long later, Aleric was dressed and ready to go. When he was exiting the room, another breeze came through the window. This time it came with a lot more force and it blew scattered straw and anything loose around the room. Aleric turned to close the shutters and glanced into the distance. He could see that a large storm was brewing in the distance, and the wind was blowing it towards the kingdom. Lightning flashed through the distant rain in and the wind blew harder again. He closed the shutters to keep out the cold wind then turned and began towards the door.

To his surprise, Thearbuc and Brodel were already standing in the otherwise empty corridor.

"Late hour for a meeting, don't you agree?" Thearbuc said glancing towards Aleric entering the hall. "Is it odd the king wants to meet with us this late in the day?"

"He is the king," Aleric replied with a shrug. "He eats supper when he chooses."

Thearbuc and Brodel also shrugged then followed Aleric down the long corridor back to the stairs then back down toward the dining hall.

The massive wood doors of the dining hall swung open and the three entered into the dimly lit hall. King Victus sat at one end of the long table, Maub near him, and three other men who Aleric did not recognize sat scattered between the many empty seats at the table. Castle servants stopped mid-stride to see who had entered the room, paused for a glance, then continued on with their trays and duties. Other servants could be seen going about their duties in the shadow of the dimly lit upper corridor of the hall.

"Ah! There are my friends," the old king said, jumping up from his seat and making his way towards them. The three noticed instantly that he was much livelier now compared to the groggy, sick, old man they had seen days before. "Come, tell me about your quest. Tell me about this mage in the woods you mentioned.

Tell me everything!" he said, putting his hand on Aleric's shoulders and escorting them back toward the table.

The king motioned for them to take their seats at the long table as he took his at the head. Thearbuc sat to the king's left side, Aleric to his right, and Brodel sat next to Aleric. A few chairs down sat Maub, quietly staring in the darkness of the dimly lit room. The three strangers were scattered randomly at the far end from the king and watched in silence. A fire burned low and pleasant at the far end of the hall, giving some light to the dim room and casting dancing shadows across the high stone walls.

The king loudly requested the servants to bring ale and food to his friends and they began discussing what had happened in the woods with the mage. Aleric told him everything from the start, how he was ambushed by a powerful mage and hunted by the mysterious beast that almost killed him and Thearbuc's daughter. And how they ambushed the mage and killed him then found Brodel in the woods the following day. When Aleric came to the part of the story where he described the dragon and wizard's staff tattoo on the mage's wrist, Maub made an uncomfortable adjustment in his seat that did not go unnoticed by Thearbuc sitting across the table from him. He also noticed that Maub was continuously glancing at Brodel throughout the conversation and staring too long with an obvious scowl from the shadows. Brodel was fixated on the food and did not notice the unwelcoming glares.

"That mage knew I was coming," Aleric said raising his voice and arms and holding eye contact with the king before turning to Maub. There was a thick awkward silence and tension hung in the air while he studied their reactions. "He was waiting for me in that field. Tell me how he knew I was coming," Aleric insinuated an accusation.

"He didn't *know* you were coming," Maub interrupted with a touch of irritableness and indifference in his voice. "He most likely just stumbled upon you and didn't want anyone in his territory."

"I'm sure that's it," replied the king. "No one but me, Maub, and our counsel knew you were going out into the far woods."

"Then explain this," Aleric said, standing up and slamming down the wrinkled parchment paper that they had found on the mage which had the timing and description of Aleric's journey. "He knew I was coming!" King Victus picked up the paper and his mouth dropped as he read the description of Aleric and the timing of his arrival. He attempted to speak but was choked up for a moment, and the words did not come out.

"We have a spy," the king finally mustered. "A spy in our midst, Paladin." Aleric sat back down and watched as the paper was passed around the table. He glared at Maub and studied his reaction to the note.

"I serve the castle as much as you, Paladin," Maub said sternly, noticing the unfriendly glare. "Do not pass your accusations at me," he warned, tossing the paper aside.

"Maub has only done good for this kingdom," the king said, jumping to Maub's defense. "He is not a spy nor an assassin." The wizard nodded in thanks at the old king.

As the king spoke about his unwavering trust in his counsel, more food and drink was brought to the table, which broke some of the tension in the room and redirected the conversation, leaving Aleric still frustrated that he had been unable to shed any light on who set him up for an ambush.

Soon after, between bites of food and heavy gulps of wine, the king leaned in and motioned to the others to listen.

"Aleric," he said with a slight slur from the wine. "We have decided what your next task shall be." Aleric and the others leaned in to hear what the king had to say. "Over the mountains and to the west lies the kingdom of Haberlorn." He paused and the others nodded, indicating that they knew of the place. "My younger cousin is King Haberlorn, and he rules there." The others nodded, they too knew of this place and King Victus' cousin, King Haberlorn. "Since the arrival of the brigands and their control over the mountain passes, no one has been able to reach our sister kingdom in years. Besides cutting off trade between the two kingdoms, they have also cut off families from one another, and most importantly, cut off the two armies from coming to one another's aid when in need." The others nodded again; they all knew the history of the two kingdoms. Then the king continued. "An agreement between the two kingdoms has stood for hundreds of years and is now worthless because the armies of the kingdoms are unable to come to each other's aid!" The king paused again while he glanced around the room. "We shall remedy this!" he finished, raising his voice.

"What do you have in mind?" Aleric asked. A hint of glowing light flickered within his eyes.

"You and your friends can make it through the mountain passes. Slip by the brigands and send word to my cousin about our plans. Together, our kingdoms will use our combined forces and The Paladin to rid the mountain passes of the brigands and restore trade and communication with our sister kingdom." The king's face was lit up and filled with excitement and life as he spoke. His mind raced at the possibility of seeing his cousin again and rejoining their alliances to create a vast, safe, prosperous kingdom—one never seen in either of their lifetimes. "The power we could create!" The king shouted, waving a clenched fist, which struck his goblet of wine and pushed it off the table.

Aleric, who was sitting next to him, instinctively leaned over to pick up the spilled goblet. Then, as he was bent over in his chair, an arrow came silently speeding out of the darkness of the wings, and without any warning or sound, stuck with a heavy thud directly into the back of Aleric's chair. The room instantly went silent as their cumulative minds raced to process what was happening. Then, without any more hesitation, Thearbuc pushed hard from his seat and laid his right shoulder into the king, tackling him to the ground. Just as they landed heavily onto the floor with a crash, a second arrow whistled past the king's chair and stuck in the thick wooden table. Aleric was already on the ground behind the table, anticipating a second arrow directed at him.

"Assassin!" he yelled. "Up in the corridors!" Everyone collapsed to the ground and took cover behind the chairs and table. They peered into the dark corridors above the dining hall to see a shadow fleeing from the scene. It was barely visible in the darkness, but the movement was noticeable as the shadow retreated further into the darkness.

"He's getting away!" grumbled the king from the ground, pushing Thearbuc off him.

The shadow was escaping quickly. He was just a few strides away from the exit and the concealment of the labyrinth of hallways and corridors of the castle when suddenly a blinding blue light appeared in the room and shot quickly like lightning toward the shadow. It was Maub. He stood tall near the table with his hands held in front of his face, blasting a blue-colored energy toward the fleeing shadow. It enveloped the assassin immediately and he was lifted into the air, engulfed by the ball of energy. He was suspended there in midair as the rest of the room watched in amazement and confusion, still trying to gather and grasp what was happening all so fast. There was a moment of pause from the others while they watched. Loud clacking and snaps of electricity filled the room as they watched the man suspended helplessly in the air.

"Guards!" the king finally managed. "Get him!" The guards at the far end of the room quickly started to make their way up the stairs towards the assassin. Aleric, Thearbuc, Brodel, and the king were also on the move, not far behind. Maub's face crumpled with concentration as he held the man with lightning-like energy flowing from his hands. As they climbed the stairs and moved closer to the assassin, they could vaguely hear muffled screams of pain and agony over the sound of crackling electricity and energy. Then, when the group approached the assassin, Maub dropped his hands, and with a heavy sigh of exhaustion, he ceased his magical attack on the assassin and slumped heavily onto a chair.

The others along with the guards moved hastily to the assassin to apprehend him, but he was not moving. A moment of inspection showed he was not breathing, and his body smoked like a log in a fire left smoldering until morning. Quickly, they pulled the cloak from the assassin's face and one by one they all looked at each other for some sort of affirmation if anyone knew him. But no one recognized the man. Beneath the cloak he wore the uniform of the castle's guards.

"I don't recognize him," Aleric stated. "He must have used the uniform to gain entry to the castle."

"Maub," Thearbuc said between deep breaths, quietly to Aleric. "I think we owe him an apology for the accusations. He just saved the king. He saved you. That was amazing!" he said, still breathing heavily from the attack and pursuit of the assassin. Aleric paused in silent thought for a moment.

"Maub, I thought you said you couldn't do magic anymore?" he yelled out from the upper corridor. Maub, still breathing heavily and with a look of exhaustion, raised up from his chair with anger in his eyes.

"Just get the king out of here!" the old wizard yelled. "There could be more of them!" The men looked at each other, still huddled around the assassin, when another arrow came from the darkness and stuck in the wall behind them. They glanced up. More shadows were moving in the wings. More than one. "Now!" yelled Maub, so loud that his voice echoed off the stone walls.

The guards readied to defend the king while Aleric, Thearbuc, and Brodel helped him up from inspecting the assassin and rushed towards the darkness of the wings and away from the dining hall. As they fled, they saw flashes of light illuminating the walls as Maub continued the assault on the hidden assassins, giving the others time to flee. They raced away until finally they were away from the hall and into the great maze of corridors and hallways of the castle.

"There's no time to rest," Aleric commanded, grabbing the king's arm when he paused to catch his breath. They hurried on. Running as fast as the old king could, he led them down the different corridors towards his wing of the castle.

Exhausted and out of breath, finally they arrived at the king's quarters. They flew into the large entrance of the wing then turned and slammed the heavily fortified doors closed and locked themselves inside. Leaning on their knees and against the walls, trying to catch their breaths, Aleric, Thearbuc, and Brodel finally had the king safely fortified in the castle's east wing. Not long after the doors had slammed closed came a pounding at the wooden doors. The four exchanged glances.

"Guards," Aleric said flatly. "We can't trust anyone wearing guard uniforms right now," he said to the king, who nodded that he agreed.

"Keep watch and guard the wing from outside the door," King Victus ordered through the doors. "With eight men, until I say otherwise. No one is to come in or out of these doors." His voice was trembling from adrenaline and fear as he spoke. "I have many of my own guards in here already," he lied.

"Yes, sir" could be heard on the other side of the doorway followed by the sound of movement and voices giving orders from down the hallway.

"Come with me," motioned the king, walking toward another end of the large corridor. This wing of the castle was his living quarters. His personal home that no one ever ventured to, except his own personal guards and Maub. The walls towered above them and large tapestries hung from above, stretching from the high ceiling and down to the floor. A large fireplace stood at each end of the room and the hall was lined with great windows overlooking the kingdom. The finest furniture, made by Mazeron's finest craftsmen adorned the entire wing, and long beautiful curtains hung from high above the large windows.

As they walked through the wing, they passed a dark room that was two floors high and filled with beautiful, glossy, wooden bookshelves that stretched from the floor to the high ceiling. Every inch was filled with various books. This part of the castle was magnificent compared to the rest of the cold drafty castle. "My personal library," the king mentioned after seeing the others gaze in amazement at its beauty and craftmanship. Then the king led them into a small dining area with a small table in the center of it. He motioned them to sit down.

"Paladin," the king spoke, standing up and placing his hands on the table. "After the events of this evening, I feel it is imperative that we speed up the timing of your next quest." Aleric nodded as the king spoke. "You have proven yourself capable and I am confident you can succeed. Our next mission, as we spoke about earlier, is to rid the mountain passes of the brigands. We have been cut off from our sister kingdom and my cousin's land for far too long. Here we stand tonight, shut away in our own castle, unable to trust our own guards. I am trapped and fear for my life in my own home. I will barricade myself in this wing until you return with help from my cousin. You must reach the kingdom of Haberlorn and seek help from him and his army. We must tell them the time has come to reclaim the mountain passes. With you and our combined armies, we will destroy the brigands, joining our once prosperous kingdoms once again." The king clenched his fist and slammed it hard onto the table as his frustration with the world and their predicament grew.

Aleric, Thearbuc, and Brodel exchanged glances as they each contemplated the idea. It was a good plan, and defeating the brigands to reopen trade and travel between the two kingdoms was imperative. They all knew it. After a long pause, they nodded in agreement one by one. No words were spoken between them.

"With these new developments," the king finally spoke again, "Assassins in my own castle, we cannot wait for an ideal time." He paused and glanced at Aleric with heaviness in his eyes. "I hate to say it, but—"

"We understand," Aleric interrupted, knowing what the king was going to say. "We set out tonight. We must go in secret, so whoever is trying to assassinate us cannot follow, and all the guards will still think we are in here with you."

The king nodded silently. "It has to be," he said, lowering his head. Thearbuc walked to a nearby window and cracked open the shutter. Fierce winds blew in with a loud howl and whistled through the chambers, blowing curtains, and tipping small objects on their side. The storm had set in already and was here to stay. He closed the window slowly, pulling heavily on the shutter against the wind until he finally overcame the wind's force. He looked at the others with a worried look in his eyes.

"We need to at least prepare," Brodel chimed in nervously after seeing the severity of the storm. "We can't just go out in these conditions unprepared. We can't pass through the high mountain tops unprepared," he said, raising his arms. There was a noticeable worry in his voice. "How can we—"

"There are secret corridors through the castle, known only to me," the king interrupted. "I will lead you to your rooms to gather your gear. Then you will sneak out of the castle and head to the stables, then slip away into the darkness. No one will suspect you left to travel in this storm." There was a moment of pause as the three others thought it over. Aleric sighed a deep breath, as if it was the last breath he would ever take.

"Where are these corridors then?" he said, moving towards the door.

"This way," replied the king. He led them into the dark library they had passed before. In the center of the library there stood a large podium. "Help me move it," he said, wrapping his arms around the podium. Thearbuc gripped the podium as well and the two slowly moved it from its heavy resting place. The king knelt down, and feeling around the darkness, he grabbed a small metal ring. Then, with a heaving motion, he moved a large stone tile out of place and revealed a set of stairs that descended into the darkness. "Torch," he commanded, outstretching his hand.

"I can help with that," Brodel said with a smile. He grabbed two torches off the adjacent wall, and with a motion of his wrist they were both magically lit. The king watched in amazement as the sparks and colors danced excitedly off Brodel's body then floated softly into the air until disappearing into nothing.

"Well, I'll be…" the king trailed off in amazement. "I think you boys are going to do just fine out there. Let's go," he said with haste.

They started down the stairs and into the dark passageways. Soon they were moving quickly through the secret passages, between the castle walls and floors. There was darkness in every direction except for the immediate glow of the torches. There was no direction in the darkness—no left or right, just blackness and a maze of stone walls and thick, stale air. They felt lost, but the king seemed to know where they were going. After what felt like hours of claustrophobia, trapped in the stuffy, cramped, darkness of the castle walls, the king suddenly stopped.

"Hold this." He shoved the torch at Thearbuc. Then he began feeling around the base of the stone walls with both hands. "Found it!" he said eventually, pulling an old rope out of a stone casing. A cloud of dust came with it. The king pulled hard and the stone wall before them began to open. Once the crack was large enough, the four slipped through it and into another dark room. It was completely silent in the room besides the distant howling of wind finding its way through the drafty castle beyond.

After a moment gathering their nerves, they began making their way towards a door at the other end of the room. They slowly cracked it open, which let in a small beam of light. Aleric peered through the crack and found that he was in the hallway near their living quarters. They waited to be sure, but the hallway was empty and quiet.

"It's clear," he announced as the rest crept through the doorway and into the hallway. "Quick. Gather your supplies, just the necessities. Twenty minutes and we meet back in this room." The others nodded then headed off to their rooms. The king followed Aleric into his quarters.

"I didn't know you had brought another magic user into the castle," he stated with intrigue as the door closed behind them. Aleric was taken back as the king had seen Brodel and his visible magic just days before, in his groggy state. Did he not remember?

"We were going to tell you. We didn't get the chance until tonight," Aleric replied slowly while gathering his things.

"How many others like him are out there?" the king asked aloud, mostly thinking to himself. "What have I done?" he buried his head in his hand, visibly regretful.

"No matter now," Aleric replied, resting a hand on the king's shoulder. "He will be a great asset to the kingdom, and he's a good boy—I mean, man. You will see."

"I believe it," the king replied, regaining his composure. Aleric continued gathering his supplies as the king gave him directions to the high mountain passes and the roads that lead to the kingdom of Haberlorn. He reminded Aleric of the danger the brigands posed and their guerilla tactics that were so effective.

"You must find a way to get through their checkpoints without being seen," he reminded Aleric again. "Get to my cousin for help. I fear all our survival depends on your success of this mission." Aleric nodded that he understood as he buckled the last of his armor then threw a large pack over his shoulder.

"We move!" he said picking up the longsword from off the bed. They made their way back toward the door, checked that the hallway was clear, then moved stealthily back to the open door at the end of the hallway where Thearbuc and Brodel were already waiting.

"I can find my way back from here," the king said in a hushed whisper. "You three will want to make your way down that corridor until you come to a set of stairs. Follow them down as far as they go then you will come to a door. The door leads to a closet near the kitchen. That part of the castle should be empty this time of night. Find a window and sneak out into the night, then make your way to the stables."

They all nodded that they agreed. Nothing was said, but they all knew it would be some time before they would all meet again, and that the road ahead would be difficult and treacherous. With a hard pat on the king's shoulder, Aleric turned quickly and started down the hidden passageways once again.

They followed the king's directions and made it to the window for their escape as best as possible and using the secret passages between the walls of the castle they were near the kitchen in just minutes. Out of the passageways the three crept through the darkness of the empty castle. Through the kitchens, past the great hall, and to the far end of the castle, closest to the stables. Thearbuc opened the shutters of a window for them to make their escape where the three peered out into the darkness of the night. The wind blew heavy and cold from the high mountains beyond. Trees shook and swayed loudly as the wind rushed through their leaves and the sound of the wind blew loudly into the quiet room.

"At least the wind will conceal our sound," Thearbuc stated. "If we hurry. The night is dark, there is no moon tonight. We should be able to slip away unnoticed if we are careful." The three stood in silence for a moment, looking for any movement or sign of guards patrolling the perimeter of the castle. There was nothing.

"Let's go," Aleric broke the silence. "We are still two stories up; we'll have to jump." The three looked down. It was a long way down, but in the dark shadows they saw a row of shrubbery bushes hugging the castle at the bottom. "Jump for the bushes. It will help the fall," Aleric instructed, climbing up onto the window ledge. He looked right then to his left for sign of any guards. And without hesitation, he jumped into the blackness of the night and was gone. The other two hurriedly peered out to see what had happened. Looking down, they saw movement in the bushes, but they could not see Aleric through the darkness. They waited intently until eventually a shadow made its way from the bushes and onto the flat ground. He was okay.

"Be quick," Thearbuc motioned to Brodel. He climbed into the window and was gone into the night. Then Brodel carefully climbed outside of the window and stood up tall, holding his balance with one hand on the rock wall of the castle. The wind blew harder, and because of his smaller frame, he was almost blown off the ledge by the wind. Carefully, he reached inward and closed the window shutter, hiding their escape route. Then he turned about, gazed into the darkness beyond, and jumped. Through the darkness and rushing wind, the three fled into the night. The sound of the wind was deafening in their ears, and small, cold raindrops pelted their faces hard as they ran toward the stables. It was late into the night; the stables would be lightly guarded, if at all. Coming over the hill, nearing the stables, a small light broke through the absoluteness of night and the three men stopped, then crouched low to the ground to observe the area.

"There are four guards!" Brodel whispered to the others sounding a bit worried.

"Why are there four guards at this hour?" Thearbuc asked.

"Horse thieves have been troublesome lately. Or perhaps they are expecting us?" Aleric replied. He looked down at the ground while he thought and tried to come up with a plan.

"I'll handle this," Brodel said while crawling away from the others. Then he made his way to a large hump in the ground, positioned out of view of the stables, and crouched and took cover behind it. Aleric and Thearbuc watched him crawl to the spot but could barely make him out in the darkness. They could see his movement, but he was a vague shadow in the night.

Then, a brightness began to illuminate around him. They could see his shape through a dim ball of light. The other two instantly figured out what was going on. He was working his magic. A moment later, a light appeared in the distance in front of the stables. It danced and flickered like a torch.

Within moments they heard voices and commotion coming from the stables. Through the darkness and dim lights of the stables, they could see the guards assembling their weapons, but they did not approach the light. Instead, they stood and watched, still closely guarding the stables.

"More, more!" Thearbuc yelled in a hushed tone against the heavy wind to Brodel. "They aren't taking the bait." Then, with a flash of light, something soared high into the sky and exploded into the air. The guards crouched and stayed in defensive positions, not budging from the stables. With a bang, another stream of light shot directly toward the guards and exploded all around them.

"That will make them angry!" Thearbuc said with a grin. Brodel's dancing flame of light began to flee away from the stables and the guards. Running fast into the dark fields beyond.

"Get him!" They heard yelling through the wind as the guards began to run from the stables, chasing the imaginary culprit that was fleeing into the night.

"Now!" Aleric said, and the three sprang up from the ground and rushed toward the stables. In just moments they were unlashing three strong horses. Aleric left his personal horse behind as to not give any suspicion that he had left the castle. As far as anyone else knew, he was secured in the wing with the king as his personal protection.

Not even a minute later they were off, riding fast into the night with the heavy wind and black night concealing any evidence that they were ever even there. The guards left in the distance were still wandering around the fields, trying to find who had agitated them.

The three rode fast and hard for miles until they felt they had safely fled the kingdom without being followed. Aleric stopped his horse first and the others gathered around. They had reached an area closer to the mountains that had more hills, so the wind had died down to a smaller breeze.

"We can't take the normal roads and follow the river into the forest. Anyone hunting us will assume that's the route we will take," he said, commanding and confident.

"What do you suggest then?" Thearbuc replied, his horse pacing around the others.

"We make straight for the mountains from here, then traverse the foothills until we meet up with the road again in a few days. Then take the road over the mountain passes, avoiding the brigands however we can. Then back down into the valley and the kingdom of Haberlorn." There was silence while the other two pondered the plan.

"That will add three or four extra days at least," Thearbuc mentioned.

"I know. But getting there later is better than not getting there at all. Stealth and secrecy are our only advantages. We are unprepared and outnumbered." There was another pause while they thought about any alternatives. But alas, they could find none.

"It is the best plan of action," Brodel said, breaking the silence. "Let's get to the hills and concealment of the forest before sunrise."

There was a nod of agreement between the three, then they were off again. Riding towards the great mountains in the distance, they could see towering white snowcapped peaks surrounded by hundreds of stars showing through the scattered clouds in the dark night. Soon they would be up there, Brodel thought to himself. The thought of it made his heart wretch with overwhelming intimidation. He had spent his life in the woods and had never been high up into the treachery of the great mountains. But he remembered who he was traveling with, and the long quest began to feel less heavy on his shoulders. Fear turned to the excitement of the unknown as they rode through the night, and the thought of returning to the safety and overall mundaneness of his hut disappeared. If he returned to his normal life, he thought, he knew exactly what awaited him. If he rode on into the unknown, his life's possibilities were endless.

Chapter 9: The Witch's Woods

The three companions rode through the night, begrudgingly fleeing the warmth and comfort of their beds in the large castle toward the wilderness and unknown. Calm but icy cold air nipped at exposed skin until it became numb to the cold. It was one of those nights after a storm has passed, where there isn't a cloud in the sky and the stars seem so clear and close that it feels like you can reach out and touch them, or almost feel what it would be like to be way out there among them.

Without the blanket of cloud cover, this night was also exceptionally cold, and it grew colder as their horses carried them to higher elevations and closer to the snowcapped mountains ahead. The white, snow-covered mountains against the black sky still towered like giant gods always watching over the valley, silently judging the lands below with their usual conceited indifference. Choosing who they would allow to pass through to the other side and who they would not.

In the late hours of the night, the ground became too steep for direct travel, so they picked up a small deer trail in the foothills and began to traverse flatly across the mountain range, which would take many days, until they met back up with the road that would lead them through the mountain passes. They were all exhausted and no words were spoken for hours as the horses trudged slowly along the damp trail. It was almost morning when they came across a small opening in the mountain. It was a cave. The foothills of Mazeron were littered with small caves from men searching for gold in years long past. These men either dug before the discovery of the magical Stone Gnomes, which could move freely through the mountains and easily discover veins of gold for miners. Or, they were men who were unable to acquire the services of the Stone Gnomes for whatever reason and were forced to search for gold the traditional way.

The caves along the foothills were most certainly not created recently though. The disappearance of the Stone Gnomes after the banning of magic had put a halt to gold mining, and no one had since seemed to care enough to even try to mine the difficult, old-fashioned way. The work was too hard and backbreaking compared to how easy it once was, so no one seemed to have the gumption for it in these modern times, and all the mines were eventually abandoned. In fact, there hadn't been a nugget of gold mined in the hills of Mazeron since the last sighting of a Stone Gnome over twenty years ago.

Thearbuc and Brodel had dismounted their horses and were already beginning to explore the cave. With a motion of his hand, the orb atop Brodel's staff began to illuminate a bright blue light, and the two entered the cave and were gone into the darkness. Aleric stayed behind and began to tie up the horses near the mouth of the cave. He looked up again at the calm night sky and marveled at the many stars. The valley below was calm and peaceful and mostly covered with green forest as far as he could see. Out of the corner of his eye, he caught a glimpse of a greenish-blue glow off in the distance that grabbed his attention. He peered into the distance. Out of the forest below came three large beings, almost as tall as the trees. He could see them clearly now. They were tall and slim and shaped like humans. They did not walk and did not have legs that he could see, but floated, suspended in the air. Long cloaks reached a few feet off the ground, but nothing was below them but air. Upon their necks all three of them had necklaces adorned with a large green glowing disc that illuminated the forests surrounding them. They moved through a clearing while Aleric watched from the distance with nervous intrigue. As they moved, one of them stopped, turned, and deliberately faced directly at Aleric. His heart was pumping in his chest. He could feel the giant staring at him from the distance, and he clenched his fists in nervous tension. The giant continued to stare with unseen eyes at Aleric up on the hillside for some moments, then simply turned and continued floating into the woods, ignoring him until they were gone. Their green glow and all signs of them completely vanished into the woods.

"Did that just happen?" he mumbled aloud to himself. It was almost a dream. Then the calmness of the night returned and his tensions from the encounter began to ease. Any threat of the mysterious giants disappeared with the passing quiet moments on the peaceful hillside of the cold mountain.

"It's safe," Thearbuc said, returning from the depths of the cave behind him. Aleric made no response, still staring off into the distance. "Did you see something?"

"Uh, no," he replied. "I guess not." He lied, not wanting to alarm the others as he turned and followed them into the cave for a much-needed rest.

In the darkness of the cave there was a small thud followed by a grunt from Thearbuc. "I hit my head again!" he grumbled. The other two could see him patting his head, observing the damage in the faint glow of Brodel's staff as they moved deeper into the cave. Thearbuc had had a run of bad luck since leaving Brodel's hut. Aleric noticed Thearbuc's string of bad luck wondered if the man always had bad luck and mild injuries or if he was just sometimes clumsy. Either way he had noticed that since he had known Thearbuc, he had stubbed his toe to the point where it was possibly broken, his boots developed a hole that made travel wet and uncomfortable, his things would randomly go missing, and his horses—no matter which one he chose—would occasionally try to toss him off. Something in the universe seemed set on constantly making his life just a little bit harder than it needed to be. Aleric shrugged and figured the man just had bad luck for some reason and continued into the cave.

"We'll rest in here during the day while there are spying eyes that may be out there searching for us," Aleric announced finally. "We will travel under the concealment of night as much as we can." As he finished, he started digging through his pack for food and a blanket. Not much else was said while the three individually ate and prepped their corner of the cave as comfortably as they could for a few hours of sleep. In the glow of Brodel's orb, Aleric observed his changed face. His eyes were not deceiving him before; the boy had definitely aged. His shoulders were wider. The stubble on his chin earlier in the day had already turned to a definite shadow, and soon would be a full beard.

"Brodel, have you…" Aleric stuttered to find the words. "Have you seen your face since you used magic to rebuild my house?" he asked quietly.

"I haven't seen it myself," Brodel replied cheerfully. "But I knew it would happen eventually, and I can feel it. I told you before that magic takes a toll on the body. I can work all the magic I want with no effect for who knows how long, but eventually it catches up to you, and even a small task can cause vast physical changes."

"How do you know all this?" Thearbuc asked from the far corner of the cave.

"Books," Brodel replied. "Years ago, I found some journals and books hidden in the foothills that were written by another magic user. Whoever wrote them was very experienced and powerful. His name was Barreston something. They've helped further my magic abilities and understand them better without having a real mentor. In a way, he was my teacher even though I've never met him." The other two nodded silently in understanding.

"Do you think you will grow young again?" Aleric asked continuing to pry, somewhat worried about the young man's older appearance.

"No, I don't think so," Brodel replied slowly. "It feels permanent. I feel older." He paused in thought for a moment. "Older and a lot more tired actually. I'm going to get some sleep." And with that he laid down in the cave and pulled the warm blanket over him. Aleric and Thearbuc did the same, and soon the three tired travelers were asleep and safe deep in the cave.

They awoke at midday to the sound of grunts and frustration coming from Thearbuc from his end of the cave.

"What is going on?" Brodel said, rubbing his eyes.

"Water. Water everywhere," Thearbuc said in frustration. "It must be coming from the ground above us. I woke up half covered in water, and it's drenched all of my gear." Another minor nuisance for Thearbuc, Aleric thought, also waking up. The poor guy can't catch a break.

Brodel waved his hand and re-ignited the orb of light. Thearbuc was standing up in the cave trying to shake his hands dry. There was a large puddle of water at his feet that went up to his ankles, and some of his gear was floating in the water with the rest sitting in the cold mud around it. There was also a gash on his forehead with dried blood from it from hitting the cave the night before.

"You're hurt. What happened to your head?" Brodel asked.

"Gah. I hit it on the cave in the darkness last night. I'm not having the best luck in here. I'm leaving," Thearbuc started gathering his gear from the puddle that had formed in the corner of the cave. The other two slowly began to get up and do the same. They could see daylight coming from the far end of the cave and the shadows of the horses still there near the mouth.

"It's still daylight out. Can we travel?" Brodel asked, glancing at Aleric. Thearbuc didn't seem to care and continued to make his way angrily from the wet cave toward the warm light.

"I suppose we're rested enough. We can't sit in here all day." Aleric shrugged. The two followed Thearbuc out of the cave.

Not long later, the three were mounted on their horses and once again trotting the deer trail across the foothills of the large mountains. The day was cool in these higher elevations, even though the sun was shining bright. The ground was slightly wet from the cold night, and short green grasses and green moss grew across almost every surface they could see.

They rode westward along the foothills above the valley for hours until they came across the merchant's road that would take them north and through the mountains. The mountains surrounding the kingdom were so magnificent, steep, and prominent that the few merchant roads were the only way in or out. The roads would wind through the canyon floors, usually following a river, and connected Mazeron to the kingdom of Haberlorn and other faraway and mysterious lands. These limited routes in and out had also been the kingdom's downfall, as the brigands knew exactly where merchants and travelers would be and it was easy for them to cut off the high defenseless roads and besiege the kingdom.

The small party approached the road with discretion and sat atop their horses in silence, listening and watching for signs of any followers or an ambush. Thearbuc dismounted his horse and began searching along the ground.

"No fresh tracks," he said quietly to the others. "In fact, I don't see any tracks at all. This road has not been used in some time. I think we're clear to continue for now."

"If we keep our speed, then no one who may be looking for us will catch up to us by now anyway," Aleric replied. "We move!" he commanded loudly as he began quickly galloping up the merchant road.

By midday they had gained a significant amount of elevation and were now deep into the forests that lined the bottom of the canyon. The large rolling hills on each side of them gave way to towering, sharp, snowcapped peaks in the distance. They traveled quietly, not speaking to each other and doing their best not to step on loud piles of leaves or felled trees, and always listening for any sign of danger or the brigands.

They knew they were in Brigand territory now, and they expected treachery and traps around at any moment. The question was, with the little number of travelers and merchants these days, had the brigands moved on to richer lands by now? Or were they still here, lying in wait? Either way, there was no sign of them yet. Aleric had instructed that they would stay on the merchant road for now because it was the fastest route. Once they saw tracks in the dirt or any sign of the brigands, they would get off the road and travel slower in the concealment of the thick forests and trees.

Later in the day, the three were riding silently through the thick, damp forests, each deep in thought, when they came across the first evidence of the brigands' occupation of the area. There was a fork in the road ahead, the main road veering right and then a smaller trail going off into the woods towards the left. The trail to the left was blocked by destroyed wagons, and the road was littered with evidence of a horrible and violent ambush. There were multiple wagons and carts destroyed, burned, tipped over, and pushed off the trail. Wooden debris, broken wheels, empty chests, and ransacked goods were strewn everywhere. This scene painted a perfect picture of an innocent wagon train being ambushed. If it was a merchant, train, or an innocent family traveling from one kingdom to the other, they could not tell. It was, however, clear that it had been some time since the ambush had happened. Weeds had grown around the debris and scattered clothes were dirty and destroyed by the elements. The three carefully and quietly inspected the scene. There were no signs of any bodies or survivors. After some time of searching the area, Brodel finally broke the silence.

"Are we in danger here?" he asked.

"I don't think so," Thearbuc replied. "Still no tracks. I can't hear or see any evidence of people being here in quite some time." Aleric mounted his horse again and stared at the wreckage in silence as the horse paced in circles.

"They want people to keep to the main road." He pointed at the roadblock of wagons, clearly preventing passage to the left.

The road veering to the right in front of them was open. "The whole reason we were sent out here instead of another large garrison of troops is so we could slip past the brigands undetected. It is time we left the main road." He paused again. "That way." He pointed to the blocked trail on the left. Just past it, a faint deer trail wandered steep up the mountain and disappeared completely from the sight of the main road. "We stay off the trail, but we make through the forests that way. It will take longer to cross the mountains, but we will be closer to the castle when we come down to the other side."

"We probably won't even make it to the other side if we stay on the main road," Thearbuc said in agreement. "Trying to pass unnoticed is a good plan."

"Then it's settled," replied Aleric, already carefully picking his way through the roadblock. As the three made their way into the woods past the roadblock, Brodel stopped and looked back.

"If we leave that roadblock there, then the next people to come through will get ambushed just the same." There was a pause of silence, then Aleric gave Brodel a nod.

Brodel turned back, set his staff on the ground, then raised his arms. A magnificent ball of blueish white light began to appear between his arms. It grew and began to radiate so much heat that Aleric and Thearbuc yards away had to shield their faces like they were standing too close to a campfire. With a motion of his arms he heaved the energy toward the roadblock. It soared slowly and quietly through the air until it connected with the roadblock then exploded into it with surprising violence, but with hardly a sound made and no fire or smoke following. In just an instant, the wagons of the roadblock were destroyed into a million bits of wooden shrapnel, but no nearby prying ears or eyes would know that it even happened.

But touch, sound, sight and smell were not the only senses that people had in these magical lands. An unperceived shockwave of magic rippled from Brodel's explosion through the air like a rock into a calm lake. It raced silently and invisibly through the trees of the forests and down the canyons then rushed into the valley below, expanding outward like exploding water breaking through a dam. Then, it was picked up.

A cloaked man, tall and lanky, stood in the foothills against a dark gray clouded sky. The tall green grasses surrounding him blew hard in the growing wind. He was a black shadow walking among the green tapestry of the land. He sensed the ripple of magic immediately, as if he had been hit by a soft shockwave of force. He turned northward and stared with soulless eyes toward the mouth of the canyon far ahead. Another ripple came; he felt it in his chest. Slowly, he raised his right arm and pointed a long, bony finger at the canyon. Nearby, four beasts raised their heads from the tall grasses. Seemingly appearing out of nowhere. They were the Morghvile and they had been scouring the grounds, searching for a scent or trail to pick up. They also looked toward the canyon. They were the same type of beast that Aleric and Thearbuc had fought in the field near Thearbuc's cabin. They were large and thick like an ox but had fierce faces and snarling teeth like a wolf. Their long black hair dripped with red sweat, and a foul stench filled the air around them.

There was a moment where time seemed to stand still as the cloaked man and the four Morghvile gazed motionless northward. They studied the mountains and canyon ahead. The ripple of magic came again. This time they had pinpointed where it was coming from. The cloaked man slowly raised a whistle-like instrument made from black bone to his lips then broke the silence with a horrible and shrieking howl as he blew into it. Instantly the Morghvile were off, charging at full speed toward the canyon and vast mountains beyond. They were trackers, and they had picked up a trail.

A day's hike northward and deep into the mountains, Aleric, Thearbuc, and Brodel were still following the small trail steeply upward to a false summit that had no trees atop it. They recognized the bald peak from when they were far down the mountain below and had used it as a waypoint throughout the day. The trail was too steep and strenuous to ride atop the horses, so they walked the path, leading the horses along. As they approached the peak, they all simultaneously breathed a sigh of relief as the steep ground gave way to easier, flatter ground.

One by one, as they reached the top of the peak they turned around and took in the glory of the view that lay before them. They had earned it. The vast valley below stretched outward to the horizon and seemed to go on forever. It was such a clear day that they could see everything. The castle far in the east reflected the sunlight from its golden roof like the ocean reflecting a sunset. It was so small from here it looked like a child's toy abandoned in a field. Endless forests stretched far into the horizon, and great rivers meandered peacefully throughout the valley. Clouds dotted the sky at almost eye level from this elevation, and it seemed to those who beheld the view that they had ascended into the peaceful afterlife.

"Let's stop here for lunch, shall we?" Aleric suggested.

The others nodded and began to gather their things from their packs. The horses were exhausted from the climb, and they too welcomed the rest. Together the group sat and ate atop the peak in good spirits. A cold, crisp wind blew softly through the air, as refreshing as the food. Soon, the horses were roaming the area, freely and peacefully grazing off the green lands. After a quick lunch and some much-needed rest, the sun was past its high point in the sky and was already well on its way back down toward the horizon.

"We should move on, deeper into the woods," Aleric said, pointing out what the others were thinking. "We will need to find shelter before it gets dark." He stood up and began to pick up his things.

"We are going to need to forage for food before we get into the high mountains and snow," Brodel said, looking through his satchel. "I am almost out of rations already."

"Same here," Thearbuc agreed, also gathering his gear.

"We will do that after we find a safe place to camp," Aleric replied. "That is the priority. Daylight will be gone soon, and we will need shelter for the night. We are already getting high into the mountains, and with this cold breeze forming, it wouldn't surprise me if the frost or snow came down to us by morning."

Thearbuc and Brodel nodded that they agreed as they slung their packs over their shoulders and began to move again. After they left, the false peak behind the trail began to dip downward and into the shade of the high mountain peaks around them. The trail would rise again sometime far in the distance as the next group of peaks grew closer, but those peaks and the trail were hidden in a deep fog that rested on the high valley ahead of them.

Not long later they descended into a thick forest of brown and gray trees, which appeared to have already shed most of their summer leaves to prepare for fall, even though the fall season was still months away. They trotted slowly atop their horses and tried their best to find their way through the narrow trail that wound through the thick trees. These trees were all short, and low-hanging, dead branches scraped across their foreheads and arms, leaving tiny scratches as they rode. As they got deeper into the woods, a fog started accumulating across the ground and began to envelope them. There was no sound in these foggy, dead woods. The silence was deafening and felt like wads of cotton had been placed over their ears.

"This forest is unnaturally quiet," Thearbuc said with a hint of alarm. "No birds. No wind." He paused as he scanned the area with observant eyes. "I don't like it," he concluded. The two others nodded that they were thinking the same thing, but no words were spoken, and the silence continued to consume them.

As they delved deeper into the eerie forest, the scrub and brush started to overtake the trail and it became too hard to follow from atop the horses, so they were forced to dismount and walk. The thorny brush and uneven. Rocky ground made travel slow and miserable. There was no end in sight to this misery, as the fog only allowed them to see past four or five trees before everything disappeared into a gray nothingness.

Brodel was making his way through the knee-high brush when suddenly something sprang up from near his feet and dashed quickly towards his face. Startled, he fell backward, flailing his arms and losing his breath. He wanted to let out a cry, but it was lost as he was gasping for air at the sudden startle. He fell backward and landed hard onto the ground as a large bird flew just a few feet into the air, then being too heavy to fly very far, it landed back in the concealment of the tall brush. Brodel rolled his eyes and threw his head to the ground in embarrassment, still recovering from the moment of fear and trying to catch his breath.

"It was just a pheasant," Aleric replied from somewhere in the fog.

"Scared me half to death!" Brodel replied, brushing the dirt from his arms.

The mood was steadily getting more tense in the thick, foggy woods. They hadn't seen the sun in some time and couldn't tell which direction they were going or where the trail was going to lead them. On top of that, this area was not fit for making camp for the night.

"We need to find our way out of these woods before it gets dark," Thearbuc said in a worried tone, with a hint of annoyance. "We are sitting ducks to whatever is out here in this sea of brush and dead trees." Drawing his sword, he pushed his way toward the front of the trail and helped Brodel back to his feet along the way. They began to move again, towing the horses through the fog. The snarled trees looked like hunched, limbed monsters. The sunlight barely showed through, making everything ominous tones of gray. A slight breeze began to set in while they traveled and blew whisps of fog past the trail like circling ghosts tormenting them. There was no direction in these woods. Only up or down existed. They couldn't see the sun or any landmark to figure out which direction they were going. The ground was mostly flat with slight ups and downs, so they didn't even know if they were going up the mountain or not.

"We've lost the trail," Aleric spoke out of the quietness of the fog. They hadn't heard a single sound besides the wind or seen a single life form, not even a bug, in some time.

"No, this is the trail," Thearbuc replied, pointing at a small clearing between the dead brush.

"It's not a trail, we're just wandering aimlessly through the woods," Aleric replied.

"Doesn't look like an actual trail to me," Brodel agreed with Aleric.

"Well! Where the blast did it go?" Thearbuc said angrily, turning in circles looking for any sign of a trail or way out of the maze of dead trees and fog.

"We have to backtrack again," Aleric said.

"Okay, to which way?" Thearbuc snapped back, throwing his arms into the air in frustration.

There was a pause again while they thought about their predicament. The three peered through the fog and trees, each looking for some sort of recognizable landmark or change in the scenery that would tell them which way to walk toward. The silence was deafening, and there seemed to be no way out of these endless woods. They had been winding through the trees and brush for hours, but neither of them really knew which way they had come from.

"We have to just keep moving at this point," Brodel said nervously. "We can't stop in here!" He was beginning to panic and raised his voice as he demanded to get out of the woods.

"It's okay," Aleric said calmly. "Stay calm. What is wrong?"

"It's these woods!" Brodel snapped back. "There is something here. Something about them. You can't feel it, but I can. Something evil. We must get out of here!" Brodel started to run in a random direction. He didn't care where he went as long as it was away!

Thearbuc and Aleric followed, all three aimlessly wandering quickly through the dead fog, snarled trees, and wet brush. Then suddenly, the silence was broken. A large crack in the distance came from somewhere in the fog. Was it a twig snapping close by or a tree crashing far away? They couldn't tell. Then there was another crack, then another, and another. They were getting faster and closer. The three stood helpless in the blinding fog, unable to see anything. Quickly they drew their weapons. Aleric grabbed his longsword, Thearbuc grabbed a hatchet and mace from his horse's satchel, and Brodel readied his staff in one hand and a ball of energy appeared in the other.

The crashes were getting closer. Something was charging through the trees, somewhere in the foggy distance. They still couldn't tell how far away it was or what direction it was coming from when they began to feel heavy thumps in the ground. It was clear now, something fast and heavy was coming their way. The heavy thumps gave them about three seconds of warning before a large beast came crashing through the forest of dead trees, exploding wood debris as it barreled toward them.

There was no time to react. By the time they even saw the beast, it had locked onto Brodel and was lunging through the air, coming in fast for the attack. It came down heavily on top of him and pinned the young wizard to the ground. Large fangs of teeth were chomping toward Brodel's face. Saliva oozed from the beast's mouth and dripped onto Brodel's frantic face as he attempted to deflect the bites without letting the jaws get hold of his arm. Then, without hesitation, Aleric ran fast toward the beast and laid his shoulder into it with all his force, chucking it off

Brodel and to the ground. The beast rolled over once but was back up in an instant. It wasted no time and lunged back toward Brodel, who was able to roll over and pick up his staff just in time. He pointed it at the animal and blasted a ball of heat and energy at the beast. It was blown back with magnificent force then came to rest after smashing heavily into a nearby boulder.

The three men watched and waited for the beast to move again—Brodel still on the ground, Aleric standing up and raising his sword, and Thearbuc wielding his heavy and sharp weapons, all readying for the next attack. They studied the beast as it lay in the haziness of the fog, waiting for movement.

"This is the same type of animal that stalked you to my field," Thearbuc said to Aleric, glancing at him quickly so as not to take his eyes from the beast for too long.

"Have you seen these before, Brodel?" Aleric asked quickly. "In your woods maybe? I don't think I've ever seen such a large animal besides the trolls." Brodel shook his head no. He was still shaken by the attack and unable to force words from his mouth.

"We need to get out of here," Thearbuc interrupted. "Now!"

As they began to run through the foggy and dead forest, the beast slowly disintegrated into ash, just like the last one had in Thearbuc's field. Skin and sweaty fur turned to ash and blew away into the wind until only a black-boned skeleton remained. They started rushing through the forest in no particular direction, towing the horses and supplies behind as fast as they could safely go.

"Stay close together," Aleric warned, leading the group as he bounded over a fallen tree.

Then there was another sound, again coming from somewhere in the forest. They couldn't see a thing through the thick fog. The trees cracked again followed by a bone chilling, loud bark that sent chills through the men and caused the horses to rear up in fear. Their packs and gear fell from the horses and scattered on the ground as the horses fled. In an instant they were gone, lost in the fog and maze of craggy, dead trees.

"Get the gear!" Thearbuc yelled, kneeling onto the ground and grabbing what he could. He threw Aleric's pack to him. Brodel grabbed his and they began to run again. They could hear something approaching. The sound of more breaking trees and branches came through the fog. The sounds of pursuit seemed to come from all around them, and they couldn't pinpoint which direction it was coming from or where they should run to. So, they just ran.

Dodging through the trees and jumping over branches and rocks, Aleric saw a shadow in the corner of his eye. There was a beast running through the fog alongside them, and he saw another one off to his left. Silhouettes of giant animals through the fog. Then it hit him. They were being herded into a trap!

"Stop!" Aleric yelled, coming to a quick stop in a small clearing. "We can't outrun them," he said, raising his sword. The other two stopped and drew their weapons as well, all three of them panting heavily from the run.

Then, the faint shadows in the gray fog slowly turned into large black masses as the beasts came closer, until they were visible through the dense forest and fog. Terror gripped the men as the beasts moved in, waiting for the perfect time to attack. Two of the beasts visualized at the edge of the clearing. Their large fangs dripped foul smelling saliva to the ground and big huffs of their breath turned into small clouds in the cold air. They were massive.

"The Morghvile," Brodel said, so stricken by fear he almost couldn't get the words out.

The animal nearest Aleric attacked first. In a moment, it had lunged farther than The Paladin thought possible, and caught him off guard. He managed a fireball from his free hand as the beast came down on him, which seemed to absorb most of the impact from the beast's weight and saved him from a fatal blow. Morghvile and Paladin fell to the ground and a scuffle ensued. The Paladin had dropped his sword in the impact, so he grabbed the beast with both arms around its thick neck and tried to wrestle it to the ground, but it was too heavy and strong. Then he began a series of quick, inhumanly strong punches to the Morghvile's side. The punches connected so hard that the impact sounded like horse hooves on the ground.

Brodel and Thearbuc took quick glances over at The Paladin but could not help him because they were preoccupied with the other beasts. Another Morghvile dove at Thearbuc who almost dodged the attack with his incredible agility, and he was able to slice it once down the side with his hatchet while it slammed into him broadside and threw him to the ground. Brodel, seeing another beast coming from the woods, simply went to

Thearbuc and huddled over him protectively and with his staff he created a magical forcefield around them, which he knew he couldn't hold for too long. It bloomed out like a gold umbrella and surrounded them in the shape of a dome.

"Wake up!" Brodel said, shaking Thearbuc as two Morghvile slowly circled them, looking for a weakness in the magic and a chance to attack. The situation had become dire far too fast, and the three friends were outnumbered and outsized. Thearbuc groaned and stirred, indicating consciousness was coming back, but he could not get up. Aleric was still dealing with his own beast. He had gained the upper hand by getting an arm around its neck when suddenly, the entire forest and sky was filled with a terrible shrieking sound that seemed to engulf and encompass everything.

Immediately the Morghvile stopped their attacks and backed away slowly. With lowered heads they kept eye contact on their prey, still ready to attack at any moment as they backed away. After they had backed up to a safe distance, the ferocious animals stopped and held their positions at the edge of the clearing, panting heavily, licking their lips, and gnashing their teeth, as if they desperately wanted to continue their attack, but couldn't.

Aleric used the sudden retreat to scramble back to his feet and pick up his sword from the dirt. He pointed it at the hungry beasts. Brodel was on one knee, still hovering over and protecting Thearbuc. He glanced frantically back and forth, wondering and waiting helplessly for what was going to happen next. No one said a word, but they were all thinking the same thing. Why did the animals stop their attack? What was that horrible shriek that filled the forest? They looked at each other in nervous anticipation, their eyes darting back and forth, peering into the deep fog of the forest. Then suddenly, without any sound or warning, someone stepped out from behind a tree in the fog, right next to Aleric.

"I can control them," a high-pitched and raspy voice screeched.

Aleric was startled by the voice, not having seen anyone near him. Quickly, he turned to look. It was a woman. She was short and frail, half hiding behind a tree in the fog near him. Her clothes were rags, and her face was badly weathered. He peered through the fog, looking closer as she stepped out from behind the tree. Her face wasn't just weathered, she looked like a corpse. Her skin looked mummified—brown, leathered, and tight against her cheekbones. He could make out the shape of her skull. Rotten yellow and black teeth showed through wrinkled and blistered lips, and her eyes were solid glossy black. She was so horrifying to look at that Aleric scurried away backwards while goosebumps rushed over his arms and up the back of his neck.

"Yesss. I have been to the land of the Morghvile," the old scary woman screeched, showing yellow teeth through a threatening smile. "Through the portals between lands I have been many times. I'll tell them what to do. I'll tell you what to do!" she said, pointing at Aleric. She spoke fast, in uneven tones, and seemed nonsensical and unpredictable. Then, unexpectedly, she let out another horrifying shriek that filled the woods. Her mouth unnaturally wide open resonated the horrifying and inhuman sound so loud that it seemed like it was originating inside of their ears. The Morghvile took more steps back, creeping away into woods, then laid down attentively on the ground. Snarling fangs turned into panting breaths as they took a less threatening stance. Even the vicious Morghvile feared the old haggard woman.

The others looked at each other with worried eyes, waiting for what was going to happen next. Then out of the silence a voice filled the forests again. They couldn't tell where it was coming from. It was everywhere and nowhere all at once.

"Kallliinndraaa," the voice in the air whispered, though it seemed to fill the entirety of the forest. Then the woman in rags began to hop and clap her hands together in an odd and terrifying display of excitement. She laughed madly for a moment as the others watched.

"The soul of the woods!" she screeched. "It is happy I'm out. Misses me here." She looked around the forest and into the foggy sky like an amused child.

"She's gone mad," Thearbuc said, finally able to stand on his feet.

"No!" the woman screamed, pointing her finger at him. "No! No! No! You can't say that to me." Her mood changed in an instant from bizarre to hostile, and she charged quickly into the clearing. Aleric backed away as she advanced aggressively.

"Do you need help?" he asked. "What are you doing out here in these woods?"

"Ha!!" she cackled. "Me need help?" She glanced around at the many beastly shadows in the fog surrounding them. There was a pause of silence. No one wanted to speak as it seemed every word made the woman more upset and unpredictable. It was as if most of her mind had been worn away by substance abuse and time, and only deranged aggression and instability remained.

"Trespassing!" she finally yelled loudly out of nowhere. "You. Are. Trespassing!" She pointed her finger at the three one by one as she lowered her voice to a whisper.

"We didn't mean to," Thearbuc replied. "We were…"

"Doesn't matter!" she snapped. "Doesn't matter if you mean to break the rules. You still must be punished for breaking the rules. That's what rules are for. Punishing!" she said it almost playfully, lightly giggling as she said it.

"Enough of this," Aleric said, having lost his patience and thinking that a show of force would sway the woman into being rational. Suddenly, he thrust his right arm forward and launched a fireball towards the old woman. But before the fireball reached her, she was gone, simply disappeared into thin air, and the fireball exploded into a gnarled dead tree, splitting it violently into pieces of shrapnel. The nearby Morghvile howled towards the sky and their snarled, snapping teeth showed they wanted to attack the men again, but still they stayed at the edge of the clearing.

The woman reappeared in a different spot, near the edge of the clearing. She opened her mouth wide, showing her sharp, rotted teeth and hissing threateningly like a cornered animal. Aleric threw another fireball at her, and she disappeared again before it struck. His eyes darted back and forth looking for her through the fog. Then she appeared again, this time right behind him, her face so close that he could smell her before he even saw her.

"Monster!" she screamed directly into his ear with thick saliva spitting onto him. Then with a long sharp fingernail she stabbed him in the neck before he barely even knew she was there. Aleric dropped instantly. Lying on the ground and unable to move, she towered above him, breathing heavily with anger and hate in her eyes. Behind her Thearbuc and Brodel both began to move.

"No!!" she yelled, turning about with an outstretched hand. A blast of energy that looked like lightning came from her hand and both Thearbuc and Brodel were stopped, frozen in place and unable to move.

"Kallllinnnndraaaa," the voice from the woods filled the sky again. There was fear in Brodel's and Thearbuc's eyes as she approached slowly toward them through the fog.

"What? What is this?" she whispered to herself as she quickly approached Brodel, noticing the magic radiating off his body. The colorful sparks and pops emanating from him were not as pronounced as they used to be before he had visibly aged, but they were still there and constantly rising from his body. The old woman tilted her head back and forth like a child trying to understand a new concept as she studied him, and the look on her face changed from anger and hate to bemusement and awe. She went to Brodel, who was still frozen in place, and touched his face. Then she put her face close to his, smelling his skin and licking his cheek up to his forehead. Her rancid breath pulled him away in disgust, but even with all his might he could only slightly move his head. Something about Brodel clearly excited her.

"Magic!" she hissed. "Lots and lots of magic. Magic to play with. Never seen so much magic," she continued looking him up and down. "New plans!" she yelled into the forest while pushing Thearbuc down to the ground. "Take him," she shouted into the fog. She turned and looked towards Brodel again while smacking her blistered lips.

Through the fog and silhouettes of snarled, dead trees, the shadows started to move. Only swaying at first but then growing in size as they came closer. Thearbuc and Aleric looked on, helpless from the ground. Brodel lay on the ground frozen in fear as the shadows approached. When they came into the clearing, finally they could make them out. A dozen or more goblin soldiers came hobbling through the fog. They were just over waist height on the average man. They had green, thick skin with pointy ears and noses, and sharp, stained teeth protruded from their lower jaws. They were armed with curved, rusted swords and wore rags and thick, oversized, weathered boots.

Their large boots stomped heavily as they came into the clearing then began to bind Brodel with lengths of rope.

"No, no," he begged as they bound him. There was a noticeable fear in his eyes that was almost too much for Aleric and Thearbuc to bear. Even though he looked older recently, they still saw him as a younger boy, and they felt an obligation to take care of him and keep him safe. After all, they were the ones who convinced him to leave the safety of his hut, hidden safely in the forest.

"Stop it! Who are you? Why are you doing this?" Thearbuc shouted helplessly. The old woman turned from Brodel and violently rushed towards Thearbuc with alarming speed. She bent down towards him, grabbing his hair and raising his face towards hers.

"I am the witch Kalindra," she hissed in a tone that suggested he should already know who she was. "These are *my* woods that *you* are in. I can take what I want in *my* woods!" she yelled, like an angered child in a tantrum.

"Please!" Thearbuc begged. "There must be something we can get you. We can help you! Please show mercy." He waited for the witch to reply but she turned her attention back to Brodel, who was being bound and lifted by the goblin soldiers. Suddenly, she was petting his face, almost frantically. She leaned in again and sniffed near his hair over and over. There was something about Brodel that she was clearly drawn to. Something about his magic. Finally, the witch Kalindra turned away from Brodel and motioned with her hand for her goblin soldiers to take him away. Brodel struggled to move, trying to conjure anything, but the witch's magic was too strong and he was overpowered and helpless, still unable to move.

"We'll come for you, Brodel!" Thearbuc screamed out. "I give you my word! I promise!" Then the witch Kalindra turned and crouched low to the ground and came face to face with Thearbuc.

"He's mine now!" she hissed with anger, hate, and psychotic instability. Then she raised an old craggy finger with long, dirty, yellowed nails and waved it slowly and threateningly in front of Thearbuc's eyes for a few moments. She slowly put her finger in her mouth and licked it once before plunging the nail softly into his neck. The pain lasted only a moment for Thearbuc. Then all was dark.

Chapter 10: High Mountain Trouble

Thearbuc awoke from a dreamless nonexistence to the sound of heavy wind and the feeling of biting cold on his face. He had no energy to rise or open his eyes, so for a moment he just laid there knowing that when he opened his eyes, he would have to face the consequences of whatever the witch Kalindra had thrust upon him. Finally, the cold became too much, and he was forced to open his eyes and begin to move.

He was lying face down in the snow, wrapped in a blanket. Very slowly, he struggled to push himself up into a sitting position. As he sat up, his blurry vision began to fade and he was able to look around. Aleric was there, sitting in the snow, huddled close to a giant wall of stone and ice with a small fire burning near his feet. There was a blizzard blowing around them, and the sound of wind howled loudly in his ears. But he was only subjected to a light breeze, as they were huddled close to a steep mountain wall that provided some protection from the wind and snow. Aleric watched Thearbuc silently as he surveyed the situation looking bewildered and confused.

Thearbuc turned about to see that they were high up, atop a great mountain. He could see where the ground gave way sharply beneath them, and far down below them the mountain was hidden behind a layer of clouds that stretched out as far as he could see, showing no land or valleys below. All around them was white. The snow, the sky, the blizzard. Everything was a whiteout.

“What happened? Where are we?” he managed to ask between chattering teeth.

“High up in the mountains somewhere, it appears,” Aleric replied. Thearbuc looked even more confused now. “Which mountains, I don’t know. I can’t see the valley below to know where we’re at.” Aleric shrugged then pulled his blanket tight around his neck for warmth.

“Why would she drag us way up here to just let us die?” Thearbuc thought aloud.

“I don’t think the witch Kalindra cared too much about us after she noticed Brodel,” Aleric replied. “She seemed infatuated with him for some reason. Plus, I don’t think they brought us way up here. There are no tracks in the snow. I think she used her magic to just place us up here and out of her way."

"How are we going to get out of here?" Thearbuc asked, looking around at the steep walls of snow and ice towering above them and descending into the abyss below.

"Luckily we had put our packs back on," Aleric replied tossing Thearbuc's pack to him. "We have blankets, some food, and one rope." Thearbuc crept to the ledge and looked down.

"Aleric, one rope isn't long enough to get us down to even the next ledge. It's too far."

"That's why we go up," Aleric replied, rolling the rope into a circle around his hand and elbow. Thearbuc looked up at the towering wall of ice before them then tried to trace the outlines of the peaks in the distance through the whiteout of blowing snow. Even the icy rock right in front of them seemed impossible. Icicles hung from every ledge, and the rock had been smoothed out from millions of years of wind and ice.

"It's impossible," Thearbuc exclaimed with hopelessness in his voice.

"We still have to try. We must get back to save Brodel." Aleric stood and looked up at the icy granite rising out of the whiteout that towered above them. "Tie this to your waist." He tossed the rope to Thearbuc. "That way you can catch me if I fall. If I can get over this ledge that we are on, then I can pull you up behind me."

"All the way to the top?" Thearbuc asked, shaking his head at the impossible plan. "I think it will be a little more difficult than that." He rolled his eyes and sinched the knot tight around his waist. With that, Aleric grabbed his pack and threw it over his shoulder and began to look for a way up. The icy rock in front of them was light gray and smoothed over from weathering and ice. He surveyed the area for a good place to start climbing for many minutes, then finally jumped and clung to a handhold that was high above his head. Slowly, he pulled himself up then lunged to the next one. With glowing eyes and an impressive show of strength, he was off the ledge and making progress.

Thearbuc watched in amazement as Aleric climbed upward by finding handholds that he couldn't even see. Like a fly stuck to the side of a wall, Aleric made his way slowly up the mountain while the violent blizzard howled around him. Finally, he came to a ledge where he was able to stand up and help Thearbuc up by pulling some of his weight on the rope while he climbed. When they were both finally on the higher ledge and not exerting so much energy by climbing, the bitter cold set in almost instantly. They were very exposed here. The wind blew so hard they could barely hear each other speak, and the blowing snow nipped at exposed skin like sand against their faces. Aleric knelt down low, and using his magic, he created a fireball in the palm of his hands. The snow and ice covering his hands began to melt away as well as the pain of frozen fingers. Thearbuc huddled near the fire as well, and they spent some time catching their breath and thawing out their hands from the first pitch of the climb.

"We need to get moving again," Thearbuc exclaimed as he noticed the wind picking up.

"Indeed," Paladin replied, getting up and surveying the next pitch. The ledge they were on was only the length of two men and was topped with an icy overhanging ledge above them. It only took Aleric a moment to realize he had gotten them into a worse position with possibly no way out. He jumped up to the overhang and grabbed onto the rock. Hanging there, he lifted his feet with incredible strength and wedged them into the rock, turning himself completely upside down, hanging from the ledge. Then he reached for the next handhold, but as his hand slipped against the ice, he fell heavily to the ground with a loud thump. Luckily, the deep snow somewhat padded his fall.

He rolled around in pain for a moment then pushed himself back up and tried again. Then again. And again. He couldn't get over the overhang and back onto the vertical face of the mountain. They were stuck. Frustration set in as they both inspected the area, looking for a way out, but neither could come up with anything.

This went on for such a long time and they were losing all hope of escaping the ledge when Aleric noticed movement in the distance. A gray shadow against the white blizzard slowly came into view. Silently and out of the whiteout blizzard, a wise-looking mountain goat came toward the ledge, walking on almost the completely vertical face with ease. He had large, curled horns and a long, white goatee. His fur was all white as well, but his eyes looked human and were filled with emotion and a hint of sympathy. The mountain goat stood there on the steep face like he was defying gravity and studied the two very out-of-place men stuck on the ledge. Thearbuc also noticed his eyes were very human-like and showed emotion and intuitiveness. The goat walked closer to the ledge until he was just a few feet away from it, and while staring intensely at Aleric, he made a sound.

"Hmmmmmm," the goat said slowly and drawn out, as if he was trying to speak to them. Then, with mighty strength he turned and lunged onto a seemingly invisible foothold that Aleric and Thearbuc could not see from their position on the ledge.

"He's showing us the way!" Thearbuc said excitedly, hurrying over to get a better look. He could see the foothold better now. "There!" he pointed to a small outcropping of rock where the goat had recently stood.

Aleric walked to the edge of the outcropping as well then faced the icy and almost vertical wall with outstretched his arms like he was hugging it. He shimmied out onto the exposed face of the pitch. With hands and feet struggling to cling to the icy mountain, he began to make his way onto the steep face and toward where the goat had previously stood. The wind howled in his ears and his fingers burned as they scraped along the ice and snow. He looked down and almost lost his footing as his head whirled about at the sight of the steep drop below him. He was barely clinging to the mountain, and the only thing besides air and clouds below him was the small foothold he was standing on. Regaining his composure, he went on and passed a death-defying traverse. He looked up and saw the wise mountain goat was only a few arms lengths away now.

"Hmmmmm," the goat said again, before jumping onto another footing. Aleric saw the route and followed. Below him, Thearbuc was shimmying out on to the mountain face as well, making his way toward the first footing. Already the strong warrior of a man was showing signs of shot nerves and crippling fear as the ground dropped away into the nothingness below. But despite the fear and cold, they went on. Slowly, the three made their way across the steep face of the mountain. The wind and ice of the blizzard howled around them, and travel across the steep face continued with the wise mountain goat as their guide. Eventually, with fear gripping them, Thearbuc and Aleric both took solace in the fact that, because of the blizzard, they could not see all the way down the steep mountain or how far up they needed to go to get to safety. The few steps in front them were all that mattered. Everything else was blocked out by the violent, swirling snow.

This steep, nerve-racking climb went on for two or three hours, and the hours feel like days when every movement you make could be your last. Each time they moved on, the mountain goat would look at them with his humanlike eyes and call to them with the same sound before moving to the next position.

Finally, after hours of misery, cold, and trembling fear on the vertical face of the icy mountain, Aleric pulled himself up onto flat ground. He rolled onto the flat surface with an enormous sigh of relief to be off of the cliff. In the moment, it was the best feeling he had ever felt. Not long after, Thearbuc came up over the steep ledge and also collapsed on to the flat ground. They were panting and out of breath from the altitude and strenuous climb. Their faces were red, burnt by the cold and snow. Aleric lay exhausted in deep, powdery snow when the wise goat came from behind him and stared down at him.

“Hmmmmm,” the goat said again, just as he had been doing for the past many hours as he led them safely off the face of the giant cliff.

“Pay him!” Thearbuc said chuckling. “He wants to get paid!”

“Of course,” Aleric replied, reaching into his bag. He pulled out a pack of vegetables and gave the goat all of the carrots he had picked from a farmer’s field along the way out of the kingdom.

The goat carefully set each carrot down in a straight line in the snow, then laid on his belly and slowly ate them one by one. He ignored the other two as he ate, as if he didn’t have a care in the world. His mouth slowly and lazily chomped in a circular motion while his humanlike eyes gazed into the snowy distance. When he had finished all the carrots, the goat stood back up again and turned to Aleric and Thearbuc.

“Hmmmmm,” he said one last time before wandering off into the whiteout blizzard until he was once again a gray shadow against a white backdrop. Just as quietly as he came.

Aleric and Thearbuc, alone on a mountain once again, began reassessing the situation immediately. They stood on flat ground, high up on the mountainside. The blizzard still raged all around them and visibility was low. They peered through the storm and saw that just beyond them the mountain began to slope upward again and led piles of seemingly endless deep, powdery snow. The snow seemed from here to be at least shin deep, and the terrain ahead seemed significantly easier than the face they had just scaled.

"We could climb straight up," Thearbuc yelled through the wind, pointing at the tall mountains ahead. Aleric peered through the blizzard and scanned the terrain.

"It's steep as far as I can see!" Aleric yelled back through the roaring blizzard. "Definitely not safe!"

"Well, we can't stay here!" Thearbuc yelled back. His beard was dripping with small, frozen icicles, as were his eyelashes and knitted cap.

After gazing upward silently for some time with a look of defeat and frustration, Aleric began to climb. One foot in front of the other. Slowly pushing through the thick snow, Thearbuc followed behind. The snow was heavy and deep. It took mounds of strength for Aleric to take one step in the unbroken snow. He trudged upward into the steep whiteout, kicking a step, taking a pause, then kicking another after he had mustered more strength—strength which was quickly running out. Climbing the icy cliffs in the fierce cold was already more than most any other man could have accomplished, and he did not have much more energy or nerves left to give. But here they were anyway, stuck high up on a mountain in a blizzard, unable to rest or find shelter.

Travel was significantly easier for Thearbuc as he followed. His energy was also waning, but Aleric was breaking the trail through snow and making footprints for Thearbuc to step in. He peered up ahead into the blinding whiteout. The footsteps looked like an endless staircase climbing up into the heavens and disappearing into the whiteout. One foot in front of the other, he thought.

"How did I end up here?" Thearbuc grumbled aloud to himself, unable to turn his thoughts away from the constant agony of the situation. "I should be at home with my family, warm by the fire. Not up here about to freeze to death on some mountain because of a hateful witch."

His mind continued to wander through negative thoughts as the hours rolled on. Step by step, they climbed the steep and snowy mountain. *Why was the witch Kalindra so infatuated with Brodel?* Thearbuc kept wondering, going back to Brodel and his circumstance over and over again in his head. They had become good friends along the trails and through the adventures they had shared. He had grown to care about and admire the young man. Suddenly Thearbuc's thoughts were interrupted by the sound of enormous cracking thunder, coming from high up on the cliffs. The sound rumbled with such ferocity that he felt it in his chest and bones. Then it faded softly away, back into the sound of the howling wind of the blizzard.

"Avalanches," Thearbuc stated worriedly." Aleric gazed upward from where the sound had come from. "We are dead men standing," Thearbuc said as he fell hopelessly into the soft snow, sinking until he sat upright on the slope like he was sitting on a throne of snow. "There's nowhere to go, our energy is gone, we're frozen to the bone. We'll just die tired if we keep climbing." Aleric stared at him with hopeless sadness in his eyes. He knew Thearbuc was right. He wanted to argue the point with him and encourage them to go on but could not find the energy for it. He scanned the area, gazing into the gray that surrounded them. It was a darker gray now, indicating that the sun was setting, wherever it was, blocked off by the storm that prevented warmth and light for what had seemed like days.

Thearbuc looked back with sorrow heavy in his eyes, waiting for encouraging words from Aleric or some sign of hope that his superhuman strength or magic could get them out of this hopeless mess. But Aleric just stared back somberly. He had nothing else to give either. Soon it would be night and they would be stuck, exposed high up in the great mountains where they would surely freeze to death or be swept off the side by an avalanche, never to be found. But just when things seemed like they couldn't get any worse, a whispered voice filled the sky.

"Kaliiiindraaaa." It came from everywhere and nowhere all at once.

"Oh no," Thearbuc said quickly, his eyes bulging with alarm. Out of the darkening blizzard there was a sudden bright flash of lightning that soared just over their heads. It was traveling up the mountain from down below. It passed not far over their heads, causing them both to duck in reflex. They heard another monstrous crack of thunder and rumbling coming from high on the mountain above as the lightning struck the mountain. But this time the rumbling sound of thunder did not stop. One crack led to another, then another. The cracking sounds filled the air and began to grow louder and closer until it seemed like the whole mountain was coming apart one horrifying crack at a time.

"AVALANCHE!!!" Aleric yelled, as he grabbed Thearbuc from the snow and pulled him quickly to his feet. They began to run to their right and downward, traversing away from the sound of the crumbling mountain. They leapt and bound through the whiteout and deep snow. They couldn't see more than a few feet in front of them, but they could hear the avalanche bearing down behind them. The roar became deafeningly loud as it came crashing down upon them, and when it completely overtook them there was suddenly a feeling of weightlessness and free falling as it swept them off their feet. Aleric couldn't see anything and just succumbed to the situation. He felt like he was in a dream—flying but unable to control the direction. It seemed to go on forever, then finally he began to feel the weight of the avalanche and snow surround and bear down heavily on him. His mind was blank. No fear, no anxiety. Just weightlessness in the blinding whiteout as he was lifted by the avalanche and swept over a ledge and into the unknown.

Then the odd feeling of weightlessness he was experiencing was abruptly ended as he landed hard on the ground, on to his back, which painfully knocked the wind from him with an audible thud. He squirmed in agony trying to catch his breath but was unable to breathe. While gasping for air, fluffy snow filled his mouth. Outside of the pain there was cold, and…soft snow. He had landed on soft snow that broke his fall!

Between gasps of air and realizing he was still alive, Aleric began to assess the damage to his body. His hands moved, his legs moved, his toes moved. Soon his breath came back to him, and he sat up taking a giant gasp of air. He was covered in snow and partly buried, but he could see now. It wasn't a complete whiteout anymore. He saw shades of gray and icy rocks just behind him. They were sheltering him from the river of snow and avalanche that was falling from the cliffs above. Then he saw Thearbuc. One leg stuck out from deep in the snow, not far from Aleric. But he was not moving. Aleric tried to move toward him but was buried too deep in the snow and was still unable to take a normal breath.

Another crack of thunder echoed high up the mountain as another bolt of lightning from the unseen valleys set yet another avalanche loose. To Aleric, it felt like predators were circling them and moving in for the kill. The witch Kalindra and the mountain were not letting up. Aleric dug frantically around his legs to free himself. They began to move an inch back and forth as he struggled to get free. Finally, he was up and moving toward Thearbuc. He began to dig again to free his friend. He couldn't see him at all besides the one leg that stuck out of the deep snow. He dug and dug but the snow was quickly turning into ice, which made the process slow and strenuous. It felt even longer knowing that Thearbuc was under there, most likely unable to breathe.

Finally, Aleric had dug enough of him out to where he could see his torso. Aleric grabbed on to Thearbuc's leg, and with a mighty pull he yanked him loose out of the hardening snow. Thearbuc wasn't moving and his mouth was packed with snow. Aleric removed as much of it as he could, but he was out of time. The next avalanche of snow came pouring violently over the cliffs, about to consume them. He grabbed Thearbuc who was limp and lifeless and drug him closer to the shelter of the rocks below the cliff. Then, as Aleric got closer, he noticed there was an opening in the mouth of the rock.

"It's a cave!" he yelled aloud in excitement as he dragged Thearbuc inside the small opening and collapsed just inside of the entrance. Thearbuc lay there unconscious, and Aleric sat catching his breath as he watched the river of snow slowly close off the entrance of the cave, until he sat in complete darkness. They were trapped now, but at least they were safe from the avalanches. Aleric was too tired to care about being trapped in the cave, or anything else for that matter. He fell heavily on to his back, spilling his arms to his sides, and lay quiet and exhausted until sleep overtook him.

Later, Thearbuc awoke in the dark cave. It was very cold, and he could see his breath in the faint glowing light. He wondered where he was and how long he had been out. Rolling over and sitting up with a loud, heavy grunt, he saw Aleric sitting near the wall of the cave with crossed legs. His eyes were glowing like embers and he had a small orb of fire floating between the palms of his hands, which radiated heat onto his hands and into the cave.

"Thanks for that," Thearbuc said, sitting up and rubbing his arms for warmth.

Aleric looked up at him with his glowing eyes but said nothing back, then lowered his head towards the orb of fire once again.

"Where are we?" Thearbuc asked. Aleric picked up an old branch from the ground that had been drug into the cave sometime in the past and placed the orb of light next to it until the makeshift torch ignited. Then his eyes dimmed back to normal as the orb went out.

"We were swept over a cliff in the avalanche. I pulled you into this cave. It's been a day or two as far as I can tell. The storm is still raging outside. We're trapped in here until it stops, and there is no sign of it letting up." Thearbuc turned toward the blocked entrance of the cave and heard the whistling of heavy wind outside as the storm tried to blow its way into the cave.

"Do we have any food?" he asked. Aleric rummaged through his soggy pack and produced a morsel of bread from a dry napkin. Thearbuc reached for it and nodded in appreciation. "We need to find a way off of this mountain," Thearbuc continued while nibbling on the bread and noticeably shivering from the cold. He pulled his damp cloak tighter up to his neck.

"There's no way off of the mountain in weather like this," Aleric replied flatly. "The mountain makes its own weather this high up. We would watch the storms while visiting the foothills when I was young. The storms would linger around the peaks for weeks at a time. They were so high and far away that they wouldn't even affect us down in the valley. I always wondered what it was like way up there, high in the mountains during a storm. Now I know, and I wish did not."

"I remember them as well," Thearbuc confirmed. "They would last for weeks. What does that mean for us?" Aleric stared back with a blank look in his eyes.

"We wait and we hope. That is all we can do." He shrugged then pulled his blanket up over his knees and leaned back against the damp wall of the cave. Without another word, he closed his eyes and began to sleep.

But Thearbuc was not tired. He spent his time trying to get warm by the torchlight and fidgeting around and exploring the cave. It was a large cave. They sat four or five horse lengths from the entrance, back in a corner where they could keep as much warmth as possible. Beyond that, the cave hooked to the right, where all light was lost and gave way to an endless and empty blackness. Thearbuc could hear the echo of dripping water coming from somewhere deep in the cave, and he wondered just how deep it went. Then, after hours of tinkering around, sleep found him once more and he too dozed off.

Later, Thearbuc awoke to The Paladin and his glowing eyes still sitting quietly in the corner of the cave, seemingly unmoved. Few words were exchanged between the two, and Thearbuc again found himself exploring the cave and pacing back and forth while Aleric sat quietly in his corner. For the next many days, this is how time passed. Thearbuc steadily grew more anxious and angry at the confinement, but Aleric had seemingly succumbed to the cave life and remained calm and collected. As time wore on, the morsels of bread became smaller as the loaf ran out and the smell within cave grew worse, as humans were not meant to live in such confinement. Their torch also dwindled away slowly, and they were forced to spend more and more time in the darkness to preserve it. Time passed like a bad dream but with little sleep inside of the cave. Days and nights bled together as the misery and impatience grew within Thearbuc. Had it only been a few days, or had it been a few weeks? There was no way to tell here in this place where time stood still.

At one point, Aleric found that he had a leather pouch of smoking leaves in his pack and offered them to Thearbuc. He graciously accepted and tried to pass some time with some smoking, which only made the cave smell worse than it already did. Leaning against the cold stone walls of the cave, smoking a pipe, Thearbuc tried to strike up conversation with his Paladin friend, but Aleric sat quietly in the same spot, ignoring his anxious friend and occasionally conjuring up a ball of energy for warmth. Eventually Thearbuc's patience snapped.

"Say something!" he demanded Aleric, who simply raised his head up, made eye contact, then slowly lowered his head back down without a reply. "You smug…You are enjoying this aren't you!?" he stood up as he raised his voice. Thearbuc, in a fit of anger, reached over and grabbed Aleric by the shoulders and lifted him to his feet. "Do. You. Feel. Anything!?" he yelled, shaking Aleric violently and grinding his teeth together.

"Get your hands off me," Aleric said quietly, his eyes turning from normal to an ominous amber glow that illuminated their corner of the cave.

"What are you going to do about it!?" Thearbuc replied, shoving The Paladin. The Paladin didn't say anything back. Instead, he pushed Thearbuc so forcefully that he flew backward and landed heavily on the cave floor. Thearbuc stood up and brushed the dirt off his hands and trousers. His teeth were clenched behind his frozen beard. Then he let out a cry and charged at The Paladin. Lowering his shoulder, he made contact directly with Aleric's torso and tackled him into the back wall of the cave. The wall crumbled and gave way from the force of the blow, and the two fell hard onto the floor in a mess of rock and rubble.

A cold breeze instantly grabbed their attention, and there was a pause until Aleric shoved Thearbuc aside angrily. They both stood up to inspect what had happened. There was a breeze coming from somewhere and the sound of wind whistled from far in the distance. The air was cold but refreshing, not stale like the air of the soggy cave they had been stuck in for so long. Around them lay a mess of crumbled boulders and rocks.

"These rocks were placed here," Aleric said, observing the ground. "They were stacked to conceal this room."

"And we smashed through it," Thearbuc interrupted. "I didn't notice the stacked rocks before. They were hidden in the darkness of the cave. Aleric began investigating the new area of the cave, feeling along the stone walls as he went. He stumbled upon a torch in a sconce along the stone walls. He picked it up with one hand, made a ball of energy in the other, then lit the torch with ease. The room lit up instantly. Immediately they realized that this was not just another corner of the cave. There was a pile of used and unused torches in the back corner, along with remnants of leather clothes that had deteriorated into almost nothing in the damp cold of the cave. There was no way to tell how long it had all been there, but it had been left intentionally at some point. Aleric nodded toward the pile of torches and Thearbuc picked up one of his own then lit it with Aleric's burning torch.

“Hang on,” Thearbuc said, rushing back into the cave to gather what was left of their possessions. He grabbed his small bag, which contained an axe, a blanket, and a few trinkets, including the armlet that Brodel had given him at his hut in the woods. Then he rushed back into the room to see The Paladin slowly ascending a set of stairs that let into the darkness of the mountain. Thearbuc followed cautiously. As they climbed the dark stairs, the breeze, the echo, and the darkness seemed to grow. Although they could only see a few steps in front of them, their other senses told them that the stairwell was vast and long.

Thearbuc kept one hand on the stone wall to his right, but the wall on the left would come and go. He leaned to the right to keep from falling and wondered how far down below the fall would be if he were to lose his footing. There was something about the darkness in here. It was dense and seemed to swallow up the light. The torches were brightly lit but would only illuminate a few arms lengths from the torch. Like the days spent in the cave, time seemed to stop in here. They climbed into the darkness for what seemed like an eternity. At some points, Thearbuc felt like they would be trapped in this endless darkness forever. But there was nothing else they could do besides keep climbing.

Their legs began to burn, and the pace slowed to almost a crawl. One step, pause and wait for more energy, then take another. The pace was agonizing, and the two only wished to be through this quest and back home—not even home, just back into the light would be a magnificent exodus from this misery. It had been days of nothing but cold and darkness. Over the hours the two took turns collapsing in exhaustion upon the stairs until they once again could muster the energy to continue on. Finally, and without any warning, the stairs ended at an old wooden door that was rusted with age. Aleric, in a daze of exhaustion and hopelessness, didn’t even notice it at first and almost bumped into the door before stopping just in front of it.

“What’s that?” Thearbuc asked, peering through the darkness. Aleric didn’t reply but raised his finger to his lips indicating quietness. The two leaned in, trying to listen through the door. Many moments passed, but there was nothing to be heard on the other side of the door. Aleric handed Thearbuc his torch, and his eyes began to glow like embers once again as he unsheathed his longsword. Slowly he pushed the door open, which was surprisingly quiet against the loud drafts of wind blowing through the mountain caverns high above them. They crept through the door and slowly closed it behind them, shutting out the sound of the howling wind and leaving them standing in a deafening stillness. Days of hearing the storm made the eerily still room uncomfortably quiet and stuffy with stagnant air.

Aleric moved in the darkness to the far door and cracked it open, still with the longsword in hand, and peered through the crack. Before him he saw a magnificently large hall that was as large as a building and as tall as two of them. It was all made of stone. There were walkways around the perimeter on the upper level, which had windows with thick shutters. One of the shutters had been left open or blown open and banged against the wall in the wind. Outside of the window the sky was blue and the sun was showing, but the breeze coming through was heavy and cold. He listened and watched but heard or saw nothing besides the constant banging of the shutter in the breeze.

"I think we're in the clear," Aleric finally spoke. "I can see the sun. I believe the stairwell took us to the top of the mountain."

"That is great," Thearbuc replied as they moved through the door. They stood in the center of the giant room, surrounded by stone walls. The shutter banged loudly in the wind as it howled through the building. It was enormous. "This must be some sort of military outpost or fort," Thearbuc said, thinking aloud.

"At one time anyway," Aleric replied, wiping the dust from a nearby shelf and picking up an old book that nearly crumbled away at the touch of it.

"Doesn't look like anyone has been here in some time." Thearbuc dumped a heap of dust out of an old stein that had been set on the ground, probably by some bored, drunken guard back when this fort was manned.

"Still." Aleric paused mid-sentence. "I feel something. As if someone has been here recently."

"Let me guess," Thearbuc replied with a hint of annoyance. "We can't seek shelter here? Not even for the night?"

"It would do us good to explore the area before we decide," Aleric replied after some thought.

"Alright then," Thearbuc nodded firmly. "Let's get it done." Slowly and stealthily, they began to explore the large room, then up the stairs, then back down. Listening intently through the wind and banging shutter. There were no objects of interest, just scattered old texts, steins, bottles, and half-used candles. Nothing indicated that the place had been used in any recent memory.

Later, creeping toward the back corner of the large main hall, a wooden door slowly appeared from the shadows as they approached. It was a double door, and one of them was cracked slightly open. They slipped through without having to creak open the old door and entered what appeared to be a large kitchen or dining area. A long wooden table ran down the center of the room. Wooden chairs were strewn about the room in no particular order. A candelabra adorned with melted candles and dripping wax hung above the table from a rope. A length of cabinets filled the back wall and was piled with uncleaned pots and pans. There were four doors in the room, one on each wall, including the one they just came through. The heavy doors blocked out most of the howling wind from beyond, and the banging shutter became a distant clack. It was there in the newfound silence that they finally heard something. Aleric heard the sound first and in a panicked motion raised his opened hand to Thearbuc, who froze in place at the warning. Holding his breath they waited…

Then they heard it again. The sound of voices. Quiet voices echoing off stone walls. The two intruders waited until they could pinpoint the direction the sound was coming from. Aleric pointed toward the door against the left wall, and they crept forward. The voices got louder as they approached, and the two leaned in toward the door to listen.

"They were supposed to be here days ago," one voice said. "That's what I was told."

"I heard the same. Maybe they got lost in the woods," another voice began. "Why do you care though? This watch is better than fighting and arresting people down there. I think it's peaceful." There was a faint thud that sounded like a stein being set down.

"Yeah, well, my shift is up in three days, and I need to start tending to my land if I want to make anything of it. But here I am, way up here, a week's worth of travel away from it while the growing season is almost upon us."

"Land!? Where did you get land?" the other voice asked. "Nobody gets new land in this kingdom. You either have it passed down to you, or you don't have land at all."

"Oh, uh," the other voice grunted. "It's part of my contract. An incentive they have for the more seasoned men who have been on for a long time. They lease me the land at a good price as long as I stay here and pledge my loyalty to... well, you know."

"How long until I can get that?"

"Note sure. 'Nother ten years maybe? Just stay loyal and they'll take care of ya'. Well, better than any other grunt job this old, soggy kingdom has to offer." Then there was a pause. Only the sound of steins being set on the table and some breathing could be heard by Thearbuc and Aleric as they continued to listen through the doorway.

After a moment, the younger voice asked, "How long do we have to wait up here if they never show?"

"Until they say to come down!" The other raised his voice in annoyance. "No one is to get through the passes and down into the Haberlorn. No one! That's the orders. I don't make 'em, I just follow 'em. Learn that boy." Aleric and Thearbuc looked at each other. They knew they were the ones that the men were talking about. They had been delayed by Kalindra, marooned high upon a mountain, almost swallowed by an avalanche, then trapped in a cave for who knows how long. Their late arrival was not expected by those lying in wait.

"Tell me more about this land you are getting," the younger voice started again.

"I told you, I'm not getting it!" the older man replied, sounding more annoyed. "I get to lease it and live on it—farm it. They want me to. At least I'll be able to live away from the barracks and all you godforsaken swamp rats. Toiling in the mud and cold all our lives just to have a roof over our head and food to eat. All that hard work just to have the opportunity to *borrow* some land." The man's tone was filled with frustration as he began to rant under his breath about the harsh life in the kingdom. "I have half a mind to march right through the forests and find my own land. Take my chances with the creatures of the forests. Wait all my life just to borrow some land. Hmph!" he finished.

"What was that?" the younger voice asked mischievously.

"What was what?" the older man answered slowly.

"Thinking about deserting, was that?" the younger man continued. "I heard if we inform the higher ups of treason or desertion, breaking our oaths, then we get their commission. Or in your case, some land for me-self!"

"You wouldn't," the older man replied slowly.

"Wouldn't I?" he snickered. "Wait another ten years toiling in the cold with the likes of you just for the chance to borrow some land? I don't think so. I take our oaths seriously," he chuckled mischievously. "And it sounds like you don't!" Suddenly there was the sound of heavy wood crashing against the stone as a chair was thrown.

"Stay back!" the younger man shouted. Their voices were getting closer to the door, so Thearbuc and Aleric each moved to the sides of the door, weapons drawn, and readied themselves. The door creaked open slowly, but only a crack before it was slammed shut again with a loud bang, followed by the sounds and grunts of a scuffle.

"I'll kill you!" The man's voice bellowed through the door. Faint thuds of impact could be heard as the men punched and fought each other. The door banged loudly over and over again and almost swung open as someone was thrown into the door and smashed against it repeatedly. Luckily, it held shut as the fight raged on inside the room. Then finally the banging door stopped, and the room fell silent. Aleric and Thearbuc could hear faint footsteps on the other side of the doorway as the men circled each other.

"Aaaaah!" one voice screamed out, followed by the sound of a shattering chair against the wall. Then it fell silent once again. Aleric and Thearbuc looked at each other, wondering what was going to happen next. Their weapons were still drawn at the ready when out of the silence there was loud slam and a crushing bang as the door blew from its hinges and two men rolled out onto the floor, taking massive swings at one another. A larger and older man was on top, and he was already swinging at the smaller, younger man's face. Then he noticed the two strangers in the room. They made wide eyes locked for one quick moment.

"Guards!" the large man yelled without hesitation as Thearbuc's sword swung to his neck. But the attack was blocked as the large, burly man raised both hands, holding metal gauntlets, and deflected the sword, falling backward with the force of the blow. The smaller guard scurried from the floor and started toward the adjacent doorway, but Aleric was already moving toward him. The sharp end of Aleric's sword made its way easily through the man's chest, just as the adjacent door blew open with a half dozen incoming guards. Aleric dropped his sword, which was still stuck in the dead guard, turned about, then slammed his body against the wooden door, pushing the incoming guards back out. The large, burly guard was making his way toward the other door, running as fast as he could. Aleric and Thearbuc exchanged quick glances.

"Let him go," Thearbuc said as he frantically looked around the room then glanced up at the wooden candle chandelier. Aleric instantly knew his plan. Thearbuc ran from the corner of the room and leaped high from the ground toward the chandelier. The Paladin couldn't hold the door much longer. The group of guards was pushing in, overpowering him even with his extra strength. Suddenly, he stepped back from the door and let the guards spill in. Thearbuc was in midair when Aleric swiftly cut the rope to the heavy chandelier, just in time for Thearbuc to grab it and thrust the chandelier toward the incoming guards with his heavy forward momentum. The chandelier blew out of the ceiling and hit the group of guards with the force of a falling tree. An enormous thud sounded, followed by gasping from those who were directly hit, and the rest were thrown to ground hard by the impact.

Aleric and Thearbuc glanced at each other, again looking for reassurance that the other was thinking the same thing. It was decided with just a glance and a shrug. This was no time for an uneven fight, they must flee this fortress. Aleric hurriedly pulled his sword from the dead guard's chest and pushed through the fallen guards in the doorway and the few more who were still standing. Thearbuc followed, fighting with fist and axe to push through the doorway after Aleric.

Finally, they were out of the small room and found themselves in another large hall. It was empty where they stood on the ground floor, but all the commotion had caught the attention of more guards who were in the corridors of the upper level. There was a door at the far end of the room from where Aleric and Thearbuc stood.

"Run!" Aleric yelled, already sprinting towards it. An arrow clanked at his feet, narrowly missing him, shot by the guards on the walkway above. Thearbuc was close behind. As he ran, he realized there was no point in trying to watch for incoming arrows and trying to dodge them. There were simply too many. So, he just run as fast as he could, straight for the far door.

As they reached the doorway, at full speed Aleric jumped forward and slammed his shoulder into the door, plowing it open and flying through it to the other side in one acrobatic motion. He landed with his feet firmly on the ground, unexpectedly, outside in the snow. Thearbuc came barreling behind him and almost plowed into him as he, too, rushed through the door and out of the fortress.

The two took a quick moment to look around. They were standing at the base of a large stone fortress. There was snow on the ground, but it was not deep. The sky was blue, but the wind was freezing cold and bit at their exposed skin as it whirled the snow around. In the distance, they were surrounded by tall, prominent mountain peaks, sharply pointing to the skies and capped with snow and icy rock. The peaks went as far as they could see. They were high and deep into the mountains. Clouds and whirling snow made it impossible to see any valleys below to gauge where they might be or which direction to go.

Aleric looked up to survey the fortress and any immediate threats. It was a large block, like a fort made completely of stone, that sat atop the mountain summit. To their left and right there were ramparts above for patrolling guards, and at the ends of each rampart were towers that were built another two stories taller than the rest of the massive structure. To his right, Aleric saw a bridge extending from the fort, which indicated that it was most likely the front gates.

"This way," he motioned as he started toward his left and to the rear of the building.

Thearbuc followed quickly. "We can't hide!" he yelled through the loudness of the wind howling around them. "We are leaving tracks in the snow!"

"Just run!" Aleric yelled back from the lead. They ran across uneven rocks, ice, and snow toward the front gates. They were almost there when Aleric glanced back and saw the group of guards burst through the door and instantly spot them. As he ran, he noticed the snow began to blend into white the fog ahead—the fog that was growing severely thick quite fast. As they ran past the back wall of the fortress, Aleric stopped quickly and flailed his arms about. It wasn't fog they were seeing; it was the sky and clouds ahead. They were standing atop a giant couloir, a steep drop-off and chute that went down the mountain as far as they could see. It was a smooth gully with jagged rocks jetting out on either side of it. The top of the chute, near where they stood, was almost purely ice. The wind blew hard up the mountain and funneled through the chutes, which blew ice and snow fiercely into their faces, stinging and biting and making it difficult to see.

They peered over the edge. The chute seemed to go down forever, getting lost in the clouds far below. Then they turned back, looking for other options. The stone fortress, majestic and powerful, towered against the harsh environment here at the top of the mountain. The brigade of guards was advancing through the rocky ice and snow steadily toward them, readying their bows and drawing swords as they advanced. There were no more options. Without speaking, Thearbuc drew both of his hatchets from his belt and tossed one towards Aleric, who caught it and looked at it confusingly. Then Thearbuc turned toward the chute, took one last look down, and leapt feetfirst into the chasm.

He landed hard on the ice and immediately seemed to pick up speed as gravity took over. Aleric peered over the edge, watching his descent. Barreling down the mountain, unable to see anything with snow and ice blasting into his face, Thearbuc let out a primal scream of desperation. He was sliding fast and uncontrollably and picking up speed as he went. His body weight in the snow left a half-tube shape behind him, like a bobsled track in the snow. After he had slid past the first, icy part of the chute, he seemed to hit a patch of soft snow that exploded into a cloud of white and slowed him down some.

In the snow, he was able to shift his weight to his left side, and with all his strength he dug his hatchet into the mountain. It yanked hard as it caught the ice and was almost pulled clean from his hands, but he held fast. The axe bit hard into the layer of ice below the snow, dragging down Thearbuc's momentum but would not bite through the ice hard enough to slow him enough, and he continued to slide uncontrollably fast. Fear began to take over as he realized the axe was not slowing him down, and he was heading violently down the mountain. He rolled over onto the axe and pushed heavily onto it, trying as hard as he could to get it to bite.

Meanwhile, with the group of guards approaching fast, Aleric turned from atop the chute to find any other option besides jumping into the steep, icy chute. He was outnumbered but stronger than the guards and falling down the mountain meant almost certain injury or death. He lowered his head in frustration at the situation until his survival instincts took over, and when he looked back up, his eyes were glowing bright, raging amber. He turned and glared at the approaching guards, and they hesitated after seeing his glowing eyes for the first time. The Paladin drew his sword and readied himself to fight the group of now-timid soldiers.

Just then, the sound of a massive horn bellowed from the ramparts high upon the fort. It echoed back and forth through the surrounding peaks and filled the air with its monstrous and deep sound. As the horn faded, Aleric could hear commotion all around him. It was the sound of many guards being alerted to his presence. This is no time to fight, he thought again to himself, feeling the tides turning against him. The horn bellowed through the mountain peaks again. He turned back, and with no other choice, he leaped into the icy chute. Just as he disappeared, an arrow from the approaching guards whisked over his head, narrowly missing him.

He hit the ice fast and began his uncontrolled slide. As he tried to stabilize himself, he could see movement above him on the jagged rows of rocks lining the long chute. It was the soldiers, moving into attack positions after having been alerted by the alarm. Another arrow struck silently and out of nowhere just mere feet from The Paladin's leg as he slid fast down the mountain. He was defenseless in the chute, and the cliffside was lined with soldiers and archers. The only option was to slide down the mountain as fast as possible and hope they weren't good enough shots to hit him. Sliding on his back, he curled his legs up towards his chest to reduce drag, then covered his face and torso with his arms. He felt the speed pick up immediately as he was whisked down the steep mountain. Arrows shot past him everywhere. Some soaring past his face, some landing in the chute near him, but most landing safely behind him as he was sliding too fast for even the most skilled archers to hit. But there were just too many. Eventually one of the arrows would surely find its mark.

Thearbuc was halfway down the mountain now and almost out of the long, icy chute. As he slid past the last jagged rocks of the thin chute, the mountain opened up into a large mountain face that looked like a vast, steep meadow covered white in snow. There were no trees, just a smooth, wide-open mountain face. Random guards and tents were strewn across the entire face of the mountain. They had been lying in wait for them, scattered about the mountain so the incoming Paladin and his group could not make it down into the valley without being seen. Arrows rained down on him as he continued to slide down the face at incredible speed.

Thearbuc had made a smooth track down the mountain from his slide, so Aleric was gaining on him fast and sliding too fast to stay in control. He had to slow down, or he would surely begin tumbling like a tomahawk down the mountain to his death. Risking being hit by an arrow, The Paladin followed Thearbuc's lead and dug his hatchet hard into the ice then leaned over until he was almost on top of it, then drove all of his weight down on it. It bit loud like thunder as it crunched into the ice. Just then, another arrow whisked past his head, so close to his ear that he could hear it whistle by. Turning and looking upward and behind him, he saw the guards that had been chasing him had leaped into the icy chute after him. Another nearby soldier fired an arrow from standing atop the chute, and in one motion The Paladin swung his axe around in an amazing display of strength and agility and batted it out of the sky with one hand. The Paladin grinned even in the face of insurmountable danger as the powers that were coursing through him made him feel strong, alive, and more than human. Even he was impressed with his newfound strength and fast reflexes.

Finally, The Paladin also made it through the long, icy chute, and he too saw the mountain open up around them and the number of tents of guards that were patrolling the large snow-covered meadow, high in the mountain. Frustration and rage rose up from deep in his chest seeing how outnumbered he and Thearbuc were. All this hard work and misery just to find themselves in a situation where there was no way out. The numerous guards were all making their way towards Aleric and Thearbuc and one by one jumping into the chute to chase after them, all while a hail of arrows rained down from the others.

The Paladin, with rage and frustration coursing through his veins, and doing his best to control his balance and speed, suddenly saw an opportunity as he noticed a large rock tower covered in snow and ice, jetting out from the mountain above him. Quickly The Paladin threw a fast fireball at the steep mountain face. It was a direct hit on the tower and made a loud thunderous crash as it struck the ice and snow. In an instant the ice face was crashing down onto the snowy mountain with a thunderous sound and immediately cracks started to open up across the mountain face while the sound of thunderous cracking all around filled the sky. Then a massive slab of snow gave way and began to slide. It came slow at first but quickly built momentum until it was a raging avalanche barreling down the mountain above him. The archers and soldiers in and near the chute tried to run away, but their efforts were futile in the deep, slow snow. In just moments they were engulfed in a river of violent snow and were swept down the mountain in an enormous cloud of white powder, never to be seen again. Aleric and Thearbuc could barely hear their screams through the magnificent thunderous sound of the avalanche above.

Further down the mountain, the hail of arrows had stopped as Aleric and Thearbuc continued their glissade down the mountain. Eventually the slope leveled out at lower elevations and the snow softened until they both came to a stop, one after the other. Then they stood up, brushed the snow from their pants, and turned about to see one lone, brave guard who had jumped into the chute after them and was far enough ahead of the others to be spared from the avalanche. Frantically, he tried to stop himself before reaching the powerful Paladin and his large, black-bearded friend, but it was too steep to stop completely, and he slowly and comically slid until he bumped into their feet.

The two glared down at the small man who hurriedly got up and began to scurry away up the mountain to escape. They watched with large grins as he frantically tried to claw and kick his way up the mountain, but the soft snow broke away below him and he made little progress despite the massive amount energy that he was putting into it.

"Do you want to handle this?" Thearbuc chuckled looking toward Aleric, whose eyes had returned to normal.

"Sure," he replied, walking over to the man, his feet crunching loudly in the snow. "Come 'ere you!" he said loudly, grabbing the man by his clothes and picking him up with one hand. He gave him a quick look over then tossed him with ease into the soft snow. The soldier was frozen in fear as his eyes darted back and forth, waiting for what was going to happen next. He had a red tunic on which was draped over light armor, and on the tunic was the symbol of a dragon wrapped around a wizard's staff. The same symbol that was tattooed on the Mischief Mage and the soldiers who came to Barreston's home all those years ago.

"Who sent you up here? Who do you work for?" Thearbuc asked, pointing his sword at the man's chest where the insignia was.

"We are the Keepers of the Dragon's Flame," the man replied after some hesitation, trying to be defiant. But his voice was shaking, so all intimidation was lost in the presentation. "We are everywhere and nowhere. You will never stop us. Mazeron is already ours," he said, forcing a laugh. "You will all be slaves!" As he spoke, he glared at them with hate and anger in his eyes.

"Will we now?" Thearbuc said, smacking his sword heavily into the soldier's armor. He jumped, visibly frightened at the motion.

"You already are," the soldier continued, speaking angrily through his teeth. "You work for us every day for pennies. Not even enough pennies to do anything but survive. You can't leave; you can't have peace; yet you still need us to live. We own ALL OF YOU!"

The guard slowly got onto one knee and was brushing the snow from his leg when without warning he drew a small blade from his boot and lunged toward Aleric, aiming the dagger directly towards his torso and lunging in swiftly for the kill. Aleric pushed the soldier's arm aside, but the blade still found its mark and slashed the lower part of Aleric's stomach. As the man fell back in the snow, Thearbuc was already in action and his swift sword came down hard and fast across the man's back. It all happened so fast, and in one quick moment, the soldier lay there lifeless in the red snow. Aleric backed away from the sudden attack and inspected his wound.

"Are you ok?" Thearbuc asked worriedly.

"Just a small cut I think," Aleric replied, poking around the wound with blood on his fingertips. "It's okay."

Thearbuc let out a sigh of relief. "That was too close. I didn't expect him to be so fast." There was a pause. "Who are these Keepers of the Dragon's Flame?"

"Never heard of them before." Aleric kicked the body over and examined the dragon and wizard's staff emblem. Then they searched the soldier's body but found nothing else of interest. No notes, no orders. The two peered up the steep mountain they had just slid down and saw the fort looming high above, half hidden in the clouds. There was no more movement or activity that they could see, so they began to head down the rest of the mountain toward the kingdom of Haberlorn.

As they trudged through the ankle-deep snow, they wondered about the events that had just unfolded. They knew the guards were at the fort lying in wait for them. The only question was why. And who was this secret society that was after them? Clearly it was the same group who attempted the assassinations in the castle, but who wanted them dead and why still remained a mystery.

The clouds overhead broke as they trekked down the mountain and the warm sun was a welcome feeling upon their cold faces. After so long in the cold and darkness, it felt to them like there was hope in this world again.

They walked for hours down the snowy slopes until they came to a canyon that led into the flat valley below. On the snowy, treeless slopes, they stood high in the mountains and looked down upon the valley below. The valley was mostly large, green fields dotted with small cottages. The sight of civilization after so long in isolation gave them relief from the heaviness of their mission and their missing friend Brodel, who had been taken by the witch Kalindra.

It was nighttime when they finally reached the foothills of the enormous mountains. They could see the dotted lights of different villages off in the distance to the northeast, so they began to trek along the foothills heading northward and toward the rising moon. The snow was still ankle-deep here as they walked along the hillsides in the soft moonlight. There were no tracks in the snow anywhere to be seen, and it reflected the moon like an endless sea of smooth powder. The wind blew lightly, and the temperature was much warmer now that they escaped the cold air from a higher elevation. It was more comfortable than they had experienced in quite some time. As they walked, they breathed the crisp air deep into their lungs and wondered what was going on in the peaceful villages down in the valley below. They imagined friends sharing drinks in dim firelit pubs across large wooden tables. Families in their cottages with the little ones playing on the floor by the warmth of the fire.

The night was still young, their spirits were high, and the moon reflected peacefully in the snow, making visibility clear and the trekking easy, so they opted to continue on for the night until they were off the mountain. They followed the bright moon until they were adjacent to and just above to a small village below.

“We should camp here before we get too close to the village,” Aleric suggested finally, out of the peaceful silence of the dark night. “We don’t know what kind of village it is and bandits are known to scour these lands. We don’t want to wake up robbed,” he said with a slight chuckle. Thearbuc nodded that he agreed, and they began to make camp. They were below the tree line, but the trees in the area were still sparse. After a little bit of exploring in the moonlight, they found a spot under a lonely tree and made a quick wind break out of snow, then tucked away in the silence of the foothills they quickly fell into a deep sleep.

Chapter 11: The Stray Fox Inn

The next day came quickly to Aleric and Thearbuc, and by the time they were awoken by the sound of a nearby traveling wagon, the sun was already high in the sky. Aleric sat up and rubbed his eyes as Thearbuc looked around from his laying position. They had made camp just fifty yards from a road and didn't even know it. The kingdom of Haberlorn was known to have better trade and commerce because they had open routes in and out of the kingdom for merchants to travel, unlike the kingdom of Mazeron, which was cut off from the world by large mountains to the east and south and vast forests filled with beasts and Brigands to the north and west. The kingdom of Haberlorn was by no means a booming center of commerce, but it was far better off geographically. Besides the mountains to the west, there were vast farmlands and lakes to the east. People could trade more freely, and although the kingdom was not rich, it provided many with a comfortable existence for their time here on earth.

The two watched the wagon go by from the concealment of the tree. It was a large, heavy thing and was loaded high and tall with goods that clanked and creaked about as it went along the bumpy road. Thearbuc and Aleric quickly broke camp and followed the direction of the wagon heading toward the village they saw the night before.

By midday they were off the foothills and firmly down in the valley. Any remnants of snow had long turned into wet grass and mud, which in turn became green grass and trees the farther down the foothills they went. When they reached the valley floor, they followed the damp dirt road toward the village, the wagon lazily clanking along still ahead of them. They saw an old wooden sign planted on the side of the road that read in faded red letters "Tillsboro."

"Sounds like a nice place," Thearbuc said cheerfully.

"I need a bath and a bed" is all Aleric replied before he continued making his way up the dirt road.

"There should be an inn," Thearbuc continued. "I am ready for some sanctuary and a hot meal." Aleric nodded and they both continued onward to the small village of Tillsboro.

As they came upon the village, it seemed peaceful to them. Well-kept homes and gardens and fruit trees and orchards dotted the route to the main street. It reminded Aleric of home, but cleaner and more peaceful. Most of the cottages were made of wood and had thatched grass roofs. Smoke rose lazily from their chimneys and filled the air with the pleasing smell of pine. There were not many people to be seen on the dirt paths as they walked toward the center of the village, and they quickly concluded this was mostly a farming village, and most people were off somewhere tending to their own lives. From time to time, they could hear the distant laughter of children playing being carried by the wind, which to them seemed like a good sign.

After some time of wandering through the village, they found that what they thought was the “main street” was really the only street. This village was mostly scattered homes and some businesses randomly strewn about. In between two houses you would see a wooden sign hanging out front that read “Blacksmith” or “Baker.” They continued to wander the quiet village until they finally heard some commotion and the sound of life off in the distance. They followed the sound around corners and down a street until it eventually led them to a large wooden building. It was two stories tall with a wooden walkway wrapped around the outside of the second floor. One man walked out of the swinging door as two others walked in. The loud commotion was coming from the inside. The word *inn* was carved above the door and the sign hanging on the building read “The Stray Fox.”

“This must be the place,” Thearbuc said as he peeked through the closing door to see the many people inside.

“Finally,” Aleric replied. “Let’s just hope they have rooms for us.” The two exchanged a glance then entered the Stray Fox inn.

As they closed the door behind them, the place seemed to swallow up all light from the welcoming sun outside and instead was filled with dark, musty, candlelight and smoke. The ground floor of the Stray Fox seemed to be a large tavern and eating hall. The room was stuffy and so loud the patrons inside had to almost yell at one another to have a conversation, and that was exactly what they were doing. There were so many men inside that there was hardly room to walk or stand without bumping into another person. Aleric and Thearbuc looked at one another, puzzled.

"Why do you suppose there are so many people here in the middle of this tiny village?" Thearbuc yelled to Aleric.

Aleric shrugged. "Something must be going on. Let's find out what it is."

As they pushed farther into the tavern, most of the patrons paused their conversations and stared at the two weary and dirty travelers. It was just then that Thearbuc realized they must be a miserable sight to see and painfully stuck out among the crowd. They had been ambushed by a witch, thrown into the depths of the mountains, had lived in a cave, and spent many more days walking through the soggy snow. They were a mess—clothes tattered, wet, and smelly, their hair disheveled and ratty. Even amidst this rough bunch of travelers at the inn they looked unpleasant. The room got eerily quiet as the many eyes gazed upon them.

"We've traveled many nights," Aleric spoke loudly and confidently to the onlooking crowd. "We are not vagrants nor beggars." He halfway unsheathed his longsword as he spoke and pointed at the large red ruby that adorned the bottom of the handle, indicating he was or worked for royalty. "We seek room and board."

Many of the onlookers nodded in acknowledgment and the room quickly grew loud again as the other travelers and men went back to their food, drinks, and conversation.

"Aye!" a man spoke as he approached the two. "I can help ye with that," he said it with a noticeably different accent than they were used to hearing in the kingdom of Mazeron. "Follow me." He pushed his way through the crowded tavern. They followed him to the bar counter, which also doubled as the front desk, and they could see a few room keys hanging loosely on the wall behind him.

The man was burly and tall with thick red hair. He was definitely in charge here and seemed to be someone that even the rough crowd of travelers would not want to contend with. His hands were calloused, thick, and hammy. Aleric wondered how the man could pick anything up with such thick, blocky fists. It looked like you would fare better being hit with the business end of a sledgehammer.

"Can't remember the last time the place has been so busy," the burly innkeeper said. "We have a few rooms left. One or two?"

Without replying, Aleric reached into his tunic and pulled one large, gold coin from his pouch and set it onto the bar. The coin was stamped with King Victus' young face and the word *Mazeron* was minted in arched letters across the top.

"Ahhe," the innkeeper said curiously, then paused as he looked the gold coin over. "Okay then," he finished, with a glint in his eye. "Two rooms it is. All you can eat and drink while you are here. You boys just let me know if you need anything from me or anyone else here at the Stray Fox. I hope ye enjoys your stay." And with that he handed two keys over then pushed two large steins of beer across the bar after them. "Enjoy!" He nodded and turned away to tend to the rest of his patrons.

"I needed this," Thearbuc said, staring at the foamy beer with a look of love in his eyes. "Shall we?" He nodded toward the busy tavern, then the two weary travelers navigated their way through the crowd of men. It was all men, they noticed, as they walked through the tavern. No women.

"Oi!" a man shouted from a far table, raising his glass toward Aleric and Thearbuc, indicating for them to come over. They nodded at the man and made their way to a large, wooden, picnic-style table and sat down with a group of travelers.

"The name is Winton." The man introduced himself by clanking his stein hard into Thearbuc's. Winton was dressed in dirty clothes that seemed to have been very nice at one point but now were weathered and tattered. He wore a red cape that was muddy at the bottom from dragging on the ground. His hair was curly and golden, and his face was badly sunburnt. The three other men he sat with shared a similar look, and all had sunburned faces, indicating they, too, had recently been on the road for some time.

"You men here for the hunt?" Winton asked. "They're even sending royalty out for it, eh?"

"He's not royalty," another chimed in with a rough voice. "He only works for royalty. Look at 'em."

"What is going on here?" Thearbuc interrupted. "What hunt?" The four men exchanged glances and confused looks.

"You haven't heard?" one man asked.

"Then why are you here in Tillsboro?" Winton asked. Thearbuc shrugged, not knowing what was going on or what they were talking about. "The hunt! The Stone Gnome! Winton said, throwing his hands up. “There’s been a Stone Gnome spotted here in Tillsboro!” he said finally.

“A Stone Gnome?” Thearbuc replied. “Above ground? Here?” The others all nodded in unison.

“Aye,” another traveler continued, leaning in close to the others with excitement in his eyes. “Been a few sightings of him in these parts lately.”

“Do you know what this means?” Thearbuc asked, glancing at Aleric. He nodded back but stayed quiet. It was a big deal. There hadn’t been a Stone Gnome sighting in almost twenty years. They were magic beings that had returned to their natural habitat underground when the humans of the surface world started to become hostile towards magic and magic beings.

The Stone Gnomes were happy underground. That is where they belonged. They could move freely through stone and rock just as a fish could move freely through the water. It was rumored that they had vast cities under the mountains that stretched deep into the earth and rose as tall as the highest mountain peaks. The cities were lined with veins of gold and diamonds, which were so commonplace for the Stone Gnomes that they ironically couldn’t care less for them. They were a simple and proud species. They enjoyed eating, drinking, and the simpler pleasures of life: good company and love. When it came to love, they spent almost their entire lives with the same partner. The fact that there had been multiple sightings of a Stone Gnome above ground was a very big deal for everyone who dwelled above ground.

“If we could catch that Stone Gnome…” another gold-haired traveler said, trailing off in thought. “We’ll all be rich. We’ll use him to open the mines again. Not an ounce of gold has been pulled out of those mountains in near two decades!” he said in a frustrated tone, hitting the table angrily with a meaty fist. This was an unstable bunch, Aleric thought to himself. He rested his left hand on the hilt of his sheathed sword as the table of rough travelers grew louder and more intense.

“We’re going to catch ’em!” Winton exclaimed. “Everyone here has been on the hunt for him for weeks now. No one is giving up. We were one of the first groups to get here.”

“Place was almost empty when we arrived,” the other hunter explained. “More people arriving every day. Trickling in one group at a time." The others nodded; they seemed frustrated about all the arriving competition. "Bastards are after our prize," the hunter continued, eyes darting back and forth, examining the other hunters. "They don't have a chance with Winton on our side here," he said, slapping Winton's back. A small cloud of dust puffed into the air from Winton's dirty cape. "He almost had The Gnome. Not far from here. Chased him down a fox hole, he did." Winton grumbled something inaudible as he buried his face in his stein and gulped down a large amount of ale.

"Well, we should get some rest," Thearbuc said, finishing his ale and standing up. "It's still a two day's journey to the castle."

"Three days," Winton said with a hiccup.

"Great. Three days it is then," Thearbuc replied, motioning to Aleric that it was time to leave the rough bunch of Gnome hunters to themselves. Aleric and Thearbuc excused themselves and began making their way upstairs to the inn part of the Stray Fox establishment. As they found their individual rooms, they both commented on the dichotomy of the seemingly perfect village of Tillsboro and the rough crowd of hunters converging on the inn.

"I hope all these hunters don't cause the villagers any trouble," Thearbuc mentioned as he unlocked the door to his room.

"That seems unlikely," Aleric replied flatly. "There's nothing we can do, though. Our mission lies to the north. We need to reach the castle and King Haberlorn as fast as possible. We are already delayed. King Victus and Maub have probably already abandoned hope on our mission and have given up on us." Thearbuc sighed heavily, and with that they retired to their individual rooms for a much-deserved rest and the first real bed they had seen in weeks.

Aleric awoke the next morning to the warm sun shining peacefully through the open shutters. Both Aleric and Thearbuc had been able to wash and dry out their clothes through the night, and they felt rejuvenated after a good night's sleep. The Stray Fox was able to outfit them with new horses and supplies after Aleric produced another solid gold coin, which was given to him by King Victus to aid them on their quest. By early afternoon they were equipped, rested, and off toward the castle.

They galloped at a brisk pace through the farmlands of Tillsboro northwestward to the castle. They passed many travelers and merchants along the way, which was a welcome change from the desolate, lonely, and dangerous roads on the outskirts of Mazeron that they were accustomed to. Aleric and Thearbuc, the two experienced travelers, made record time and the three-day journey to the castle turned into one day plus one morning. By the afternoon of the second day, they had spotted the castle in the distance. A magnificent structure in the center of vast flatlands and farmland. The nearest village was beyond the castle more than a mile away, making the castle a prominent and awe-inspiring structure, surrounded by beautiful greenery and gardens. As they approached the castle, they suddenly heard a voice call out.

"Who goes there?" a guard yelled from somewhere behind the gate as the two warrior-looking men approached the castle gates. The gate was made of metal bars, and a beautiful courtyard with wandering residents and guards could be seen through it. And just beyond was the large stone castle.

"I am the king's Paladin, Aleric of Mazeron. We have come at the request of King Victus to speak with his cousin, King Haberlorn."

"You don't look much like a Paladin," the guard said in a snide tone, commenting on their dirty appearance.

"We have passed through the mountains. It has taken many weeks," Aleric stated. "The witch Kalindra ambushed us in the woods and took our friend. We are lucky we made it here." Aleric paused but the guard did not reply or say anything. "No one has been able to successfully cross the mountains from Mazeron in nearly ten years," Aleric said, raising his arms. The other guards looked down mockingly at the shabby pair of weary travelers and whispered to one another for some time. Eventually, Aleric produced another gold coin and wrapped it in the flag of Mazeron that he was carrying then tossed it through the gate as proof of where they came from.

"King Victus requires the help of his cousin, King Haberlorn. He sent us to give him a message," Thearbuc said, reinstating what Aleric had already said. The guards examined the flag and coin then handed it back to Aleric through the gate.

Then one of the guards atop the rampart yelled down, "Leave your weapons on the path behind you. Then you may enter. The guards will escort you inside and send word to the king. It will be his decision if he wants to meet with you or not."

With that, the large iron gate sprang to life. Creaks and clanks filled the air as the massive gears began to move, hoisting the thick bars into the sky. They entered the courtyard as the steel gates closed behind them and were instructed to wait there until someone came to escort them to the king. As they waited, they instantly noticed that this courtyard was much livelier than their castle's courtyard was. Many people were coming and going, and two men were practicing sword fighting off in the distance. One was an instructor and the other the student. Stables could be seen in the distance, and the stable boys were bringing in new bushels of hay. Guards walked to and fro, and natural flowers that lined the perimeter grew up the stone structures. The guards atop the ramparts did not take their eyes off the two strangers, and the castle's archers stood ready with notched arrows in their bows.

"No lack of security," Thearbuc mentioned with a chuckle.

"They don't believe we are who we say we are," Aleric replied in a serious tone. "And why would they? We look like transients."

"We are transients!" Thearbuc replied. "We haven't had a home in weeks now. I am not accustomed to looking like one," he replied grumpily.

Just then a well-dressed man approached from the far end of the courtyard. "Follow me," he said, turning and walking away briskly. He said no other words and led them quietly through the courtyard and into a side door of the castle. They were expecting to be led through the large front doors and into the king's great hall but were instead shuffled through a side entrance. Aleric and Thearbuc glanced worriedly at one another as they entered through the small door into the castle. "The king is unavailable at the moment," the guard finally said, directing them to a thin, dark flight of stairs. Aleric and Thearbuc's hope dropped instantly, and their stomachs lurched at the thought of coming all this way and losing their friend for absolutely nothing.

"His Majesty will see you tonight," the man finally continued, while motioning them down dimly lit hallway." Aleric and Thearbuc both breathed a large sigh of relief. "Here are your rooms. You can get cleaned up." The guard looked them up and down condescendingly. "You can't be expected to meet a king looking like…well, this." Then he turned and opened a wooden door with a massive creak and motioned Aleric in. "Your room is next door, sir," he said to Thearbuc and motioned in the other direction.

The two retired to their rooms where they each found fresh clothes and a large bucket of water to clean off with. They were both ecstatic about having a warm room to sleep in and warm water to wash with. Aleric was just laying down for a much-needed rest when there was a knock at the door.

"His Majesty King Haberlorn will see you now," a voice on the other side said. Aleric got up with a tired grunt and made his way to the door to find the same man who had escorted them to their rooms waiting for them in the hallway. "Follow me," he said, beginning to walk down the corridor.

As they walked along, Aleric noted the similarities between this castle and the castle of Mazeron. This castle was greatly lacking in fashion comparatively. The floors were rough wood with no rugs lining the hallways and no tapestries adorning the walls. It was a simple stone building, and it was left just at that, with no decorations or warmth at all. This castle was livelier though, he did notice. Instead of the long, empty corridors he was used to, there were people constantly coming and going to their rooms and duties. It felt more like an inn than a castle, he thought, as they walked along the halls and back down to the ground level where King Haberlorn would be waiting.

Finally, they came to a set of large doors that reached high toward the sky. Their guide reached for two large iron circles and pulled heavily on them to open the large, magnificent doors. Walking through, they entered a great hall. Wooden candle chandeliers lined the tall ceiling, and a long, wooden table sat in the center of the room before them. At the far end of the great hall a large throne sat on an elevated platform. There were people sitting at the table, presumably waiting for their guests. King Haberlorn sat proudly at the far end of the table with a dull-colored crown atop his head.

"Come sit," he bellowed from far across the table. His commanding voice echoed along the stone walls. He did not stand up. The guide nodded to Aleric and Thearbuc then took a step backward and closed them in the great hall. King Haberlorn motioned to some empty chairs at the far end of the table near him. As they took their seats, they were able to get a good look at him. King Haberlorn was one very large man, both tall and wide. He had a round face, red in color, with thick, curly red hair and a big red beard to match. He outstretched a bulky hand to welcome the two guests. Their hands looked like a child's compared to his when they shook, and his hands completely engulfed theirs.

"Now, to what do we owe the pleasure of my cousin's kingdom?" he bellowed. "After all these years, why has old King Victus sent ya? Or should I say, what does he want from me? Ha ha ha." His large belly bounced from his deep laugh. There was a faint chuckle from the other guests at the table.

"I am no simple messenger, King Haberlorn," Aleric said with confidence. "I am the king's Paladin. I have been sent to deliver the message that change has come to Mazeron and all nearby lands. That peacefulness and prosperity are soon to be restored. And with your help, the roads between our great kingdoms and the trade routes will be opened once again."

"Haaa ha ha!" the large king bellowed, with so much bass that Aleric felt it in his chest. "Is that so now?" he continued, still laughing. "And with what magic and army is your king accomplishing that with?" He chuckled as the others joined in, laughing at Aleric's statement.

Aleric was not amused by the king's arrogance and held eye contact sternly on him. "With my magic. And your army," he said firmly.

King Haberlorn quickly fell silent. He stared back at The Paladin, examining him. "This is no time for games, boy," he said quietly. "What is your play here? What do you want?" he snapped.

"We want your help and to join armies to rid the forests of the brigands," Thearbuc chimed in, sensing the tensions beginning to rise. Aleric and the king still held their stare at one another.

"Is that so?" King Haberlorn replied. "You…you abandon us for decades! Closing the mines and leaving us out in the middle of nowhere to fend for ourselves. No word or contact for years! Then you come to me with this? Tales of magic and power as long as I sacrifice my army for it. And what am I to do when the brigands inevitably destroy my army? Pick them off one by one in the forests. We will be sitting ducks here. Overtaken and enslaved!" He paused to catch his breath. In the silence there was great tension. "No, knight. I don't believe your tales of magic. We are fine here. We have trade routes to the east. We have commerce that doesn't rely on pulling gold from the mines."

Aleric was clenching his fists as the rage grew inside him from the king's insolence and condescension. He slammed his hand down on the table, and when the king looked back toward Aleric his eyes were glowing a bright amber, casting a threatening glow onto the king's surprised face.

"It is not a tale." The Paladin's voice was changed. It was deep with a slight echo that struck fear in those who heard it. "We *can* rid the forests and trade routes of the brigands," he said, this time banging his fist on the table once again. King Haberlorn was taken back. The sudden sight of The Paladin's force left him speechless for a moment. But that quickly turned to anger and rage, as he was not accustomed to being intimidated in his own castle.

"Out," he muttered quietly under his breath. "Get out of my sight. You come here and try to intimidate *me*?" His voice grew louder and angrier as he spoke. "You tell my cousin, King Victus, to use his own army if he wants the merchant roads to open between our lands. He has abandoned us before. I'm sure he just wants to use us then abandon us again. Tell him we are fine here on our own and we will never use our army to protect his kingdom!" The king pushed angrily back from the table then stood and began to walk away while shaking his head.

"But we've come so far," Thearbuc said pleadingly, "with such sacrifice. How can you write us off so easily?"

The king paused and looked back over his shoulder. "You can rest here for five days," he said calmly after a long sigh. "We will send you with new supplies and horses. That will make your trip back home less…eventful."

"Please reconsider, or just think about it," Thearbuc begged again as the king walked away. He gave one last glance at the two as he exited the great hall, noting that The Paladin's eyes were still glowing as he sat motionless at the table like a statue.

"Great tactic," Thearbuc said angrily to Aleric. "Intimidate a king at his own table?"

Aleric took some time to reply. "I thought if I proved I was who I claimed to be then he would understand that we have a real chance of succeeding," he said with a sigh.

Aleric and Thearbuc sat in silence for the rest of the meal. The other guests at the table tried not to look at or make eye contact with the two guests who had angered the king. The mood was tense and awkward for some time, until the doors swung open, and their guide returned once again.

"This way," he said condescendingly as he turned on his heels quickly and began to walk away, without even waiting for the two. "I will show you back to your rooms."

Aleric and Thearbuc followed in silence back through the stone stairwells and corridors. The castle was quiet this time of night, and they saw no one else as they walked along. They retired to their rooms without saying much and bid their guide goodnight. Although frustrated at King Haberlorn's stubborn stance towards his cousin, Aleric remained hopeful that he would come to his senses after sleeping on it for a night. He had to realize the mutual benefit of ridding the lands of menaces and thieves. Those were Aleric's thoughts as he fell asleep in the dark quiet stone room.

It was late into the night when under the cover of darkness, a wizard cloaked in black approached the castle of Haberlorn. He stood in the dark night, unseen, and stared at the castle in silence for some time. The wind blew softly around him, and the tall grasses blew lazily, brushing against his thick cloak. The wizard was far enough away from the castle that the guards or any prying eyes could not see him through the darkness. He was only a black shadow against the black night. He sniffed the air like an animal on the hunt, then with a thin grin he turned toward the castle and raised both arms. Like a musical conductor, he slowly started to move his raised hands as his magic began to gather.

From deep in his sleep, Aleric was awoken by the faint sounds of yelling far in the distance. It stirred him awake so slightly that at first, he lay there wondering if he had actually heard anything or not. Then, there it was again. The definite sound of commotion coming from outside the castle window. A faint yell in the distance, then another, and another. He got up to investigate and slowly moved toward the window. He quietly cracked open the shutter then peered out into the darkness. At first, he saw nothing of importance. The gray stones of the castle walls glowed cold in the gray moonlight. Beyond the castle was almost complete darkness.

"It's on the roof!" a voice yelled out from out of the darkness.

"Shoot it!" screamed another. Aleric darted his eyes back and forth, peering through the darkness, but he couldn't see anything. Then, suddenly, a loud scratching and thumping pounded on the roof above him. Dust fell from the ceiling into eyes as he looked up. Something large was on the roof of the castle, and it was moving fast. Hurriedly, he ran to the other end of the room and grabbed his sword just as Thearbuc came charging into the room, sword drawn and ready to fight.

"What is going on?" he asked with confusion and sleepy eyes.

"I'm not sure," Aleric replied. Then there was another sound at the window. Quickly, they ran to it.

"On the wall!" a guard called out from below. Aleric and Thearbuc peered out to see an enormous shadow on the side of the castle. It was dark, so they couldn't make out what it was and could only see an outline of its shape. It had at least four legs and lay flat along the castle walls, motionless for the moment.

"What is that thing?" Thearbuc asked sounding worried. Arrows came out of the darkness from below as the guards fired on the shadow. The shadow moved with unnatural speed and agility, and the arrows clanked and sparked off the walls as they hit the castle's stones then bounced harmlessly to the ground. The shadow danced back and forth as the wave of arrows continued. Aleric and Thearbuc both thought they witnessed at least one or two arrows make a direct hit, but those, too, bounced from the castle's walls, apparently missing their mark.

"There's more!" the guards could be heard yelling from the ramparts below. The sound of scraping and the thud of movement on the roof started again. The entire room seemed to jolt with the force of whatever was moving up there. Dust fell to the floor from the impact.

"Watch out!" Thearbuc yelled, pointing to the window. Aleric turned to see another shadow heading straight for them, crawling on the side of the castle like a fast-moving bug. He pushed Aleric to the side, grabbed the shutter, and slammed the window closed just as the shadow was approaching. An arrow flung through the closing shutter and stuck solidly into the wood ceiling just as the shutter closed and Aleric and Thearbuc fell backward on to the floor. Instantly, it fell silent. From their spots on the floor, the two men pointed their swords at the window, waiting for the beast to blow through at any second. But it did not come.

The commotion continued outside with the sound of arrows hitting the walls and the scratches of unknown beasts climbing across the castle walls and roof. It sounded like there were many of them, scrambling all about the castle like a spider-infested rock.

Aleric and Thearbuc were heading toward the door to find their way outside to help, when suddenly the door slammed open with a loud bang and King Haberlorn entered the room. He was covered in weapons—swords, knives, and a mace hung loosely from his belt. He was red with anger and rage.

"What have you brought upon my castle!?" he yelled out. The two visitors from Mazeron stared back blankly, unable to find an answer, not knowing if they were about to be attacked by the king or if they were all going to join the fight against the castle's unknown assailants.

"Aaah!" King Haberlorn yelled in frustration as he took out the spiked ball and swung it heavily toward the wooden door, splintering a hole in it and knocking it from its hinges with a powerful blow. "No time! Those things are going to die by my hands!" he yelled in a rage as he turned to take off down the hallway and join the fight. Thearbuc and Aleric followed, running fast behind.

Exiting the castle, the three were met with several guards. all immersed in the battle and shooting arrows at the creature. Only one could be seen by Aleric, Thearbuc, and King Haberlorn as they exited the castle, and then it scurried away quickly and was gone just as fast as it had come. The guards waited in silence for another wave of attacks. Confusion was on their faces as to what they were fighting and where it had gone.

"Fill me in!" the king demanded loudly.

"They can't be hit, sir," one of the commanders responded. "Almost all our arrows have been used and not one single hit. Some sort of magic beasts they are."

"Nothing I ever seen before either, my lord," another guard chimed in. "They can't be of this world," he continued with a shaky voice.

"Magic," the king grumbled angrily. "You!" He turned toward Aleric. "This is not a coincidence! What have you brought upon my castle?"

"We have brought nothing." Aleric stood his ground angry at the accusation. The king and the guards continued to look toward the dark sky, but all was quiet now. The mysterious shadow creatures seemed to be gone for the moment. King Haberlorn turned back to Aleric quickly and angry.

"Be gone from my home, Paladin!" he yelled, pointing an angry finger. "We were fine before you came here. We've survived and made a life without the help from your king and Mazeron's gold. Tell my cousin that he abandoned us long ago and we are fine here on our own now." And with that King Haberlorn turned about and stormed off back towards the castle.

"You can't leave us out here with those things still out here!" Thearbuc pleaded as the king walked away, but he ignored his pleas. "They'll kill us! Someone clearly wants us dead!" But still his pleas fell on deaf ears and the king slammed the castle doors without even glancing back. Aleric and Thearbuc stood in silence among the few remaining guards on the watch.

"You can stay in the barracks for the night," one of the guards finally spoke. "But not past sunrise or the king will hear of it and have my hide." Aleric nodded and told the guard thank you and how much he appreciated the offer. Spending the night in the barracks surrounded by guards on duty was a far better option than wandering the open land in the pitch dark in the dead of night. They were escorted quietly to the barracks and hunkered down for the night in the commons area. They kept watch at the door and the weapons at the ready, as they felt extremely exposed and vulnerable here, like bait left out to lure a predator.

But alas, the morning sunrise did come. The warmth of the rising sun was a welcome feeling and great relief for the guards, who had stayed awake all night waiting for another attack. There was a shift change at the barracks and news of the mysterious wall crawlers began to spread quickly throughout the kingdom as the night guards returned home to tell others what had happened.

Chapter 12: Skerlin

At first light, Aleric and Thearbuc were shuffled quickly from the barracks to the stables, where they were told they must leave the lands of Haberlorn at once. But upon entering the stables, they found that leaving may not be as easy as they had thought. In the stables was an unfathomable and grotesque sight. Some of the horses had been slaughtered during the night, and the rest had been let out and were scattered all about the lands, grazing in the early morning hours.

"I didn't see anything!" one of the stable boys pleaded with the head guard on duty, who was questioning him heavily. "I didn't fall asleep at my post. I didn't hear anything! I was standing right there, then the next thing I knew, I was awakened over there in the hay."

"There was magic afoot last night," Aleric mentioned, trying to help the boy.

"The king will not allow me to give you any of his horses," the guard said to Aleric and Thearbuc. "Too many of the horses are gone and I will lose my job if I allow any more of them to go. I'm sorry. You must flee these lands on foot."

Aleric nodded and lowered his head. Heavily defeated and completely out of hope, Aleric and Thearbuc conceded to the predicament they found themselves in and thanked the guard for his help. They began to walk away heavyheartedly from the castle of Haberlorn after having come all this way for nothing. Gaining nothing and losing a friend in the process. The only thing they knew for certain now was someone or some*thing* was after them. Trying to assassinate them in the castle then stalking them for great distances across the mountains and valleys. Now they were alone, left to walk across the vast lands, defenseless against whatever was coming for them. They were basically sitting ducks out here on foot.

"Make for the village of Skerlin," the guard yelled to them as they began to walk down the dirt road away from the castle. "It is directly east from here. If you're lucky, you can get there by nightfall!" The two nodded and waved at the guard as they faded slowly into the distance and began their journey back to somewhere safe, then hopefully back to Mazeron.

The morning was uneventful as they trekked along the Haberlorn countryside. "Beautiful country," Thearbuc mentioned more than once. But Aleric could not enjoy himself. The feeling of an attack coming at any moment had him on edge, and he rested his hand on the hilt of his sword most of the journey. By midday, a wooden sign appeared at a fork in the dirt road. "Skerlin," it read.

"Sounds like a skeevy place to me," Thearbuc said, thinking aloud.

"Indeed," replied Aleric. "I believe it is. I have heard telling's of it. Rampant thievery and shady gambling are what it's known for. Still, we have no other options. Let's go. If we're lucky, we'll make it before nightfall."

They continued throughout the day, taking minimal breaks. Although on edge from their predicament, the day was peaceful and quiet. The road was mostly empty, and travel seemed to go by quickly. The two spoke about being stalked by their unknown assailant from one valley to the next and made assumptions about who or what was behind it.

"They are scared of how strong we are," Aleric noted.

"What makes you say that?" Thearbuc replied.

"Because they won't confront us head on. Whoever it is, is always waiting in the shadows or sending beasts to stalk us. If they weren't afraid of us, they would have just come for us long ago. They are trying to outsmart us and wear us down."

Thearbuc nodded that he agreed. "I think other magic users are threatened by your power and you being here. What was the name of that secret society the guard mentioned?"

"The Keepers of the Dragon's Flame," Aleric replied. "Their insignia of the dragon wrapped around a wizard's staff was the same emblem as the tattoo on the forearm of the mage."

"Where should we start looking for these Keepers of the Dragon's Flame?" Thearbuc wondered aloud. "Maub? He is the only other magic user around, besides you."

"Only one we know about," Aleric replied with a shrug. "He did, after all, save us from the assassins in the castle. If he had sent them, why wouldn't he have helped them instead of saving us?"

Thearbuc threw up his arms, frustrated. "I don't know. I give up."

"The truth will present itself to us eventually," Aleric said. "Hopefully we can survive it when it does."

Later in the day, the sun was just getting low in the sky when multiple dirt roads came together at a crossroads. At the side of the crossroads there was another sign that read "Skerlin" except the *k* and the *l* were missing as the sign was old and unattended to. In the distance, against the setting sun, they could see the silhouettes of wooden buildings and smoke rising into the sky from chimneys. It looked much larger than the previous village they found, and more used to visitors.

"We are here," Aleric spoke, stating the obvious. "The town of Skerlin."

As they descended upon the town, they found heavily-used, muddy streets with large puddles of stagnant water. The citizens of Skerlin did not seem to travel by horseback, and most wore tall boots to protect themselves from the mud. Everyone seemed to walk with their heads down, facing the mud, and no hellos, greetings, or nods were given to one another.

"People here like to keep to themselves it seems," Thearbuc said, noticing the unfriendly vibe.

"Less likely to run into trouble or get robbed if they keep to themselves," Aleric noted. "Don't talk to anyone. If someone comes up to talk to us, you can bet it's a scam to distract us while someone else picks your pocket."

"Nice place." Thearbuc rolled his eyes and moved his money pouch from his pocket to inside his tunic.

"Just keep an eye out for an inn. We need to find Skerlin's version of the Stray Fox."

"Hopefully an inn that isn't lousy with gold miners." Thearbuc laughed and tried to lighten the mood by making jokes about the place. "I wonder if they've captured their Stone Gnome and are on their way to riches by now."

"Those miners will never catch a Stone Gnome," Aleric said matter-of-factly. The two continued to walk as the sun dipped down past the horizon. "We've got to get off these streets before dark," Aleric said, picking up the pace.

"There!" Thearbuc eventually pointed down a small street as they walked by. "That wooden sign. That must be an inn." They walked towards it in the quickly approaching darkness. It was an inn, a small, two-storied building with a simple sign hanging out.

They entered the establishment to find a surprisingly pleasant mood. It was much different from the loud hustle and bustle of the Stray Fox. This inn was clean, quiet, and only had two people sitting in the lobby, both smoking on pipes and minding their own business. Relief washed over Thearbuc and Aleric as they realized they would finally be able to find some sanctuary and rest.

"Two rooms please," Aleric asked the innkeeper as they approached the counter. The innkeeper looked the two over with a stern look while he silently investigated and judged the two weary travelers.

"One gold," he replied after a long pause, most likely keeping one hand on a weapon behind the counter. Aleric produced the coin from his leather pouch and noticed the innkeeper leaning in and taking a long glance at his coin pouch. His eyes darted away quickly when he noticed Aleric watching him. The innkeeper slowly slid two separate keys over. "We are a nice establishment here," he said. "We don't tolerate any trouble."

"You'll find no trouble from us," Thearbuc replied, cracking his token bright white smile behind his dark black beard. The innkeeper nodded in a respectful manner and pointed the two travelers to the stairs that would lead them up to their rooms. As they turned the corner and were out of sight, the innkeeper glanced at the man sitting alone in the corner of the lobby smoking his pipe. The two exchanged a mischievous nod in unison. The man in the corner got up from his seat, pulled a hood over his head, and exited the inn quietly into the darkness at a brisk pace.

Even though it was early in the evening, Aleric and Thearbuc decided it would be safest if they retired to their individual rooms and ate the bread that they had in their packs for supper instead of going out where they would more than likely become prey to a thief. They were both incredibly tired from their travels anyway, and both hastily agreed to the plan then retired to their rooms for hopefully a long rest and peaceful night of sleep.

Entering his room, Aleric locked the door from the inside. The key jiggled loosely in the lock, but with a little effort he got the lock to click. The room was nice and quiet. The wooden shutter was opened, and he could hear the citizens of Skerlin going about their evening. They were a noisy bunch. Every few minutes there was yelling of some sort in the distance. People angry at each other, someone who had too much to drink, or someone's coin purse being snatched. All these scenarios played out in Aleric's mind as he quietly nibbled on his bread. It was definitely a good idea to stay in tonight, he thought to himself. He closed the shutters for safety and to shut out the unpleasant sounds of the dangerous city.

"How are we going to get out of this city and back over the mountains?" he said aloud, pondering to himself about their situation. *Getting through the mountain passes almost killed us before*, he thought. *Now we have no horses, no gear, and are expected to do it again somehow?* He pulled the coin pouch from his tunic and looked inside at the coins King Victus had given to him before they set out on their journey. Only one coin remained. His heart sank again, and he rolled his eyes heavily at his predicament. Thoughts of living here in Skerlin, homeless on the streets, taking odd jobs until he could build another life here ran through his mind. "That won't happen," he assured himself. Thearbuc had his family to get back to and Aleric had allies and people counting on him back at the castle. They *must* find a way to get back over the mountains to the lands of Mazeron. Even if it almost killed them again.

The severity of their situation was setting in and the dread began pushing him down into the bed with an invisible yet enormous force. Laying in the bed, in the dark room, his thoughts once again turned to Briss. He wished there was a way to blame this horrible situation on anyone else but himself, but he knew deep inside it was him who had torn them apart and his actions alone that put him here in a cold, dark, lonely inn. These dark thoughts accompanied him to sleep and soon were turned into dark dreams.

Suddenly, Aleric stirred awake in the middle of the night. He could see the moon shining brightly outside, coming in through the crack in the shutters. It was high in the sky and no sounds could be heard outside besides a soft wind blowing by. He rubbed his eyes and tried to remember where he was from his deep sleep. Then, out of the silence, he heard a click and the sound of movement. I will never get another full night of sleep, he thought to himself, rolling his eyes.

The clicking sound seemed to be coming from his door. He reached over quietly and put one hand on the hilt of his sword, which was still lying in the bed with him. Then the faint clicks stopped before he was able to pinpoint what they were. Quietly, he listened, but the room stayed completely silent, save the soft wind. Eventually he rolled over to go back to sleep, but a nagging suspicion kept him from relaxing. He needed to know what was going on and where the sound was coming from. Slowly, he got out of bed and crept quietly towards the door. He cracked the door and peeked into the dimly lit hallway.

At the end of the hall, he saw the figure of a person kneeling in front of the door of the room three doors down from his. In the sconce's dim light, he could see that they were well-dressed in a clean, brown leather tunic, leather boots, and had a dark woolen hood pulled over their head, concealing their face. A leather toolkit lay on the ground in front of them. Aleric knew instantly that this was a thief in action. Then, just as he got a glimpse of the thief, he heard the lock click open and the thief quietly entered the room. Aleric sprang into action. He hated injustice and thieves with a burning passion. He rushed quietly back into his room and quickly put on what remained of his light leather armor, then grabbed his sword and exited the room. He lightly tapped at Thearbuc's door before moving down the hallway toward the room the thief had entered.

He peered through the cracked door. He could see them inside, kneeling near the bed and rummaging through the person's belongings. Suddenly, Aleric burst through the door and yelled, "Stop thief!" He grabbed the thief from behind and locked his arms together to detain them.

He didn't know how it happened, but the thief was thin and metaphorically slippery, and in an instant, they had wiggled from his tight grasp and ducked out and under his locking arms. Aleric didn't even see it happen, but out of the shadows a massive kick came and struck him directly in the chest, knocking him over. And suddenly he was lying on the ground realizing this person was a lot more to handle than he had first assumed. He shook off the pain and began to stand back up just as Thearbuc came rushing into the room.

"What is going on?" he yelled. The man in the bed was sitting up and rubbing his eyes, having no clue what was causing all the commotion in his room.

"Thief!" Aleric cried out, pointing toward the open window. Thearbuc just barely saw the shadow jumping through the open window and into the night before they were gone. In just seconds, the thief would be concealed by the blackness of the night and escape, just to return to another victim tomorrow and the next day and the next. Thearbuc and Aleric gave each other a quick glance, nodded to one another, then both were out the window in chase.

They ran through the dark streets and down small alleyways after the would-be thief. Luckily it was a full moon this night, and the thief was not able to disappear into the shadows easily. However, the thief was shockingly fast, with long legs that carried them swiftly and quietly into the night.

"He's strong! Be careful," Aleric huffed at Thearbuc as they sprinted after the assailant. They were losing ground, and before they knew it, they were standing in the center of a crossroads of two quiet streets and did not know which way the thief had gone. Frustrated, Aleric threw his hands into the air while he paced in circles around the intersecting roads. Then they heard a bang and a scuffle coming from the street to their right. They turned quickly and began to run into the darkness.

Turning a corner from one dark alleyway to another, they stumbled across what all the commotion was. It was dwarves. Drunk dwarves! Dozens of them were exiting two pubs across the road from each other with ale steins in their hands and started to meander all in the same direction down the road. There were so many that they acted like a slow, rushing river, pushing along anything and anyone that got in their way.

This was a common occurrence for dwarves in these parts. They would gather in massive groups to drink, sing, and be merry. But when they were good and drunk, they had a tendency to wander. Because of their smaller size and preference for stronger ales, this tendency to wander drunkenly happened more often than not. By now, the people of Skerlin were used to it, and it was just a part of life in these parts. They would drunkenly shuffle out of a pub as slow-moving mob—thick, sturdy bodies, shoulder to shoulder, too drunk to notice anyone else. And anyone or anything in their path would get swept up in the current as they hobbled through the streets. They were never looking for trouble; they weren't even actually very loud. They just wouldn't notice anything else besides great conversation and the taste of good beer and would scoop up whatever got in their way as they went.

Before they had time to realize what was going on, Thearbuc and Aleric were caught in the center of such a congregation. Heavy dwarves thudded and pushed against them as they bumped on by. There was more commotion up ahead and they saw the shadow of the fleeing thief down the road in the distance. It was easy to spot, as Aleric and Thearbuc towered over the sea of shorter dwarves. Aleric pointed and yelled out to Thearbuc, then they began pushing and shoving through the crowd of heavy dwarves to get closer. The thief was significantly slimmer and lighter than Aleric and Thearbuc and quickly began to get washed away in the sea of wandering drunken dwarves. The thief was pushing frantically, but they weren't much taller than the dwarves and began to stumble and get swallowed up by the crowd, likely to get trampled to death without the mob of dwarves even knowing.

"Ayye yuuuu!" a dwarf's voice rumbled out. There was a lot of stirring and laughing up ahead and suddenly the thief was hoisted up and pushed on top of the meandering river of dwarves and carried away with them as they went. The thief rode swiftly on top of the mob of dwarves compared to Aleric and Thearbuc, who were still trying to push and shove their way through it, which only caused a lot of push back and angry grumbles from the drunken dwarves..

"Watch it! Where do you think you're going, skinny bones boy?" one dwarf said, while shoving Aleric surprisingly hard. There was a glaze in his eyes and ale foam dripping from his thick beard.

"I don't want trouble," Aleric replied, trying to keep an eye on the thief as they were swept away. "They're going to kill that person!" Aleric pointed up towards the thief.

"You're going to kill me, eh?" the drunk dwarf replied, rolling up his sleeves exposing thick arms and hammy fists. Before Aleric could speak again, the wind was knocked out of him as a heavy punch from the dwarf found his sternum. He bent over in pain, then in an instant more dwarves were jumping all over him, punching and kicking. All looking for a fight and ready to protect their drunken friend. The lazy procession quickly turned into a brawl. There was chaos everywhere as Aleric and Thearbuc tried to break free of the crowd. The dwarves were too sturdy and heavy. Blows were coming in from everywhere. It happened so fast and there was so much confusion that Aleric didn't even think of using his powers to break them up. He just kicked and flailed as the mob attacked them.

Then his frustration set in, and not even realizing what he was doing, his eyes began to glow, and he let out a massive yell and started throwing dwarves out of his way. He raised both hands and created a ball of energy that he slammed into the ground, creating a massive boom! The river of dwarves broke up in fear and confusion and began to scatter and scurry every which way into the night. None of them were sticking around to find out what was going on or what had created the loud boom.

As the crowd dispersed, Thearbuc spotted the thief once again. They were no more than twenty feet away from each other. For some reason, the thief had stopped fleeing and instead was standing still, staring silently at Thearbuc. He stared back, looking confused. It was just a moment that they stared at each other before out of the darkness of the alleyways, a massive beast came charging into the crowd. It smashed through the dispersing crowd like a bull, taking many dwarves and the thief down with it. The thief was thrown heavily onto the ground and lost in the darkness of the streets.

A roar rose up from the dwarves as most of them began to flee, while others who saw the beast come raging in stayed to fight it. The beast rolled to the ground and smashed into a wall after first ambushing the crowd of dwarves, but it was quickly back on its feet again and looking around, seemingly searching for something. It didn't take long for it to spot The Paladin, and the two locked eyes. Without hesitation the beast began to pounce, going in for the kill. But from out of the darkness, the moonlight reflected off the blade of a knife, almost too quick to see before it found its way directly into the side of the beast's throat. It was the thief, who after slicing the beast tumbled to the ground having used their last bit of energy. The beast flailed in pain for one moment then too came crashing to the ground where it came to a rest and never moved again.

Aleric and Thearbuc looked at each other, bewildered. It had all happened so fast. The dead beast began to draw a crowd of the few remaining dwarves, but it began to evaporate into black ash then blew away into the wind. With the scene being over, the remaining dwarves scattered, leaving Thearbuc, Aleric, and the thief alone in the dimly lit alleyway.

Thearbuc quickly ran to the thief who was breathing heavily with both hands on the ground, trying to hold themselves up. He bent down and ripped off the thief's hood. In the moonlight, a woman turned to meet his eyes. Taken aback, Thearbuc stood up and took a step backward. Like a wounded animal, she lay there looking back at him, breathing heavily, waiting to see what her pursuers would do next.

"You're…you're a woman," Thearbuc said, not being able to find any words for the chaotic situation.

"A woman who saved us from another beast," Aleric said, approaching the two. He outstretched his arm and helped the woman to her feet. Her hood fell to her shoulders, and they could see her more clearly. She had wavy dark brown hair just past her shoulders, a thin nose and neck, and she was dressed in the finest leather. Her tunic had many straps filled with daggers and miscellaneous tools. She had fancy brown leather boots that were laced up past her ankle and had almost no heel, which partly explained how she was so nimble and fast during the chase. Thearbuc stared at the woman in silence and seemed to make no facial expression behind his thick black beard.

"She's clearly a thief," Aleric said, changing his tone as he looked up and down at the tools and daggers she wore.

"I'm not," the woman snapped back quicky and nervously. "I mean, I don't want to be. I can explain."

"Explain it to the watchmen," Aleric replied.

"She just saved our lives, Aleric," Thearbuc chimed in. Then he turned to the woman. "These Morghvile beasts, they have been tracking us, hunting us since we set out from Mazeron."

"Mazeron!" The woman's eyes lit up. "You are from Mazeron? How did you get here?" she stopped mid-sentence, cutting herself short. "Please, please let me come with you," she continued. "I can help you if you let me explain myself. I've needed to get back there for years, but the mountain passes and all the roads are blocked. I have been stuck here in Skerlin, forced to steal just to survive." There was a pause while she awaited their reply. Aleric stared at the woman and Thearbuc stared at Aleric.

"I believe her," Thearbuc decided, still holding eye contact with the woman. There was a commotion stirring somewhere down the nearby alleyway that was growing louder by the minute. The drunk dwarves were regrouping, most likely looking for a fight, and this time with a bruised ego from The Paladin and the mysterious beast that ruined their merry parade.

"We need to get off the streets," the woman said urgently. "I know a place. If you follow me, I can explain everything and get us out of here."

Aleric glanced at Thearbuc and sighed. "If she leads us into a trap and robs us in a dark alleyway, then it's on you."

"Fine with me," Thearbuc said, already starting to follow the woman as the dwarves grew louder behind them.

Quickly, the three started down a dark alleyway, with the woman thief leading the way. She was like a shadow that defied the laws of physics. Leaping and bounding in the darkness over barrels and carts, agile and weightless. The two could barely keep up, and her agility and focused, smooth movements showed that she could have gone a lot faster if she needed to. Running clunkily behind and breathing loudly and heavily, Aleric and Thearbuc were spotted going through the intersection of two roads.

"There!" a bystander shouted, having gone outside for a smoke in the disturbance. The clatter in the streets grew and they could hear yelling and cursing behind them, echoing down the otherwise quiet streets. Up ahead, the shadow of the woman thief stopped. This street was extra dark with no lanterns and no candles in any windows. Aleric and Thearbuc nearly ran past her, she was almost invisible in the darkness.

"Here," she whispered as they caught up. They stopped running to see that she was kneeling near a merchant's wagon, which was cluttered and unkempt, like it had been there for some time. Quickly she opened a trapdoor that was concealed behind the merchant's wagon. She ushered them in, warning them to be careful on the dark steps. One by one they ducked into the trap door and stepped down in the complete darkness under the streets of Skerlin.

Aleric stopped in the darkness a few steps down and heard the soft clunk of the door closing, leaving them in complete darkness. They stood in the dark silence, listening only to their breaths until the sound of the angry dwarves outside rose to a thunder of heavy, stomping feet then slowly faded away again into the quiet of the night. The three breathed a sigh of relief to be off the streets and safe from the hostile mob of drunken dwarves. The strike of flint broke the silence then a soft light illuminated a dark passageway of stairs ahead.

"Follow me," the woman said, pushing past the two others and leading them down the stone stairwell deeper into the underground. Eventually they entered a small room with old, crude wooden floors where they could see the dirt of the ground between the gaps in the wood planks. There were multiple other doors lining the walls of the secret room. In the center stood a simple wooden table, some books, gold and silver coins, pearl necklaces, and other trinkets that looked like they were worth decent value, and Aleric and Thearbuc wondered why these items were forgotten here in this old, simple room. The woman took her small light and lit the torches on the walls, illuminating the room in a comforting glow.

"Okay, talk," Aleric said in his usual blunt attitude. "Why did you save us from that beast after we chased you through the streets?"

"Ha!" The woman rolled her eyes. "You probably wouldn't believe me if I told you," she said calmly.

"Why is that?" Aleric asked.

"Because it has to do with magic. Which I have. Just. Like. You." She pointed at Aleric with a mischievous playful grin as she spoke. She was clearly a confident person and comfortable here on her home turf beneath the streets of Skerlin.

"No more games," Aleric replied. "Why did you save us from the beast instead of just running off and letting him at us?"

"Because of him," she said quickly, pointing at Thearbuc. "He's a very good person. I can tell."

"Stop being coy!" Aleric snapped.

"Fine, fine, alright," she replied, shying away. She sighed a heavy sigh. "You won't believe me."

"Try me."

"Alright. I have a gift like you. Well, not like yours, though. I can see…I can see energy." Aleric and Thearbuc looked bewildered. "Energies around people," she continued, "the energy of a room, or whatever. Something that you can probably feel in your gut, but I can actually see. It's another sense that we all have, mine is just more…advanced."

"What does that have to do with Thearbuc?" Aleric asked, still somewhat annoyed and not sure if he was buying what she was saying or even where the conversation was going.

The woman sighed again and rolled her eyes like she was embarrassed. "I've never seen anyone with such positive, loving energy." She glanced sheepishly at Thearbuc. "He has a bright, warm light around him like I've never seen. You are one good person, Mr. Thearbuc," she laughed.

"But as for you…" She trailed off as she moved closer to Aleric, looking at him up and down. "Well, you are a confused one, aren't you? A good person filled with sadness and rage. You have bright light being engulfed by clouds of blackness that snuff out the light." Aleric stepped back, insulted as the words hit far too close to home. "What a power struggle it is too," she continued. "Enough energy to fill any room. Which character trait is going to take over? The light or the darkness? Only you can decide that, Paladin."

"What is your name?" Thearbuc interjected, seeing the pale uncomfortableness wash over Aleric's face.

"Lamora," she replied quickly, turning from Aleric. "My name is Lamora and, yes, I am part of the thieves guild, as you have probably already guessed. But I use my powers to justify my profession. I only steal from bad people. As you now know, I can see bad energies in people, so I only steal from them." She paused "Karma in the flesh." She grinned and gave a slight courtesy. "I've been stuck here in Skerlin since I had to flee my home in Mazeron, many years ago. During the magic purges, it wasn't safe for me there. People close to me started to catch on to me and were beginning to realize that I had something special. I had to leave for my own safety."

"So, you became a thief?" Aleric rolled his eyes. His deep-seated hatred for injustice and people who hurt others was not completely swayed by her story.

"I did what I had to do to survive," she snapped back. "And trust me, there is no shortage of bad people worth robbing here in Skerlin." She spit on the ground as she said the dirty city's name. Then the room fell silent, and she purposely left Aleric and

Thearbuc alone in their thoughts to absorb all she had told them before speaking again. "If you are going back to Mazeron, please let me come with you," Lamora finally spoke again. "I take care of myself, always have. I will be no burden to you. The passes are far too dangerous for me to go alone. I have a brother there. I must get back to my home somehow."

Just then, there was more commotion outside on the street. It sounded like the dwarves had regrouped and were out looking for a fight, tossing things around and looking for the three fleeing humans.

"We need to get out of here," Thearbuc said to Aleric anxiously.

"I can lead you safely out of Skerlin through the thieves guild's tunnels." She glanced at the many doors leading out of the room. "Without my knowledge of the route, you'll be lost in the tunnels for days," she said, starting her sales pitch again when Aleric interrupted.

"Fine. You can come with us." He glanced at Thearbuc for reassurance, who nodded that he agreed. "Let's go."

Lamora gave them a big smile and moved toward a door at the far end of the room. "Follow me," she told them again, handing them small torches then lighting them with hers.

The three made their way through seemingly endless, long, dark tunnels. There were doors everywhere. It was like the entire city was connected by underground hallways, built by the thieves guild. Aleric grew dizzy at the enclosed space and numerous quick turns. Lamora was right. This place was a labyrinth that only a few knew the way out of. Aleric noticed as they scurried through the tunnels that there were etchings along the stone walls at many of the junctions. No doubt they were secret codes for the thieves guild to communicate with one another. Which houses had the most loot, where the watchmen were, and directions through the tunnels telling one another how to find each other. It was a very complex system they had created, and all here under the city where no one even knew.

Eventually the three stopped taking twists and turns and began walking straight for some time. Two of their torches had already burnt out, so the mood became nervous and urgent.

"We're almost there," Lamora assured them, confidently leading the way.

After what must have been over two or three miles of walking, the ground began to slant slightly upward until they came to a small wooden door above their heads. Putting her hand through a small slot in the rock, Lamora unlocked a mechanism of some sort, and the door clicked open. She opened the hatch, and they emerged from under a large, felled tree into the blinding light of the sun. Aleric and Thearbuc shielded their eyes and pulled away in discomfort.

"It's morning already?" Thearbuc said, trying to hide his eyes from the blinding light. They were in the woods, on the outskirts of Skerlin. Grass, wildflowers, and trees surrounded them. They could see the village off in the distance. It looked peaceful and nice from this far away. No signs of drunken mobs of dwarves or thieves setting traps for unprepared travelers.

"Let's head for the mountains southeast of here," Aleric said, surveying the landscape. "As far east as we can go. The mountains are steeper over there, so the passes may not be controlled by that many Brigands, if any at all. If we can find a pass, we can drop right back into Mazeron, near the orchards of Briardale, not far from the castle."

"Those ranges can be incredibly high and steep," Thearbuc replied in a worried tone.

"Yes, but there are tales of marauders making their way through them and attacking the villagers near Briardale in the past. If they found a way through, we can find it too." Aleric didn't know it, but the tale he was telling was how his own father had been murdered so many years ago, working the orchards near Barreston's home.

"He's right," Lamora chimed in. "The direct passes to Haberlorn are too dangerous. Nobody that attempts them is ever seen again. The brigands have them locked down. The mountains are almost just as treacherous to the west, and there's rumors of an evil witch that occupies the forests there as well."

"Yes, we know," Thearbuc said sadly. "Kalindra. She has our friend. When we get back to Mazeron we will put together a party to get him back. He was a good friend; we just hope he is still alive."

"Let's keep moving," Aleric said, trying to push the negative thoughts about Brodel out of his mind. "We can get to the mountains by nightfall, get some rest, then tomorrow we start looking for a pathway up the mountain."

So, the three set off. It was a beautiful day as they journeyed along, and Thearbuc commented multiple times how much better these open lands were than the fields and valleys of Haberlorn. Before the end of the day, they had reached the foothills and mountainous areas once again. The mountains here were significantly taller and steeper than the rolling hills of the valley. They gazed in awe at the enormous snow-covered peaks that lay before them, stretching high into the dimming sky.

There were cliffs and waterfalls all around this mountainous region as they traveled. Some waterfalls were hundreds of feet high, and the water would crash down with a thunderous sound. Others were small with a pleasant pool at their base, where one could swim and cool down on a hot afternoon. Thearbuc was in his element here in the forests and mountainous regions. He hiked fast and confidently, sometimes picking up tracks or signs of animals and other travelers along the way. He was a true tracker and a great mountain man, but by the time they reached the steeper parts of the mountains, the light of the day was fading and they were unable to search the area for a trail into the mountains. As they gazed at their next obstacle from a clearing in the trees, their hopes were dashed upon seeing just steep the mountains here were.

"This climb will be tougher than I had thought," Aleric said, sounding concerned.

"There may not even be a pass at all," Thearbuc replied, looking up at the high cliffs that seemed to block the way in every direction. "It may end up costing us many days."

"What other choice do we have?" Aleric snapped back in frustration. "We will surely be captured or killed if we try the main passes again. We barely made it out alive last time, and you can be sure they are looking for us now. Those mountains to the west will be impassable. Searching here to the east is our only option."

"I know, I know," Thearbuc backtracked.

"Maybe we should settle in for the night?" Lamora chimed in, sensing the growing frustration. "I know I'm tired, and if we start looking now, we could rustle up a decent supper." Aleric made a mental note of her choice of words and thought to himself that they seemed a bit rough, as did her personality in general. She was rugged physically and strong mentally. She seemed comfortable and confident out here on the road and never asked for or needed any help from her travel companions.

Aleric paused in thought, trying to think logically through the frustration he was feeling upon seeing the impassable mountains. Then, through the silence, he heard running water. Most likely a waterfall in the distance, somewhere nearby through the woods.

"Okay," he agreed. "Let's make camp and pick up our search for a trail tomorrow." He picked up his pack and started walking. "Follow me."

Aleric led the other two through the scattered trees of the forest toward the sound of running water. Not long later, they came to a clearing that opened up into a soft, flowing waterfall and small pool at the base of it, all surrounded by cliffs and forest. "This should be safe for the night," he remarked.

"I'll find dinner," Thearbuc volunteered, pulling two daggers from his belt with a grin.

"And I'll find dessert," Lamora replied flirtatiously, emptying a small carrying pouch. "I saw some berries not far back." She turned and began to swiftly make her way back into the woods.

"Make sure to return before dark," Aleric said as the two disappeared into the darkening woods. "I'll make the fire."

The three parted ways. There was a lot of work to do before sundown if they were to have a comfortable evening like they wanted. Aleric began to gather firewood, and not long later he had it stacked as high as his shoulders. He knelt down to the teepee of branches he had stacked and put his hands together in the shape of ball. A flame appeared between them which he slowly and carefully placed under the wood to light the fire. Within seconds it began to roar in the soft wind. He grinned at how easy it was to start a fire now and wondered if he would ever get used to having these mysterious powers.

The sun had already dipped below the horizon somewhere, and last bits of sunlight were licking at the high clouds in the sky while Aleric comfortably leaned against a felled tree in front of his warm fire, enjoying the peacefulness of the forest. Finally, Thearbuc returned with two fat jackrabbits and a big smile.

"Dinner is served," he laughed tossing them next to the fire. Lamora came back into the clearing not long after, holding a full bag of berries and fruits. The three gathered around the fire and began to cook and enjoy each other's company. Later, they ate a large, delicious meal and talked late into the night.

"Explain your magical powers to us, Lamora," Aleric asked politely as they sat near the glow of the campfire in the surrounding darkness of the late night. "You mentioned them briefly in the tunnels under Skerlin. What did you mean by you can see energies?"

"Okay," she said somewhat nervously from suddenly being put on the spot. "Well, you know when you meet someone and you get a gut feeling about them? How you can almost instantly sense if you trust them or not?" Aleric and Thearbuc both nodded that they understood. "That is the same thing I have. People and places have an energy about them, and we can all sense it. My sense for it is just a little more advanced than yours. While you can only feel it and hope your gut is getting the correct feeling, I can actually see it with my eyes, as well as feel it strongly in my body."

"Amazing," Thearbuc said, sitting up and giving Lamora his full attention. "What does it look like?"

"The energies around us? They're like whirling clouds circling a person or filling up a room. Some people have dark energy. It engulfs them, blocking out the light from ever reaching them. The dark can be so intrusive that when they are near others, I can see it begin to swallow up their light too."

"That is depressing," Aleric chuckled.

"It's not all bad," Lamora rebutted. "People's light can rub off on others too. Unfortunately, it takes a lot more brightness to block out the dark than it does the opposite. I think the best example is music," she continued as the light from the dwindling fire cast a soft red glow across her face.

"I remember when I first made it to Skerlin. It was a dark time for everyone. It had been a bad year for the crops, so most people had been eating mush and pumpkins for as long as they could remember. The mood was bleak at best." She chuckled and threw a small pebble into the fire. "I remember walking into this pub and the negative energy just consumed the room. I mean, it was just dark, black clouds swirling around everyone, and the whole room was full of negative energy. You could see it on people's faces too. Glum and sad, all of them—expressionless, just staring into their ales. Then a traveler dressed in brightly colored clothes came in, and he had a metal horn instrument with him. Later in the evening he started playing it, and suddenly there were these bright wisps of light coming from the horn and rising into the sky, filling up the room. I remember watching as the wisps of light circled the people one by one and snuffed out their darkness. I watched them smile and pep up almost instantly as it happened. Within minutes the entire room was lit up with happiness and joy. The sound of laughter and conversation filled the room once again as the musician played and danced in the corner of the room." Aleric and Thearbuc sat in silence around the crackling fire, contemplating what Lamora was saying. "I guess it's not that great of a power," she said shyly, in an attempt to take the attention from her. "I mean, if you guys were there you would have been able to feel it anyway. The only difference is I can see it."

"That's incredible," Thearbuc replied. "It must be a burden to see everyone for who they really are and still have to be cordial to them, or not let on what you know about them."

"Well, I'm not all of the time." She chuckled and pulled a fine silver necklace from around her neck. "Sometimes I make sure they get what they deserve," she said. "I told you before, I'm karma in the flesh."

Aleric wasn't amused. "A thief is still a thief," he grumbled.

"That's just his job in law enforcement talking," Thearbuc said jokingly to Lamora. "He worked as one of the castle guards in Mazeron before…Well, before all this."

"I assumed he did," Lamora said, looking Aleric up and down. "The sword and armor kind of give it away. Oh, and the flag he carries with the family crest of King Victus on it." She and Thearbuc laughed together.

"Well, I'm going to turn in," Aleric said, patting his belly to say he had eaten too much and was growing tired.

"Wait," Thearbuc said pushing his shoulder back down before he could stand all the way up Aleric looked at him confused. "Talk with us a bit." Aleric didn't realize it in the moment, but Thearbuc asked this of him because he could sense the flirtatious nature Lamora had towards him, and although Thearbuc enjoyed her company he was not interested in being romantic with her, or anybody for that matter. The wound of losing his wife, although long ago, was still too fresh and he couldn't imagine himself ever being with anyone else. He often wondered if he ever would. He was content with his children and his simple life in the woods. The last thing he wanted was to lead some poor girl on or get himself into an awkward situation with her, as he was a simple man and hated the notion of even the slightest bit of drama. He gave Aleric a pleading look as he squeezed his leg.

"I guess I could stay a little longer," Aleric replied. Lamora seemed to pick up the hint and chimed in, "It's okay. I'm tired too." She stood up and brushed the dirt from her hands and pants. "See you boys in the morning." And with that she walked away from the fire and into the darkness without saying another word. Thearbuc sat with a confused look on his face for a moment.

"Guess you don't need me now," Aleric said with a grin. "I'm turning in too."

Chapter 13: Sophie the Stone Gnome

The next morning Thearbuc awoke to a calm forest. The air was fresh and had a crisp coldness to it. The birds and squirrels and all other types of creatures were out gathering their morning breakfast, and the forest was loud with their songs and chatter. He was enjoying the peacefulness of the morning when suddenly he heard a sound that seemed unnatural to the forest, and it grabbed his attention. He paused, listening intently. Then he heard it again. Thearbuc sat up. It sounded like faint taps in the distance, like something hitting something else. Then he heard a voice. Or at least he thought he did. It sounded like humming or singing in the distance. Quietly, he got up and alerted Aleric and Lamora. Talking only in whispers, they gathered their weapons and put on their shoes to go investigate the sounds.

They crept away from their camp and went into the woods. They could all hear it now, a sporadic sound that forced them to stop and listen for minutes on end before hearing it again and continuing in its direction. They crept silently through the woods until they came upon a clearing, where they saw movement in the distance. Within the concealment of the forest, they ducked behind a large fallen log and peered into the clearing.

It opened into a small field of green grass and wildflowers and was at the base of large cliffs, like their camp the night before, except there was no waterfall or pool of water here. There was a small deer trail that led away from the clearing and into the forest on their left. At the far end of the clearing, nearest the cliffs, they saw a small man moving about. He moved quickly, flitting nervously from one place to another. He hopped up onto a small boulder and jumped toward a tree, grabbing a nut from it. Then he scurried over to a large, felled tree and sat on it. He stared at the nut for a moment then set it on the tree and wacked it hard with a large rock. It made a loud thud as the rock came down and cracked the nut. Aleric, Thearbuc, and Lamora exchanged silent glances. That was the sound they had been hearing.

The small person, who was the size of an older child, swung his legs back and forth from atop the felled tree while he nibbled on the nut he had cracked. Then he began to sing a song. It was a goofy song that made Aleric, Thearbuc, and Lamora curl their brows and silently wonder what was going on. The song was reminiscent of yodeling, and there were many “fiddley-dees” and “fidely-dums.” It was gibberish. Fast gibberish. The small man could really do a tongue twister, the silent observers thought from their hiding place.

“Aleric,” Thearbuc said quietly, tapping him on the shoulder. “I think that is the Stone Gnome those hunters were looking for.”

“A Stone Gnome?” Lamora whispered with doubt and a grin. “Stone Gnomes live underground, my dear. That cannot be a Stone Gnome.”

“There’s been a sighting of one above ground,” Thearbuc replied in a whisper. “There are a bunch of rough gold miners assembling in Tillsboro to hunt down and capture him.”

“I think you might be right,” Aleric whispered back. “Look at his face—he looks old but is the size of a child.”

As the others gazed on, The Gnome continued to enjoy his playful morning in the woods. He wore a small pair overalls with large golden buttons and had large tufts of fur coming out of his ears. He would prance from his large tree and tiptoe across a row of rocks, keeping one foot in the air at a time like he was walking across a balance beam. Then he would jump high and tap his heels together and prance away all while singing his silly song. At one point, he scurried to a fruit tree and did a full summersault before taking a quick hop and picking some fruit from it. Then he went back to his log to eat it, all while singing and swinging his legs gleefully.

“That is our way through the mountains,” Aleric whispered. “Our only way. We can’t go over them. With him we can go *through* them.” Thearbuc and Lamora both looked at Aleric like he was crazy.

“You can’t be serious,” Thearbuc questioned. “The depths of the mountains are no place for our kind. Not to mention Stone Gnomes are notoriously hard to catch. And by hard, I mean impossible.”

“Hard to catch?” Aleric whispered back with a smirk. “Look at him. We’ll just pick him up. He’s basically a child.”

“You can’t just take him,” Lamora interjected. “Just go out there and talk to him. Make nice and offer him something. He might be willing to help us.” Aleric and Thearbuc looked blankly at one another. It barely registered in their brains that you could accomplish things in other ways besides brute force.

"That's actually a good idea," said Aleric after moment's pause. Thearbuc shrugged and agreed "Okay then," Aleric continued in a whisper. "Just in case, Thearbuc, you go over and guard that trail to the right. And Lamora, you guard over there by the cliff. Don't let him get by if he runs off!" The two nodded, then, without warning, Aleric arose from behind the fallen log and began to calmly walk into the clearing.

"Well, hello there!" Aleric announced his presence from far off with a wave of his hand. The Gnome jumped in startlement and dropped his fruit to the ground. He looked at the large man approaching him, looked down at his fallen fruit, then looked back up to Aleric again with a look that was both angry and frightened at the same time.

"Hello to you too, I guess," The Gnome said quickly, his eyes darting back and forth looking for possible escape routes.

"Are you a Stone Gnome?" Aleric asked in a friendly voice, yelling from a distance.

"Who's asking?" the little man snapped. "I mean, no. No, I am not a Gnome. Have you ever seen a Gnome this tall? I don't even wear a hat. Of course I'm not a Gnome," he said in a shaky but irritable voice.

"Don't be scared. I am not here to capture you or hurt you," Aleric said, reassuringly.

"They all say that!" the Stone Gnome snapped again, taking a few steps backward. "They always trying to get old Sophie. Take him away is what they want," he trailed off as he said it, still sizing up his escape routes.

"We are trying to get passage through the mountain," Aleric announced. "King Victus will reward you handsomely if you can help us. We are stuck in this valley and need to get back home to the other side of these mountains, back to the kingdom of Mazeron."

"We?" The Gnome asked. "Who is we?" His eyes were darting about, his arms out wide and knees crouched, ready to be pounced on. "No, you don't! You don't get Sophie!" he suddenly cried out. He turned and ran quickly down the deer trail to flee the approaching man. His legs were small, but he was unnaturally fast. As he made for the trees, Thearbuc stepped out of the shadows and blocked the way. He raised his hand calmly, motioning for The Gnome to stop. The Gnome shrieked then turned and ran back toward the clearing where Aleric was closing in. The Gnome was only a few feet away from Aleric when it stopped mid-stride. "Oh, no you don't!" The Gnome said angrily. Out of nowhere, lightning type bolts burst from his fingertips and struck Aleric. In just a flash the magic bolts engulfed him, and within mere moments he was completely turned into stone.

Where Aleric once stood there was now a statue of him, frozen in time with an outstretched arm, forever to be a stone statue here in the forest. Thearbuc and Lamora, both watching from a distance, were shocked and frightened at what they had just witnessed. They weren't expecting any sort of attack from the small, innocent-looking gnome. They did not even know Stone Gnomes were hostile when confronted. One moment their friend was there with them, and now they stared blankly at the statue that resembled him in complete shock.

"Not so tough now, are we knight?" The Gnome laughed hysterically. "You think you can just take old Sophie? No, you can't! None of them can. They all think they can, but they can't take old Sophie. Only Sophie tells Sophie where Sophie can go!" he said, spitting on the stone statue of Aleric and continuing his angry rants.

"The Gnome is losing his mind," Thearbuc mumbled aloud, in shock and suddenly quite terrified of the little creature.

"You never take Sophie!" The Gnome finished his ranting, as he had begun to tire out. Then, finally, he turned to walk away from his victim when there was the sound of cracking that echoed off the cliffs of the small clearing. Thearbuc and Lamora's eyes darted back and forth, waiting for what was coming next. Then the stone encasing Aleric began to crumble. Small cracks turned into large chunks of stone that crumbled to the ground until The Paladin stood there once again with glowing eyes of fiery amber. He shook the stone dust from his body.

"Very clever," The Paladin said, moving toward The Gnome, clenching his teeth in anger and ready to wring his little neck.

Sophie shrieked in alarm. "Aaaah!" he yelled out in his high-pitched voice. He sent another burst of magic from his fingertips toward The Paladin and once again turned him into stone. The forest was quiet again for a moment. The Gnome, Thearbuc, and Lamora all held their breath as to what was going to happen next.

Then the stone began to crumble around The Paladin once again. He shook it off within moments this time, then began his advance towards The Gnome. So, The Gnome fired again, turning The Paladin into stone a third time, only for him to break free moments later. Then again, and again. Every time he turned The Paladin into stone, the thinning layers of stone surrounding him would shatter and he would break free and take one more step closer. He was slowly closing in on The Gnome. Pushing him further in towards the cliffs and cutting off his escape routes.

Finally, The Gnome was backed against the cliff. There was nowhere else for him to go, and The Paladin's strength had overpowered his magic. The Paladin grabbed The Gnome by the throat and lifted him up to his glowing eyes.

"I give up! I give up!" The Gnome yelled in a terrified voice. "What do you want with me? Please don't take me into the mountains. I will make you diamonds. I will make you rich. Don't make Sophie go into the mountains!" he wailed out in utter distress.

"Why are you so scared of going into the mountains?" The Paladin asked, shaking The Gnome in anger, still very upset from being turned into stone multiple times. "You are clearly a Stone Gnome, after all."

"Sophie can't! Sophie can't!" The Gnome cried out. "It's so dark, so scary," he said between panting breaths. "Sophie gets stuck. It's so dark. So dark." Tears streamed from his frightened eyes. Aleric's glowing eyes returned to normal as his anger faded, and in frustration he dropped The Gnome in the dirt with a heavy thud.

"Tie him up, please," he said, rolling his eyes to Thearbuc who was approaching from the woods. "So we don't have to go through all that again." Thearbuc pulled a rope out of his pack and began to tie up The Gnome. "So, we've come all this way and you can't help us get through the mountains?" Aleric asked Sophie again, going back to their original plan of trying to be nice to the odd, little creature.

"Sorry, sir," The Gnome replied sheepishly. "Small dark spaces, small dark spaces," he began to mumble to himself repeatedly.

"You're claustrophobic?" Aleric asked, wrinkling his brow. Sophie nodded yes as he sat nervously on the ground. "Well, aren't you a sad case. A claustrophobic Stone Gnome." Aleric continued as Lamora approached from the forest, "Afraid of your own domain? Well, I am going to help you get over your fear. You will take us through the mountains, or I will cut off your head right now and put you out of your misery. How do you like that?" He winked at Lamora as he unsheathed his longsword and showed the sharp blade to Sophie who began to panic and squirm at the sight of it. "Death might be a gift for someone in such a sad case as yours," Aleric continued to threaten The Gnome. "What do you say, hmmm?" He stared heavily at The Gnome, who tried to look away from the intimidating large man.

"Don't hurt Sophie. Don't hurt Sophie. Sophie will help. Sophie will take you through the mountain," he finally answered.

"I believe you will," Aleric replied. "I think it will be good for you. Who knows, after this you might become a pro at it. After all, they do say what doesn't kill you makes you stronger."

"This *will* kill us," muttered The Gnome.

"What was that?" Aleric asked.

"Nothing, sir. Sophie will take you. Don't hurt Sophie."

"You will receive payment from King Victus when we get to the other side. You have my word, Gnome. There is no time to waste, let's get at it."

The three began to gather their things and get ready for the trek through the mountains. Sophie was tied up to Aleric so he couldn't escape, and the unlikely company started making their way toward the tall cliff at the far end of the clearing.

"This should be a good place to enter," Aleric spoke loudly to the others.

"It is, it is," The Gnome replied. "But Sophie hasn't moved the rock in a long time. Sophie needs some time."

"Take all the time you need, Sophie," Lamora said nicely. "We will wait for you to be ready."

With that, Sophie turned towards the mountain and raised his arms, and a ball of light and energy began to form in front of him. The other three could feel the energy moving through the air, and it shook their clothes like a slow, invisible shockwave. The rocks in front of them began to vibrate like an earthquake. Then suddenly, The Gnome and Aleric were gone. Just disappeared into thin air. Thearbuc and Lamora gasped and stepped back in disbelief.

Just inside the mountain, Aleric and Sophie stood near the mouth of what looked like a cave. Sophie dropped his arms and stared at his hands in disbelief.

"See, I knew you could do it, Sophie," Aleric said, patting The Gnome's back. Looking back at his friends, he could see they were still standing outside the entrance of the cave. "Come on in!" he yelled out to them. But they were looking bewildered and confused, and it seemed like they could not hear him. "I said it's okay!" Aleric yelled toward the cave entrance with cupped hands. "Come on in!" He was yelling loudly but Thearbuc and Lamora couldn't seem to hear him. Aleric looked at Sophie who had a frustrated and angry look on his face. The Gnome was looking at the rope tied him to Aleric, then The Gnome threw it angrily to the ground.

"You were going to ditch us, weren't you?" Aleric said, shocked.

"Stupid rope," Sophie muttered. "Makes you come with me."

"Okay, back out we go then. We are not leaving my friends."

Sophie sighed heavily in frustration, and with a sudden burst of light the two appeared back outside the mountain and in front of Thearbuc and Lamora again.

"Here, you have to tie up too." Aleric tossed a length of rope to Thearbuc. "If you aren't connected to Sophie, then it won't work. He tried to sneak one past us, didn't you?" he said, yanking the rope hard on Sophie.

Thearbuc and Lamora tied up, and after checking that all the knots were tight and secure, they were all tied together and ready to try again. Aleric began giving Sophie a threatening speech about what he would do to them if he tried to evade them again, but The Gnome was simply not interested. He just folded his arms and looked away, occasionally spitting on the ground to show his distaste for the situation.

Seeing that threats against The Gnome would not work, Lamora made her way over to Sophie and gently pushed Aleric to the side. “Let me try,” she said to him. She crouched down in front of Sophie and gently cupped his face.

“Sophie, please don’t hurt us. We need you to get to the other side of the mountains. You can come back here as soon as we are done. Aleric says the king will give you whatever you want for helping us.”

Sophie’s hardened face slowly softened, and eventually he looked towards Lamora. “Sophie will help,” he said in a defeated tone.

She patted him on the head gently as she stood up. “See, Paladin, brute force isn’t always the best way to get what you want,” she said with a smirk.

“Okay then,” Aleric announced aloud, indicating they were ready. “Sophie,” he said with a nod toward The Gnome. Sophie stepped up to the cliff and once again raised his arms until a bright light emitted from them, and in a snap, they stood inside of the mountain.

From where they stood it looked like they were at the back of a small cave. Light illuminated from the entrance, and they could see the clearing where they had just been. The cave walls pulsed like a wave from the remnants of the magic that had pushed them through the stone. Lamora walked toward the cave entrance with bewilderment on her face, but only made it a few steps before she smashed into an invisible wall and hit her head on an unseen stone. “Ouch!” she cried out.

“Don’t stray far from Sophie,” The Gnome said, realizing she had gone too far away from his magic and ran into a wall.

“I see that,” she said, rubbing her forehead.

“Follow Sophie now.” The Gnome began to move forward. Into the darkness of the mountain, they went. The bright entrance grew smaller and smaller behind them until it was just a dot of light then gone altogether. Sophie led the way with arms outstretched before him, carrying two balls of magical light that allowed them to move freely through the rock and illuminated the small area around them. Inside, the mountain the air was heavy and stagnant all around them, suffocatingly calm, and not even a wisp of a breeze was felt. The cold rock surrounding them dripped with cool water that trickled through the earth. Lamora could see now why The Gnome did not like it in here. Claustrophobia was the norm, and it felt like at any moment the mountain could swallow them up and leave them to die slowly, encased in stone and unable to move in this dark tomb, never to be found.

Hours and hours went on as they made their way through the mountain. Not much was said to one another here in the dark depths, and the mood was tense and frightening. One by one, they realized they had no idea how long this journey would take, and it began to feel like they would never see the light of day again. They also started to realize just how much trust they were putting into the kidnapped Stone Gnome. If he wanted to, he could take them deep into the earth to wander lost forever.

Miserable minutes bled into miserable hours as they continued through the darkness. As they delved deeper into the mountain, the stone walls around them started to change. Large veins of quartz gave way to thick veins of shiny gold. At one point, something in the walls and ceiling began to flicker, reflecting the light from Sophie's magic. They were diamonds. Countless diamonds. Like a million stars on a dark night, they glinted and glittered in an awe-inspiring display of natural beauty. Lamora, naturally, tried to pick some from the stone but could not.

"They are buried in stone, they are," Sophie remarked. "We are passing through them. They only look like they can be moved, but they are still buried deep in the mountain. Lamora rolled her eyes in frustration, leaving a giant diamond half the size of her fist behind and continuing on, deeper into the mountain.

More hours passed. Had it been over a day by now? Despite the long, exhausting trek, little rest was had. Deep inside a dark mountain was no place to stay any longer than needed, and it was unknown if Sophie's magic was infinite or if it could run out any moment, and they'd instantly be crushed by the weight of the mountain. Either way, all of them just wanted to get out of the mountain and back to the surface world as soon as possible. Time seemed to stand still down here. There was no way to tell how many hours or days it had been, but it felt like months. Like a bad dream when your movements are slowed down and you are stuck for eternities on end, only to wake up and find that it had only been a few minutes.

At one point, it began to feel warmer. Alot warmer. The rock and air around them felt hot and thick, like a room filled with steam. Their lungs gasped for air, and although they were breathing, it felt like nothing was going in. It enveloped them like a heavy blanket and began to smother them, only making the claustrophobia and anxiousness worse.

"Sophie!" Lamora spoke between heavy breaths, gasping for air. "We have been down here for days it seems. Aren't the mountains only several miles from one side to the other? Maybe a half day's travel?" Sophie suddenly stopped in his tracks and began to think.

"Ooooooh," The Gnome wailed out in distress. Aleric, Thearbuc, and Lamora exchanged worried and confused glances at one another. "No, no, no!" Sophie yelled out frustrated and angry, pounding his fists along the stone walls and pulling his hair.

"What is going on?" Lamora asked worriedly.

"Sophie took us down. Down too deep. Sophie hasn't been inside the mountains in so long, Sophie can't!" The poor Gnome was about to be in tears.

"Are you telling us that we have been going down instead of straight through the mountain?" Thearbuc asked.

"Ooooooohs!" The Gnome wailed again, falling to the ground in despair. "Too deep!" he wailed. "Too deep!!"

Aleric reached into his tunic and pulled out a small coin, which he raised to his head and dropped to the ground. Sure enough, the coin did not fall straight down but rather at an angle, and landed not at his feet but a few strides away.

"We've been going downward at an angle," Aleric stated with frustration.

The three began to panic and shout questions to the despairing Gnome. "Can we go straight up?" they asked. "Have we gone through the mountains already and are underneath the valley?" The questions began to roll in to the frightened Gnome, who was just lying on the ground, tucked in a fetal position and shaking.

"Sophie, can we start going up again!?" Aleric asked sternly.

"Sophie can't control it!" he wailed in reply.

"Are you saying we can't get out? We can only go downward?"

"Oooohs!" The Gnome wailed out again in despair.

"He told us he hadn't mastered his magic," Lamora stated, reminding the others that this had always been a possibility. Then finally The Gnome stopped whimpering and all was silent again, just for a moment.

"Uh oh," Sophie said slowly, looking at a hole in the rock, down near their feet where he lay. He put his hand up to the hole and paused…

"Ruuuuun!!!" The Gnome screamed out, jumping to his feet. He threw his hands into the air and his ball of magic grew large and bright, illuminating and showing them further into the distance than before. He began to run and yanked on the rope hard, pulling the others along. They followed The Gnome, not knowing why until suddenly they felt the air around them getting extremely hot and heard a blast of noise from behind them. They turned back just in time to see a blast of hot, steaming air blow through the hole like a cannonball. Then hot lava followed it, spewing through the vents in bubbles and burps.

"We would have been cooked!" Aleric said, still shocked. "You saved us Sophie."

"I wouldn't say that just yet," Thearbuc replied, pointing into the distance where Sophie's increased magic was illuminating. They turned to see a sea of holes and vents scattered all through the ground and walls.

"The vents," Sophie said with a whimper. "I led us right into the vents." He lowered his head in shame and defeat.

"Thermal vents," Thearbuc continued. "Each one ready to blast lava or steam hot enough to melt the skin from our bones at any given second." Some of the vents were filled with lava, which appeared to them as thin towers of lava, flowing upward in the mountain.

"Those will be easy to avoid," Aleric said, pointing at the upward-flowing lava. "It's the vents that blast the heated air and steam that will get us."

"Can we just back out?" Thearbuc asked.

Sophie turned around and illuminated the area behind them. It opened up into a vast area of just the same. They were trapped in the middle of a field of thermal vents.

"Well at least we know where we are," Aleric said in a somewhat joking manner. "There are pools of naturally heated hot water at the west end of the valley, just a few days journey from the villages. I suspect these vents are what heats them. If we can just get out of here, I know we are close to the edge of the mountains." As he said it, the ground beneath them began to rumble, and in an instant, Aleric looked down to see that he was standing directly on top of a vent. Without thinking, he pushed, tucked, and rolled away from the hole just as a powerful blast of hot steam exploded from the vent. The droplets burned the group as they rained down around them, but the bulk of the hot blast was avoided.

"That was close," Thearbuc said, as lava began to slowly burp up from the hole and spill onto the floor surrounding them.

"This isn't safe," Lamora's shaky voice added. "We need to get out of here!"

"Agreed," they all said in unison and started to run. Not knowing where, just away from here, they ran aimlessly into the minefield of thermal vents, dodging from side to side as blasts of air, lava, and steam burst all around them. As they fled, the anxiety within all of them grew as they realized the vents and climbing lava seemed to go on as far as they could see, with no end in sight.

"Which way do we run?" Lamora cried out, dodging a blast of steam near her hip.

"One of these is going to get us!" Thearbuc yelled as they ran through heat and stone. "We can't doge them all!" He jumped high over a large crack in the floor. As he looked down in midair, he could see the glow of flowing lava coming from far down below.

"This whole place could blow at any moment," Lamora said, gasping for air. She noticed the number of blasts and vents around them was increasing, and the situation had become alarmingly more dangerous very quickly. Running fast, she jumped over a large vent just as a blast of steam blew through it and caught the back of her leg, burning her badly. She fell to the ground and grabbed her shin, trying to pull the melting leather away from her skin. In the moment of extreme pain, she rolled right over another vent. But before another explosion of steam could blast through it, Aleric lunged toward her and lifted her off the ground. The two stumbled backward and Lamora realized she had almost been cooked. They stayed for a few moments to catch their breath, making sure neither of them were near any more vents. The smell of sulfur filled the air around them so thick they could barely breathe, and almost didn't want to breathe it smelled so bad. Hot steam dripped down the stone walls, and the sounds of flowing lava, gases, and steam gurgled around them.

"I'm okay," Lamora assured the others, who were investigating her burnt leg. "Let's go." She helped Aleric to his feet, and soon the group was off again.

Fear gripped them as they ran through the field of thermal vents. The thought of coming to an untimely end here in the dark depths of earth consumed their thoughts, and the only thing anyone could think of was running—running as far away from here as possible. They had almost given up on ever seeing the sun or feeling a cool breeze again and succumbed to the fact that they would most likely become entombed deep in the earth forever. But Sophie, who had been silently running in a sweaty panic, yelled something inaudible ahead of them. The others looked ahead to see Sophie pointing at something in front of them with an excited look on his hot, red, sweat-covered face. There in the distance was a large half-circle carved into the wall of the stone. As they got closer, they realized that it was a large tube, slanting upward.

"A dormant vent!" Aleric yelled out.

"Let's hope it's dormant," Lamora replied. As they approached the tube, it began to stand out more and more from the surrounding stone. Sophie stopped in front of it and suddenly seemed to act scared, cowering away from it. Aleric realized what was going on, and with no other choices left, he turned and pushed his arm through the invisible stone surrounding them and into the vent.

"It's not hot," he said to the others. Without another word, Sophie jumped into the vent, with the others following close behind. In an instant everything around them went dark, and they all collapsed onto the cool ground in complete darkness.

Thearbuc took a large, heavy breath. "The air is cool," he said, saying what the others were thinking. "Can we get some light?" Then there was a glow of light against the cave walls as The Paladin's eyes began to glow and an orb of light formed between his cupped hands. Sophie was lying on the ground panting for breath and looking like he had spent every bit of nerve he could muster to get them out of the field of hot vents.

"You did it, Sophie!" Lamora said, thanking The Gnome and reassuring the poor little guy that things were going to be okay.

"You take Sophie into the mountains. Sophie says no. Sophie hates mountains…" The Gnome trailed off and quietly continued with his upset rant in low mumbles.

"This vent continues upwards," Aleric said, ignoring the distraught Gnome. "We can follow it up and straight out of the mountain."

"I need a minute," Thearbuc said, leaning against the wall and holding his side, indicating he was in pain. His face was black with soot from the run through the vents. The air in the tunnel, although stale, was welcomingly fresh compared to the feeling of moving through solid stone. The small party was in no rush to move on and took some time to rest before continuing.

After a quick rest, they were on the move again, and once again the journey was more difficult than first expected. Aleric led the way with glowing eyes, as they always were when he used magic. Between his hands the orb of light illuminated the path ahead. Behind him walked Lamora then Sophie then Thearbuc in the rear. They were all still tied together as to not get lost or let Sophie disappear. Although the tunnel was large, they had to crouch as they walked, and some areas became so steep or tight to where they had to crawl to get through to the other side.

More hours went by as they climbed upward. It was like climbing a mountain but with no sun or breeze upon the skin. They breathed in the thick, stagnant air and tried to fight off fatigue to keep going.

"How deep were we?" Lamora asked, panting for air. "We've been climbing forever."

The newfound hope they had gained once they entered the tunnel had long gone, and it once again felt as if they would never see the light of day or feel the fresh air upon their skin. No one replied to Lamora, as no one really knew how deep they had gone. The time just continued to slog on miserably as they hiked upward in the darkness.

Finally, after hours of climbing, Aleric broke the silence as they had trudged along. "Look!" he said excitedly, pointing ahead. The others looked to see that along the wall of the tunnel, there was a very faint light flickering on the stone. It was small and faint, but it was there. Upon further inspection, they found a small crack in the wall above their heads with light illuminating through it. Standing on his toes, Aleric peered through…

"We're out!" he whispered to the others in the dark tunnel. "I can see a lit torch and a hallway on the other side. As he turned to peek through the crack again, the black shadow of a cloaked person went past the crack and startled him. "There's people in there," he whispered to the others. "Sophie, we need you one more time." The Gnome reluctantly accepted Aleric's outstretched hand, and he pulled Sophie up from the ground.

Sophie was already sweating nervously again about going back into the mountain when he raised his arms once again to create the magic that would allow them to move freely through the rock. Suddenly, a large hole opened in the tunnel wall, and they stepped through and into the mountain once again. The air changed in an instant, and all their hearts dropped at the same time to be back in the dreadful situation again.

"It's just for a moment," Aleric said, reassuring the others. "We are almost out of here." Then he led Sophie around the hallway, but they did not cross into it. They stayed inside the mountain until they could explore the area and make sure they did not drop themselves into the den of an unfriendly cave dweller of some sort. After some time, Aleric gave them the go-ahead and the four tumbled through the stone wall and onto a corridor floor. Fresh air once again engulfed them, and they gasped deep breaths to feel its refreshing coolness on their lungs.

One by one, they stood back up and observed the area. The hallway they stood in was well-lit with evenly spaced-out torches lining the stone walls. The ground was dirt and showed evidence of high use as it was patted down firmly. Somewhere in the distance they heard the low sound of voices bouncing off and echoing through the stone chambers beyond.

"People!" Aleric whispered. "That way." He pointed, and the party began to quietly move toward the low, echoing sound. As they made their way through the stone corridors, they twisted and turned like a maze through the mountain. They began to wonder again just how long they would have to wander to get where they needed to be. But there was at least hope now, as the sounds they were hearing were getting louder and closer.

"It sounds like chanting," Thearbuc whispered to the group. It did. It was harmonious in tone and reverberated and echoed smoothly through the corridors. The hallway they were in seemed to be spiraling inward, they noticed, as the pathway veered right in tighter and tighter circles like it was taking them to the spiral center. Then ahead of them appeared a wall in the hallway and an open doorway to its left. They approached stealthily and quietly then peered inside.

It was a large chamber room, deep in the mountain. The far end from where they stood was well lit, but here in the back of the chamber they were concealed in the shadows. Looking in, they saw a small group of cloaked men.

"Sorcerers," Lamora said. "Bad ones. The room is filled with dark energy." The sorcerers were all wearing thick, dark wool hoods and hats that concealed their faces and draped down to the floor. They were standing in a circle, looking at something, but the circle was closed tight and Aleric and the group could not see through from their position. Then the sorcerers began chanting again. Low and slow, it reverberated through the chambers like a ghostly song.

"What are they saying?" Thearbuc whispered.

"Not sure," Aleric replied. "It's either another language or echoing too much to understand." They continued to watch from the back of the room as the chanting grew louder. Eventually, one of the cloaked men moved to the front of the room and, they could see a stone podium with a large book on it, which the sorcerers appeared to be reading from. Aleric and his group of friends did not know it, but this particular book was actually two books, and they had once belonged to Aleric's grandfather, Barreston. Near the podium stood what looked like a round water well made of stone, built up to about waist height.

"Weird place for a well," Thearbuc mentioned. "There's no water here in the center of the mountain."

As the chanting grew louder, a blue light in the shape of an orb began to hover above the well and started to float above the cloaked sorcerers. It grew quickly in size into a large sphere, larger than two men's arm spans. The center of the orb was bright, but the edges were foggy like clouds, wispy and fading from bright to dim.

"This is black magic. Dark magic," Lamora said quietly with a shakiness in her voice. "Banned in these parts for decades. How are they doing this?" she whispered.

"The stone walls," Aleric whispered back. "They do magic here, concealed in the depths of the mountain, so no one else can sense that they are doing it. This is some secret society that has survived the times of the magic ban, probably by hiding in plain sight among us and only working magic here underground."

"What is that emblem on the far wall?" Lamora asked, squinting. Thearbuc and Aleric peered past the cloaked men to the emblem that was carved into the stone walls and illuminated by the floating orb of light. It was a dragon wrapped around a wizard's staff. The same emblem that they had seen before. They both turned to look at each other at the same time and their stomach's lurched. They knew instantly. It was the same emblem that they had found tattooed on the forearm of the mischief mage out near Thearbuc's woods, and the same emblem that the guards atop the mountain wore on their shields and armor.

"What was that name that soldier in the mountains said he worked for?" Thearbuc asked in a whisper.

"The Keepers of the Dragon's Flame," Aleric replied as his stomach lurched.

"We found them," Thearbuc whispered, as they ducked back behind the concealment of the wall.

"Could there really be a secret society of sorcerers that survived all this time? And that are after us?" Aleric asked, thinking aloud.

"After *you*, you mean!" Thearbuc replied, trying to whisper. "You are a magic user. New in town. They don't want you upsetting the balance of things. It's plain as day—they see you as a threat," he said, slightly raising his arms. Aleric reached to unsheathe his sword, but Thearbuc grabbed his arm and stopped him. "You really aren't thinking about fighting a group of powerful sorcerers, are you?" he asked, as a worried look washed over his face.

"We have all the evidence we need that these are the people who have been trying to kill us. We can't just walk away and let them continue coming after us," said Aleric.

"We have no idea how powerful these sorcerers could be," Thearbuc replied. "Their magic could overpower you instantly. If they see us here, then we're all dead. We need to get out of here alive, then we can come back with the king's soldiers," he pleaded.

"Yes, we need to get out of here," Lamora interrupted, starting to panic. No one else could see what she could see, but the entire room had just filled with a dark cloud of energy. It came spewing from the well like black fog then dropped low to the floor and began filling up the room. It whipped and swirled around the cloaked, chanting sorcerers and crept towards Lamora's face, taunting her as she was unable to do anything about it besides witness it. Then, before anyone could reply, the glowing magical orb began to change. Within the center of it a shape began to form. A dark shadow, small at first but growing quickly, until it was almost the size of the entire orb.

"It looks like a bull running toward us," Thearbuc said aloud as the shadow started to take shape, but no one else heard him. With an explosion of blue light, a large shadow burst forth from the orb. Then, moving as fast as the wind, it came towards them with frightening speed then suddenly turned and whisked past them, disappearing down the corridor. None of them had time to say it, but the shadow had the shape of the Morghvile that had been stalking and hunting them across mountains and valleys.

It all happened so fast, and the beastly shadow exploding from the orb was too much for Sophie's nerves to handle. He let out a giant uncontrolled shriek as the Morghvile blew past them. Sophie's shriek pierced the room, and all in one moment the sorcerers ceased their chant, and the magical blue orb collapsed on itself and disappeared. Simultaneously, all the cloaked sorcerers turned and stared straight at the four spies watching from the shadows.

"Save me! Save me!" Sophie screamed out suddenly. "They've kidnapped me! Save me!" Thearbuc grabbed the squelching Gnome that had given them away and tucked him under his arm like a child, and they all began to run. The cloaked men were already making their way toward the trespassers. To buy some time, The Paladin blasted a fireball into the group, but almost in unison all the cloaked men waved their arms and destroyed the blast with some sort of invisible force. Three blue-colored blasts were returned to The Paladin as he ducked behind the entryway and started rushing down the corridor. He felt the heat and shockwave on his back as they exploded into the wall behind him.

They ran hard and fast, twisting and turning through the stone corridors. They narrowly avoided being hit by a barrage of magic blasts from the pursuing sorcerers every time the pathway took a turn. Just as they were getting tired, wooden doors began to appear in the stone walls.

"Get us out of this deathtrap!" Aleric shouted ahead to Thearbuc, who was already trying the first door. He pushed and pulled hard on the doors as he ran, not even fully stopping as he checked it.

"It's locked!" he yelled back.

"There!" Lamora pointed. "Try that one!" It, too, was locked. They smashed into doors as they ran, all the while losing headway on the pursuing sorcerers. Every door seemed to be locked. Then, finally, Thearbuc laid a heavy shoulder into one of the doors and it crashed open, Thearbuc falling hard on the floor inside. Lamora and Aleric followed close behind and slammed the door shut behind them. Just moments later they heard the commotion of the sorcerers rushing past the door, and for a moment they felt like they had lost and outsmarted them.

They stood in the dark silence for a few moments, then The Paladin created a ball of light in his right hand so they were able to look around the room. There was a large table in the center of the room and a few unlit torches along the walls. Besides a few scattered books on the ground, nothing else was in the room.

"Quick, the table," Aleric whispered in a hushed voice. With a heave and a shove they pushed the table in front of the door to block it.

"We're trapped," Thearbuc said as he paced the perimeter of the room, pounding on the stone to find an exit. "Sophie, you got us into this, you've got to get us out of it," he said angrily to The Gnome.

The Gnome folded his arms, tucked his chin low, and slightly turned away from the large man scolding him like a misbehaved boy. "Sophie doesn't care," he grumbled like a pouting child.

Aleric snapped at the phrase. "You make me lose my temper, Gnome!" he said, standing tall over him and unsheathing his sharp longsword. It glinted in the torchlight as it moved across

Sophie's frightened face. Smooth, cold steel—as sharp as any object could get. The Paladin's eyes were glowing with the rage he had built up from their long, exhausting journey that ended in nothing but being trapped once again. He raised the sword above his head, and just as it seemed he was about to strike The Gnome down, Sophie gave a frightened shriek, waved his arms, and dove headfirst into the stone walls.

Then it was dark. Almost completely dark and silent. And the stuffiness of the air was back. The four looked around at the same time and found themselves a few feet inside the stone walls. The portal from Sophie's magic showed the room they were just standing in, empty, only a few feet away.

"You saved us again, Sophie!" Aleric said with a smile on his face while grabbing The Gnome by the shoulder in a playful, friendly manner. "You thought I was going to kill you?" he laughed aloud. "I just had to scare you back into the mountain. I am truly sorry, my little friend."

Sophie gave Aleric a look that he would gladly kill *him* if he could and humphed once again, like a child throwing a tantrum. Then soon, there was a commotion coming from the room, and a loud thud as someone on the other side of the door slammed hard against it.

"That table should hold until we can get out of here," Thearbuc mentioned. He hadn't even finished the sentence when the door suddenly exploded into pieces and sent a shockwave into the room, blowing everything about in a violent explosion. A large sorcerer, taller than the doorway, entered the room, ducking under the doorframe. The other sorcerers followed. One by one, they entered the room and looked around bewildered.

"No one is here," one hissed low under his cloaked hood. "It could have been a decoy, created by magic. Search the caves. Find them!" His voice hissed like a snake and the hair stood up on Lamora's arms as she saw the evil surrounding him.

"Please get us out of here," she said, shaking Aleric's arm with a worried look. "These people are not good. They'll find us here. They are magical too."

"Sophie, let's go," Aleric whispered.

So once again they made their way through the mountain with the use of Sophie's magic. They only had to walk a short distance this time until they came to the edge of the mountains where they could see the forests and clearings beyond, out in the open world. But they did not immediately exit the mountain. They wanted to be sure the area was clear, and they would not be found by the secret society of sorcerers who they now knew were known as The Keepers Of The Dragon's Flame, whoever that may be. So, still inside the mountain, they continued on, as the direct roads into the kingdom were surely being watched. The plan was to walk away from the main roads through the outer forests, even if it meant taking a few extra days journey, then loop back into the kingdom, hopefully unnoticed by The Keepers Of The Dragon's Flame..

After they had walked a few hours with no sign of the sorcerers, Aleric announced, "Take us out, Sophie. I think we've gone far enough." In just a moment they were transported from the claustrophobic, stuffy mountain into the freshness of the forests of Mazeron. Lamora collapsed to the ground in relief, breathing deeply, taking in as much fresh air as possible.

"I'm never doing that again," she said exhausted, flailing her arms over her head. She sighed heavily. "Oh, Mazeron. It feels good to be almost home again."

"Sophie!" Aleric snapped unexpectedly. The Gnome jumped at the sound and looked helplessly at the large knight. Sophie's heart sank as Aleric unsheathed a large knife from his ankle and raised it to The Gnome's face. Sophie's eyes got large, and he was unable to speak he was so frightened.

"You're free!" Aleric chuckled, and he cut the rope binding them together. "I told you I wouldn't hurt you. Here is part of your reward." He held out his leather pouch and gave Sophie his last gold coin. Sophie looked around for a moment then snatched it quickly from the mean Paladin's hand. He spit on the ground at Aleric's feet once more for good measure. But Aleric seemed unoffended by the act and simply said, "King Victus will reward you more if you stop by the castle sometime. Take this flag with you; it will get you in with no trouble from the guards." Then Aleric handed him his small flag with the Deer of Mazeron on it. Only the king's workers were allowed to carry them. Sophie snatched it as well and grumbled something inaudible.

"I'm never seeing your king," The Gnome pouted. "Have Sophie as a slave, they would. Sophie gone." And with that, The Gnome turned and walked away mumbling angrily to himself as he went. As he exited the clearing, he kicked a fallen tree with one last angry grunt before he entered the forest and then was gone.

Chapter 14: The Brigands

"Let's stop here for a moment," Thearbuc announced. He slumped down from exhaustion against the brush on the side of the trail. "I need to rest."

They had been trekking through the outer woods for two days already, making sure to keep away from the direct and predicable routes back to the kingdom, which were more than likely being watched by spies from The Keepers Of The Dragon's Flame who they had stumbled upon deep within the mountain, only days prior.

The outer woods were vast, unexplored, thick forests filled with treachery and the unknown. Dangerous and unpredictable fairies thrived in the woods, so many that they could illuminate the entire woods in some areas at night. A soft, red glow that could be seen through the trees, but always at a distance. Well, the hope to every traveler was that they were always in the distance. If they came upon you, then you would never be seen again. The fairies, along with other unknown monsters and beasts that called the outer woods home, was why these parts were rarely traveled to. Aleric, Thearbuc, and Lamora had not seen any signs of other travelers in the past two days, as they made their way southward through the vast forests. No wheel tracks in the dirt, no footprints. Nothing but vast, thick, forests and the unknown as far as the imagination could wonder.

"We should have taken our chances on the main roads," Lamora said jokingly, sitting down next to Thearbuc and shaking pebbles from her boot. Aleric was quieter as usual as he led the group from far enough ahead to not be part of their endless conversations.

Around them, the forest was so thick that they couldn't see more than a few stride lengths in any direction around them. The overgrown road had been cut through the forest so long ago and was so rarely used that the forest was beginning to take it back, and the path was no longer clear enough to follow. It carved and wound through the forest for untold miles into mysterious faraway lands that most people of Mazeron had only heard about in fairytales and bedtime stories. In the opposite direction lay

Mazeron. Another two- or three-days' journey by Aleric's and Thearbuc's best assumptions.

"We should get moving," Aleric announced finally, standing up once again and pulling on Thearbuc's arm to help him up from his rest. In turn, Thearbuc helped Lamora to her feet and they brushed the dirt from their pants to continue the journey once again. The three were tired, but they were also friends who enjoyed one another's company, so the trek was not completely unbearable. The mention of a bath, decent food, and a soft bed did come up often, as they were all ready to be rid of the long, dusty road.

Not long later, the trail suddenly took a sharp turn through thick woods at brought them to a crossroads. They walked cautiously up to the intersection, where there was a wooden sign that had been carved into a point to show the way to… somewhere. But the sign was old and faded, and the arrow was slanted, pointing more downward than any other direction.

"That's helpful," Thearbuc mentioned, as he spun the sign around with a light push.

"Are we lost?" Lamora asked.

"We're not lost," Aleric remarked. "We just need to get to where we can see the sun setting then walk the opposite way to know we're going east. Eventually we'll pick up the river and it will take us right back to the kingdom."

"Possibly past my lands as well," Thearbuc mentioned. "I would love to see my children, should we pass near there." He lit up at the thought of reuniting with his children after so long.

"You left your children out here in the woods all alone?" Lamora asked worriedly.

"Nah," Thearbuc grumbled in his deep voice. "My eldest boy and his missus are watching over my daughter. They could use some time without their old man anyway. It's good for them. Good for all of us if we can help the kingdom. I can't keep my daughter cooped up out in the forest her whole life anyway. They will want to see the villages and towns soon and make families of their own. It would be nice if Mazeron was a prosperous place again by then, where they could thrive and be happy."

Lamora noticed the joy on his face when spoke of his family. He truly cared about them. She imagined what they were like and hoped she could see such a peaceful place as he had described his land and home on the great river to be. But her thoughts were abruptly interrupted by a faint yell in the distance and the sound of clanking metal. The three turned quickly toward the sound and saw a person off in the distance, slumped on the ground against the side of the trail. They were clanking something small, like a cup, against something else metal that looked like a dagger.

Quickly but cautiously, they ran to the person and came upon them in moments. It was a man. He was half off the trail, sprawled in the dirt, with his head in the bushes. He was clanking the metal cup and knife together to get their attention. Aleric reached him first and pulled the man from the bushes then leaned him up against the trail. It was one of the king's guards! Aleric recognized the blue tunic and Mazeron deer symbol instantly. The man's helmet and sword were missing. His nose had dried blood on it, and his face was caked in dirt. He had been out on the trail for some time, it looked like.

"What happened? Are you okay?" Aleric said, shaking the man, who seemed to be almost unconscious. "Where is your sword and helmet?" The man's eyes just rolled back, and his head flopped lazily to the side as Aleric held his shoulders up.

"Brigands," the man finally mumbled, but it was barely audible.

"Did he say Brigands?" Thearbuc asked, immediately reaching for his sword and scanning the surrounding thick forests.

"You won't see them if they don't want you to," Lamora said, reaching for a rag and wiping the man's forehead.

"Let him speak." Aleric knelt down close to the soldier's face to hear the garbled and muffled words better.

"Half-day west," the soldier whispered. He was pushing to get the words out, but it was slow and visibly painful to speak. He motioned down the path with his eyes and a nod. "Careful," he continued slowly. "They have the roads blocked. Trees. Everywhere. Ambush…" The soldier trailed off to catch his breath.

"It's one ambush after another," Aleric said in a frustrated tone while trying to get the wounded knight some water. "The king keeps sending soldiers out here to get slaughtered, almost like eventually the brigands will tire of it and flee these lands.

Brigand territory

Half of the king's guards are dead or missing by now. The most fruitless endeavor I've ever seen." He shook his head, clearly frustrated.

"Why does he keep sending them?" Lamora asked, concerned.

"I don't know," Aleric replied. "The king is not well-versed in the arts of war. I've been waiting for my luck to run out and to be sent out here to get slaughtered for years. It cannot go on!" He finished clenching his fist in frustration.

"Knight, where were you ambushed?" Thearbuc asked. "How many of them were there?"

The wounded knight flopped his head over to his other shoulder and looked down the forest road. He raised an arm to point, but it fell heavily back to the ground. Aleric noticed he had an arrow in his side that his arm was covering.

"Lamora," he said, getting her attention and motioning toward the wound, trying not to bring attention to it and worry the wounded soldier.

"Crossbow wound," she replied. "Let me bind it," she said to the soldier. "We can get it out when we get back to the kingdom." The man grunted in pain and shielded the wound with his hand.

"He doesn't want to be touched," Aleric said, placing his hand on hers to stop her. He leaned into Lamora's ear as the wounded man slumped to the ground.

"He's too far gone," he whispered. "He wants peace." Aleric turned back to the wounded guard and pulled him up, so his face wasn't lying in the dirt. His head flopped lifelessly from one side to the other as he was moved.

"He's gone…" They waited in silence for some time, listening for any sign of breath, but the soldier had passed.

"We have to do something!" The Paladin said eventually, visibly upset, his eyes glowing of raging amber. "They must be stopped. I'm going after them!" he said angrily, standing up and stepping back from the soldier's lifeless body.

"We need to get out of here," Lamora said worriedly again. "Not go *to* them!"

"More lives will be lost," Thearbuc chimed in, surprisingly in agreement with The Paladin. "We have an opportunity here. We somewhat know where they are from here. We don't have to walk aimlessly around the forests waiting to get ambushed. A half-day west." He pointed down the overgrown road that cut through the thick forest. "With Aleric, the element of surprise, and a little bit of luck, we might be able to at least set a trap for them and catch one alive."

"One is all we need," The Paladin bellowed in his deep, inhuman, and ominous voice. Not one Brigand had ever been captured alive. This made them an incredibly difficult enemy to counter, having no real intel or information on them, besides what those who fight and live to tell the tale can share. They are like ghosts of the forests, unable to be found or seen until it is too late. "All we need is one to gain an advantage," he continued. "We may even be able to inflict some real damage to those rats. I'm sorry, Lamora, we must try. You are free to head to the kingdom alone, if you choose."

"No. I'm coming with you," she said bluntly. Her attitude seemed to have changed quickly, or she just didn't want to leave her newfound friends. "Besides," she continued while spinning a dagger in each hand, then sheathing them with a sassy style, "you might need someone to bail you out of trouble."

"Let's get moving," The Paladin motioned. "We're coming for them."

Before leaving the area, they rounded up the soldier's armor, which was lying near him on the trail, and his horse, which was wandering aimlessly on the road not far away. They placed the soldier's body near the worn-down sign, where it would be most visible, as a warning to any others who may be traveling on the road. Then the three friends and the horse began to make their way west down the road. A faint fog hung low to the ground and gave an eerie look to the dense trees, which blocked most sunlight down here under the thick forest canopy. Not long later they came across the old wreckage of a destroyed merchant cart, burnt and ransacked on the edge of the road.

"That's our cue," Aleric announced, leading them and the horse off the road and into the woods. From then on, they walked in silence, choosing their footsteps carefully and staying as quiet as possible as they hunted the brigands. Luckily for them, sound did not travel very far in these woods. The air and leaves were wet and thick, which dampened any sound that was not in the immediate vicinity. The stillness of the sleepy forest made their journey feel eerie as they traveled in the ever-deepening silence and thickening fog.

"If I was going to hide in the woods to ambush people, this is where I would do it," Thearbuc mentioned quietly at one spot, hours later. Visibility through the fog and trees had become so bad that they could see almost nothing past a few horse lengths in front of them. "We might end up walking right past them at this rate," he said, scanning through the deep woods. The day already seemed to be getting away from them, and their morale was sinking as fast as the evening sun. Their clothes were soaked from trudging for hours through wet brush and leaves. The fog started playing tricks on their minds as the light began to fade, and innocent tree stumps took on ominous shapes of would-be assassins or monsters lying in wait.

Lamora noticed more than the others the growing eeriness and unease, as she could actually see it building. Shadows and wisps of black and gray circled the fog, just barely noticeable out of the corners of her eye, but they disappeared when she turned to see them.

"I feel as if we are being watched," Thearbuc said, just as Lamora was about to speak.

"There are ghosts in these woods," she replied quietly. "Don't interact with them and they can't hurt you," she said calmly, pushing through the fog. "But beware, they can take on many forms." As they continued on, the wisps and whirls circling through the air grew in number and thickness in Lamora's magical sight. Dark, motionless shapes stood staring in the fog. Lamora could see them, and the others could feel their piercing stares.

"This is not a good place to be once the sun goes down," Thearbuc said with a hint of panic.

"We can only continue on at this point." Aleric replied stoically. There was nowhere else to go either way. Then, not long later, the ground seemed to rise. "Up." Aleric motioned, quickly turning and changing direction. "It's our only option." They continued on as the ground kept climbing steadily upward until the travel was noticeably more difficult on the steeper ground.

"Maybe we can climb out of these cursed woods?" Thearbuc mentioned as they hiked along a faint deer trail through the fog. The trail was so small that the trees and brush on both sides of them scraped along their shoulders.

"I hope so," Lamora said nervously. The ghosts of the forests were everywhere. Whipping past her face and through the trees. Staring threateningly through the fog, toying with them, ready to consume them at any moment. And she was the only one who could see it. The others could feel it, but to her, it was a living nightmare. She picked up the pace and placed her hand on Aleric's shoulders, pushing him forward.

Time seemed to stretch on forever, with them getting nowhere as they climbed, and the thick fog showed no sign of letting up. The sun had sunk below the horizon, and although it was not late in the evening, the forest floor had become very dark. "We aren't getting out of this," Aleric announced eventually. "Let's hunker down for the night here." He pointed to some large boulders that were outlined in the fog, not far off the trail. "They'll protect us from the wind."

Lamora's heart sank. She didn't want to spend the night in these cursed woods, filled with lost spirits and wandering souls. But she knew they were exhausted and out of options. Even if she tried to explain what she was seeing to the others, they would either not believe her or not realize the severity. She drew upon memories of when she was younger and had been in similar situations. She always survived, she told herself. This exact situation was why she had never dared to travel through the mountains alone. Instead, she became a creature of habit, always sticking close to her home and the areas she knew were safe. But now she found herself lost in thick woods, with spirits and energies whirling around her and through the forest fog.

Aleric led them to the boulders, where the three tucked in as close as they could. The loud howling of the wind was softer under the shelter of the rock and made a soft whistle as it blew by. The sound of the leaves blowing in the distance was ominous and a constant reminder of the harsh conditions away from their temporary shelter. There would be no fire on this night to heat any food, as they knew Brigands could be around any corner, so after they had unpacked their sleeping gear, they ate cold bread in silence.

"Our best bet is to just sleep through this misery," Aleric mentioned at one point, noticing the others struggling through the cold storm as well. "Maybe this wet fog will let up by morning and we can dry out in the sun before we continue on?" He thought the comment would give the group a small amount of hope, but the others just looked at him and half-nodded.

Soon, they had all eaten and were huddled under their blankets to sleep through the harsh and windy night. Aleric and Thearbuc, exhausted from the trail, fell asleep quickly, but Lamora could not sleep. She was tormented all night long by the wandering spirits that the others were unable to see. She would close her eyes to block them out and would almost be asleep, but then she would hear a loud scream from a lost, angry soul that would startle her awake. It was terrifying. It sounded so loud, like someone screaming in her face, but no one was there, and the others could not hear it. She had always wondered why the spirits would torment her and not others. They must hate her for being able to see into their realm, she figured. She didn't want to. Her powers let her see all kinds of energies as well, living and dead, dangerous and harmless. She couldn't control it.

She attempted to ignore the howls and screams throughout the night, but very late into the night she heard something that she could not ignore. It started out as a clanking. Like a cowbell off in the distance, she thought to herself. Then it got louder as it approached very slowly. She didn't want to, but she dared to open her eyes and peered into the darkness. An old man was approaching their makeshift shelter. Hunched over, thin and frail, he was banging a metal spoon on a tin cup and hollering something into the howling night.

"Have you seen Ataleen?" he said, not speaking to anyone or anything in particular. "Ataleen!" he cried out. The pain in his voice was picked up and carried away by the heavy winds. The hair on Lamora's neck and arms stood up at the sound of the old man's ghostly wails. There was something devastating about his voice, and her heart wretched inside her chest. "Ataleen," he called out again as he limped closer, clanking his tin as he went.

"Maybe he will just pass me?" Lamora whispered aloud to comfort herself as he crept along. Then, suddenly, the man turned and looked directly at her. Her heart sank, and her stomach lurched. She clenched her fists together in fear.

"Ataleen, is that you?" the ghostly man asked as he reached for Lamora.

"Please leave, please leave, please leave," she whispered through tears dripping from her fearful eyes.

The ghost was so close now. "Ataleeeeen!" he screeched through the midnight fog and wind. Instantly, he appeared directly in front of Lamora's face. His yellow teeth almost touched her mouth, and she could smell the stench of death on his breath, which seemed to engulf her. Lamora was too frozen in fear to move away. "Ataleeeeen," he hissed one more time, so close to her face that it felt like he was going to burrow inside her and consume her from the inside out. Lamora tried to scream out in fear. Kicking and flailing, she tried to scream, but there was no sound. Nothing came out. She clawed and scratched at the apparition, but it did not care and would not leave her. Finally, she was able to let out a horrifying scream that pierced into the night and awakened her from her sleep. She quickly sat up from her place of slumber, still shaking. Aleric heard her cry out and woke up also.

"What is going on?" he said sleepily, rubbing his eyes while they adjusted to the darkness. For a moment, Lamora thought she had just had a bad dream, but then to her returning horror, she watched as the old man shuffled slowly away into the dark and windy forest, still clinking his tin and calling out for Ataleen as he faded away.

"Do you see that?" Lamora asked, trembling in fear.

"See what?" Aleric replied, still rubbing his eyes. "Bad dream?" he asked.

Lamora paused before she answered, still watching the ghost until he faded into the blackness of the forest night. "Yeah," she finally replied. "Just a bad dream." She knew that no one else could see the lost ghost, so it wasn't worth bringing up. Despite her fear, she couldn't help but wonder how long the poor soul had been wandering the woods in search of his lost Ataleen.

Lamora and Aleric both lay back down on the cold forest ground, and she spent the rest of the night thinking about who Ataleen was to the wandering apparition. Was it his first love? His daughter? Someone he needed to find to pass to the other side and find peace? She tossed and turned all night, tormented by the spirits of the forest. The others were tormented as well, but on a level that they barely realized. Their sleep was plagued with odd dreams and visions of doom as the spirits whirled around their sleeping bodies on the cold ground. At one point, Lamora peered out from her blanket to see an apparition floating near Aleric, holding his hand. Then a violent scream pierced through the night, and he awoke suddenly with a jerk from a nightmare. He took a deep breath as he realized it was just a dream. His arm was dead asleep, cold, and tingly. Lamora could see him rubbing it to bring sensation and life back into it. She didn't say anything, but she knew it was from the cold spirit holding on to him.

As Aleric lay there, still feeling uneasy from his nightmare, he caught a whiff of something. It was the faint smell of smoke in the wind. He turned in the direction and peered into the blackness of the howling night. Nothing was there, no fire or light out in the distance. Then he smelled it again, stronger this time. He was sure now that something was there. Someone had a fire somewhere nearby in the forest…

"Lamora." He shook her gently. She was not asleep, still tormented by the spirits of the forest. "Follow me," he whispered, motioning with his finger. "Smell that?" he asked. She turned her head to the sky for a moment and breathed in before nodding. Soon they were both out of their place of slumber and quietly creeping around the camp. Then, Aleric spotted something through the trees. A faint light, like a star in the dark distance. He pointed in the direction, and they continued toward it. The ground slanted downward steadily through the trees until they came to an opening in the forest. Everything around them was black. Lamora took one more step just as Aleric grabbed her arm and pulled her back before she walked out into open air and tumbled off an unseen cliff.

"Careful!" he whispered through the howling wind. Lamora fell backward with her hand on her chest, gasping to catch her breath from the scare of an almost certain death. The wind howled extra hard here at the edge of the cliff. Lamora's imagination was running wild thinking about how far down it could have been. "Look," Aleric whispered, pointing off into the distance. The faint glow was coming from a valley below. Definitely a fire, but they could not tell how far away it was. It flickered in the night, wincing out then coming back every few moments. "Someone is down there," Aleric continued, whispering against the howling wind. "Let's get back to camp."

Quietly, they ducked back into the trees and crept away from the cliffside. When they got back to camp, they awoke Thearbuc and informed him of the news. After Lamora's scare, they knew it was too unsafe to wander around in the dark night, so the three tucked back into their capes and blankets and awaited the dawn. No one slept.

Finally, the sun began to creep over the horizon, and blackness turned to dark blue then golden light as the sun awoke. The winds stopped howling, and the forest came to life with the sound of all types of wildlife. Birds sang their beautiful songs in the peaceful morning, and that is when Aleric knew it was time to move. The others sat up as they heard him stir.

"No time to eat right now," he said, still whispering. "Let's check out that valley." So, the three companions rose from their makeshift beds once again and ventured back into the forest. This time, they could see the large cliff clearly in the light of day. As they approached it, they laid on the ground and crawled to the edge of the cliff, not wanting to be seen yet by whoever held camp at the bottom.

"Whoooooa," Lamora marveled, as she gazed over the edge and saw a vast hidden valley open up before them. There were over two dozen fires going, with tents and men everywhere. Men with spears. Soldiers! Their morning fires stretched across the large fields below. They were huddled in small groups of five or six, cooking their collective breakfasts. A slow river trickled through the field and ended in a small lake, which settled off to their right. Two men seemed to be spearfishing in the lake, while one other on the far side was swimming or taking a morning bath in the fresh water.

In the center of the field there was a large stone building with a wooden roof. The stone structure was old and run down, but it was two stories tall with a massive chimney on one end that stretched up to the sky and leaned to one side, ready to succumb to its age and fall at any moment. The wooden roof was rotted with holes. No windows or doors adorned the long stone walls. What was it doing out here in the middle of the unknown forest? Who built such a structure so many years ago, and why?

"The brigands," Thearbuc mumbled with disgust. "This must be their camp!" Gazing out along the large field, their hearts sank at the sheer number of men inhabiting this hidden valley. Among the trees and brush there must have been five hundred of them scattered throughout the valley.

"We can't fight all of them. Hope is lost," Thearbuc mumbled to the others. The entire king's army couldn't outnumber all these men, which meant that the three tired companions were hopeless to do anything on their own besides not get caught. "No wonder they can patrol every corner of the forest," Thearbuc continued with his pessimistic thoughts at the sight of so many soldiers. "How are we going to get out of here without getting captured? It's a miracle they didn't see us on the way in."

"We aren't leaving," Aleric replied with a grin slowly stretching across his face.

"What do you mean we aren't leaving?" Lamora and Thearbuc both said in unison whispers.

"You're right, Thearbuc. The king's army cannot defeat this enemy," Aleric continued, rising from the ground.

"Get down!" Lamora begged. "They'll see you!"

Aleric grinned as his eyes began to glow. "I'm counting on it…"

Back down in the thick forest, the wind was blowing loudly through the trees even though the sun was out, and the day looked seemingly pleasant. It was midday when they reached the forest floor again, and Thearbuc and Lamora bade Aleric farewell for the time being. He looked tall and proud atop his horse, adorned entirely in the fallen soldier's armor. It was a full armor suit—gauntlets, chest and leg armor, and a helmet, along with Mazeron's flag waving proudly above him and the horse. His longsword hung sturdily from his waist and went down past the horse's torso, making him a menacing sight.

"Well, they'll definitely notice you," Thearbuc said jokingly, trying to hide the worry he was feeling.

"Is there no other plan?" Lamora asked. The look of distress and worry on her face was obvious.

"The king has tried the other options. This is the only one left," Aleric replied sternly, with seemingly increased confidence as he stood tall, strong, and proud in his glistening armor upon his steed. The others nodded and patted the horse for reassurance and good luck. "Camp below the ridge and meet me back here in three days. If I don't come back, then return to Mazeron and tell the king of this location. Come and rescue me if you can, but *do not* let them be simpletons about it. Make sure they have some sort of plan and don't come blaring through here loudly to get ambushed." Thearbuc and Lamora nodded that they understood.

"Three days, below the ridge," Thearbuc affirmed.

"We move!" The Paladin said boldly as the horse started to gallop forward. The two bade him goodbye, but he did not look back. Briskly, The Paladin trotted into the forest, his armor glinting in the sunlight along the winding tree-lined road

It wasn't long until he came across more evidence of the brigands. More burnt and plundered wagons lined the road as he went further into the brigands territory. Most were left abandoned so long ago that the earth had overtaken them again, and grew green grasses inside the wreckage. What havoc these monsters have wreaked for so long, Aleric thought to himself as he trotted past the destruction of people's lives.

Not long later, his senses started tingling, and he felt as if he was being watched. At one point, he thought he heard some sounds coming from the thick forests surrounding him. He stopped in the center of the road and stood in silence for some time but heard nothing except the soft breeze blowing through the trees.

"Brigaaaaands!!!!" he yelled so powerfully that it echoed through the forests and birds flew from their nests. Aleric waited for a reply to his battle call but there was nothing. So, he yelled again, "Brigaaaaaands! Show yourselves." As he said it, he slowly reached down to his side and unbuckled his longsword and let it drop loudly to the ground. There it lay between the horse's hooves, and he was noticeably disarmed to anyone who may be watching. Then he raised his arms up above his head. "I'm not here to fight!" he yelled aimlessly into the woods. "I come from the Kingdom of Mazeron as a steward bearing a message. I am but a humble servant." He trailed off as he began to feel like he was just yelling at the trees.

Then, just when he was about to gather his sword and give up, the whole forest around him seemed to come alive. His eyes darted back and forth nervously as he tried to make sense of what was going on, and before he could comprehend it, he was surrounded by Brigands on all sides. Men pointed spears and arrows pointed directly at him appeared from the forest all around him. Panic quickly set in, being helpless against so many enemies, and Aleric wondered if he made a horrible mistake in coming here.

"How in the world?" he mumbled to himself while trying to steady his startled horse. "Hold! Hold!" he yelled nervously, holding out the palm of his hands in a show of defense and friendliness. "I don't come for a fight! Please hear me." The horse was dancing back and forth nervously in circles. The brigands stayed steadfast and silent from their positions around the forest. Aleric was expecting a hail of arrows and the end of his days to come at any given moment. He was far too outnumbered and vulnerable here for any hope of a fight or escape.

"Dismount!" a strong voice called out from the trees, loud and demanding.

Aleric paused for a moment, glancing at all the arrows and spears pointed toward him, then swung one leg over and dismounted the horse quickly and without argument. He slapped the horse hard on its rear and it fled fast down the road and was quickly gone into the forest, its hooves still thudding long after it was out of sight. Aleric was left standing there alone on the road, with his hands raised above his shoulders. For a moment there was no sound, and he awaited nervously what would happen next.

"Men," the same voice yelled again. Then the group of Brigands emerged from the edge of the trees and formed a large circle around Aleric. They stood there silently with their bows drawn. Though Aleric couldn't see past the men, he heard the thud of heavy footsteps approaching from somewhere in the woods. Thump, thump, thump.

"Geh!" a loud voice grumbled as a large, burly man pushed two archers roughly aside and appeared before Aleric in the circle.

He was massive, tall and very round with bushy black hair and a big beard. He lumbered more than walked, swinging his arms wide from side to side, his body leaning left and right as he took heavy steps. The dirt plumed beneath him as each foot stomped toward Aleric, but he moved briskly for such a large beast of a man. He wore a thick silver necklace, and his knuckles were lined with fat silver rings with emblems and jewels on them. A round gold earring adorned one ear.

As he approached, Aleric instinctively put his arms out to protect himself. The man did not slow but instead swatted Aleric's arms down, and in one motion, placed a massive leg behind Aleric's ankle and shoved his chest, tripping him backward to the ground. In an instant, Aleric lay flat on the ground, staring up at the trees. Then without a word, the man gracefully swiveled around and placed one heavy foot atop Aleric's neck and chin, pressing down until he was tightly pinned. Aleric grabbed the large foot by the ankle and tried to break free, but it was too heavy and did not budge.

"What's the word, knight?" the man's loud voice bellowed as he began to laugh. The other men who surrounded them began to laugh as well. *They're crazy*, Aleric thought as he lay helplessly pinned and squirming on the ground. His plan had gone out the window, and his only thoughts now were of survival.

He couldn't threaten them, so smarting his way out was his only hope.

"Did you come looking for your friends?" the large man yelled, obviously trying to entertain the others. "Maybe we can find one of their heads somewhere around here? Haaaa!" His wild laugh bellowed from low in the belly and resonated through the forest. The men were laughing and enjoyed their leader taunting the helpless trespasser. Then the large, bearded man turned his head down, and his smile quickly vanished as his eyes met Aleric's. "Really, knight. What brings you here?"

"I have a message from King Victus," he forced out, struggling to breathe from the man's heavy foot upon his neck. "A proposition for the brigands," he squirmed.

"Oh, do you now?" the burly man said sarcastically. "You're really not in a position to be making deals now, are you?"

"Hear me out," Aleric grunted, still trying to lift the heavy foot from his neck. But he couldn't let himself get too upset or his eyes would glow and reveal his powers, likely leading to a fruitless, angry rampage. "I'm just doing my job."

"Tell me then. What is your proposition? We can get this done quickly. You tell me, we'll kill you, then we'll go back into our merry woods."

"I can only tell the leader of the brigands," Aleric said, still squirming. These words visibly upset the man, and he pushed harder into Aleric, who felt the pressure driving him into the dirt and crumpling his armor. Then, just when it seemed like his armor and throat were about to cave in, another voice spoke from the crowd.

"We should hear him out!" the voice said loudly. "He is but one unarmed man." The burly man wrinkled his face in disgust behind his black beard.

"It is proper procedure, Vidor," another voice from the group yelled. The burly man was silent for a moment, then with a shove he let off Aleric and turned to face the other men.

"I know the procedure," Vidor yelled commandingly. "Tie him up!' he snapped as he walked away from Aleric, who was still gasping for air. In a quick moment, multiple Brigands were on Aleric, and he was rolled over so his hands and feet could be tightly bound. With great strength, he was hoisted to his feet by the brigands, both hands and feet bound and barely able to move.

"Come with us!" Vidor waved his arm forward with a laugh. "Welcome to our forest!" Aleric was shoved forward as the group began to march. There must have been twenty men or more, all tall and strong and well-equipped with weapons. Bows, spears, and daggers—each one deadly in their well-trained hands. Upon their chests they had leather armor, which would defend against indirect arrows or slices from a dagger. But the most interesting of their armor was their helmets, which only some of the brigands wore. They were bronze with two horns upon them. The center of the helmets was adorned with a tall, red, plume-like mohawk, which made the brigands a very intimidating bunch to see. As they marched along, Aleric noticed the discipline and professionalism the group shared. They marched in almost perfect unison in rows of three. They communicated with passing scouts along the way by hand signals. *They have this forest completely locked down*, Aleric thought to himself. *No wonder they are impossible to counter.*

"Sorry, mate," a voice from behind Aleric spoke just as a bag was pulled roughly over his head. "No one can know the way," he laughed as he hit Aleric lightly in the back of the head. Aleric rolled his eyes to himself beneath the heavy, damp bag. He already knew where the brigands made their camp. They must be getting close, he thought, but what would his plan be once they arrived? Why hadn't they killed him yet? He had so many questions about the mysterious bandits.

They pushed through the forest; Aleric being guided by the shoulders. They were on a small deer trail, he could tell. Twigs and brush rubbed against his legs, and tree branches whipped across his chest. The trail twisted and wound through the forest until finally they stopped their long march. There was silence in the air and Aleric heard shuffling around him. Then the sack was pulled from his head, and he finally saw the brigands' camp up close. There was the large run-down stone building that he had seen before across the field. Beyond that were the makeshift huts and dozens of small firepits scattered about, most still smoldering from the morning's breakfast. Beyond the stone building, far in the distance, were the tall cliffs that he had stood upon earlier that morning.

Suddenly, Aleric was shoved forward, and the group started marching again, single file this time, with their prisoner in the center of the group. As they wound around the huts and numerous firepits, the other Brigands stood up to watch the prisoner be forcefully marched through their camp. Stone-cold faces of hardened soldiers peered at him behind thick, bushy beards. No words were said by any of them, and Aleric got the feeling he was the only outsider to ever set foot within the brigands camp.

Through the fields and up the hill they went, until finally they reached the stone building in the center of the valley. It was rather massive up close. It had zero windows and one giant wooden door in the front. Bits of stone lay piled around the perimeter from where they crumbled off the walls who-knows-how-many centuries before. The building was ancient, Aleric could tell just by looking at it. But who could have built such a large building so far away from civilization and so long ago?

Two Brigands stepped forward to the door and leaned into it, pushing heavily with both hands to force it open. It swung heavily inward, and Aleric was shoved forward and marched inside. Even the old door was incredibly thick, Aleric. The place was a fortress.

Inside, the room opened into a single massive area, like a large dancing hall. But the inside was not the simple, ancient architecture Aleric was expecting. No, the inside was covered in splendor and only the finest materials. Beautiful tapestries hung from high upon the stone walls and draped beautifully down to the floor. Amazing candle-lit chandeliers lined the ceilings, and the room was bright, warm, and welcoming. The floors were beautiful, polished limestone and giant wooden beams lined the ceiling. There were no holes in the roof like it had seemed from the outside. It had obviously been painstakingly repaired by the brigands at some point.

Nearest the door were many circular tables that men stood and sat around, mostly with ale and meat, with one long table down the center of the room. *It could easily fit 100 soldiers*, Aleric thought. How could this rough group of murderous bandits afford such elegance? But he quickly remembered how many merchant trains they had ambushed over the years, and he rolled his eyes at their stolen splendor and luxury at the cost of the countless unfortunate souls who happened to cross their path.

Aleric was pushed ahead again, now toward the magnificent table at the center of the hall. As they marched, he saw a raised platform with a magnificent throne at the far end of the hall. There sat one man, an enormous blazing fire in a large marble fireplace roaring behind and three armed guards standing on either side. It was more of a large chair than a throne, with a back that stretched toward the ceiling and padded armrests. The center of the chair was a deep-red, soft-looking fabric. No doubt a chair made for a king at one point then taken by the band of Brigands, only to end up here in the company of thieves.

"Stop there," the man in the throne said calmly as they approached. He didn't have to yell. The sound of his voice carried easily through the stone hall.

"A prisoner set for trial, Commander," one of the men escorting Aleric said.

"Aaah. Good work, men," the man on the throne said. "No mindless killing. Disarm and bring him in." Then he turned to Aleric and made eye contact with him as he spoke, "We are civilized men here. Once the threat is gone, we take prisoners and set them for trial."

"I am no threat," Aleric spoke, sensing he was out of line, but needing to say it anyway. "I have been sent from King Victus of Mazeron to deliver a message to the brigands of the forest."

"Brigands!" the man yelled in offense with a chuckle. "We are not mere Brigands, thieves, or beggars of the forest. We are an army of highly skilled warriors!"

"My apologies, sir," Aleric said, holding back a sarcastic remark and his instinct to antagonize any man who lies so blatantly.

"Leave us," the leader commanded the others. "The trial will be set for tomorrow morning. Until then, I will discuss whatever matters at hand the prisoner has brought to us." The others shuffled out, leaving the six guards at the head of the room and a few of the other Brigands nearby. The large and abrasive Vidor was one of the men who stayed behind. He had been glaring at Aleric like a wolf ready to kill for most of the march over and was not about to let up any time soon from the looks of it. He wanted a fight, that much was clear. Vidor seemed more animal than man. Abrasive, rude, loud, mannerless, and always ready for a fight.

"Come, sit," the Brigand leader said as he rose from his throne and motioned to the long table. "We can speak here while we dine. It is, after all, almost supper time." Aleric, still bound at the wrists and ankles, shuffled to the large table.

"I am Commander Rune," the man introduced himself, standing next to the seat at the head of the table. He was a tall man of thin build but looked strong. His black hair was combed, and he was well dressed, making him look sophisticated and clean. Not the rugged forest warrior that Aleric was expecting, like other Brigands were. As Aleric sat down at the table, he noticed a large map laid out across it. It was a map of the surrounding forests, complete with deer trails, roads, and rivers.

"Aaah, you didn't think we were just some renegade band of thieves, did you?" Commander Rune said, studiously observing Aleric's reaction to the detailed map. "I bet your king never even bothered to map his own forests, did he?" he said condescendingly from the head of the table as he picked an apple from a basket. "Guess that's why they became *our* forests, right?" He took a bite, not waiting for a reply.

Commander Rune was confident and professional; it was apparent to Aleric. Unfortunately, that was not the foe that he had envisioned when he set out on this quest that led him straight into the lion's den. He had hoped for a brute who was easily manipulated and overpowered. This would most likely not be the case with Commander Rune.

"So, knight," Commander Rune continued, taking another bite of the apple. "What message does your king have for us lowly band of thieves?"

Aleric paused, choosing his words wisely. "A truce and a gift," he finally spoke. "You have cut off the kingdom's trade routes and the people there are suffering from it. The kingdom has fallen into ruin. You have been out here for over a decade, as far as any of us can tell, and we are guessing that by now you may want to leave your primitive hiding place in the forest and return to civilization."

"A bold assumption," Commander Rune said, "but go on."

"The king is prepared to give you and your men large swaths of land on the west side of the kingdom. It is fertile farmland. You could make peaceful lives there. Take jobs in the kingdom, mine for gold, build instead of destroy. Become part of civilization!"

Commander Rune leaned back casually and raised his hand high and motioned to the luxury surrounding him. "We are already civilized, sir knight. As you can see."

"Our lands are fertile," Aleric interjected. "You will have more food than you can eat."

Commander Rune again motioned toward the table, which was filled with food, and picked up a large turkey leg, then bit into it exaggeratively. "We have food," he said as he finished the bite.

"The land is large and spacious," Aleric tried again. "Enough room for everyone to build homes and new lives."

"We have plenty of land," the commander smugly motioned at the large map strewn across the table.

"We have gold!" Aleric sat forward raising his voice as he began to lose his patience with the commander.

"What use do we have for worthless metals?" Commander Rune snapped back, also sitting up in his chair and leaning in closer to Aleric.

"There is culture and entertainment in civilization!" Aleric said, leaning further in.

"Have it here," the commander motioned to one end of the room where various instruments hung along the wall. He leaned in more and so did Aleric. The two were almost face-to-face as the conversation picked up speed, and they threw reason after reason and excuse after excuse at one another. The tension in the room was building fast as the fire behind them roared.

"There are honest jobs, honest work!" Aleric yelled out.

"Who needs that?" Commander Rune roared back, putting his hands on the table and standing up to lean in toward Aleric with threatening posture. Aleric, too, stood up and slammed his hands on the table. The two men stood face to face, just inches apart. Aleric paused and they glared at each other angrily, each waiting for the other to blink or give up the argument.

"We. Have. Women," Aleric said finally. A thick silence suddenly washed through the room, and the commander, for the first time, had nothing to say in return. Aleric slowly sat back down in his chair, knowing he had won the argument. The commander stayed standing, still glaring at Aleric while anger burned inside of him.

"Would be nice, sir," a shaky voice said from across the room.

"Nobody speaks out of turn to the commander!" Vidor yelled from near the table and in an instant was moving toward the guard.

"Just because they don't like you…" the guard said laughing as Vidor thumped forward, again ready for a fight.

"Enough, Vidor!" another voice rang out. It was the man from the forest who insisted they take Aleric to trial. Vidor stopped his advance on the guard and huffed at the other man, then walked away still clenching his fists.

"My younger brother, Visko," Commander Rune motioned. Aleric hadn't noticed before, but the two could be twins. Both tall, strong, and thin for their height. Visko was holding his horned metal helmet now, and Aleric could see their facial features and hair were almost identical.

"He's right about the women, you know," Visko said calmly to his brother, coming to stand beside him. There was a long pause as he thought out the situation.

"We are not trusting some foreign king with our lives," Commander Rune finally spoke again as he calmed from the argument.

"It's not a trap, if that is what you are thinking," Aleric interjected.

"Sir knight," Commander Rune said to Aleric, "we thank you for your offer, but we must decline. Your trial will go on as planned, and your sentencing will commence at sunrise on the morrow. I hate to be so harsh, but it is for the safety of all my men. Being someone who is familiar with the nature of these engagements, I'm sure you can understand." Aleric nodded then lowered his head as despair washed over him. He said nothing in return while the guards, Commander Rune, Vidor, and Visko stared back at him. "We might as well get our prisoner his last meal," Commander Rune finally said aloud. "Come, fetch some food for us." He motioned to the guards and two of them filed off, then returned moments later with plates of food. "Tell us, knight, all about this kingdom of yours," Commander Rune said, sitting back down near Aleric and picking up a chicken drumstick from the plates of food.

Aleric quickly described the kingdom but made no mention of his powers or the king using him as a tool to restore peace and prosperity to the land. He only explained that he grew up on a farm and took a job as a castle guard when he was old enough, and that he was only the king's messenger.

"Fascinating," Commander Rune said dryly, clearly expecting a more spectacular story about knights of honor living in a once-magical kingdom.

"What is your story?" Aleric asked. "How did you and your people end up out here in these mysterious forests?

"It's a long one," Commander Rune started. "We were once a proud army for a proud king. Our lands were beautiful and prosperous, and we were at the forefront of civilization. No barbarism or unjust kings. We had democracy and industry."

"Why did you leave then?" Aleric asked.

"It was our duty to defend our new civilized way of life and expand it across the known world. Our king sent us south for an offensive against a barbaric nation that constantly attacked and threatened our way of life. We marched for months and months to reach their lands. When we got there, we found civilization well beyond ours. They had an incredible amount of people and thousands of soldiers."

"They were populated, but they were not civilized," Visko chimed in. "Basically animals, the lot of them. I think their favorite pastime was beheading people. A violent and tyrannical culture. Exactly what we were trying to stave off from our own lands."

"We were met with an enormous defensive force," Commander Rune started again. "Many conquered nations all serving under the one leader. Our offensive fell apart before it even started, and we were ambushed. In the retreat, we lost our king. Not sure if he ran away in fear or if he was slain, but we were lost without him. I took over command at that point and made it my duty to get these men back to their homes. We wandered through these forests for what seemed like an eternity. It was like there was some kind of wicked magic keeping us in. Never getting anywhere, surrounded by trees as far as anyone could ever see. The fairies… it must be the fairies or wicked magic in these cursed woods. We would climb mountain passes only to end up back in the same valley again. Eventually we gave up hope of finding our way out and set up a new life here. There were plenty of merchants to pick off and live comfortably. Life is simple now, and we are a lot better off here than wandering through these cursed woods for all eternity."

"Why didn't you just come to the kingdom for help? Make a life there?" Aleric asked.

"Ha!" Commander Rune snarked. "A foreign army marching on a defended castle? That would have gone well…" he trailed off and was silent for a moment. "We are free men, knight," he continued. "We will not be bowing to a king and his oppressive laws. I'm sure your dungeons are full enough as it is, and your king doesn't need our help to fill them."

Everyone sat in silence after hearing Commander Rune's sad tale of the once-proud army now lost in the unforgiving forests. Finally, the commander stood up from the table and pushed his seat in.

"Well, I'm sorry, but our meeting has come to an end. Your sentence will be handed out at dawn. Guards…" he motioned them to secure the prisoner and take him away. Commander Rune stood aside as four of the guards secured the ropes binding Aleric's wrists then escorted him from the long hall.

"I'll give you one more chance to change your mind," Aleric said as they marched him away.

"We will have to decline, good knight. For our own safety. I hope you understand," Commander Rune said in solemn tone as the doomed prisoner was escorted away.

As they approached the exit, the guards walking behind Aleric did not notice his eyes begin to glow their bright amber color. Cupping his bound hands together, he created a small ball of fire, which he used to singe the ropes that bound him, and in just a few moments he was able to pull them apart.

"What is that smell?" one of the guards asked. He grabbed Aleric's shoulder from behind, making him stop while they investigated the smell, but as soon as his hand touched The Paladin's shoulder he swung around and swatted the guard's arm aside. He laid a powerful blow to the guard's stomach, which dropped him to the ground with barely a sound. Then The Paladin lowered his shoulder and shoved another guard heavily to the ground, using the moment of chaotic confusion to run to the door.

"Guards!" one of the men yelled out for help. But he was too late—The Paladin was already slamming the large wooden beam down between the thick doors, locking all the other guards outside.

As he turned around from the barred doors, one of the escorting guards was already on him, mid-thrust with a sharp spear. Just in time, The Paladin dodged the attack and with his left arm slammed down hard on the spear, shattering it to harmless bits. His other fist met the guard's face, and he too went down. Four guards remained, all attacking at once with swords, spears, and shields. It was an uneven fight, but not for The Paladin. In an instant he raised his arms high above his head and formed a large ball of fire. He hurled it at the ground in front of the attacking guards and the subsequent explosion and blast blew all four of them into the air. They landed hard, rolling a few times before they came to a lifeless stop.

At the far end of the hall, The Paladin saw Commander Rune, Visko, Vidor, and the remaining guards scrambling for weapons and putting together a quick offensive against him. Quickly he grabbed and put on his gauntlets that the guards had carelessly left on the table then jumped atop the long wooden table that stretched across the hall and began running fiercely towards them. Arrows came from the far end of the room but were swatted away by The Paladin's arms and sturdy metal armor. They bounced harmlessly aside to the floor as he ran quickly toward them.

Two guards ran toward the attacking Paladin and tried to take out his legs with large swings of heavy clubs. The Paladin dodged them easily, and one by one he picked up the attacking guards and tossed them aside before moving on, stomping on plates and glasses as he went. Vidor, who was standing near the end of the table was the last to engage. The Paladin didn't miss a stride and gave the lumbering bully a swift kick to the face, felling him hard to the ground with an audible thud.

With no pause or hesitation, the Paladin jumped off the table and made his way to Commander Rune without even breaking eye contact. The commander swung his sword hard at the paladin, but he blocked it easily with metal gauntlets he had snatched from the table. The Paladin grabbed the sword and with enormous strength tore it from the commander's hands, leaving him helpless. With just one hand, The Paladin grabbed Commander Rune by the throat and pinned him against the wall, lifting his feet from the ground. The Paladin's glowing eyes met the fearful and angry eyes of the commander. Visko, who was about to come to his brother's aid, dropped his weapon and took a few steps backwards when he saw The Paladin's inhuman strength and glowing eyes. None of them had ever encountered a magic wielder like this, and they weren't sure just how powerful he might be.

"One more chance," The Paladin spoke. His voice was deep and came with a faint, eerie echo. Commander Rune squirmed. "Come with me, swear allegiance to our kingdom, or die right now." He let his grip on the commander's neck loosen so he could speak, and he gasped for air.

"They will rip you apart," Commander Rune said, gasping for air, his eyes glancing back to the army of Brigands currently trying to break down the barred doors at the other end of the hall.

"Not before I snap your neck," The Paladin replied, without missing a beat. He leaned in so they were face-to-face. His glowing eyes illuminated the defeated commander's stoic determination. There was a pause as The Paladin held eye contact as he awaited the commander's final reply.

"We'll do it, we'll do it," gasped the commander, still struggling to break free.

"Marvelous," The Paladin echoed in his inhuman voice. He let the commander down slowly until his feet were back on the ground but did not loosen his grip around his neck just yet. "Once I let you go, I know you will try to undermine me," The Paladin spoke again. "Believe me, mortal, it will not work."

Commander Rune's eyes bulged, and his mind raced with fear. He knew he was overpowered and out of options. Defeated by someone seemingly not of this world.

"No tricks," the commander gasped under The Paladin's strong grip. Then instantly The Paladin let his hand loose and stepped away from the commander who fell to one knee, gasping for air. The Paladin stood motionless, watching him collect himself and regain his breath once again.

"Partners?" The Paladin asked, extending his arm out in a friendly manner to the commander.

"Aye" was all Commander Rune could muster. But it was enough. Aleric grabbed him by the arm and helped him back to his feet, and they stood face to face once again.

"Tell them…" The Paladin motioned toward the ruckus at the other end of the hall, the guards outside still trying to breach the barred doors.

"STOP!" Commander Rune yelled out. "Surrender!" He motioned to his brother Visko, who was still standing nearby watching helplessly at the events unfolding. "Get them," Commander Rune barked at his brother. Visko unbarred the door, then informed the guards that everything was okay.

"We need to see the commander," one soldier stated. The others nodded in unison.

"Let them in!" Commander Rune yelled from the far end of the hall. His eyes met The Paladin's as he spoke, "It's okay. I will inform the men on what has taken place here." Aleric, with his normal eyes, stepped back and stood close behind the commander as the many Brigands shuffled into the great hall to be addressed by their leader.

Then Commander Rune stepped up onto the long table to address his soldiers.

"Men," he said loudly, standing above them. His voice carried through the great hall. "We have been made an offer that I cannot refuse. This generous knight, sent from the Kingdom of Mazeron, has brought word that the king, King Victus, has granted us large swathes of land inside the kingdom and granted us all pardons if we vacate these here woods."

The great hall fell deathly silent. Aleric expected a cheer or applause or something, but there was no reaction from the men. "We can finally start new lives. Live again!" the commander continued. "Build farms and families." There was another pause as the men exchanged confused glances to one another, quietly mumbling to each another.

"But we are not farmers, sir," one man spoke. "We are soldiers!" The crowd of Brigands erupted in agreement. It was clear to Aleric now that they did not want to leave their lives in the woods either.

Aleric walked forward and shouted out, "The king has need for soldiers too. You can take any job you'd like. There is gold in the hills, rich farm soil in the valleys, strength needed at the castle and in the king's army." The soldiers fell silent again, exchanging more glances and whispering to one another.

"There are women..." Aleric continued bluntly. "Two women to every man, as it stands right now." And he wasn't lying. Since the initial banning of magic and subsequent tyranny, many men in the kingdom had been locked up or disappeared, especially those who owned desirable land. Not to mention the countless men who had been sent into the forests only to be ambushed and killed by these Brigands.

Slowly the men began to exchange glances and one by one began shaking their heads and shrugging, silently suggesting that this idea might not be so bad after all. Their attitude on the matter seemed to change almost instantly and soon enough they were being loud and talking amongst each other as if the tense situation going on had never happened.

"Women." Commander Rune shrugged at Aleric. "They do make the world go round." His voice could barely be heard over the loud chatter "Gather your things, men!" he yelled loudly. "We march to Mazeron at dawn!" The men erupted in cheer and fists were thrown into the air at the exciting thought of a new life somewhere. Aleric knew he had convinced them, and there would be no trouble from the Brigand army, for now.

But Aleric couldn't help but wonder what he would do if the king didn't agree to letting them stay in the kingdom. None of this had been cleared by the king, but he would have to understand that this was the only way to rid the forests of their enemy.

Aleric's thoughts were interrupted when a large brute of a soldier with thick red hair and matching beard slapped Aleric on the shoulder and shook him as a sign of comradery.

"Thank you, good knight," he said with a smile. "You've given us hope. A second chance at life..." he said, then walked away with no other words.

"You have their support," Commander Rune said to Aleric, still yelling over the commotion from the men. "Now if you don't mind, I am retiring to my quarters." It was apparent that Commander Rune was angry at the entire situation. He had been outmatched and forced into something that was not his decision.

"Visko!" he called over to his brother. "Let's go." The two made their way out of the hall. Aleric let them go, as he knew he had the support of the soldiers at this point, and even if

Commander Rune tried to go back on his word, the men would not support it.

Later that night there was a great celebration. Fires raged and cheers cut into the cold, quiet night of the forest. Thearbuc and Lamora could hear the celebrations from atop the nearby cliffs, but they did not know if Aleric had succeeded or if the brigands were celebrating his execution.

But their questions were answered the next morning, shortly after the sun rose from beyond the horizon. They were awakened from their uneasy rest by the sound of a large horn. It echoed through the valley proud and deep. Thearbuc and Lamora opened their eyes instantly at the sound, then scrambled back to the cliffs to see what was going on.

Down below, they saw the large army of Brigands assembling. Long rows of soldiers filed in perfect lines, some atop horses and others standing in line. There must have been two hundred of them or more. Then the horn blew again, and they began to march. Thearbuc spotted Aleric toward the front of the congregation. His shiny armor was easy to spot, glinting proudly in the morning sunlight. Next to Aleric and also atop large horses were Commander Rune and his brother, Visko.

Vidor was back among the troops riding an enormous horse, necessary to carry the weight of the burly soldier. He was abrasive as usual, harassing and picking at the troops to keep them in line as they began their march.

"He's all right!" Thearbuc exclaimed happily to Lamora. "He's okay! He's getting them to leave the forest!" Lamora smiled and happiness washed over them, both knowing their friend was okay and his mission was accomplished. "Let's get down there," Thearbuc continued. The two hurried from the cliffs down to camp to get ready to depart.

At camp, Thearbuc and Lamora repacked their things for the long journey. Thearbuc, wanting to rearrange his things to fit more comfortably in his pack, dumped its contents onto the ground. As he was sifting through it, placing things carefully back into his pack, Lamora suddenly gasped and pointed. She couldn't speak, but Thearbuc could see something was the matter.

"What is wrong?" he asked. She shook her head and bulged her eyes but said nothing. "Lamora?" he asked again.

"That trinket," she finally said, pointing to the armlet that Brodel had given Thearbuc back at his hut in the woods. "Where did you get that?"

"Our friend Brodel gave it to me," Thearbuc replied after a pause. "Back in his hut. It was a gift. I thought I would give it to my daughter when I got back home. A little keepsake from the road." Lamora was still looking for words, but they did not come easily.

"You…You need to get rid of that," she said in a low whisper.

"How come?" Thearbuc replied with a chuckle. "I do not. It's a pretty trinket."

"Do you believe me when I tell you that I can see energies?" she asked.

"Well, sure, I guess," Thearbuc replied.

"That armlet, it is surrounded by bad, evil energy. Very bad. Blackness surrounds and follows it. Please, get rid of it," she begged.

"Oh, it's just a harmless trinket, Lamora. I hardly doubt it's a problem." And with that he shoved it back into his pack.

"You don't understand!" she cried out.

"It's not your place," he said gently. "Let it go." Lamora breathed a heavy sigh, seeing what the object meant to him. If she had to, she could steal it and get rid of it later, she thought, so she dropped the matter for now.

She knew how objects like that worked, how they silently destroyed people's lives, which only fed their blackness and made their evil stronger. The seemingly insignificant item would seem pretty enough to keep so that unaware people would bring them into their homes and forget about them. That is where the dark object would sit unnoticed in people's cluttered cottages for years. Slowly tearing their lives apart with sickness, tragedy, and disasters that would rip happy families apart. Once the person's life was thoroughly destroyed by an endless string of bad luck they would be forced to move or sell all their belongings which would unknowingly send the bad luck charm to its next victim. The only way a person could save themselves from a bad luck charm was to constantly throw out unused items and keep their cottage uncluttered from unused junk. Keeping windows open to let in breeze and sunlight to blow and snuff out their negative energy would also help, but to only a certain extent.

"Let's go," Thearbuc said, standing back up and throwing his pack over his shoulder. "Hopefully they have some extra horses down there for us. Would be a shame if we had to walk the whole way back to Mazeron."

Instead of trying to catch up with the army, Thearbuc and Lamora planned to go back down the deer trail to the main road, where they would meet back up with Aleric and the brigands. They arrived much quicker going down the hill than it took them to go up it, so they waited for the large group to arrive. Finally, Aleric came around the bend, leading the army of Brigands, and the three friends met up again.

"These are my friends, Thearbuc and Lamora," he introduced them to Commander Rune and his brother Visko as they approached on their horses. Thearbuc and Lamora could tell the tension was tight and uncomfortable between them. But the army of Brigands were on the move, and that is all that mattered.

Soon Thearbuc and Lamora were outfitted with a pair of horses, and the army marched on through the forests to Mazeron. Aleric quietly explained to Thearbuc and Lamora what had transpired down in the Brigand camp, and the empty promises that he had made, still unaware whether he would be able to make good on those promises or not.

"You will have to persuade the king," Thearbuc whispered as they spoke about it.

"It shouldn't be hard with an entire army standing outside of his door," Aleric replied.

"Or you just brought war to our own doorstep…" Thearbuc trailed off.

"Either way, it is in motion now," Aleric continued after a long pause. "All we can do now is reach the kingdom and hope for the best."

The army marched on throughout the day. It was cool and damp in the depths of the forest. The blue sky was overhead, but the trees were so thick all around them that they never saw the sun. Awkward tension arose every time the group passed by a burnt wagon or ambushed merchant train from long ago. They knew they had committed these crimes while living as renegades in the forests, and now returning to civilization the guilt of their brutal lives seemed to hang over their heads.

The march was accompanied with the sound of a thousand footsteps, horses trotting, and of course the constant noise of Vidor barking orders at the marching soldiers.

"Get in line!" he would bark. "Pick up the pace. Look straight forward soldier." He did not carry a whip or ever assault the men but just barked orders constantly.

"Vidor is like a small dog," Aleric laughed at one point, talking to Commander Rune. "Why do you let him treat the men like that?"

"Gah," the commander grunted, clearly unhappy. "He's harmless, and it makes him feel better. He has nothing at home. Military is his entire life. He is the king's cousin…"

"Yes, but it is your army," Aleric interrupted.

"Aye. But I am replaceable just like anyone else," the commander replied. "We let him do his thing and as long as he doesn't get out of line, it doesn't matter to anyone. The men don't even care at this point." Aleric looked back from his horse as they trotted along. Vidor was going up and down the rows barking orders, and he could see that the commander was right. The men weren't even looking at the large, round tyrant doing his best to get under their nerves.

The group continued their march through the woods until the sun began to dip low in the sky and the forest floor darkened once again. As they marched into a clearing, Commander Rune stopped the convoy to notify them they would be spending the night here, and to get ready to make camp and their own suppers. They broke rank instantly, and like a well-oiled machine, they had tents up and fires started within no time.

"You run a tight ship," Aleric complimented the commander on his troops.

"They are good men," the commander replied. "I just hope they fit in with your kingdom and this new lifestyle." As he said it, he met Aleric's eyes and stared with a look of desperation, and Aleric understood that the commander was just as nervous about the situation as he was.

That night the fires raged tall and loud against the black night, and the shadows danced across the forest's tall trees from the large flames. The mood was all around good, and the men drank and sang for hours. It was clear that they enjoyed the forests and were very comfortable out here living in them. The forest was like a big home to them. They could find food and have a large fire going within a matter of hours, and every one of them seemed very comfortable, warm, and prepared for the cold night.

Later that evening, Aleric, Thearbuc, and Lamora found themselves sitting on the ground near a roaring fire next to Commander Rune and his small group of trusted friends and advisors. Thearbuc began taking items out of his pack while looking for his ale cup so he could pour himself a drink. Without realizing it, he set the armlet that Brodel had given him on the ground, then continued digging through his pack. By complete coincidence, Vidor walked by at that exact moment and noticed the armlet sitting on the ground. The gold band and small shiny jewels reflected the flames brightly, and it glinted beautifully in the dark night. Vidor stopped in his tracks at the sight of it. Then he took a large swig of ale from his stein and sat down beside Thearbuc, offering him a friendly handshake and making conversation. As they spoke, Thearbuc did not notice the burly man lay one foot over the armlet, pull it toward his lap, and pick it up and quietly slip it into his pocket. Thearbuc did not give it much notice, but after the armlet had been stolen from him, the fire shone brighter, and a weight seemed lifted from his shoulders. "Must be the ale and the fresh forest air," he said aloud to himself at one point.

The group sat by the roaring fire drinking ale, eating, and engaging in good conversation as the night wore on. It was starting to seem like the tensions had eased, and everyone was beginning to trust one another a little more. Around the main fire sat Thearbuc, Vidor, Aleric, Lamora, Commander Rune, and Visko. The other Brigands were close by and scattered throughout the woods around their own fires. Some of the brigands attended to the main fire and brought them food and drink. After a few ales, Aleric noticed that Vidor was talking more than normal, jabbing insults at everyone around the fire or anyone who dared walk past.

"The man is a brute," Aleric whispered to Lamora, disgusted at Vidor's boorish behavior.

"What about you, knight?" Vidor said drunkenly as he pushed Aleric with more than just playful force. "You do, huh? You think you're strong and tough behind that armor, don't ya?"

Vidor continued to prod. “Only scaredy boys wear armor if you ask me,” he said after a big gulp that left ale running down his beard.

“No one asked you,” Aleric replied in an annoyed tone, but it did not slow the drunken brute. The men just ignored him, shaking their heads as they walked away. It seemed they were used to him by now and treated him more like an annoying fly that wouldn’t buzz away.

But Aleric was not used to him. His blood had begun to boil long ago, and it was only getting worse as the night and beratement wore on and Vidor became more drunk. The man was an abrasive troll and a spoiled child all rolled into one. Later, when he turned toward The Paladin and with wretched breath to antagonize him once again, Aleric was done.

Without a word or any sign of aggression at all, he rose calmly, grabbed Vidor, and gave him one solid punch to the face, then another to the stomach. Caught off guard, Vidor fell backward hard into the ground, spilling his drink all over himself. Blood started running from his nose. The other soldiers quickly turned their attention to Aleric, and some rose to their feet as if they were going to advance on him, but no attack came. Not one soldier attempted to help Vidor. They just stood silently, staring at The Paladin and the bloodied nose of Vidor who was rolling on the ground and grunting in pain. Aleric met the eyes of Commander Rune and waited for a response, but the commander simply gave a short nod and took another sip of his ale. In fact, no one said anything at all about Aleric knocking Vidor to the ground. All they could do was stare at Aleric and hope they weren’t the next ones to be on the receiving end of his unforgiving temper and quick fists.

Aleric wanted to break the tension but all he could muster was “I’m going for a walk” as he made a hasty retreat into the dark woods. He was in no mood for eating, drinking, and being merry anymore, so he made his camp out in the woods and retired for the night

The next morning nothing was said of the incident. Breakfast was light and fast. Shortly after the sun began to rise, while it was still early morning, the convoy of Brigands began to move again

The day wore on and the march towards Mazeron was uneventful. The long road through the seemingly endless forests, along with the constant nuisance from the Leedles, began to wear on the men.

"We must be close to water," Aleric mentioned, pointing out the Leedles and trying to make small talk with the commander. He did not reply. Commander Rune did not much care for Aleric, and even though they kept up the façade that he was in charge, the commander was still upset that his army had been taken away from him, and they were currently marching toward unknown lands and an unknown future. For all he knew they could be marching straight into an ambush.

Later in the afternoon, the forests began to give way to grassy fields and rolling hills. The road became wider, indicating they were getting closer to civilization. Then, passing through a small valley of green grass and small cliffs on either side, Aleric noticed something.

"What is that?" He pointed out into a green field near them. The men stopped and peered into the distance.

"It's a dead sheep," Thearbuc spoke loudly from a few rows of soldiers behind Aleric. Thearbuc was an experienced hunter, and his eyesight and ability to recognize different animals from a distance was superior to the others. The small army halted for a few moments and waited for the shape in the field to move, but it never did.

"I think he's right. Carry on, men," Commander Rune yelled to the others as he began to trot on. But just a few feet further they saw another dead sheep, then another, and another.

"This is peculiar," Thearbuc said to Lamora as he trotted up next to her. "I don't like it." The others were thinking the same.

Finally, the road bent slightly behind a small hill and suddenly they came upon a small cottage. It had a grass thatched roof and faint smoke rose lazily from the chimney. In front of the cottage, they saw a man down on one knee who was leaning against a small wooden fence outside of the cottage. His face was buried in his hands, but he eventually looked up as the sound of the battalion alerted him.

"Good sir!" Aleric announced their presence from afar as he rode towards the man. The man stared at the large group but did not move. Aleric took this behavior as a sign that the man was not scared of them, nor was a threat, so they continued to approach him. Riding up to the man slowly, Aleric could see the man's face was red and his eyes were puffy. He had been crying. "Good sir, are you alright?" Aleric asked looking down at the old man from atop his horse. The man wiped his nose and sniffled. His head turned from side to side then he motioned towards the field near his cottage.

"My sheep. My flock…" he trailed off. The group turned to examine the field and there they saw more bodies of dead sheep. Lifeless heaps strewn about the field. Flies buzzing around them in the midday sun.

"What took place here?" Commander Rune asked directly. The old man was clearly distraught and was having trouble finding the words to speak.

"Wolves." He spoke. "Wolves got them all." He motioned to another section of the field behind the hut where a lifeless wolf lay with two arrows sticking out from it. "Many wolves…" the man said, staring blankly into the field. "We've never had wolves here…"

Commander Rune dismounted his large horse and went to the distraught man and offered him his leather bag of water which the man took and drank from. "What is your name sheep herder? Where are your guardian dogs?" Commander Rune asked looking around the fields.

"Addison" the man replied with a grunt, clearing his throat. "My name is Addison. We've never needed guardian dogs for the herd." He continued as he slowly regained his composure. "We are surrounded by cliffs on either side and the river. My family have been sheep herders in these parts for three generations. Never needed no sheep dogs. There just haven't ever been wolves in the area."

Aleric looked confused. "No sheep dogs?" He mumbled in bewilderment.

"No sheep dogs?" Commander Rune continued. "Every herd needs to be protected." He was thinking aloud more than making conversation.

"Don't you think I know that now," Addison replied holding back tears. "Now that it's too late! The whole heard is gone." He trailed off as he gazed around at the slaughter that had taken place. Commander Rune patted Addison on his shoulder to comfort him. Aleric noticed the gesture. He was beginning to realize what a good man the commander was. Not just a brute, strong military man. But smart, civilized, and respectful. All traits that should be admired in these unrefined times.

"Hang on…" The commander said. "We will help where we can. Commander Rune began to walk away. "Vidor!" He said calling to his general. Vidor came out of the shadows, slowly trotting atop his horse. "Have the men leave three dogs and a barrel of ale for this man," he ordered. Vidor nodded but did not speak. He trotted slowly back toward the wagons in the rear and began relaying the orders to the men. Soon a small group came forward, two carrying a barrel of ale and the others coming up with three leashed dogs.

"We have many good dogs. They are from a proud breed and have kept our flocks safe for many years. Please take them to help rebuild your flock. As far as the sheep, we had to leave ours behind so you will have to obtain those on your own and begin to rebuild. A good shepherd never lets his guard down and you must use force when needed, to keep foes at bay." With that the commander gave Addison one last pat on his shoulder then returned to his horse.

"We move!" he called out. Then the battalion began their march once again. One by one they filed slowly past the distraught shepherd. Addison nodded in appreciation behind puffy eyes as they filed past him. After they all went by, he kneeled down to greet his new dogs and one began licking his face. Looking back, Aleric saw a smile on the man's face just as the road took another bend and continued on into the forests once again.

"It's hard to imagine someone being so naïve. A man not having anything to protect his flock," Aleric eventually said to Commander Rune. "Just hoping for the best when there are so many threats out there" There was a pause as they trotted slowly along.

"Why is it so hard to believe when your king has done almost the exact same thing?" Commander Rune replied with a snarky tone. Aleric was taken aback.

"What could you possibly mean by that?" he said in defense.

"Well…Your brilliant king banned magic, the kingdom's best weapon against a world filled with threats, in a land fraught with monsters and adversaries. He's no different than a sheep herder without sheep dogs. What did he think was going to happen when he left the whole place defenseless? Do you just hope that wolves won't be wolves?" the commander chuckled at the analogy as he said it. "No, no, Paladin. It is ignorant to expect wolves to not be wolves. They don't change. It's nature. One must simply prepare for them, for their aggressive behavior is very predictable."

Aleric knew he was right. As a soldier himself, he knew that pacifism was not the way to counter most threats. Loyal to his king, he had nothing more to say and just nodded at the commander as they rode on into the forests.

It was mid-afternoon the following day when the battalion reached the outskirts of the kingdom. It had been raining all day, and it was still coming down. The men were drenched and a miserable sight to see. Their usual thick, proud hair was matted in front of their eyes and dripping wet with rain. Soggy clothes and soggy shoes made for a heavy and uncomfortable journey.

As they passed various cottages and farms along the main road on the way to the castle, they did not go unnoticed. One by one the inhabitants of the cottages saw the battalion of Brigands making their way through the kingdom and came to their doors to observe the procession. The villagers knew exactly who these men were, and a warm welcome was not given. The only reason there was not a full-on panic from the gathering villagers was because Aleric flew the flag of Mazeron from his horse at the front of the procession.

"Why did you bring them here!?" one old woman asked Aleric as he trotted slowly along in the drizzling rain.

"They'll kill us all," one man mentioned as he watched them file by.

"They killed my uncle," another replied. "Ambushed our family's merchant train. We lost everything!" he cried out.

The villagers weren't sure whether to be angry that Aleric was bringing them here or fearful of what they might do, but more and more continued to gather as the battalion marched towards the castle. The brigands mostly ignored the villagers, as instructed by Commander Rune, but with so much disparity and fear in the air, the mood felt like a powder keg about to ignite.

Word of their arrival must have spread, because every guard was assembled and at the ready by the time Aleric, with his Brigand army in tow, reached the castle's ramp. Slowly they marched up to the ramp and shuffled into the castle's courtyard, which was lined with the castle's guards, weapons drawn at the ready. No words were spoken.

"Stay here," Aleric said to Commander Rune, marching up the ramp to the waiting guards.

"I thought you said the king had already arranged us to come to the kingdom," Commander Rune whispered sharply. "You've led us into a trap," he said in a hushed tone, so that others could not hear the worry in his voice.

"I'm a man of my word. Let me negotiate the terms of your surrender of the forest with the king. Then, you will be welcomed," Aleric simply replied. Reluctantly, Commander Rune held his position and kept the soldiers in line.

Aleric dismounted and walked to the castle's main entrance, nodding at the guards at the door as he approached. The massive doors swung open before him, and he entered the castle to see Maub standing tall, threatening, and angry before him.

"What have you done, Paladin!? he hissed, standing tall and craggy, leaning heavily and hunched on his staff in the castle's main ballroom. His old face was wrinkled with anger, and hate burned in his eyes.

"I did what I was tasked to do, wizard. Rid the forest of the brigands," Aleric replied. He had learned not to fear the mysterious and powerful wizard, but he couldn't help but notice his stomach lurch and heart begin to race at the sight of him. "Where is the king?" Aleric continued, walking past the angry wizard. His eyes met one of the castle's guards, who motioned to him then led Aleric up the stairs to the king's wing of the castle. Maub followed closely behind. Inside the king's chambers, King Victus was standing near his bed, peering out one of the small windows at the large army that had gathered at the foot of his castle.

"What is going on!?" the king snapped at Aleric as he entered the room. Maub was standing uncomfortably close behind him and he felt trapped and cornered.

"Sir, I have rid the forests of the brigands, just as you asked," Aleric replied, trying to sound confident behind his worry and nervousness.

"By bringing them here!" the king cried out. "You'll have us all killed. What are we supposed to do with them? How are the villagers supposed to react!?"

"You brought the wolves right to our door," Maub hissed. Aleric began to lose his temper and became defensive almost immediately.

"There was no other choice!" he snapped back unexpectedly. "We went to Haberlorn and they refused to help. So, what did you want to do? Keep sending the men into the forest to be ambushed and killed one by one?" The three exchanged glances and neither King Victus nor Maub had a reply. "I saw their camp and their tactics. There was no way to beat them by force, I can assure you. I have done my part. I rid the forests of the brigands. Now it's time for you to do yours."

"What do you mean?" Maub snapped back, answering for the king.

"Give them land. Give them a place to live and build new lives. It will keep the forest roads open, and together we can all rebuild!" Aleric said with compassion and conviction.

"Never!!" Maub yelled, answering for the king again. "I will destroy them all right now." As he said it, he rushed toward the closed balcony doors in anger and his staff began to glow an eerie blue.

"Stop!" King Victus finally chimed in, catching the wizard mid-stride. "Aleric may be right. They are a strong, capable force. Fighting may not be the best option. What did you have in mind, Aleric?" Then he turned to Maub, who was glaring back in anger. "Let's hear him out, wizard," King Victus said calmly. Aleric made his way toward the large map of the Kingdom of Mazeron that hung on the far wall.

"Here." He pointed to an area on the south end of the map. "Give them this land. Nothing is there anymore, and it is fertile farmland. They can farm the land and harvest food for the entire kingdom." The king stayed silent for some time, contemplating Aleric's words. "Imagine, my lord," Aleric continued, "the forest roads open for trade and goods, the kingdom with an abundance of food."

"It is not going to happen that way!" Maub interrupted. "They are thieves and murderers. They will destroy the kingdom." King Victus, still lost in thought, did not reply.

"Those are my lands!" Maub yelled out, finally losing his temper.

"Your lands?" King Victus replied, taken aback and insulted by the wizard's choice of words.

"Our lands, sir. I meant *our* lands," he snapped quickly, backpedaling.

"Those lands belong to the farmers and settlers," the king continued.

"Not anymore," Aleric replied. "All of the farmers and settlers in those lands have been locked in the dungeon or have mysteriously disappeared. The land is completely vacant. Isn't that right, Maub?" Aleric knew the area was open land from when he had stumbled in to one of Maub's secret court sessions in the dungeon and had seen the map of land now owned by the kingdom. Apparently, the king did not know anything about this, Aleric was now realizing. King Victus held an angry stare at the wizard, demanding some explanation.

"The kingdom has worked hard to rid these lands of conspirators and law breakers, my King," Maub said. "The villagers in that area united as a group conspiring against you. They were trying to obtain the use of magic to do it," he continued in defense.

"And you didn't tell me?" the king asked, bewildered.

"We handled it, my King," Maub replied slowly. "We were only doing our jobs." The wizard trailed off, then waited for the king's reply. The king started to pace back and forth, with one hand on his chin as he thought about the situation.

"Sometimes I don't know who's side you are on, wizard," King Victus said, frustrated. Then after a long, uncomfortable silence he spoke again. "Aleric," the king finally spoke. "Tell your Brigands that they have the lands south of the river and up to the foothills."

"Thank you, sir," Aleric said, as an enormous sigh of relief washed through his body.

"But they are your responsibility. Do you hear me?" King Victus continued. "You will oversee their settlement and keep a close eye on their behavior. If they become trouble, they will be rounded up just like any other criminal. But if they can assimilate and behave, then they can stay."

"I will do my best, sir," Aleric replied. "This is the right decision, my King."

"The only decision," King Victus grunted in stressed annoyance, then turned toward the balcony and held his hand to his forehead as if pushing back a headache. He paused at the doorway and took one last giant sigh before opening the large double doors of the balcony above the courtyard. As he walked out, the commotion coming from the villagers and Brigands below fell silent as they waited in anticipation for what the king had to say.

"People of Mazeron," King Victus yelled out to the crowd. His voice was surprisingly loud as he addressed the courtyard. "Today we celebrate. Today, thanks to our paladin, the forests and merchant roads are open and free of Brigands and thieves!"

The villagers below instantly erupted in anger and the castle's guards poured out of the barracks just in time to separate the villagers and brigands from a full-on battle. The king tried to continue his speech with reassuring words about prosperity and opening trade again, but against the nearly violent commotion no one was able to hear him, so he turned quietly and walked back into the castle and slowly closed the doors behind him.

Maub was glaring at Aleric hard in anger as the noise from outside became muffled. At this point he knew that Aleric had been snooping through the dungeons of the castle. Without a word, he turned quickly, his long robes flowing through the air as he stormed out of the room, the door slamming hard behind him. King Victus sighed again after the wizard left.

"Tell your new friends they can camp out past the village tonight. Tomorrow we will begin discussing jobs throughout the kingdom and their lands. If they don't end up fitting in here and cause us trouble, then this whole kingdom will be thrown into chaos. Either way, Paladin, you did the impossible. The merchant roads are open!"

Chapter 15: The Witch Kalindra

The weeks had steadily rolled by since Aleric brought the band of Brigands, a lost army from the north who had made the forests their home, back to the kingdom. There was a lot to be done. Land had to be divided up, rules established, new positions in the castle's ranks appointed. The last thing the kingdom needed, King Victus had said, "was a bunch of violent beggars roaming the streets." So, he had taken it upon himself, with the help of his counsel to help the new members of their kingdom find work and begin to build and grow.

Fields were beginning to be cleared, and seeds planted by new farmers. Small dwellings were popping up around the old gold mines as some of the men took to prospecting. The brigands mostly seemed to keep to themselves, and the villagers, although still skeptical of the once-renegade bandits, seemed to have calmed down and put them mostly in the back of their minds.

Six small groups of former Brigands were sent out into the mountains to find any trace of Brodel and the witch Kalindra. The weeks passed slowly and agonizingly for Thearbuc, who wanted nothing more than to find his friend and get him home safely. But none of the search parties had returned with any news yet.

Thearbuc moved into the castle just down and across the hall from Aleric. Lamora had moved back into her childhood home, which was apparently still in her family.

One morning, while Aleric and King Victus were on the castle's balcony overlooking the kingdom and discussing the growing commerce, they noticed two of the king's guards off in the distance, riding quickly towards the castle. At first, they paid no mind, but once the riders got closer, Aleric spotted it. One of the riders was carrying Brodel's staff. He knew it was his because it radiated magic just like Brodel did. Even from a distance Aleric could see the small flicks and sparks of magic radiating and glowing.

"That is Brodel's staff!" he called out with an excited jump before turning and heading toward the door. King Victus followed, and they ran down the castle's steps and corridors as fast as possible. Because the castle was so large, it took some time to get down to ground level and out to the main gate. But by the time they got down to the castle's entrance, the two riders were nowhere to be seen.

"Where did they go!?" he called out to King Victus, who was just now coming out the castle doors.

"Try the stables," the king replied. Quickly, they ran down the ramp and to the stables. Aleric noticed one of the guards on the ramp was sweaty and his hair was a mess.

"You there!" he announced as he walked aggressively towards the guard. "Did you just ride in? Where is the staff you had?"

The guard stuttered and tripped over his words, obviously trying to hide something. "I…I'm not—I can't say," he stuttered.

"Maub…" Aleric mumbled under his breath. He turned from the guard and quickly ran back to the castle. The king followed behind him but could not keep up. Aleric ran to the side of the castle, up to the dungeon's doors. The guards stepped in front of the doorway and stretched out their arms, forcing him to halt as he approached. But instead of slowing, he ran faster, and before the guards knew what was happening, Aleric slammed one of them aside with his shoulder then heaved open the dungeon door with a giant shove. There, just a few steps in front of him in the dark hallway leading to the dungeons, was Maub, with Brodel's staff in his hands, softly illuminating the dark hallway with its glowing magic.

"Stop there!" Aleric commanded the wizard. Maub turned about quickly, and with fire in his eyes raised the staff. It began to create a ball of energy at its tip, and he pointed it directly at Aleric, who could only tense and wait for the blast to hit him.

"What are you doing!?" the king suddenly interrupted, approaching the now-open door out of breath.

Maub quickly lowered the staff, trying to hide it. "Just…I was…taking this…." The wizard stumbled over his words. "The men believe they found your friend's staff. I was taking it to the king."

"Through the dungeon entrance?" King Victus asked.

"I was near the dungeon door when the men arrived," Maub replied slowly. "Ater all, it is where I work," he snarked. "We have trials set for today."

"Let me see the staff," Aleric demanded, approaching cautiously. He knew the power the staff could wield in skilled hands such as Maub's, and he still did not fully trust the wizard, even though he had saved his life from the assassins in the dining hall just months before.

"It is yours," the wizard conceded with a bow, handing Aleric the staff.

"This is it! Brodel's staff!" Aleric announced. "We must find the riders and put together a rescue party at once."

They left Maub standing in the dark hallway and rushed away. The king fetched Thearbuc to tell him the news, while Aleric found and questioned the riders about the staff. They knew the location of where the staff had been found and that was about it. There was no other evidence of Brodel or the fight they had in the woods against Kalindra and the Morghvile beasts.

The riders who found the staff were given two days to rest before the search party was to set off and they were to show them the way to the area where they had found the staff. A party of twenty men was assembled. Among them were Aleric, Thearbuc, Lamora, and the rest were Brigands who would be led by none other than Vidor. Commander Rune and his brother Visko were too busy getting the brigands settled into their new lives and jobs to go off and leave them leaderless in the tense kingdom. Vidor was their sergeant, and the men were used to following his orders. Commander Rune had promised Aleric that the abrasive man would behave on the road. Plus, Vidor had not forgotten the beating Aleric had given him the last time they traveled together.

So, two days later, the party was assembled on horseback and supplied well enough to be on the road for an entire moon cycle looking for Brodel. Vidor and the brigands had specific orders to kill the witch Kalindra if the opportunity presented itself, but Aleric and Thearbuc's only goal was to get their friend back. Soon, they were heading down the castle's ramp even before the sun rose above the distant mountain peaks. Two by two, they filed down the main road and out of the kingdom, once again adventuring deep through the outer-woods and into the mountains.

On the second day of travel, when they were already deep into the woods, they came across a curious little creature. They heard him before they could see him. It sounded like someone talking angrily, like an argument, but with only one voice. Then they spotted where the voice was coming from: It was a small gnome sitting next to a large tree. He was a smaller gnome, about the height of a grown man's knee. He was well-dressed and smoking a pipe. The tree he sat against had a wooden door carved into it, and little bits of clutter and clay pots sat scattered near the doorway.

As the group approached The Gnome, it became clear that he was very grumpy and was, in fact, arguing with himself. Cursing, grunting, speaking fast, and calling out names and unpleasantries. When The Gnome noticed the battalion approaching on horseback, he grunted in annoyance and took a big puff on his pipe, then blew it casually and arrogantly into the sky.

"Gah. What ugly bunch of trough-drinkers do we have here, eh? And I'm not talking about the horses." The Gnome spat on the ground in disgust, then began to mumble quickly to himself, "Dumb knights, lost in the forests. They can't find their way anywhere. Always need help. Incapable nincompoops."

"Are you done?" Aleric asked the small gnome, who then took another puff of his pipe and blew it directly into Aleric's face.

"Done with you," The Gnome replied as he scratched his long white beard that just barely grazed the ground when he was sitting.

"Why are you so angry, gnome?" Aleric asked.

"Why are you so stupid?" The Gnome replied. Aleric couldn't help but let out a bewildered gasp that the tiny gnome was so insulting to people five times as big as him.

"What is your name?" he asked.

"Wellington," The Gnome replied. "That is Sir Wellington to the likes of you." It was becoming clear to Aleric that The Gnome was looking for a fight. But why, he could not imagine.

"Well, we are in hurry so we will let you be, Wellington. I hope you have a good afternoon," Aleric said, beginning to ride on.

"I hope you die," Wellington The Gnome grunted in reply. "Hope your big horse trips and fall right on your big dumb head." Aleric just scoffed again and began to trot on. Best to leave the unpleasant gnome alone he figured. Why The Gnome had such an unpleasant disposition was none of their business.

The search party passed by Wellington one by one, and he made it a point to taunt and harass each and every one of them as they passed. Wellington had a very sharp tongue and somehow knew exactly what to say to each man to cut them the deepest. Some things even started to seem personal, as if Wellington had known the person their entire lives and knew just what to say to be as mean and hurtful as possible.

"She didn't leave you because you weren't rich enough, laddie," The Gnome said to one man as they shuffled by. "She left you because you couldn't satisfy her."

"What a mean little devil," Lamora remarked to Thearbuc after The Gnome commented on Lamora not having parents and Thearbuc "looking like the type of man who would abandon his children in the woods." Most of the men ignored Wellington's sharp tongue and just let the angry gnome be. But then Vidor approached The Gnome.

"Have you ever seen a piece of food and not eaten it?" The Gnome said to the burly sergeant.

"What did you say?" Vidor challenged, leaning down from his horse and getting close to The Gnome's face. Wellington took a large puff from his pipe, held in the smoke, then slowly blew it in Vidor's face, making him cough on the smoke and stench.

"What foulness are you smoking, gnome?" Vidor asked tauntingly.

"It smells like flowers compared to your breath," The Gnome snapped back without missing a beat. Vidor's blood was beginning to boil after being taunted mercilessly by such a small creature. He slowly shook his head back and forth, clenched his teeth, and began to dismount his horse.

"Best to let him be!" Lamora called out from the front of the caravan. "There is magic in these forests; you don't know what he is capable of!"

Vidor ignored her. He was already frustrated and angry after a string of unfortunate incidents had hit him since coming into possession of the bad luck charm that he had stolen from Thearbuc, and he was ready to take it out on anyone smaller than himself. "You need a lesson in manners," he said to Wellington, still clenching his teeth and fists as he went at The Gnome.

"You need a lesson in healthy eating," Wellington replied calmly as the angry burly man approached him. "Maybe you sh—"

The Gnome was cut short as the massive foot of Vidor met his body and he was punted from the ground. Wellington soared through the air with a faint scream, spinning end upon end into the distance, through the trees and sky, then finally out of sight.

"Haaaa ha ha!" Vidor leaned backward and held his hips as he laughed at the sight of the tiny gnome being kicked away into oblivion.

"Nice kick!" the men congratulated the burly sergeant with laughter and applause.

"You kick like a sissy," a voice announced suddenly. It cut through the laughter like a knife, and everything fell silent instantly. Vidor turned around to see The Gnome standing there as if nothing had happened.

"I've seen mild winds pack a harder punch than that," a voice came from another direction. Vidor looked back the other way. It was another gnome. An exact copy of the other and was standing calmly by the door in the tree, casually smoking a pipe. Vidor looked back and forth in confusion upon seeing two of the exact same gnomes. The two Wellingtons were talking to each other, making jokes about Vidor like two bullies picking on a smaller child.

"You think he'll try to eat us?" one Wellington said to the other.

"Is there anything he won't eat?" the first Wellington replied between puffs on his pipe.

Vidor's face was bright red, and his blood was boiling over. With clenched teeth, he took quick steps and again punted The Gnome with a massive kick, sending him flying into the woods. Then he turned and picked up the other Wellington and threw him through the sky fast and far into the woods. The men nervously chuckled again at the faint screams as The Gnomes flew through the air. Vidor rubbed his hands together, patting off the dirt with a look of accomplishment on his face when he heard another taunting voice. It was Wellington again!

He turned back towards The Gnome-home tree to not see not just two gnomes but four gnomes this time, all perfect duplicates of Wellington and all making fun of him, taking jabs at his appearance and his weaknesses.

"Devils!" Vidor cried out in a fit of anger, flailing, kicking, and hurling the four small gnomes away. When they were gone, he fell to one knee and panted heavily to catch his breath.

"That all you got, missy?" Wellington's voice pierced through the quiet forest. The hair on the back of the onlookers' necks stood up at the sound as eight unharmed gnomes were suddenly surrounding Vidor, seemingly out of nowhere.

Vidor drew his axe and tiredly swung at one of the Wellingtons, who easily hopped out of its path. Then The Gnome came charging at Vidor fast and jumped on top of him, just as another two jumped on him from behind. Vidor let out a cry of anger and pain then stood up fast and tried to shake The Gnomes off. Frantically, he grabbed them and hurled them off into the distance and hard onto the ground. Finally, when the eight gnomes were gone the helpless onlookers could see blood running from Vidor's neck and arms. He leaned heavily onto his axe for support as he tried to catch his breath. The woods were silent once again, but only for a moment.

"I could do this all day, tiny man," a new Wellington gnome said, casually leaning against a tree with a small pipe in his mouth. Vidor clenched his teeth in anger.

"You don't have to fight!" one of the onlooking Brigands cried out from where they were watching from a safe distance.

"Just stop!" Lamora yelled through the trees.

Vidor was surrounded now. Sixteen gnomes were scattered throughout the trees, encircling him, casually smoking pipes and waiting for his next move. Every time Vidor attacked, the Wellingtons would double, clawing and biting at the large burly man.

This cycle continued as the horrified onlookers watched helplessly until it seemed the whole area of the forest was occupied by small, angry, foul-mouthed harassing gnomes. Vidor lay on the ground bloodied and exhausted, gasping for breath. One of the Wellington gnomes approached him slowly. He took a long, slow drag from his pipe and casually blew it in Vidor's face, which was now lying in the dirt.

"I've seen my grandmammy use a blade better than you," The Gnome said snidely, while casually nudging Vidor's axe with his foot. Vidor, with his last bit of strength, swung his axe blade pitifully at The Gnome but before he could even finish the swing

The Gnomes were on him. Piling on in droves, The Gnomes covered Vidor in just an instant. His screams were slowly muffled as more and more Wellingtons piled on.

"We've got to get out of here," Thearbuc said to Aleric with fear and disbelief in his eyes. "This sorcery is too powerful for us." Aleric agreed, and quickly the group hurried away into the woods. The last thing they saw of Vidor was a small stream of blood flowing away from the pile of angry gnomes. None of the onlookers who witnessed the attack were able to wrap their head around what had just happened, but they now had a fresh reminder of the dangers of these magical and unknown woods.

The days passed quickly as the group journeyed from the valley's forest floor up into the mountain canyons. The terrain started to look familiar to Thearbuc, and he became anxious about confronting the witch Kalinda for a second time. The closer they got to the area they last saw her, the more dead the trees around them became. The hair on the back of Thearbuc's neck stood up just thinking about her wretched voice. The trees seemed to wither and die here, and the fog floated low to the ground, making it difficult to see far into the distance. Thearbuc's heart continued to sink as they went along.

The group was already deep into the witch's woods and was making its way up the steeper, rockier, terrain when they were called to a stop. It was drizzling rain, and the low-hanging, dead trees made ominous shadows in the thickening fog.

"It was right around here where we found the staff," one of the brigands announced, standing under a small rock outcrop, just about as tall as two men. "I recognize these rocks."

Just as he said it, out of nowhere a goblin-like creature jumped from atop the outcrop and in an instant stabbed the Brigand through the chest with a rough, bronze-colored sword. It happened so fast that almost no one moved until the man slowly slumped over and fell to the ground. Before them stood a small green goblin, just above waist height on a normal man. He had oversized brown leather boots and a leather tunic. His nose was long and arched downward into a tiny point on his rough green face.

Without saying a word, the goblin advanced quickly on to another nearby Brigand, who was too slow in drawing his sword and was also cut down by the swift creature. His oversized clunky boots made it seem like he would be a clumsy foe, but his agility was a surprising sight to see. In an instant, he was on to his next victim, but the brigands had readied this time, and the next one blocked his swinging sword and deflected it aside. Another Brigand swung hastily at the goblin, but his attack missed as the goblin hopped aside with amazing agility. Another swing of the goblin's sword was deflected, but it caught the Brigand off guard, and he tripped backward on an exposed tree root. With a quick leap, the goblin was already on him before the man knew he had even fallen. But just as the goblin raised his sword to finish the attack, he was pierced through by another Brigand. The goblin made horrible gasping sounds as he tried to wiggle free from the skewered situation he was in, but it soon fell limp and silent. The Brigand pulled the sword back to himself, and dark green blood sizzled and burned the blade.

"Careful with that," Thearbuc said to the guard. "It'll burn right through your armor and skin." The guard had a panicked look on his face, still in shock from the sudden attack. He carefully wiped the sizzling blood from the blade while the others checked on the two fallen soldiers.

"They're gone," Aleric announced, closing one of the fallen man's eyes. "We should stick close together, but we must split up to find out where the witch's lair is. Let's fan out, but no more than a carriage length apart from one another. Keep your weapons drawn."

After a short rest, the group disbanded and began walking through the foggy witch's woods. The fog was so thick that they were just shadows, and the only sound was the drizzling rain patting slowly onto the dead leaves and mud. As they searched, the wind carried a sound through the air that some noticed but most did not. "Kallliiiiindraaaaa," it whispered through the trees. A few of the men stopped and looked up but quickly shrugged it off before continuing on.

Then, in the thick of the fog, one of the men felt something on his shoulder. He stopped quickly but did not dare turn around as a large, wretched hand slowly rested on his shoulder and long bony fingers slowly clamped down hard on him. He was so suddenly overtaken by an unnatural fear that he froze, and every muscle in his body tensed up. He gasped for air but could not breathe and was unable to move, unable to scream. The fear engulfed him like death until his mind was overtaken by blackness and then ultimately a dark nothingness. There his body stood in the foggy woods, frozen in the mist to stand like a statue as a warning to others for the rest of time.

Then the witch moved methodically, and silently through the fog to her next victim. One by one, she gripped them with deadly fear and turned the men into frozen like statues with the touch of her grotesque, large fingers. No one saw her; no one heard any screams for help.

Finally, after realizing he was alone in the woods and turning back to find the others, one of the men eventually came upon a shadow of one of the other brigands in the fog. He could not make out any details in the gloom, so he approached him slowly. "What are you doing?" he asked as he approached. "Have you found anything? We've been wandering around in these woods for too long." As he got closer to the shadow, it became clearer through the fog. It was one of the other men, except he was frozen solid in fear with his mouth agape and a look of agony upon his forever motionless face. His dead eyes were iced over, frozen in time forever. The man cried out in fear upon seeing the frozen Brigand's body. Instantly, the others came running. Aleric, Thearbuc, Lamora, along with five other guards. Only five others…

"She's here!" Aleric announced, darting his eyes back and forth through the fog and raising his sword in front of him.

"Another one!" a voice from the fog yelled, announcing he had found another of the witch's victims.

"She'll pick us off one by one," Thearbuc said in a shaky voice.

"What do we do?" One of the brigands asked.

"Stay together. Back-to-back," Aleric replied. They were helpless here in the foggy woods. Like fish in a barrel, they could only wait for the inevitable attack.

Then, through the fog, Lamora noticed something. Large, thick wisps and whirls of black fog and dark energy were spewing out of a section of rock in a nearby cliff. To her, it looked like a portal of evil. She paused, unable to speak or process what she was seeing.

"There!" She pointed to the cliff. Then suddenly, a high-pitched scream pierced through the woods. No one could tell where it originated from. Quickly, Lamora ran towards the dark energy spewing from the cliffside. "Follow me!" she yelled out to the others as she ran. Soon the group came upon the small cliff. The base of it was covered in shrubs, and there was seemingly nothing special about this area of rocky cliff to anyone else besides Lamora.

"What?" Thearbuc asked. "What are we looking at?

"Do you feel it?" she turned to ask Aleric.

"I do. What is it?" he replied.

"Give me the staff," Lamora yelled. To her, the energy engulfed them. The others looked at each other with confused looks. "Brodel's staff!" she yelled. One of the guards turned to the horse he had in tow and untied the staff before handing it to Lamora. The round end of the staff began to glow a bright blue as she held it near the cliff. Then she gently put it against the stone and pushed. Out of nowhere, a small door opened up from the side of the cliff. It was so small, maybe three feet at most. Even if the hidden door was left open, the group most likely would have missed it without Lamora's eyes and unique magical ability. With a flicker of The Paladin's eyes, he quickly lit a torch and held it inside of the opened entrance into the mountain.

"It's a stairwell," he announced. "Who knows how far it goes down, but the air smells rotten and carries the stench of death. I think the three of us should go and the rest of you wait out here. If we aren't back by nightfall, then mark this location and head away from here and back down into the valley. Then come back with the entire king's army."

The brigands nodded and took Brodel's staff back, stowing it safely away. Then, with torches in hand, Aleric, Thearbuc, and Lamora made their way into the dark, dungeon-like mouth of the mountain and began slowly descending the dark stairs into the earth.

"How did we end back up inside a mountain again?" Lamora whined.

It was just like before. Stagnant air hung heavy in the dark corridor and was thick and suffocating as they breathed it in. The stairs were thin, wet, and slippery, and there wasn't a handrail to hold on to keep stable. They tried using their torch hands against the wall to stabilize them as much as possible, and it felt like one misstep would mean certain death from falling who knows how far down into the belly of the earth.

Then, amid the silence and darkness, Aleric saw a reflection of light from his torch in front of him. Two eyes! He stopped just in time as a yellow sword glinted in the torchlight and narrowly missed him, striking the wall with a spark. Instinctively, he returned a swing and felt his sword hit flesh. A dark green goblin fell to his knees and slumped forward on the stairs. Using his torch, Aleric could see the goblin was dressed similarly to the last one, with the same type of bronze sword and oversized leather boots. He pushed it aside with his foot and they continued.

After descending the steps in the dark for what seemed like forever, the three finally reached flat ground. Aleric tossed his dying, flickering torch to the ground and created a ball of light from his left hand to illuminate the room. This cave did not seem like a powerful witch's lair. There was nothing on the walls and no seats or tables or books. There were two wooden doors at the far end of the room.

The Paladin motioned at the other two and they walked to the doors to investigate. Before they could reach them, three more goblins ambushed them from behind. One of them struck The Paladin, but the small weapon of the goblin bounced off his sturdy armor with a loud thud. The three turned toward the goblins and countered their attack immediately. Lamora, seeming to defy gravity, jumped up and pushed off the wall, landing directly behind one goblin, and she stabbed him. Thearbuc, taking a more direct approach, swung his sharp sword directly at another goblin and cut through the goblin's neck in one fell swoop. In just a few moments, the goblins were lifeless on the cave floor.

"Impressive," The Paladin commented on Thearbuc and Lamora's fighting skills and Thearbuc's sharp sword.

"New steel I invented," Thearbuc said with a smile behind his thick beard. "Told you it was better than any other."

"This one," Lamora pointed to the door on the far right and began to move towards it, already forgetting about the goblin attack.

"Why that one?" The Paladin asked, his eyes still glowing and illuminating the walls.

"It's different," Lamora replied. "I'm not sure how or why yet, but there's nothing coming from this door. We should try it first."

Slowly they pushed the door open, and Aleric stepped through. He raised his bright light to illuminate the room and investigate. But the moment he stepped into the room, the magical light he was casting suddenly went out. Bewildered, he was unable to summon it again and asked for the others to light his torch instead, which they did after a few moments.

They found themselves standing on a platform midway up a tall room that must have been as the height of three cottages. The ground was far below them in the darkness, and the ceiling was high above. Something was hanging from the center of the ceiling, and Aleric raised his torch so they could see it better.

"Brodel!" Thearbuc cried out. He began to make his way toward the steps then looked again. "Is that Brodel?" he asked the others. They looked up at it; it was definitely a person, in a cage hanging from the ceiling. The person looked was dressed like Brodel, but he looked much older. Not like the young man they were looking for.

"We need to rescue whoever we can while we are here," Aleric stated, making his way down the stairs. The others followed. As they went, they noticed the cave walls glinted and reflected light like they were spotted with gold.

"What is on the walls?" Thearbuc asked.

"I don't know," Lamora replied. "I've never seen anything like it.

Finally, they reached the bottom of the rounded stairs and found themselves standing in a circular room. There was nothing in the room besides a rope tied off near the ground, which was connected to the cage that was suspended from the ceiling. Without wasting any time, Aleric untied the rope from the cleat on the wall and all three held fast to the rope and slowly lowered the cage down to the floor. As it came into view, they got their first good look at the person who was trapped inside it. He was an old man, dirtied and hunched over. Long, gray hair covered his face. The man was not moving. Then they heard a faint voice say, "You came back."

Despite the scratchiness of the muffled voice, Thearbuc recognized it. It *was* Brodel! Thearbuc smashed open the lock that held the cage shut and Brodel fell limp into his arms.

"Brodel, is that you?" Thearbuc asked, overcome with joy and excitement. But his heart sank again when he brushed the old man's gray hair aside. Thearbuc took some time and studied the old man's face.

"Give me that torch!" he yelled and motioned toward Aleric. They passed it over and held it near the man's face so they could see him better.

"Thearbuc," the old man whispered behind cracked lips and obvious agony.

"It is Brodel!" Aleric said joyfully. "It's this room! I think it is snuffing out his magic. I can feel it too. The second I came in here my magic was stifled. We've got to get him out of here."

"That makes sense," Lamora chimed in. "I can't see any energy around us."

"Get him to his feet. We have got to get out of here," Aleric said, standing up and lifting Brodel by his arm. Just as they got him up, they heard a noise coming from far above in the room. Aleric held his torch up and saw the wretched witch Kalindra standing in the doorway. For a moment, she stood there motionless, staring down at them. Her evil eyes were glowing in the torchlight, staring blankly like a predator would stare at their prey. Emotionless, indifferent, and uncaring as it killed without remorse.

Then her mouth opened wide, and she screamed a horrific screech, unfathomably loud in the echoing stone room. Her jagged yellow teeth were horrifying, and the four could do nothing but clench their fists and eyes closed until the horrific scream stopped. Brodel slipped back onto the floor into the fetal position and shrunk away in fear. But when the piercing scream stopped, the witch turned quickly away into the darkness and slammed the door closed—gone just as suddenly as she had appeared. The four were left trapped in the dark room, engulfed in silence, fear, and darkness.

After a moment of gathering themselves and assessing the situation, Aleric stood up and attempted to muster a fireball to explode the door open. But after many attempts, he announced that he was definitely unable to conjure any magic in this room. It was like he had Forgotten how to use it.

"Magic doesn't work. The walls…" Brodel mustered, still slumped on the ground, barely able to speak. Whatever the witch had done to him, he was horribly aged and barely clinging to life.

"We need to get out of here," Thearbuc said in a panic, his eyes darting around the dark room for any way of escape. "Our torches won't last much longer."

"I've got this," Lamora chimed in. "Come with me," she motioned toward Aleric. He followed her up the stairs with his torch, and when they reached the platform in front of the door she knelt down and began going through her pack. She pulled out a leather pouch and unrolled it on the floor. Glinting in the torchlight were several shiny metal tools.

"Thieves guild. Remember?" She rolled her eyes at Aleric's judgmental face. "You'll thank me in a minute." She began to get to work with her tools, jiggling them around the keyhole one by one, listening intently to the sounds they were making and feeling which ones worked best on the large door.

"It's not going to work," Aleric said, expressing his doubt.

"It must work. There's no magic in here, right? Lamora replied. Aleric nodded; she had a point. "Well, then the lock must be a normal one," she continued. Just as she said it, there was a click and the door slowly creaked open. The four friends held their breath, waiting for Kalindra to shove her way in or slam the door on them once again. But the attack did not come. The air was silent and still. Aleric pushed open the door and peeked through the other side where he found the room dark and empty.

"Get Brodel!" he said in a hushed whisper. "I'll watch the door."

Thearbuc lifted Brodel to his feet and basically dragged him up the stairs. Brodel tried to help but could not carry his own weight. But with Lamora on his other side, they had him out of the dark torture chamber in no time. As soon as he passed the threshold, Brodel took a deep, satisfying breath, like someone who had been held underwater for too long. As he breathed, his body began to radiate and sparkle magic very slightly. His grayed hair and beard slowly darkened and the heavy bags around his eyes seemed to tighten up somewhat as some color returned to his face.

"Can you walk?" Thearbuc asked, witnessing the transformation.

"I can try," Brodel replied. His voice was almost unrecognizable. He took a step and stumbled, so Thearbuc and Lamora helped him forward as Aleric led the way up the long stairwell that would take them out of the mountain.

As they got closer to the exit of the chamber, Aleric raised his torch in the darkness only to find the way blocked by a half dozen goblins. Oversized boots and rusty bronze swords flickered in the torchlight as they stood at the ready, drool dripping from bloody fangs. The mischievous looks on their faces glared at the four trespassers, and they licked their dirty lips in anticipation of being able to eat them. The goblins pounced with no hesitation and simultaneously charged Aleric at alarming speed. He dropped the torch on the ground and almost instantly he had conjured a fireball from the palms of his hands before hurling it towards the attackers. The ball exploded into a magnificent light and blew heavy heat through the cave as it blasted the goblins aside and cleared the path towards the exit.

"Hurry!" he said, picking up the torch and moving forward again, stepping through the fallen goblins who were either motionless or rolling around in agony. As quick as they could, they began to climb the long corridor of stone steps. It was slow progress having to carry most of Brodel's weight, but he continued to improve at an alarmingly fast pace. By the time they could see a dot of light far above them at the end of the tunnel, he was taking steps on his own, leaning against the wall for balance as he went.

Step by step, they climbed, though expecting an attack from Kalindra at any moment. Why hadn't she come yet?

Then their questions were answered. From far down below them. there came the terrible shrieks and battle cries of many goblins. Looking down the seemingly endless steps, Thearbuc could see their small torchlights assembling at the bottom of the long stairwell.

"They're coming!" Thearbuc cried out. "Go!"

They hastened their pace. Brodel pushed on hard, clenching his teeth and using his hands against the walls to help push himself up. As they got closer to the end, the light from outside began to beam through the cave entrance, and Brodel seemed to bask in the sunlight between panting breaths as he struggled to move forward. It was like the light of the outside world and the fresh air were breathing new life into him.

"We're so close! Come on, Brodel, you can do it!" Lamora cried out. Finally, they had almost reached the exit, but the goblins were right on top of them. Lamora, being at the back, cried out, "Thearbuc, help!!"

He turned to see the events unfolding behind him. The goblins were so close that he could see their arched, pointed noses in the torchlight. They were only a dozen steps from Lamora when he sprang into action.

"Take Brodel. I'll stall them," he said, pushing Lamora aside to stand and face the onslaught of goblins. Lamora and Brodel clamored to reach the final steps and hoped that the surviving Brigands, those who had not been turned into statues by the witch Kalindra, were still outside waiting for them.

Outside, the forest was quiet, and the sun shone down nicely onto green moss and grasses. Then, out of the peacefulness, the heavy stone door of the witch's lair burst wide open with a loud slam as it hit the rocks and Aleric came bursting through. He was followed by a massive amount of commotion and fighting coming from inside the cave. Soon, Lamora and Brodel also came bursting through the door, panting heavily in the newfound fresh air. Still inside the doorway was Thearbuc, valiantly fighting off the small army of goblins one by one in the small stairwell to buy the others more time. Brodel and Lamora collapsed, panting for breath, just outside the exit, unable to find the strength to go on. Then, with impressive grace and agility, Thearbuc rolled out of the cave, leapt back to his feet, then slammed the stone door on the approaching goblins. He pushed heavily with his back on the stone door. Seeing this, the others knew they had just a moment of time to decide what to do next. Their eyes darted around the forest, adjusting to the brightness of the outside world.

There was hope! A handful of Brigands, at least three of them, stood nearby in the forest. And they had the horse! Aleric, Thearbuc, and Lamora looked at one another in disbelief at the sight of the brigands and the thought that they might actually be able to escape and save Brodel.

But their moment of hope was dashed almost as quickly as it was found, as suddenly, a horrible, screeching wail pierced the forest sky. So fierce and miserable that it pierced not just their skin but through their very souls. The wretched scream made all who witnessed it writher in fear to the point that they would rather be dead than endure such agony for a moment longer.

Aleric turned, following the sound, and he saw her first. The witch Kalindra was standing atop the small cliff, directly above the cave entrance behind them. She was wretched and weathered in the plain daylight. Her clothes were tattered, her wrists and bones skinny, and her cheeks sunk in like an addict who was one needle away from the grave. She ground her yellow teeth together and licked her blistered lips as she glared with a deep hatred at the escaping trespassers.

"Run!" Aleric cried out to the others, just as they, too, spotted the witch. Lamora and Brodel were soon on their feet. Lamora was surprised to find that Brodel was now able to lift himself and didn't require much of her help.

Aleric pushed them forward and away from himself, then turned and stood on the forest floor below the witch, ready to take a stand against her while the others fled. He began to draw his sword with his right hand and conjure a fireball in his left. But before it was more than just a spark, the witch had already made her move, and he was struck heavily with such a powerful force that he was blown into the sky, flipped head over heels, and landed lifelessly with a thud onto the ground. The others watched it happen and waited for any sign of movement from Aleric, but he was still.

"Get my staff…" Brodel mustered to Lamora as they continued to flee again toward the surprised Brigands, who had survived Kalindra's first attack but were now thinking they might not survive another. Brodel raised his weak arm and pointed toward the horses. "My staff…" he said again, louder this time. Lamora began to run quickly towards the brigands who were only a dozen carriage lengths away. She could make it.

Thearbuc, seeing the Witch Kalindra's attack on Aleric and his unmoving body on the forest floor, knew he couldn't hold the cave entrance any longer, so he let the door free and ran. Hoping to draw the goblins and the witch away from Lamora and Brodel, Thearbuc ran away from the remaining Brigands across the forest.

The goblins spewed from the cave entrance like rushing green water. Their anger showed fiercely in their eyes and clenched teeth as they came piling into the forest with weapons and torches, ready to kill anything that moved.

There was another terrible screech and the witch began to float down to the forest floor toward Brodel. Brodel's gut wretched in fear at the sight of her coming for him again, and his hobble began to turn into a slow, unstable run as he did his best to escape. Behind the witch, the goblins were also approaching. Aleric was still unconscious on the forest floor, and Thearbuc was too far away to help. They were outnumbered and overpowered. Their hope of escape was slim.

But despite their predators closing in for the kill, Lamora kept running. She was fast and agile as she leapt through the forest, over logs, stones, and closer to Brodel's staff. She finally got to the horses and pushed aside the still-bewildered Brigands watching the scene unfold. She quickly untied the leather straps holding the staff, then turned to see Brodel half limping, half running away from Kalindra.

"Brodel!" Lamora cried out. He looked up to see Lamora running toward him with the staff. He stretched out his hand to her as she approached and begged her, "Get it to me!"

But the witch Kalindra got to Brodel first. Lamora saw she was almost on top of him, so Lamora tossed the staff into the air towards Brodel. As the witch came down on Brodel like a hawk to its prey, Brodel caught the staff in the air and in one motion turned toward the falling witch. He bowed his head, fell to one knee, and slammed the staff hard into the ground.

Instantly, the ground shook. A shockwave of force originated from the staff, and a beam of gold light emerged from the top and created a translucent dome that surrounded him. It happened in slow motion. Just as the witch came down fiercely from the sky, her sharp yellowed teeth showing and her long dead fingers like claws ready to tear into her prey, she hit the magical forcefield and let out a terrible shriek. The witch's eyes changed in an instant in shock and surprise. Brodel could see her face just inches from his, but she could not get to him. He turned his head away and clenched his eyes in fear as she descended upon him.

At the same moment, the shockwave from the staff reached the goblins and sent them flying into the air with a powerful and thunderous bang. As soon as the witch hit the forcefield, she disappeared into thin air. Her evil, piercing scream suddenly ceased, and she was gone.

Brodel was left in the middle of the calm forest with the sun shining down on him. The only sound was a faint buzz emitting from the staff. The witch had disappeared somehow. Most of the goblins lay motionless, strewn around the forest among scattered oversized boots and bronze swords. The few remaining goblins that were not hit quickly scurried back into the cave from whence they came and closed the stone entrance behind them.

Lamora and the brigands stood in shock at what had unfolded right before their eyes. Thearbuc ran to Aleric and rolled him over, so his face wasn't in the dirt. His armor was singed and smoking from the witch's blast, and a large black impact mark was burnt on to the side of his armor where the blast had hit him. Thearbuc shook him, and Aleric slowly opened his eyes.

"Haaa!" Thearbuc laughed. "You're alive! Knocked you out pretty good, she did. Let's get you up. Brodel is okay." Thearbuc helped Aleric to his feet and the two slowly limped over to Brodel and Lamora. As they approached Brodel, they stopped and gasped at the sight of him. Aleric and Thearbuc's mouths dropped in awe and confusion. Brodel's smile slowly washed away from his face upon seeing their reaction to him.

"What?" he asked with a worried tone. "Aren't you excited to see me!? I am sure happy to see you two."

Aleric and Thearbuc couldn't find words. They just stared for a few moments. From the bottom of the stairwell until now, Brodel had turned from an old, haggard man into a middle-aged, strapping, healthy man. The bags under his eyes were gone, as was the pale, droopy skin. His tangled gray beard was now short and black. He stood tall and proud with wide shoulders and white teeth.

"You're young," Thearbuc finally managed to speak. "Well, you're older than you were before, but you're young! We thought we'd lost you." As he said it, Thearbuc showed a big grin behind his bushy beard. He could still recognize the boy even though he had now grown into a man since he had last seen him. "It's great to see you." He came forward and embraced Brodel.

"You look good!" he continued, holding Brodel at arm's length and looking him over, trying to make sense of the whole situation.

"This is probably what I'm supposed to look like," Brodel said in his familiar shy tone. "I told you I wasn't as young as I looked back when you first met me. Magic is curious like that."

"You were an old man just an hour ago," Lamora stepped forward, observing him with a perplexed look.

"Well," Brodel continued. "Magic ages you. The witch… she…" he trailed off.

"You don't have to tell us. You don't have to say anything if you don't want to," Aleric rested a hand on Brodel's shoulder.

"No, it's okay," he replied. "The witch…She liked to toy with me. Like a cat playing with its prey. I think she was drawn to me because of my magic. No one else could counter her like I could. But it was relentless…" he trailed off and sadness was in his eyes.

"She knew you were a powerful magic user, much like herself, I'm sure," Thearbuc added.

"She did," Brodel continued after a moment. "She liked that I could put up a fight. Someone on her level that she could challenge herself with. But she always made sure to keep the upper hand. She was more powerful than me. And when I was finished, when I couldn't go on, instead of destroying me she would lock me in that dungeon where no magic could penetrate. She could rest and recharge while I was left to rot. The magic I had to use against her just to stay alive aged me into that old man you saw down in the dungeon." Brodel dropped his head and looked sadly at the ground as he recalled the horrors of the witch's cave. The others patted his shoulders and gave words of encouragement.

"We're all back together and we're all alive—that is what is important," Thearbuc said. "You made it. She's gone. Let's get out of these cursed woods…"

And with that, the group began to prepare the horse for their journey home. The sun started to fade as gray clouds moved in and covered up its warm glow. As they rode away, they passed the ominous dead trees of the witch's woods and the dozens of scattered, frozen Brigands who had been turned into statues by the witch Kalinda.

"Do you think they'll be there forever?" Lamora asked as they rode past them.

Aleric nodded. "As permanent reminders. Warnings of the witch's woods," he replied.

"Let us never come back to these cursed woods," Thearbuc announced, as the group of friends who were finally together once again trotted slowly away, never to look back.

Part II

Chapter 16: The Morghvile

Weeks later, torchlight dimly illuminated the inside of a cave, and the shadows of hooded men danced and flickered across stone walls while Sophie the Stone Gnome crouched quietly and observed them from inside the mountain. He had been observing the comings and goings of the hooded men through the cave and caverns for some time. Sophie didn't know whether it was night or day, or even what day it was at all. He had been under the mountain, hiding, ever since The Paladin had captured him and taken him hostage. But in the mountain was where he belonged and his fear of dark enclosed spaces was quickly fading. Sophie was beginning to feel like himself again. He had needed that push to force him back into the mountains, where his body and natural biology knew what to do. He was safe down here inside the earth.

And he had been busy. Busy creating a new home within the mountain, away from the exposing sun, would-be kidnappers, and people who wanted to hurt Sophie. That's when he began noticing something was amiss within the depths of the mountain. Footsteps and whispers from men going in and out of the cave, cloaked in dark red robes, hiding their mysterious faces. Sophie had seen them before. The day The Paladin brought him into the mountain against his will. "He hurt poor Sophie," The Gnome whispered to himself, thinking back on the day and wincing from the pain of the memory. Sophie was a sensitive soul. Sophie would not be caught again, not down here. But now, even down here in Sophie's domain, there were men intruding again.

Sophie, still safely concealed within the mountain using his natural magic, crept closer to the cloaked men to get a better look. Then more cloaked men entered the cave from the caverns beyond. There were about seven or eight of them in the cave by now, all huddled in small groups whispering to one another.

Sophie noticed one of them had an eerily painted face beneath his cloak. Half blue and half red, he looked like he was not from this world. His jagged teeth and soulless eyes made Sophie shiver. Then he noticed another strange person, one with no arms or legs. Instead, only a smoke-like substance wafted through the air where his limbs should be. He knew this to be an apparition of some sort, most likely not even a man at all.

Minutes later another cloaked man entered the room. He was taller than the rest of them and wore a black cloak instead of red like the others. He carried two large, leather-bound books in his arms, and his fragile, boney fingers looked as if they struggled to hold the weight of the books. The cave fell silent as he entered. The whispering ceased as the cloaked men turned to see the new stranger. He walked to the far corner of the cave, toward the round stone well that came out of the ground and stood about waist height. The others gathered in a circle around the stone well, then one of them spoke, “We have lost control of the kingdom.” The words were barely audible to Sophie, who was just on the other side of the stone wall.

“The Paladin is too powerful,” one of the others added, sounding worried. “Can he be defeated?”

“It’ssss not jussst him anymore,” the smoke-like apparition hissed. “He’ssss brought an army with him.” Something in the apparition’s voice made Sophie’s skin crawl, and he clenched his teeth and fists trying to fight his urge to flee deeper into the mountain.

“Enough of your worries!” the tall, hooded man yelled out angrily. It was clear he was the leader. “Yes, the kingdom is prospering once again, and a vast swath of our lands has been taken from us. We’ve had obstacles before, and this is no different,” he said, trying to calm the others.

“Where did this magic-wielding Paladin come from anyway?” the painted man whispered, as they all huddled closer around the stone well.

“No one seems to know,” the other replied. “I don’t think even he knows. Be that as it may, he is too powerful to risk fighting, and he and his army have the support of the king. So, we repeat what put us into power in the first place.”

“What are you proposing?” one of the others asked.

“Instability!” the leader raised his voice again. “We regain our power and control with instability, just like before. We create a tragedy, and humans who are notorious for their knee-jerk reactions and lack of foresight for the future will do the rest for us. They will happily support giving us full control over the laws and enforcement of them for their own safety, just like when we got magic banned. And just like when we were able to rid the kingdom of magic wielders, the brigands will be gone too. Thrown in jail or disappeared altogether.

We're like godssss to them," the smokey apparition laughed behind his cloak. "Let'sss toy with them more. I welcome their misssery."

"Our soldiers will pick them off one by one just like before. By this time next year we will have no more opposition, our lands reclaimed, and everyone will be slave to our will," the tall man finished.

"With no land of their own they will be forced to work for whatever crumbs we decide to throw at them for their entire lives, and once again we will rule and control everyone and everything," the painted man said, laughing under his breath as his rotted sharp teeth showed in the torchlight.

"But this time we take the castle!" the taller man interrupted with anger and frustration in his voice. "No more relying on the whims of a dying king."

"Why haven't you just killed the king?" the painted man asked with an evil look in his hollow eyes. "Why do you keep that weak old man around?"

The taller sorcerer paused and breathed deep. "You know why," he said in an annoyed tone. "The lands belong to his family. If he were gone, then his cousin, King Haberlorn, would just come in and take over the kingdom, our lands and power along with it. Plus, King Haberlorn dislikes me, and I would be banished from the castle along with any power or sway almost immediately. It's just easier to control him than to get rid of him."

"How are you so sure you can control him?"

"The man is depressed!" He's lost his family and has taken to the drink. All I have to do is bring in a barrel of wine and someone for him to talk to and he is out of commission for a week, and I have the run of the place and the king's guards at my disposal. Although I must admit, he has been more and more hesitant to drink as of late, now that the things in the kingdom have been looking up," he trailed off.

"Won't, King Haberlorn just come take his lands if we take the castle now?" the painted man asked.

"Not with what I have planned," the other said ominously with a snicker. "Now, let's proceed with creating this tragedy."

As the others nodded that they agreed, he set the two large books down on the side of the stone well and began to flip through the pages, arranging them in a seemingly specific order. After he laid page over page the books began to glow, and the wizard pointed at the text. "You all know your parts and what to do. Let us begin."

In unison the others put their hands and staffs towards the center of the well, then suddenly, it began to spark. Small and almost unnoticeable at first, there was a small flash of light that even Sophie was not sure he had really seen. Then it happened again. He did see something! More flashes and sparks surrounded the well. The books began to glow a deep purple, growing brighter and brighter. Then the men began to chant. Quiet and mumbled at first, it echoed eerily off the stone walls. In the center of the well a black and white smoke spiral started to form. Wisps of fog and whirls of black whipped up into the air, nipping at the group of sorcerers. The chanting got louder. Sophie slunk back into the stone as fear began to grip him.

The chanting was so loud now that it echoed and reverberated off the walls, radiating a constant ominous bellow. The well sparked and flashed, the spiral around it getting faster and the chanting louder. When it was so chaotic that Sophie almost couldn't take it anymore and was ready to turn and run away, the men started slowly raising their arms in unison. A black shape started to take form and rise out of the well. Their arms collectively began to shake, like they were lifting something heavy. The black wisps of smoke and fog came further and further out of the well, materializing into the recognizable shape of a wolflike head, thick body, and long legs of the Morghvile. It floated in the center of the well, which was still popping and flashing a magnificent light show. The floating materialization hovered above the well and seemed to turn its head. It scanned the room slowly, looking at each of the men individually before stopping at the man in black. The tall sorcerer whispered words in a language Sophie had never heard before, then with a motion of his hand the ghostly apparition flew out of the room as fast as an arrow. It shrieked a horrible, wailing sound as it exited the tunnels of the mountain and out into the night.

Sophie, frozen in fear, could not believe what he had just witnessed. He could feel the darkness of the apparition that had been summoned by the cloaked sorcerers. He felt the absolute blackness and death that surrounded it. He had never felt anything so horrible. Still, he watched the room. The tall sorcerer at the podium closed the books, and slowly, the bright light above the well faded out. The cloaked men broke their circle, then nodded at one another in unison. A few whispers were muttered. Then, in a single file line, they quietly shuffled out of the room and exited through the cave. The dark well was left lifeless, cold, and still once again.

The following day, in another part of the kingdom, new friends Thearbuc, Brodel, and Lamora were enjoying a pleasant afternoon near a small mountain lake in the foothills near the orchards of Briardale. The grass and trees were green and swayed lazily in the afternoon breeze. There wasn't a cloud in the sky. They were expecting Aleric to arrive when he was finished with his morning meetings with the king.

They all had been taking a lot of leisure time of late. The kingdom was thriving, and the best thing anyone could do was just leave it alone and let the economy and trust in the kingdom build itself back up. Some of the ex-Brigands had taken up farming and were already seeing their first crops. Nuggets of gold were being mined from the mountains by others. A group who did not want to give up military life had found jobs as the castle's guards. Villagers had ceased being arrested for minor infractions, and tyranny in the kingdom seemed to be at an all-time low. In fact, the king's guards were quite often bored because of the lack of crime in the kingdom.

Thearbuc was still staying in the castle near Aleric's quarters and would visit his grown children in the countryside often. Lamora was living at her family's property in her childhood home. She was living there alone, as far as anyone could tell or assumed. And Brodel occupied Aleric's old house, which he had rebuilt with magic. But it was assembled without a door and had askew windows and roof. A door was eventually put in the old-fashioned way, by cutting a rectangle out of the house, and it was livable enough for now.

Brodel had retained his handsome, middle-aged look. No one knew if he would soon revert to his younger-looking self or grow even older, since his magic was unpredictable after being held captive by the witch Kalindra. But he looked the same now as he did when he escaped her grasp: middle-aged with a close shaved, dark-black beard. He normally wore a thin, black, hooded cloak and walked with his wooden staff, which had a glowing orb upon its top that changed colors depending on his mood. That is what most assumed anyway. The snaps and pops of magic that once radiated from his body had mostly ceased. But by all accounts, he seemed to be just as powerful a magic user as he ever was, perhaps more. It just wasn't as visible now. He preferred this look, as he finally looked the age that he believed he was. Also, people didn't stare at him everywhere he went for looking like a walking sparkler anymore. Now, he just blended into the crowd, and besides his magical staff, no one would know he even had magic unless he chose to show them. Life seemed good in Mazeron. For the first time in a long time.

It was midafternoon when Aleric finally arrived. He trotted slowly on his horse to the lake to meet his friends. Thearbuc and Lamora were stretched across a large picnic blanket lined with food and drink, while Brodel sat reclined and relaxed on a large rock.

"Take off your boots," Lamora yelled as he approached. "Let the grass cool off your feet." She wiggled her bare toes as she said it.

"Are you guys sipping on wine?" Aleric asked, reaching his hand out to ask for some.

"Indeed," Brodel replied, taking a large bite of food and holding a glass in the other hand. "We have fresh-baked bread to eat too."

"Do you like the taste of honey?" Lamora asked, tearing a piece of bread off a loaf for Aleric.

"Too much honey hurts your belly," Thearbuc groaned as he rolled onto his side with a smile, holding his full belly.

Brodel set down his glass of wine and licked the remaining food from his fingers. He then picked up a guitar-like, stringed musical instrument from the rock next to him and began lightly strumming a tune.

"Sing a song to me, then I'll play one for you," she said to Brodel cheerfully as she started dancing. She softly waved her thin hands in the air while methodically moving her hips. She danced in the calm breeze while Brodel provided the music. Thearbuc and

Aleric watched the beauty of the moment unfold in a content calmness as they sipped on their wine and ate their bread. This was the perfect afternoon for a group of good friends.

The day wore on and the bottles of wine became empty. They took turns swimming in the lake and napping in the grass under the shade of the trees.

"I could live like this forever," Thearbuc said aloud.

But the moment was not meant to last, as they were soon to find out. Life always seems to find a way to complicate itself. For some reason, it is always harder to make a simple, happy life than it is a hard one.

Aleric heard it first while he was half asleep resting under the shade of a large tree after a refreshing swim in the lake. It was the heavy thud of a trotting horse. He sat up and waited calmly as a rider came up over the hill and approached them.

"Paladin!" the rider announced as he approached.

"That's me," Aleric replied calmly.

"The king requests you return to the castle at once. There have been happenings, and he requests your counsel."

"What is going on?" Aleric asked. The rider took a big breath, then sighed heavily before he started again.

"There has been an attack. Something. Someone…Something has attacked some of the farms in the southwest lands."

"What do you mean some*thing*?" Aleric replied.

"It doesn't seem another human could have done it, sir," the messenger said with a shaky tone.

"Trolls?" Lamora asked, sitting up from her blanket nearby.

"Doubtful it's trolls," the messenger replied. "It's too gruesome. Unless they were very mad trolls. I think you'd better come have a look for yourself, Paladin," the messenger continued. "The king requests you accompany him and his counsel to the area. In case…"

"In case what?" Aleric asked with a loud voice.

"In case it's still out there, sir."

Aleric and Thearbuc both looked at each other and grumbled in discontent at the same time. They were both thinking the same thing: What if it was another one of those beasts that had stalked Aleric to Thearbuc's cabin? And again through the mountains, which pushed them directly into the hands of Kalindra.

"I better come with you," Thearbuc said, beginning to stand up.

"I will too," Brodel chimed in.

"It's settled then," Aleric said, walking slowly toward his horse. "We meet at the castle. We ride at dawn."

No more words were said. The messenger nodded at The Paladin, then made his way hastily down the trail to deliver the message to the king. The others geared up and rode away from the peaceful lake and secluded orchards.

The next morning came quickly, and Aleric found himself at the stables in full armor, readying his horse for the upcoming ride, before the sun had even come up over the horizon. Brodel slowly trotted up to him, his glowing staff acting like a sort of headlight for his horse.

As the sun crested the horizon, the group had grown to Aleric, Thearbuc, Maub, and a handful of the king's guards.

"Where is the king? I thought he was joining us?" Aleric asked aloud.

"The king…" Maub spoke slowly and eerily as was his usual tone, "will not be joining us today. His counsel suggested it would not be safe, and he should stay within the castle walls this day." Aleric rolled his eyes where the odd wizard could not see and slowly trotted away toward Thearbuc.

"Looks like we get to take care of the old man today," Thearbuc whispered quietly to Aleric with a joking tone.

"You take care of him," Aleric whispered back. "If he falls behind, it's not my problem."

"Ahem!" Maub cleared his throat loudly. "Sunrise is almost here," he nodded in the direction of the rising sun. Already the beams of light were illuminating the large morning sky. "We must make haste," he continued. "Try to keep up." He glanced at Aleric with a mischievous grin.

Maub wrapped his long, gangly fingers around the horse's reins and gripped them tight. "We ride!" he shouted with a kick of his horse, and then was off. The others hurriedly did the same, and the group was moving, with Maub already far ahead.

The wizard rode unnaturally fast. His tall, dark steed was thick and burly, but it was quick and agile. No one could keep up, and soon the party was following a small dot in the distance as Maub rode far ahead.

Finally, in the middle of the afternoon, the group approached a small farming village. They trotted slower now as the horses were run down and tired. As they approached from the fields on the outskirts of the village, they saw gray smoke in the distance rising high into the air. There was no sign of people, no children to greet them or waves from the farmers, as was usual when approaching the small outer villages.

Right away, they spotted a burning cottage. Half of it had burned and the wood planks were only smoldering by now. Aleric and Thearbuc dismounted and slowly peered inside the already opened front door. Inside, the room was filled with hovering gray smoke and was cluttered as if someone had tipped it on its side and spilled all the contents of the bookshelves and tables onto the floor. A half-melted pot sat in the stone fireplace, and all the wood surrounding it had been burnt away. There were large claw marks gnashed into some of the wood planks that were strewn about.

"Looks like they left while the fire was still raging and it grew out of control," Thearbuc announced to the other riders waiting out near the yard. "What could have done that?" he mumbled to Aleric and Brodel looking confused.

"Maub is signaling to us," one of the king's guards interrupted, pointing off into the distance. Maub had ridden to the nearest cottage, which was a field length away and was waving them to come his way. He looked like a raven again from this distance with his thick feathered cape on.

As the group rode up to the cottage, a gruesome scene unfolded. There were signs of a massacre and blood. Lots of blood. The occupants of the cottage were mostly still there for all to see. Pieces scattered about here and there. Glancing around, they could see more cottages in the distance, all smoldering or half torn apart. The other guards that had inspected them rode up and their faces told the others everything they needed to know. The whole settlement had been ravaged by something viscous.

"Trolls?" one of the guards asked aloud as they all stood dumbfounded and traumatized after assessing the scene.

"Not trolls," Thearbuc replied. "Trolls don't leave damage like this. Trolls are more thump you on the head with a giant club than they are rip and tear, like this is."

"What could have done this then?" the guard replied, his voice still shaking.

"Something not of this world," The Paladin said loudly. "A beast that was conjured by magic. A Morghvile..."

"Nonsense." Maub, who had been mostly quiet the entire day, jumped in surprisingly quick with a sarcastic drawn-out tone. "Such things do not exist."

"We were chased by them on our last voyage," Thearbuc chimed in. "They do exist."

"Just because you have never seen anything like the animal you saw before does not mean they are from another world or are the mythical Morghvile," Maub replied with a snark. "It doesn't matter where it came from. What matters is it's still out there," Maub continued, changing his tone. "You two." He raised a bony finger at Aleric and Thearbuc. "Wander about and see if you can find any signs as to which direction this beast went. If you can, track it and kill it." Then Maub turned his horse and slowly trotted away toward the other guards.

Oddly enough, Aleric did not know or recognize any of the guards on this journey with them. They were "new at the castle," they had mentioned.

"Alert the High Elves," Maub said in a hushed tone. "It is time..."

"Did you say High Elves?" Aleric turned his horse and yelled toward the wizard.

The wizard Maub turned his horse and had a look of surprise and shock on his face. "This doesn't concern you, Paladin," he replied in an annoyed tone. Aleric motioned his horse and began trotting toward the wizard.

"Surely you didn't say High Elves," Aleric questioned as he approached.

"There are no elves here, Paladin," the wizard replied angrily. "I need not remind you again that you do not question me. You do not question a wizard, and you do not question the castle's authority. Know your place!" he said, clearly losing his temper. Aleric conceded for the moment and raised his hands non-threateningly. "If you get out of line again, I'll have you arrested," Maub said menacingly.

Aleric glanced at the other guards. "I would like to see them try." His eyes flashed brightly in a warning, like a cobra flaring its hood, and the other guards sheepishly looked away. Aleric turned his horse and trotted back across the field to Thearbuc.

"Guards!" Maub yelled loudly. "We must deliver word of what has happened here to the rest of the kingdom. We ride immediately, back to the castle." Maub glanced at Aleric, Thearbuc, and Brodel again. "You three. Track the beast, but no later than the evening, then make your way back. Do not be caught out here in the dark. Good luck to you." And with that, the wizard, with his guards in tow, took off eastward back to the kingdom, leaving Aleric, Thearbuc, and Brodel standing alone near the bloody scene of the crime.

"He doesn't seem to have much hope that we will find whatever did this," Thearbuc mentioned as they watched the party ride off.

"We already know what did this," Aleric replied.

"You think it's another one of those beasts. The Morghvile?"

"It has to be, doesn't it?" Aleric asked. "Have you ever seen anything capable of doing something like this? These poor people were torn to pieces. Not eaten or cooked by a dragon, not thumped by a troll."

"You don't think…" Thearbuc trailed off.

"What?" Aleric asked. "Say it…"

"You don't think Maub is behind all this do you? The cloaked sorcerers in the cave, they were conjuring up something in there. And one of them was tall, just like Maub, who is also a wizard."

"I still don't think it's him," Aleric replied. "We would have recognized him, even with a cloak on. Plus, he rarely practices magic anymore in his old age."

"He seemed practiced enough when killed that assassin in the castle," Thearbuc pointed out. "His lightning bolts came out of nowhere. He is more powerful than he lets on. He hides behind his old, frail body."

"You mean in the castle where he saved us from an assassins arrow?" Aleric chuckled as he said it. "You would've had an arrow go through the back of your neck if it wasn't for him." Aleric paused and looked around as the wind blew lightly through the tall grass. "No, I don't think the old wizard is behind this."

Thearbuc stayed quiet, pondering the events of late. "I suppose you are right," he finally said. "Let's see if we can find any footprints and track down whatever did this."

"Agreed," Aleric said, turning his horse towards the woods that surrounded the fields of the small village. "But let's not take long.

The three scoured the countryside for many hours, looking for clues as to what had killed the villagers and where it might have gone off to. But the only evidence they found besides large claw marks on the victims and scratches through the walls of some of the cottages were some large footprints leading into the forests beyond.

"We just have to hope that it keeps wandering in that direction, away from the kingdom," Aleric said eventually. "There is a chance we may never see or hear of it again."

"Hopefully," Brodel replied. "Too hopeful most likely."

Eventually, they lost the tracks in a clearing where the ground was too hard to leave a mark, and they were forced to turn back empty handed. The sun was beginning to dip low in the sky, so Aleric called off the mission, and they returned to the castle. The ride home was quiet, as the two were exhausted from being out on the trail all day and their minds were filled with unanswered questions. They rode in silence as the sun dipped away and finally gave way to the night.

Chapter 17: Jace

Later that night, on the outskirts of one of the villages, the night was calm and quiet. The kind of night that was so still that if you closed your eyes, you felt like you were floating in the air. The only sound was the crickets. The only light was from the waning crescent moon. Tomorrow the moon would not be visible at all, and the lands would be too dark to work in. This was the best moon cycle to for Jace, the head of the thieves guild' in Mazeron.

He crouched against the stone walls of the manor, relaxed and staring up at the stars, listening for the sound of movement and enjoying the peacefulness of the night. He calmly tossed up and flipped a dagger while he waited. The score on this night could be monumental. The manor belonged to the head of the king's guard. A large, beautiful property in the countryside at the edge of a small lake. It was minimally guarded, three stories tall, and from what Jace imagined, filled to the brim with jewelry, silver, and magnificent works of art. The anticipation was almost overwhelming. He rubbed his eyes, as he was still somewhat groggy from sleeping all day, knowing he would be up all night working.

He looked up at the sky again. The grouping of stars that looked like a large frying pan was almost completely upside down, which meant it was near midnight. *Time to shine*, he thought with a grin.

Jace slowly stood up from his crouched position by the wall and made his way to a nearby tree. With one quick motion he jumped, grabbed a large lower branch, and pushed his way on top of it. Within seconds he was standing on the branch and staring directly at a cracked window on the second floor of the manor. Weeks of reconnaissance was already paying off. He crept slowly toward the cracked shutter and peered inside.

It was dark, but his eyes were used to it. Inside, he saw what looked to be an office. A wooden desk stood at one end of the room, one of the walls was lined from floor to ceiling with filled bookshelves. The general would spend many evenings here studying and reading in the glow of candlelight. He would crack the window to let in a small breeze from the lake while he studied, but when he was finished, he often forgot to close the window, thus leaving an opening to infiltrate the manor. The fact this room happened to be near a sturdy tree was pure luck. If it was a bedroom, his plan most likely would not work, and Jace could be found out before he even started his work.

He pushed the shutter open slowly without even a creak, then hopped from the tree and landed quietly inside the room. Already, he was eyeing the place. The silver candlesticks on the desk, the painting on the wall behind it, a golden amulet in the shape of a heart—most definitely a beautiful anniversary gift for the general's wife, but now a quick payday for the quiet thief.

He unraveled a length of rope with a large, thick sackcloth tied to one end. He quickly and quietly started placing items on the cloth, and once he had successfully cleared the room of all treasures, he pulled the cloth around the goods and tied a slipknot on one end, closing up the sack around the stolen goods. He carried it to the window then slowly lowered it down.

Jace had a special kind of mind. He could think fast, and his mind processed quicker than most people. His motions were precise, like a surgeon, but also quick. With his intense attention to detail, the large sack of valuables didn't make a single noise as he lowered them from the window to the ground. Once the sack was on the ground, he released one end of the rope very slowly, which opened the sack onto the ground, then slowly started to pull the empty contraption back up. "One room down," he whispered to himself as he began to move to the next.

He crept silently into the hallway. All still. He then found himself on the second level, looking down into the living room. A small flicker of fire still burned in the large fireplace, giving some light to the room. A single empty ale stein sat on the table. Someone had been here not long ago. His eyes darted back and forth, looking for anyone who might still be up. But the only sound was the occasional pop and crack from the smoldering fire. He crept on to the next room.

Entering silently through the half-closed wooden door, he found a cluttered room filled with different clothes and many dresses. Some were hanging from mannequins; some were strewn about on different furniture. The general's wife's or daughter's clothing room, he thought. Jackpot. He could already see the jewelry boxes against the far wall.

Atop a working desk sat different necklaces adorned with pearls and gems that looked to be imported long ago at great expense .They were Jace's now. He slipped them silently into a large pouch and claimed them for his own. The jewelry boxes were also emptied, save for some useless heirlooms, clearly handed down from grandma and worth little money to the professional thief.

As he entered back onto the landing that overlooked the living room and the still-smoldering fireplace, he noticed how tidy it was. The place was spotless except for the single ale stein on the table. Someone here was a clean freak. That's why the off-centered picture frame at the bottom of the stairs stood out so much. A crooked painting in a house this immaculate? No way…

Jace stealthily made his way downstairs to the slightly crooked painting in the living room. When he got to it, he stabilized it with one hand and pushed the corner with the other. He couldn't hide his mischievous grin as he exposed a wall safe hiding behind the painting. He gently set the painting on the ground, reached to the leather pouch in his belt, and pulled out his tools.

Within minutes the lock clicked and the safe swung open, revealing three large pouches. He looked inside…Gold coins! All of it, gold coins! His heart raced as he held a bag close to his chest and looked up, with a feeling of great relief. An enormous weight was instantly lifted from his shoulders and a feeling that everything would be alright swept through him. This loot would last him years. Years of laying low and enjoying the easy life instead of hustling and running every night, making a living in the shadows of people's homes.

But the blissful feeling was short lived. As he regained his focus, he saw a beautiful dagger with an inlaid red gemstone in the handle displayed over the fireplace. The feeling of contentedness washed away instantly. He had to have it. He looked down at the pouches of gold coins and lightly shook them. They were heavy—too heavy to be walking around with. They would make noise and give him away. He needed to get the gold out, then he could come back for the dagger.

Jace quietly crept back up the stairs and to the open window in the library. *Just leave the dagger and get out with the rest of the loot*, he tried to convince himself. He already had enough to set him up for quite some time. He tried to put the dagger out of his mind as he crept back out onto the branch and climbed down the tree to the pile of stolen goods he had lowered down earlier. "Have to get these out of here first," he mumbled to himself, then got to work.

Piece after piece was taken quietly away from the chateau and stashed in a small cave he had dug out weeks prior. It was under a small outcropping of natural rocks, and when the hole he had dug out was covered with branches it was completely unnoticeable. He spent the next few hours stashing the goods, until the late hours of the night. It was still completely dark, but the sun would be coming up soon and he still had two trips left. He had to hurry. But he also had to have the dagger.

As he approached the chateau this time, he made his way to the front to see if he could find another open window, one that would be closer to the living area or on the ground floor. As he crept to the front of the chateau and surveyed the area, he did not notice that one of the gargoyle statues perched high above the front entrance followed Jace's every move with dark eyes.

"No windows open," Jace mumbled softly to himself before continuing back to the rear of the property. High above him, the gargoyle's head followed. Jace picked up the last handful of goods and headed back to the cave. The worry of being caught had all but left his mind after his many hours of freely walking around the property.

He looked up at the sky as he walked, then he thought he heard something far off in the distance behind him. A faint clatter. He turned around quickly, scanning the area behind him. There was nothing. Then he brought his gaze back up to the sky. Against the dark night there was a small section in the sky that was blacker than the rest. There were no visible stars in one spot, he noticed almost immediately. And it was growing larger! He turned around and ran, but it was too late. The large gargoyle crashed down upon him, wings spread, coming down fast and quiet like a hawk. Its large claws ripped into his shoulder blades and threw him hard into the ground. Even after the initial attack, there was no mercy. The gargoyle was on top of him, floating with slow flaps of its wings to stabilize itself while its talons ripped into Jace. He rolled over to defend himself and started swatting and punching at the beast. Eventually he was able to reach an arm up to the beast's face and shove it off him. He scrambled to his feet as the gargoyle came at him again. It was relentless in its attack.

Jace reached for the sheath on his leg as he fell forward from another attack from behind. This time when he rolled over to face the beast, he was ready, and he slashed a sharp blade unexpectedly at the creature and sliced its side with a deep cut. The gargoyle shrieked and flapped backwards to put distance between itself and the blade. Jace stood up quickly, still holding the dagger out in front of him in defense.

"Back up!" he yelled at the beast, swinging the dagger through the air. The gargoyle flapped and took one more hop back before landing on its feet. The two circled each other in the dark night. The gargoyle, a large shadow in the night, followed Jace's every move, slowly circling him and staring at him through the darkness. Jace was trying to walk backwards to leave the area, but the gargoyle followed. One step back, then the beast would take one slow step forward. It was patient and methodical. Jace was filled with fear and didn't know if he could escape the stalking beast.

Then, while stepping backwards, Jace stumbled on an exposed rock and slightly lost his footing. It was just for a second. Still holding the outstretched knife, he peeked behind his shoulder to get a quick glance at the terrain behind him and regain his footing. Then the attack came. The gargoyle leapt into the air and was on top of Jace again in an instant, claws digging into his chest and pushing him hard into the ground. The impact of getting slammed so hard on his back knocked the wind out of him and made him drop his dagger.

The gargoyle went crazy. It ripped and clawed violently at the thief, tearing his arms that were up in defense. Jace tried hopelessly to get a hold on the beast to shove him off again, but it was moving so frantically and violently that he couldn't get a hold on him. He turned and saw the dagger just an arm's length away. As he reached to grab it, he felt a claw rip into his exposed ribs where his arm was now outstretched and not guarding his body. His instinct was to pull it back in and defend himself, but his mind knew better. He couldn't win if he only played defense. He rolled toward the dagger, winching in pain and further exposing his body to more attacks, which the gargoyle took immediate advantage of. Finally, he had his hand wrapped tightly around the dagger, and in one motion, he rolled back over and plunged it deep into the gargoyle's side.

It let out a horrific gasp. It probably would have screamed in pain if it could, but Jace must have hit its lungs, because the only sound it made was frantic gasps as it flailed and flopped off him. Jace scurried backwards on his hands in a sitting position and watched the beast flail for a few more moments until it finally came to rest and slumped over.

Jace sat, once again, in the silence, breathing heavily and covered in his own blood, his shirt and skin scratched through. He scanned the horizon waiting for the next attack, holding the dagger tight in anticipation, but nothing came. Slowly, he regained his breath and made his way back to his feet.

He watched the chateau from far off, waiting for the lights to come on. Someone must have heard the commotion. But after some time, nothing happened. He must have been far enough away to where no one heard the battle. His confidence started to come back to him, and he jingled a few of the gold coins in his pocket. *The dagger…*, he remembered. One quick trip in through the window and back out. It was simple. In a few minutes, he could be gone into the night and have a trinket that he would cherish forever. Not to mention the status it would give him. A golden dagger with an emerald inlay. It was the ultimate trophy for a thief.

He argued with himself in his mind for a few moments about whether it was too risky, but his mind was already made up. He couldn't help himself. It was in his biology, and there is no fighting that.

Stealthily, he crept back toward the chateau, this time scanning the rooftop as he went. No movement. He climbed the tree with ease and quicky was back inside the chateau, creeping down the stairs. The fire had all gone out by now, and only glowing coals were left, so it was darker in the room now and only a soft glow remained. He felt his way down the stairs, relying mostly on memory of the room, and found the dagger that hung proudly over the mantlepiece. Its gold blade flickered brightly even in the dim light. He softly reached for it and lifted it carefully from its hold. As he pulled it, he felt the slightest resistance against it, then heard a faint jingle of some bells on the other side of the wall.

His heart sank, and for a moment he lowered his head and closed his eyes, wishing more than anything that he could turn back time. The heaviness of remorse washed over him. The dagger was booby-trapped, and he had fallen right for it. There was the faint sound of a thud or two on the other side of the wall, then in just moments, the door next to the fireplace burst open with incredible force and slammed against the wall so hard it almost shattered.

Out came a large ogre, barreling into the living room. He was massive, roughly three times the mass of Jace, who was thin and of average height. The ogre stopped past the doorway to peer in the darkness for the intruder. Jace should have known, he thought to himself. Ogres were common home protection for the wealthy. They were dumb, loyal, huge, and violent.

Jace was standing still, with his hand still on the dagger, his mind racing about what move to make next, when his thoughts were interrupted. He had been spotted. The ogre came charging at him, thumping huge steps across the wooden floor, shaking the house as he came. He was fast, but Jace was faster. With nimble agility, he ducked and rolled past the ogre as he came clomping by. The ogre smashed heavily into the mantelpiece and slammed his fists down in frustration, breaking through the wood. He turned toward Jace again. He was cornered now; the ogre stood between him and the stairs. As the ogre started for him again, Jace took three fast steps towards the ogre, and just as he was near him, Jace stepped sideways up onto the wall then flipped over the ogre's shoulders, and he landed firmly on the ground with two planted feet.

The exhibition of acrobatics was impressive, but the ogre was quick this time. Before Jace could regain his balance, the ogre swung around, grabbed him by the collar, and threw him easily across the room like a doll, smashing him hard against the wall. Jace slumped down to the floor, marveling at the ogre's strength through the haze from such a hard blow. He started to shake it off, but the ogre was already coming at him again. Jace tucked and rolled and grabbed the dagger from his ankle sheath again, and in one quick motion sliced the ogre just above the ankle.

The ogre wailed out in pain at an alarmingly loud volume, then fell heavily onto the floor, grasping the wound. Jace rose to his feet. He was a killer when he needed to be, but the ogre had been subdued. Just then another shadow appeared at the doorway. Jace recognized him immediately as the owner of the chateau, the general of the King's Guard. Jace did not want to fight anymore, he just wanted to escape. So, he turned and ran for the stairs.

"Guards!" the general yelled from the doorway dashing to tend to the wounded ogre. Jace leapt up the stairs and was gone in seconds. He climbed down the tree with quick, smooth agility and made his way swiftly into the night. In mere moments, he was just another shadow.

He was already a good distance from the chateau by the time he noticed the candles being lit and all the windows lighting up. The guards and a search party were no doubt being organized and would be outside scouring the area soon. But by the time the line of torches came marching outside from the front gates, he was already long gone.

Far enough away, he finally slowed his jog to a comfortable walking pace. The first sign of the morning was beginning to creep over the horizon, and small beams of light cut their way through the darkness of the early morning. Jace pulled out one of the pouches of gold and ran his fingers through it, jingling the coins as he walked through the forest. He couldn't help but grin. The gold was his.

Chapter 18: Evicted

The next morning, Aleric was awoken in his castle chambers by a loud commotion in the courtyard below. A massive crowd of villagers and guards had gathered, and there were hostile sounds of yelling back and forth. Aleric got out of bed slowly and tiredly, then made his way to the window and opened the shutters. Down below, in the market, one of the guards was standing on the courtyard steps above the crowd.

"Back to your homes!" he yelled. "By order of the king. Anyone out wandering shall be arrested immediately!"

"You can't do that!" someone in the crowd shouted.

"It's for your own safety," the guard snapped back. "There is a beast out there roaming the villages, ready to rip your face clean from your soggy bones!"

"Who gives you the authority to tell me what to do?" another peasant shouted angrily. "I am not scared of some mysterious beast."

"The authority comes from that we are stronger than you and can easily throw you into the dungeon," the guard replied condescendingly. "So do what we say or that is exactly what will happen to you. All of you!"

"How long do we have to stay in our homes?" another peasant cried out.

"Until the beast is found and killed," the guard replied. He was losing his patience with the unruly crowd. "Get them out of here!" he yelled to the other guards, motioning toward the mob with his hand.

The many other guards who were surrounding the courtyard began to close in on the crowd, and they pushed and shoved each other, trying to clear the courtyard of the villagers.

"Go home!" they shouted. "We will start arresting anyone on the streets—by order of the castle!"

Aleric could see that things could turn violent at any moment. The whole kingdom was pitted against their own neighbors, the castle guards, all because of something the old king had decided. He must go talk some sense into him, he thought. Aleric changed quickly and headed out the door and down toward the great hall.

At that same moment, Thearbuc and Lamora were downstairs, entering the castle through a side entrance after an early morning walk through the gardens. They did not know about the commotion that was going on in the courtyard, and they made their way to the great hall for breakfast without any cares in the world. As they turned from a corridor and entered the hall, they saw Aleric rushing down the stairs in a hurry. Just then, Maub also entered the hall, with a group of guards following him. Lamora had never seen the wizard Maub before, as she usually either entered the castle through an open window or met Thearbuc outside in the village. She stopped suddenly and gasped at the sight of him. Her breath was taken away from her like she had been punched in the stomach. She quickly stopped in her tracks and stared at the wizard with a look of horror on her face.

"What is wrong?" Thearbuc asked worriedly upon seeing her behavior change. Lamora couldn't reply. She couldn't speak. What she saw was a sea of blackness and evil surrounding the wizard. Like a thick, black cloud, it engulfed him and filled the entire room. She had never seen anything so evil, except for once. In the mountain cave where the sorcerers were conjuring magic. Her mouth dropped and her body was gripped with fear upon seeing such an all-consuming darkness.

As she stood there, mouth agape, Maub turned and spotted her. He looked at her curiously for just a moment, then his bewildered expression quickly turned into rage, and he rushed towards her and Thearbuc.

"Who are you?" he demanded. "Why are you in this castle?"

Just as he was about to grab Lamora by the wrist, Aleric interrupted the wizard. "Where is the king?" he asked loudly, storming into the main hall. Maub was taken back at The Paladin's interruption, and the look of anger on his face only seemed to get worse.

"The king…is ill," the wizard Maub spoke, with an annoyed tone behind clenched teeth. "What is it that you want today?"

"You are closing down the markets?" Aleric replied. "Over something that isn't even here?"

"It is for everyone's safety," Maub replied slowly.

"I told you all when we got back that the beasts tracks were leading away from the kingdom and into the outer forests. Has there been more murders?" Aleric asked.

"I guess our Paladin friend here doesn't think wild animals can turn around and walk in different directions," Maub said exaggeratedly while the others in his entourage snickered. "There have not been any more murders—yet."

"I need to speak with the king," Aleric said urgently.

"We need to get out of here," Lamora whispered to Thearbuc with a look of fear in her eyes.

The wizard turned toward Lamora and studied her. Somehow, he knew that she knew what he was, but he couldn't quite pinpoint what magic she was using on him. "Is this your friend?" he asked Aleric, ignoring his previous question.

"This is Lamora," Aleric replied. "A friend. I am going to find the king," he said, turning away from the wizard and heading to the stairs up to the king's quarters. The wizard glared at Lamora constantly while she turned her head away, trying to escape his hateful gaze.

"There is something else, Paladin," Maub said loudly, motioning to the group of guards as Aleric walked away. Aleric ignored him and continued walking. But as he approached the steps leading to the upper levels of the castle, the group of guards moved forward from both sides and blocked the way with readied weapons. Aleric was taken aback. He reached for his longsword, but it was not there. He had left the sword in his room.

"What is the meaning of this!?" he shouted angrily.

"As I was saying," the wizard Maub approached slowly, "before I was so rudely ignored, is that under these new circumstances, where there is either a murderer or a beast on the loose, ravaging the countryside—Wait, didn't you say you were stalked by these beasts not long ago and are familiar with them?" Maub said accusingly. Aleric stayed quiet and did not reply to the insincere question. His fists were clenched and ready to attack the guards if they moved on him. "We cannot risk the king's safety if you are being stalked by these beasts. You will lead them right to the castle! It is for everyone's safety that you and your friends be expelled from the castle immediately."

"That is absurd!" Aleric yelled, throwing his arms up.

"King's orders," Maub rose his hands as if there was nothing he could do. "Not mine. I just follow the rules, just like you or any of these men." He gestured at the guards. "We are a kingdom of laws, and we must follow them."

"Let me hear it from the king then!" Aleric said angrily, making his way towards the steps again. The guards doubled down, raising their weapons, and taking combat stances. Aleric stopped short, his eyes glowing as he clenched his fist in frustration and anger.

"Don't!" Lamora cried out, running to The Paladin. She ran up to him and grabbed his forearm with both of her hands and looked into his glowing eyes. "We need to get out of here," she pleaded, with a look of desperation in her eyes. She quickly glanced back at the wizard. "Please!" she begged, tugging on his arm. "It's for the best."

"Now, now," Maub interrupted calmly, towering over Lamora and resting his long, withered hand on her shoulder. She could see and feel the blackness begin to surround her, and it sent chills through her body. "What would the king say if you were to kill a bunch of his guards inside his own castle? Has your loyalty to the castle turned, Paladin?" But The Paladin stood fast, eyes still glowing and ready to fight. "Why, you would be banished from the castle forever. Locked away or hanged for treason. You do not want blood to spill in the king's castle. Walk away with your dignity and your friends, save some face and leave."

The Paladin stood defiant and silent for a few more moments, then his eyes slowly began to dim until they were normal once again. A look of relief washed over the guards' faces, and Aleric stood back up from his fighter's stance and looked around. "I will need to collect my belongings," he said finally.

"Your sword, you mean," Maub said with a mischievous chuckle. "I should think not. Your belongings will be delivered to your cottage in the countryside this afternoon. The one without doors or windows, if I remember correctly." Now the wizard was just taunting him. Outnumbered and outplayed, the king's Paladin had no other option but to comply. Aleric stood down, took a step back, and raised his hands above his head showing the guards he was backing off.

At his peaceful concession, a group of guards suddenly tried grabbing Thearbuc and Lamora to escort them out of the castle. Aleric turned to see Thearbuc being shoved and pushed by the group as he pulled away, and Lamora was grabbed by two others. She was irate, yelling at them and trying to fight back while Thearbuc was trying his best to de-escalate the situation.

"What are you doing?" Aleric yelled at the guards, who began to let up their aggression upon hearing his powerful voice. Lamora ripped her arm away from the guard's grasp and showed the palms of her hands, indicating she wouldn't fight anymore. She brushed her hair back and acted calm, while innocently and slowly backing up closer to Maub, who was watching the chaos unfold.

Aleric was busy arguing with the guards, and Thearbuc was trying to calm him down, when Lamora saw her chance. Amidst the chaos, Lamora turned quickly and grabbed Maub's old, craggy hand. He tried to pull away in reflex, but she was strong, and she held fast to his boney fingers. She quickly threw the wizard's cloak sleeve up past his elbow and twisted his arm to see the underside of his forearm. But to her surprise nothing was tattooed there.

"Lamora!" Aleric yelled, pulling her away from the wizard. "What in the world are you do—"

But before Aleric could finish, he was shoved aside with great strength, and by the time he turned to see what was happening, Maub was standing face-to-face with Lamora, towering over her with a raging scowl on his face. He wrapped his craggy fingers around her neck and slightly squeezed her throat with clenched teeth, like he was holding back destroying her right then and there. Aleric, seeing what was happening, immediately pushed himself between the wizard and Lamora. "Hey! Stop!" he kept saying, trying to get Maub to let go. But Lamora was at the complete mercy of the wizard. She held a threatening and defiant stare at him even as he gripped her. Finally, Aleric was able to pry the wizard's fingers from her neck and pull her away. Not wanting to push the wizard any further, the three hurried away from the situation while being shoved out by the overly aggressive guards.

In what almost didn't feel real, the three of them suddenly found themselves standing outside the castle with the door slammed in their faces, locked behind them, and shut out for good. It seemed like just as they had gotten comfortable in their own beds, they were evicted, standing homeless in the castle's courtyard.

"What were you thinking?" Aleric turned angrily and barked at Lamora. "Assaulting a wizard like that? The king's head counsel, I might add. You could have gotten us all locked up or worse!"

"I'll explain later," she replied quickly, her eyes darting back and forth. "We need to get out of here."

"Is everything alright, Lamora?" Thearbuc asked upon seeing her prolonged anxiousness. "You've looked pale and scared ever since you saw Maub." Lamora didn't say anything, but she didn't have to. She gazed into Thearbuc's eyes with a pleading sadness that he could see right away. "Alright," he spoke, "let's get away from here."

Then the three stepped away from the castle doors and exited out into the courtyard. They came upon another scene of complete chaos: the angry mob that Aleric had seen from his window earlier had turned into a full riot! A large brawl between dozens of villagers and guards. The shouts and curses at one another and the sound of weapons striking against metal armor were deafeningly loud. Aleric, Lamora, and Thearbuc could not believe their eyes. How had the kingdom turned back into chaos in just one day?

"Let's steer clear of this mess," Aleric said, taking the lead and trying to walk around the outskirts of the fight. As they tiptoed around the perimeter, they came to a group of guards beating on a small group of older villagers.

"It is for your own safety!" the guard yelled, while clubbing a man across the face with a heavy plank of wood. The man fell hard to the ground and did not get up. "Can't you see we're trying to help you!" the guard continued, then spit on the motionless villager.

"Get back to your cottages, you," the other guards were yelling. Aleric raised up his hands and showed his palms to the guards, showing that he meant no threat as they went peacefully by. Paladin or not, he could not stop this situation while defenseless, outnumbered, and unarmed.

Finally, they made their way through the brawl and back down to the stables, where it was quiet and normal. All the guards must have been busy fighting in the courtyard because there was no one there watching the horses.

"Alright, what was that back there with Maub?" Aleric asked Lamora once again, not letting it go. She sighed heavily, not sure if Aleric would believe what she was about to say.

"I was looking to see if had that tattoo on his forearm, like that mage you encountered in the woods. The emblem we saw in the cave of sorcerers."

"Why would you do that? Are you crazy?" Aleric replied throwing his arms up.

"He's evil!" Lamora snapped back. "Pure evil. He is not a friend to us, the king, or the kingdom."

"Oh, we've decided he's just odd," Thearbuc chimed in. "Most old wizards are."

"Not like this," Lamora snapped again with a nervous and shaky tone. "Don't you two remember that I can actually *see* these things? He is pure evil. It whirls and flows around him so thick that it fills the entire room and surrounds anyone around him. You know you can feel it!" she pleaded. Aleric and Thearbuc exchanged glances but did not say anything in reply. "I've seen that dark energy before," Lamora continued. "But only once. I saw it in the cave of sorcerers when we came through the mountain." Aleric and Thearbuc were taken back at the statement.

"We're in a lot of trouble if that is true," Aleric said, sounding worried.

"One of the wizards in the cave was pretty tall and thin, and I've had doubts about Maub before" Thearbuc said, scratching his beard. "And you did see how corrupt he is in the dungeons."

"We'll need more evidence than the dungeon keeper being overly strict before we start assuming he is the head of a secret society of sorcerers out to kill us," Aleric stated. "We need to figure out a way to get back into the castle and investigate some more."

"We need to get out of here first!" Lamora interrupted, pleading again. "Getting out of that castle is probably the best thing to happen for you two."

"Why are you just telling us this now?" Aleric asked.

"I've never seen him before," she replied. "I always stick to your side of the castle. I only saw him for the first time just now." Whatever she had seen, it was apparent to the other two that it had rattled her deeply.

"Okay. Let's get out of here," Aleric announced finally, throwing his leg over his horse. "Thearbuc, I am going back to my cottage to discuss this with Brodel and see if we can figure out what is going on. Something about the whole kingdom locking down and the king kicking us out without talking to me first does not feel right.

"I'm coming with," Thearbuc offered, without having to be asked. "I'm with you to the end of this."

"You two are looking for trouble," Lamora said angrily. "I don't want anything to do with that old wizard in there, and I suggest you two stay far away as well. I'm going home." She jumped onto her horse with a scowl.

And with that, the three rode as fast as they could away from the stables before anyone could stop them. When the road split, they parted ways, Thearbuc and Aleric off to Aleric's old cottage to meet Brodel, and Lamora in the opposite direction toward her village. Later, as Thearbuc and Aleric approached his odd-looking cottage, with its crooked door and sideways window, they heard a loud boom, and a plume of pink and purple smoke puffed out the window and chimney.

"Brodel!" Aleric yelled angrily. Suddenly, the wizard appeared in the window with his token black robes and his staff topped with a glowing blue orb.

"Uh-oh," he said, then rushed back inside. Aleric made his way to the door, pushed it aside, and entered the dwelling, which was filled with pink smoke.

"If you blow up my house again, I swear." Aleric shook his head with disappointment.

"I'll fix it again if I do," Brodel laughed. "You will love what I am working on." He held out a glass ball with a cork in one end. Inside swirled pink and purple smoke, the same that seemed to be swirling the room. "Magic smoke bomb. In case you ever need to sneak away in a hurry. Take it," Brodel said, giving the orb to Aleric. As he handed the gift to him, he could tell his cheerful attitude was not shared by either of the men. Brodel furrowed his brow. "What's wrong?"

"We got kicked out of the castle," Thearbuc said solemnly from the other side of the room. "The whole kingdom is being confined to their homes until they can find the beast, or whatever it was, that killed those farmers at the edge of town."

Brodel looked bewildered. "How will they ever do that? The villagers outnumber the king's guards ten to one." He scrunched his face in thought. "Why would they even want to try to keep everyone confined?" He trailed off. "There must be something more to it."

"That's what we were thinking," Thearbuc added. "But what?"

"Brodel," Aleric said, "I need to get back into that castle to figure out what is going on. This whole situation is not sitting right with me. Something Lamora said about the wizard Maub. And where is the king? Why wasn't he the one to tell us to leave the castle? He wouldn't do this to us," Aleric reassured them and himself.

"I've got just the thing," Brodel smirked. He went around the room, which had gotten fairly cluttery in the short time he had been a guest here. He threw a pile of trinkets and papers from a wooden chest and opened it, then began rummaging around inside. "Here it is," he said, pulling a shiny silver tunic from the chest. As he held it up, the light seemed to change the silver mesh to different shades of purples, blues, greens, and reds. "Invisibility cloak. I believe I've shown you this before." He handed it to Aleric.

"Indeed, you have, my friend, "Aleric replied. He did not know that, once again, he was holding the very item that saved his life as a child, so many years ago. "I'm going back to the castle tomorrow night. I'll sneak in through the dungeons and find out what is going on. I'll tell the king what has happened to us, and at the very least ask for an explanation.

Thearbuc nodded that he agreed. "Brodel, you have a solution to everything, don't you?" He grinned in reply.

The three friends spent the rest of the evening discussing the matters at hand and what they could possibly do about it. In the end, they figured nothing could be done until they knew what they were dealing with. All they knew was the three of them were now roommates.

The next day, a rider came to the house. He carried the flag of Mazeron and was going to every cottage in the area nailing a notice to their front doors. Aleric, Thearbuc, and Brodel happened to be outside when the rider approached.

"What is it you have there?" Aleric asked nicely as the rider slowly approached.

"That had better be an apology letter from the king," Thearbuc said in a low chuckle. The rider dismounted and handed the paper to Aleric, which he read out loud to the others…

NOTICE FROM THE KING

THE KINGDOM IS HEREBY CLOSED UNTIL FURTHER NOTICE

MURDEROUS BEASTS ROAMING THE LANDS

Gold mines: CLOSED
Food markets: CLOSED
Town hall: CLOSED
Playhouse: CLOSED
Castle and courtyard: CLOSED

STAY IN YOUR HOMES
VIOLATORS WILL BE ARRESTED ON SIGHT

"Apparently it's not important enough for you to stay in your home, eh old chap?" Thearbuc mocked the rider with a mischievous grin.

"Rider, what is this all about, do you figure? What do you make of it?" Aleric asked with a friendly tone, trying to change the tension that was quickly building.

"Not sure." The guard spit crudely onto the ground and let it drip from his lip. Many of the guards were known to be uncivilized at best.

"Is there any more word from the castle?" Thearbuc asked.

"What of the king?" Brodel chimed in. There were so many questions. Especially from out here in the countryside, where they could get no whisperings or gossip from the townspeople.

"Haven't seen the king," the guard replied, hocking up mucus from deep within his nose and throat. Brodel recoiled in disgust. "There's a rumor, though. You didn't hear it from me. Rumor is a High Elf arrived at the castle this very morning."

"Oh god, not the High Elves," Thearbuc said, rolling his eyes. The others grunted in mutual disgust.

It was well known that the High Elves were almost always trouble. They were once a proud race of elves that dwelled high in the mountains far away, hence their name. They were known for their craftmanship, classy nature, and ability to build magnificent civilizations far more advanced than any others around at the time. But the earth was experiencing a thaw from a recent ice age, so as the centuries rolled on and the land grew warmer, a type of mushroom began to grow in their lands. This mushroom, when consumed, was a potent drug that gave the user a euphoric and out of body feeling. The official name for the drug was Psytic. But it was usually referred to as "Eleven Moonroot." For some reason, the High Elves took to it more than other races, and they quickly became addicted. Consumed by it, Elven Moonroot was the only thing most of them cared about at this point. Some theorized that it was something in their biology that made it so addictive to them. Others thought that after centuries of such strict living, they wanted badly to rebel from their straight and narrow ways. Whatever the reason was, this mushroom had all but destroyed their once-great civilization.

Psytic grew in warm, wet climates. The part of the mushroom that was visible above ground was not the part that they consumed, but instead the bulb that grew half an arm's length below the soil. Wherever they went, they would dig through the ground looking for and harvesting the bulbs at the root, always leaving a trail of destruction and destroyed earth. On top of that they were almost all always on the stuff. Too belligerent and burnt out to build or create, they would wallow in their own dirt and filth, basically only caring about the drug and on occasion their next meal. Once all the mushrooms in the area had been dug up and consumed, they would move on to the next area. And being so debilitated by the drug, they wouldn't bother to raise animals or farm and instead would hunt and gather everything they needed to survive, leaving the once-lush area a complete wasteland, void of any vegetation or wildlife. They were destructive and by all accounts, a nuisance and a plague upon any land they came across.

"Did you say a High Elf?" Thearbuc said in a disgusted tone.

"That's what I heard," the guard replied.

"Did you see him? How could a High Elf be in these lands, and you are not sure?"

"No one is allowed around the castle grounds right now," the rider continued. "Everyone is gone. It's eerie quiet. No one is there to see him. Could be a rumor." He shrugged.

Aleric walked over to Thearbuc and handed him the notice. "We need to get in there. See what is going on," he whispered.

"Aye," Thearbuc agreed.

Aleric turned back toward the rider. "Thank you for coming by good sir. That will be all from us."

The rider nodded and made his way back to his horse, then was off in the direction of the next cottage.

"I'm leaving now," Aleric said flatly. "I will return by morning." And with that, he went back inside and started gathering his things. He grabbed his dagger instead of the bulky sword and thin leather shoes instead of his metal armor battle shoes and gauntlets. Lastly, he grabbed the invisibility cloak. This was a stealth mission.

As Aleric returned from inside the home, Thearbuc spoke, "I'm sure they have heard that the kingdom is mining for gold once again. They come to lands where they can beg and leech of off others' hard work, all while they stay lazy and drugged."

"I know the stories," Aleric replied, sounding somewhat disinterested.

"Anyone but the High Elves," Thearbuc continued. "If the rumor is true and one of them is here to visit the king. He better not let those leeches come here to destroy all we've worked so hard to build."

"You really hate the High Elves, don't you?" Brodel chuckled.

"You just don't know what they are capable of," Thearbuc replied. "You're too young to have seen it. Others build, create, and advance. They can only destroy. And the worse thing is that they are pretentious about it too!"

He was right. Although their civilization had crumbled to pieces, the High Elves had retained their deep-seated belief that they were better than everyone else. At one point, they were. For hundreds of years, in fact, they were the pinnacle of civilization and progress. It was so ingrained in their nature to look down on others that their superiority complex had stuck with them to this day. It was, to say the least, an annoying combination for anyone who had the displeasure of coming across them.

"I need to get going," Aleric cut in.

"Do you need backup?" Thearbuc asked, always eager to help his friend.

"There's only one invisibility cloak," he replied. "You being there will only attract attention. This will be a quick mission. I'll get in, scope out the castle and figure out what is going on with this closed kingdom and these High Elves, then get out fast. I also need to check in on the king. Once we know what is going on, we can come up with a plan." Thearbuc and Brodel nodded that they agreed then Aleric was off, riding hard away from the odd-looking, magic-built cottage.

It was already almost dark when The Paladin approached the castle grounds. He left his horse tied to a tree a good distance away, then approached the town and castle on foot. He waited as long as possible to slip the invisibility cloak over his head, as no one knew exactly how the cloaks worked or if wearing one for too long would wear off the magic and expose the person wearing it.

"I hope this works," he mumbled quietly as he slipped the colorful glittering tunic over his head. When he popped his head out of the neck hole, he looked down and could no longer see his hands, body, or legs. "What an eerie feeling!" he thought aloud, trying to suppress the panic that washed over him. It was an unnatural feeling to say the least, not being able to see your own hands. He took a moment to calm his breath and nerves, then continued on toward the castle.

Walking along the main road up to the castle was eerily quiet. The usually crowded dirt road was completely empty. The market had not even been set up this day, and there were no merchants selling their wares anywhere. Up ahead, in the middle of the road, two large shadows came out of the growing darkness. Aleric stopped in his tracks and his heart skipped a beat, as he was sure they were about to spot him. He jumped to the edge of the road and tried to hide in a doorway. Slowly, the shadows got larger and closer until they were right in front of him. Two large horses with guards atop of them slowly trotted on by and paid him no attention. *It must work*, he thought to himself. *Time to get going.*

As he approached the castle, Aleric noticed the large siege doors atop the ramp had been closed. It was the first time he had ever seen them closed. “There must be a way if Lamora can sneak in so often,” He thought to himself. *But no way I can spring up walls and trees to an open window like she can.*

Then it hit him: the dungeons. The entrance there was his best bet. He hurried around the side to the back of the castle. It took some time as the castle was massive. He crept quietly when he came across any patrolling guards, so as not to make a noise or raise any alarms. Finally, he was there. He stood just a few yards from his old post where he worked as a castle guard for so long. It felt like an eternity ago, he thought to himself. Like another life. So much had changed since then. He stood aside, then waited and observed. The dungeon entrance was more heavily guarded than usual. Six guards stood in front of the door. Who knows how many more were inside.

“I could probably take them all,” he mumbled to himself, concealed in the darkness. *Especially with the invisibility cloak on*, he thought. But he quickly brushed away that plan because he did not want to hurt any of his old friends who were just doing their jobs. Plus, six bodies lying in front of the entrance would most definitely give him away. He needed another idea. The minutes kept rolling by. At this rate, he would run out of time and waste the entire night crouched here in the darkness. Then finally, he caught a break…

“Open the gates,” a voice called out from the darkness and fog. Then shadows became visible from the darkness and approached. It was two guards dragging a villager—a young man. Too young for the dungeons. So many memories from when he used to work here came flooding back at the sight of it.

“Caught one!” the approaching guard yelled as they walked past Aleric. “A whole bunch of them out playing night games. Only could catch the one though, the rest scattered and fled.”

"We'll get 'em," the other guard said. "Only a matter of time if they keep it up."

The other guards did not reply but turned and slowly pushed open the heavy doors to the castle's dungeon. This was Aleric's only chance. He sprang from his hiding spot and tiptoed quickly behind the guards, then slipped right through the door behind them. As he did so, he got a bit too close and brushed against one of the guards. The guard turned around and reached for his sword.

"What was that!?" he said, turning about quickly.

Just in time, Aleric crouched down low, and the guard looked right over his head.

"What was what?" the other guard asked mockingly.

"Never mind," he replied, still glancing around. Then the two guards proceeded to drag the boy away into the darkness.

Aleric stood motionless for as long as he thought was safe, then began to advance down the corridor. As he got deeper into the belly of the castle, he rushed quickly past the cells. Every cell had multiple people in it, many moaning in agony or cold. He had never seen the dungeons so full. Then he started seeing prisoners chained to the walls outside of the cells. They had overfilled the dungeon in a single day. What was going on? This had clearly gone too far already. The threat the town faced did not justify this level of brutality. He wanted to unshackle every prisoner and set them free while he could, but that would do no good in the long run. He had to reach the king and find out what was going on in the castle.

Soon he was on the stairs, climbing out of the dungeon and into the food storage area of the castle, then into the great hall. It was dark and empty. No one was around anywhere. The castle seemed to be just as locked down as the rest of the kingdom. Aleric crept quietly up the dark stairs toward the king's chambers. But when he reached the king's wing, he heard something coming from the other direction. He turned away and peered down the hallway to see a light coming from one of the doorways.

"I'll check out what is going on in there first." he mumbled to himself. "Get back to the king's wing afterwards." He crept toward the door and heard voices inside as he got closer. When he approached the door, he found it slightly ajar and peered inside.

It was a meeting room where he had met with the king and his counsel countless times. At the head of the long wooden table sat Maub. Aleric did not recognize the other men. *Friends or counsel of the king?* he wondered. They were speaking to Maub, but Aleric was too far away to hear what they were saying. He very slowly crept through the cracked door, sucking in his chest to fit through without bumping it. He was holding his breath, moving painfully slowly, then finally he was through.

The moment he stepped through the door Maub stopped speaking. "Stop!" the wizard said loudly, raising a single bony finger to the others at the table. The others immediately went quiet as well. Maub looked around the room with intense eyes but said nothing.

"What is it?" someone at the table asked eventually.

"Shhh!" snapped Maub. "I sense something." He paused again. The silence of the room was so heavy that Aleric felt like he was in a pressure tank. The weight of the air pressed down all around him. He was found out. How could he not have thought of this? Of course the wizard would be able to sense the magic of the invisibility tunic at work. Aleric recoiled down and against the stone walls, waiting to be found. Maub stood up to investigate. He was silently looking around the room, listening to what his senses were telling him, when suddenly the door to the room swung open fast and slammed hard against the wall, almost hitting Aleric where he crouched. He instinctively shuffled further away from the door, still hugging the walls.

There were shadows in the doorway. They were tall and stood higher than the doorway itself. They stayed in the darkness for a moment, then stepped forward and into the light. Three elves entered the room with visible confidence, their chins held high and proud.

Aleric observed them as they entered. The lead elf wore a sleeveless leather tunic exposing trim, muscled arms. He carried a large sword on his back and his hair was light blue, down to the middle of his back, and tucked behind his sharp ears. It had become common for the High Elves who were all naturally blonde to dye their hair bright colors. It was believed that it was a way for them to stand out and show their uniqueness in a sea of identicalness, or possibly to ward off others and show they were a threat, like a bright-colored venomous snake, or a more apt analogy for the elves would be a striped skunk.

The elf stood silently in the doorway for a moment, staring at the others with a look of condescension, then came forward into the room. The two other elves followed close behind him, both with a similar look and build and both armed with long swords and bows.

"I am Aghasty," the High Elf announced as he entered the room. "Leader of the High Elves and commander of its army. Thank you for inviting me into your…" He paused and looked around with a look of disgust upon his face. "Your home," he continued. "If that is what you can call it."

"It smells rather wretched," the second elf said condescendingly.

"Indeed, it does," Aghasty replied, making a scrunched face.

"What is it that you want?" Maub bellowed from the back of the room, while sitting back down in his tall chair. "Our meeting was not to be held until tomorrow."

"We know," the elf replied loud and snooty. "We just cannot bear to stay another minute in this squalor you live in. We will have the meeting now, then we will leave."

Maub took a moment to reply and had a look of deep thought upon his face. "So be it," he finally replied to the elf. "Take a seat."

Aleric knelt quietly against the wall. *Why is Maub allowing them to treat him this way?* he wondered. In his own home even? This was completely out of character for the usually short-tempered and impatient old wizard.

"We will not sit," the elf replied loudly. "This will only take a moment."

"Have you no manners at all?" one of the men sitting at the table next to Maub shouted at the elf. Aghasty slowly rolled his eyes, but no other emotion was shown, and the comment seemed to fall flat on the floor rather than pierce him as the man may have hoped.

"Heel your dog, wizard," Aghasty replied in an annoyed tone. "He does not speak to us, and we do not speak to animals." The man began to lose his temper and stood up, reaching for his sword.

"Sit down!" Maub yelled at the man, while raising a threatening hand. "Let our guests speak." The room fell silent once again and Maub motioned with his hand for Aghasty to continue.

"The High Elves have heard your call and are already on the move," Aghasty spoke. "We will reach the borders of your kingdom on the morrow."

"Why thank you," Maub replied. "That is very fast of you. How did you reach these lands so quickly?"

Aghasty rolled his eyes again. Questions seemed to annoy him. "We were already not far off," he replied to the wizard. "It seems that years of not defending or tending to your lands will give dragons the idea that they can nest wherever they please. They took over the western foothills and high mountains long ago and their runoff of gas and acidic poison flowed into our lands and destroyed everything in its path. I'm sure there's a lesson in there for you if you are wise enough to heed it: leaving things be, or being idle, will only allow room for destructive forces to move in."

Aleric pondered the accusations from the elf. It could be true, but he knew it was mostly a lie. Yes, roosting dragons would destroy the surrounding earth, but only the High Elves and their endless digging for mushrooms would destroy so much earth that an entire area would have to be abandoned for more prosperous lands.

"We had already crossed the mountains long ago and have been living near your borders for some time," Aghasty continued. It was merely a few days ride to your lands, and the first groups shall be arriving in a matter of hours. Which brings me here. What of our payment?"

"Your payment will be as promised," Maub replied, standing up and leaning across the table to the large map of the kingdom that always lay across it. "You get all the lands west of the river and up to the foothills. In return, we get the services of your army for as long as your people dwell there.

"Where are the rivers?" Aghasty replied, wasting no time. Maub and Aghasty both leaned in towards the map.

"There are rivers here, here, and here," Maub said, pointing to locations on the map. It was no doubt Aghasty was securing land by the river for his people to dig for Elven Moonroot and secure their mushroom supply for the foreseeable future. But in exchange for their entire army? *What could Maub need that many soldiers for?* Aleric thought to himself. A feeling of dread washed over him.

Then, in an instant, it all started to come together. Maub was selling out the kingdom's land and using the people's own taxes against them. Using their own money and land to hire mercenaries to oppress them, arrest them, and steal more of their land.

As far as Aghasty went, his plan was much simpler. It was commonly known that the High Elves had kept a piece of their once-civilized nature and were a democratic type of society. Aghasty was voted into his position and kept it only as long as he kept his people happy. Therefore, he was not a leader who cared about what was best for his people or advancing or improving their situation. All he had to do was give them things they wanted, and in turn, they would vote for him. By securing the land and a temporary supply of Moonroot, he would stay in power and keep his position as leader and commander of the High Elves.

As the pieces of the puzzle began to click in his head, he sat, crouched down along the wall. Aleric noticed a quick flicker of light that immediately grabbed his attention. For a split second, he didn't know what it was, or even if it had really happened. But then that very moment, Maub darted a glance in Aleric's direction, and he realized what it was. The invisibility tunic had momentarily stopped working. Was it running out of magic? Was it a one-time glitch? Aleric sat still in hopeless desperation, praying he would not be found out. Then it happened again. He flickered into existence, then disappeared again. He was sure of it this time, as he saw his own hands appear.

Maub saw it too. At least he thought he did, but the look on his face said maybe he wasn't sure. The menacing wizard slowly stood up from the table as Aleric darted for the door. The motion of Aleric moving must have made the invisibility tunic give out even faster, because as he dashed away, he flickered into visibility many times, like a candle flickering out in the wind.

To Aghasty and the elves surprise, suddenly a man appeared, running directly in front of them. Aleric noticed the look of surprise on Aghasty's face, so he smashed heavily into him, knocking him over as he ran towards the exit then out the door.

"Intruder!" the entire room yelled almost simultaneously. "Guards! Get him!"

Aleric ran into the dimly lit hall and headed fast toward the stairs, which were also in the direction of the heavily guarded king's wing. He could hear the commotion growing behind him as the others gave chase.

Aghasty sprang up from the ground with impressive agility and was already to the door in just a moment. He grabbed a bow from one of the other elves and snatched an arrow from his quiver, then turned and darted into the hall. In another second, he had the bow drawn and aimed at Aleric, who was fleeing down the corridor oblivious to the fact he was on the wrong end a silver-tipped arrow. Aghasty let the string go, and a twang rang out from the bow's heavily drawn tension. At that very moment, Aleric darted left and down the stairs. The arrow missed him by only a finger length, even though the shot came from such a far distance. The arrow rang so fast and true that it flew right past him and continued down the corridor, striking one of the approaching king's guards above the knee. He went down with an agonizing howl. Aleric kept on running, glancing back only to realize they were shooting more arrows directly at him and the invisibility tunic had stopped working completely. His hopes sank at the realization that everyone could see him now, and the entire kingdom was covered with guards enforcing the king's orders.

But there was no time for dashed hopes, he thought as he ran. Just survival. He ran as fast as he could, through the empty great hall and down a long corridor of (hopefully) empty rooms. These hallways were dark, only lit by random torches along the walls. He heard the commotion of guards in pursuit behind him and knew he had to make a decision quickly. Without thinking much about it, he chose a random room and quickly opened and closed the door behind him, trying to catch his breath. Quickly, he hurried over to a window and opened the shutter. Down below, he could see the torchlight of the patrolling guards. He could tell by the flames' sporadic and fast movements that they had already been informed and were on alert for the intruder inside the castle. To his right, Aleric noticed a large tree that grew near the window. He was still high up, but if he could jump down and land or hang onto a larger branch, then he might just be able to use it to climb down to the ground level far below.

Doors could be heard opening and slamming shut loudly down the hall as the guards began searching the rooms. He could hear them getting closer, and soon they would open the door to this room to find him standing here, cornered and outnumbered. So, Aleric quickly climbed onto the windowsill, looked down, then jumped. The thick branch he jumped to came at him fast as the wind rushed past his face, the cold biting at his skin. He landed chest-first with a heavy thump, then wrapped his arms around the branch and squeezed tight. His arms held and he did not fall to the ground. Slowly, and with the wind knocked out of him, he raised himself onto the large branch, then began to shimmy towards the trunk. He heard the guards above enter the room he had just jumped from, and they immediately saw the open window.

"In here!" he heard one say as he began climbing down the tree. He was almost down when they spotted him.

"Guards! Guards!" they shouted and waved their torches in the air to bring attention to the other guards on the ground. Aleric could see their torches turn and come towards him quick. He was done for. Then it hit him…He was The Paladin. Out here, not cornered or too outnumbered, this shouldn't be a problem.

Finally, he hopped from the tree and onto flat ground, then ran away from arrows reach and toward the incoming horse-mounted guards. As they approached him, riding fast and hard, he continued to run directly at them. As he got closer, his eyes began to glow, and the strength and confidence of The Paladin took over. He knew no fear at this point, and was driven solely by instinct, like a predator charging at its prey.

As the first rider approached, he began to draw a longsword from its sheath and readied to strike the oncoming fugitive. But The Paladin was too quick. He jumped inhumanly high and used his momentum to crash into the rider before he could swing his sword. They impacted with an audible thud, and the rider came crashing down to the ground with Aleric on top of him while the horse rode on, seemingly unaware that it had just been relieved of his rider. One punch from The Paladin and the guard was unconscious. The others were attempting to turn their horses in a hurry, but the attacking Paladin was already up again and coming toward them.

Approaching from behind, The Paladin reached up and grabbed the next guard by the collar and ripped him from his horse and threw him heavily onto the ground with ease. The Paladin quicky took the rider's sword and mounted his horse then turned to face the next guard riding toward him. The Paladin raised his sword in anticipation to strike down the last guard, but the man had no fight left in him and simply threw himself from his galloping horse and rolled along the ground to a stop. With no one left to fight, The Paladin spurred his horse, and they were off and fading into the black of night

When Aleric was a far distance away from the castle, he pulled the invisibility tunic off and studied it. It looked like tattered old cloth at this point. No more colorful glimmering in the moonlight. Instead, it had become dull gray and dotted with holes like an old garment. He tucked it into his belt for safekeeping and wondered if magic or a spell could ever revive it. He turned north, spurred the horse, then they were off again, riding fast into the night. But this time riding away from home…

It was still late in the night as Aleric approached the small village—the nearest village to the castle, besides the market and huts that surrounded the castle grounds. From the dark road leading into the village, he could see the torchlights of patrolling guards up ahead.

"You will draw too much attention," he mumbled aloud to his horse as he dismounted then shooed him away in the opposite direction. Aleric approached the village on foot now. He steered away from the main road and weaved his way through the cottages and establishments, deeper into the town. It was extra cold this night, and the wind chill bit his ears as he went. Luckily, thick clouds were covering the moon, so it was dark and ominous out. A feeling of anticipation and urgency ran through Aleric's veins as he snuck in and out of alleyways, around small homes, and through muddy streets.

Finally, he approached a small wooden house. It was single level but had steps up to the front door. The lower portion of the home was raised above the ground, as many of the homes built here were. As he climbed the steps, he noticed how worn and weathered the home was. The dark wood was rotting, and planks were slanted and falling off here and there. One of the planks on the steps was completely missing. The home was in despair. Through the shutters, Aleric could see the flickering of candles, indicating that someone was home.

He knocked softly at the door. No reply. Inside, he could hear the faint sound of creeping footsteps, then it seemed to get darker as whoever was inside doused the candles.

"It's okay, it's Aleric," he whispered at the door. Moments later the door swung open. It was Lamora.

"Aleric?" she asked with a look of shock on her face. "What are you…How do you know this place?"

Aleric ignored the questions. "I need to speak to your brother…" he said flatly.

"My brother…." she trailed off. Her eyes darted back and forth as if she was looking for an escape or a lie to tell in reply, while a look of confusion washed across her face. "I don't have a bro…"

"It's okay. I know," Aleric cut her off. "I wouldn't ask unless it was important. Take me to him."

Lamora stood in silence for a moment. Then she backed up and looked over Aleric, studying him. Her ability to see energies helped make up her mind. She could see it plainly with her eyes that his intentions were not ill-willed. "Okay," she finally said slowly. "Hang on while I gather some things." She returned to the home, doused out the remaining candles, grabbed her dagger, and in minutes they were off.

They snuck through the village quickly, again, weaving in and out of the alleyways to avoid the main roads. They kept close to the walls as they went, and Lamora constantly looked over her shoulder as they moved like shadows through the village.

"No one is following us," Aleric reassured her, noticing her worry.

"Okay. This is it," Lamora said, leaning in towards an old wooden door on a rundown, closed-up tavern. She looked around to make sure no one else was around or watching, then softly knocked at the door in a specific pattern of seven knocks. Not long later a slide opened on the top of the door and a pair of eyes and a dark nose appeared on the other side.

"What is the password?" the voice said gruntingly, low, and rough.

"Hembibble," Lamora whispered back. There was the sound of multiple clicks and bolts and the sliding of a large wooden bar from the other side of the door. Finally, it swung open.

"Come in," the grumbled voice said, still hiding behind the door as it slowly swung open.

Rays of warm candlelight poured into the dark street as the door swung open and the two entered to find a candlelit, sparsely occupied but inviting little tavern. Maybe a half dozen patrons sat around a beautifully built wooden bar. The bar was stocked with the finest liquors, rarely ever seen in these parts. Bottles of this and that of every color, fancy labels, and corks in the bottle tops. Most taverns around the kingdom just had barrels of ale or reused bottles containing potato or corn alcohol. Aleric was taken aback after stepping into such a fancy place when the outside looked so tattered and worn. The barkeeper and the patrons of the establishment were very well dressed for the villagers of Mazeron. They were adorned with bright-colored accessories, warm furs, and gem-studded jewelry. The bartender wore a clean white shirt and fancy suspenders, as opposed to the dirty apron you would see most barkeepers around the lands wearing.

"This is the thieves guild?" Aleric asked Lamora sounding bewildered.

"Not quite," she said with a grin. "Follow me."

They continued on past the barkeeper, who glanced at Lamora and gave her a friendly nod as he walked by. Then they walked past the bar and down a dark corridor into an even darker room. The faint candlelight from down the hall barely illuminated a filled bookshelf along the side wall of the room. Lamora halfway pulled out a seemingly random book.

"The password," a voice spoke from a dark corner of the room behind them. Aleric turned toward the voice, startled, just as a small match was lit and showed a glowing face in the darkness. He stood motionless in the darkness. As Aleric's eyes began to adjust to the dim light, he could see a row of daggers lined up with blades stuck in a wooden table, ready to be picked up and thrown by the hidden man at an instant.

"Three daggers in the moonlight," Lamora replied to hidden man. He slowly nodded his head downward.

"This way," he said quietly. He moved away from the corner of the room, still staying close to the shadows on the wall.

Then, Aleric heard some sort of noise—the click of a lock—and suddenly the room lit up slightly as a square trapdoor was opened from the ground. The hooded man gestured toward the hole in the floor. Lamora went first. There was a ladder leading down into an illuminated room below. Slowly, she went down the latter, then the hooded man nodded at Aleric to proceed after her.

On flat ground again, Aleric looked around to see a large, dimly lit room with men scattered about, none of them paying any attention to the two newcomers. Along the back wall was a bar, where hooded figures stood quietly with their drinks. Some alone, some quietly speaking to another. Aleric noticed quickly that everyone here was thin and wore a black or dark purple hood that concealed their faces.

Thunk. The sound of a dagger hitting wood drew Aleric's attention. He turned to see a small group of three hooded figures playing daggers against the far wall.

"I win again," a quiet voice said from the corner. "Pay up this time or they'll find your body in an alleyway before morning." Another hooded shadow pulled a pouch of coins from his person, and Aleric saw the glittering coins reflect the dim candlelight as they were passed over to the winner.

"Over here," Lamora whispered. "Follow me."

Quietly, the pair roamed past the hooded patrons through the dark establishment and to the other side of the room, where Aleric saw a long wooden table stretched across the length of the wall. One man with a black hood sat alone. He tossed a dagger slightly into the air, then watched it flip and come down tip-first, sticking into the wooden table. He slowly and methodically did it over again, handling the dagger lightly and elegantly, like it was an extension of his body.

Lamora approached the hooded man with Aleric in tow. The man stopped his dagger play and looked up at her as she stood before him.

"What brings you here this late? Bringing trouble, I'm sure," the shadowed man said calmly. "That's okay. I like trouble." His eyes glinted in the dim candlelight as he said it.

"Aleric," Lamora spoke with a sigh. "This is my brother," she said, outstretching her hand towards the hooded man. "This is Jace..."

Chapter 19: The High Elves

"Well, look what the cat dragged in," Jace said slowly from behind the darkness of his hooded face. "A square..."

"You can trust him," Lamora said to Jace.

"Well, you don't seem to know me at all, sis," Jace continued, calm and cool. "I don't trust anybody." He picked up a dagger that was stuck in the table and began swirling it around his fingers before picking his teeth with it. "What is it that you want, Paladin?" he asked. "I already know who you are. Everyone does."

"I need the help of…" Aleric began. No, those were the wrong words in this delicate situation. "I need to hire the thieves guild for some work," he said.

"Thieves aren't for hire," Jace replied quickly.

"They will be once every pocket in Mazeron is empty or in jail," Aleric replied. "You'll want to hear me out. There is lots of gold in it for you."

"Gold, you say?" Jace replied, lifting an eyebrow. "Well, consider me all ears."

"The kingdom is facing a problem, and I believe only the thieves guild can fix it," Aleric started. "Maub is selling out the Westland to the High Elves. They are already moving this way. It is his intention to give them the kingdom's land in return for the use of their army against us."

"High Elves?" Jace said behind his dark hood. He clenched his teeth and fist, which seemed to be the only indication of his distaste for the subject. "As loathsome as they are, many of them are still strong fighters. I'm afraid the thieves will be no help against them,"

"Not if we catch them by surprise and on our terms," Aleric replied quickly. He had already gone over the conversation in his head a dozen times and had the talking points and questions down. "The thieves are the only chance to push them back from our lands. We can't march a loud, heavy army at the High Elves. They would cut right through us. But the thieves…" Aleric continued with a mischievous grin. "Well, they are quiet and nimble assassins. A group of them in the right conditions, say a field of tall grass at night, could take down dozens of elves without them even knowing it, picking them off one by one." Jace perked up at the compliments The Paladin was showering the thieves with. "But it's the payoff that will make it worth your while," Aleric continued. "Me and my men will provide backup support for the attack, but the thieves get all the spoils. Any item in any pocket. All the gold or anything in any wagon is yours. A thief in a candy store," he grinned.

The promise of riches was too much for the master thief to ignore. "Okay, let's talk," Jace agreed.

"If you can round up three hundred men and women from your guild, then we could have them cleared out of our lands in two nights. Can you have them ready for a fight by tomorrow?" Aleric asked.

Jace threw his head back and laughed. The first sign of real emotion Aleric had seen from the chief thief. "Three hundred!" he laughed again.

"What is funny about that?" Aleric replied. Growing up in Mazeron, the thieves guild was always one of the largest problems the kingdom faced. Every night, and sometimes even during the day, there was evidence of the thieves guild around. Homes robbed, pockets picked, treasuries looted. They were everywhere…

"Friend, there are only fifty of us, maybe," Jace snickered as he said it. "This is not exactly the type of membership that we go around advertising."

"There is no reason to lie to me," Aleric replied, seemingly losing his patience with the thief. "Are you telling me that maybe fifty people have wreaked so much havoc on this kingdom all this time?"

"What can I say?" Jace leaned back and outstretched his arms in triumph. "We are good at what we do." Aleric lowered his head in disappointment. This was his only plan, the only way to counter the elves, and it was already dashed. "Don't fret," Jace said in his sly, cool tone after pausing for a moment. "The thieves are assassins by nature and would love to get our hands on some of that elven treasure."

The look on Aleric's face changed instantly. He knew the thieves couldn't resist the promise of treasure. It was well known throughout the lands that although the High Elves' society had collapsed, the soldiers who were not addicted degenerates had accumulated and still possessed the finest elven treasures. Family jewelry laced with rubies and diamonds and the finest quality garments. But the most enticing for the thieves would be the gem-studded daggers and trinkets. Anything that had been hocked or traded was in the High Elve soldier's possessions, and it was all heading right this way. Right to Jace and the thieves guild. Aleric couldn't help but notice the glint in the thief's eye as Jace's mind wandered and marveled at the riches he could claim. Not to mention the thieves hated the High Elves more than most. There was only room for one group of moochers in this kingdom. If no one was producing and everyone was leaching…well, even Jace knew that the resources would run out quick.

"Where and when?" Jace snapped back from deep within his thoughts. With a grin, Aleric pulled out a seat and leaned in, then the two began to create a plan to stop the High Elves.

"It may already be too late," Aleric finished. "Their leader, Aghasty, said they are already marching on these lands."

"Well then," Jace said slyly from behind his dark hood, "I'd say there's no time to waste then. Allow me…"

With that, the sly thief got up from behind the table and walked through the guild. Aleric noticed his body was thin beneath the cloak but taller than average. He moved with a confident sway and his left arm hung loosely and cool at the wrist as he strutted away. "Watch this," he said with a smirk. He produced a key from his cloak and unlocked an old wooden cabinet that was covered in dust on the wall. He reached inside and Aleric could hear the clicks of locks unlocking. Then, Jace picked up the entire cabinet and set the whole thing on the floor. What was left against the wall was a large brass tube, like the small end of a trumpet or a horn. Jace went up to it, winked at Aleric, then blew into the brass.

The sound traveled from Jace's lips through the brass into the brick wall and up a fake chimney, where a giant horn had been built, hidden in the brick. Outside, the whole sky was suddenly filled with the bellowing sound of the large horn. It was so loud and deep that it filled the ears of anyone who could hear it and rumbled in their chests. It resonated through the sky, past the castle, and on to the nearby villages. Everyone heard it.

People of the kingdom glanced at each other, wondering if they had really heard anything at all. But the thieves throughout the kingdom knew exactly what it was. It was their call. Immediately, every member of the thieves guild in the land stopped what they were doing, put down the jewels they were stealing, and made their way back to the guild. This calling was only ever used at times of the utmost importance. It either meant the heat was on to them or there was a big score to be had. Either way, the thieves were to make their way back to the guild and consult with their leader, Jace.

"Now we wait," Jace said, putting the cover back over the brass horn. "Have an ale." He offered a stein to Aleric. "I know even the squares like the stuff sometimes." He turned to Lamora. "So, sis. How do you know the infamous Paladin?" he asked.

The three began to engage in light discussion, but it was not long until different men and women came trickling into the guild. One by one, heeding the call until the dark tavern was filled with hooded thieves. Most leaned cool and calmly against the walls with an ale or tossing a dagger in hand. Others quietly spoke to one another while they waited.

When it seemed everyone was present, Jace addressed the room and informed the guild of the approaching threat to their lands and riches. The thieves simultaneously spit on the ground in disgust at the mention of the approaching High Elves. The thieves were all more than happy to have a shot at what treasures may remain in their possession.

"There's not much time to waste," Jace said as he finished the briefing. "We need to leave the village tomorrow night under the cover of darkness. We'll rest in the outer woods by daylight and travel under the cover of dark until we find where the High Elves are camped. Get your weapons, get your rest. We meet on the outskirts of town at sundown tomorrow. You know the place."

The thieves nodded in understanding, then one by one made their way to a room at the back of the guild, which Aleric soon realized was their armory. Then they exited one by one, loaded to the teeth weapons—bows, arrows, daggers, and throwing stars. Not a lot of swords, he noticed; sword fighting was too loud and brutish for the thieves. They weren't necessarily the strongest fighters, but they were the smartest fighters. Which is why The Paladin had come to them for this particular problem. The thieves shuffled out of the guild and into the night to prepare for their battle. Aleric and Lamora stayed at the guild for the night and the following day with a handful of other thieves. There was a makeshift bunk house for thieves who may need to lay low for some time until the heat on them died down, but tonight it would house a different kind of fugitive.

The next evening, Aleric and Lamora found themselves armed and standing in the cool forest night in a clearing under the stars, waiting for the rest of the thieves to assemble. The guild had horse-drawn wagons hidden in the woods, which the thieves climbed into one by one as they arrived. There were also multiple well-fed, strong horses at the ready. This was their rendezvous point to get from town to town. It was manned and guarded at all times and contained horses and supplies for any thief who might need it to flee. These rendezvous points were usually hidden in the woods on the outskirts of every village. Again, Aleric marveled at how organized and advanced the thieves actually were for such a small group.

Soon, they were off. Jace, Aleric, Lamora, and a handful of thieves on horseback, while the large, covered wagon filled with the rest of the thieves trotted behind, powered by a team of five horses. It was a slow caravan, but they traveled only by night, quietly and with no lighting. They were ghosts in the forest.

Hours later, the sun began to rise, and the company veered off of the trail and pushed into the woods. Tracks were covered and they sought the concealment of the forest for the daylight hours. Here, they were safe from all prying eyes that may be on the road. Scouts were sent ahead to scope out the next day's journey and attempt to find the whereabouts of the migrating High Elves. At this point, all they knew was that the elves were coming from their lands in the west. Camp was set up quickly, and after a cold meal, the group of tired thieves were all quickly asleep.

Later that day, Aleric was awoken abruptly by a commotion coming from not far off in the forest. He rubbed his eyes as he sat up to see the sun had not set yet but was already dipping low into the sky. They had slept all day, but that was the plan, so no time was lost in his deep sleep. He peered through the forest from the large tree he slept under to see a group of hooded thieves having a conversation with Jace. Aleric could tell by their body language that something was up.

He rose from his resting place with stiff joints that cracked as he stood. "I'm going to feel tired the rest of my life at this rate," he mumbled to himself. He took a moment to ponder all the traveling and fighting he had been subjected to lately. "I wish I was warm in bed with Briss," he said quietly aloud with a sense of sadness. The memory of her would jump into his head far more often than he cared to admit. It was something he couldn't help, and she was never far from his thoughts. He shook off the thoughts then advanced through the woods to Jace. Jace made eye contact with Aleric as he approached, and he could see worry in his eyes.

"We have to leave now," Jace said quickly.

"What's going on?" Aleric asked.

"The High Elves are already upon us. Their closest camp is just hours from here. There are hundreds of them, maybe thousands," Aleric sighed heavily. He had hoped the High Elves would have sent a military group first, ahead of the others to secure their lands before bringing in the whole population. He was not prepared for the news that women and children would be traveling alongside the soldiers. He was already conflicted about what to do.

"Let's get going," Jace said with a flip of his dagger as he sheathed it into his belt with the others.

After a quick late-afternoon breakfast, the thieves were off again. The sun was still up, but it was a risk they had to take, and it would be going down soon.

Later that evening, when the sun was setting, they pulled off on the road once again because the scouts informed them they were already getting close to the High Elves camp.

"We'll go on foot through the woods from here," Jace announced, tying up his horse. He left instructions for the scouts who had been out all day and night to watch the wagon and horses and rest while the rest of the group went on.

They hiked away from the road and straight up a ridge. The ridge had a steady incline, and progress was quick and easy for the strong and agile thieves. Jace led the way, and as he approached the summit of the ridge, Aleric saw him stop and freeze in his tracks for a moment before instantly dropping to the ground in a crouched position. He turned back to make eye contact with Aleric, and the look on his face immediately told him that something was wrong. Jace was white as a ghost as he gasped and stared with blank eyes and confusion on his face.

"What is it?" Aleric hollered ahead in a hushed tone. But Jace just stared blankly toward the ground. Aleric and the rest of the thieves hurried toward Jace, and as they approached, the frozen thief was finally able to muster some words.

"Get down! Get down you fools!" He motioned with his hands. The thieves, like a trained flock of birds, collapsed to the ground in unison. Then, when Jace motioned with his hands to come to him, they crept up to the ridgeline, crawling on their stomachs. Aleric reached the ridgeline first and peered out over the edge into the vast valley below. The sun was just setting, so he was able to see it perfectly. An unexpected and horrifying sight lay before him. So awful that it took his breath away momentarily as he gasped at the horror.

Outstretched before him, off in the distance was the High Elves camp. Thousands of them dotted the landscape. The land was already gutted, dug up and torn all the way to the other end of the valley. It was utterly destroyed, mudded and void of anything green. Small groups of elves could be seen wallowing in the filth. Some groups were high and blissful rolling in the mud and onto each other. Other groups were frantically digging through the soil, looking for their next root to consume.

"How long have they been here?" Lamora whispered.

"Can't be longer than one or two months," Jace replied. "We were out here in these lands not long ago and they were not here."

"They destroy that much land that fast?" Lamora gasped.

"Apparently," Aleric replied. "We can't let them get to Mazeron." As he said it, they studied the different groups of elves below. They could see some groups assembling in a large group of wagons. Some of them carried swords and others bows.

"Look," Jace pointed them out. "I think that is part of their military there. They are already getting ready to move out. Probably to find the next place to secure and settle into."

Peering down into the valley, Aleric followed the road that the wagons were assembling on. "Look at the road." He pointed. "It leads right out of the valley between those two mountains and into the forest there."

Jace gave a sly grin as he realized the opportunity that The Paladin was pointing out. "Ambush," he said mischievously. "This is going to be almost too easy." He turned to his sister Lamora and winked. “Let’s get it,” he said quickly, then was up and moving back down the ridge.

That night, under the bright glow of a full moon, two elves spoke to one another as they marched on the road through the forests.

“Aghasty and the rest of the army will march tomorrow,” the battalion leader said to the other. “We will march through the night, then set up the next camp. The battalions will join us there tomorrow night.”

“And the civilians?” the other elf asked.

“They will be escorted by the soldiers like always,” he answered. The elf stopped and stared up at the stars in the sky. The calm night breeze blew softly around him as he rested his legs for a moment. They had just exited a thick part of the forest and into a grassy field, where the sky opened up so large above them that he felt like an ant under its vast magnificence. He sighed at the beauty of it all—the sky above, the large grassy field before them. The dew drops that glinted in the moonlight on the shoulder-high grass. Aleric was there too, but he was not watching the stars and the sky. He was watching the elves.

Perched low on hill at the edge of the grassy field, he stayed concealed and hidden from the elves’ sharp, prying eyes. To them he was just another shadow in the night. He watched the battalion of elves advance, one by one, exiting the forest and entering the field of tall grass. He saw their bright-colored red and blue hair in the moonlight. Different styles of long, smooth, silky hair were tucked behind pointy ears and others with fierce-looking bright mohawks and their once fabled, fair, pale skin now mostly dirty with grime and damage from living in the dirt and sun.

This was the first time he had seen the regular High Elves. Until now, he had only seen their leader. These elves were adorned with a plethora of gawdy jewelry—different rocks and beads around their neck, ears, and wrists. So much that they clamored as they walked. Not very sneaky, he thought, for the military. This group was not expecting any confrontation, it seemed like. Simply marching from one camp to the next in a land they technically had been invited to, as far as they knew.

Soon, the entire elven battalion was spread throughout the large grassy field. Closed in by low-lying hills on either side, they marched through the tall grass, unable to see more than a few feet in any direction. Aleric knew what was about to happen next. Although he couldn't see them, he knew the thieves were also in the field, concealed by the tall grass.

Down in the tall grass, one particular elf wandered carelessly. His mind was blank and at peace as he walked, enjoying the cool night air. Suddenly, he heard something in the grass near him. At least, he thought he did. He turned quickly but saw nothing. Then a shadow moved in the distance through the grass in front of him. He turned again, but nothing was there. He didn't even hear the twang of the bow or the whistle of the arrow speeding through the tall grass before it struck him right between the eyes, dropping him instantly without a sound.

Aleric watched him drop silently from his concealed position above the field. Then there was more movement in the tall grass. It started as some faint rustling of grass, then quickly moved forward at an alarming pace, straight towards an elf. Aleric could see his soft-skinned, stupid elf face glowing in the moonlight. This elf, too, disappeared, and the tall grass was motionless once again. Besides the wind blowing softly through the tall grass, there was not even a sound.

"My turn," Jace mumbled to himself, as he slowly maneuvered a dagger through his fingers while he crouched unseen in the tall grass. He made a faint but high-pitched whistle, so faint that even though the marching elves heard it, they paid no attention to it. But the thieves recognized it immediately, as they had trained on this extensively. The faint whistle told them to find a target now. Jace gave a five second pause, then gave the faint whistle again. Suddenly, from his concealed spot above the field, Aleric saw ten shadows appear in the grass as the thieves stood, drew back their bows, and let loose a speeding arrow at each of their targets before disappearing back into the grass. It took less than three seconds for all of them to fire, and Aleric watched as about ten pale elf faces disappeared into the tall grass without a sound.

This plan was working. The thieves were picking off the High Elves one by one at an alarmingly impressive rate. This wasn't even a fight. It was a massacre! He watched it unfold as the elven soldiers emerged from the forest and into the killing field. So carefree in one moment, then gone the next.

But after some time, his untethered optimism grew worrisome as the High Elves kept coming and coming. The number of elves he assumed they had to contend with tonight had come and gone twice by now, and yet still more came. He watched the thieves in the grass moving ever backward as they struggled to keep up with the assassination of so many elves. There were too many bodies to hide at this pace, and the thieves were so optimistic about the outcome of the massacre that they never even discussed a plan of retreat.

Then, an elf cried out in alarm as he found the slain body of another elf in the tall grass.

"It's an ambush!" he cried out to the others. "We're under attack!" Just as he said it, an arrow struck him in the chest and knocked him to the ground. But it was too late. The alarm had already sounded. Immediately, the elven soldiers sprang into defensive battle positions, all running back and joining forces at the center of the field near one of the large wagons carrying supplies. Hard, steel shields were emptied from the wagon and formed in a seemingly impenetrable circle around the wagon, like a dome guarding all the remaining elves inside.

Then slowly, the joined group of elves began to make its way across the field, moving as one large, circular, defended unit. The elves' sharp eyes peered out from behind the shields, scanning the tall grasses for their attackers. An arrow came from somewhere in the grass, aiming for an opening, but it missed and bounced off. Just moments after the arrow hit, a group of elven archers stood up quickly from behind the shields and simultaneously released a hail of arrows in the thief's direction. A scream cried out from the darkness as they found their mark on the doomed thief. Aleric watched in horror at how precise the elf archers and their eyesight were. They were fortified behind a dome of shields and would pick off the thieves one by one as they tried to flee the killing field.

"There!" An elf shouted from the group. A group of archers appeared above the shields and fired upon their target, once again finding it before disappearing back behind the cover of shields. Aleric saw the thief try to turn and run as they drew their bows, but the thief barely made it a few steps before his back looked like that of a porcupine from the many arrows.

"What do we do?" one of the thieves asked, crouching in the tall grass near Jace. Unable to provide an answer and not willing to make a noise, Jace just shrugged. But it was enough to move a few blades of tall grass, which caught the attention of the elves' sharp eyes. The thief near Jace saw the group of elves simultaneously glance his way, and he panicked. He turned to flee, but again did not get more than a few steps before he came crashing face down in the grass next to Jace. The sweat beaded off Jace's hooded head. He knew he was done for. It wasn't a surprise to him that a life of thieving and risks would end up like this. He was almost calm about it, like it had been expected to happen sooner or later all along.

As Jace and the remaining thieves sat helpless in the field, awaiting their deaths, Aleric's eyes began to glow with rage and frustration as the scene unfolded. He wasn't about to let the High Elves of all people kill his friends, then come destroy his lands. His last thoughts before The paladin took over and he sprang from his hiding place was "I didn't want to let them have all the fun anyway."

He sprang up from his hiding place. His glowing eyes were the only thing visible against his black-painted armor he had been given by the thieves guild. His sword was already drawn, so when he began to move, taking enormous strides toward the elven battalion, he was almost completely silent. He was off the hill and bounding through the grass before the elven battalion even noticed him. In the confusion, their line began to break. Some archers were able to get a shot off, but The Paladin turned his head away from them and they bounced harmlessly from the reinforced armor with a loud clink as metal arrowhead hit metal armor.

The Paladin moved so fast that most of the High Elves didn't even have time to grasp what was happening before he crashed through their defenses and sent many of them flying to the ground. Thuds and clanks were the only thing the remaining thieves could hear as The Paladin's sword struck one High Elf after another, cutting through light armor and flesh. In a matter of moments, The Paladin alone had broken up the defensive dome and the elves were scattering back into the tall grass. The thieves saw this and took full advantage. Instantly they were up again and moving through the fields. Assassins in the night, they made quick work of the scattered elven battalion. The elves' sharp eyes were no match for the speed and agility the thieves had in the tall grass under the darkness of the night. Like snakes in the grass, Jace and the thieves moved from one victim to the next, disappearing under the tall grass only to reappear moments later in a new location to take a new victim.

Meanwhile, The Paladin was engaged in close combat as well. The elves could not keep up with his quick movements. By the time one would draw back a bowstring, he was on them, and most arrows went unfired. As the battalion was dwindling down to the last few elves, Aleric was engaged in a swordfight with one extremely strong and talented elf he was struggling to bring down. Jace, just a few yards away, had been overrun by a group of elves and one was on top of him, struggling to stab him through the chest. Jace held the elf's arm tight but was losing strength, and the dagger came closer and closer to his skin.

Then, another elf seemingly appeared out of nowhere standing on the rear of the wagon. He drew his bow; he had a perfect shot at Jace standing there above the tall grass. The Paladin saw the imminent danger to Jace, so he shoved his attacker then tucked and rolled away. Within an instant, The Paladin conjured up a fireball and sent it exploding from his hand. It sped through the sky, finding its target on the torso of the elven archer. The fireball exploded into a brilliant flash of fire and light that illuminated the killing field, and when it was gone, so was the archer.

Distracted by the magic-wielding Paladin, the elf attacking Jace let his guard down and was easily shoved aside by the thief, who then stabbed him through the neck. Jace jumped back up from the ground and went to The Paladin to help subdue the few remaining elves, including the battalion leader, who Aleric was thus far unable to subdue by himself.

"Your land is ours," the battalion leader laughed as he circled with The Paladin and the thief. "You'll never stop us all. Besides being outnumbered, humans are too stupid to stop us. It is an elf's world now." Aleric and Jace exchanged a glance. The infamous elven condescension was true after all. They rolled their eyes, then attacked simultaneously. Jace moved in first, forcing the elf to swing, but he hopped backward with agility, causing the sword to miss. This exposed the elf's backside to The Paladin, which he took full advantage of and stabbed the elf through. The elven battalion leader dropped to his knees, defeated. He examined the wound with a bloodied hand. “Jagged and rough metal,” he mumbled between labored breaths, feeling the wound. “You humans can’t even make a sword right. Is there anything you take pride in?” The elf leaned and fell to the ground while attempting to laugh. Again, Jace and The paladin exchanged glances and Jace rolled his eyes at the condescension once again.

“Finish this scum,” Jace said to The Paladin, who came forward and towered over the dying elf. Aleric raised his foot and slammed it hard against the elf’s head, crushing his skull. Suddenly the night was still. The only sounds were the wind pleasantly blowing through the tall grass, and the faint sound of gurgles as the last of the elven battalion lay dying in the field.

“No one takes our land,” The Paladin said aloud. “For Mazeron!” he yelled out, raising his sword to the sky.

The remaining thieves yelled back victoriously in reply, “For Mazeron!”

“Now,” The Paladin continued, “collect your spoils.” He indicated the coast was clear for the thieves to collect all the loot they could from the bodies.

The thieves instantly went to work, pillaging the large elven wagons and stripping the bodies of anything of value. The elves were plentiful with jewelry and goods, especially their military, which kept the utmost quality in almost everything. Their weapons were inlayed with rubies and gems, their armor and garments were only the best quality and woven with the most rare and exotic materials. Inside one of the wagons was a chest filled with gold coins. There was no doubt it was meant to be wages for the elven army, but now it was the property of the thieves guild.

Throughout the night, the thieves’ wagon was brought in and loaded to the brim. It wasn’t even near midnight and the wagon was already loaded and off, heading back to conceal the loot safely at the guild while the thieves stayed behind to ready for the next group of elves to come through the pass and into the vast killing fields on their way to Mazeron.

As the wagon slowly faded into the distance, Jace gave Aleric a look of appreciation and outstretched his hand. “Thank you, knight,” he said as they shook. “You will always be welcome among thieves.”

Aleric nodded in appreciation. "Let's clear these bodies before the next group comes through," he said, changing the subject.

Jace paused in confusion. "But there are so many elves," he said sounding worried. "We will never be able to kill them all. Not to mention women and children. I won't…We won't be part of that."

"Don't fret," Aleric replied calmly. "The elves know they are vulnerable and helpless without their soldiers to protect them. If we take out the battalions, the rest will leave on their own."

Jace thought quietly for a moment then nodded in agreement. "Okay, but let's move forward and into the woods for our next attack. It will take us all night to clear this field, and the thieves need rest."

Aleric agreed. Jace was right. The fields were too littered from the last battle to mount any sort of surprise attack again. "Assemble your assassins," he said.
"Let's move."

Within minutes, the group of thieves was on the move. Agile and fast, hooded shadows bounded through the forest in the night. Darting between trees, jumping over the brush and felled logs, they moved like the wind through the woods. But it wasn't long until Jace called out for their halt with his token high-pitched whistle. The thieves immediately stopped in their tracks and awaited directions from their leader.

"Something up ahead," he whispered as the group gathered near him. "Look…" He pointed through the thick woods, and the group of thieves peered into the dark forest. At first there was nothing—just the shadows of trees in the dim moonlight. Then, a faint and sudden flicker of light.

"I saw something," Lamora said in a whisper.

"Me too," Aleric added. "Quick, get to the high ground. This way." Aleric turned to his right and led the thieves away from the forest floor and up a hill, where they could be concealed but still able to see anything moving on the road below. As they climbed the hill, more lights came into view. Then more and more. Dots of light flickered through the forest. The group of thieves stopped at a large boulder and took cover no more than fifty feet above the forest floor. There was no time to go further as the lights seemed to be advancing fast and growing in number quickly. The thieves darted behind trees and an outcropping of boulders, concealing themselves and blending into the hillside. Then they waited…

"Do we attack?" Jace asked in a whisper to Aleric.

"Wait," The Paladin replied. "There are too many. We might have to wait for them to pass then pick them off from the back, one by one." Jace nodded, impressed with The Paladin's strategic quick thinking.

The thieves did not have to wait long before they were able to observe what was coming their way. Out of the darkness, the elves began to appear. Illuminated by large torches, they came into view from the deep forest. Most were on horseback, some were walking, but all carried torches. There were so many that they illuminated the forest as much as the approaching morning sun would. The line of torches seemed to stretch like a long snake into the forest, as far as any of them could see.

"There's so many of them," Lamora whispered as her stomach lurched at the sight

"They aren't all soldiers," Jace replied to his sister. "Look," he said, pointing. "Only the front portion is armed. Most carry only a torch."

As the massive convoy of elves approached, Aleric was the first to notice and recognize one of them. There was one in the lead of the convoy who rode on a tall, strong horse, slow and confident ahead of the others. He held a torch in one hand and a white bow with a golden string in the other. A long, golden-colored sword with an ivory handle swung from his hip. "Aghasty," Aleric whispered aloud. "Leader of the elves."

"We'll never be able to stop them," Lamora whispered back.

"We don't need to stop all of them," Aleric replied. "Just the front few. Cut the head off the snake, the rest will go running. Here is the plan…" Then, after a small huddle and formulating a whispered plan, the thieves crept through the forest and took their positions for the attack. Aleric told them they would know when it was time to strike.

Meanwhile, trotting through the forest with his people behind him, Aghasty was lost in thought. He was tired from the day's march but never showed it. He made it a point to never show weakness to his people. He held his head high and proud as he led them to their new lands.

Then, suddenly, a light appeared on the road before him. "Hold!" Aghasty said aloud to his convoy, raising his torch to better see what lay before them. He peered through the moonlit night, and there in the middle of the road stood a knight, clad in black armor. He had a tall shield, so tall that it rested on the ground and went up past the knight's stomach. It was The Paladin of Mazeron. In the palm of his hand, he held an orb of magical light that illuminated himself and the road and pierced through the darkness of the thick woods and tall trees surrounding them.

"We've no time for games, knight," Aghasty yelled aloud. "Move or we will shoot you down. Archers, step forward!" he yelled. Aghasty wasted no time asking questions or trying to figure out what the knight's purpose was. He was known to be ruthless, and he was already showing it. He didn't care what the knight wanted, all he knew was that he was in the way of his people's progress. Dozens of elven archers stepped forward from the wagons. As they raised their bows at The Paladin, he threw the fireball from his hand and launched it towards the elves. It exploded into a wagon near Aghasty and caused his horse to rear up, nearly throwing him off. Without hesitation, the archers let their arrows loose. A barrage of silent and nearly invisible arrows in the dark night sped toward The Paladin. He stood seemingly uncaring as the arrows rushed towards him, but then, just as they approached, he crouched down behind his large shield. He listened as dozens of arrows clanked off the shield and fell harmlessly to the ground.

"Now," whispered Jace from somewhere concealed in the forest. The thieves, who were scattered throughout the forest, began shooting arrow after arrow into the thick grouping of elves. The elves were completely unaware, focused solely on the knight blocking the road. Elves dropped like heavy bags of sand one by one, silently in the night. This went on far longer than the thieves or The Paladin had thought was possible, as The Paladin kept them distracted with his own attacks on the convoy. Eventually one of the elves, struck with an arrow through the chest, cried out in pain, and amongst all the noise and confusion, the elves realized that they were under attack from the surrounding forest.

"They're in the woods!" Aghasty yelled, rearing up from his horse. "Pay no mind to the knight, he is a distraction!"

"I'll show you a distraction," The Paladin mumbled to himself. He sprang from his concealment behind the shield and launched another fireball toward the elves. It struck near a large group, scattering them about, and sent four of them through the air and into the surrounding brush. Aghasty instantly sprang into action. Teeth clenched with anger, he reared his horse around and grabbed a long jousting pole from the nearby weapons wagon, then he aggressively charged at the Paladin at full speed atop his enormous horse.

The Paladin did not see what was coming until it was too late. He saw the elf leader charging him but assumed an attack from his bow or sword. It wasn't until Aghasty was right on him that The Paladin saw the long pole speeding toward him. Instinct took over and The Paladin swung the shield toward his attacker and tried to tuck behind it. The pole slammed hard into the shield, with the weight and speed of the horse behind it, and with enormous force sent The Paladin violently crashing to the ground. The pole shattered to pieces as it struck the shield, but the plan worked. The Paladin was knocked to the ground and the shield thrown somewhere into the forest.

With beautiful agility, Aghasty leapt from his speeding horse high into the air, landed softly on the ground, and within a few large strides came to a stop. Then he turned back quickly and came toward The Paladin who was still on the ground, shaken from the blow. The Paladin saw him approach, but it was all happening so fast he couldn't do much about it. The violent elf unsheathed his sword as he ran at him and raised it high above his head, ready to strike The Paladin again. As the sword came down, The Paladin rolled aside quickly, and the strike just missed him. The sword made a heavy clank and sparked as it hit the dirt road. The Paladin was defenseless. He could not carry both his longsword and the large shield, and the shield had been knocked away in the initial blow. He did not count on the elves being such aggressive fighters. He rolled away from the attacking elf leader once again, and kneeling, he conjured a quick fireball into his right hand. But before he could launch it, Aghasty swung his sword and knocked The Paladin's hand aside, along with the magic fireball with it. The ruthless elf advanced again. Then, an arrow clanked on the ground near The Paladin and bounced harmlessly to the side of the elf. "Too far away," The Paladin thought aloud. The thieves' bows were too small to reach him from this distance, so they could offer no help to the defenseless Paladin. If he could just hang on a little longer, he thought to himself, then they could get closer and rescue him from the attack.

The Paladin's thoughts were soon interrupted as Aghasty's golden colored sword came crashing down onto him once again. He raised an arm in defense and the sword struck the armor with alarming force. Again and again, the elf struck The Paladin, but the armor held. Finally, getting tired, Aghasty took a moment too long to take his next swing, and The Paladin took full advantage of it by swinging a left hook at the elf's ribs. This gave The Paladin the moment he needed to rise back from his knees and to his feet once again. He struck the elf one more time in the ribs before noticing something out of the corner of his eye. Aleric and Aghasty both instantly took a step back from each other and gazed into the forest near the group of elves.

A soft, greenish-blue light was illuminating through the forest, slowly growing brighter and brighter somewhere in the forest. It was like the sunlight was coming through the trees, casting large shadows of them through the rest of the dark forest. Everyone—the elves, the thieves, The Paladin, and Aghasty—stopped their fighting to gaze at the oncoming greenish light and wondered what it could be. Then, out of the forest stepped a giant being, almost as tall as a tree, then another, and another. Three giants emerged from the forest. They must have been at least three stories tall, and all three of them had a green glowing medallions hanging from around their necks and down to their chests. The three giants moved smoothly and silently, without noticeable feet below their long robes that adorned their bodies. They appeared to be floating as they moved slowly and methodically to the center of the forest for all to see.

Aleric recognized the giants immediately. He had seen them from the hillside on his journey to Haberlorn. As they floated through the forest, he found it hard to discern any facial features behind the bright light of their illuminating medallions. But he could tell the giants were looking around, studying the elves and the thieves who trespassed in their forest. Everyone stared in awe as the giants slowly and silently passed through the forests.

"It's the giants of Hazy Hollow!" someone yelled fearfully from the forest floor.

"The legends are true," another whispered in awe at the eerily silent and ominous giants.

While all the fighting in the forest had stopped, the giants continued on in silence, floating smoothly through the hordes of elves that were trespassing in their forest. Then suddenly, one of the giant's behavior seemed to change, and his movements went from slow and calm to sporadic and alarmed. Then, without any warning, the green medallion around his neck blasted a laser-like energy beam of light into the group of elves that exploded onto the ground and sent dozens of them flying through the air with a magnificent, bright, blueish-green explosion. The giant turned and exposed a long, lanky arm from beneath his cloak, and with one strong swoop he sent one of the elven carts into the air with so much force that it flew away like a child's toy.

The elves scattered immediately at the sudden and unprovoked attack. Then, the other two giants began attacking the elves just the same, blasting them with their magic medallions and throwing them and their wagons haplessly into the dark forest. The blasts from the medallions were so bright that the forest surrounding the giants became as bright as day, and the forest beyond looked like a black abyss against their ominous, violent brightness.

Through the beams of light, a barrage of elven arrows rained down on the giants, but they barely seemed to notice them. It was like the giants were on another plane and the arrows flew through them, leaving them unharmed.

"They don't want us in their forest," Aleric mumbled to Aghasty, watching one of the giants scoop up a group of elves into his enormous, lanky hands, and burn them to a crisp by holding them in front of his beaming medallion. In mere moments the giant cast their ashes aside and continued its attacks on the others.

"I'll deal with you another time, knight," Aghasty said, running back toward the giants to help his people. "Run! Scatter!" he commanded the elves with his booming voice as he ran. "Get into the concealment woods, now!"

As he ran, a beam of energy from the giants raced towards Aghasty, but without hesitation, he hopped spryly and light over one then ducked and rolled under another and was up again racing towards the giants without losing any speed as the forest exploded behind him from the blasts.

The thieves had already scattered and disappeared, leaving the brunt of the attack to be taken by the hordes of elves in the woods. Aleric was about to flee as well when Lamora and Jace came rushing to him.

"Should we pick them off as they flee?" Jace asked.

"No," Aleric replied. "The giants are too dangerous; we need to get far away from here as fast as we can. We'll have to think of a way to stop the elves at another time." Just as he said it, one of the giant's medallions, which was blasting a steady stream of light and energy that destroyed everything in its path, came right toward Aleric, Jace, and Lamora. The three instinctively jumped aside as the blast tore through the forest, exploding everything in its path and felling a large tree next to them.

"Let's get out of here," Lamora yelled in a panic. Quickly, the three began to flee down the forest road, leaving the attacking giants and elves to fight one another. The last thing Aleric saw as the road turned around a bend was Aghasty on his horse with a group of elves, defending his people from the giants while the rest of the elves scattered through the forests. There was no telling what the outcome of such a fight would be. For now, the fate of the elves and them reaching the lands of Mazeron was out of Aleric's hands.

Chapter 20: Tyranny

Larsolen Gall sat at the supper table with his family over two decades ago. His wife and two boys. The table was silent, and the air was thick with tension. His wife's spoon shook as she nervously attempted to eat her evening stew but most of it spilled from the spoon and onto the table.

"It's going to be fine," Larsolen said with frustration in his voice and a tinge of anger. "We haven't done anything wrong," he said squeezing his fist, clearly anxious as well.

But they had done something wrong. They had used magic beans to grow their crops during a long season of drought and word had gotten out about it. His wife had harmlessly and accidentally mentioned it to one of their neighbors. Then in turn she told her friend and notorious gossip, Abigail Frain. Once Abigail heard of the infraction it was all over and soon word spread to the wife of one of the castle's guards, then inevitably to the castle itself. The king's guards would most likely be coming for them soon.

"How did we get to here?" Larsolen mumbled aloud, wiping the sweat from his brow. He began thinking to himself about it. He thought of a time not long ago, before magic was banned. He thought of one extra peculiar wizard named Owlister.

Owlister the wonderous he called himself. But this wizard was not very wonderous at all. In fact, he was rude and mostly trouble. An old and disheveled curmudgeon who lived near the woods on the outskirts of town. He seemed to always be in a quarrel with someone or another despite living mostly in seclusion. His notable troubles varied anywhere from killing peoples livestock that wandered harmlessly onto his land, to getting drunk at the local alehouses and performing cruel magic on unsuspecting patrons. On top of that, he would constantly falsely accuse people of owing him money while also never paying his own debts. He would lie so often that he would tell people a dishonest version of something that they had witnessed themselves just days after it happened. If someone didn't agree with his made-up stories, false accusations, or numerous conspiracy theories, he would show up to their property and just not leave for weeks at a time. Basically, setting up a messy camp near them for the sole purpose of being rude and trying to make others angry. He would spend some time in the dungeons, but he never seemed to stay long. Usually because he annoyed the guards so much that they would let him go free to be someone else's problem, or by freeing himself with the use of magic. The biggest problem with the troublesome wizard is that he never showed any remorse for anything he ever did or displayed even the slightest hint of fear of going back to the dungeons. He was by all accounts an entitled, selfish, nuisance.

At one point, after a more serious infraction that he was acquitted of because of a technicality, the local villagers went to Maub who was the new leader of the king's guard and upholding the laws and they begged him to change the laws to make it easier to arrest Owlister and get him thrown in jail more easily and for good. They were sick of the wizard slipping through the cracks of their imperfect system and being allowed to be set free again and again. They were ready to do anything to get him locked up forever and rid the kingdom of his constant trouble.

So new laws were drawn up that cancelled out the old laws which gave people many of their rights. These came to be known as "The Owlister laws." A group of laws that waived the right to a public trial and gave ultimate power to the kingdom. This group of laws were so trivial that even words became criminalized with them. Anyone could be arrested for almost anything. Finally, the wizard could be locked up.

The townspeople at the time should have been wearier about how easily Maub agreed to the Owlister laws. But instead, they were blinded by their very short-sighted victory and finally being able to rid the lands of the abrasive wizard. Not long later, Owlister was inevitably accused of more infractions. Nothing serious, mostly just being a disturbance and a generally rude wizard. But with the laws changed he was quickly rounded up, not granted trial, and was never seen or heard from again.

"No trial," Larsolen mumbled to himself as he thought about his part in getting the Owlister laws passed and ridding the kingdom of the dreadful wizard. That seemed like such a short time ago, and now here he was about to meet the exact same fate. "I guess you could call it ironic or poetic justice," he said quietly to himself as a heavy knock came at the door.

When the Owlister laws were passed the villagers thought they would be the ones saying who the laws were used against, but inevitably and surprisingly fast they were used against the very people who asked for them. After that the term Owlister became synonymous for changing ones morals for a quick, short-sighted victory that would eventually come back to bite you in the long run, or someone who only thought about the present, and never the future. "Alright Owlister," people would say exaggeratively with an eyeroll when someone was about to do something incredibly stupid or short sighted.

Larsolen was one of many villagers who disappeared without trial over the years, since everything from talking poorly about the king to the use of magic had been banned through the abuse of the Owlister laws. Larsolen's last thoughts as he lay starving in a dark, wet, cold dungeon were the irony of how he supported the very thing that put him there.

Now it was the present day. It had been a week since Aleric and Lamora had fled the forest and The Giants of Hazy Hollow and their seemingly unprovoked attack on the migrating High Elves. Now they found themselves sitting quietly with Brodel and Thearbuc in Lamora's run-down home. Their thoughts were heavy, since they were unable to stop the advance of the High Elves into the kingdom, and their frustrations were high as the kingdom was still closed, and they were forced to be confined to the safety of their cottages most of the time because of the mysterious and violent beasts attacking the countryside.

"Here they come again," Thearbuc mentioned quietly as he peered through the window. Two guards slowly rode by on horseback, patrolling the streets and enforcing the afternoon curfew. The villagers were only allowed out for two hours every morning to trade food and supplies, then were expected to spend the rest of their days "safely" inside their cottages. "About every fifteen minutes," Thearbuc continued. "Easy enough to sneak out of town if we need to get out of here. If things get bad enough."

"I'm not abandoning my lands or our people," Aleric replied with a tinge of anger. Thearbuc just looked back blankly with a hint of sadness in his eyes. He could see everything they had worked for crumbling right before them and wondered if Mazeron would ever see peaceful, prosperous days again.

Soon there was a commotion outside, and the four friends looked out the window to see some villagers coming and going. Two of them were talking loudly, not even trying to be discreet about breaking the curfew. It wasn't long later when the two riders patrolling the area came galloping quickly down the small road. The two villagers ran and scattered as the guards approached. But a third villager came out of hiding and ran up behind one of the guards and smacked his horse hard on the rear end. The horse took off immediately and almost threw the guard off as he tried to control the animal.

"That is why Maub wanted to bring in the High Elves' soldiers," Thearbuc said, watching the unrest unfold. "To help police the kingdom. More soldiers. More ruthless ones too," he trailed off. "Do you think the elves will still make it here after those giants in the forest? No sign of them yet anyway, and the elves could have made it two days ago if they recovered from the attack. Maybe the giants destroyed them all," he hoped, just thinking out loud. The four friends sat silently thinking about the possibility of the High Elves invading their lands.

In the quiet midafternoon, a sound cut through the calm and echoed through the village: *Baawoooooo!* The melodic sound of a horn filled the air. The four friends' eyes darted back and forth from one to another with confused looks on their faces.

"That's the sound of an elven battle horn," Brodel pointed out, as a second sound resonated through the sky. "I know because I have one."

The others glanced at each other with perplexed looks. "The elves can't make anything that sounds that beautiful," Thearbuc argued.

"Not anymore," Brodel replied. "But back in their old civilization, they were masters at building and creating. Their horns now are just passed down from then." The four got up and went to the doors and windows to see what was going on. Other villagers were stepping outside their cottages, and more were walking down the streets cautiously toward the sound. Among the confusion, the two guards on horseback came trotting down the main road. They were yelling something as they went.

"Town meeting! Come all! Town square! King's orders! Town meeting!"

“Lets’ go,” Aleric motioned to the others, and they shuffled out into the street with the other villagers and made their way to the town square. Anticipation grew as they approached the town square. Had the beasts ravaging the countryside been killed and life could now return to normal? Had the elves made it to the kingdom after all?

But as they approached the town square, they could see a few men, standing tall, high above the villagers, on horseback. As the group of villagers came closer, it became more and more apparent through their thin stature and long and colorful hair.

“Bloody elves,” Thearbuc mumbled to himself, just as Aleric was thinking it.

“Aghasty,” Aleric whispered back.

“What?” Thearbuc replied.

“That is the head elf I was telling you about. His name is Aghasty,” Aleric explained. “We met in the castle and again in the forest. He is a strong fighter; I was unable to subdue him.”

“Obviously…” Thearbuc replied with a grin and friendly wink.

“I don’t want him to recognize me,” Aleric said worried. “Stand in front of me. I’ll lean here against the wall out of sight.” The two shuffled away to the side of an old wooden cottage and blended in with the other villagers. Then, Aghasty spoke from high atop his horse.

“People of Mazeron!” he said loudly, speaking down to the villagers from atop his horse. “There is a threat to your lives or our lives, roaming these lands.” Some of the villagers nodded their heads, understanding where the elf was going. Others glared at him with disgust as the High Elves’ bad reputation was well-known throughout all lands. His long hair blew lightly against the white bow on his back. He had changed his hair color again since Aleric had seen him last. It was red on one side and blue on the other, divided down the center. “These beasts…We do not know much about them besides they kill everything in their path. Ripping and shredding…” He paused. “It is our hope that you never have to see the carnage they leave behind.”

“What does that have to do with elves?” a villager yelled out angrily.

"Elves," Aghasty snapped back quickly with his condescending tone, "have some of the greatest hunters and trackers to exist. Your wise king has brought us here to help."

"So, you're going to kill the beasts?" another villager yelled excitedly.

"We will. In time," Aghasty replied calmly. "We are also here to make sure these villages stay safe. That no one gets themselves or others killed. That you don't lead the beasts here by carelessly wandering around and get every last one of you killed! We will be policing these lands for the time being, for your own safety."

"We don't listen to no elves!" a villager heckled, then spit on the ground in disgust.

Aghasty stayed calm high upon his horse. "Elves!" he called out, pointing to the villager. Suddenly, a group of elven soldiers appeared from an alleyway. They had weapons drawn and they immediately pushed through the crowd, shoving some villagers to the ground as they made their way through. They grabbed the villager who spoke out by the arms and began to haul him away. Some of the other villagers stepped up to stop the elves, but they were unarmed and the elves quickly had sharp swords pointed at the villagers' necks. The villagers slowly backed away as the man was taken, his screams of resistance fading into the background as they went. Then Aghasty spoke again.

"There will be no leaving your homes during curfew. No sneaking about. No leaving the village. No visiting your friends or family. And most importantly, no disobeying orders from the elves. We are here on behalf of your king. If you speak poorly of the king or the elves, you will be arrested." As he said it, dozens of high elves emerged from the streets and alleyways behind Aghasty. They outnumbered the villagers two-to-one, it seemed. The villagers all knew it immediately. Even if they were armed, there was no fight to be had here. They were at the complete mercy of the High Elves, a degenerate, pretentious, and condescending group that had taken over their village. "I am sure even your simple brains can comprehend this," Aghasty continued. "Go to your homes. Stay there. If we catch anyone getting out of line, they will be arrested and taken to the dungeons."

With that, he turned his horse and walked away, through the large group of armed elves that accompanied him. Their multicolored hair in bizarre styles blew slightly in the wind. They did look like a rough bunch for being so fair-skinned and thin, Thearbuc thought as he watched the events unfold. Unhinged, altered brains from years of mushrooms left them short-tempered and angry. He could see it in their eyes and their overall look.

In the wake of this unfavorable news, the villagers were talking amongst each other, and the town square was loud with frustration. Once again, Aghasty's loud voice broke through the air, "Anyone out on the streets in ten minutes is getting arrested!" he announced loudly but calmly. "Or worse…" The villagers knew what that meant. They could see the elven soldiers were seething for a fight. They even started barking like dogs to intimidate the civilized and peaceful villagers.

"Could they be any more degenerate?" Thearbuc asked quietly, still watching with Aleric from the corner of the cottage.

"An ounce of class might just kill them at this point," Aleric replied. "Let's get out of here. They want trouble now, while we are unprepared. We are not going to give it to them." Quickly, they made their way back into the crowd of villagers scattering this way and that to return to their homes. The sun was setting. There was a feeling of urgency and panic in the air, like something bad was coming that no one could see or do anything to stop.

Aleric, Brodel, Thearbuc, and Lamora hurried back to Lamora's home to hunker down for the night. They agreed to start making plans in the morning about what to do about their predicament, but for now, all they could do was comply with the High Elves' demands. They had been abandoned by their own king—alone, jobless, confined to their homes. The mood was dreary at best, and they concluded that the best idea for now was to try and get some rest.

But sleep evaded them. The night was plagued by the sound of pounding on doors, doors being broken down, and screams in the distance. Aleric lay on the floor of Lamora's cottage, only able to imagine what was going on in the kingdom he had sworn to protect.

"They're probably rounding up people who are critical of the king," Thearbuc whispered in the darkness from across the room. "That's my guess anyway. Getting rid of the competition before they can act out."

"Let's just hope they don't know I'm here," Aleric said glumly. "How is this happening? If I was only stronger," he trailed off.

"We can't take on an entire regiment of soldiers, just the four of us," Thearbuc reassured. "For now, all we can do is wait."

"Why is it that kings and governments are always trying to lock up as many people as they can?" Aleric wondered aloud. "It's the same story throughout every land and tale you have ever heard about. Someone gains too much power, turns tyrannical, and people suffer until it gets so bad they finally overthrow them. For a while it's good again, then inevitably the cycle repeats itself."

"It is in their nature for people with power to want to control others," Thearbuc chimed in from his chair in the corner of the room. "In fact, maybe it's just plain human nature in general, but those in power are the only ones who can actually act on it? Either way, it will never change because people never change."

"What about in say eight thousand years?" Lamora asked with a slight chuckle. "You would think they would be so smart and advanced by then that they wouldn't allow it to happen."

"They won't be," Thearbuc replied. "This cycle of tyranny and revolution will go on as long as humans exist. The best anyone will ever be able to do is stave off the tyranny part."

"That still doesn't explain why they always trying to lock up as many people as possible," Aleric replied, leaning back.

"These people are rule crazy, so they want to see who will jump through their hoops and follow their rules. Anyone who won't comply is their enemy and must be dealt with," Brodel chimed in.

"Well, with all these strict rules they will be able arrest pretty much everyone eventually. Anyone they want," Thearbuc laughed.

"Maybe that's the whole point?" Aleric replied. "Once someone is arrested, the authorities can get at their land and gold. It's just unfortunate that people aren't more compassionate and will not care about the injustice happening right next door until it is happening to them. I've seen how they act; people are vengeful and want people locked up over the tiniest infractions and even technicalities. I think the villagers like watching people get thrown into the dungeons just as much as the authorities like doing it."

The following weeks went by like a dream. Every day was the same: being allowed to gather food in the mornings, then being confined to their cottages the rest of the day and night. There was no word of the beasts ravaging the countryside, which was supposedly causing all of this mess. Only whispers of missing family members and friends—people who had gone missing without a trace.

Rumors flowed from one village to another, spread by those who dared to sneak out during the nights. It was rumored that the entire castle was surrounded by the High Elves' soldiers and the king's guards, and the king himself had not been seen for some time. Other rumors said the king had been spotted surveying his kingdom from his balcony as he always did, but he was always motionless, staring off into the distance and never moving.

One morning, Lamora awoke to find Aleric putting on his full armor in the living room.

"What are you doing?" she asked, bewildered.

"I am sick of waiting around here for someone else to do something about these beasts," Aleric replied, snapping a gauntlet in place with a clank. "I am going after it myself. To put an end to all this madness."

Lamora was taken aback. "You can't!" she gasped. "You'll be arrested on the spot as soon as you leave."

"I am already arrested, Lamora," Aleric replied in a frustrated tone. "Look at us! We've been locked inside here for weeks!"

"You still don't understand, do you?" Lamora snapped back. "There are no beasts out there anymore. And if you did find one and tell everyone you killed it, they would just conjure up another one to make sure this keeps going on like this."

"You're crazy," Aleric replied, mostly ignoring her.

"You don't understand," she pleaded. "You can't see Maub for what he really is like I can. He's a powerful and evil wizard; you have to trust me!" Aleric rolled his eyes and reached for his helmet. He mostly didn't care because there was nothing he could do about Maub at the moment anyway.

"Is it so hard to believe?" Thearbuc asked calmly, entering the room. "The castle is granted extra powers over us when there is a crisis in the kingdom through the Owlister laws. Would it not make sense for them to create crises to hold on to that extra power over us? Especially since they can't arrest people for magic anymore ever since you came along."

Aleric stopped and made eye contact with Thearbuc. "I suppose you are right," he sighed. "What do we do, then? We can't sit in here and rot forever."

Just then, they were interrupted by a hard, heavy knocking on the door. Aleric hurriedly stepped back into the rear of the home and hid while Lamora went to the door. She opened it to find no one there, but a notice had been hammered to the door...

<u>NOTICE FROM THE KING</u>

TAX INCREASE

PER ARTICLE 3, ALL CITIZENS WILL HENCEFORTH BE SUBJECT TO A TAX INCREASE OF 15%

TAXES WILL BE PAID TO THE HIGH ELVES FOR THEIR SERVICES DURING THIS TRYING TIME

Signed, your king,
King Victus

Lamora's mouth dropped as she read it, and the others could see the concern on her face.

"I can't believe it," she said, bewildered. "They are stealing our money and giving it to our enemies!" She shook angrily as she said it. "This is the most evil thing I've ever heard of."

"Let me see that," Thearbuc asked, taking the notice from her hands. He took a moment to read it and turned red as he did. "Just when you thought things couldn't get any worse for the kingdom." He shook his head and handed the notice to Brodel.

"They can't just take other people's money and give it away to their own friends," Brodel yelled out, losing his calm and collected composure for a change.

As Aleric stared at the notice his blood began to boil and the rage from a lifetime of unfairness and endless toil began to boil over. "The meek will go extinct," he mumbled under his breath with trembling lips and clenched teeth. Those words that were burned into an old wooden table under a large tree in the foothills of Briardale had never made more sense than now. That warning from Barreston all those years ago. Just then, there was the sound of a scuffle outside and Aleric turned to see a large raven snatching up a smaller, beautifully colored bird then fly it to the side of the cottage and begin to eat it. The small, beautiful bird had no chance against the large, disgusting raven. Aleric thought more about it. This happens constantly, and now there are hardly any pretty birds left in the villages anymore, while the disgusting ravens are everywhere and flourishing. What kind of world rewards cruelty and mindless aggression? This world does, he thought. "The meek will go extinct." he said aloud to the others.

"What was that?" Thearbuc asked.

"The meek will go extinct!" Aleric yelled out. "If we lay down in the face of tyranny we will not survive. But we are not meek. We are going to fight and survive!" he said angrily, standing up. "We leave the village tonight. We need to get to Commander Rune and the brigands in the village of Emoras-Graum."

"Emoras-Graum? What for?" Lamora asked.

"We need allies. We have more strength in numbers. Which is most likely why they have locked us all up like this. They can pick off who they want, one by one, until they have anyone who is disobedient and a threat to them locked up, and can steal all their lands for themselves, because there will be no one left to stop them," Aleric paused before picking up his sword. "You can stay or come with me. I am done waiting. It is time to fight."

Chapter 21: Emoras-Graum

That night, the four friends snuck out from Lamora's cottage like shadows through the alleyways, hiding from the patrolling elves until they made their way outside the village. Not long later, with the help of the thieves guild outpost, they were mounted on horses and riding hard into the night to the south of Briardale to the settlement of Emoras-Graum, where most of the brigands had made their homes in the lush farmlands surrounding the settlement.

It was a long ride there, too long to be made in one night, so as the sun came up, they veered off the main road and into the woods to hide out for the day. This was a very welcome change, being outdoors in the wild once again after being caged inside Lamora's home for longer than any of them even really knew. Their mood was already significantly better, and they went from constantly being agitated at one another to laughing and having friendly conversations once again. The birds chirped above, the sun was warm on their skin, but most importantly, the air was fresh and blowing lightly across their faces.

Once the sun dipped below the horizon, they were on the road again, galloping hard but staying vigilant as to not stumble across any elven patrols along the way. The night was still young when they exited the woods and gazed upon the magnificence of Emoras-Graum.

The fortified village was nestled comfortably at the base of the enormous mountains where dozens of towering waterfalls flowed from the cliffs high above. Pine trees and a cozy blue, darkening sky adorned the skyline as they approached.

Emoras-Graum. It's odd name could be attributed to the fact that long ago it was once a proud fortification built and inhabited by a race of trolls that had been settled in the area for longer than anyone could know. At some point in history, thousands of years ago, they disappeared or abandoned the village for one reason or another, but their odd and somewhat terrifying architecture and the name of the village still remained. The beautiful crashing waterfalls not only brought water to the settlement but occasionally flooded the nearby flatlands which brought nutrients to the soil. Naturally the area became lush farmlands, which had recently been settled by the brigands.

As the group approached the village from the lesser-known side trails, they noticed the crops withering in the fields that they passed by.

"Don't tell me they aren't even letting people farm their own fields," Brodel said aloud in disgust.

"Let me guess. It's too dangerous to be outside, and the mysterious beasts will get them," Lamora said exaggeratively with a slight giggle.

"You laugh, but you know that is exactly what is going on," Thearbuc said bluntly.

"Shhh, you two," Aleric interrupted, motioning his hand for them to slow down. "Look. There are no lights on in most of these cottages."

"That is odd," Lamora agreed.

"Do you hear that?" Aleric asked.

Brodel nodded. "Voices in the distance," he answered. "Lots of them. Like a meeting or something."

"Quick!" Aleric said, pointing ahead and slightly picking up the pace.

As they came to the village, they got their first look at the fabled troll architecture. Craggy and bent, dark and black were the structures. Most with some sort of crooked, pointed roof.

"They must not have been very good builders." Thearbuc mentioned as they rode past the odd structures."

"Then why are they still standing after thousands of years?" Aleric replied with a laugh.

Then they heard the sound of commotion again and it seemed to be coming from the tallest building in the center of town. It's craggy bent roof towered high above the others and a small lantern was lit towards the top of it, showing the way in the fading sun.

"That must be the center of town," Lamora mentioned, as they rode on.

When they got there, they found the town square completely lit up, which was opposite almost every other dwelling they had passed along the way. The entire village must have been gathered here at the center of town. There were dozens of horses tied up around the square and a loud commotion was coming from inside the angry-looking town meeting hall. The four friends tied up their horses a block away and crept toward the town hall, being careful not to be seen until they figured out what was going on. After that point, the plan was to blend in until they found Commander Rune.

Slowly, they crept up to the town hall. The door was slightly ajar, so Aleric peered inside. The hall was filled with so many men and women they were standing almost to the back door. Aleric motioned to follow him, and one by one they crept inside and stood at the back of the room with the rest of the villagers, who were yelling about something.

Once inside, they got a good look around. The room was filled with the once brigands and some other villagers and families. At the front of the room stood dozens of High Elves, all soldiers armed with bows and swords. Once again, Aghasty stood before the crowd. He spoke assertively over the commotion of the angry crowd.

"You all agreed to Article 3 when you agreed to build your lives in the kingdom," he shouted calmly over the angry crowd. "The castle has the right to tax you, and you don't have the right to decide where it goes. I can dig out each and every one of your signatures if you want me to."

The crowd grew quiet, and the villagers all mumbled to one another in frustration as they knew Aghasty was right. Not morally right, but technically right, according to the law.

"We want to keep our money and get rid of you!" a villager yelled. "Go home, we can govern ourselves." The crowd grew loud in cheers of agreement.

"We were fine before you got here! We don't need you!" an old farmer yelled out.

One of Aghasty's soldiers stepped forward. "Why is it that you are fine with these immigrants coming into your lands," he motioned towards the once brigands. "But not ok with our immigrants coming here?" he motioned towards the elves.

"Because these men came here to build and create!" The farmer snapped back without hesitation. "You only come to take and destroy. Once our lands are of no use to you anymore, you will go your way and leave our lives destroyed. You don't care about this land; you only wish to exploit it."

"Quiet!" Aghasty stepped in and commanded. He controlled the room, no doubt, with his confidence, poise, and not to mention the small army behind him. "Now, I have a solution. But you have to agree to it, whatever the outcome is, if you will hear me out."

The villages looked at one another. "What is it?" one man yelled out impatiently.

"We have here an advanced civilization, no? Are we not a democracy on most matters?"

"Aye!" the crowd cheered in agreement. The citizens of Mazeron had always been proud of their (almost) democracy, which was rarely, if ever, heard about in these lands and in the times of old.

"Then let's put it to a vote," Aghasty said. "All in favor of the High Elves leaving these lands, raise your hands." All of the villagers raised their hands; it was completely unanimous. Aghasty took a moment to count the hands. "Now," he continued, "who is in favor of the High Elves staying in these lands?" Immediately the dozens of High Elves in the room raised their hands in unison behind Aghasty.

"Hey, they don't count!" a villager yelled out. "They don't live here. They aren't citizens of Mazeron."

"Of course they do," Aghasty replied in his usual condescending tone.

"They don't even live here. They don't care about these lands," another villager yelled out.

"But they are here now, are they not?" Aghasty motioned behind him towards his large battalion. "Democracy at work," he said with a smirk. "You have the smaller group, so you don't get to decide. Sorry," he shrugged.

"But we are the smaller group by only a few people." one of the ex-Brigands yelled out. "How is it fair that all of you get to decide what happens to all of us just because you have a few more people?"

"I don't make the rules," Aghasty said sternly. "That is democracy for you. Now!" he raised his voice, seemingly taking to anger in an instant. "Taxes will be collected in three days from now. You pay them or you spend time in the castle's dungeon equal to the amount owed."

"How can we make money while we are locked in our homes?" an angry farmer yelled out. "Our crops are dying because you don't allow us to tend to them."

"Not my problem," Aghasty snapped back. "My problem is keeping you from getting your guts ripped out by the beasts roaming the countryside. You should be thanking me." Again and as always, the castle was using people's safety as an excuse to bring tyranny upon them.

The commotion erupted again as the crowd grew angrier at the injustice happening to them. Aghasty stepped down from the platform he was on and walked slowly over to the farmer who had last spoken. The room grew quiet again as the elf towered over the man, who barely went up to the elves' chest. Aghasty looked down upon him, standing so close that his red and blue hair touched the farmer's face.

"Thank me," Aghasty smirked. The farmer looked up at him with fear in his eyes, and his body shook slightly with nervousness. But the farmer said nothing.

"Say it," Aghasty said quietly. But the farmer still stood silent. "Thank me now!" he screamed angrily. "Thank me or take your last breath right now!" Then quickly and angrily, Aghasty drew a shiny silver dagger with a bright-white hilt from his belt, grabbed the farmer's hair, and pulled his head back, exposing his neck. He thrust the knife up and held the blade up to the farmer's neck. "Thank me for keeping you safe, farmer. Thank me now or die."

"Th…th-thank you," the man finally mustered, pushing out the words with force.

"Enough of this, you elven swine," an ex-brigand said from nearby, abruptly charging at Aghasty with fists swinging. The anger of the room finally boiled over and exploded. Everyone charged the elves to fight and the elves, without hesitating, charged back.

Suddenly, the room erupted in a fight. Aleric and company stayed toward the back of the room. They were unarmed, and fighting was not their mission tonight. As they observed the commotion, one thing quickly became apparent: the brigands were unarmed. They must not have been allowed to bring weapons into the hall. The villagers didn't stand a chance. The sound of screams pierced the room as men were run through with swords and blood splattered against the walls. The fight did not last long, as the brigands and farmers quickly realized they were outmatched without any weapons and crept back toward the rear of the hall, crowding Aleric and the others.

Aghasty walked toward the retreating group of men, not missing a step and looking unshaken from the fight. His small army, too, approached, quickly behind him with all weapons drawn.

"Him." Aghasty pointed at Commander Rune, who had been observing the meeting and unrest from the side wall. "He is their leader. Arrest him." The room erupted again with commotion and distaste. "Your commander is hereby arrested for disturbing the peace," Aghasty continued loudly over the angry crowd. They attempted to push forward and fight back, but Commander Rune was already surrounded by the elven army and his hands were bound before he could even process what was going on. "Get back to your homes, now!" Aghasty called out, drawing his longsword, and retreating backward to create space between the angry villagers and his soldiers holding Commander Rune. As the elves backed up, the Brigands stepped forward.

"Stand down!" Aleric finally shouted from the back of the room. Everyone in the hall turned to see where the powerful voice had come from. "Can't you see they *want* you to fight right now? They are antagonizing you because they know they'll win. You have no weapons! Use your heads!" His voice boomed through the room, causing everyone else to stay quiet. "There isn't a fight to be had," he said, raising his arms in surrender.

"At least one of you has some sense," Aghasty said, not recognizing Aleric as he had never seen him without his armor on. "Elves!" He motioned, and in a moment a large group of elves were gone, taking Commander Rune with them.

A portion of the large elven army stayed behind to guard the hall, and Aleric helped usher the brigands, villagers, and farmers back out the door away from them. As they exited, Aleric mumbled under his breath to each one, "Meet at the old grain storage, west of town. Tomorrow, when the sun is just above the mountains. Bring your weapons."

He said it over and over to every person leaving. Thearbuc, Brodel, and Lamora heard it as well and began doing the same thing. They relayed the message to every villager who exited the hall, making sure everyone heard. "Bring your weapons. Bring your weapons," they emphasized. Soon the hall was empty, and only the four friends remained standing outside.

"Let's get out of here," Aleric said hurriedly.

"Where?" Lamora asked. Some of the eleven soldiers from the town hall were approaching them at brisk pace and with angry glares.

"Anywhere but here," Thearbuc chimed in. "We can find an empty cottage for the night. It looked like there were plenty to choose from."

As they turned the corner to run away, Commander Rune's brother, Visko, came out of the darkness of the night and startled Aleric. "Come with me," he whispered. "Hurry!" Quietly, they followed Visko and made their way away from the town hall just as the elven soldiers approached the front doors.

"Why are you telling everyone to meet outside of the village?" Visko asked nervously, once they were safely away from the town hall. "We need more time if we are to mount an offensive against the elves."

"We don't have time," Aleric replied quickly. "Half of the elves stationed here will be gone tomorrow, marching your brother to the castle dungeons. If we attack tomorrow, then we only have half as many to deal with."

Visko stood silently in the darkness as he thought about the plan, then nodded his head in agreement. "We'll need weapons," he whispered.

"Aye," Thearbuc replied.

"Follow me," Visko whispered. He led them to an old, craggy, rundown, cottage on the outskirts of town. It was dark and looked empty inside and from the looks of the yard, no one had been here for quite some time.

They entered the cottage through a side window, one by one, until all five were inside. Visko lit some candles to illuminate the room. It was clear it had been vacant for some time. The smell of stale air and dust filled the room. It was cluttered with seemingly worthless knickknacks and nothing of importance, like whoever had fled the home had taken everything that was worth anything with them long ago.

Visko started moving again through the cottage, holding a large candle to illuminate the way. They followed him into a room at the back of the cottage, where he bent down and tossed a dusty rug spread across the floor hiding a trap door. With a loud creak of old hinges, it opened, and they followed Visko down a set of rickety stairs into the darkness. Visko lit a torch that hung along the wall and illuminated the large room. The whole area beneath the house had been dug out and was filled wall to wall with weapons and armor. Aleric and Thearbuc gasped at the sight of it. The brigands were not supposed to have weapons, per their agreement with the king.

"We know we weren't supposed to bring our weapons with us," Visko said sheepishly, avoiding eye contact with Aleric. "But you must understand, a group of people letting themselves be disarmed is just about the most reckless thing a group can do." He turned away from Aleric's glare as he said it. "We smuggled them in, little by little, these last few months. But now aren't you glad now that we did?" Visko said with a smile, trying to ease the tension.

"I suppose you are right," Aleric grinned back, his face slowly softening. "It will give the villagers a fighting chance. We will need to start meeting them early in the morning and arming everyone."

"How far do you intend to take this?" Brodel asked.

"All the way," both Aleric and Visko replied simultaneously.

"This tyranny has gone on long enough," said Aleric.

"They have my brother," Visko added.

"They are stealing my money and giving it to the bloody elves," Lamora added in disgust, then spit on the ground, as was becoming tradition when speaking of the High Elves.

"We'll never take the castle with some farmers and old swords," Thearbuc replied. "Your cause is lost before it has begun."

"But we have him!" Lamora interjected, excitedly pointing to Aleric. "His powers can breach the castle's gate. And Brodel has just as much power."

"If they can get close enough maybe," Thearbuc replied with doubt, folding his arms.

"I've got one more thing to show you," Visko interrupted. "Follow me." Quickly, they followed him back up the stairs and out the window again, into the woods just beyond the cottage. There in the pale moonlight they saw a large hedge tower in front of them, blocking the way further into the woods.

"Look!" Visko said as he started pulling large tree branches and shrubs away from the wall. A large chunk of the foliage fell away and exposed multiple large catapults and piles of what looked like steel metal balls and heavy rounded rocks. "We confiscated these from a passing army years ago," he said excitedly. "They'll launch these explosive balls three field lengths way. They'll blow through your castle walls. Believe me, they'll breach it and more." He stopped, then hesitated for a moment. "You are willing to attack your own castle? The one you were sworn to protect?" he asked, turning toward Aleric.

"I swore to protect the lands and my countrymen," Aleric snapped back. "Not a corrupt government who has taken over the castle and sold out their own people."

Visko nodded firmly, impressed by the sternness of Aleric's reply. "Okay then," he said. "Let's rest up. In the morning, we rid Emoras-Graum of elves."

The following morning came quickly, and soon the sun was peaking up from behind the towering mountains. As far as the elves occupying Emoras-Graum knew, the day was normal and had been quiet. But in the shadows and outskirts of town, the villagers had been busy. Busy arming themselves and drawing up plans for their attack.

Midday arrived as the elven patrols trotted slowly along the dirt roads of the village, making sure everyone stayed inside and no one caused any trouble. The only life that seemed to be around were the birds. It was eerily quiet except for the sounds of their chirping. Then eventually, a large group of Brigands and farmers appeared, marching toward the center of town. They emerged from a nearby hill and made their way, so far, unnoticed through the village. A village that may have seemed unimportant and insignificant to the occupying elves, but was everything to its inhabitants.

The villagers came armed. Heavily armed. They descended upon Emoras-Graum with large spears, tall shields, swords, and bows. The brigands were dressed in primitive leather armor. Padded leather breastplates hung from their necks and draped down, protecting their torsos from slashes, debris, and slower arrows. Leather gauntlets and shin protectors were tied to their arms and legs. They came ready for battle, and battle was their expertise. Although they had succumbed to the domesticated life as of late, they still longed for the blade. And finally, they could use it…

Not long later, a large group of Brigands had gathered near the town square. Without making a lot of noise, they were able to march through the village unnoticed for a lot longer than expected before any elven patrols finally happened upon them.

"What's this?" a horse-mounted elven soldier yelled at the large group of assembling men. "Did a horse leave a pile of dung in the road that has drawn you all to it?" he said with a condescending snicker.

Without wasting any time, the second elven guard drew a small flute-like instrument that hung from his neck and blew into it. No doubt it was to sound the alarm and bring the rest of the nearby elves to help. It made a beautiful, high-pitched sound. So high that most of the brigands could *feel* it inside their ears more than hear it. The elf was quickly moving his fingers up and down the flute, making pretty, fluttering sounds, when suddenly the breath was stolen from his lungs by a Brigand spear that hit him hard and rammed through his chest. The eleven soldier was thrown from his horse and landed heavily on the ground, never to move again.

The other elven soldier immediately turned to flee on his horse as the brigands roared into battle behind him. The brigands gave chase on foot, pursuing the elf toward the far end of the town square. Then, just as they neared the town hall, a whole group of elven soldiers appeared from the alleyways and blocked the way from their attack. The brigands stopped quickly and turned to retreat away from the new group of elves, but another group of elven soldiers arrived and blocked the roads to their right and left. They were surrounded in the town square on all sides by tall, horse-mounted, armed elven patrols. The brigands shrunk back and grouped together into a battle formation and waited.

"You are surrounded, and we have the high ground," the elven battalion leader said, calmly approaching from atop his horse with sword drawn. The other elven soldiers had already drawn their bows, and dozens of sharp arrows were pointed directly at the group of Brigands. "And if you choose to march on the castle, you will find it is guarded by the most advanced weaponry known in these lands, and beyond. You have no chance!" the elf yelled out, raising his arms. "We will give you one opportunity to surrender. Go back to your cottages or we will be forced to use… force," he trailed off, letting the brigands marinate in the threatening words he was saying. "Look at your old little weapons compared to ours. You don't stand a chance," The elf finished. The brigands stayed quiet, contemplating their situation. They were leaderless without Commander Rune and surrounded. The seconds of nervous tension ticked by. Their hearts pounded hard in their chests, and they gripped their weapons nervously awaiting what would happen next.

Then, Aleric stepped forward from the group. "You may have the best weapons," he said to the elves with his booming voice. "You may have the fortifications. We may be just a poor group of villagers. But none of that really matters, you see. *We*!" he emphasized, "have the most important thing of all."

"And what would that be?" the elf soldier said condescendingly, acting like he was barely listening or caring enough about the situation to pay attention.

"We have the numbers," The Paladin said ominously, as his eyes began to glow bright like embers. "Now!" he yelled out quickly, drawing his sword.

Immediately, the brigands charged the mounted elves and suddenly, dozens more Brigands came charging in from the side roads and alleyways, sneaking up from behind the elven soldiers and surprising them with a flank attack. The elves let loose their arrows as the brigands descend upon them and every single one of them found a mark. Dozens of Brigands fell wounded to the ground, but still it barely mattered. Dozens upon dozens more appeared from the shadows, charging towards the elves. Spears flew overhead and were buried into the elves' chests or struck their horses, bucking them off to be consumed by the attacking mob.

The initial surprise attack was a success and many elves fell, but the battle was far from over. The surviving elves retreated where they could, regrouped and joined with other battalions, then charged again. They rode hard and fast through the scattered Brigands, stabbing and slicing as they pushed back. Their arrows were the deadliest weapon they had as they could fire one arrow almost every two seconds, and every one was accurate.

Led by The Paladin, the battle raged on through the once-quiet streets of Emoras-Graum nearly the entire day. Both sides were exhausted and wounded, but neither backed down. The brigands had the advantage as they knew every nook, alleyway, raised position, and corner of their village, so they could regroup and surprise the elven soldiers from new positions. But the elves had superior weapons and genetics.

At one point, after single-handedly cutting down a group of elves that had ambushed him, The Paladin found himself at one end of the courtyard with a large group of Brigands behind him and the remaining attacking elves at the other end in front of him. Without hesitation, he raised his sword again and commanded the charge. The brigands followed him into the clash, just as they had throughout the day. The once poor, simple, castle guard was now in charge an entire army and leading them into battle. It was a surreal moment for The Paladin, but it didn't last long as they crashed together with an enormous thunder of clashing weapons. The Paladin cut through the line with glowing eyes and inhuman ferocity and speed. The Brigands followed and protected attacks from behind him and cut down the fierce elves as they went.

The fighting was intense, but in the end of the scrum, the brigands still had their numbers while most of the elves lay strewn about the village, defeated. The Paladin took it upon himself to make sure he was the last thing that the condescending elven battalion leader ever saw, and when he turned back from the killing him, he saw the army of Brigands all cheering him. "Paladin, Paladin!" they yelled out, banging their spears and swords together. A group of them came to Aleric and surrounded him, patting his back and congratulating him on the magnificent display of force he had shown throughout the day.

"We couldn't have done it without you," some said. "He killed five elves to our one," said another. Thearbuc and Lamora watched the celebration from a distance with large grins, happy for their friend, the brave Paladin.

"You don't think he'll let this go to his head, do you?" Thearbuc said with a chuckle as drops of splattered elven blood dripped from his body.

"How could it not?" Lamora laughed as Aleric was praised over and over.

"The village is ours!" Aleric yelled out to his army. "But they will be coming back to reclaim the village," he said, changing his tone. "We will have to defend it if we want to keep it. There is not time to celebrate just yet. We must clear the bodies from the streets. Then, we must fortify the village for their inevitable attempt to take it back."

Soon the celebrations were over and after some conversation and confirming that everyone agreed, the group of Brigands broke up, and with Visko shouting orders to the different groups, they immediately got to work in fortifying Emoras-Graum. Luckily the village had once been a fortress so the sides were lined with tall walls, and the front gates could easily be rebuilt.

At one point Aleric approached Visko. "We need to send word to the rest of the citizens in the neighboring farmlands and mining villages to tell them what is happening here and to join us. Send messengers for them to come here if they want to fight to retake the kingdom from these tyrants."

"Aye," Visko agreed, then turned to give the orders. Soon messengers were sent out in every direction while the other Brigands cleaned up the village and started making fortifications to defend their liberated village.

The following days were pleasant but busy in Emoras-Graum. Everyone had a job to do. Crude walls with pointed ends were being rebuilt around the village where they had fallen over the years. Large trees were moved onto the roads that led into town to slow any advancement of large weapons that may be coming their way. But the best part was, throughout the days, different groups of Brigands began trickling into the village, ready to join and fight. Their numbers were growing. Then, within a matter of days and after an enormous amount of hard work, the town was secured and manned with an impressive army.

Then, the brigand army waited with anticipation for the castle's army to come marching up over the horizon, but after a few days, they never did.

After that the days seemed to drag on and on, and the waiting was agonizing. The village was lifeless, day-in and day-out with everyone standing at the ready, just waiting impatiently for battle to come.

One particularly slow afternoon, Aleric stood staring toward the horizon when Visko approached him.

"It must have been two weeks by now, sir," Visko said drearily. "I don't think they are coming."

"You may be right," Aleric replied. "Any word from the scouts?"

"None have returned," Visko replied with a sigh.

"Something is amiss. Twenty scouts sent out and none of them have returned? It's only a one- or two-day ride to the castle."

"They must have been captured. The king's army could be watching the roads and forests. The way must be blocked."

Aleric stayed silent for a moment, deep in contemplation. He growled a low grumble under his breath. "Well," he finally spoke. "If they won't bring the fight to us. We will take the fight to them."

Visko nodded that he agreed. "It makes sense, I suppose. Just letting us rot here. It doesn't hurt them any to have us sitting around. I agree, let's take it to them."

"Gather the men," Aleric replied. "Tomorrow, we march on the castle."

Chapter 22: The Battle of Mazeron

After painstaking preparations, the morning finally arrived, and the brigands were ready to take the fight to Aghasty and the elven army defending the castle. Aleric stood atop the ramparts that had been assembled at the gates of the village and surveyed the army they had created. His army. Hundreds of Brigands lay before him, armed and ready for battle. The giant catapults had been constructed as well and stood towering among the men. Dozens of carts filled with supplies, food, and weapons were ready for a long siege. Aleric turned to his army.

"Today is the day!" he bellowed. "If the cowardly elves won't come to us, then we will take it to them!" The men erupted in applause as he said it and raised their spears to the sky. "Note this!" he continued. "Tyranny will never have a home in these lands again." The army roared once again. "For freedom!!" Aleric yelled.

"Freedom!!!" the army replied, so loudly that it echoed through the lands and rolled across the fields. They started beating their spears against their shields, making an enormous racket as they slowly began to march forward. The heavy catapults creaked into motion and the horses pulled the carts filled with supplies. Many of the brigands had started families since arriving in Mazeron, and they bade their loved ones farewell before setting off and marching towards the castle.

They moved slowly because of the heavy equipment and carts, but by afternoon, the army had cleared the villages and the farmlands, and they were well on their way to the castle. As the army marched through the farmlands, they spotted elven scouts along the way—small dots on the hillside in the distance, observing the army as they marched ever forward toward the castle.

"They know we're coming," Visko said to Aleric, staring at one of the scouts in the distance.

"Our mission is the castle," Aleric replied. "There was never an element of surprise with this battle. Let them know we are coming. There is no hiding this army." As he said it, they trotted by an abandoned checkpoint on the road. Wooden barriers had been left in a hurry, and they simply pushed them aside as they went through.

"Seems like all roads leading to the castle were being patrolled," Visko said, thinking aloud. "They really did have this place locked down pretty good."

"Not anymore," Aleric said ominously with a slight laugh.

They continued on, unimpeded for the entirety of the day and the entire army of angry citizens and once brigands slothed along with heavy catapults and equipment being pulled by teams of horses. Along the way, the road took a turn up a small hill. As Aleric summited, he stopped to observe his surroundings. Before him lay the long and vast road ahead. Around him was tall grass blowing peacefully in the afternoon breeze, and behind him marched a vast army that was at his control.

His thoughts raced back to not long ago, when he was a poor servant to the castle with no meaning in life. Hardly anyone even knew he existed, and he had no hope for a future. Now here was, not even a year later, commanding an army and marching toward a better life for all of them. Instantly, he was overrun with a feeling of joy and accomplishment. The feeling of purpose. It started in his fingertips and rushed through his veins and up his shoulders, giving him goosebumps and a quick shiver. It feels good to have purpose, he thought. "This is my purpose," he whispered as he gazed across his army. People search their entire lives for their purpose and most never find it. At that moment, Aleric, The Paladin of the people, had found his. *I may not be where I want to be, but I am where I am meant to be*, he thought to himself.

He turned from the vast army stretching out along the road before him and gazed once again toward the castle. He could see it in the distance, beyond the vast rolling hills. The golden roofs were concealed partly by the haze from the distance between them. *What awaits us there?* he thought to himself. A feeling of doubt began to creep into his mind, and it immediately washed away all feelings of comfort and confidence. What if he was unfit to lead these people into this battle? What if the elven army and the wizard Maub were too powerful to defeat? He thought again of the vast army behind him, his friends next to him. *I am not alone in this*, he continued in his thoughts. Suddenly, the fear and negativity washed away from him again. That reassurance was all he needed. "We move!" he commanded loudly as he spurred his horse and continued onward, the others following beside him.

The day slogged on as the army marched forward. Eventually the sun had reached its peak in the sky and was making its daily descent back toward the horizon. "We should camp here for the night," Aleric eventually announced. "We don't want to make camp too close to the castle and risk getting ambushed in the night."

It was agreed upon, and the large army halted their march and made camp for the night. As the sun went down, they noticed that there was a bright glow coming from the direction of the castle. It lit up the horizon like the rising sun. The army stared into the distance with worry, wondering what force could make such a bright light.

"Could be the wizard and his evil sorcery," Thearbuc mentioned aloud. "Making a glow that bright."

"Maybe they have set fire to the surrounding forests to keep from being ambushed in the night," Lamora added.

"Stop speculating," Aleric interrupted. "It will only bring worry and doubt. We will find out tomorrow when we approach the castle." The others nodded. He was right. No sense in worrying at this point. "Visko, set the watches for the night," Aleric began giving orders. "No large fires, only small ones for cooking, and once the men have eaten, they are to be doused. I want everyone fresh and strong on the morrow."

Visko nodded, then turned and repeated the orders to the generals. Aleric was always impressed and still somewhat surprised at the professionalism and discipline the once-renegade group of bandits was capable of, and he was quite interested to see what they were capable of on the battlefield.

Later, as the sun faded away and the night grew darker, the tension grew with it. The men's mood's became somber, and the camp was depressingly quiet. Everyone ate in silence and pondered what the next day would bring them. How fortified was the castle? Would they survive to this time tomorrow? So many unanswered questions daunted their minds and the impatience of wanting to know grew uncomfortably within them. Still, they were hopeful, and they found solace in the fact that their cause was just and soon, god willing, they wouldn't have to live under the strong arm of the castle and would be free men once again.

"I guess if you want a peaceful life you have to fight for it." One man said half-jokingly to a small group sitting around a dwindling fire.

"When we came here you never told us the place was corrupt," Visko stated his thoughts with a quick scowl at Aleric.

"When you came here it wasn't." Aleric replied.

"Using us as your own personal little army to overthrow the castle," another brigand said snidely. "How convenient," he said rolling his eyes.

"I didn't plan any of this," Aleric snapped defensively. "When it's over, you'll all go back to your farms and your jobs. Peace and freedom will be restored. Then I'll be waiting for your apologies."

"Cheers to that. 'Visko said, raising his stein and purposely changing the mood away from attacking Aleric.

"Cheers!" The others joined. And clanked their steins together. Aleric did not raise his cup and stayed quiet for some time as the others grew louder around the growing fire.

"You're thinking about her again, aren't you?" Lamora eventually asked Aleric after noticing his solemness. He quietly nodded his head yes. "I think you should try to find comfort in the fact that you and Briss' love happened, and it was wonderful. How empty would your heart and life be without those memories?" she stated more than asked.

"Ha!" Aleric snarked. "Losing true love is like losing an arm. You know how horrible life is without it. But if you never had it in the first place you wouldn't even know any difference. It might be better at the time you have it, but it is most definitely worse after it is gone."

Lamora realized then that she didn't have answers or solutions. No one did. It was just the way things were. "I hope you find peace," she said eventually, resting a comforting hand on Aleric's shoulder.

The rest of the night passed calmly with no issues, and to most of their surprise, there was no ambush from the High Elves or the castle guards. Aleric and the brigands awoke to a peaceful mountainous scene with birds chirping and a light cool breeze upon their faces. It was like the world didn't even care or know what plight they were facing and the hardship that awaited them this day. Little creatures everywhere went about their daily business while the unfortunate large group of men prepared to march into chaos and battle, not knowing if they would survive the day or what fate awaited them.

Finally, after days of marching, they got their first up close glimpse of the castle. Aleric, Thearbuc, Brodel, and Lamora saw it first as the road exited the thick trees near the castle's lands. Lamora's jaw dropped as she observed the scene before her.

Outstretched before them was a vast green and brown field of rolling hills leading up to the enormous castle. The green grass blew lazily in the wind, and the castle towered in the distance, its gold cones reflecting brightly in the sunlight. The ramparts and the ramp leading to the castle gates were lined shoulder to shoulder with the High Elves' army. Another large group of at least two hundred elves stood at the base of the ramp, outside the castle walls as the castle's first line of defense. Atop the large balcony above the castle's courtyard was a dark outline of a man. It was Maub, standing alone on the balcony with his massive army of elves sprawled out below him. The flags that flew over the castle had been changed from the green flags with the white galloping deer of Mazeron to red flags adorned with the dragon curled around the wizards staff. The emblem of the Keepers Of The Dragon's Flame.

As Aleric's army exited the forest and slowly and somewhat clumsily shuffled their way onto the battlefield, they were baffled that the first group of elves did not rush and attack them before their defensive lines were set up.

"Why aren't they attacking?" Brodel asked Aleric, who was stoically and silently observing the battlefield.

"I don't know," he replied slowly. His eyes glowed as he surveyed the land and imagined the battle unfolding before him.

Meanwhile, at the other end of the field, a large group of Brigands had entered the battlefield, and one extra burly man, who was notorious for his loudmouth and disdain for authority, began to get too riled up and excited for the fight. He galloped back and forth quickly on his horse, yelling strong quips and slogans about slaughtering the weak elves and all the glory to be taken on the battlefield.

Aleric heard the commotion, but before he realized what was going on or had a chance to stop it, a group of Brigands broke free from the lines and charged the battlefield straight at the group of High Elves that were guarding the ramp to the castle gates. They roared loudly as they went, and they rode so fast and hard that the others could feel the horses' hooves rumbling the ground as they charged forward.

They were more than halfway across the battlefield when, suddenly, it seemed like the entire castle sprang to life. A hail of arrows and multiple large, fiery projectiles from catapults soared into the sky in almost perfect unison—so many that it turned the blue sky dark with the shadows of arrows and fireballs. The charging Brigands didn't have a chance. They saw the attack coming but had no time to turn back or escape. The arrows came down from the sky with ferocious speed, and more of them found their mark in the brigands' body's than anyone could count. The crash and explosion of the fireballs followed almost immediately after. It was a spectacularly horrifying sight, one that none of the Brigand army had ever seen before, and they gazed in fearful amazement as the heat from the fireballs warmed their faces even from the other end of the battlefield.

"Elven ingenuity," Thearbuc mumbled to the others. "Their wartime technology has far surpassed ours."

"That is why they didn't charge us," Aleric replied. "They don't have to. They'll wait for us to get near the castle, then annihilate anyone who approaches."

"They're hoping we'll just give up and go away," Lamora said sounding hopeless. "They probably don't even care that we are out here."

"How do we get past the field?" Brodel asked.

Aleric didn't reply right away, and his silence hung heavily over them. Had they come all this way for nothing? Was their plight in vain and they never had any chance of regaining their freedom in the first place? Finally, with glowing eyes, The Paladin spoke.

"I have a plan," he said with a faint grin. "Wait here," he commanded, as he turned his horse quickly back toward the woods and rode away.

The brigands held the line across the field from the castle. Neither side made a move. The bodies of the overly eager Brigands smoldered at the far end of the field, the grass scarred and burned from fireballs the living marveled at the precision of the strike.

Then out of nowhere, three enormous fireballs rose from the concealment of the forest and hurdled high overhead with incredible speed at the castle. It was Aleric and the brigands' catapult teams, concealed within the forest trees. The fireballs sped towards the castle and each one found a mark. One exploded marvelously against the castle's stone wall, leaving a mark but not breaching it. Another crashed to the ground near the castle's ramp, sending heat and debris toward the High Elves. Only a few fell. The last fireball made it over the castle wall, but as it hurled toward impact it unexpectedly exploded in midair from a large bolt of energy suddenly colliding with it, sending small harmless ashes floating lazily to the ground.

"Maub!" Thearbuc yelled angrily, his horse pacing back and forth. "He destroyed the projectile!"

"How are we going to hit the castle with him defending it?" Lamora asked nervously as the concealed catapults continued hurling burning ball after burning ball towards the castle.

"We won't," Brodel replied, hanging his head low. He knew of the wizard's powers and what he was capable of.

They could see Maub, high atop the castle's balcony shooting energy as the fireballs approached their mark. The brigands could only launch so many projectiles at a time, and the wizard was so quick with his magic that he made destroying them look easy. None of them got through.

Soon after they decided to try more offensive tactics. The brigands were the best spear-throwers in the land, so the plan was to charge the battlefield as a large group under the cover of shields, then launch their wooden spears high into the air and over the castle's walls. When they tried it, many elves were hit by the spears and some of the brigands fell victim to well-placed arrow in the process. Eventually, by the end of the day the two armies stood at a stalemate on their respective ends of the battlefield, and they stayed that way until the day turned to night.

In the darkness of the night, they began testing each other's defenses. Small groups of Brigands charged quietly to one end of the castle or another, then quickly retreated or got hit when the hail of arrows arose from the castle. So far, no weak spots could be found.

The High Elves were playing their own games, looking for weak spots of their own. They sent small groups of hit squads out into the countryside, trying to flank the brigands through the forest, only to be met with a superior hand-to-hand fighting force which defeated them and forced them to retreat over and over again. But each time, a few Brigands would fall to the attacks. They were being withered down slowly and methodically.

"We won't last a week if this keeps up," Aleric said angrily. "We need to change the pace of the battle to our favor. We are playing right into their hands, doing exactly what they want us to do while they just wait us out."

So, in the early hours of the next morning, Aleric gave the order for his army to retreat from the battlefield and into the protection of the surrounding forest. They needed rest and they wouldn't make any progress in the daylight with a tired army. As he watched the last of his army slip into the forest, he gave one last look at the castle as the sun came up over the horizon. There, atop the high balcony, stood Maub. Motionless and stone-like, he observed the battlefield with unwavering purpose. Aleric knew the wizard was staring back at him. His heart sunk. How was he supposed to defeat such a powerful wizard and large army? His powers as a Paladin were useless at this distance. He felt hopeless, and even worse, he felt ashamed that so many people had put their trust in him and come this far, only for him to hit a wall and be unable to proceed. He slipped quietly into the forest with a heavy heart, knowing there was only one thing they could do if they wanted to have any hope of breaching the castle walls.

It was now midday on day two of the siege. The battlefield was quiet and the only sounds that could be heard were the birds playing carelessly in the fields. Swooping high and fast as they chased each other through the air. On one end of the battlefield was the quiet forest, with no sight or sound of Aleric's army. On the other was the massive fortress of the castle and the unwavering, unmoving army of disciplined High Elves ready to defend the castle at any and all cost.

Eventually the morning silence was broken by a faint but heavy rumble in the ground, then out of the concealment of the forest the entire Brigand army came rushing out all at once. None of them screamed or yelled out any battle cry as to keep the element of surprise for as long as possible. The only sound was the increasing thunderous booms beneath their feet as the large army charged the battlefield all at once. The men in the lead had made it halfway across the battlefield before most of the elven army even noticed they were coming.

The evil wizard Maub was absent from his perch overlooking the battlefield and started to scrambled out from within the castle as soon as he realized he was being taken by surprise. As he rushed out on the balcony, he saw the large army was already nearing the castle's ramp, and suddenly a hail of spears came over the walls from the brigands below. He went to work immediately, his quick reflexes throwing lightning bolt after lightning bolt, trying to intercept the bombarding spears. But there were too many to destroy them all. He was too distracted by the spears to see the incoming catapult projectiles that were already quickly approaching. He barely saw one out of the corner of his eye and destroyed it just in time, but missed the second and third projectiles, which crashed with magnificent explosions among the elven army which were helpless to them. Dozens of soldiers were tossed into the air like they weighed nothing, and others were sent scurrying about, engulfed in flames and screaming in a frenzy of confusion and pain before collapsing to the ground.

"It's working!" Aleric mumbled to himself from behind his metal helmet, as he and the first wave of Brigands reached the castle's ramp and made ready to fight the legion of elves that came charging down the ramp to meet them. There were hundreds of them, far more than it looked from afar. As they came charging down with fierce battle cries and weapons drawn, Aleric readied for hand-to-hand battle. Another fireball from the catapults hurled above his head and into the castle. He could hear the explosion and screams that followed it.

Suddenly, in the middle of all the chaos and fighting, the castle launched a barrage of their own projectiles. Aleric and the brigands watched as they, too, flew far over their heads and landed haplessly out in the battlefield behind all of the charging Brigands.

"They can't hit us if we stay close to the castle walls!" Thearbuc roared out as he fought elven soldiers at the foot of the castle's ramp. The thin elves were no match for the girthy, fiercely strong man in hand-to-hand combat. He could grab their clubs and swords mid-swing with his armor and toss them aside.

The Paladin was also faring well in battle. Clad in his shiny armor, the elven blows bounced right off him, leaving him only to feel heavy thuds in the chest from each blow. He wielded his longsword so powerfully that the massive weapon seemed to weigh almost nothing to any elf who witnessed it. Behind his armored helmet his eyes glowed a bright amber as he pushed towards the charging elven army.

He followed one swing of the sword by a powerful fireball into a group of elves, exploding them from the ramp before they could even reach him. He was overpowering the elves with an incredible display of strength.

Their hope was rising as they fought their way up the ramp, getting closer and closer to the castle. Then the castle gates slowly crept open. Two enormous wooden doors creaked loudly as the old metal and wood mechanism pulled the heavy doors. The brigands saw it open, and out spewed hundreds of more elves like a river washing away a dam.

"Retreat!" The Paladin roared loudly, seeing his army scattered across the ramp and the battlefield. They could easily be picked off if they were to be outnumbered and overwhelmed by the charging elves. "Regroup!" he shouted again with a booming voice.

Soon, The Paladin, Thearbuc, Lamora, Jace, Brodel, and a large group of Brigands found themselves back down at the bottom of the ramp. Arrows were falling all around them, along with bolts of electricity from the wizard Maub and flaming projectiles from the catapults. But they found if they stayed close to the high castle walls, most of the elves could not get the angle down on them to be much of a threat.

Down the ramp the next group of elven soldiers came charging. Hundreds upon hundreds of them. This time, they were prepared and clearly had a plan of attack. The ones in front came fast with open weapons and charged directly into the line of Brigands, who had their large, almost body height shields and spears at the ready. In the rear came the elven archers. Away from the attacking Brigands, they were able to take their time finding their targets and let off arrows by the dozens into the enemy. Some hit their large shields, but some made their way through.

The battle was gory and chaotic. Elves and Brigands were dropping left and right, and the field was already red with blood, yet the castle gates were still far away. The catapults, concealed in the forest, were still hard at work, but Maub was effective at destroying the fiery projectiles. Among the chaos and fighting, The Paladin found Lamora and Jace.

"Lamora!" The Paladin yelled over the fighting, with his ominous and magical echoing voice and glowing eyes. "I need you to find your way into the castle. Use your secret ways in." Lamora and Jace quickly glanced at each other. The thieves always knew their way into any important building. "You must get in and stop that wizard!" The Paladin commanded.

"Stop the wizard you say?" Brodel chimed in from hurling blue bolts of energy from his staff. "I'll go with you."

The four nodded at each other as if they had silently or telepathically developed a plan in a matter of seconds, then Jace, Lamora, and Brodel were off. Like shadows, they were quick to blend in and weaved in and out unnoticed until they quickly found themselves at the mostly unguarded rear, east side of the castle.

"The entrance to the tunnels must be two miles from here," Jace said worriedly, talking quickly and nervous while trying to catch his breath.

"We don't need the tunnels," Lamora said with a grin. Suddenly, she burst from their hiding spot behind a rock and large tree, then charged at the few guards that were guarding the unimportant, rear side of the castle. The guards had barely even noticed her coming before she was midair, landing heavy kicks to their faces and dropping them both instantly. Then without missing a beat, she went to a nearby tree and began to climb it. "Follow me," she said in a hurry as she scrambled up.

"That tree just goes up to a stone wall," Jace said with confusion and doubt. He was right. The castle wall towered above them. Nothing but stone. It was no wonder this end of the castle was not guarded. A giant with wings could not breach this enormous stone wall.

"Trust me," Lamora said again with a grin. She climbed out onto a long branch of the tree, and with the castle wall towering above her, she jumped. She soared through the air and somehow clung like a spider to the side of the castle wall. Looking far down at the others on the ground below, she yelled back, "There are a lot more holds than it looks like from down there. Hurry, get up here."

Jace and Brodel followed. Each scrambled up the tree, Jace obviously the quicker of the two as he was right at home scaling walls. Then, each made a leap of faith directly onto the castle wall and grasped for dear life for something to hold on to. They all found it. Lamora was right. The rocks up high on the wall were not placed with the care that the lower rocks were. They were jagged and easy to grip and step on.

"Let's climb," she said, starting to move upward. The three scurried along, high up the enormous wall, climbing ever higher and higher. The wind began to blow hard as they gained elevation, and they could see the battle unfolding in the distance below.

"Someone is going to see us up here," Brodel worried. "We need to hurry."

"I'm working on it," Lamora replied, approaching a closed shutter and locked window high up on the wall. She pushed and examined it for a minute, then moved on.

"What are you doing!?" Jace cried out as she ignored the window.

"That's not the one," she replied. The two others were confused but put all their trust in Lamora and continued to follow her. They passed another closed window, then another, and another. Each time, thinking they were finally getting off the wall only for Lamora to keep moving higher and on to other closed windows. Finally, they came to a seemingly unimportant window high up on the castle wall. Lamora pushed the shutters, but they were locked from the inside and did not budge.

"All this way for nothing?" Jace said, worried again.

"No faith, little brother?" Lamora grinned. Then, straddling the window with one foot on a hold and hand gripping the wall, she took her right foot and slipped it into a knot in the wooden shutter. With one easy lift of her leg the shutter came up from its hinges inside and dropped to the floor, opening the castle to them. She looked at Jace and winked. "Beat that," she chuckled as she swung inside like a carefree acrobat.

Jace and Brodel quickly followed, and as they landed inside the castle, they all held their breath and listened. For the first time today, it was silent. Dead silent. They stood in a small, empty stone room and listened to the silence. The heavy wind that only moments before felt like it would blow them off the castle wall to their deaths e now sounded like a calm, friendly breeze from within the safe walls of the castle.

"Let's find that wizard," Brodel said, pulling his wizard staff out from its holder on his back. The orb atop the wooden staff glowed a bright blue, brighter than usual, and his eyes were wild with anticipation. Lamora and Jace both noticed the orb and the crazy look in Brodel's eyes. "It's excited," he said, glancing at the orb and noticing the curious looks on their faces. "No time to waste." Brodel turned and hurried toward the door.

"Wait!" Lamora whispered. "Sneaking around castles is our expertise. Follow us," she said with a grin. Brodel nodded that he agreed and took his place behind Lamora and Jace as they opened the door slowly with a faint creak and peered out into the long, empty hall of the castle. "It's clear," Lamora said. Then the three exited the room and began to make their way through the castle.

Outside the castle, the massive battle raged on. Hundreds of Brigands faced hundreds of elves, neither side making any noticeable headway against the other. The brigands' massive catapults were effectively neutered by Maub's magical defenses and the hordes of elves were blocking Aleric from getting anywhere near the castle gates.

More and more elves emptied onto the battlefield as their places on the ramparts proved vastly ineffective as they ran out of arrows and traditional defenses. The brigands, too, had taken up mostly hand-to-hand combat now as their spears had been destroyed. It was a ground war now—a slug fest. Swing to swing, punch to punch, and blade to blade, the armies fought with rage and anger against one another.

Thearbuc and The Paladin stayed close together. The Paladin was always near the front of the lines, close to the castle's ramp, just waiting for an attempt to get close enough to explode the doors and gain them entry to the castle grounds. Dripping with sweat and about to collapse from exhaustion, The Paladin saw a glimmer of hope. As he threw a slain elf to the ground, he noticed he had a few moments to catch his breath before another was on him. The battalion of elves was thinning! A newfound store of energy pulsed through him.

"Charge the gates!" he roared. The others looked up and quickly came to the same realization: The elven numbers were dwindling while the brigands still numbered in the hundreds.

"Charge!" they roared in unison. Like a wave of destruction, they roared up the ramp, cutting down any elf that stood in their path. In just minutes the towering castle gates stood before them.

The Paladin wasted no time. Eyes glowing, rage and life pulsating through him, he dropped his sword to the ground and conjured a large fireball of energy with both hands. Then, he instantaneously blasted it thunderously at the castle's doors. The fireball hit with incredible energy, and the boom that it produced brought many nearby Brigands to the ground, holding their ears as the sonic boom from the blast was too much for the human body to handle. The door exploded into a million pieces and sent shrapnel inward, dropping dozens of elves who were lying in wait to ambush.

The scene was surreal, and nobody who witnessed it had ever seen anything like it before. There, standing alone in front of the most well-constructed castle gates known to anyone, was one man. One Paladin standing before the now destroyed towering doors. A breeze of hot, dry air from the burning wood blew slowly past the onlooking Brigands as they marveled at The Paladin and his magical strength. Before, they saw him as their leader, but at this moment, they saw him differently: He was a god.

But the incredible moment passed quickly as Thearbuc, who was always levelheaded and observant, didn't want to waste this rare element of surprise. He rushed past The Paladin with his large sword held high above his head and led the charge into the castle's courtyard. The brigands followed him by the dozens, and soon the majority of their army was within the castle walls.

From the highest rampart, Aghasty watched The Paladin as he exploded his way into the castle. He watched with no emotion and had no reaction when it happened. Surrounded by hundreds of elves who were ready to defend the castle, he quietly picked up his longsword, sheathed it, then grabbed his ivory bow. Still staring blankly into the distance at The Paladin, Aghasty began making his way toward him.

Aghasty

Aghasty slowly raised his right hand high into the air, his fist in a ball. The hundreds of elves that lay in wait watched him in anticipation. Then, he calmly opened his fist, exposing the palm of his hand, and dropped his arm fast and purposefully. This was the sign the elves had been waiting for— their sign to charge and attack, holding nothing back. Suddenly, the army of elves was on the move. Charging around Aghasty like a rushing river around a large rock, they bellowed into the courtyard of the castle to meet the incoming Brigands. The war erupted with a newfound energy and hate as the two armies clashed together once again.

As The Paladin made his way through the courtyard cutting down elf after elf, he briefly thought about how odd this situation felt. It was not long ago this was his home.

The window in his quarters overlooked this very courtyard, and he started every day gazing out into it. Now it was filled shoulder to shoulder with armies cutting each other down and fighting for control of the castle and lands that were all so peaceful not long ago.

But his thoughts were quickly interrupted by the sound of Thearbuc yelling beside him. "Duck!" he yelled. The Paladin noticed Thearbuc moving fast toward him, so he immediately ducked his head in defense and covered his face, just as an elf's sharp sword swung fast above his head. Thearbuc was already swinging over The Paladin's crouched head, and he sliced through the attacking elf and instantly dropped him to the ground. The Paladin nodded at his friend in thanks, and they were back to the fight. The two together were a powerhouse of energy and destruction, cutting their way through elf after elf, ever nearing the castle's entrance.

Within the castle, Lamora, Jace, and Brodel stealthily moved through the corridors, making their way to the king's quarters. So far, the halls had been empty, and they had gone unnoticed. It seemed like King Victus and Maub had thrown everything they had at defending the castle from the outside and left the interior largely undefended.

After what felt like an eternity of wandering the large castle, they finally heard some commotion from a corridor and went to investigate. As they followed the noise, they noticed this part of the castle was extra lavish compared to the rest. Red carpet lined the hallways, tapestries hung on the walls, and tables with gold trinkets adorned the hall. This was the king's corridor.

As they entered the far end of the hall, they came to a large door that was barely cracked open. The commotion they heard earlier was coming from within this room. It was the sound of the war raging outside accompanied by sporadic, deafening cracks of thunder.

Lamora peered inside. Before her was the king's chambers. It was an enormous room with fancy furniture and a large bed. Beyond the furniture, out on the balcony, she saw the tall wizard Maub. The deafening cracks of thunder were the magic that spewed from his wretched hands. Lamora slowly pushed open the door. Its old wood and hinges creaked loudly but went unnoticed against the commotion of the battle raging outside. The three crept into the room, looked about, then glanced at one another as if saying "What do we do now?"

Jace crept over to one of the large couches that adorned the room and crouched behind it. He was only ten feet from the wizard now. He could see a large, oversized book opened before the wizard. "Spell book," he mouthed to the others as he watched the wizard unleash spell after spell onto the battle below. Lamora crept up behind Jace.

"We need to get that book!" he whispered hastily. "He's using the spells to destroy the army." Lamora nodded quickly in agreement.

Just then, they heard a muffled sound coming from the other end of the room, and the three quickly turned their heads in unison to see where it was coming from. They spotted it immediately. There, at the far end of the room, was King Victus. He was tied and bound to a chair with a cloth tied over his mouth. He was mumbling through it to get their attention.

"The king!" Jace exclaimed in a whisper.

"You get the king, I'll get the book," Lamora replied without hesitation. Jace crept over to the king, who was bound to the chair by thick ropes. He put his finger up to the king's mouth, telling him to be quiet as to not draw attention to them. Jace slipped a knife out from under his tunic and cut the cloth that bound the king's mouth.

"Thank you, boy," the king said, gasping for air.

"All that powerful magic and the wizard just tied you up?" Jace asked, confused. "No paralyzing spells or mind control? Just simply tied you up?"

"Rich and powerful people rarely have any imagination," the king explained. "Quick, cut me loose."

Jace and his sharp knife made quick work of the thick ropes, and soon the king was almost free of his binds. At the other end of the room, Lamora and Brodel were devising a plan to stop Maub and his relentless attacks on the army below.

Outside, near the courtyard, Thearbuc and The Paladin were still fighting against the seemingly infinite number of elven soldiers. One would fall, two would attack. Their energy was wearing down, and although The Paladin didn't show any sign of fatigue, Thearbuc was nearing a point where he wouldn't even be able to swing his sword anymore.

Aghasty, from the tower high above the battle, was raining arrows down on the courtyard, wreaking havoc on the Brigand army. Maub, adjacent to him on the balcony, was conjuring his own attacks. Lightning bolts would strike out of nowhere and take out multiple Brigands at a time. The crash and booms filled the air like thunder.

"We can't hold this much longer!" Thearbuc yelled at The Paladin as they fought side by side. A crash of lightning hit just a few arm lengths away and more Brigands dropped lifeless to the ground. Another arrow from Aghasty's white bow and golden string struck another Brigand nearby, and he screamed out in agony as he stared in horror at the arrow in his chest.

"We need to fall back!" Thearbuc said with panic. "We'll never reach him! He'll pick us off one by one!"

Just as hope was dwindling away on the ground, up in the castle, Lamora jumped from the rafters high up by the ceiling and swung from a long rope that was used to pull the massive curtains closed. The wind rushed past her face and her stomach lurched from escaping gravity as she gained speed toward the ground. The fall was long, but the rope quickly ran out of slack and swung her outward—out toward the wizard Maub. With one hand she held tightly to the rope, and with the other she reached out as she swung past the wizard from behind, and in one motion, she grabbed one of the large book's of Abborell from the pedestal in front of him and swooped away with it.

The wizard was dumbfounded for a moment. The book was there right in front of him, then in the next moment it was suddenly gone, whisked away in an instant. He turned to see Lamora hop off the rope, landing firmly on the ground and running away with the oversized book of Abborell as fast as she could. She was already making her way to the side window to escape with the sacred texts before he even fully realized what had happened. But the wizard was quick. He threw his robes aside, making sure his hands were clear of any obstruction, and he began to conjure an energy bolt. Lamora saw it coming out of the corner of her eye as she ran as fast as she could to the far window. The feeling of fear gripped her body as she realized she was still too far from the window and the wizard was just a mere moment from blasting her down.

Then, just as the wizard was casting his spell, a countering bolt of energy came from across the room and struck him. It was Brodel. The blast was thick and made a thunderous crack as it hit the wizard. Dry heat filled the room, and the energy made the hairs stand up on Lamora's arm.

But Maub had seen the bolt coming just as it happened and was able to direct his blast at it instead of Lamora, diffusing most of the energy that would have surely killed him had it hit him directly. The wizard was pushed heavily to the ground at the impact, but he was back on his feet again in a second. He was agile, fast, and strong for an old man. Then he returned the blast at Brodel, but it was also easily deflected by the magic user. Lamora was long gone with the magic book by now, having leapt from the window like an acrobat and scaled down a tree outside. Maub ran to the window, dodging attacks from Brodel just in time to see her land firmly on the ground and sprint into the distance with the book of spells gripped firmly under her arm.

"Curse you!" The wizard Maub turned his attention back to Brodel and threw a hastily created fireball, which was off-mark and easily dodged by the young wizard Brodel.

Outside, the soldiers from both sides immediately noticed the cessation of magic raining down from the castle's balcony, and there was a simultaneous pause as they all looked to the sky and observed the newfound silence and calmness. But it was short lasting, and moments later the elves and Brigands were back, fighting more ferociously than ever.

After defeating one particularly strong elf, The Paladin looked to the sky and spotted Aghasty, still high up on the ramparts with his ivory bow and golden string firing arrows down on the brigands.

"Now is your chance! The magic has stopped!" Thearbuc yelled, also seeing the opportunity as he blocked an attacking elf from charging The Paladin. The Paladin nodded with bright glowing eyes, then was off. He jumped over bodies and shoved elven soldiers aside as he went. He was not going to waste any more time killing random elves; he was going after Aghasty.

Aghasty would have seen the large, armor-clad Paladin rushing toward the stairs to the tower, but he was momentarily distracted trying to see what had happened to Maub. Inside the castle, he saw Maub and Brodel locked in a fierce battle of wits and magic. They both had their left hands up near their faces, palms facing outward, and streams of energy were coming from their staffs. Although the battle did not look magnificent or intense in any way to the outsider, Aghasty knew well the abominable severity of wizard battles.

Inside their heads, they were both using magic to twist and torment the other. Finding pathways and weaknesses through their minds, dredging up past and painful memories and even creating new ones to break each other's minds through extreme mental anguish and agony. There were no rules in a wizard battle. Nothing too off limits or below the belt. Only those who had experienced it could attempt to describe the agony and torture they would have to endure.

The two wizards paced slowly in a circle, locked in a battle like two adjacent spokes on a wheel. Brodel grimaced in pain and let out a small whimper of agony. The sides of his hair turned gray as he winced, then moments later the hand that held his staff began to wrinkle and became spotted, like it had aged fifty years in a matter of moments. Jace and King Victus watched from across the room, both knowing they could do nothing as the wizards continued to torture, twist, and torment each other's minds.

"I have to help the boy," King Victus whispered suddenly, as he watched Brodel fight the older and more experienced wizard with all his might.

Outside, on the tower, Aghasty watched the wizard battle unfold. He knew he could help Maub from this distance, so the elf slowly reached into his quiver and pulled out one of his last arrows. In an instant he had it pulled back to his cheek and Brodel in his sights. He only took one second to pause and exhale, then he let the arrow loose. It flew through the air fast with a slight wobble as arrows do. Ever following the sharp tip like a snakes body follows its head through the grass. The arrow was through the balcony doors, heading straight towards Brodel's chest when the king abruptly came running into view, lunging at Maub to help Brodel.

As the king closed in on Maub, the arrow found its mark directly in King Victus' chest. It hit with such force that it stopped the king's forward momentum and dropped him instantly to the ground. The arrow was buried deep in his chest, just under the heart. In shock, the wizards broke off their mental assaults on one another and their attention went quickly to the king, who had collapsed onto the floor.

Outside, the Paladin had scaled the tower stairs and finally Aghasty was close and within view. He saw the elf wince and the shock on his face as his arrow struck the king, but at that moment, The Paladin did not know why the elf was so taken aback. But he took advantage of the moment of confusion and charged the elf leader from behind. The Paladin was coming upon Aghasty at full speed, still with the element of surprise. But elves are hard to surprise. Aghasty felt the approaching footsteps with his fine-tuned senses. In an instant, he saw the Paladin bearing down on him and reached for his dagger and braced for impact.

The two clashed together with incredible force, and the elf was able to block The Paladin's swinging sword with the hilt guard of his dagger, and the two fell hard to the ground. They rolled twice before they came to a stop, and The Paladin found himself on top of the elf. He grabbed him by the wrist, disabling his dagger strikes, and used the other hand to punch him hard in the face repeatedly. The elf took the beating as he tried to squirm his arm free. He reached, grabbed his dagger, and plunged it into The Paladin's side. The sharp elven dagger went easily through the armor and into the flank of The Paladin, who yelled out in agony and rolled off. Aghasty quickly scrambled away toward his bow, which was laying on the ramparts from being thrown by the initial impact.

As Aghasty hobbled to the bow, blood dripping from his face, The Paladin rose to his feet and assessed his wound. He pulled out the dagger sticking from his side and blood squirted out of the wound. His chest armor clanked heavily to the ground as he unbuckled it and dropped his helmet. Then, almost immune to the pain thanks to his adrenaline, he plunged his finger into the wound and grimaced for a moment as he felt around inside.

"Not too deep," The Paladin mumbled to himself. "I'm okay." He exhaled heavily and brushed the blood from his finger as he realized the wound was not mortal. But Aghasty had reached his bow and was already nocking another arrow and drawing it back, pointing it directly at The Paladin.

Before Aghasty could let go of the arrow, The Paladin hurled a small but fast fireball at the leader of the elves. The arrow let loose but only traveled a short length before striking the fireball and being instantly singed to the point it could not fly straight and flew haplessly aside and down onto the courtyard. Aghasty quickly reached for another arrow, but he was too slow. The Paladin had already sent another fireball at him, and it struck him hard in the torso, making a large and hot explosion that cracked like thunder and sent a heatwave across the ramparts. The impact burned the elf badly and threw him back onto the stone ground. After a moment of pause to assess the situation, The Paladin approached the felled elf slowly. Holding his bloodied side, limping in pain, and dragging his large sword, he hobbled forward. When the Paladin finally reached him, he got his first good look at the elf. His once silky and perfect hair was singed and smoldering from the blast. His tunic had burnt open, and his fair skin was burned almost down to the bone. Aghasty squirmed in pain as he lay on the stony ground.

"You could have just gone home. You could have just stayed in your lands," The Paladin said ominously, with anger in his voice and a burning hate in his glowing eyes. "We just wanted to be left alone." He towered above the wounded elf. "But no," The Paladin continued. "There's always someone who won't just let you live your life. You just can't help yourselves but try to mess with everyone else!" He raised his voice loudly as he kicked the wounded elf hard in his burnt chest.

"I was…I was just," Aghasty gurgled, trying to force the words out. "I was just helping my people."

"You think you are the good guy when you hurt other people just because it helps you?" The Paladin asked exaggeratively, clenching his teeth and trying to hold back the anger. The Paladin released his hand from his wound and glanced at it as blood quirted from his side, then he grabbed his sword with both hands and raised it above his head. The elf squirmed in pain and reached above his head, seemingly to protect his face from the incoming blow. The Paladin did not notice the elf's hand slip underneath his singed hair, and before he could drop the heavy sword and strike down the elf once and for all, Aghasty had thrown a dagger that was concealed behind his back before The Paladin even knew he was in any danger. In the last second, he saw the dagger racing toward his face and quickly leaned aside and brought his arms up, deflecting the dagger with his metal gauntlets. The Paladin clenched his teeth in anger at the surprise attack and with rage pulsating through his veins and his eyes glowing bright amber, he struck down the leader of the High Elves with his longsword so forcefully it nearly cut him in two.

"Raaaah!!!" The Paladin roared out in anger. He stood over Aghasty's body in a victory stance, huffing his chest heavily as if to let the spirit of the elf or anyone who witnessed the fight know that he was not one to be trifled with. Then, he bent over and picked up the body and hurled it over the side of the wall and down into the courtyard below.

There was an eerie silence that followed the sound of the body hitting stone. The noise of battle had permeated the air for the past two days, so the silence felt odd and awkward to those on the battlefield. Aleric peered over the edge of the rampart walls and down into the courtyard. Having seen the body of their fallen leader, the remaining elves all begun to surrender. One by one, they laid down their swords, daggers, and bows. The brigands roared and chanted in unison at their victory and for the lands that would now be returned to them. They looked to the sky to see their leader, the great Paladin, and they roared and cheered as he raised his arm in a fist, declaring victory over the elven army.

But the moment of victory was short lived for The Paladin. As he turned away from the ramparts, he caught a glance inside the castle through the adjacent balcony. "The king!" he audibly cried out in shock. Inside, he could see the king hunched over in the corner and Jace kneeling over him. There was blood all around him. Lots of blood. Maub and Brodel were once again locked in battle, cloaks swooping back and forth like fire as they dodged one another's blasts. The room was a disaster of destruction, and the curtains and furniture were on fire. Jace looked up from the king and saw The Paladin outside through the door.

"Help us!" he screamed out, pleading to anyone who would hear him.

Aleric jumped into action immediately and bounded down the stairs and toward the castle, dropping all of his heavy armor along the way and keeping only his sword. He ran through the courtyard at alarming speed, ignoring the congratulations and celebrations going on by his fellow army. Jumping over debris and bodies, he ran to the side entrance of the castle and smashed into the door so hard it crumbled inward. Thearbuc knew something was wrong and followed close behind.

The two ran unobstructed up the steps to the king's chambers. As they entered the hallway, they could hear the crashes of thunder and see the flash of lights illuminating the hall as the two powerful wizards fought inside the king's chambers. They wasted no time and came barging in with weapons drawn.

The scene was unbelievable. The room was filled with static electricity and dry heat from the lighting, flames, and fireballs, and the room had descended into complete chaos. They choked on the smoke as they burst in, and there they were—two powerful wizards pitted against each other. Flames and lightning came from their staffs and a beam of energy from their hands joined them together, each one trying to get inside the other's mind to twist it into submission. Aleric got a quick glimpse of Brodel's face underneath his black hood and saw that his face was old and weathered once again, just like when they had saved him from the witch Kalindra. He barely recognized his good friend, and the shock of it sent his stomach lurching and his heart felt broken and sad.

But the sadness quickly turned to anger, and The Paladin's eyes began to glow again as his rage pulsated and started overtaking his body. He clenched his teeth as he focused all his hatred on Maub. He channeled all of the energy into a ball of fire, and he launched it at the wizard. But Maub knew an impulsive attack was coming from the man overcome with his emotions. In an instant, he released his attack on Brodel and blocked the fireball coming from the Paladin, redirecting it into the wall where it exploded with ferocious heat that blew everyone's hair back with a powerful gust of dry wind.

Instantly, it was clear that Maub was not pleased with the show of magic used against him. His teeth clenched as his anger began to boil over, and he quickly turned all of his attention to the Paladin. Before he could muster up another fireball, the wizard outstretched his hand and staff toward him and the Paladin was lifted from the ground. He rose helplessly into the air with arms and feet flailing, unable to defend himself or do anything to counter it.

As he felt the invisible energy build around him, he glanced helplessly towards Brodel, hoping his friend could come to his aid, but the young wizard had collapsed to the floor after what felt like an eternity of fighting Maub. That was the last thing Aleric remembered before being hurled at the wall and being knocked unconscious.

Seeing this, Thearbuc attempted to go after the wizard next. He charged across the room with his sword thinking he could strike down Maub if he could just get close enough. But he didn't have a chance at that without magic. He was nearly halfway across the room when he, too, was lifted from the floor and suspended helplessly in the air. Maub circled the room slowly, toying with the large man and taunting him from the floor below.

"What makes a mortal like you think you can best a wizard," he hissed from beneath his dark hood. He slowly rotated his pointer finger in a circular motion, and it made Thearbuc spin in slow circles in the air. Thearbuc flailed his hands, trying to grasp at the wizard or anything he could get his hands on, but it was fruitless. Slowly, he began to realize that the day could not be won after all, and he and his friends would be defeated by the powerful wizard. The king lay dying in the corner and the only two people who could even compete with Maub's powerful magic were lying unconscious on the floor.

"Why?" Thearbuc mustered sounding defeated.

"Why!?" Maub replied, his craggy and wrinkled face scrunching up. "Because of power. Absolute, beautiful power. The moment I first felt the power radiating from the magic books of Abborell I knew I had to have them. Then once I had a taste of such power, I had to have more. So, I got rid of anyone else who could use the books and became even more powerful! The people here. They are so weak without magic to defend them. I can do absolutely anything I want to anyone and no one can even try to stop me. If a villager bumps into me in a crowd or looks at me in a way I don't like, I can do whatever I want them. Turn them into anything, torture them in ways you can't even imagine, just for fun."

"You're sick," Thearbuc grumbled, spitting at Maub from his position floating in the center of the room. "Your soul is blackened by greed and power."

"Oh, it's not my fault," Maub replied condescendingly. "For I am only a living creature on this planet, and desiring power and control over others is just human nature. Not just human nature, but all of nature. It's a survival mechanism to try and control your environment to ensure one's safety and survival. From the moment they are born humans crave power over others. As soon as a child can walk steadily, it will show dominance over anything that is smaller than itself and begin to assert it onto the family pet and farm animals around the home."

"This primitive behavior you are speaking of is rooted in fear," Thearbuc snapped back. "People who try to control others like that are just scared of the world, and it is their pitiful survival attempt to try and control everything goes on around them. The more scared someone is, the more they try to control and dominate other people. You're just scared and weak."

"Ah, but it is not just me," Maub cut him off. "If one group of people is stronger than another, they will assert dominance over them every time. In fact, almost every living thing in nature will gladly hurt another if it benefits them. Knowing these facts of life, it is the citizens own fault for granting one person so much power. What did they expect when they agreed to let ONE person in the entire kingdom have all the magic and power? Did they think I would suddenly care about each individual person and personally take care of them? That is not human nature, and it is ignorant to pretend it is! I am a wolf, and they let me right in!" Maub yelled, seeming to get angrier and more unstable as he ranted. "I am merely a victim of evolution." He said more calmly. "Not as much a victim as you are about to be, but a victim nonetheless," he continued with an evil grin. "Plus, I hate to admit it, but I hate you mortal humans. You can't seem to survive unless there is someone out there that you think you are better than. If every single one of you were exactly the same, you would still find the most miniscule difference to think you are somehow superior and begin to fight over it," he said, raising his voice again and flailing out his arms. "It was my pleasure to steal your lands and control how little coin everyone made. The more land I acquired the easier it was for me to acquire more land, until eventually I controlled it all. I rigged the salaries and land value so no one could ever quite make enough to stop working or be able to buy and own their own land. Forced into a lifetime of leasing from me. Like a squirrel that is unable to store nuts for the winter, their entire lives were wasted on toil and survival. Never able to rest. And a population just trying to survive has no time to fight among each other, uprise against oppression, or want more from life when they are focused solely on finding their next meal. Maybe I did them a favor, keeping them in squalor instead of out fighting each other? Either way, they were my slaves. The control and power are addicting. I am a god to these people! I control everything! And no one could even try to stop me. Not until your absurd Paladin came along. He threatened to ruin everything, and once you have tasted that sort of power over others…" Maub trailed off. "Well, like I said before, it would be hard to let go of." Suddenly Maub snapped back from his angry rantings and turned to Thearbuc who was still suspended in the air. "Your time is up, mortal!" the wizard yelled out, raising his staff.

Thearbuc thought of his children and his peaceful life in the forests, and he questioned his decision to ever leave that life. *I had to try. I had to help,* he thought as he waited for the attack. Then it came. The sudden disappearance of gravity. His stomach lurched as his body began to move fast through the air and he landed hard on the ground. The ground! He suddenly realized. Not hard against the wall! Then he heard the cracking sound of thunder and felt the hot air and electricity in the air of another blast as he saw the wizard Maub being thrown violently across the room. Then he saw Brodel, standing up once again, leaning heavily against his staff, which had just delivered a brutal blow to the evil wizard. The distraction from Aleric and Thearbuc had given him just enough to time to break free from Maub, regroup himself, and strike again.

The loud crack of electricity and hot blast of air shook Aleric back into consciousness just in time for his blurry eyes to see a second bolt of energy hitting the wizard directly in the torso, without even a hint of deflection or defense. It only took two direct hits for the old wizard's body to lay lifeless, slumped onto the floor, smoldering from the heat of the blasts. On the other side of the room, Brodel collapsed to one knee.

"Brodel!" Aleric yelled, picking himself up from the floor and rushing to his friend. Thearbuc was close behind. Putting their hands on his shoulders, they watched the young wizard gasp for air, and they knew he was severely hurt.

"Are you okay?" Thearbuc asked. "Say something!"

"You did it, Brodel," Aleric offered some encouragement. After a moment, Brodel made an inaudible noise from underneath his cloak. It was raspy and dry, like an old man's voice, and the others did not recognize it.

"What happened?" Aleric asked worriedly, then he pulled Brodel's hood back and revealed his face. Aleric and Thearbuc both leaned away in shock as they laid their eyes on him. His skin was wrinkled and spotted with sunspots. His veins could be seen through frail old skin, and his hair was grayed and thin. Large bags adorned his eyes, making him look old and sad.

"It's still…me," the old man mustered between breaths.

"Brodel?" Thearbuc asked, concerned.

"I told you guys before," Brodel said, sitting up slowly. "Magic ages the body."

"I can't even imagine what you just had to go through," Aleric said, patting his friend on the back.

"The torment," Thearbuc agreed, shaking his head. "I've heard tales of wizard battles. I wouldn't wish one on anybody, let alone my best friend." There was sadness in his eyes as he said it, seeing his friend age an entire lifetime in a single day, so many years robbed from him. He wanted nothing more than to help, to change him back.

Suddenly, the three were distracted by a noise coming from the far end of the room. It was Jace and the king, both stirring back to consciousness. The king was gasping for air. The arrow was still sticking out of his chest and blood ran down from his mouth.

"Oh no," Aleric whispered at the sight of the wounded king. He rushed over to the far side of the room. "What happened?" he asked Jace, who was still slumped on the ground, leaning against the wall, having just regained consciousness.

"Elven arrow," he replied with a cough. Aleric took the king in his arms and propped him up. He was weak, barely holding on to consciousness, if at all, and his body was dead weight. Aleric stared at him for some time, assessing the wounded king. Blood pooled on the floor from the wound in his chest, just below his heart. Aleric looked around at each of his friends, Thearbuc, Jace, and Brodel—all were wounded from the battle.

"I think I can save him," Aleric announced. The others glanced up. "I do have healing powers, remember?" Aleric stated. "I helped bring Brodel back after he rebuilt my house with magic." The others nodded. It was still unknown if it was the Paladin that had brought Brodel back, though, or if Brodel had done that on his own. But it was worth a try. The others nodded. "See what you can do," they agreed.

"We'll need some space. Some time," Aleric told them. "Let's get him to his bed chambers." Thearbuc and Jace helped raise the wounded king to his feet, and the three of them dragged him across the hall to his bed. They gave Aleric a nod of good luck as they closed the doors behind them.

There, in the king's chambers, for the first time in days, it was finally quiet. After such a long and loud battle, the silence felt odd. It engulfed Aleric and settled on him like a thick cloud. He stood at the door and stared at the wounded king, who would sometimes let out a gurgle as if he was gasping for air or wincing in pain, then would go back to motionless unconsciousness again. Aleric sighed heavily as he saw the man who took him in and change his life look so frail and helpless. He was pale and was almost unrecognizable. Aleric's heart dropped for the king. That title had brought the man nothing but pain. His family was stolen from him, his son murdered or lost and his wife disappearing without a trace. He was a broken man even before the arrow pierced through his skin. Aleric went to the king and knelt down next to him.

The Paladin's eyes glowed as he sat beside the king and the magic began to flow through him. He sat and stared at the king, and the longer he stared, the more upset he got. The king was a broken man, and somehow, it led them all to this point. Years of misery and pain. The downfall of the kingdom and the subsequent wasted lives of hundreds of people who were just unfortunate enough to be living in these lands at this time. Being weak had let so many evils into the land to leech off the people's hard work and prosperity. And in a desperate attempt to lean on someone strong, the king had chosen none other than a purely evil wizard who only wanted the kingdom's land, riches, and power for himself.

"I would have never had let any of this happen," the Paladin whispered despairingly to himself and the unconscious king. He thought about the past and his hardship-filled life in these lands. But surprisingly, a feeling of peace began to wash over him as he realized something. There was a once-in-a-lifetime chance presenting itself at this very moment. No, a once-in-a-*hundred*-lifetimes. He began to think of his future and possible future children. The peaceful and rich lives they could have, void of pain and worry. Just one decision could change it all, for not only his family but for countless others too. One decision could mean no more toiling, no more lying awake at night in fear of where the next meal would come from, no more resorting to horrible and miserable things just for some food and a roof over their heads. All of that could change.

The Paladin's eyes grew a brighter, fierce glowing amber as he thought of it. He gazed at the glowing green Medallion of Mazeron on the king's wrist. He knew it had to be taken or given, and if he passed away without giving it to anyone, then the kingdom would be thrown into worse turmoil as the remaining nobles fought and squabbled over who was entitled to the castle and lands of the kingdom.

This chance will never come again, he thought to himself. Then suddenly and without any further thought, he reached down to his ankle and pulled out his dagger and slowly pushed it deep into the king's chest where the arrow had struck. He felt the dagger go in smoothly, and the king abruptly opened his eyes to meet a The Paladin's as he gasped in pain and horror.

"Why…?" the king gasped with his last breath. It was only an instant, then the moment was over. The king's eyes closed softly, and he was at peace.

Aleric dropped his head as the torment immediately set in and rested it on the arm that still tightly clenched the dagger, then screamed out silently from within against the unbearable anguish over what he had just done. Did he even want this? And what would he do without the king, an almost father figure, to guide him on his path through this new life? He had just killed the one person besides Briss who ever put any faith in him.

"He was gone anyway," he mumbled to himself with trembling lips, wiping his nose as his eyes returned to normal and began clouding up with tears. "I couldn't save him, but I can save the kingdom," he tried reassuring himself. He had to do it, and deep down he knew that. He pulled the dagger from the king and wiped the blood from it before quickly stowing it back in its sheath.

As the lifeless king lay there, Aleric pulled his sleeve up and exposed the green, glowing Medallion of Mazeron. Aleric gazed upon it. He had never seen it up close before. Instead of its usual glow, it was pulsating like a lamp running out of oil. It flickered green for another few moments, then went dark. Aleric knew that meant the king had expired. Now the final decision was in Aleric's hands. He waited another moment, but its light did not return. He grabbed the arm of King Victus and carefully slipped it off. After a moment of examining the medallion, Aleric put it on his wrist. Suddenly, the stone at the center of the medallion began to glow again and a newfound feeling of life pulsed through his veins. He breathed heavily, trying to catch his breath at the sudden feeling of bliss and strength. It almost tickled, and he let out an audible laugh as a feeling of strength, comfort, and peace washed over him like a soft blanket placed on by a loved one.

Then there were footsteps coming from down the hall and the door swung open, slamming against the stone wall. Thearbuc and Jace and a few of the king's guards burst into the room. They were breathing heavily from the sprint.

"We heard a yell!" Thearbuc exclaimed with his weapon drawn. Then they laid eyes on Aleric and the lifeless king. In unison, Jace, Thearbuc, and the guards' mouths dropped in shock and awe. Aleric slowly raised the palm of his hand, exposing the glowing medallion on the underside of his wrist. He tried to say something, anything, to break the tension, but the words would not come out. The others were speechless as well, and they exchanged looks of shock for a long moment.

"He…" Aleric tried to push out the words. "He gave me this," he finally exclaimed.

"Oh my goodness," Jace said slowly, in almost a whisper. "Do you know what this means?" Aleric barely moved his head with a slight nod, but the tension and nervousness of being found out was still gripping him.

"You are king," Thearbuc said slowly. "The king!" he continued excitedly.

"I couldn't save him," Aleric said, dropping his head as the others rushed to his side. Thearbuc patted him hard on his back.

"I can't believe it," Thearbuc said in awe. He reached down to the king and pulled his shirt aside, exposing the wound with the elven arrow still sticking out of it. He looked at the wound then a bewildered look came upon his face. He glanced up at Aleric, scanning his face for a moment and looking back and forth at Aleric and the wound. As he stared at Aleric in silence, their eyes met, and each held a long stare at one another. The moment felt so tense that the entire room's mood changed in an instant.

"What is going on?" one of the guards asked, taking a step forward. Thearbuc and Aleric held their stare at one another.

"Nothing," Thearbuc finally broke the tense silence and fierce glare. He covered the wound back up with the deceased king's shirt. He forced a soft, friendly smile behind his thick, bushy black beard. "Nothing at all." Aleric looked down and away as the others moved closer and helped Aleric to his feet.

"Can I talk to you outside?" Thearbuc asked Aleric.

“Alright then,” he replied as the two began to exit the room. Soon the two stood alone in the silent hallway.

“I know what you did in there,” Thearbuc stated with a scowl.

“I didn’t have much of a choice,” Aleric replied defensively after a long pause. “You would have done the same thing if given the chance. Anyone would have. He was going to die anyway.”

“Then you should have let it happen that way!” Thearbuc snapped back. “What you did was wrong.”

“I don’t see it that way,” Aleric replied. “They tell us that taking what we want is wrong so the people who already have what everyone wants are less likely to have it taken from them. Everyone goes around pretending to be so righteous, but you know as well as I do that if they were given the chance like I was, every one of them would take it. They only say things are bad or immoral because they weren’t the ones who were given the chance. Its jealousy.” Thearbuc stood bewildered, he didn’t even know what to say. “He was going to die without transferring the medallion to anyone,” Aleric continued explaining with a pleading tone. “His son is missing! The kingdom would be thrown into chaos and war for the rest of our lifetimes. Judge me if you must, but it had to be done. Now, for the actual first time in my life my future is secure. Yours is too. We can actually make a difference now!”

Thearbuc did not reply for some time and the tension hovered thick and uncomfortable as the two looked silently at one another with solemn faces. “You won’t get any judgement from me,” Thearbuc finally broke the tension with a sigh. “You have an army of people out there and a lot of worried citizens who need a strong king,” he said, forcing a grin. “They are waiting for you. Go to them.”

Aleric smiled and rested his hand on Thearbuc’s shoulder as the others shuffled into the hallway. From down the hall, Brodel the old, crippled man came slowly shuffling forward from resting on a chair and immediately saw the glowing medallion on Aleric’s wrist. The old wizard smiled as he approached and followed as the group entered the king’s living quarters, where the body of the wizard Maub still lay on the floor. They stopped to glance at the body, then all breathed a sigh of relief that the fighting was finally over.

Aleric stepped out onto the large balcony, overlooking the courtyard of the castle. Down below, the army of Brigands were already celebrating and going about clearing out the bodies and destruction from the battle. Aleric stood over them from the balcony above like a conductor to his symphony. He went largely unnoticed for some time, until someone below yelled out. It was Commander Rune, rescued from the dungeons by his men.

"All praise the Paladin!" he yelled out, throwing his hand to the sky in a clenched fist of victory. The army roared in unison, and it echoed across the stone walls and ramparts as the sound of victory permeated the air.

"He is no Paladin," Thearbuc yelled out, stepping toward the edge of the balcony. "He is KING!" As he said it, he grabbed Aleric by the wrist and raised his arm high above his head, exposing the Medallion of Mazeron to the army below. The people instantly erupted in cheer. The sound of applause and happiness was almost deafening. Aleric stepped up to the balcony to address his army, but in the moment of celebration and distraction, they did not notice Maub begin to squirm back to life inside the castle.

Many don't know, but a powerful wizard can move freely from plane to plane. Although the wizard's body had expired, his spirit had not, and it had found its way back into this plane among the living. As Aleric started address the soldiers, he was cut short by Brodel.

"Look out!" he yelled from back inside the castle. Aleric swung around to see a fireball from Brodel explode against the wall, missing its mark, and Maub already running fast toward a large, swirling dark fog in the center of the room.

"It's a portal!" Aleric yelled out. "Stop him!" Brodel cast another fireball, but it was too late. Maub had moved too fast, and with one giant leap he jumped straight into the portal and disappeared from the room. Aleric was halfway to the portal when the wizard disappeared into it. He stopped in the middle of the room, unable to decide on what to do next. Suddenly the portal began to flicker and get smaller. Bolts of electricity pulsed from the portal and it roared like thunder. "He can't get away!" Aleric yelled, and that was the last thing any of them heard from him as without further hesitation the new king of Mazeron jumped into the portal just as it closed behind him.

The room was once again eerily silent, and Thearbuc, Brodel, Jace, and the others looked at one another shocked and confused looks upon their faces.

"He's gone," Brodel whispered. It had all happened so fast. "He was just here. He was just announced king, and now he's gone."

Chapter 23: The Keep

In another land, Aleric burst through the other side of the portal, confused and disoriented. He had never traveled through time and space before. Stepping out of the portal was like taking a misstep down a flight of stairs, and he came out falling to the ground hard on his hands and knees. He shook his head and rubbed his eyes, trying to orient himself and figure out what had just happened to him.

Waiting for his eyes to adjust and his senses to come back to him, he looked up and realized he was in a cave. He saw the stone walls around him and felt the cool, stagnant air. Rubbing his eyes, he began to look around, and there across the room he saw the wizard Maub. For a moment, he wondered how the wizard was so far away from him considering they both went through the portal just seconds apart. But portals bent time, so a few seconds on one side could be minutes on the other. With his craggy hands, the wizard waved his staff through the air and mumbled something inaudible. Aleric instantly knew it was a spell being cast by the wizard. Suddenly, a blast of light came from the orb end of his staff and another portal opened up in mid-air above a stone well in the center of the cave. Aleric then realized where he was. He had been here before and had seen the group of wizards summoning the Morghvile from that very well with the exact same type of portal.

“No!” The paladin shouted as he attempted to throw a fireball at the wizard, but it was small and puttered out before the wizard even needed to dodge it.

Maub looked back at The Paladin like he wanted to attack him, but he winced in pain at every movement from his badly burned body. He gripped his side in pain, then decided he was in no shape for another fight. As The Paladin still crouched on the floor on his hands and knees, the wizard fled down one of the corridors of the cave and was gone, leaving The Paladin alone in the cave with the swirling portal there in front of him.

The Paladin’s head was still swimming. Apparently traveling through space and time was not for the inexperienced. Eventually he regained enough strength to stand on his feet, and he tried walking it off until the rest of his strength came back to him. As he paced around, he started hearing growls, howls, and screams coming from the portal.

"The Morghvile," he mumbled aloud. One could only imagine what horrific and nightmarish plane the portal led to, and now it was open. "I have to close it," he said aloud with a grimace of pain from his stab wound. His mind raced and he began to panic. The nightmarish sounds from the portal were growing louder. Without further hesitation and with no other plan in mind, he conjured a large fireball in his hands and launched it at the portal in hopes that more magic would possibly destroy it.

Schluuuurp. The fireball made a noise like a heavy lead ball moving through a thick liquid as it went into the portal, then disappeared. The Paladin backed away and stood motionless, awaiting what would happen next.

But instead of the portal closing as he had hoped, he heard a loud, horrifying scream from inside it. A scream of pain followed by more and more roars. Scared for what he had done and what was on the other side of the portal, he moved stealthily towards the wall of the cave and drew his sword in anticipation. Then, before he could sneak out of the cave, something burst into the room from the portal. It came in roaring with a deafening scream, flying erratically like a bat. Angry, sporadic, and mad, it flew around the room with smoke trailing behind it. It was obvious that this thing had been struck by the fireball, and it was scared and angry all at the same time.

At first, Aleric couldn't make out it was. It was flying, spinning, dipping, and diving so quickly that it was impossible to see. But then it saw Aleric and came right for him. A giant batlike creature with a wingspan as long as two men. It bared its large fangs, and its black eyes locked on him. The Paladin ducked and rolled as the monster smashed into the wall, just adding to its disorientation. The Paladin watched with glowing eyes as it circled the room again, trying to find a way out. He swung his sword at the creature as it flew by but missed time and time again. Then, as it came back around a fourth time, he swung hard and fast and his sword finally made contact and struck it down to the ground. It screamed out in pain and gnashed its sharp teeth. Its wounded body was unable to reach The Paladin, even though it tried viscously to get at him. Then, with one last swing of the sword, the creature fell limp and silent.

Sweat poured from The Paladin's forehead, and his hands shook from the fear and adrenaline. Instinctively, he moved away from the portal and to the far end of the cave where the wizard Maub had disappeared off to. He stayed for just a moment longer to see what else would happen with the portal, hoping that maybe it would close by itself now that something had come through it or that the magic would wear off. But the portal roared to life once again with the deafening sound of beasts, growls, and screams that only got louder and louder. As the screams hit its peak, another giant beast came through the portal. It was large and thick, with long legs like a horse. Aleric recognized it instantly as another Morghvile. He knew it then. The portal led right from the land of the Morghvile and into the kingdom of Mazeron. The animal landed on the ground in front of the portal, and without any hesitation, it ran at full speed like a horse straight for the open corridor in front of the portal, and it was gone from the cave in an instant.

Aleric's heart sank and his stomach lurched as he realized the tunnel led straight out of the mountain and into the forests of Mazeron. They had followed that tunnel out of the cave system the last time they were here. Aleric collapsed against the wall. What was he supposed to do with a steady stream of viscous, murderous, Morghvile heading directly toward the kingdom? There could be hundreds of them at the other end of the portal. Maybe thousands.

His dreaded thoughts were interrupted by the portal coming to life again. He groaned aloud, sounding defeated. Then his survival instinct took over. "I'm not staying around to find out," he said to himself, turning and running from the cave, out of the tunnel Maub had escaped down. He did not see the next Morghvile emerge from the portal, or the next, or the next. A stampede of murderous beasts were coming through the portal at an alarming rate, heading straight for the kingdom.

Deep inside the cave walls, surrounded by magnificent stone structures and towers of gold he had built, sat Sophie the Stone Gnome. Crouched behind the stone walls, hidden from the beasts, he trembled in fear at the sight of them. "Can't hurt Sophie. Not in here," he reassured himself. He put his thumb in his mouth for comfort, like a child, then bit nervously at the nail. More beasts emerged from the tunnel, each one either frantically or lazily making its way down the tunnel that lead straight into Mazeron. Eventually Sophie's nerves couldn't handle any more of the hellish sight, and he turned around to retire back into the mountains where he would be safe again.

In the meantime, Aleric was making his way through the tunnels, still deep inside the mountain. They started out small and he had to duck as he moved, but soon the sound of the portal and beasts behind him faded into nothing and the tunnels opened up to a normal height. He walked and walked through the tunnels, always keeping his right hand on the wall. He wondered constantly about how deep or how far the tunnel system would go, or if he was going the right way at all.

Eventually, he saw a small dot of light far in front of him. "An exit!" he said aloud excitedly. He doused the fireball he had conjured in his left hand, which had been illuminating the dark path, and began to walk freely, feeling more at ease with each and every step. As he made his way to the light, he realized that the tunnel was now very large, as wide as a road and tall enough for two wagons to fit through. There was no sign of any threats, and a sudden and out of place feeling of calm washed over him the closer he got to the large exit of the tunnel.

The feeling of blissfulness became stronger and stronger as he got closer to the exit, and he was more inclined to skip than to walk. At one point, his head began to swim, just for a few moments, but to the point where he couldn't orient himself. He paused and thought he had almost blacked out for a second. From that moment on a soft breeze was on his face and the feeling of calmness and peace was the most intense. He didn't know it for sure, but he felt as if he had just passed into another dimension.

Finally, he reached the exit of the tunnel, and when he stepped into the light, he found himself standing on a green hillside with enormous mountains towering high above all around him. Mountains he had just traveled under, no doubt. He looked down from the mountainside upon a valley, green with forest trees and grass as far as the eye could see. In front of him he saw a path of dirt carved through the green grasses. He followed it with his eyes as it wound down the mountain and into a clearing in the forest. In the center of the clearing stood a large, fortified stone structure—a keep.

Then he saw something move in the distance. He covered the sun with his hands to help his adjusting eyes and saw the wizard Maub down near the keep, hunched over and shuffling as an injured person would. The wizard, who was far in the distance, went around the side of the stone structure and disappeared inside the keep.

"He got away." Aleric clenched his teeth and fists as frustration took over. "I will burn that thing down with him in it if I have to," he said as his eyes began to glow.

As he walked down the path to the keep, he wondered where he was and what lands he was in. He had traveled over the mountains to Briardale and Skerlin in the past, but he had never seen such a beautiful place as this. There was a peace about it. A feeling as if no one had ever stepped foot here before and all the animals lived harmoniously together. The sun was out, but it wasn't hot. There was a soft breeze, and it made a pleasant sound as brushed through the leaves and grasses of the forest. He also noticed the sky looked different than usual. It was a deeper blue, almost a purple color. And the mountains surrounding this valley were monstrous. Aleric didn't remember the local mountains ever being this towering. *It must just be my mind playing tricks on me*, he concluded, and maybe he had just never seen the mountains from this angle before. He knew where the portal was, based on stumbling upon it before, and he knew he had taken the tunnel opposite the one that led to Mazeron, so common sense dictated that he was somewhere on the other side of the mountains from his kingdom. Somewhere near Skerlin or Briardale. Still, this place was nothing like one he had ever seen or felt before.

To get to the keep he had to pass through a thick patch of forest and cross the valley floor, but he made the trek quickly. As he stepped out from the thick trees, he got his first up close view of the keep he had seen from the mountainside before. It was enormous. He gazed up toward the sky and marveled at its high stone walls. There were only a few windows very high up and no balconies or any other discerning features. Just thick, impenetrable stone walls. The odd feeling of bliss he had been feeling since he entered this land seemed to disappear as he approached the keep, and a feeling of darkness and dread settled over him, and seemingly the entire area around the keep.

"What is this place?" Aleric thought aloud as he looked for a better vantage point while trying to stay hidden near the woods. Then he saw movement in the sky, and far off in the distance a dragon glided lazily, high above the snowcapped mountaintops. It was calmly riding the wind with no particular place to be. But his attention to the dragon was interrupted when, out of the corner of his eye, he saw movement at the top of keep. Or at least he thought he saw something. He gazed upward, trying to protect his eyes from the sunlight and get a glimpse of what was going on. Then suddenly, a fireball came speeding toward him from atop the tower. He saw it and tried to escape, but it was coming fast. Instinctively, he took two lunging strides then jumped away and rolled behind a large rock just as the fireball exploded on the ground next to him. The blast of hot, dry air singed the hairs on his arms, and the smell of burnt hair wafted through his nose.

For a moment, The Paladin stayed behind the safety of the large boulder then peeked out from behind it. There, atop the keep, he could see the wizard Maub pacing back and forth, trying to gain a vantage point on him. Then The Paladin sprung out from behind the boulder and launched a fireball of his own, fast towards the wizard. But it hit the protective wall around the ramparts and caused no harm to the wizard or the keep. The wizard had the advantage of the high ground. There was no way for The Paladin to launch an effective attack from way down here.

Then another blast came at him. He dove back behind the boulder and rolled to cover just as the blast slammed hard into the boulder making a thunderous crack. The boulder exploded into pieces, exposing The Paladin, who quickly rose to his feet. He knew another blast was coming, so he immediately started to run. The wizard threw fireball after fireball at him, and The Paladin had to jump and roll to avoid each blast. He tried to return the attacks, but the height advantage of the keep was just too much to overcome. He could not hit Maub from down here. The only plan he could think of at that moment was to flee!

Rising back to his feet, The Paladin took off in a sprint toward the rear of the keep and the safety of the woods at the far end of the clearing. Dodging blasts of fire and lighting, he eventually reached the concealment of the woods and collapsed from exhaustion just inside the tree line. As he regained his strength, he gazed out from the trees and watched the wizard pace the ramparts of the impenetrable keep. Abruptly, the wizard stopped pacing and turned to face directly at him. The Paladin was too far away to see the wizard's eyes, but he knew the wizard was staring directly at him, waiting for the time to strike and taunting him from the safety of the keep.

But The Paladin was not going to engage in another unfair fight, no matter how much he hated and wanted to destroy the wizard. *I need to get some help*, he thought. He tried assembling a plan in his head to come back with the army of Brigands and catapults. Then it was decided. The wizard launched one more fireball at the trees for good measure as The Paladin slipped away and escaped into the woods.

Meanwhile, back in the kingdom of Mazeron, the army of once-brigands were now reunited with their leader Commander Rune and had their hands full clearing out the mess and destruction caused by the battle. Bodies of elves and brigands had to be carried away from the castle and buried. Ramparts and structures had to be rebuilt, and debris cleared out. The undertaking was massive and would take weeks at least. Commander Rune and his brother Visko were atop the ramparts surveying the damage and giving orders for rebuilding when suddenly two men came running up the stairs, breathing heavily and sweating. They approached him but could not catch their breath to speak.

"Speak!" Commander Rune barked. As he said it, he could see fear in the men's eyes, and his callous tone changed quickly. "What is it? What has happened?" he asked worriedly.

"Sir…" one of them finally spoke between gasps for air. He pointed east, still panting. "Beasts," he finally muttered.

"Beasts?" the commander replied. "What beasts?"

"Huge beasts, sir. Wandering the countryside. Coming this way."

"We were ambushed. They are so strong…so fast." the other man finally spoke. "Beasts like I've never seen before."

"They are the Morghvile," the other exclaimed with fear in his shaking voice, still trying to catch his breath. "The legends are true."

Suddenly they were interrupted by a bloodcurdling scream from out in the fields surrounding the castle. They turned to the tree line and saw the group of men who were digging graves on the battlefield now fighting a large animal. It pounced from one victim to another. One group ganged up on it with spears, but it seemed to swat them away easily before going for the others.

Commander Rune peered out over the field from the ramparts to try and better make out what was happening. The attack was quiet from here, but they could hear the faint screams coming from the distance. The commander did not waste any time. "Men!" he yelled, stowing his sword and beginning to run. "Get the horses! There is an attack on the battlefield."

Almost instantly, the nearby Brigands sprang into action, collecting their weapons and horses and quickly making for the battlefield. They rode hard and fast across the field, following Commander Rune into an unknown foe. In a matter of minutes, they were across the battlefield and slowed their horses as they came upon the scene. It was a bloodbath. Gore and bodies were strewn about, and a large black beast with the girth of an ox and head like a wolf was digging into the body of a fallen Brigand. It snarled its bloody teeth as the others approached, and they saw that its black eyes had no pupils or soul and was hollow and unremorseful.

"Kill it!" Commander Rune yelled from atop his horse. Immediately, the brigands were throwing spears at the Morghvile, but it would not go down without a fight. It was so fast that most of the spears missed it, and the ones that did hit it only seemed to make it angrier. The smart Brigands jumped from their horses and surrounded the animal, attacking it on all sides, confusing and outnumbering it. Many were bitten and wounded, but finally, the Morghvile was defeated. It lay there on the battlefield, wet with blood and sweat. Flies and bugs seemed attracted to it even before it was dead, and its thick black hair crawled with all different sorts of unpleasant bugs and insects.

"The thing is massive!" one Brigand finally spoke between heavy breathing as he wiped his forehead.

"What is it?" another asked.

"Nothing of this world," Commander Rune replied ominously. "It's from another plane. It is the Morghvile. Most likely the work of that infernal wizard."

"It took thirty of us to bring it down!" another Brigand said with dismay and worry.

Then out of nowhere, the air was filled with a horrific, high-pitched screech that pierced into the souls of all those who heard it. Commander Rune and the brigands winced and clenched their teeth in fear and repulsion at its horrific sound.

"It came from the forest!" Visko said, pulling on the reins of his horse. The others peered into the forest, their eyes darting back and forth, looking for any sign of movement.

"Well, don't just stand around!" Commander Rune yelled, jumping back onto his horse. "Get to the castle! Get inside the walls!"

Immediately, the group started back for the castle, racing as fast as they could with fear in their hearts as the horrible screech pierced the air again and again, getting closer and closer. They were halfway across the battlefield, halfway back to the castle, when Commander Rune turned around and saw the Morghvile explode into the clearing from the forest.

"Riiiiide!" he screamed out to the others. "It's behind us!" They rode like they had never ridden before. The horses galloped so hard it shook the ground as they approached the castle. Up the ramp they went as the monstrous beast gained on them. At the top of the ramp, they could see the rest of the army, eyes wide with fear and weapons in hand as the beast approached. "Get to the gates!" Rune screamed out again. "Close the gates!"

It was a good idea, but the gates had been exploded open by The Paladin during the great battle, so the large entryway remained open as they sped toward it, the Morghvile almost on top of them. Commander Rune, Visko, and the others raced through the open gates of the castle, but the Morghvile leapt forward and caught one of the brigands right before he passed through the safety of the gates. He was torn to pieces in just seconds, but it was enough time for the large group of Brigands waiting at the gate to launch a full attack on the beast. As it turned his attention to his kill, he was riddled with arrows and spears and soon collapsed to the ground, lifeless, right in front of the castle.

Commander Rune hopped off his horse and turned back, immediately giving orders to secure the castle. "Get those gates closed!" he yelled out as approached the dead beast.

"They gates have been destroyed," a man shouted back.

"I know!" he snapped. "Figure out how to barricade these walls." Quickly the men got to work, moving rubble and debris from the area. They found two largely intact pieces of the original gates and were soon rebuilding, hammering other pieces of wood together to make some sort of semblance of a gate to close off the castle's entrance.

As they worked throughout the day, more Morghvile wandered from the forests, and each one, upon seeing the men, was thrown into a sudden fit of rage and attacked. Each time one attacked, the ramp where the carpenters were trying to fix the gate would descend into complete chaos and madness as the soldiers fought and killed one after another. The plight was unsustainable, and at this rate the gate would never be rebuilt.

"Get out there on the field and hold them there!" Commander Rune yelled eventually. "Every one of you." He sent his entire army outside the safety of the castle walls to defend it. "Carpenters," he said with a worried look, "you really need to hurry."

The soldiers spent the day fighting the Morghvile beasts as the carpenters secured the gates. It was an efficient system, and the gates were almost completed.

The sun was setting low in the sky and the soldiers out in the battlefield were black silhouettes behind a bright orange sun, casting long shadows across the corpse-strewn battlefield. The last finishing touches were being put on the gates, and for a quick moment, Commander Rune felt like things might just be okay.

But that moment quickly changed. As the sun dipped lower, the air was pierced by yet another horrific scream. But this time it was not just one scream. It was followed by another, from a different end of the battlefield, then another, then another. There were dozens of them.

"They are calling to each other," one of the men stated in a shaky voice.

Commander Rune ran to the gates and out onto the ramp. "Retreat from the battlefield!" he called out. "Retreat!"

Soon, the entire army of Brigands was riding and running hard back toward the castle. The piercing screams were growing as the sun was setting, and the sound was now almost constant. Fear gripped the men's souls as they ran. There was something about the piercing screams that seemed to suck all hope from those who heard it. Still, driven by instinct, they ran for their lives back to the gates of the castle. Commander Rune stood just outside, shuffling the men inside one by one as they ran through. As the last of them gained the ramp and was safely behind the castle walls, he gave one last look to the battlefield. He had to squint, as the sun was low in the sky, but what he saw took his breath away.

It looked as if the entire tree line was moving. Black outlines headed right towards them. Hundreds of Morghvile were exiting the forest, coming right for the castle. "Have mercy," Commander Rune mumbled to himself in disbelief. "They'll overrun us all," he whispered, unable to move and gripped with fear.

"Commander!" Visko shouted, getting the commander's attention and breaking his thoughts. The commander snapped out of it and ran inside the gates.

"Get them closed!" he said in a panic. The carpenters and workers were already on it, but the gates were heavy and had been thrown together quickly throughout the day. Dozens of men pushed on each side as they slowly scraped heavily along the stone floors.

"Close it!" Commander Rune cried out again in a panic. He was standing back in the center of the two doors, and he could see that the herd of Morghvile was approaching fast. He knew that if even just a few got inside they would all be slaughtered. "Close it. Close it now!" he cried out.

"It's caught!" a man yelled. "It won't move anymore!" The first Morghvile were already at the bottom of the ramp when the commander rammed his full weight and momentum into the stuck door, breaking it free and finally moving it once again.

Then, with fear in their eyes from seeing the Morghvile and their viscous teeth and soulless orange eyes just a few arms lengths away, the men slammed the gates closed right on the Morghvile's snouts. Outside the gate, the monstrous beasts slammed heavily against the thick wooden gate, which jarred it open once again, just enough for one to slip through. Those who were able were on the Morghvile right away, and the whole group of them had it slain quickly while the others pushed all their weight on the gates until finally the crossbar was slammed into place and the gates were closed and secure. Commander Rune and the workers collapsed to the ground in exhaustion and relief. There was heavy pounding at the gate as the Morghvile outside tried to force their way in, but the crossbar was thick, and the gate was holding.

After finding the strength to stand again, the commander and his brother returned to the ramparts to survey the battlefield. The sun had dipped below the horizon now, but there was still just enough light to see. As they walked out onto the ramparts, their hearts sank. There were hundreds of Morghvile surrounding the castle. Snarling, drooling, and screaming their hideous shrieks. It was havoc and chaos all around. They watched as more and more wandered out of the forests and into the fields. The castle was besieged and the portal was still open.

"What can we possibly do?" Visko asked his brother solemnly. There was no hope in his words.

"The only thing we can do, my brother. Fight until our last breath. Just keep fighting." The two walked away from the hellish scene and Commander Rune gave orders for the archers and footmen to line the ramparts, because some of the creatures were able to fly and were becoming a dangerous nuisance as they swooped in and picked off soldiers one by one. "If the gate holds, those flying ones are the only ones we have to worry about for now," he explained.

Meanwhile, Brodel stood high atop one of the castles towers. Concealed from the flying beasts by the golden conical roof over his head, he spent the entire evening casting fireballs and lightning down onto the Morghvile below. One by one or two by two, he could pick them off, even though it hardly made a dent in the ever-growing number of them surrounding the castle.

Inside the castle walls, after a day of fighting, Lamora and Thearbuc held each other close while the fear of being devoured by beasts gripped over them. They felt helpless but found solace in the fact that they had each other in these final hours. But deep inside they both felt a small glimmer of hope. Somewhere out there was The Paladin. Maybe it was blind, false hope, maybe it was just comforting to think about, but something told them that as long as he was out there, they could still be saved.

Chapter 24: The Lake of Dreams

The day wore on as Aleric delved deeper and deeper into the unknown forest. It was unlike any forest he had ever been in before. It was so thick with large trees that the forest floor was almost black, and it looked as if it was dusk all the time. He would stop in the clearings and look to the sky but could see no sun or moon. The sky was not yet black but there were many stars in it.

"What a peculiar place," Aleric said aloud. Although it was darker than he was used to on the forest floor, he felt no fear but rather a constant pleasantness surrounding him. Still, the thought of being caught outside without any supplies in an unfamiliar place loomed over him, so he picked up the pace and continued on, deeper and deeper through the forest. Luckily for him, the path that wound through the forest was easy to see, indicating that it was well-traveled, which gave him hope that it would eventually lead to somewhere.

After many hours, Aleric noticed that the sky was still about the same color as it was before. It should be night by now, he thought to himself. He was exhausted. He had been making his way through the deep forests for endless hours by now, and still there was no change of scenery or sign of any civilization. In fact, this area of the forest looked pretty much exactly the same as the area of the forest that he was in many hours ago. Or was it many days by now? He shook his head, trying to stave off the tiredness.

"This forest is messing with my head," he said aloud as he continued on begrudgingly. Still, it was a beautiful forest, he thought to himself, one that you would read about in fairy tales.

Finally, the trek had become too cumbersome to bear, and he collapsed to the ground and leaned against a large tree. "I'm giving up for the day," he said aloud with a large sigh. He looked around the calm forest, trying to find any ideas for getting food and water for the night. He was mysteriously not hungry or very thirsty for having traveled so far. "I'll figure that out later," he grunted, then laid his head back against the tree and closed his eyes.

As he rested peacefully in the silent forest, his attention was suddenly startled awake by a sound. He opened his eyes and sat quietly, listening. He heard it again right away. It was the sound of singing. A beautiful woman's voice, far in the distance was being carried off by the wind. The song was high pitched and smooth and felt soothing and pleasant to his ears. His spirits immediately lifted at the sound of someone else here deep in the forest. He sprang quickly to his feet with a smile on his face and began to follow the sound. He went off the trail and into the thick forest brush toward the beautiful voice.

He went quickly, pushing aside large plants and foliage that grew thick on the forest floor, and the beautiful singing grew louder as he got closer and closer. Finally, he pushed aside the thick brush and stepped into a clearing of green grass surrounded by tall trees. There before him stood a large wooden cottage nestled deep in the forest.

The cottage was made of large wood planks, but over time the forest began to take it back, and most of the walls and roof were covered in green plants, grasses, and flowers, as if the cottage itself was part of the woods.

The singing was just around the corner, so he crept quietly around the perimeter of the clearing to see where it was coming from. Then, off in the distance in a clearing behind the cottage, he saw a woman.

She was waltzing through the grass, singing as she went. Aleric was frozen in awe at such a beautiful sight. He crouched at the edge of the tree line to watch for a moment. She seemed to float through the tall grass as she sang. She spun slowly and gracefully and made waving, flowing motions with her thin hands. She wore a long dark-blue dress that sparkled like magic as she moved through the sunlight. Her hair was light brown and cut short and curled inward just below her ears. There was a black sash wrapped around her thin neck that she threw playfully into the wind as she twirled about. Her voice resonated through the forests like it was amplified somehow, and her mouth would barely open and with ease an enormous and beautiful sound flowed out and envelope the entire forest.

The hair on Aleric's arm stood up as the music sent chills of happiness and awe through him. What a beautiful sight, he thought to himself, and wondered how any person could possess such talent and beauty.

Finally, he stepped out into the clearing and cautiously made his presence known to her. As he stepped out, she turned toward him right away. Then, as if she was floating, she came towards Aleric, still singing while holding eye contact. Aleric stopped in his tracks as she advanced.

"I knew you were there," the woman said softly, still playfully whirling and dancing as she moved toward him. Her voice was cheerful and upbeat, and Aleric was at ease even though he was in an unknown and odd situation. She danced and twirled toward him with bare feet then outstretched her hand to greet him.

"I am Solaris," she said as Aleric shook the ends of her petite fingers. She curtsied as she introduced herself. "And you are The Paladin, Aleric," she continued.

"How do you know who I am?" he replied, bewildered.

"I just do," she giggled playfully. "I know everything." Aleric was speechless and fumbled for words. "Follow me," she said, softly taking his hand and leading him toward the cottage.

As they rounded the corner to the rear of the cottage, he got his first glimpse of how large it actually was. It was the length of three regular cottages, and the back portion had no walls which made it look as if the cottage just blended into and was part of the forest. As they proceeded, Aleric saw many small children running about, playing in the trees and surrounding forest, happy and free. The sounds of their laughter permeated the air and brought a smile even to the hardened Paladin's face. There was also another woman there watching over the children. She gave Aleric and Solaris a soft smile as they approached.

"This is Amaris," Solaris introduced them. Amaris was tall and slender and had perfect pale skin. She wore a simple black dress that went down just above her knees, and she had her black hair up in a simple ponytail that bobbed playfully when she moved her head. Aleric noticed that both Solaris and Amaris were barefoot in the grass and wondered what kind of free and peaceful place this could be. Aleric glanced at the many children playing in the clearing and the surrounding woods. The sound of their playful laughter filled his heart and forced a calm grin.

"Where are the men?" he asked, gesturing toward the children.

"There are no men," Solaris said with a playful laugh. "It's just us here."

"We get them when we need them," Amaris laughed along.

After a pause, the two women said nothing further on the matter, so, bewildered as he was, Aleric thought about dropping the subject. But he needed answers about this odd, peaceful place.

"Are you two, uh, lovers?" he asked sheepishly.

"No," Solaris laughed. "We are mothers. These are the lost children of Mazeron," she said motioning toward the dozens of playing children. "Orphans who have lost their parents and children whose precious lives were cut short by the reckless decisions of your king and the subsequent tyranny brought on by Maub.

Solaris seemed unnaturally carefree, despite the subject at hand, and she began to dance and twirl her way into the clearing toward the children whilst humming soft music to herself. She found a small bird and outstretched her hand until it flew to her and landed on her finger. She brought the bird in close to her face and spoke to it as if she was speaking to a friend. Bizarrely, the bird chirped in reply, as if the two were having a conversation. After what seemed like a long, awkward moment to Aleric, Solaris finished the conversation with the bird, and it flew away. How peculiar, he thought to himself.

"What is this place?" Aleric asked. The questions were growing faster than the answers were coming, and he found himself more intrigued and confused than he was before.

"There is no name for this place. This place just…is," Solaris replied between humming notes aloud.

"How can it not have a name?" Aleric replied, beginning to lose some patience with the vagueness of the two women of the forest.

"Places don't have names," Solaris replied. "People give places names. Birds and the forests creatures do not give places names. We have not given this place a name. This place just *is*."

"The place that just is, huh," Aleric replied dryly, trying not to roll his eyes.

"That is what you can call it," Solaris replied softly and peacefully. "Would you like to hear a song?" she asked. Then, before he could answer, Solaris began to float upward into the sky with her arms outstretched until her feet were higher than Aleric stood.

He watched in awe as she floated beautifully through the air toward a large tree that seemed to have grown around a piano. He could have sworn it was not there before. Aleric shook his head like he was going crazy and told himself he just must not have seen it before.

As his mind wandered, Solaris floated down gracefully to the piano that the large tree had partially consumed. One of the older children was standing near it, and she kissed her forehead before sitting down at the piano and beginning to play the most beautiful music. Her fingers ran up and down the keys effortlessly, and Aleric watched in amazement. Just when he thought he couldn't be any more impressed, she opened her mouth, just barely, and the most beautiful voice came out and filled the entire forest with peacefulness and beauty.

The hardened Paladin got goosebumps along his arms again and wondered how it was possible that such a cruel world could create such a goddess. He watched her play for some time, as did Amaris and the other children, until his questions came back to him, then Aleric had to interrupt.

"No. No, please," he interrupted. "That was beautiful, but I need to figure out where I am and get back to my kingdom."

"Yes, you do," Solaris replied, changing her tone to as she stood up from the piano tree. "But first your quest lies farther away from your home. For if you go back now, you will have no home to go back to."

"What are you talking about?" Aleric asked, beginning to grow tired of the games and riddles Solaris seemed to speak in.

"We know of the wizard, Maub," Amaris chimed in. "We know of the gate he has opened and the Morghvile that spill from it."

"We know, and you know, that you do not have the power or magic ability to close it," said Solaris.

"Are you mocking me now?" Aleric replied dryly.

"Just stating the facts," she continued. "The facts are your kingdom is being overrun as we speak. The countryside is being ravaged by beasts from another world and the castle is under siege. Soon the Morghvile will find their way here, too, just as you did." Solaris paused, lowering her head.

"We need your help as you need ours," Amaris finally broke the silence. Aleric quickly began to appreciate Amaris's straight to the point style over Solaris's playful vagueness.

"A few beasts cannot overrun the strong kingdom of Mazeron," Aleric replied with a smirk. "Stop playing games with me. Direct me toward my home and I will be off."

"I will show you," Solaris said, turning and coming quickly towards The Paladin. Her sudden intense speed made him flinch and back up in fear. Still, she came closer, and she stopped just in front of his face and raised her hands. As she motioned her hands, a smoke-like fog and lighting grew between them. *Another portal*, Aleric thought to himself as he watched her magic unfold.

"It is not a portal," Solaris replied, reading his thoughts. "It is only a window." Through the smoke and flickers of light, an image began to appear, and Aleric was able to make out a large structure. It was the castle! He peered into the image as it became clearer and clearer. It was surrounded by large, horrible beasts.

"The Morghvile," Aleric whispered in disbelief. They stretched through the vast fields and countryside's. Fireballs and lightning strikes of magic rained down from the ramparts onto the beasts that were attacking the castle gates. "Brodel!" Aleric said alarmed. "That is Brodel!"

"The gates will not hold for long," Solaris said calmly. "And at this point, all other options have been depleted. You are their only hope. Our only hope as well." As she trailed off, Aleric noticed a pleading sadness in her eyes and a worry on Amaris' face as she lowered her head. Aleric sighed and looked at the ground feeling overwhelmed as he contemplated the heavy situation and the sadness that was washing over him.

"Okay," he said finally. "What can I do?"

Solaris closed the magic window with a wave of her arms then stepped back from Aleric. "There is a place," she said. "A lake, not far from here. This lake is the absolute far edge of this world and our plane. It is controlled by the spirits of another world that lies beyond, and its purpose is to ensure that none from this world cross through the veil into the other.

"The fairies?" Aleric asked. "I've heard of the tales."

"You can call them that if you like," Solaris answered. "But they are spirits. Neither living nor dead. They torment the living, and none who have stepped a mortal foot into their waters have ever come back to tell about it."

"And you think I can?" Aleric replied, almost laughing with a tremble.

"It is said that a strong mind with a good heart can enter the waters of the lake and return to tell about it," Amaris chimed in. Aleric tried to reply but was cut short by Solaris.

"Collect the waters from the Lake of Dreams, Paladin," she said, ominously. "The water from the lake has more power than any magic of this world. To ensure that no one can pass from one side of the veil to the other, the waters of the lake will douse and destroy all magic it touches. So, douse the portal with the waters of the lake and it will close." Aleric dropped his head as he listened, trying to absorb the information and what was being asked of him. He was to go to magical lake at the edge of the world, which was controlled by spirits of another, and somehow make it back, even though no one else ever had? He felt hopeless and defeated already.

"There is one more thing," Solaris said worriedly.

"What else now?" Aleric asked, rolling his eyes at the already nearly impossible task.

"The waters of the lake," Solaris continued. "As someone who possesses magic, if the waters touch you, it will kill you."

"How am I supposed to collect water from a lake without touching it?" He threw his arms up in frustration.

"Very carefully," Solaris replied softly, handing The Paladin four bulb-shaped, glass potion bottles with corks in the tops. "Just know that it if you choose not to go, then the ravenous Morghvile will overrun this world, and you will be dead anyway."

"Great pep talk." Aleric rolled his eyes as he took the four potion bottles from Solaris.

"We would love for you to stay the evening," Amaris said nicely in a more upbeat tone.

"But," Solaris interrupted, "time is not on our side. Your friends and the castle do not have much of it."

"How do I get to this mystical lake?" Aleric asked.

"Follow the path that I illuminate," she said, waving her hand outwards. As she did, a small trail opened through the forest. The nearby trees seemed to fade away into a ghostly outline, and the horizon opened up before him where he could see a long trail that ending at a large body of water. The only thing beyond the water was the horizon and stars. "Now you know the way," Solaris replied as the forest began to close back up and the magic wore off.

Aleric said nothing, and the forest was suddenly filled with a thick silence and feeling of dread. He thought about his friends back at the castle and the gruesome demise they would have if he failed to close the portal. He waited for Solaris or Amaris to speak again, offering some sort of hope or kind words. But instead, they, too, stayed silent and let the severity of the situation sink deep into Aleric's mind.

Finally, Aleric lifted his head and began to say goodbye to the two forest goddesses, Solaris, and Amaris. He had made up his mind that he would go and was instantly in a hurry to complete the task and save his friends. He nodded at the two as he stepped into the forest, following the path as they waved goodbye behind him, and in just a few steps into the thick forest, he could no longer see the women or the cottage. He paused for a moment. Trees surrounded him so thick it felt like they were hugging him. Claustrophobia began to creep in. He looked at the empty potion bottles one more time, then stepped forward and began down the long path through the woods toward the Lake of Dreams.

The day grew late as he marched through the thick woods. Just as before, the sky was difficult to see through the thick forest canopy, but when he did catch a glimpse of it, it was never changing—always the same light purple color, like the sunset was approaching, though it never did.

As the trek wore on, Aleric tried to keep his pace up, and a sense of urgency pulsed through him even though the peaceful forest surrounding him begged him to be at ease. His feet were screaming, his joints aching, his back sore from the long trek, and every bone in his body was begging him to collapse to the ground for a much-needed rest. But the thought of his friends and his castle under siege kept him going. He pushed through the pain and marched onward through the forest. It felt like the path went on forever, and he began to wonder if this was a trick to make him wander these magical forests alone and tired for the rest of eternity.

Finally, through the thick forests, he saw a soft blue light coming through the trees. He took one more step and his feet landed on soft sand as the trees seemed to disappear and give way to a new scene.

His jaw dropped as he gazed at the magnificent beauty surrounding him. The sky before him seemed to stretch on forever. It was purple and blue and filled with stars, and Aleric could see. swirling galaxies and moons and nebulas so magnificently large that he felt as small as a bug. The sky was so clear and open that it felt like he had left the world and was floating in the vastness of space. He reached out slowly toward the stars and felt like a god, almost like he could touch the faraway galaxies swirling above. Every fear and negative thought he had ever known washed away from him, and it felt as if gravity itself had ceased to exist.

He breathed a long sigh of calm as the peacefulness washed over and surrounded him. In an instant, all the worry and fear for his friends and kingdom had washed away. And although it wasn't possible, he thought he could stay here forever.

Almost gleefully, he took giant strides down the sand dune toward the vast lake and away from the forests. A cool breeze brushed across his face as he went. It didn't look much like a lake at all, as it reached all the way to the horizon and further. Massive galaxies and millions of stars sat on the horizon so clearly that it looked like they were sitting on top of the lake. Never had he seen such beauty.

Soon Aleric reached the shores of the lake and stood there for some time, marveling at the beauty surrounding him. Then he remembered the task at hand, so he bent down and slowly and carefully began to fill the glass potion bottles with the waters of the lake. Of course, being extra careful not to let the water touch his skin. *This isn't such a hard task*, he thought to himself as he started on the fourth potion bottle. Then, something appeared in the distance in the lake. A small dot at first which soon began growing in size and clarity.

"A boat," he whispered to himself with wide eyes, standing back up. In moments, the object was close enough to make out. It was, in fact, a boat, and it was coming calmly and steadily towards him. As it approached, he could see a single large red sail, which reflected brightly on the glassy calm water. It was not a large ship, but a smaller boat. Small enough for one sail to push. He could see there was someone on it. They stood motionless, staring back at him on the shore as they approached.

Finally, the boat arrived, and the bow pushed heavily through the sand in the shallow waters until it came to a stop just a few arm lengths away from Aleric and the beach. He could hear stirring on the boat and got a quick glimpse of someone's back as they secured the lines. Eventually, a woman emerged from the boat. She stepped towards the bow and made a playful laughing sound as she dropped a long plank onto the beach. Aleric recognized the laugh immediately, and he lit up with more excitement than he had ever known. In an instant he was running toward the boat, and as he got closer, he saw a smile that he could never forget. It was Briss!!

He ran up the boat ramp as fast as he could, narrowly missing the water as he bounded from the shore onto the plank, then rushed up it and leapt like a playful child into the boat. He grabbed Briss by the shoulders and their eyes met. In an instant, a lifetime of memories and happiness came back to him as he held her shoulders and felt her red hair brush across his fingers. She gazed into his eyes and smiled back at him, then he pulled her in close and squeezed hard, as if he wanted to imprint the feel of her onto his body, so he would never forget her touch again.

"I'm so sorry," Aleric whispered behind tears as he held her close. She wrapped her arms around him tighter as his eyes began to water. "Please don't leave me again," he begged. As they pulled away from the embrace, Briss gave her husband a soft smile and kissed him gently on the lips. The smell, the taste of her brought him back to when they were young and in love and frolicking in the orchards of Briardale. He could see in her eyes that she still loved him deeply, and in that moment, he realized that there was no better feeling in the world than a deep shared love between two people. “I didn’t want to let you go,” Aleric said, pulling her in once again. “I know it’s my fault. It’s all my fault. I’m sorry. I’m so sorry.” He collapsed to his knees in grief and happiness as she hugged him again.

Eventually Briss smiled again, then turned around and picked up the lines and swung the sail. Out of nowhere, there was a strong gust of wind and they were cast off from the beach and were sailing out into the open waters. A cool, comfortable breeze blew across Aleric’s face as they sailed into the calm and endless waters. He gazed from the front of the boat and scanned the horizon, the galaxies and stars seeming to surround and envelope them.

“This…” he said softly aloud. “This is my heaven.” A magnificent shooting star stretched across the sky above them, and as his eyes followed it back down toward the horizon and the bow of the boat, he saw that the small boat had turned into a large wooden ship. He gasped in awe as he stood at the large helm, seeing numerous large sails pushing them fast through the calm waters. He heard Briss’ wonderful laugh once again and turned with a smile to see her sitting near the starboard side of the ship at a small table filled with various food and drink. He went to her and sat down.

“I have so many questions,” Aleric said as he sat down next to Briss and grabbed her hand. She squeezed his hand gently and rubbed it softly, as she always had when she wanted to portray affection.

“The universe wants us to be together, but the world wants to tear us apart. But I think despite all that we both know we are destined to be together forever,” she said with a loving smile.

“I’ve always known that,” Aleric replied. “It is so hard to live without you. Every little thing reminds me of you. Every smell, every location in Mazeron brings back memories. I get excited about something, and my mind instantly wants to tell you all about it, even after all this time, but when I go to tell you, you aren't there. It's been so hard, Briss. I can't tell you how painful it is"

"I know," she replied. "It's hard to survive a love that's gone. But we are together now, and that is all that matters."

As the night wore on, the two fell in love all over again. Not only did they talk about old times, but it felt like they were reliving them all over again, and they picked up right where they had left off.

Aleric was consumed with a joy that he had never experienced as they sailed away past the edges of the world. The air was warm and calm, yet the sails were filled with wind that sailed them fast through the calm waters. He and Briss talked and laughed for hours, as if they had never been apart from each other at all. Or was it days? Or had it been weeks since they had left the world behind? He did not know and did not care. Time was a blur now, but he knew in his heart he could continue doing this forever. Time stretched on perfectly as they sailed away into endless happiness.

Unfortunately, Aleric had all but forgotten about the kingdom and his friends who were fighting for their very lives. It went unnoticed that the sight of land had disappeared past the horizon, and he was completely at the mercy of the Lake of Dreams.

One morning, or was it evening? Aleric awoke from a deep, peaceful slumber in the captain's quarters of the ship. He knew this place and even though his mind seemed cloudy about how long he had been asleep, he felt comfortable and knew this was his home. He knew Briss should be close by, but she wasn't there with him, so he got up from the bed, dressed, and exited the captain's quarters to search for her. They had been sailing on the open seas in a blissful existence for what felt like years. For as long as he could remember really. In fact, outside of the ship, there were no other thoughts or memories.

He stood by the helm for some time and let the crisp, morning air blow gently across his face as he stared out from the ship. He saw enormous, jagged mountains jetting up from the waters and towering into the sky just a short distance from the ship. As they sailed by the steep mountains, he could see snowdrifts and snowcapped peaks through the wispy fog of the cool morning.

Eventually, Aleric made his way back from the helm, down the wooden steps, and into the main area of the boat to find where Briss had gone. He turned about and suddenly the sky had gone dark, and he saw a warm, welcoming light and the sound of laughter coming from inside the belly of the ship, so he followed the steep steps down into the boat. Ducking his head as he went below the deck, he saw a long wooden table full of people eating, drinking, and being merry. There were cards on the table along with coins, lots of food, and wine. Their shadows danced happily across the walls as the lanterns that hung from the ceiling swayed back and forth with the rocking of the boat. Their laughter and lively conversation boomed throughout the hull of the ship, and Aleric couldn't help but crack a smile. There must have been a dozen or more people, none of whom he recognized except for Briss, who was sitting at one end of the table.

"Briss!" Aleric gave a large sigh of relief. "There she is," he mumbled aloud to himself as he made his way over to the large table.

"Sit down, friend," a stranger interrupted him as he approached the table. The man gestured toward an empty seat at the opposite end of the table from Briss and nudged Aleric towards it. Aleric looked over at Briss, hoping to find an open seat near her, and their eyes met, but she just stared back at him blankly for a moment. She gave no expression, then quickly turned her eyes downward, as if she had just glanced at a stranger in a crowd.

Odd. Aleric thought to himself as he was nearly pushed into his seat. Almost every memory he had was in the comfort of Briss' love then out of nowhere she was acting like she didn't recognize him or barely even knew who he was. Aleric's thoughts were quickly interrupted when another stranger slapped him hard on his back and threw a leather bag of wine into his arms.

"'Ere ya go, mate!" the stranger said with boorish loudness and drunken enunciation. The man was large with thick, hammy fingers and calloused hard hands. He had the unkempt stubble of a beard and reeked of stale smoke and wine.

By then the room had already erupted again in loud drunken conversation and laughter, and Aleric had seemingly already been forgotten about. He gazed at the people around the dimly lit, hazy room as he sipped his wine. The people seemed familiar, but he did not recognize any of their faces. Except for Briss and one other woman, they were all men. Almost a dozen of them. He listened and watched their mannerisms and noticed they were all loud, boorish simpletons who could barely put together an audible sentence. What a rough-looking crowd, Aleric thought to himself, wondering who these people were and how they all ended up here, and what in the world someone with as much class as Briss was doing with such a rough group.

The night wore on, and Aleric continued to sip his wine, trying to enjoy the gathering but mostly going unnoticed at his end of the table. He tried to strike up a conversation with one or two of the strangers, but his questions were mostly ignored until they slapped him on the back with hammy hands and shoved the bag of wine back into his arms. He also attempted to get up and make his way towards Briss multiple times, even though she never even glanced at him once throughout the night, but he would always be stopped by someone who would throw the wine bag back in his chest and begin telling bad jokes or stories Aleric wasn't the least bit interested in.

Deep into the night and through the haze of wine, the room had become even more lively, and most of the people had gotten up from the table to talk together in smaller groups or sing together with a man who played a stringed instrument. Aleric stumbled about; the effects of the wine were being exaggerated by the swaying of the ship. He wanted to talk to Briss but hadn't gotten the chance to get close to her all night. He saw her turn and leave one small group to walk toward another. Finally, he saw his chance and rushed over to her.

"Briss!" he yelled out excitedly as he reached her. She stopped and looked at him with a blank stare. As he advanced, Aleric opened his arms to embrace her, but after seeing her blank look he stopped short and stood in front of her. "Where have you been?" he asked. "I've missed you so much."

"I…Uh…" She paused and hesitated, but no real words came out.

A look of confusion came across Aleric's face. "What's wrong?" he asked with a hint of pain in his eyes. But Briss did not reply; she stared back at him blankly, like she didn't even know who he was.

"Um, I have to go," she eventually said flatly, then turned away from him and hurriedly disappeared into a group of friends, almost like she was scared of Aleric. He was left alone in the shadows with a group of people he did not know, none of whom would even acknowledge him. He stood lonely in the dark, staring at the ground and trying to wrap his head around what had happened. What was going on, and why had Briss suddenly decided to ignore him?

Soon, the wine began to make him feel heavy, like there was a weight was on his shoulders, and he could not keep his head straight. Slowly and with a feeling of defeat weighing over him, he went back to the stairs and climbed out of the hull of the ship and stood alone on the dark deck. There were no stars in the sky tonight, and the feeling of darkness hung over him like impending doom. Finally, he turned and walked back into his captain's quarters and fell heavily onto the bed.

Morning came again and Aleric once again woke up alone in his captain's quarters. He didn't know where she was, but he knew Briss should be there by him, and she wasn't. A dark heavy feeling hung over him as he wondered why she wasn't there with him. Every morning for as long as he could remember she had woken up next to him, so he knew there must be an explanation for why this morning she was not there. He got dressed and exited the captain's quarters and slowly made his way up to the helm of the ship to get his bearings. The helm was tied off and no one was steering the ship. A cool breeze bit at his face as tall, icy mountains jetted out of the dark waters just yards from where the ship sailed. He saw snowcapped mountain peaks and snowdrifts through the fog as they sailed by.

"Have I been here before?" he thought aloud as a feeling of deja vu swirled through his mind. Everything about this morning seemed familiar: the mountains, the air, the feeling of dread pulsing through his veins as he wondered where Briss had gone to.

After scanning the deck of the boat and seeing that he was alone, he began to wander about the ship. Slowly and methodically, he wandered the deck, then went down below into the dark belly of the ship. He looked behind barrels and boxes in the dank darkness and scoured every bit of the ship but eventually found that he was the only person aboard, so he returned to his captains quarter's with an even more intensified feeling of dread and loneliness.

The next morning was the same. Then the next and the next. Day after day, he woke up alone and searched the ship for Briss only to find he was alone in a sea of emptiness and loneliness. Every day he woke and wondered if this was the first day since he had seen Briss or the hundredth day. Some days he had memories of her appearing on the ship but not acknowledging him. Or were they just dreams? Vague, dark, cloudy memories of people he knew from his past being on the ship in a group with Briss but never acknowledging or welcoming to him. Other days he would see shadows of someone through the fog, but when he ran to them, they were gone.

This seemed to go on for ages and the heavy despair that pulsed through him was growing and growing. There wasn't much left of him at this point. He would wander the deck for months at a time, wondering how long he could go on like this while secretly wishing for the sweet release of death and nothingness.

Finally, one day, while standing near the helm of the ship gazing out into the emptiness of the fog, he turned to see someone standing at the other end of the deck. It was Briss! She was facing away from him, motionless and gazing off into the emptiness of the foggy sea. A feeling of hope rushed through Aleric's body, and he ran quickly to her, bounding across the deck with large strides. When he got to her, he grabbed her shoulders and swung her around fast, then quickly pulled her in and embraced her with a long and hard hug.

"I've been looking everywhere for you!" he said as he hugged her tightly, pulling her in close and taking in the familiar smell of her soft hair. "Please don't leave me again," he begged.

"You're hurting me," Briss said in an angry and annoyed tone as she pushed him back and stepped away from his embrace. She folded her arms and took a step away, looking at the ground and avoiding eye contact as she did.

Aleric looked her up and down as the feeling of hurt came rushing back. "Why are you turning away?" he asked with a trembling voice. But Briss did not answer. She stood like a shy deer and kept her distance from him. Her arms were folded, and she stared at the ground, avoiding all eye contact with Aleric.

Normally, he towered over Briss, but in that moment, he felt small and helpless. It was more pain than he could control, and despair quickly turned into anger. He grabbed Briss' shoulders and shook her in frustration.

"What has happened to you!?" he cried out and pleaded. But she did not reply. She looked up at him with sad eyes that met his and held the gaze. For just a moment, Aleric felt a glimmer of hope, some happiness stirring deep in his stomach. But it was quickly doused as Briss broke the gaze and began staring at the ground once again. Aleric pushed her away by the shoulders in frustration. "I hate you!" he screamed. He was filled with a rage and anger that had been building, and without thinking about it, he began to yell a slew of hurtful, mean words at Briss. The insults came spilling from his mouth like bile as he tried to provoke a response from her. Any response at all. Horrible things he didn't mean or want to say came spilling out in an attack of frustration, loneliness, and anger. "I wish I had never met you!" he said multiple times. When he was done ranting, he paused and waited for Briss to say something. Anything...

The two stood in silence on the foggy deck of the ship for some time. Her gaze was fixed safely on the ground, away from his angry stare. "Are you done?" she asked snidely with a hint of annoyance. Aleric was taken aback and could not even find words to reply. How could someone who loved him so much at one point act so indifferent and uncaring to him? He raised two trembling hands to the side of his head, then, looking defeated, he slowly backed away from her. She turned slowly from the rails of the ship and began to walk away.

"I'm sorry!" Aleric cried out, falling to his knees. "I didn't mean any of that!" he said, filled with despair. Briss did not look back as she slowly walked away, and he collapsed to the ground on his hands and knees while tears trickled into the corners of his eyes. "Give me one more chance," he begged. "I'm lost in this world without you. You are part of who I am," he sobbed, choking on tears. Briss faded into the fog, a gray shadow that could barely be seen. "It's so lonely without you," he whimpered. "So lonely."

Finally, Briss stopped and turned back toward him. He could barely make out her face through the thickening fog. She glanced back, and for the first time in what seemed like ages, she had a show of emotion on her face. Aleric looked up with begging eyes. Begging for any sign of adoration from her. But the look she gave back was only one of sorrow, and her lips curled into a frown as if she, too, was trying to hold back tears.

Aleric's mind raced and he could almost feel the words *I'm sorry* coming out of her mouth, which he so badly needed to hear. *Just say it*, he thought to himself as she held her gaze. *Just say you're sorry and come to me so we can be one again.* He begged the universe to make it happen. There was nothing he had ever wanted so badly in his entire life.

But the words did not come. The look of sadness was all that Briss gave him, and it lasted for only a few moments before she turned and walked away, fading into the thick fog and leaving him utterly alone in this vast emptiness once again. Aleric collapsed completely to the ground, sprawling out along the cold wooden deck while tears flowed from his eyes. He was utterly defeated. Never had there been such a broken man living through such despair, and he knew that there was only one thing left to do. He knew he could not wander this lonely existence forever.

Eventually, Aleric attempted to muster the energy to climb back to his feet. The world was heavy on his shoulders, and any movement at all was tiresome, almost too difficult to accomplish. But finally, on one knee, he pushed as hard as he could and stood back up on two feet again. He slowly shuffled his heavy feet toward the railing of the ship. Every step was agonizing, and the air felt so heavy and thick that it would not go into his lungs, making every breath difficult and painful.

Finally, he came to the thick wooden railing of the ship, and putting his hands upon it, he leaned heavily onto it. He gazed at the slow-moving, dark waters below, barely able to see it through the thick fog surrounding him. "I just want peace," he mumbled to himself as he wiped the dried tears from his face. Thoughts of how the world had turned so cruel to him whirled through his mind, and he tried to think back on how he had ended up here in such a dark predicament. Finally and without making a conscious effort, his mind went completely blank. For the first time in as long as he could remember, he felt a glimmer of peace.

"I just want peace," he mumbled aloud again. And that was the last thing he would ever say. He let loose his grip on the railing and leaned his head forward. He felt the weight come off his feet as his body flipped over the railing. The weightlessness of falling from the ship was a welcome change to the heavy burden he had been carrying for so long, and he floated in a blissful thoughtlessness for his last moments. When he hit the water, everything went dark.

As his body slowly sank into the darkness of the sea, the spirits that kept this place watched from their plane with a rare, deep sadness. This was not a feeling they were used to, and toying with mortals who dared venture into their side of the veil was usually a welcomed pastime. But for some reason this time was different.

"He has suffered enough." One being transferred a thought to other nearby spirits who were also watching The Paladin's suffering. The sentiment was acknowledged by the others.

A millennia had gone by when Aleric was thrust back into the pain of consciousness. Born again, he found himself lying face down on a beach in the sand. Slowly, he pushed himself up onto his hands and knees. Rubbing his blurry eyes, things began to become clear again. Behind him was a forest; in front of him was a vast lake. Millions of stars blanketed the sky above, even though it was not the black of night.

"I know this place," he mumbled as his thoughts began to come back to him. The Lake of Dreams, he thought to himself. It was all coming back to him. Including his memories of Briss and the realization that he had lost her for good once again. He broke down into the heaviness of the grief.

"Glad to see you made it back," a soft voice arose from seemingly out of nowhere. He looked up with blurry, watery eyes to see the forest goddess Solaris kneeling down on the beach next to him.

"What in the…" he trailed off trying to find the words to describe the heavy despair that was bearing down on him. "What in the world was that!?" He managed between gasping breaths.

"That was the lake," Solaris replied softly, trying to comfort the distraught paladin.

"Why? Why does it hurt so much?" he asked, squeezing a fist of sand in pain and anguish.

"Because it was real," she replied rubbing his back. Your love for each other was real and no matter what else happens in this life, you had it. You shared and experienced it together. Even a catastrophic cosmic event cannot take that from you; for it happened, and it is yours to treasure forever."

Slowly the grief started to fade away as Aleric realized where he was and the memories of the lake started to become more distant.

"The kingdom. My friends!" he said aloud.

Suddenly, his memory was coming back, and he scrambled to find the satchel of potion bottles that he had flung around his neck after filling them. But the satchel was gone. He felt frantically around his neck and chest, but it was not there. All of this trouble and anguish for nothing? Then he turned, and lying on the beach just a few feet away, there it was. He scurried towards the satchel and opened it frantically and clumsily. Inside were four bulb-shaped glass potion bottles, all filled with soft, blue glowing water. He had done it! He had returned from The Lake of Dreams with its magical waters. He sprung to his feet with newfound energy and brushed off the despair from what seemed like an eternity on the lake.

"How long have I been gone?" Aleric asked quickly.

"You have been gone only one day," Solaris replied.

"A day!" Aleric said, confused. "How is that possible? How…I mean—How can that be?

"The lake is mysterious," she said calmly. "You are lucky you made it back at all," she said it with a smirk.

"I've got to get back to Mazeron. I need to get to the well!" He turned and began running up the beach, but progress was slow in the steep, soft sand.

"Take my horse. His name is Felanador," Solaris offered and gestured down to the beach. Near the forest line there was a brown horse quietly grazing on the tall grass. Aleric looked at her with a thankful expression upon his face.

"He won't run when you go to him, Just hold tight when he rides. He is a fast one," Solaris winked as she said it. "There is also a full set of sturdy armor in the large sack near him. You'll see it."

"Thank you!" Aleric yelled back as he was already making his way towards Felanador. Aleric strapped on the armor quickly then hopped onto Felandaor with ease, and in just moments they were off. As they sped away into the forest, he gave only one look back and promised himself that no matter what happened in his life, he would never return here to The Lake of Dreams.

Chapter 25: Wizard's Last Stand

Leaping and bounding through the forests over fallen trees and large rocks, Aleric atop Solaris's horse Felanador raced back toward the keep and the opened portal that was spewing deadly beasts into the lands of Mazeron. Aleric held as tight as he could and let Felanador do the steering, as he was the easily the fastest horse he had ever been on. He grabbed the reins tight, tucked low near his neck, held tight, and hoped for the best. Every so often he would take the risk of letting go of the reins with one hand to tap the satchel at his side to feel that he still had possession of the magic waters from The Lake of Dreams.

"Still there," he said aloud, crouching back down low near Felanador's neck. He could hear him breathing heavily as he sped through the woods at a continuous and fast cadence. Never slowing down or speeding up, he was the most focused and fast horse Aleric had ever known. Finally, they burst through the heavy brush and back onto the main road through the forest. Aleric breathed a sigh of relief that he instantly recognized this place and knew they were on the right track, back toward Mazeron. There was only one problem. There was still the keep, guarded by Maub, the powerful and evil wizard, and the large dragon guarding the mountain pass back to the portal and the tunnels that led back to Mazeron. But he would have to deal with Maub and the dragon when the time came, for there was no time and nothing he could do to prepare.

They sped through the forest and somehow Felanador never seemed to tire, even after what felt like miles upon miles of strenuous galloping. As they rode, Aleric noticed again that the day never grew later or darker in this forest. It stayed a peaceful evening constantly. *I'd like to come back to these magical lands,* Aleric thought to himself as they rode, and he wondered what other playful creatures called these lands home. But soon his thoughts were broken as he began to smell smoke in the air. He looked around and noticed he couldn't see far through the trees. As they continued on, the smoke began to thicken and build around them, so he stopped and dismounted Felanador, threw the reins around a tree branch, and walked through the forest to investigate.

As he walked, the smoke grew around him, engulfing the forest, and it began to burn his nose and throat. He covered his mouth with his shirt, but it did not help much. His eyes burned and he began having trouble seeing. Then, through the thickness of the smoke, he began to see flames through the trees ahead. Enormous, tall trees and brush were on fire. Others nearby them had already been scorched black and slowly smoldered as the smoke was carried away by the soft breeze.

Then, from somewhere in the distance, Aleric heard a thunderous clap and boom. It echoed through the forests, making it difficult to figure out which way it had come from. Still, he kept to the road, advancing ever more towards the keep. Finally, pushing through smoldering brush and trees, he got to a clearing on a hill overlooking the keep. He made his way off the road, through the trees, then hid behind a large rock and peered out from behind it.

What he saw was mayhem. The entire forest surrounding the keep was on fire or had been on fire and was already destroyed. The sky was blood red from the sun trying to shine through the thick smoke, and the flames of burning trees licked upward to the sky. Then he saw movement from atop the keep. "Maub!" Aleric whispered to himself. Suddenly, a large fireball shot from atop the keep and blasted into the forest, exploding and setting fire to multiple trees in the distance.

"Is he really going to burn down the entire forest just to find me?" Aleric said aloud, bewildered and disgusted. Another fireball exploded in the distance, coming from atop the keep, nowhere near where Aleric was concealed behind the rock. It was clear the wizard did not know where he was hiding, or the blasts would have been directed at him. Aleric continued to watch the scene unfold, surrounded by an apocalyptic hellscape as the forests around him burned and smoldered and the wizard shot out blast after blast.

Then all of the sudden a large shadow rushed over Aleric's head. Silent and sudden, it came and went in an instant. He jumped as it came across him and quickly turned his head to the sky to see what it was, just in time to see a large dragon swoop down toward the keep, then level out, flying fast above the trees. The dragon was focused. Its head was straight like an arrow as it sped toward its mark. Then abruptly it opened its mouth, and a volcanic-like eruption came forth. Spewing fire and flames, it strafed the forest and in a magnificent display of power it destroyed an entire section of the forest in just mere moments. Aleric watched in fear at the amazing power of the animal. He slumped heavily behind the rock, holding his chest and panting, trying to catch his breath. Behind him, the dragon gracefully flew high, back into the sky and began circling around. It blocked out the sun as it passed, scanning the forests for his next attack.

Aleric closed his eyes hard and clenched his teeth, wishing he was anywhere else besides in this situation with seemingly no way out. He could smell the sulfur from the dragon's breath wafting through the wind. A very distinct smell compared to the rest of the smoke that surrounded him. It was that smell of sulfur that instilled the most fear in him. Dragons from a distance were almost mythical and didn't seem real. They usually stayed far away from humans. But here, close enough to smell it, it became very real. An emotionless, unthinking, powerful animal that was ready to scorch anything it saw moving in the forests below into oblivion.

"I've got to get out of here," Aleric mumbled to himself. The urge to flee came over him powerfully. He knew there was no fight here and nothing left to do except run. He sprang from his hiding place behind the large rock and dashed into the forest without any further thought. He hadn't made it more than ten steps when a blast of heat suddenly exploded near him, sending shrapnel and bits of tree and dirt into his face with a rush of dry heat. Maub had seen him. His stomach lurched knowing he had been found out by the wizard, but hope grew with every step further he took into the forest. One more step, one more tree between him and the powerful wizard until he was far enough away to be safe from the wizard's blasts. But not safe from the dragon.

Finally, Aleric got back to Felanador, who was patiently waiting for him. He was peculiarly calm considering the area was filled with burning smoke and flames. He untied the reins and hopped on fast. He knew he couldn't stay here, and the dragon would be swooping down from the sky at any moment to decimate this area of the forest and him too if he didn't move fast. There were no options, he thought to himself, as Felanador swayed back and forth while he tried to decide which direction to go. It only took a moment for his mind to be made up. "We can't stay here. We can't go deeper into the woods and outrun a dragon," he thought aloud to himself. The only option was to charge toward the keep. Get closer to danger and hope that they can outrun and counter the wizard's attacks well enough to get to the concealment of the cave on the other side of the valley. "It's the only option," Aleric said aloud, reassuring himself. He patted his satchel to check that the glass containers of magic water from the Lake of Dreams were still there and intact.

Then they were off, darting fast through the burning forest. The trail ahead of them grew more difficult to see due to the smoke and flames growing around them. Felanador was magnificently fast as they burst from the burning forests and down into the valley to the keep where the wizard was lying in wait. Among the chaos, Aleric glanced up toward the sky. No sign of Maub! Luck was on their side, at least for the moment. The wizard either had his attention directed toward the other side of the keep or had given up his attacks and gone back into the belly of the large stone structure. Either way, they had a head start, the element of surprise, and speed on their side.

Soon the trail leveled out at the bottom of the hill, and they raced past the keep, far too close to it for comfort. So close that they rode through its shadow. Still no sign of Maub. They raced on, getting closer and closer to the other side of the small valley. Aleric could see the trail in the distance ahead of them, leading upward back into the burning forest and concealment of the trees.

They had almost made it past the shadow of the keep when the first blast hit. A booming explosion crashed behind them and threw hot air and rock debris in their direction. Aleric felt the rocks ping off of his armor and Felanador jumped at the explosion with a newfound speed that burst them forward. Aleric felt the sound of the wind blowing harder across his face as they gained speed. He must be the fastest horse alive, he thought again. As they sped adjacent to the keep, another blast hit near them, then another, and another. But they were too fast, and Aleric kept Felanador zigzagging to throw off the wizard's aim. Blasts from the wizard landed and exploded all around them, blowing pieces of the forest apart but missing the horse and its rider.

Finally, they reached the other end of the gulley, and the trail began to climb up once again—back to the well and opened portal where Aleric could cast the magical waters of the Lake of

Dreams and close the portal for good. His determination grew with every passing step as fireballs and blasts crashed around them, until eventually they found themselves finally out of reach of the wizard's attacks, the blasts landing far behind them and safely out of range.

Aleric slowed Felanador to a stop, and they slowly turned to look back at the keep and the chaos of the burning forest around it. He could still see Maub in the distance, standing silent and motionless staring at them from atop the keep. Aleric waved his hand at Maub in a gesture of defiance, then with a big grin on his face he turned and began to make his way up the mountain trail and back to the cave.

As he rode up the trail, getting closer to the burning tree line of the forest, unexpectedly a great shadow passed overhead, and before Aleric had the chance to look up and see what it was, an enormous roar exploded from the skies and filled the valley with a horrible and powerful boom. It was the roar of the dragon.

Immediately, Felanador reared up in fear and threw Aleric hard to the ground. His heart jumped and he was filled with anxiety after the fall, and he frantically felt for the pouch carrying the magic waters to make sure the bottles hadn't been broken. He patted the satchel and looked for water, then took a long sigh of relief when he found they were unharmed. But the relief did not last long as he gazed up into the sky to see the large dragon at the other end of the valley circling back around to make its way toward him. Aleric looked for Felanador, but the last he saw of him he was racing into the forests, fleeing from the dragon's roar. Aleric hopped to his feet quickly and began to run, but he found he could not. The fall had injured his right leg, and he could not make a full stride. He could only hobble as quickly as possible toward the tree line and back into the concealment of the forest.

He could not help but glance over his shoulder again and again as he slowly but frantically made his way toward the woods. The dragon grew from a small dot in the distance to a large monster on the horizon in only a matter of moments. Aleric glanced back at the trees, then back to the dragon again. He knew he couldn't make it. And even if he did make it to the tree line, there wasn't enough time to hide or find concealment from the dragon's rage and fire.

The dragon was too close already. Aleric gave up hope of outrunning and hiding from it and stopped in the center of the trial, frantically reaching for anything to fight with. He drew his sword. *How am I going to stop a dragon dozens of feet above me with a sword.* he thought to himself, releasing the handle. Then he felt the satchel and the glass bottles of magical waters from the Lake of Dreams. "Not much of a shot, but still a shot," he mumbled aloud, frantically trying to get the bag open as the dragon flew silently closer and closer. It was almost bearing down on him now, and he could see the red eyes and stained teeth as it opened its wretched mouth, readying it's interior furnaces for the attack.

Then, without any hesitation, The Paladin with glowing eyes hurled a glass potion bottle of the magical waters at the flying beast with inhuman strength and speed. Just as the animal was opening its mouth, the gas churning and igniting inside, the bottle smashed into one of the dragon's teeth and exploded the magical waters from the Lake of Dreams across its face and into its mouth. The beast reared upward in reflex, motioning away from the attack and bellowing out a horrific and loud roar of pain as it flew high and away from The Paladin. The Paladin turned and followed the dragon with his gaze, wondering and watching what would happen. And what was happening, he could not understand. It started at the face where the magical waters struck the dragon. The dragon appeared to be disintegrating right in front of The Paladin's eyes. Large teeth and scales turning into a pink ash-like substance that blew away in the wind.

The Paladin watched in amazement and confusion as he could not understand why magical waters from the Lake of Dreams worked at destroying the dragon. But it did either way. Was the dragon a mirage, created by a spell from the wizard Maub? Are dragons magical creatures that would be destroyed by the waters of the lake? Or were they normal animals but used magic to spew incredible amounts of fire from their mouths? It didn't matter, in the end, to The Paladin. He watched as the dragon, unable to control itself, flew frantically toward the mountains slowly disappearing into the wind until what was left of its body ultimately crashed hard into the side of the mountain and exploded into a magnificent fireball. He watched in awe as the glow of the explosion illuminated his face.

Then he heard a powerful yell coming from behind him and turned to see an enraged Maub blast another fireball at him. Aleric turned and sprinted to the concealment of the forest and looked back to watch the fireball explode harmlessly in the distance. The wizard was in a fit atop the keep. He haphazardly threw fireball after fireball to explode harmlessly in the forest, then Aleric slipped quietly into the trees, leaving the wizard in a fit of rage, far away atop the keep.

Meanwhile, back in Mazeron, the castle was still under siege by the violent and viscous Morghvile. The last three days of defending the castle had been exhausting for everyone, and there wasn't much left to give. Commander Rune and his brother Visko tried to keep the troops fighting in shifts so they could all rest, but there was always a new attack that called all hands to defend the walls. The soldiers were almost out of arrows and had already exhausted every trick and trap they had to keep the creatures back from castle's gates.

Brodel had been their saving grace, barely sleeping and using every ounce of magic he had to keep the Morghvile at bay. But even he was now showing signs of giving up. His movements were slow, his body hunched over like an old, crippled man. His black hood covered his face, and he would not turn around to speak to anyone. But his hands were visible, extending from his cloak, and they were old and withered like that of an old man's. Finally, he had nothing left to give. His magic and strength depleted, and he collapsed atop the ramparts, hunched against a wall. Thearbuc, who was fighting nearby defending the castle gates, took immediate notice of the sudden quietness as the fireballs and lighting strikes from Brodel ceased. Him and the men paused and looked to the sky at the sudden onset of silence. There was a pause…

Then abruptly, the large wooden gates of the castle burst open as the weight of dozens of Morghvile slamming against them was finally too much to hold and whatever protection spell Brodel had casted had failed along with his strength. Thearbuc thrust his sword forward, stabbing one deep as many rushed the castle grounds and began choosing their victims to gnash and gnaw. The archers from the ramparts did what they could, firing arrow after arrow down at the Morghvile, but there were just too many and the arrows quickly ran out.

"Retreat!" Commander Rune cried out with a booming voice the moment the doors broke. Everyone that could, began fighting their way back to the castle as the courtyard and grounds were soon to be overrun. Thearbuc fought like a madman as he made his way back from the failed gates. Lamora was fast and agile, hurling over beasts and striking them with her dagger along the way. She dove and slid under others, cutting their bellies. They ran for their lives surrounded by death, watching the less fortunate be torn apart and devoured by the sharp teeth and claws of the Morghvile.

Brodel, still slumped over on the ground, watched from the ramparts above. He peered over the edge under his black cloak, unable to even move his head. He had done all he could, but in the end, it wasn't enough. He watched as the grounds and courtyard below began to fill with the beasts now pouring through the open gates. He closed his eyes; it was only a matter of time now.

Back in "the land that just is," smoke burned Aleric's lungs as he ran up the burning trail. Fire and smoldering trees surrounded him, and his eyes burned as he squinted to see the trail through the smoke. He was exhausted and had almost nothing left to give, but still he pressed on in hopes that he could close the portal in time and save his friends and the kingdom.

Finally, through the smoky haze, he could see the mountain not far in front of him. He followed the trail with his eyes and there in the distance, not far off, was the opening to the cave. His heart leapt with joy as he could finally see something tangible for all his recent battles and hard work. He was so close now. The weight of the armor and fatigue seemed to wash away with newfound energy, and he sprang forward faster and faster until he stood at the entrance of the cave. He turned to give one last look at the burning valley. No one was following him that he could see. He could see the outline of the keep far in the distance through the smoke but no sign of Maub. He turned quickly and rushed into the cave.

The air immediately grew stagnant and heavy within the stone walls, and the light depleted quickly until he stood in the darkness with the heavy air surrounding him. Suddenly, The Paladin's eyes began to glow, and a small orb of illuminating light appeared in the palm of his hand to light the way ahead. He continued on with hurried steps, making his way through the winding tunnels of the mountain. They twisted and turned back and forth, sometimes turning one direction in a tight circle, making him think he was almost there, only to quickly turn the opposite direction and continue winding through the mountain. Thoughts of anxiousness filled his worried mind as he went. Am I in the wrong place? Did I miss a tunnel? Am I lost? Is it too late already? His mind raced as he rushed through the caves.

Finally, he turned a sharp corner and burst into the room where the portal was. He leaned back and his feet skidded in the dirt to a stop, and he immediately fell backwards and lost his breath at what he saw.

There in front of him was the opened portal. Hovering over the stone well, it illuminated the room with a dancing blue glow and made a loud and constant roar. In the center of it, black and gray smoke swirled about. Aleric's mind raced at what horrible lands could possibly be on the other side of the swirling veil of the rift. But that is not what made him slink in fear against the back wall, trying to make himself as small as possible.

There, across the room, was another creature. Not like the Morghvile he had seen before. He knew this mythical creature instantly as the Rabisu. It stood on two strong, human-like legs and had large, leathery wings like a bat extending out of its back. It had two sets of long, lanky arms with sharp claws at each end, and unlike all the different Morghvile beasts he had seen come from this cursed portal, it did not have any fur on its body.

Aleric peered from across the room and watched the Rabisu. He could not see its face, as it was facing away from him, frantically scratching, clawing, and digging at the wall of the cave. In a frantic fit, it was flapping its wings, raising itself off the ground to claw at the walls, then dropping back down to the floor. Shrieking and clawing at the cave walls, it was a horrific scene to behold, and Aleric wondered what it wanted so badly that it was frantically attacking the walls when the other cave exit was just feet away.

As dangerous as the mad creature seemed, he did not seem to notice or care about Aleric, so Aleric turned his attentions back towards the task at hand: closing the portal. Keeping a close eye on the horrifying looking Rabisu, he carefully reached into his satchel to pull out a bottle of the magical waters from the lake. His fingers fumbled around the bag in the darkness, and he felt their round glassy shape but could not get a good grip on one in the dark. Then, one of the bottles clanked against another in the bag, making an audible sound. Aleric clenched his teeth, closed his eyes, and held his breath in anticipation. Maybe the Rabisu didn't hear it? He waited a moment longer, then slowly unclenched his fists as he heard it continue clawing at the stone walls. So far, he had not been found out. He reached back into the satchel, more carefully this time, and firmly grabbed one of the bottles and pulled it carefully from the bag. He held it in front of his face and noticed that the light blue water glowed softly in the dark. He remembered the color of the water in the lake, and the memory of the everlasting nightmare came flooding back to him.

He tried hard and put those thoughts out of his mind and contemplated the task at hand. *How do the magical waters work?,* he wondered. He had three potion bottles left, so he concluded he would toss one into the portal first just to see what happens, then he could deal with the horrifying creature in the room afterwards.

He left the satchel where it was then crept a good distance from the portal, remembering what the forest goddess had told him about how dangerous the waters of the lake are to a magic wielder like himself. He crept quietly so as not to be heard, and when he was close enough, he reared back and hurled the glass bottle hard and fast into the portal. It disappeared into the black, smoke-like substance and immediately the portal began to flicker and roar like a loud fire being stoked by an intense wind. There was no going unnoticed now. The Rabisu quickly turned from its frantic attack on the cave walls, and without any hesitation, it flapped from the far end of the cave to the other in one bounding leap and came crashing down on Aleric, who was still trying to draw his sword by the time it was on him.

They impacted with a loud clang to the floor as the ground and beast crashed into The Paladin's armor. He raised his arm in front of his face and the Rabisu began violently gnawing at the metal gauntlet, so far unable to bite through. Aleric used the distraction to his advantage and with his other hand landed a heavy punch to the creatures face, pushing him off.

They both rose to their feet, The Paladin's eyes glowing with rage and the Rabisu already moving fast and frantic with another attack. As the Rabisu approached, The Paladin swung his sword quickly, but the beast was faster, and without warning, quickly took to the sky with a simple flap of its wings, dodging the sword and landing a counterattack on The Paladin with its large, clawed feet. Its claws were so strong that it picked The Paladin up from the ground, ripped through his metal armor, and threw him into the back wall of the cave. He hit so hard the world almost went black, and the dazed Paladin slumped over in pain. Trying to keep conscious, he saw the creature coming at him again, already preparing for a third attack. With a last effort, he threw a fireball from his left hand and slumped over to the cave floor. The small fireball was all he could muster up, but it was enough to scare the Rabisu off, and it retreated to the far end of the cave to keep a distance until it assessed what new threat The Paladin posed to it.

From the floor of the cave, The Paladin reached out and grabbed another bottle from the satchel. The portal was still flickering and roaring but had not closed yet. The viscous Rabisu was circling, waiting for the right moment to attack, and The Paladin knew that moment would come soon. He knew he was defeated, and he couldn't hold its attacks at bay any longer. Then, with the last bit of strength he could muster, he hurled the potion bottle at the stone base of the well, this time not being careful if the waters splashed back on him or not. The glass bottle shattered against the stone and splashed wide across the portal and its base just as the Rabisu made its attack. From across the room, it leapt high again and came down on The Paladin. Its gnashing teeth were just inches away when the portal exploded into a bright blue ball of heat and energy, blasting the creature to the other end of the cave and smashing it hard against the cave wall. The Paladin watched as it hit the wall and fell to the floor. Then suddenly, everything went completely dark.

Back at the castle, all hope had been lost. Brodel still laid slumped on the ramparts and watched from above as all different types of the Morghvile beasts piled into the castle grounds and filled the courtyard, ripping and shredding any person they came across. He saw Thearbuc and Lamora reach the castle and get inside, and his heart felt a small amount of joy that they might be able to live another day if they could keep the beasts out of the castle. Still, another day or two is all they could hope for. The castle was besieged, and at best, they would run out of food and slowly starve inside, as the entire land had been overrun by the horrific monsters. He closed his eyes and waited for the end. There was a calmness about it as he waited for it. He was ready.

Then suddenly, out of the terrifying screams and loud roars of the Morghvile came a large boom that jerked his eyes opened and hurt his ears. It was so loud that it filled the skies and echoed so hard that he felt like he had been hit in the chest. He pushed himself up and peered out into the fields surrounding the castle, looking for what might have caused the enormous boom. Far in the distance, coming from the mountains, he saw a large blue shockwave moving quickly toward the castle. It violently shook the trees as it raced through the kingdom, and as it approached, Brodel clenched his teeth, closed his eyes, and plugged his ears. It blasted across them hard with hot wind and came with another enormous boom that shook the castle walls as it hit.

In a second, the shockwave had come and gone, and Brodel felt the tower walls slowly sway back and forth. Then the air was filled with horrible shrieks and screams. Brodel peered down into the courtyard and saw that all the Morghvile were in a frantic frenzy, rolling violently on the ground, screaming in agony until they began to fall over and cease to move. It was like they were being deprived of air, he thought to himself. Quickly the wizard rose and looked off at the mountains in the distance. There was a blue cloud of smoke rising high into the sky above the mountains. "Aleric!" he whispered. The Paladin had closed the portal, and somehow, the life force that was coming from it was cut off and the beasts were being choked out.

Inside the castle, Thearbuc and Lamora were waiting for the beasts to explode through the doors to consume them when they, too, were shook by the thunderous boom and the subsequent screams of death. There was a pause as an odd silence settled over the castle. No one expected it to be true, but soon all of the beasts lay lifeless on the ground. The soldiers took turns stabbing the downed beasts, half expecting them to all get back up and continue their attack on the castle. But alas, there was no movement from any of the beasts. They were all dead.

Out of nowhere, the silence was broken by Commander Rune as he roared out in victory, stretching his sword high into the sky. His roar was so loud it was almost inhuman. It was inspiring, and everyone's hearts were filled with great relief, and the roar of victory filled the air as everyone raised their weapons to the sky in triumph.

Back in the cave, Aleric lay on the cold ground in complete darkness. He knew he should be getting up to deal with the creature that was still in the room, but he was too tired to care. He lay in the thick silence and did not move for some time. Then eventually, he heard the sound of something scuffling across the floor. He forced himself to sit up and conjured a small glowing orb in the palm of his that illuminated the cave, then he reached for his sword and thrust it outward.

"Hey, hey!" a scared voice yelled out. Aleric's eyes adjusted to the darkness until he could make out the shape of something about the height of a child standing in front of him. It was Sophie the Stone Gnome! He stood at the far end of the cave, near the scratch and claw marks on the cave walls from the beast. His little golden buttons on his overalls reflected the small magical light that illuminated the cave.

"Sophie?" Aleric replied. "What are you doing here?"

The Gnome sheepishly walked to the center of the room. His little legs and feet shook as he came closer to Aleric.

"Oh, Paladin," he finally said with a shaky voice. "The monsters. You should have seen them. One by one they come after Sophie. Want to kill Sophie, they do."

"Was that you he was clawing at behind the walls?" Aleric asked, looking at the lifeless body of the dead Rabisu, his wings strewn across the cave floor. Sophie nodded his head; The Gnome was still scared. "The beasts are gone now, Sophie," Aleric reassured him.

"The wizard," the Stone Gnome spoke up again. "The wizard brought them."

"Indeed, he did," The Paladin nodded, his eyes glowing bright.

"The wizard is still out there," Sophie continued.

The Paladin paused. "I guess he is," he said in his ominous and inhuman voice. He reached across the floor and picked up an old torch that had fallen from the wall and lit it. As the fire illuminated the room, his eyes began to dim and returned to normal.

Sophie shook his head and fumbled at the buttons of his overalls, clearly scared and nervous, shaken to the bone from witnessing the beasts emerge from the portal day after day. “He will open the portal again,” Sophie started again. “The wizard. Bring more trouble to Sophie. I know it.”

“I can’t defeat him,” Aleric lowered his head as he said it. “Maybe if we assembled the army and came back?” he said, thinking out loud. He knew even with an army it was a long shot. The keep was too high and strong to breach, and the wizard was too powerful.

“Sophie knows a way,” he interrupted quickly. “Trust Sophie. Come with Sophie.”

Aleric squinted his eyes and studied The Gnome. “You would help me?” he asked. “Is this a trick?”

“No trick! Sophie knows no tricks,” The Gnome replied.

“Ha!” Aleric chuckled. “I remember your tricks.”

“No more tricks!” Sophie snapped back. Aleric began to remember how The Gnome was socially inept to say the least, and impatient to boot. “Sophie wants the wizard gone. Sophie doesn’t want that again. Sophie has someone to protect.”

“You do, huh?” Aleric said standing back up, still not fully trusting The Gnome. Sophie turned away shyly and grinned. “A girl?” Aleric asked. Sophie’s cheeks turned red, and he kicked the dirt.

“That is Sophie’s business,” The Gnome finally mustered. “Follow me.” The Gnome hurried forward, and without saying anything else, he grabbed Aleric’s hand and pulled him toward the nearby wall. Aleric raised his hand in reflex as he almost slammed his face into the cave wall but stepped forward and right through it.

“Oh yeah,” he mumbled to himself, remembering The Gnome’s natural ability to move freely through stone.

“You want to see what Sophie can show,” The Gnome continued as he led the way through the mountain.

In just minutes, they were through the mountain and standing on the foothills again. It was nighttime now and the large moon illuminated the mountains and surrounding forests. It was a calm night, the fires had all gone out, but the hills were dotted with red ash from the burnt trees. The keep stood tall and powerful in the distance, a dark black shadow that ascended into the star-filled sky.

"Follow Sophie," The Gnome said as the two began their way back down the trail toward the keep.

"I'm not going down there," Aleric stopped short.

"Must trust Sophie," The Gnome said, getting annoyed again. There was a hint of desperation in his voice, and he was still shaky from what had transpired in the cave.

It took a moment, but Aleric decided to trust him. It wouldn't make any sense for The Gnome to be on the wizard's side. Or would it? "Okay, Sophie," Aleric said finally. "I will trust you. But if you betray me, I will string you up by your feet and use you as a punching bag."

"No one is nice to Sophie," the melancholy Gnome stated as he began to march forward, pouting.

The two descended down the trail. Aleric kept a very close eye on the keep, watching for any sign of the wizard in the shadows. But the keep seemed motionless and empty. So far, no sign of the wizard Maub.

Finally, Aleric and the Stone Gnome stood along what was left of the tree line and gazed at the keep towering in front of them.

"This way," Sophie said, taking Aleric's hand and stepping into the clearing.

"What are you doing?" He jerked back. "We'll be seen!"

"Trust Sophie. Remember?" The Gnome snapped back.

"So demanding," Aleric rolled his eyes as he said it. "Well, we've come this far," he said, throwing his hands up.

Aleric took The Gnome's hand and stepped into the clearing, and the two crept quietly up to the keep then around to the far corner. Sophie looked up at The Paladin. His eyes twinkled in the moonlight and his face was blank from emotion.

"What?" Aleric whispered.

Sophie did not reply but turned and faced the large stone wall of the keep, then he yanked Aleric's arm hard and pulled them both into the wall of the keep. Aleric tried to pull back, but it happened too fast. In an instant, they stood in an almost pitched black room. Aleric felt loose gravel on his feet. There was almost no light, and Aleric couldn't see his hand in front of his face. He waved his free hand and conjured a small orb of light to illuminate the room.

The first thing The Paladin saw was thick metal bars surrounding him. Two walls of jail cell bars, and behind him, two stone walls of the keep. Panic gripped The Paladin after discovering where he was, and he held The Gnome's hand hard so the little sneak could not slip away from him and abandon him here.

"A dungeon!" he said angrily. "You are trying to trap me in a dungeon! How could you?"

"No, no, no," Sophie said, trying to pull his hand away. "You're hurting Sophie!" He pulled again on his hand. "It's not like that. Sophie promised."

"Then what is it like?" The Paladin whispered angrily in the dark. Soon there was another voice that came from somewhere in the darkness.

"Who's there?" the voice called out. The voice was old and hoarse. The Paladin stood motionless and waited. It did not sound like Maub. "Who is it?" the old voice came again. "We know you're here."

"That's what," Sophie spoke up. "Follow me." He pulled Aleric's hand, and they began to move forward into the darkness. The small orb of light and the little Stone Gnome guided the way.

Then, out of the darkness, shapes began to form. At first they were shadows, then a group of men, leaning against the dungeon bars and sitting on beds of hay. He knew immediately these men, whoever they were, were prisoners of the wizard Maub and more than likely not a threat.

One man rose from the ground and slowly hobbled toward The Paladin and The Gnome. "Who is there?" the old man said as he came into view. Aleric peered through darkness at the man. He was very old, his eyes droopy and sad. A long gray beard flowed down past his chest and was ratty and unkempt. The man's voice was labored and shaky, and he coughed after he spoke. His eyes lit up as he stepped closer and was able to see The Paladin in the soft glowing light.

"A knight?" the man asked, looking over his armor. Then his eyes landed on the soft glowing orb of light in his hand. "No…" he said. "A Paladin!"

After he said it, more of the imprisoned men began to come forward. All shabby and tattered but all in peculiar clothes—long robes, pointy hats, and once bright-colored scarves now dinged with the color of dirt. Aleric stepped back as the odd-looking bunch came toward him.

"Who are you?" he asked, taking a step back.

"We were once wizards," the old man replied with dry raspy voice, motioning at the others. "Now we are just prisoners. I don't even know how long it's been," the old man drooped his head as he said it, almost as if he was ashamed. Aleric looked over him as the man spoke. There was something familiar about him, he thought to himself. Then the man reached his arm out as if to introduce himself. "What is your name?" he asked. "My name is Barreston. And these are the Brothers of Smoke and Orb." As he motioned, Ehvsund and the others came forward out of the darkness.

As he said it, Barreston looked The Paladin in the eyes and they each held their stare for a moment as they shook hands. Barreston held his gaze as if he was studying The Paladin.

"Tell me, Paladin," he asked curiously, pulling his hand back into his tattered robes. "How does there come to be a magic user such as yourself in these lands?"

"I don't…" Aleric paused. "I don't really know. I just found it out." He shook his head, trying to make sense of the situation. "Sophie, why did you bring me here?"

"Wizards!" the small Gnome replied, motioning toward the peculiar group of prisoners.

"I don't see your point" Aleric whispered back as he lit an old torch that had been cast aside and was lying on the ground.

"Who is causing all your problems?" Sophie snapped back, already losing his infamously thin patience. "A wizard!" he said, throwing his hands into the air. Aleric looked back at the small Gnome blankly. "Who can help you defeat a wizard?" Sophie urged. "Many wizards!" The Gnome threw his head back and his hands into the air as he said it. "You'd think your mind would be bigger than mine," he said, stomping as if throwing a small tantrum.

"You're right!" Aleric replied. "Sophie, you are a genius!"

Aleric turned back to Barreston and the group of peculiar prisoners. "We need to get you guys out of here. Quickly, make a line and hold each other's hands. We all need to be connected to Sophie for his magic to work. Aleric grabbed Barreston's hand and instructed the others until they were a long line of at least ten odd-looking wizards. Sophie waited by the stone wall until they were ready, then Aleric grabbed his hand as well. "We're ready, Sophie. Take us out," Aleric whispered. "Everyone, be quiet until we are clear of the keep."

Sophie the Stone Gnome turned and looked up at the tall, dark wall. He motioned his hands in front of his face while mumbling something under his breath, then was gone. Aleric's head swam and the world around him became cold as he was pulled into the rock behind the Stone Gnome. Then, one by one, the wizards slipped through the stone walls until they all stood outside. The fresh, crisp air surrounded them, and the moon and stars shone bright above. The imprisoned wizards took a deep, unbelieving breath of the fresh air and stared at the magnificence of the sky above. Some fell to the ground and rubbed their hands through the plants and grass. Although they were quiet, they were not completely silent….

"We need to get out of here," Aleric whispered. In the darkness they crept away, back toward the trail that would lead them into the forests and far away from here.

Then there was a faint crashing sound coming from inside the keep behind them. A faint glow randomly appeared in one of the tower windows. A candle had been lit. Fear rushed through Aleric and his wide eyes met the others, who were frozen, waiting to see what would happen next.

"Run!" Aleric announced and began sprinting toward the trees. The group of old wizards followed him, but they were slow and beaten by time. They were halfway to where the trail touched the mountain when suddenly an explosion of fire hit the ground behind them, sending heat and rocks hurling toward them. The light of the blast illuminated the shapes of wizards scattering around the keep.

A great yell rose up from behind them as Maub realized what was happening. Then blast after blast rained down on the area surrounding the keep. One blast hit too close to one of the wizards and he was blown aside like he barely weighed anything. Hearing the screams of the men he just attempted to save made Aleric's heart sink and stomach lurch. *What have I led them into?*

The thoughts rattled through his head, wrenching his stomach as he tried to think of a way to get the old wizards out of this mess.

Then Aleric, who was in the lead, quickly veered off the trail and motioned the others to keep running forward. “Head to the trees!” he yelled. He launched a fireball back at the keep. It exploded just below Maub and sprayed ash and fire up at the wizard. But Maub had the high ground, and Aleric knew he could not score a direct hit on the wizard. The best he could do was just buy some time.

Quickly, The Paladin jumped and rolled aside as a blast was returned directly at the spot he had fired from. The blast gave away his position, but he had no other choice. He had to distract the wizard until the others were able to get away. The Paladin threw another ball of energy at the keep, then moved before it even hit its target. Blast after blast was exchanged until The Paladin felt the others had made enough distance between themselves and the keep. Quickly, he turned and sprinted up the trail, heading for the trees.

As he ran in the darkness, the cool wind nipped his face, then a rush of smoke would pull the air from his lungs as he passed a burning tree. For a moment, the world became silent again except for the sound of his heavy breathing as he ran closer to the concealment of the thick trees. The attacks from Maub had also stopped for some reason. But that was just as alarming as hearing them, Aleric thought to himself as he ran faster and faster into the darkness. Finally, Aleric caught up with the others at a high point on the hillside, almost even with the height of the keep.

“Has he given up?” Aleric asked, stopping short of the others, trying to catch his breath.

“Maub never gives up,” Barreston replied with a cough. “We need to keep going.”

As he said it, a sudden boom filled the air and shook their chests as the shockwave of it passed through them. They turned to see a great ball of light shooting quickly toward the sky. It rose, and rose, and rose. Almost as if it was going to leave the atmosphere of the earth itself and continue on into the vastness of space.

“Oh no,” Barreston said, his voice shaking and his battered face illuminated by the blast. “We need to get to cover.”

Barreston was already moving up the trail before he even finished speaking. The others were quick to follow. They ran and ran as the ball of light blasted high into the night sky. Then, the entire forest was illuminated with a blinding white light and a thunderous boom surrounded them, so strong that it pushed the trees forward as the blast came to them.

They looked up to see an enormous explosion had taken place in the sky, and balls of fire began to rain down on them, extending out like a giant willow tree.

"The cave is just ahead!" Aleric pointed at the cave entrance, just a few dozen yards away now. The forests surrounding them were now brightly illuminated by the incoming balls of fire that were already beginning to rain down on them. "Run!" he yelled out again.

The group of wizards shuffled as fast as their old bodies and long rags would let them. They lost another one along the way as a ball of fire rained down on him and hit like a falling meteor, sending his old robes up into a frantic moving ball of flames.

Finally, Aleric reached the cave entrance, and he turned back to escort the survivors in just as the world outside became engulfed in flames from the sky.

No words were spoken as the group turned and fled deeper into the cave, farther away from the wizard Maub and his enormous attacks on them and the surrounding lands. They followed The Paladin's orb of light, twisting and turning through the caves until they finally reached the large room where the portal once was, and Aleric stopped and slumped to the ground, leaning heavily against the cave wall, exhausted from the flight from the keep.

The wizards all followed, dropping to the ground, trying to catch their breath. One nearly sat on the corpse of the dead beast and let out a shriek so loud that everyone jumped back to their feet ready to flee again. Then the room lit up as Aleric lit a nearby torch on the wall. "It's dead," he reassured them, lighting another torch. The wizards inspected the gruesome beast, as they had never seen anything like it before. Barreston examined the deep scratches into the stone that the beast had made.

"What has gone on here?" he turned to ask Aleric with worry in his eyes. "This is not of this world."

“You are right about that,” Aleric replied with a slight chuckle.

“But how?” Barreston replied. He was deep in thought about something when his eyes met the stone pedestal behind where the portal had once stood. His mouth dropped and his eyes bulged open.

“The book,” he whispered in disbelief. He scurried to it, his arms outstretched like he had seen an old friend after being apart for years. He grabbed the large book and stared at the pages with wide eyes and disbelief. He began turning the pages, scanning them quickly before turning to the next page.

“Tell me, boy,” Barreston said excitedly. “Did that beast there, did it come from a portal of sorts?”

“It did,” Aleric replied, seemingly upset. “It almost killed me. The portal was right where you are standing. In fact, it almost got the entire kingdom killed!” he said raising his voice. “Why do you seem so excited about it?”

Barreston ignored Aleric’s anger and raised voice. “It works,” he whispered to himself. “Amazing.”

“It’s not amazing, it’s dangerous,” Aleric replied. “That book needs to be destroyed.”

“Destroyed!” Barreston shouted, changing the tone of his voice and coming back to reality. “This book is our key to defeating Maub,” he said excitedly.

The other wizards came forth and began to gather around Barreston. “That book only contains half the spells,” one of the wizards said as they approached.

“Ah yes, indeed,” Barreston agreed upsettingly as he closed the book with a loud snap.

“He can’t be defeated. He’s too powerful,” Ehvsund, Barreston’s old friend, said hopelessly.

“And he’s held up in that keep,” Aleric added. “It’s a fortress, and our Stone Gnome has run off. Not that we’d want to go back into Maub’s domain again anyway.” He threw a small pebble at the wall in frustration as he said it.

“Let’s just go home,” Ehvsund said, turning to Barreston.

“With Maub still out there?” Barreston questioned in disgust.

"Maybe he'll just leave the kingdom alone," Aleric interrupted. "He's been wounded, the beasts are defeated. Let him rot in his fortress."

"The ignorance!" Barreston snapped at Ehvsund, then turned and shuffled quickly towards Aleric. "We have spent over twenty years with this madman. We know him better than anyone." As he said it, he leaned in toward Aleric, getting closer and closer, his eyes wide with madness. "He does not rest, he does not waver, he does not falter, and most importantly HE DOES NOT GIVE UP!" he bellowed in Aleric's face. "He will follow us to the ends of the earth." Barreston's voice was booming off the cave walls. "He will not stop until we are destroyed, the kingdom is destroyed, and he is the most powerful wizard on the earth, controlling all the lands and people as he pleases." Aleric pulled away and tried to interrupt as the old wizard unleashed the facts onto him. "No, boy. I'm sorry to say it, but we must destroy the wizard Maub or be destroyed trying." After the outburst, Barreston slowly turned away and dropped his head as he walked back toward the book and other wizards.

"It is hopeless," Ehvsund said sadly, resting his hand on Barreston's shoulder.

"It would appear that way," Barreston replied, looking at the others with a deep sigh.

They were all tired and needed rest, and more importantly, needed to think about their next move as to not be trapped by Maub again the moment they left the caves.

Eventually Barreston spoke, finally breaking the long silence. "Tell me, boy. How is it that you came to have magic and can use it freely in these lands? Last we knew, every magic user was being arrested or had disappeared. Did your dad have the gift of magic? Or perhaps your grandfather?" Barreston studied Aleric closely as he replied.

"Not that I know of," Aleric replied. "I have only recently discovered my magic ability."

"Odd," Barreston replied, deep in thought. "Usually, magic users pass their abilities down from generation to generation. Not common for you to have it and not your ancestors," he said, trailing off in thought.

Suddenly, the group's silence was interrupted by the sound of footsteps echoing through the chambers and stone caves. It was coming from the far cave, the one that led to Mazeron. Aleric jumped to his feet and drew his sword while rushing towards the cave entrance. Barreston and the other wizards crept forward, ready to attack or be attacked by whatever came through the corridor.

Then, as plain as day, they heard a voice. "I can see a light ahead," it whispered.

Aleric knew the voice instantly. "Thearbuc? Is that you?" He was already making his way toward the corridor when Thearbuc's bright white smile behind his dark black beard appeared in the doorway.

"You're kidding!" Aleric went toward him. "I know this man," he said to the wizards, motioning them to put their sticks and rocks down. Behind Thearbuc were Lamora and Brodel. "You're all here!" Aleric couldn't hide his excitement as he embraced them one by one. He grabbed Thearbuc's shoulders to look him over. "How did you get here?"

"We just followed the smoke," Lamora replied with a smile. "There was a large explosion coming from this area just a day ago. We thought it might be you, so we rode toward the lingering smoke. It led us right to the area where we exited the mountains coming back from Skerlin, and then we found the entrance wide open."

"Must have been blown open from the blast," Thearbuc chimed in. "A large rock, hidden behind some bushes, took us into the caves that led us straight here."

"Are you okay?" Lamora continued.

"Yes, yes, we're fine," Aleric replied. Then he turned to Brodel. He was covered by a black cloak, so Aleric could not see his face, but he knew him from his staff with a blue glowing orb atop it and his height and stature. "Brodel, my friend. Thanks for coming for me." Brodel very slowly reached out toward Aleric and patted him softly on his shoulder. Aleric could see his hands were old and withered, like an old man's hands. Brodel did not speak. Aleric knew why.

"We will never forget what you did for us," Aleric said with a smile. "You saved us all. You were the only one who could defeat Maub."

"Almost defeated," Brodel said in an old, raspy voice from under the dark hood.

Aleric turned towards the other wizards. “These are my friends.” He gestured. “Thearbuc, Lamora, and the powerful wizard Brodel.”

The other wizards paid no attention to Thearbuc and Lamora but began slowly surrounding Brodel. All speaking together in hushed whispers, they made their way across the room and began discussing something away from the others.

“I guess we’re not in the cool wizards club,” Lamora chuckled, looking at the peculiar group of mismatched wizards all huddled in a circle. Some of them were examining Brodel’s staff and orb. Barreston and Ehvsund were slowly flipping through the pages of the large book. Barreston was combing his fingers through his disheveled beard, deep in thought. Then, the wizards congregated together again until eventually they approached Aleric, Thearbuc, and Lamora, who were having their own discussion at the other end of the cave.

“Well…” Barreston announced. “We have a magic staff,” he said, pointing to Brodel’s staff. “We have the magical power and ability.” He gestured toward the group of wizards. “We have half of the book of Abborell.” He held up the large book from the podium. “But…we only have half of the book. The other half could be anywhere. Maub could have it, or it could have been lost to the world decades ago.” He lowered his head, as if defeated as he said it. “We just don’t have the power to defeat Maub. We figure the best we can do is go into hiding. Probably flee these lands.”

“What, and wait for him to come after you one by one?” Aleric interrupted angrily, waving his hand at the wizards like a parent scolding their child.

“We need the other book of Abborell,” Barreston replied, trying to explain.

“Would this book be very large, about this tall, and resemble that book?” Lamora asked pointing at the book on the stone pedestal.

“Indeed, it would,” Barreston replied. “The spells inside these books are so powerful that they were split into two books, to keep any one person from having sole power of them.”

Lamora’s eyes instantly lit up. Lamora had stolen the book from Maub on the balcony of the castle and fled with it.

"Do you still have it?" Brodel said with as much excitement as an old man could muster.

"I have it! It's in the satchel on my horse!" Lamora was already heading towards the corridor as she said it. She ran toward the cave exit and was gone.

"Is this true?" Barreston asked Brodel. "Can it really be that we can reunite the books of Abborell right here and right now?"

"I believe so," Brodel said slowly while nodding his head under his dark hood. Faint sparks of magic lifted slowly from his shoulders and popped a few inches into the air as he said it.

"I've never seen so much magic radiate from one wizard," Barreston said, grabbing Brodel's hunched shoulder. "Amazing."

Soon they heard footsteps again as Lamora returned, this time holding a large leather-bound book with magic markings stamped across it. The wizards glanced at her book, then at the one on the podium, then back at Lamora again.

"It can't be!" Barreston said, rushing toward her. "You have it!" Barreston quickly pushed the first book aside and sat the second book of Abborell next to it. They both fit perfectly on the stone podium. He took a moment to find matching pages, then intertwined the pages and pushed them together. The books began to glow a soft purple light as the pages came together.

The others gathered around as he flipped from page to page, half pages and half spells coming together as one. There were dozens of them. Fireball, ice fall, transformation, confinement, numb tongue, hypnosis, undead, and of course, open portal.

"I still think it would we swell to do this one and create an enormous limestone pyramid in the desert. Largest mausoleum ever!" Ehvsund said with a chuckle as they flipped through the pages, remembering the pyramid spell from the first time they looked through the books.

The pages of the books were weathered and wrinkled. "He must have memorized some of these," Aleric announced. "That's how he was able to open portals so quickly." The others nodded as Barreston flipped through pages of different horrific and magnificent spells.

"There!" Aleric pointed his finger to a sketch of what looked like an exploding sun and mushroom cloud of explosion.

"That's the one we'll use. Blow the keep to pieces with him in it." The other wizards nodded and grunted with agreement.

"It won't work," Barreston replied.

"How is that?" Aleric asked, taken aback.

"You don't know Maub like we do. Brute force will not be enough to destroy him."

"Well, it's a good place to start," Thearbuc chimed in, defending Aleric, who was already picking up the large books of Abborell and turning to make his way towards the exit of the cave.

"We do it now," he said with eyes starting to glow.

Some of the other wizards began to follow Aleric, along with Thearbuc and Lamora. Amongst all the commotion, Barreston motioned to Brodel and Ehvsund, who both stayed behind while the others shuffled out of the room. Lamora saw them whispering to each other in the dark corner of the cave as she exited.

.

Not long later, Aleric and the other wizards exited the cave to find themselves on the hillside overlooking the keep once again. This time the scene was horrifying. The earth had been scorched from Maub's last stand at them escaping. All the trees and brush were scorched. Black, smoldering earth filled the entire valley, and nothing was left alive as far as any of them could see. Smoke lazily rose into the air and burnt their eyes and lungs as it surrounded them. Lamora was taken aback at the destruction as she entered this side of the mountain for the first time and saw such a bleak scene. There before them, towering above the smoke and burnt landscape, was the keep.

"What is this place?" she asked, instantly noticing the sky was not like anything she had ever seen.

"It is the place that just is," Aleric replied.

Lamora rolled her eyes. "I'm not in the mood for riddles," she replied. Aleric shrugged as if he didn't know what else to say about it.

Finally, after a long wait, Barreston, Ehvsund and Brodel appeared from the cave and joined the others on a flat spot on the hillside where the other wizards had laid the magic books of Abborell down and had begun making a circle and joining hands around it.

"Nice of you to join us," Thearbuc announced as they exited the cave.

"Where were you?" Aleric studied them closely with as they replied.

"Just a little slower than you young lads," Barreston replied as he joined the others.

The wizards did not waste any time after that. Maub could spot them or be nearby for an ambush at any time. They needed to cast the spell then escape as fast as possible. One by one they observed the keep for a moment. No movement, no sign of Maub. Then they quickly joined hands together around the books of Abborell and began to chant. Aleric stood with Thearbuc and Lamora at a distance and watched with wide-eyed amazement. He had never really been in the company of many magic wielders. He had never been a part of a secret society or group of like-minded people. He admired the professionalism of it all, like they all knew exactly what to do and when to do it.

"We'll need your powers too," Barreston announced, looking up from the book and toward Aleric. "Every bit helps if we're going to bring down that fortress."

"But I don't…I don't know how to do spells," he replied, shrugging.

"It doesn't matter," Barreston answered. "You don't need to say the spell with us, just bring your power. Come now…" He smiled as he said it and Aleric felt a quick sense of belonging and warmth that he had never felt before.

He walked toward the wizard and the opening in the circle they had made for him. His eyes began to glow as he approached. In the center of them, the books of magic glowed a bright purple and illuminated all their faces. He joined their hands, and they closed the circle tight, blocking out Thearbuc and Lamora from seeing what they were doing. The two looked at each other, shrugged, then stepped back behind a large boulder for cover. Then they watched…

The wizards began chanting something. Soft and quiet at first, but then it began to grow louder and louder. The words were in a language Thearbuc and Lamora could not understand. Louder and louder the voices grew, faster and faster. Then the sun began to rise, bringing a cool dawn to the scorched lands. It came above the horizon slowly, stretching long shadows of burnt trees across the hillsides. But then it kept rising, quickly into the sky. Thearbuc and Lamora looked at each other with confused looks but said nothing. The sun was rising fast. It had just come from the horizon and was already high enough to be early afternoon in just a matter of moments.

Then, as it moved across the sky, it began to appear clearer. It was no sun after all. It was a great ball of burning light. The wizards' chants grew unnaturally louder and louder until it was deafening to hear. The sound rolled through the valley and echoed from the mountains, engulfing everything around them. Finally, the chanting grew to a roar as the large ball of light settled high above the keep.

Just then, a shadow appeared atop the keep, scurrying back and forth. It was Maub. His lanky stature a silhouette against the bright morning sky. He stared up at the magnificent ball of flames above and began frantically running back towards where he appeared. He stopped near one end of the keep and attempted to blast some sort of energy at the ferocious ball hovering over him, but it dissipated harmlessly into the atmosphere, leaving the sun like ball of flames unchanged. Then he tried blasting a lightning bolt type of blast from his staff at the gathered wizards on the hillside, but just as it got to them, their combined powers seemed to absorb it into a harmless dome that surrounded them. Maub quickly gave up trying to defend his position and frantically ran back inside, into the safety of the keep.

Then, as the wizards and their chant reached their booming crescendo, the sun-like ball of energy suddenly came hurling downward from the sky at incredible speed until it crashed violently into the keep. It exploded with unimaginable ferocity and strength and the shockwave blew the wizards backward as it crashed into a magnificent blinding fireball. Thearbuc and Lamora dove for cover as the explosion reached them, just barely saving their eyes from the blinding light, but unfortunately not their ears, as a booming shockwave of scorching heat blew past them so loud it was like they were standing in thunder.

Smoke and fire rose up toward the sky in the shape of a mushroom as bits and pieces of stone and shrapnel began raining clumsily down on the group. One by one, the wizards broke the circle and gazed toward the keep with heavy intent, waiting for the smoke to clear to see if the explosion had brought it down. There was too much smoke and debris to see clearly.

Then finally, it cleared. As the wind whipped and swirled the smoke away, they got the first look at the keep. It was a pile of rubble. Completely destroyed. The wizards erupted in excitement and cheer. Thearbuc and Lamora returned to the group, brushing the dirt and debris from their shirts and joining in the celebration.

"I can't believe it worked!" Thearbuc laughed, his bright teeth smiling joyfully behind his bushy black beard.

They celebrated and watched the pile of rubble for some time, then, as the smoke cleared, it was decided that Aleric, Thearbuc, Lamora, Barreston, and Ehvsund would go down to the rubble to investigate the damage and look for a body. Barreston was still not convinced a blast was a foolproof way of destroying Maub, so he insisted on taking Brodel's staff just in case they should happen across Maub still alive.

Not long later, the five were down in the valley investigating the damage. "I don't see anything," Thearbuc said, kicking blocks of stone from the pile. The pile of stone that was once an enormous fortress still stood the height of a two-level structure. "We can't dig here all day. He's under there somewhere, and he's dead."

"He has to be," Lamora replied, standing atop the pile and throwing large block after block from the pile.

"What's this?" Aleric yelled out. "I found something!"

Barreston and the others came quickly. Something was in the rubble. Barreston pointed as they approached slowly. Then they got a better look at it. At first it looked like a burnt, thick black branch, but then they saw the glow.

"Maub's staff," Lamora whispered. She had seen it up close before.

"Indeed, it is," Barreston replied. He knew all too well what Maub's magical staff looked like, as its magic had kept him a prisoner for decades. Aleric reached down and tossed more rubble aside until he could pull it free from its hold. He held the staff upward toward the sky and instantly felt a feeling of dread fall across him, like something was horribly wrong, but he did not know what.

"Gah!" he said, tossing the staff back to the ground. "It is pure evil." He shuddered and shook his hands as if trying to get spiderwebs off him.

"A wizard's staff should only be handled by an experienced wizard," Barreston informed him. "A powerful staff can corrupt and take over the mind of the unknowing person. Ehvsund, my friend, please collect the staff."

Aleric kicked the staff away and quickly jumped backward as he touched it, and it sent another small shock through his foot. It tumbled down the pile of rubble and came to rest on the ground, then the old wizard hobbled over to collect it. The staff seemed to have no effect on Ehvsund, who slowly walked it back to Barreston. They decided they were satisfied in finding the staff and that were done looking for the body of the wizard Maub and were ready to rest for the trek back to Mazeron in the morning.

"It will be a fine day to see home again," Barreston said to Ehvsund as they began back up the trail. Aleric, Lamora, and Thearbuc watched the old wizards fade into the distance, and a sense of joy and lightness seemed to wash over them, like a heavy weight had lifted from all around them. They could already feel the simple life coming their way. No more battles, no more long journeys. No more fighting for survival and the daily worry of being arrested for doing something wrong. Together they looked at the sky and breathed a collective sigh of relief as the sun began to sink low toward the horizon.

"Well, I'm ready to celebrate," Thearbuc finally broke the silent calmness.

"Hey, me too," Lamora smiled and nudged him with her shoulder playfully. Then the three friends began walking away from the pile of rubble that was once the great keep. They walked slowly and lightly, without a care in the world, talking and laughing along the trail and hardly noticing the scorched earth and destruction surrounding them. The day was theirs, and they were going to take it.

Later that night, back in the cave within the mountain, the room was filled with laughter and joy as the odd group of wizards and Aleric and his friends celebrated their victory and the wizards' newfound freedom. Luckily, Lamora and Thearbuc's horses were equipped with bottles of the best wine for travel as usual, and the wizards showed no shame in enjoying their first night out of the dungeon in who knows how long. The torchlight and laughter bounced off the stone walls of the cave and a warmth of comradery and victory settled comfortably around the room.

Even Sophie the Stone Gnome made an appearance that evening, appearing seemingly out of nowhere from the depths of the mountain, he came from the walls with a second Stone Gnome whom he introduced as his new wife. She was a cute little thing, wearing tattered overalls just like Sophie and two golden pigtails in her hair. She was small like a child, just like Sophie was, but her face was aged and weathered unlike that of a child. The two Stone Gnomes shared in the drinks and victory over the evil wizard that had plagued them as well, and they even took those who were interested back into the mountain for a tour of their new home. Lamora refused, as she promised herself she would never enter the mountain again, but Aleric and half of the wizards agreed to see what he was so eager to show them.

In they went, tied together in a single file line with the stony mountain closing in around them and the torchlight of the cave quickly fading away. But the darkness did not last for long. Suddenly, they exited the confinement and claustrophobia of the mountain and stepped into a vast cave that stretched more than an entire field's length and extended upward to what looked like almost the entire height of the mountain. It was the largest "room" any of them had ever stood in.

Surrounding them were beautiful towers made of stone, each lit with torchlight that softly illuminated the enormous cave system. It was a palace inside the mountain and lined with shining veins of quartz and gold.

"Sophie, did you make this?" Aleric asked, his eyes wide with awe and disbelief.

"Sophie did," The Gnome grinned from ear to ear up at the large Paladin.

It was unbelievable. The little Stone Gnome had finally gotten over his fear of tight spaces and had clearly begun to embrace his biology and created a beautiful city of palaces and towers in the mountain for himself and his wife.

"I am proud of you," Aleric said, grabbing The Gnome's shoulder and squeezing it softly. "No hard feelings?" Aleric asked, extending his hand to Sophie. "Friends forever?"

“Friends forever!” Sophie replied happily, shaking the large Paladin’s hand. Then they took one more glance at the underground city Sophie had built and went back to the cave.

After entering the cave again, the wizards went back to the wine bottles and happy conversations, and the celebration continued. But no one seemed to notice that two of the group were now missing…

Outside the cave, exposed to the windy and cold night, a cloaked figure sat cross-legged near the cave entrance, staring out at the valley where the keep had once stood. The wind blew hard, so no other sounds could be heard beyond it. The dark woolen cloak flapped in the heavy wind as the person sat motionless on the cold ground.

Out of nowhere, a soft yellow glow appeared behind the cloaked figure and a tall figure walked out from the shadows and stood between the cloaked figure and the cave entrance.

“You will suffer for thinking you could defeat me,” A raspy voice said slowly. The person sitting knew the voice immediately, and they were gripped by a sudden terror that caused their stomach to twist at the sound of the voice. There was no mistaking it. It was Maub.

Slowly, the evil old wizard advanced, holding a small yellow glow in the palm of his hand. He towered over the cloaked wizard, who still sat motionless despite being gripped with fear.

“The books of Abborell are mine,” Maub said with angry clenched teeth. “They call to me. I knew from the moment I saw you bring them together, all those years ago, that I must have them. They wanted me to have them. I won’t spare you this time,” he said as he reached out a long, withered hand from his dark cloak like the grim reaper reaching out to touch his next victim. Then, right before the wretched hand touched the wizard, he rolled aside and sprang to his feet, sidestepping Maub and dashing quickly toward the cave entrance. “Fool!” Maub shouted, swinging about and casting a fireball toward the entrance of the cave, just narrowly missing the fleeing wizard and sending ashes floating into the windy night. Maub did not waste any time and was after him in an instant.

They rushed through the cave in frantic pursuit, wizard chasing wizard. Maub was fast, with his tall legs and long stride, and began to gain quickly on the old, cloaked wizard as he scurried as fast as he could, pulling up his cloak as to not be tripped by it.

"You can't escape me!" Maub yelled out, his booming voice echoing loudly through the chambers and hallways of the cave. But the cloaked wizard kept a distance between them as they twisted and turned through the dark cave. His heart pounded like a rabbit being hunted by a fox. Predator and prey, the chase continued through the darkness. Maub was gaining and gaining. His outstretched arm was just about to grasp the other wizard's cloak when the cave turned a sharp left and the cloaked wizard burst into the room with the other wizards.

From the side of the cave, Barreston stood in the shadows, waiting for just the right moment. Then, he thrust Maub's magical staff into the air and a bright blue light burst from its tip. Then he slammed the staff downward toward the ground, creating a bright portal that floated in the center of the doorway. Maub, in pursuit of the cloaked wizard, turned left quickly and did not have time to react, and when the large burst of light and a portal opened up before him, he was unable to stop in time or avoid it. He ran straight into the portal and instantly disappeared into it.

The others turned to see the commotion that was unfolding so fast. The cloaked wizard who was acting as bait stopped at the center of the room and turned about, throwing the cloak from their head, and revealed their face. It was Lamora!

"Now!" another voice yelled out from the darkness of the cave. It was Brodel's voice. Barreston stood back and slammed the magical staff towards the ground, closing the portal like a zipper in time. The motion of the staff was so quick and powerful it smashed hard on the cave floor creating a powerful boom and a plume of dust that exploded upward around them.

For a moment, it was completely silent. Everyone else in the room glanced at each other, wondering what had just happened. They were trying to piece it together. In the span of only a few moments, a cloaked figure had burst into the room, there was a sudden flash of light, then the shadow of a person rushed into the light, and it was silent again.

"It's done," Barreston announced from the far end of the room, almost collapsing against the wall but holding himself steady with one arm. The staff he held in the other dropped to the floor, and Brodel and the other wizards rushed towards him.

"What just happened?" Thearbuc asked.

"He is gone now," Barreston said, regaining his composure with the help of the others. "Trapped forever."

"Who is? What is going on?" Thearbuc asked again.

"The wizard Maub," Barreston said slowly. "I knew brute force alone could not defeat him. Even if he was in the tower when we brought it down." He glanced at Aleric who looked away shyly.

"It's the only way I know," he replied with a shrug and a grin.

"So, we set a trap," Barreston continued. "Lamora was the bait." Thearbuc looked over at her with alarm on his face, as he had no idea of this plan they had hatched. "She was the only one spry enough to outrun the wizard," Barreston continued. "I assumed he would come for us, capturing us all again for a lifetime of enslavement. Lamora was the bait, and he took it. He ran through the portal and there he will stay for as long as he can survive in whatever cursed lands it leads to. Only he knows, I'm assuming."

"How did you know the spell, how did you know how to open the portal?" Brodel asked excitedly with his old raspy voice. He was still fascinated by magic despite his own powers, as he had still not been around other magic users much in his life.

"I used Maub's staff," Barreston replied. "It already knew this spell. A few words from the books of spells and I knew I could open it."

"Brilliant, brilliant!" The other wizards took turns congratulating Barreston. He had done it! He had finally defeated the wizard that had destroyed his life and family so many years ago.

"Well if it's safe outside now, I've had about enough of this cave and being in the mountains." Lamora eventually said. The others agreed and soon the group made their way out of the cave, back towards the valley of Mazeron.

That night they slept under a million stars and for the first time in as long as any of them could remember they slept peacefully and without any care or worry.

The next morning came and while Aleric and Thearbuc were making plans on which route to take back to the kingdom Barreston walked up to them with Maub's staff and with a large grin pointed the staff towards the sky and suddenly opened another portal.

"Why walk when you can portal?" the old man chuckled.

Aleric became quickly alarmed and worried Maub would come back through the portal, but after peering into it he could see the cloudy outline of the king's chambers.

"This will lead us right back to where Maub had opened the portal in the castle?" he confirmed with Barreston.

"Indeed," the old wizard said, motioning towards it.

"Allow me," Aleric said as he began to step through. As he did the wind from the portal blew his hair back and Barreston noticed a large birthmark on the back of Aleric's neck. One that he recognized instantly.

"Stop!" he said pushing against Aleric's chest and blocking the way. "That birthmark on your neck…" Barreston said curiously. My daughter's son had the same…" he trailed off and after a moment of pause a big smile spread across his face. "Oh, do I have a story for you, boy," he said trying to contain his happiness. I'll tell you when we get back, for it is a long one.

Aleric shrugged and soon the group began hopping into the portal one by one until they all stood in the king's chambers once again.

"Now, lets tell these soldiers their king has returned!" Thearbuc said with a smile, patting Aleric's arm.

Aleric and the group made their way to the castle's balcony and what he saw there was not at all what he was expecting. The cleanup effort from the battles was still ongoing and the state of the castle still in complete shambles. The castle gate was still broken and the grounds left wide open, and the courtyard seemed ridden with dirty, half-drunk soldiers everywhere. Some were sleeping on the ground; others were fighting amongst each other.

"What has happened here?" Aleric asked bewildered and disgusted at the scene. Quickly he turned from the balcony and made his way into the castle toward the stairs.

As he went through the castle, he saw soldiers and citizens strewn about the castle like squatters in almost every room. Quarrels were everywhere and the smell was as unpleasant as the scene. As they made their way into the great hall Commander Rune's voice could be heard booming through the hallways as he came rushing in to break up a fight between two soldiers. Aleric and the others approached him.

"What in the world is going on here?" Aleric yelled angrily.

"Oh, thank goodness," Commander Rune replied, resting his hand on his Paladin friend's shoulder. "I am so glad you are here. Everyone thought you were dead."

"What has happened to the castle? My castle!?" Aleric erupted again.

"It's the king's guards, sir. And the brigands," Commander Rune's voice was distressed as he spoke. "Neither will recognize the other as their leader and neither will agree to join forces. They have all claimed the castle for their own. There was nothing I could do."

"Nothing you could do?" Aleric nudged him aside to get a better look at the soldiers strewn about the ballroom.

"Well, nothing short of a civil war," Commander Rune replied firmly. "I don't have the authority to wage such things in a land that is not mine. It's all I could do to keep them from killing one another until you hopefully returned. The men, these people, Mazeron, they *need* you." There was desperation in his voice. "They have fought for this castle, fought for these lands. They all feel they have a claim to it now."

Aleric paused in thought for a few moments. "Maybe they do," he said finally. "Round everyone up. We are restoring order."

Within moments, the castle was abustle with the word that the soldiers and people of Mazeron were to be addressed. Some soldiers were awoken and brushed themselves off as they made their way to gather in the courtyard. Others had to be coaxed or basically pushed out of the castle, and multiple arguments and scuffles broke out. Eventually, the castle was emptied, and the courtyard was full of soldiers waiting for some sort of word about what was to happen next. It was a pot ready to boil over at any moment.

Finally, Aleric emerged from the castle's ballroom with the group of odd-looking wizards, including Barreston and Brodel, following him. They stood on the steps just above the gathered crowd and waited for the restless men to quiet.

"People of Mazeron," he announced loudly. The crowd instantly fell silent. "I am here to tell you that we are no longer the king's guards and Brigands, peasants or royalty, farmers or beggars. From this moment on, we are all citizens of Mazeron. We are one!" The words echoed off the stone walls amongst the otherwise thick silence. The soldiers gathered seemingly disinterested. They looked at one another with confusion and distrusting looks on their faces until he continued on, "We will rebuild together and make these lands prosperous and stable once again."

"Who are you to tell us what to do?" a voice yelled out of the crowd. Others followed suit and shouted in agreement.

Suddenly, Aleric's eyes began to glow, and in a visible show of force and he reached for the sky, exposing the glowing Medallion of Mazeron on the underside of his wrist.

"Your king!" he yelled out.

Abruptly, the courtyard came to life as the soldiers realized what they were looking at: the rightful king of Mazeron, the owner of the castle and all the lands that belonged to it. One by one, they began to kneel to Aleric, their new king.

"No, no. Get up," he said, waving his arms. "I may be king of this castle, but I am not king of your lives. From this day on, the decisions that affect the lands will be voted on by you, the citizens. Votes on every issue, unless it takes something away from others, then there will be no vote at all," he said recalling the corrupt voting disaster proposed by Aghasty at the Emoras-Garum town hall. There were a few scattered claps and shouts of approval, but still the rugged soldiers and villagers seemed unmoved and hard to please. They grumbled amongst each other as if they did not believe the words that they were hearing, but Aleric continued anyway.

"Lastly, I am announcing the return of magic to these lands." As he said it, he turned to Barreston, Brodel, and the other wizards and grinned. "We will embrace one of the greatest strengths we have and never again will we allow ourselves to become weak enough to be overrun by evil. Weak enough to be walked on, weak enough to be taken advantage of and controlled.

Weak enough to watch our values and lands be eroded away. We will hold the line of civility and justice, and we will hold it by being more powerful and stronger than those who want to destroy it. Strength that we can only build together!"

Finally, some of the soldiers started nodding their heads in agreement and clapping slowly while they finally felt some hope that they might have a leader who cared about them first. Cared about the welfare of the land and the people's well-being and not just themselves.

"I could get on board with that!" one man yelled aloud. The others simultaneously and loudly cheered out that they agreed. Some turned to one another and shook hands or embraced and from that moment the two groups started to become one. Joined together by the only person who could do it. The King of Mazeron.

"Aleric. I mean, uh, King Aleric," Commander Rune eventually interrupted, quietly tapping Aleric on his shoulder. "I have something to show you. You'll want to see this."

Aleric glanced back at the courtyard, and seeing the soldiers talking and being friendly to one another, he nodded to Commander Rune. The group consisting of Aleric, Thearbuc, Lamora, Brodel, and Barreston walked away from the courtyard with Commander Rune and his personal entourage. He led them down under the castle near the dungeons and Maub's corrupt courtroom that Aleric had stumbled upon that night long ago.

Winding through the dark corridors under the castle, it took some time to get there, and they all wondered what was going on.

"Where are we going?" Aleric asked.

"Here," Commander Rune finally exclaimed as they turned the corner, and he lifted a torch above his head, illuminating one of the castle's stone walls. "We found this while searching Maub's dungeons and setting the wrongly imprisoned free." The others turned and gazed at it. The wall seemed to be corroding, with holes and cracks in it and some parts gone altogether. Pieces were dropping off and disappearing before they hit the ground, and other pieces of the wall were simply blowing away in the faint gusts of air.

"What is this?" Lamora asked, gazing at the wall in awe.

"It's magic," Barreston and Brodel answered simultaneously. "It's a spell that is eroding away. No doubt one of Maub's spells," Brodel continued.

"Allow me," Barreston said. He put his staff up towards the wall, and with a poof of light the entire portion of the wall disappeared and exposed a dark room behind it.

Cautiously, the group advanced forward into the room, then raised their torches. Their eyes bulged and their jaws dropped at what they saw. The entire room glowed so brightly in the torchlight that they almost had to shield their eyes, as the room was filled with so much gold, diamonds, and precious stones that it almost blinded them with the reflection.

"Oh my goodness" they whispered in unison as their eyes beheld the largest treasure any of them had or would ever see. Commander Rune's men could not contain themselves and ran into the room like excited children, grabbing handfuls of gold coins, diamonds, and gems and jumping on the piles of gold.

"Why? How?" Aleric was trying to put together words as he inspected handfuls of thick gold coins. "This must be almost all of the gold Mazeron has ever minded. The entire kingdom's wealth! Why did Maub need so much gold? And to have it all just sit here? It didn't even do anything for him. He couldn't spend all this in ten lifetimes!"

"It wasn't about being rich," Thearbuc replied, flipping coins through his fingers. "In the king's chambers, he mentioned this. It wasn't about being rich, it was about control and stealing freedom from the people. When it comes down to it, freedom is the main thing that all humans crave; it's in our blood. And really, gold is the physical form of freedom. Freedom to enjoy life and experience what the world has to offer. Freedom from constant work and toil. Like a squirrel unable to store nuts for winter he said. By stealing their gold and keeping them from being able to own land he was forcing them into an entire life of endless toil. Stealing all their time, which in a way is stealing their very lives. Paying everyone just enough to survive, but not enough to actually live."

The wonder and celebration of discovering the room full of treasure turned solemn as the group contemplated the misery and strife for so many people the piles of gold represented.

“How can one man cause so much despair?” Barreston said, angrily throwing some gold coins back onto the pile.

“At least it’s over now,” Lamora replied, resting a comforting hand on the old wizard’s shoulder.

“I guess this is yours now,” one of Commander Rune’s men said to Aleric with a heavy sigh, implying that the new king would want all of his gold for himself.

Aleric nodded as the men started to glumly walk away from the secret chamber of gold with their heads hanging low. Then, as a faint grin slowly crossed his face, Aleric finally spoke. “What are you talking about?” he said with a smirk. “This,” he gestured, “This is all yours. This all belongs to the people of Mazeron. Take it to them.”

Epilogue: The Witch and the Wizard

Years had gone by since Mazeron was reclaimed by its people, and the lands were slowly returning to stability. The new king had thus far proven to be a man of honor and justice. Barreston had moved into the castle and was appointed the castle's wizard and head counsel. He was also put in charge of expanding magic use throughout the kingdom, and the two had forged as much of a family as they could for having been apart for over two decades.

The roads from the mountains leading into Mazeron were reopened and trade was bustling. The brigands had proven to be hard workers and had taken up and thrived in all different trades. The ones that became farmers had blessed the lands with a plethora of food. Those who stayed in the military service provided a strong defense as castle guards and upheld justice within the land. Some of the more rugged men had taken to the gold mines and with the help of a new forged friendship with the Stone Gnomes were pulling gold out of the mountains at a level that had never been seen before. The land was peaceful and prosperous once again.

Far away from the castle, in a small stone cottage deep in the woods, an old man shuffled slowly across the room with a cup of hot tea and sat down at a wooden table. It was a beautiful, sunny midafternoon, and the sound of birds and leaves in the breeze filled the air. The old man looked up and gazed out the window, and his mind wandered peacefully to more adventurous days before age had left him slow and tired.

The magic Brodel had used to survive the witch Kalindra and defeat the wizard Maub in the battle for the castle had left his body aged and broken.

"You just don't know what a blessing being young is until it's taken from you," he mumbled aloud to the trees and birds with a sigh. His body hurt as he sat with a hunched back over the table and reached his bony, arthritic hands to his cup of tea, which somewhat soothed the pain and stiffness as he gripped the warmth of the cup.

He looked around at his peaceful cottage. It looked the same now as the day he left with Thearbuc and the mysterious

Paladin, all those years ago. Magic items and trinkets were strewn about and stacked all across the floors and table. Books, scrolls, magic lanterns, bottles, wizard staffs, invisibility cloaks, and of course, the last potion bottle of the waters from the Lake of Dreams that Aleric had collected so long ago.

In his old age, he longed for companionship and the days of adventure and the unknown once again. He pondered for a moment then shrugged. Those days were long gone now, he thought to himself as he continued to sip his hot tea.

Then, a shadow moved across the table. It was quick; there one moment then gone another. He froze in place, looking at the table to see if it would appear again. Did he see a shadow or was it his imagination? He got up and peered out the window to see the trees lazily blowing in the soft wind. It was probably just the trees, he thought to himself. He turned back and reached across the room for an open book that he had been reading, then there it was again. A shadow swept across the room. Only for a moment, then gone again.

He turned back and frantically scanned the room for his staff. Where was it? He turned back to see his staff along the far wall near the door. Just as he was breathing a sigh of relief, the door began to creep open. It moved slowly and creaked as it opened. Brodel sat motionless in his chair, his old mouth agape. He instantly knew the smell and felt a familiar cold dread wash across him. The door swung open slowly and in floated the witch Kalindra.

Brodel turned immediately to grab something to defend himself with, but she was faster and pointed with one finger. "Don't!" she screamed in a wretched high screech. Brodel froze in place, his eyes turning back toward her as she came into the cottage with confidence, as if it were her own.

"I have missed you," she hissed between rotted, yellowed teeth. "Did you miss me too?" She licked her sun-chapped lips as she said it.

"Be gone, witch," Brodel demanded, still frozen in place.

Suddenly, the witch's calm demeanor changed in an instant and she snapped and screamed at Brodel. "You be gone!" she screeched at him. She rushed toward him and grabbed his old face hard by the chin, pulling her wretched face close to his.

"Don't be mean!" she snapped like an unstable child. Brodel's eyes darted back and forth for something, anything, to defend himself with. The witch Kalindra seemed even more unstable and irrational than she had been before. One second she was giggling, laughing with madness, then the other, screaming from internal misery.

Without warning, she raised her hands to the sky and lifted Brodel from his chair. He frantically tried to counter her spell, but he was frozen. Time paused for a moment as he was suspended in the air, then she threw him hard across the room and he hit the wall with a loud thud before falling to the floor. The witch howled with enjoyment and cackled with laughter as the old wizard lay motionless on the floor.

She came toward him once again, but Brodel sprang to life. Grabbing his staff and rolling over quickly, he swung his staff towards the witch and watched as an invisible force threw her hard against the adjacent wall. Brodel rose to his feet, his staff still in hand, then approached the witch cautiously.

She was only down for a second, and Brodel had no time to cast a spell, so he simply charged her and tackled her against the back wall. They fell hard to the floor, and she was under Brodel, scratching and clawing at his face like a cornered beast. Trying to protect himself, Brodel let her go, then an instant later found himself slammed against the wall once again.

They tussled and fought. Bashing around the room, causing damage and destruction to priceless magical artifacts. Neither of them was able to get an advantage over the other.

Finally, they stood in front of one another, both breathing heavily from the fight. Brodel lunged once again at the witch and tackled her hard against the wall, this time smashing into the potion bottle filled with the water from the Lake of Dreams. They crashed to the floor.

"No!" the witch shrieked, laying on the ground. She knew instantly what had covered her and what the consequence of even touching the magical waters from the lake would do to a magic user like her.

She turned to Brodel. Filled with rage and anger, she wanted nothing more than to kill him right then and there for what he had done. Then she saw it. He was covered in the water too. He leaned against the wall, looking at his hands and cloak, soaked through with the magical water. The feeling of dread came over him as he realized his fate, and he rolled from the wall and slumped on the floor next to the witch Kalindra, both covered in the deadly magical water from the lake of dreams.

Nothing more was said between the two as whisps of steam began to rise and whirl from their bodies, filling the room with magical swirls of color and smoke. Brodel wondered if it would be painful and closed his eyes as he waited for the darkness to come over him. It started in his feet and crept upward. He could feel it overtake him. He waited for unconsciousness, then waited, and waited some more, but it never came. His mind was blank, but consciousness was still there.

Slowly he opened his eyes and saw light once again. The room was clear. The smoke and sparkling colors were gone. He slowly turned his head towards Kalindra and found that she was doing the same. The two looked at each other in silence for many moments and staring back at one another were young faces. Smooth skin and bright carefree eyes.

They both burst into laughter at the same time. Rolling on the cottage floor, they laughed without restraint. Tears of joy rolled down their faces and they realized they had both become young again and they gazed in awe at one another like teenagers. The legends must not have been true, and rather than killing them, the waters of the lake had only killed the magic inside of them and returned them to the age they were when they began using magic.

They could not control the feeling of happiness and relief that was flowing through them. Pain, unhappiness, frustration, and anger at the world were already distant memories. For the longest time they lay there on the floor of the cottage, touching each other's faces and laughing. They had just been given the greatest gift in the world. One that every person longs for eventually. Another chance at life. A chance to start over. A chance to be young again.

www.ingramcontent.com/pod-product-compliance
Lightning Source LLC
Chambersburg PA
CBHW030602310726
48979CB00003B/545

9798218864101